ASHES OF WAR

BECK TODD

First paperback edition March 2024

Book design by Kelly Carter

ISBN 979-8-9862007-4-3 (paperback)
ISBN 979-8-9862007-5-0 (ebook)

For my family for your continuing support and encouragement.
Thank you.

ALSO BY BECK TODD

Dionysus Trilogy: Dionysus, Event Horizon, Prospero

Gadyeni Cycle: Ravens in Flight, Ashes of War

Contents

CEOL

SEA OF
WINDS

WALLACH RIVER

NERIN RIVER

SAETHYR

LOWYRN

TEYRNAS

JEMAYRT

VOGEL MOUNTAINS

BYYAR

AVERIL

THARYS OCEAN

KEREU

NORTHERN REALM
OF
ELTRIAR

MADAN OCH

NORTH SEA

WALLACH RIVER

GALION

COLD SEA

TIRSHAY

NOWAN

SALVATION SEA

MALLR RIVER

BRAN MARO

GULF OF MARO

TREILEAN

NERIN RIVER

TAROD

GULF OF SYKERIA

1

Unwanted Guests

The knife soared through the air, tumbling end over end, the morning sunlight glinting off the metallic edge. It hit the tree hilt first and fell limply onto the soft grass.

Realta grounded her teeth.

"This skill takes years to perfect," said Ezri Namazu. The Jemayrti bodyguard retrieved the knife and handed it back to her.

"Why can't I just use Manipulation?" Though she couldn't Manipulate anything larger than a book, Realta could hit the tree blade-first every time she used her Thane ability. Well, not quite every time. More like nine out of ten. But it was far more accurate than simply throwing the knife.

Ezri smirked, his white teeth standing in brilliant contrast to his dark skin. "Remember where we are, Realta." He pointed eastward. "It won't always be safe to use that ability."

Two months of travel had led their group to the outskirts of a small village in Kereu, about ten miles from the western shore of the Nerin River. All villages in this area were more than happy to receive visitors. The war in Teyrnas had cut off most trade from the north, and tensions within the country were high, considering that Tarod, a prominent member of the Eastern Coalition, rested just beyond the river.

Though merchant-controlled Kereu was open to Thanes, a number of people began to share their neighbors' views, wondering if Thanes truly were dangerous. Chinasa Ekene and the Thane Scholars had to lie about their abilities twice and hid away their colorful bead necklaces and bracelets. In the last village, Realta watched as a small mob attacked Minder Thane and threw him out of an inn. The Thane had read the innkeeper's mind, trying to determine if he was getting a fair price. The innkeeper interpreted the action as a threat and exaggerated the incident to the magistrate, causing the man to be thrown in jail. He was still there awaiting trial when the Scholars left the following day.

Realta's knife throwing lessons with Ezri began shortly afterwards.

She studied the knife. The handle was made of wildcat bone, smooth and lightweight, just like the knives her father had used while working as a mountain guide. Callum rarely used those knives on the farm, keeping them solely as mementos.

"Do you want to hold one?" Callum had asked Realta when she was six years old. Realta had gone into Callum's room to ask permission to visit the Tamlin farm with Master and Mistress Loy. The knives, their blades freshly sharpened, laid out on his writing desk.

She looked up at her father's towering presence and nodded.

Callum selected a knife, the smallest one, and crouched down beside her. He held out the knife hilt first.

"Feel the weight," he instructed her. "See how it balances in the middle? Right where the blade begins?" Callum positioned her hand nearer the hilt. "See? Easier to hold this way," he said, smiling.

Realta hadn't understood why Callum allowed a six-year-old to handle a knife, not until a few years ago. She overheard him speaking with Esme, wondering if he ought to train Realta to become a mountain guide, just in case she wanted to follow in his footsteps. Esme instructed him to be subtle, so Realta would not feel pressured.

Looking back, Realta noted a dozen other small lessons. Callum teaching her about the changing weather patterns, how a sunny winter day can quickly turn to freezing night or how long a storm would last based on the color of the clouds. And Esme had taught her and Charity about healing herbs. Facts a mountain guide ought to know.

When Realta and Charity began to talk about the Academy, about what they would study if given the chance, the lessons grew less frequent.

"Do you want to try again?" Ezri asked, pulling Realta out of her thoughts.

Realta gripped the knife, mirroring Callum's hand, took aim, and threw it. The blade sank into the ground, a foot in front of the tree. "Fire and smoke," she muttered.

"Close."

A twig snapped, echoing through the quiet forest.

Realta spun on her heels and saw Serena appear at the top of a low hill, dodging trees on her way down. The taller girl had the skirt of her dress bunched up in one hand, and her shoulder-length, sandy brown hair was in wild disarray. She used her free hand to slap tree branches out of the way, ignoring the growing collection of scraps on her arm.

Ezri picked up the knife and tucked it into his belt. "Lesson over for today."

Serena reached the base of the hill. She trembled from head to foot, her blue eyes wide.

"What now?" Realta asked, dreading the answer. Images of their first week on the road sprang to mind. Racing away from the war. Fleeing at a moment's notice because of Coalition movements. Many times, they fled in the middle of the night. She had lost count of the sleepless nights. Long nights seemingly without end, praying their horses could run fast enough.

They had crossed the river into Byyar last month, around the time the mountain kingdom had joined the war. King Nolfri of Byyar, Queen Isla's father, formally announced the alliance and petitioned every village to send men and women to fight. Most soldiers were stationed along the river, protecting the western shore. So far, the fighting had not reached the Nerin. Chinasa speculated it was only a matter of time.

Last week, they crossed the border into Kereu. The Merchant Council, having too much to lose by taking a side, officially remained neutral. But they vowed to attack whoever marched onto their land.

After the incident with the Minder Thane, the Jemayrti Scholars decided to camp at the edge of the forest, along a dirt-paved road, a day's ride to the nearest village and miles away from the Southern Highway. The forest, more akin to a marshy swamp than the forests in the Hinterlands, protected them on three sides, and the road allowed for easy travel, both to gather supplies at the village and to flee farther south if necessary.

As of right now, they were just another group of refugees traveling to the Sykerian Empire, a country that comprised the entire Southern Realm. Shasta Cray had invented that part of their story. Realta hoped it was just that. A story. She had no desire to travel even farther from home. But neither did she want to be in the middle of the war.

"A merchant train," Serena said, her voice shaking. "Nowani."

Realta's heart skipped a beat. She immediately looked at Ezri.

"Go to the wagons. Quicky." He drew a knife and rounded the hill.

Realta and Serena took off running. Serena, usually the faster of the two, ran a pace behind Realta, unaccustomed to running through a forest. As they reached the crest of the last hill, Realta spied a long caravan of wagons. At least twenty. Each one flew the flag of Nowan: a hawk with silver keys in its talons on a field of purple and white checks.

Guards with swordbreakers at their belts and nocked arrows in their hands surrounded the caravan.

What if they aren't guards? Realta wondered. The guards and servants accompanying Queen Gallia had been soldiers in disguise, waiting for the signal to attack.

No, they will honor Kereu's laws. They won't attack us. Seeing their camp, Realta failed to convince herself. All the way out here, they were easy prey.

Three small wagons comprised their camp. Chinasa bought them from a merchant in Byyar shortly after they crossed the river. The wagons, as always, were arranged in a loose circle with a firepit in the center. A line of fresh laundry hung between two wagons, created a barrier between the camp and the road. The horses were tied in a line next to the trees.

Realta slowed as she and Serena passed the horses. Spooking the animals would draw unwanted attention. Her mind raced, seeing the caravan drawing nearer, slowing down. What should they do? What should they say? They were merely passing through, heading south, same as the merchants, no doubt. But why did she have a sinking feeling in her gut?

Scholar Adanna, sitting on the steps of one wagon with a book in her hands, motioned for Realta and Serena to come closer.

"Quick," said the Scholar. "Hide in here."

They climbed inside. The interior was so narrow that it barely had room for three cots. One took up the back wall while the two on the sides were almost touching. A chest of drawers occupied the front wall, leaving no space between it and the door. Scholar Adanna closed the door, turning the cramped space into a claustrophobic's nightmare.

Realta sat on one bed and peered through the narrow window. The Scholars gathered at the edge of the road, waiting. Serena sat down beside her, shaking like a leaf in a storm. Realta wanted to say something to comfort her, but her throat was caught in a vise. She noticed her own hands shaking and quickly balled them into fists.

The caravan came to a halt, and the leader, a tall man with slate gray hair and a short beard, dismounted and approached Chinasa. The ambassador wore simple gray and brown clothes. He had long since stowed away his white clothes, opting for less noticeable colors. A sheathed knife rested on his belt near the small of his back. Realta wasn't the only one receiving lessons from Ezri.

Realta cracked open the window and listened.

"You're a long way from home, Master Ekene." Realta shivered, hearing the leader's Nowani accent. The lilting, almost song-like cadence was identical to Val's accent.

"We didn't expect Byyar to be caught in the fray," Chinasa replied, the lie rolling easily off his tongue. Another of Shasta's inventions. If anyone asked, the Jemayrti Scholars had traveled to Byyar to meet King Nolfri, with Chinasa acting as their interpreter. The war broke out before they reached the capital city, Artinyr. "We certainly could not risk returning north to Caman's Pass."

The Nowani merchant smirked. "Certainly not. Are you continuing south, then?"

"To the coast. Jemayrt has long wished to establish relations with Treilean. Now seems like a good time."

Realta frowned. Treilean? What happened to Sykeria? *He must be trying to throw them off our trail.*

"Really?" The merchant rubbed his chin. "I've got a man here with a Treileani servant. Maybe he can give you some advice.

Those islanders can be very fickle. Friendly one minute, and then they're pointing spears at your throat the next."

Chinasa regarded the merchant for a long moment. Realta hoped he'd be able to get them to move along quickly. "I would not want to delay anyone."

"Nonsense." The merchant lowered his voice. "He's Teyrnian. No loyalties to the Raven Throne, mind you, but a lot of folks are getting anxious. I don't want any trouble, especially not in Kereu. Do me a favor. Delay him for a couple of days. Just enough for us to get ahead. His name is Waylar Corey."

Chinasa studied the long line of wagons. "Only if you do me a favor in return. Don't mention meeting any Jemayrti."

"Deal." The merchant shook Chinasa's hand, relief sweeping over his face.

Serena gasped, her eyes growing wider.

"What is it?" Realta whispered.

"My work shirt. It's hanging on the line. The tailor's tag reads Teyrnas. What if they see it?"

Realta glanced back at the caravan. The lead merchant signaled for them to rest the horses. Over a hundred people began moving about. Some approached the Scholars, wanting to trade. Anything from bolts of dyed cloth to salted meat to ink and paper. The Scholars quickly gravitated towards the writing material.

"Do you really think they'll see it?"

"We can't risk it." Serena darted towards the door. Realta grabbed her wrist, forcing her to sit back down.

"Let me go. My Lowyrnic is better than yours." They had created this story in Byyar after a curious innkeeper asked too many questions. Realta and Serena were linguistics apprentices from the Lowyrn Academy, studying under Chinasa and Scholar Adanna.

Serena took another glance at the gathering crowd and conceded.

Realta, steadying herself, exited the wagon. She walked towards the laundry line, forcing her steps to be slow and even. One merchant, a woman with her black hair tied in a bun and wearing a gaudy yellow dress slashed with purple, was trying to convince Scholars Adanna and Leila to buy packets of seeds. Rare varieties of vegetables that grew in the cold climates of Madan Och but could thrive in warmer weather as well. The Scholars politely declined. None of them noticed Realta, thank the Creator.

She moved down the laundry line, touching a few articles as though checking to make sure they were dry, and found Serena's work shirt. Her eyes darted back and forth. No one watching. Good. She ripped off the tag. It read: *Skyla Islwyn and Daughter, Tailors and Seamstresses, Abyrthal Street, Teyrnas.*

"Hello, little girl."

Realta whirled around and stood face to face with a man. He was in his fifties, a bit shorter than Callum, with dark hair touched with gray and a strong build. His dark brown eyes were as hard as marbles, and he wore a well-tailored, dark blue coat over a linen shirt and dark trousers.

"Alo," she said in Lowyrnic, stuffing the tag into her dress pocket. She hoped the accent was passable. Callum had taught her a good bit, enough for a simple conversation, but his accent was far better. The benefit of living in Lowyrn several months a year and having a Lowyrnic wife. How fluent would Realta be if Kiana had lived?

"Excuse me. What are you doing?" Chinasa broke off his conversation with the lead merchant and stormed towards them. The lead merchant paled and quickly followed.

"Good morning, sir," the man said. "I was just saying hello to this little girl. Is she your servant?"

Realta bristled under the question and touched the bracelet covering her left wrist. As much as she wanted the servant's mark gone, they could not risk going to a tattooist and having it removed. Some were discreet, but others asked a lot of questions and required paperwork in order to remove a servant's mark. Paperwork they did not have and likely never existed. Logan had given her the tattoo out of spite.

"She is my apprentice," Chinasa replied curtly.

"Oh, my mistake." The man gave him a short bow.

The lead merchant stepped in. "Um, Master Ekene, this is Waylar Corey."

Chinasa clasped his hands behind his back. "I see."

"Ekene," Corey said. "That's a unique name. Where are you

from?"

"Jemayrt. Realta, fai a Shasta le mai amim." *Get Shasta, please.*

"Hold on a minute. That's Lowyrnic." Corey raised an eyebrow.

"You have an ear for language." Chinasa gave Realta an urgent look. "Nis, Realta." *Now.*

She ducked under the laundry line and went to the wagon farthest from the road. Shasta Cray, her face impassive, stood at the base of the steps and studied the merchants. The former head of servant's silver tongue and level head had gotten them out of several tough situations. Realta hoped she could do so again.

"Who are they?" Shasta asked. Realta told her, and her face darkened. "Why aren't you hiding? Where is Serena?"

"Well..." Realta suddenly felt very foolish. Yes, they could not risk the Nowani discovering that she and Serena were Teyrnian, but not a single one looked at the laundry. Why would they?

"No matter. What's done is..." Shasta's eyes narrowed. "What do you think you're doing?" She stormed towards the firepit.

A tall man with sandy hair stood next to the cold firepit. Several knives hung from his belt, and a long sword was slung across his back in the style of Sykerian soldiers. He had a bow and arrow in one hand.

"Who are you?" Shasta demanded.

The man smirked, looking down at her. He eased the tension on the bowstring and placed the arrow back in the quiver. "Just doing my job. Hope this isn't an inconvenience." His eyes fell on Realta. A curious look crossed his face. "Huh. Interesting."

"What is interesting?" Shasta asked, not taking her eyes off him for a second.

"Nothing."

Chinasa, Waylar Corey, and the caravan leader entered the camp's center. Chinasa frowned while the leader looked as though a heavy weight had lifted off his shoulders.

"And don't think we're imposing on you," Corey said to Chinasa. "We have our own supplies. It ain't every day you meet someone traveling in the same direction as you." He was all smiles.

"No, it is not." Chinasa scowled.

"They're going to Sykeria, too?" the armed man asked.

"Sykeria?" Corey made a disgusted face. "Let the Nowani have

Sykeria! We're sailing to Treilean with these fine people. So don't hurt anyone, Braedan."

"No problem. Not sure Elliza will like it, though."

Corey rolled his eyes. "Do they check out?"

"The man standing next to you is a Learner. High-leveled. She," Braedan pointed at Scholar Kambri as she peered around the wagons, "is a Manipulator. Very low-leveled. Nothing to get worked up over. And that other guy is also a Learner and Empath. Middle level for both. And..." Braedan glanced around the camp. His eyes fell on Realta.

Her heart caught in her throat. A Cuchasi. This man was a Cuchasi. She reached for her belt, but the knife wasn't there. Ezri had it. She quickly glanced around, hoping to see the bodyguard. No such luck.

"That's it," Braedan said, giving Realta a wink before turning back to Corey.

The lead merchant paled. "Thanes? You're a Thane?"

"Yes," Chinasa replied, "but since your caravan is moving on, there is nothing for you to worry about, Master Lagard."

"Um, right." Lagard said goodbye to Chinasa and Corey and nearly ran out of the camp. He exchanged hurried words with the other merchants, causing more than a few to turn pale. They completed their transactions and quickly returned to their wagons.

Chinasa sighed and rubbed his forehead.

"Hey, don't worry about Lagard," said Corey. "He's pretty open-minded when it comes to Thanes."

"How is running away open-minded?" Shasta questioned.

"He didn't run away screaming for the guard," Corey laughed. "Braedan, help Elliza set up camp. I think right there," he pointed between the first and third wagons, "will be an excellent spot."

"You're camping with us?" Chinasa asked. "I thought you had your own supplies."

"I do. But it's far safer for four wagons at night instead of one. Or three. Especially considering the mess they have up in Teyrnas."

Chinasa studied Corey for a silent moment, no doubt weighing the options. "Very well, Master Corey."

Shasta huffed and went into the wagon she shared with Realta and Serena, likely to give Serena the bad news.

Now what do we do? Would they be able to keep up their charade all day? And how long would Corey travel with them? A few days? A few weeks?

A shadow moved over Realta. She looked up and saw Braedan towering head and shoulders over her. He smiled.

"Those are very pretty beads. Did Mister Ekene give them to you?"

Realta touched the bracelet covering her servant's mark. Several bands of black beads interspersed with an occasional golden one. The necklace Chinasa gifted her also had the same pattern. Black beads for being a Dreamer. Gold for being a Manipulator. She nodded.

"Is he a good teacher? Great Creator." Braedan shook his head. "Do you speak Teyrnian? I was just assuming."

"Yes, I speak Teyrnian, Lowyrnic, and Jemayrti." A partial lie. Her Lowyrnic was good, but she only knew a handful of phrases in Jemayrti, and she had yet to grasp the noun case system. Apparently, words had different endings depending on how they were used in a sentence. And sentences were not always in order, with the subject coming in the beginning, middle, or end, depending on the speaker's preference. It was more than a little confusing.

"Braedan, I don't pay you to stand around," Corey snapped.

"Sir, yes, sir!" Braedan replied sarcastically, placing his fist over his heart. He gave Realta another wink and sauntered away.

Shasta watched from the wagon as Braedan walked off and then approached Realta. "Are you all right?"

"Why did he lie about me?" she whispered.

Shasta studied Corey. The man spoke with Scholars Kambri and Okorie, asking about their Thane abilities. A young woman, perhaps eighteen or nineteen years old, stood by Corey's side. She had long, black hair that reached midway down her back, and she had oval shaped, dark brown eyes and tan skin, a shade or two darker than most people in the Hinterlands.

The girl locked eyes with Realta. A strange tattoo, a circle with eight lines radiating from the center, like spokes on a wheel, adorned her left cheek. It was eerily similar to the tattoo worn by the Cuchasi in East Bridge. Was she a Cuchasi, too? The girl jumped, as though startled by a loud noise, and turned away.

"Just be grateful he did. Come along." Shasta led Realta to their wagon. The merchant caravan had already hitched up their horses, and the lead wagons started down the road. Too bad Corey wasn't leaving with them. "Might as well make our guests feel welcomed," Shasta continued. "As unwelcomed as they may be."

2

Proposals

Lok sat quietly in the hidden alcove above the Council Chamber. He was supposed to be at martial arts class right now, but Scholar Tell had introduced a new fighting style yesterday: unarmed versus armed. Lok understood the practicality of the lesson. Not every fight was fair. Students had to learn how to use their opponent's advantages against them.

Except Lok did not want to fight.

During his turn, Lok allowed his armed opponent to knock him down. And when their roles were reversed, Lok immediately dropped his quarterstaff, allowing Paul, who was both shorter and skinner than him, to tackle him to the ground.

And no amount of yelling on Scholar Tell's part motivated Lok to actually try.

"He is really pissed off at you," Zandon told Lok after class. Zandon had embraced the lesson as naturally as a bird learning to fly. That made perfect sense. Zandon was preparing to leave for the Garrison soon. He needed to learn in order to defend Teyrnas.

Lok honestly didn't care if Scholar Tell was angry. He was at the Academy to study history and master his Thane ability, not to learn how to fight.

The Premier Scholar entered the Chamber, the doors gliding open and shut without a sound. All sixteen members directed their attention towards her.

Since the coup two months ago, the Council and the nobility transformed the Academy into a new capital in all but name. Queen Isla attended meetings several times. Lok always tried to watch, even if it meant skipping one or two classes. Those meeting, however, were growing infrequent. The Queen of Teyrnas had a lot on her plate, in addition to mourning her husband, King

Logan. Lok was grateful not to be in her shoes.

"Scholar Iosaph, what are the current troop movements?" the Premier Scholar asked. Though her voice was strong, she slouched in her seat.

Scholar Iosaph stood. His white cloak was trimmed with purple. An Empath.

Lok frowned. Scholar Koranic held the Empath's seat. He had been absent during the last two meetings, but Lok assumed he was taking a break or busy with other tasks. Perhaps the Scholar was ill. Or maybe Koranic had stepped down. A lot of Scholars had suspended classes due to stress. But if that were the case, why hadn't the Council made an announcement?

"The armies of Bran Maro are now stationed along the Wallach River, threatening to cut off the road to Norgard. Tirshay positioned its army between the Academy and Teyrnas, slowing down the movement of refugees. As for Nowan's army, the soldiers are deployed in and around the capital."

The Scholars murmured, too softly to be overheard.

"What of Tarod and Galion?" the Premier asked.

"Unknown Premier." Iosaph paused. "Information from soldiers is spotty, and three of our Deirow Hawks were lost."

The Premier drummed her fingers on her chair and asked, "What are the latest numbers for refugees?"

Scholar Catrinna, a woman with no Thane ability, stood and removed several sheets of paper from a portfolio. Clearing her throat, she said, "Guards have recorded one hundred and seven refugees in the last full week. Sixty-eight were moved to camps in Norgard while the other thirty-nine were placed in the Academy camps."

Countless tents dotted the Academy's green space, inhabited by refugees who had nowhere else to go. At first, the Scholars forced Students and Journeymen to double up in order to make room. Lok did not mind, since it meant sharing his room with Jaim. But then they had to triple up, and very few Scholars still had private rooms. Many complained, but the Premier and Queen Isla quickly put a stop to it. If they did not like sharing their rooms, perhaps they would prefer sleeping in a tent while a refugee family lived there instead. Surprisingly, a handful of Scholars volunteered to give up their rooms, believing this crisis was far more important than their personal comfort.

Lok now lived with Jaim and Gareth Haar. Gareth had arrived at the Academy with Queen Isla, a handful of nobles, and all the palace servants. It took a few weeks for Gareth to adjust to the new environment, and he outright refused to talk about the coup, always lapsing into silence for hours, sometimes a day or two. Lok didn't blame him, not after seeing haunted looks on countless refugees.

And more refugees arrived each day. Some came from the capital and many others from the small farming villages surrounding Teyrnas. Coalition soldiers burned down the houses while leaving the growing crops for themselves.

What would happen after the Academy and Norgard ran out of room? Where would everyone else go?

The Premier processed the numbers. "How many of them possess a trade?"

Scholar Catrinna turned to another page. "Of those at the Academy, two are carpenters, five are seamstresses, four are bakers, and the rest are children. Fourteen of them arrived unaccompanied."

The Premier let out a heavy sigh. "Very well. Put the adults to work and find adequate shelter for the children. What of the Garrison?"

Scholar Osian, the one who had given Lok his earring during the Thane Ceremony, stood. "Recruitment levels are still high, mostly from refugees. But there aren't enough weapons to distribute to everyone. The blacksmiths are working around the clock, trying to fill quotas. Unfortunately, they're running out of supplies."

"Can they convert farm equipment?" asked Scholar Jori.

Osian shook his head. "If we do that, there won't be enough tools for the harvest this autumn. And with additional people, we cannot afford to waste unharvested food."

"What of Madan Och?" the Premier asked, tilting her head to the side. "Have their supply ships arrived?"

"Representatives from the Tribal Council are scheduled to arrive today, Premier, but with the Marish army stationed along the

Wallach…" Osian shrugged.

"Send word to the Garrison," the Premier replied after a silent moment. "Have Teyrnian soldiers escort them, waving a gray flag. The Marish might respect the Madani's neutrality. Have archers stationed at the North Gate, just in case."

"Yes, Premier Scholar." Osian took a seat.

"I will now open the floor to proposals," the Premier announced.

Scholar Sorcha proposed converting the natural science labs into armories, allowing Scholars and Journeymen to develop new weapons. The proposal contained one caveat: the lack of supplies. Supplies that routinely arrived from the capital before the war erupted.

Lok thought it was a good idea. He had studied a lot of dangerous chemicals in Scholar Dyson's class, and some of them exploded when combined.

"Be extremely careful," Dyson had instructed the class when they were working with acids. "If the acid touches your skin, tell me immediately." The Scholar then explained how acids ate away a person's flesh and often caused permanent damage.

A shiver ran down Lok's spine, imagining soldiers using acid on the battlefield. Perhaps it wasn't a good idea.

Scholar Rose, a Manipulate of middling ability, then proposed securing the walls in case the Coalition violated the Neutrality Law and attacked the Academy. The Scholars debated at length, some agreeing with Rose and others claiming that the Coalition would never break the centuries-old law. The Premier shelved the proposal when she saw they were getting nowhere fast.

Scholar Domhnall's proposal called for Students to aid refugees during their free hours, distributing food and basic supplies. The Council quickly voted in favor. Lok smiled, knowing that Charity would readily volunteer.

Scholar Lucan then stood. "I propose we use Thanes as a primary defense of the Academy and Norgard."

Uneasy murmurs echoed throughout the Chamber. The Premier fixed Lucan with a steely glare.

"The primary purpose of this Academy is to educate Thanes," she said. "Part of that education is teaching them how to use their abilities without causing harm. Do you suggest we abandon a tradition that goes back to the founding of the first Academy?"

"All due respect, Premier, but unless we take drastic actions, there won't be an Academy." Lucan paused, allowing the words to sink in. "The Eastern Coalition has already occupied Teyrnas, Hygate, and a dozen smaller cities along the Highway and the Wallach River. How many more people must die before we face facts?

"The Gadyeni gave Thanes their abilities in order to fight," Lucan continued, addressing the entire Council. "Manipulators to launch arrows. Farsights to view enemy movements hours in advance. Elementals."

Lok's heart skipped a beat. He leaned forward, pressing his face against the peephole.

"For three hundred years," Lucan said, "we believed Elementals were extinct. But the Creator and His Gadyeni have blessed us with perhaps the only Elemental left on Eltriar. Lok Tolman."

"Lok Tolman is only seventeen," Scholar Jori chimed in. "A year younger than fighting age."

Lucan fixed him with an icy glare. "Do you think the Eastern Coalition cares? You heard Scholar Catrinna. Fourteen unaccompanied children arrived at the Academy last week. Fourteen orphans of war. How many orphans were unable to escape? How many were shot with arrows as they fled? How many were run down by Nowani cavalry?"

"You've made your point," Jori snapped. He then hung his head. A heaviness descended on the Chamber.

"I propose we use the strongest Thanes among us, both Scholar, Journeyman, and Student, to aid in the war. And Lok Tolman, with his ability to control fire, is an asset we cannot afford to ignore.

"And don't discount him based on his age," he turned to the Premier. "Over the last two months, Tolman has showed remarkable improvement in his Thane ability. Scholar Kuno has proven himself an apt teacher. Tolman, according to Kuno's reports, hasn't so much as sparked a candle by accident in weeks."

"Your proposal has been noted," said the Premier. She steepled her fingers. "I will pass it along to Queen Isla this evening. In the meantime, print announcements asking for Journeymen and Scholar recruits. I will not have anyone pressed into fighting. I suggest using Scholar Kuno as an intermediary when approaching Tolman. You know how attached the boy is to his mentor."

Lok leaned against the wall. His heart pounded frantically, and an icy cold sweat coated his forehead, chest, and back. Fire and smoke, it felt like someone had dumped a bucket of freezing water over his head!

No, I don't want to be a weapon. I don't want to fight anyone!

A bell chimed the hour. The meeting quickly adjourned with a few closing words from the Premier.

Shaking all over, Lok replaced the peephole cover and half walked, half stumbled down the narrow staircase. He felt like he was going to be sick. How could Scholar Lucan propose such a thing? Thanes were protectors, not weapons. Lok did not want to fight people!

He reached the base of the stairs and slowly cracked open the hidden door. The last few Scholars exited the Chamber.

"I don't like it," said Scholar Jori, shaking his head. "Tolman is just a boy. I don't care how powerful or rare he is."

"I hate this, too," said Scholar Osian. "But we're fighting one against five. We…"

Scholar Lucan walked by, giving each Scholar a nod. Both returned the favor, Jori putting on a polite smile.

Once Lucan was at the main staircase, Scholar Jori dropped the smile and muttered, "Jackass."

"Yeah, but he's a jackass with a point."

"You honestly don't think Tolman will go along with this, do you? Tell says the boy is a complete pain to teach. Only listens to Kuno."

"I'm not talking about Tolman."

Jori's eyes went wide. "Osian, you aren't…"

"What choice do I have? I'm a Minder and an Empath, and my niece is here. I'm going to volunteer."

"But you're fifty-one years old!" Jori looked at him aghast.

Osian sighed and placed a gentle hand on Jori's shoulder. "We all have to do what we think is best." He walked down the stairs. Jori followed on his heels, trying to talk Osian out of it, but the

Scholar would not be swayed.

Lok cautiously stepped into the empty hallway. He thought over Osian's words. Fighting in the war was best for him, but what was best for Lok?

He recalled the promise he had made to Brother Malaky during his reprimand. He had sworn to learn and to do better.

I don't want to hurt anybody.

Lok squeezed his eyes shut and tried to think. The Premier or Queen Isla could reject Lucan's proposal, but if either approved, the Scholars were going to use Kuno to persuade him.

Only one course of action then.

He had to find Kuno first.

3
Numbers

Charity turned to a blank page in her notebook as Scholar Lyle walked into the classroom, a weighty textbook in his hands. Placing the book on the desk, he turned to their current chapter and wrote a series of equations on the blackboard.

A handful of Students groaned.

Charity smiled. At first, she hated algebra. Letters combined with numbers in a confusing mess. But as they progressed, patterns emerged. Instead of causing a headache, each problem was now a welcomed challenge, a puzzle waiting to be solved.

"Any volunteers?" Scholar Lyle asked the class. A few timid hands raised. The Scholar selected three.

Charity glanced over at Gareth. He, along with the royal family, several nobles, and scores of servants, arrived at the Academy two months ago. A few days after the Eastern Coalition had taken over Teyrnas. It was another couple of days before he and Charity reunited. He had been lost in the shuffle of entrance exams, class schedules, and housing arrangements. Things he did not want to do, but Isla insisted that he attend classes while here.

The boy nearly broke down when Charity asked about Kel, Realta, and Callum. They were supposed to arrive shortly after the royal household. But days turned into weeks, and then months. And still they heard no word.

And the bad news did not end there. Queen Gallia Toutain of Nowan had assassinated King Logan during the coup. Charity did not want to believe it, but Queen Isla confirmed the rumors. The people of Teyrnas had lost their king.

Gareth refused to talk about the coup, but slowly, she and Lok coaxed out his account.

"We went to the tunnels," Gareth said quietly, picking at the hem of his cloak. "No one had seen... had seen him, so Father went to look. Told me to stay with Isla, that I could trust her. Then Gregor caught up with us. He said…" Gareth paused. Charity waited for him to continue. "He said the king was dead. Gallia and her messenger killed him."

Chills went down Charity's spine. To think she had stood right next to the woman!

A few days later, Gareth confided in her and Lok that he was a Cuchasi, confirming once again the green lights surrounding Lok.

"We have to tell the Scholars!" Charity exclaimed, but Gareth begged her to keep it a secret. He was just a half Hiraethi boy from the Hinterlands who worked in the palace stables before arriving at the Academy. Nothing more, nothing less.

Gareth stared out the classroom window, one hand propping up his chin. He looked just like Kel. The light blue Student cloak was wrapped tightly over his shoulders despite the summer warmth.

Charity poked his arm.

"What?" he asked, startled.

"You should answer one." Charity gestured towards the blackboard. The three Students had solved their equations and Scholar Lyle was asking for another set of volunteers.

Gareth shook his head, shrinking down in his seat. Not that it did much good. He was almost as tall as Callum now.

"But you're good at math."

"So?"

"Charity and Gareth," Scholar Lyle said, smirking, "since neither of you need to pay attention, would you care to solve these equations?" He pointed at the board with a piece of chalk.

"Yes, Scholar." Charity went to the board. Her equation included material they had learned yesterday. Squared and cubed variables. Those needed to be done first. Nodding to herself, she started working.

"Gareth?"

Charity glanced over her shoulder. Gareth remained in his seat. His usually ruddy face was pale. Every eye in the room slowly turned towards him.

"Please solve this equation."

Gareth shook his head.

Scholar Lyle sighed. He was generally a patient man, but even the most patient people had their limits. "You will not receive full credit for the course if you don't participate."

"I don't care," Gareth whispered, so quietly that Charity barely heard him.

"You should. Isn't natural science your area of study? You need to learn math in order to properly study science."

Charity finished her equation. She double checked it, solving it backwards, a technique that Kel had taught her and her sisters. Yep, x equaled three. She returned to her seat. Gareth stared at the table, his shoulders rigid and his black hair hiding his face.

"Um, I can solve it, Scholar Lyle," volunteered Marshalee, an Empath Thane with a purple earring.

"No, this is Gareth's equation." The Scholar fixed him with a level gaze. "Gareth, please—"

"Five!" he shouted. "The answer is five!"

Charity stared at Gareth wide-eyed. She had never heard him raise his voice before. Several Students whispered to one another.

"Yes, that's correct," Scholar Lyle said slowly. "Would you please come up and show the class—"

"No!" Gareth started trembling. He pulled his cloak tighter around his shoulders, running his fingers along the hemline.

"Okay." Scholar Lyle sighed and rubbed his forehead. "Bethany, please solve this equation. Make sure to show all the steps."

Bethany did so without a word. Step by step, Charity saw how x equaled five, but how had Gareth solved it so quickly? It was the hardest one on the board.

"How did you do that?" Charity whispered. Had he inherited his father's gift for numbers?

Gareth did not respond. He remained in a hunched position for the rest of the class.

The bell rang, signaling the end of the final class period, and the Students hurried out of the room. Some had to attend study sessions with their mentors or work on assignments. Charity's only assignments were to read a chapter in her anatomy textbook and study for an Old Eltrian short exam. Two tasks that would take less than an hour.

She exited the class, a lightness to her steps.

"Gareth, a moment," Scholar Lyle said. Charity glanced back and saw Gareth standing frozen in the doorway, trembling as though a gust of icy wind had blown past him.

"I'll wait right here," Charity assured him.

Gareth just stood there.

"You're great at algebra," Scholar Lyle told him. "Why are you so reluctant to show that?"

Gareth shrugged.

The Scholar noticed Charity and motioned for her to come closer. "You grew up together, right?"

"Yes, Scholar," Charity replied.

"Has Gareth always been a good student?"

"Yeah. His father was my tutor, and Master Kel was very good at math, too."

"Is good." Gareth glared at her. "My father is good at math. Stop saying was!"

Charity blinked. Gareth never lashed out. Not even when he was angry. Most times, he was too nervous or afraid to speak, causing some people in Vala to believe he was mute. Softening her voice, Charity said, "You know I didn't mean it like that."

Tears glistened in Gareth's eyes. He squeezed them shut. "Father promised he would be here. He promised..." He gripped the edges of his cloak.

Charity almost placed a hand on his shoulder, but she stopped. Gareth never liked being touched, even when he was in a good mood.

"His father is traveling from the Hinterlands?" Scholar Lyle whispered to her, confused.

Charity quietly told him that Gareth and Kel had been in Teyrnas during the coup. Gareth made it out safely, but they hadn't heard from Kel in months.

Scholar Lyle sighed. "I suggest taking him to a chaplain. The Creator knows they have their hands full these days, but it won't hurt."

Charity thanked him and noticed that they were alone. "Gareth?"

A piece of blue fabric disappeared behind a corner. Charity

sprinted down the hallway, catching up with Gareth as he turned another corner.

"Leave me alone." Gareth kept his eyes fixed on the floor.

"I just want to help. Maybe you should talk to a chaplain."

"No." Gareth walked faster.

"But—"

"I want to be alone!" Gareth snapped.

"No, you don't."

"Charity—"

"You want Kel."

Gareth froze. Tears welled in his eyes, threatening to overflow.

"I know Kel and Esme always helped you when you…" How to phrase this? "When you didn't feel well around people. They're a lot better at it than me. I guess they just knew, being your parents. They sat down with you someplace quiet or told you a story. Something to take your mind off what was bothering you. Would either of those things help you now?"

Gareth was quiet for a minute. Then two, then three. A group of Students walked by, including Evelyn. She and Charity waved to each other.

"Someplace quiet," Gareth said once Evelyn and the others were gone.

Charity smiled. "Great. We can go…"

Gareth shook his head. "By myself."

"Are you sure? Jaim and Lok are probably at the library by now. Maybe…"

"I will see them and you later. I want to be alone. Please."

Charity relented and gave him a smile. "Very well, Master Cuchasi."

Gareth jolted, as though he had touched Scholar Maryn's lightning device. He glanced furtively around the empty hall.

Charity laughed quietly.

"That's not funny." Strangely, the Academy had no way of testing whether a person was a Cuchasi. They didn't have Auras, and even the other Cuchasi were ignorant of Gareth's ability. It was as though they were invisible.

"Just promise me you won't be truly alone. Go somewhere you can see other people."

Gareth looked at her as though she had dared him to eat raw fish coated in castor oil. "No."

"Then promise to show me how you solved that equation in your head." Scholar Lyle required them to show their work, but Gareth's method would help her solve problems twice as fast.

"It's easy. Just look at the numbers."

"Well, that explains a lot," she replied sarcastically.

"My father is the tutor, not me."

"Valid point."

Gareth glanced around the hallway once more and gave Charity a quick hug.

"What was that for?" Gareth had never hugged her or Realta. In fact, he ran away every time they tried to hug him!

"For trying to help," he said, staring at the floor. "I know you miss your family, too."

Fresh tears stung Charity's eyes. She had only received one letter from her parents since arriving at the Academy. They were worried sick and feared the worst when Callum's letter described how she and Lok were separated after Kanton attacked them. But they were relieved that she and Lok were safe. They hoped to hear from her soon.

The letter arrived a week before the war started. She wrote to her parents several times, but she doubted the letters got farther than Teyrnas. She prayed that her family was safe, that the war would not reach the Hinterlands.

Charity wiped a stray tear away and realized that she was alone. Gareth disappeared again!

"How on Eltriar does he do that?"

4

A Crown of Silver

Queen Isla wiped her sweaty palms on her dress. Two months of meetings. Two months of speaking with nobles, Scholars, and various diplomats and representatives. And she still got nervous. She'd had plenty of responsibilities as queen, and all her tutors had prepared her for the royal court and politics, both foreign and domestic, but Logan had always been by her side. Not necessarily as a source of comfort, but as someone who she knew she could rely on.

Her hands somewhat drier, she read over the documents. Premier Scholar Emera and representatives from Madan Och would arrive in a few minutes with the latest updates on the Eastern Coalition's movements and, hopefully, a way to aid the countless civilians.

A sharp knock sounded at the door. Isla bid them to enter. Una Benet, her personal scribe, and Gregor Pym, the palace's stable master, stepped inside and took their places in the small room. Formally a Scholar's room, it had just enough space for a bed, wardrobe, writing desk, shelves, and a private bath. Two small cots for Morgan and Mannix lined the far wall. The boys originally had their own room, just down the hall. But constant nightmares drove them to Isla every night. She moved their cots into her room a half week after their arrival.

Una sat at the desk on Isla's right. Gregor Pym, wringing his hands, remained by the door.

"Perhaps I can just show them in this time?" Gregor suggested.

"Nonsense. You and Una are my advisers."

"But, your Majesty, I'm just—"

Isla cut him off. "Master Pym, you have earned this position. Please sit."

Gregor did so, sitting on Isla's left.

Not a minute later, one of the Academy's guards, a man named Tyson who always had a Deirow Hawk on his shoulder, opened the door. "Your Majesty, the representatives are here."

Isla quickly smoothed down her dress and placed her crown, a simple gold circlet, over her auburn hair. It felt wrong to wear Logan's crown, but who else would wear it if not her? "Show them in."

Duke Rafael Margents, Isla's younger cousin who had arrived from Byyar a half week ago, entered first. The gangly teenager had transformed into a lean, capable nobleman in her absence. With his auburn hair neatly combed back, he looked just like King Nolfri.

Next entered the three Madani representatives: Agust, Ulfor, and Elinya. All three sat on the bed. Some sort of hospitality rule that Isla had only halfway puzzled out. The two men wore traditional brown and green hunting clothes, while Elinya wore a blue and white dress in the same style worn by Teyrnian noblewomen. All three then presented Isla with hunting knives, hilt first. She accepted each one with a short bow and placed them under her chair, acknowledging that they were here in peace.

Finally, the Premier Scholar entered and sat down opposite Isla. The two guards escorting her waited outside the door.

Isla shuddered as a bloodied axe appeared over the Premier's head.

"Is everything all right, Queen Isla?" the Premier asked.

"Nothing has been all right since the war began," she replied diplomatically. The bloodied axe obviously symbolized death. But whose death? The Premier's? Or was she about to send people to their deaths like an executioner?

At least I didn't scream.

Collecting herself, Isla said, "Premier Scholar, would you inform us of today's Council meeting?"

"I will speak last."

Isla hoped to hear the report first. "Um, very well. Duke Margents, how soon will soldiers arrive from Byyar?"

"Half of our units are a week out. King Nolfri ordered half to sail to Norgard along the Wallach River. They will transport extra supplies and reinforcements."

"And the other half?"

"About two full weeks. They're marching south, crossing the Nerin River near the confluence with the Mallr River. They plan to attack the Eastern Coalition from the south before heading north."

Isla nodded, thinking. Ten days until the first group, twenty for the second. If they both arrived on schedule. If nothing delayed one group, or both groups. If, if, if. Too many ifs.

So far, none of the fighting affected the Academy directly. Academies were neutral territory. One had not been attacked in centuries. But how much longer would the Coalition honor their neutrality? She expected little honor from the woman who murdered her husband.

"And the reinforcements from Madan Och?" Isla asked.

Elinya spoke for the group. "Settlements closest to the Wallach River have been asked for volunteers. We will not force anyone to fight in *your* war." The Madani clearly stated that these reinforcements would aid civilians at the Academy and Norgard. And they would only fight in cases of self-defense. "As of yesterday, we have approximately five thousand men and women."

Isla blinked. Had she heard that correctly? "Five thousand?"

Elinya frowned. "Is that number insufficient?"

"No. It's more than I hoped for." Five thousand recruited from villages? She knew Madan Och covered a wide territory, about as large as Teyrnas and Nowan combined, but it was mainly composed of nomadic villages. A mere handful of traditional cities existed and only for trade. "When will they arrive?"

Elinya exchanged a few words with Ulfor in Madani, speaking too quickly for most linguists to understand. She then addressed Isla, "Normally, they could sail here in a half week, but Eastern armies are posted along the river. Several scouts were killed. A large group will only be able to move swiftly at night. We estimate ten to fifteen days."

Isla nodded gravely. Help was on the way, but what happened if it arrived too late? How would she keep her people safe?

"Premier Scholar, I'd like to hear about the Council meeting now."

"Yes, your Majesty. The Council reached a decision this morning," she said, her voice sharp and clear. "We will ask Thane Journeymen and Scholars to volunteer, both on the front lines and as reserves. If the fighting reaches the Academy, we should be able to defend ourselves until the Madani and Byyarian forces arrive. We only need your approval, your Majesty."

"How many of them have fighting experience?" All the Scholars Isla had met were bookish types who likely had never raised a fist, let alone a sword. How were they supposed to fight trained soldiers?

"They will use their Thane abilities to fight."

Rafael shot to his feet. "You can't be serious. Every Thane at the Byyarian Academy swears an oath of nonviolence. You cannot allow Thanes to use their abilities as weapons!"

"Normally, I would not. But never have five kingdoms allied together to destroy one. That is why it is volunteer only. Queen Isla?"

Suddenly, all eyes were on her. Isla looked from face to face. The Madani representatives wore expressionless masks, while Una and Gregor looked at her expectantly. And Rafael... Her younger cousin looked as though she alone held the power to free or damn him.

"I need time to discuss this matter with my advisers."

Rafael breathed a sigh of relief and sat back down.

The Premier stared at her. What Isla wouldn't give to be a Minder for just ten seconds. Just long enough to know this woman's true thoughts. "Very well. You have twenty-four hours."

Twenty-four hours? For such an important, possibly historical, decision? "Well, actually—"

The Premier rose. "I expect a definitive answer no later. Too many lives hang in the balance, Your Majesty."

"You think I don't know that?" Fresh tears stung her eyes. She bit down on her tongue, fighting back the tears. *You can cry all you want in private*, her mother had said, *but never in public*.

Logan, I wish you were here.

"Good day, Your Majesty, and may the Creator guide you." The Premier left, escorted by her two guards.

The Madani representatives stood. Isla returned their knives, handing them back hilt first. The three sheathed the knives, bowed deeply, and left the room, Agust and Ulfor following Elinya.

Rafael gave Isla's hand a small, reassuring squeeze before leaving. For all the young man had changed physically, his good heart remained the same. At least Isla could count on one thing not changing.

The door opened again. Isla glanced up, thinking Rafael had forgotten something, but instead, it was Gareth Haar, Carwyn's son. The boy studied her with Esme Haar's dark brown eyes.

Isla gave him a weak smile. "Oh, Morgan and Mannix aren't here right now, Gareth."

"I don't want to see them. I want to be alone but with people." Gareth frowned, his eyebrows knitting together, and shook his head. "I don't completely know what that means, but Charity said it will be good for me."

"You are always welcome here, Gareth," Isla said. She felt something wet on her cheek and wiped it away. A single tear.

"Did you have a Farsight?" Una asked, opening her small notebook.

Isla almost told her about the bloodied axe but decided against it. She had seen too much blood this year. "No, Una. Feel free to take the rest of the day off."

"Are you sure, Your Majesty?" Una asked nervously. Relocating to the Academy had thrown the poor woman completely off. Not only did she have to memorize a brand-new layout, but she had to share it with a thousand other people. Far more than she was comfortable with.

"Of course," Isla replied with a smile. "I'm sure Amzie would love to see you."

"Yes. Of course." Una collected her notebook and pen and quietly left the room.

Isla rested her head on the desk, and the tears began to flow. Silent ones, thank the Creator. Morale was low enough. The people did not need to hear their queen sobbing.

A gentle hand rested on her shoulder. She glanced up and saw Gregor by her side. She had meant to dismiss him, too, but she was glad he was here.

"I miss him, too," Gregor whispered. "He could be a real pain in the ass sometimes, but he had a good head for these types of things. I know he really cared about you."

Cared. But not loved. Tried as they might, Isla and Logan never grew to love one another, not the way a married couple should. The price of a political marriage.

Isla blinked away the tears. She was too busy to cry now.

She spied Gareth standing by the window, gazing at the clouds. Images materialized around him. A hawk, a Deirow Hawk, judging by the white-tipped wings, rested on his right shoulder. A dagger appeared on his belt. And finally, a thin circle of silver rested over his black hair. The crown of a firstborn. Isla blinked, and the images disappeared.

"What do you see when you look at him, Gregor?" Isla whispered.

"I see Carwyn in his face, and Esme in his eyes." Gregor lowered his voice. "I see a boy who should be a prince."

"What if he had been a prince? How well do you think he would have fared?"

Gregor sighed. "I honestly don't know. I knew a boy like him growing up. Rarely talked. And he always acted strange around people, even folks he'd known his whole life. His..." Gregor cleared his throat. "His parents sent him to an asylum when he was sixteen. They tried to teach him a trade, but he either got scared or frustrated, no matter who they apprenticed him to. And the healer couldn't fix him. They didn't know what else to do."

Isla's heart ached. She could not bear to think of Carwyn and Esme's son being locked away.

She cleared her throat and said, "Gareth, how was your day?"

"Fine." He continued to stare out the window. A hawk flew across the sky, soaring on a gust of wind.

"You have four classes, right? Do you like them?"

"I hate Lowyrnic. Biology and algebra are okay. They put me in drawing. I don't know why. Callum can draw."

"Yes, I saw his drawings. Your uncle is very talented."

"Callum was a mountain guide. He knows all about plants and animals..." Gareth's voice choked off. He rested his elbows on the window ledge and wrapped his blue cloak around himself.

"Can you draw me a picture?" Isla asked.

Gareth shrugged.

"Maybe you and I can visit the stables," Gregor suggested. The man had always felt more at home with animals than with nobles and was depressed for a week after the Academy refused to let him work there. Isla promoted him to royal adviser, hoping to raise his spirits. "Biology is studying animals, right? Horses are animals."

"Your cousin is purple with gold sparks," Gareth said quietly. "The Premier is gold. One of the Madani men, the shorter one, is silver, but the lights are small. Not like Ivar. His lights are stronger. Do you think I should tell the Scholars that I'm a Cuchasi? Charity thinks so."

Isla didn't know how to respond. She never heard Gareth say so much at once. She went to the boy's side and was surprised by his height. Midway between his father and uncle's heights.

Outside, the sun blazed in the clear blue sky. Large, white clouds moved lazily across the expanse, as though nothing at all was wrong with the world. A Deirow Hawk flew from one gate post to another. And a mass of tents dominated the ground below.

"What do you think, Gareth?"

"I know what I think. I'm asking you."

Isla chose her next words carefully. "The Academy is always eager to find new Cuchasi. I know it will make the Scholars happy. But you will receive a lot of attention once they know. Attention is something you try to avoid."

"Do you think Kel will be proud if I tell the truth?"

"Yes, I think he will." Will, not would. Isla had made the mistake of speaking about Carwyn in the past tense, and Gareth broke down sobbing. Days passed before the boy spoke to her again.

Gareth nodded. "Can I be at your next meeting? I promise not to talk."

"I don't see why not. The Premier might not care for a random Student listening in, however."

"I'm not a random Student. I'm your nephew." Gareth immediately turned pale. He glanced around the room furtively, eyes wide like a deer cornered by a hunter. "I..." He ran his fingers along the hem of his cloak. "What would people do if they learned that truth?"

A pit formed in Isla's gut. Officially, Prince Carwyn O'Kelwyn was dead. If people discovered that he had run away to live under an assumed name, all manner of chaos could break loose.

Questions regarding House Kelwyn's role in the scheme. The legitimacy of Logan's reign. Inheritance disputes. A whole mess of legal trouble. Since Carwyn never abdicated, Logan's title could be taken away, and…

Logan is dead.

A shadow fell over her heart. The king was dead. The truth could not hurt him, but what about Carwyn? Chances were he was still in Teyrnas. Any rumors regarding him could put him in further jeopardy. And she had to consider Esme, Gareth, and Estrid. Revealing the truth might endanger them. More than a few nobles had been vocal about Isla's ability, or rather inability, to rule, wondering if another House should vie for the throne. If any of them learned about Gareth…

"I think that truth should be kept a secret."

Gareth nodded and relaxed. "Do you really want me to draw you a picture?"

"If you want."

The boy walked over to the desk, selected a blank sheet of paper and a pen, and sketched. The lines took shape, revealing the Academy's walls and the tents on the green in perfect detail.

Isla watched as the silver crown reappeared on Gareth's head. She reached up and touched the crown on her own head. A new weight settled on her shoulders. Not only must she protect her people and lead Teyrnas to victory, but she also had to protect Teyrnas' true crown prince.

5
Truth

Lok trudged down the hallway to his room, completely exhausted. He had searched the entire Academy for Scholar Kuno. Classrooms, the library, the sprawling tents that covered the grounds from wall to wall.

He almost ran into Scholar Lucan. The Scholar, his dark eyebrows knitted together and scowling, stormed down the hall, muttering under his breath. Lok ducked into an empty classroom, his heart in his throat, and watched the Scholar through the cracked door. Lucan's pace didn't slow for an instant, thank the Creator.

What would have happened if Lucan saw him? Would he have recruited Lok without giving him a choice?

Lok pushed open his bedroom door, fully expecting to see Gareth and Jaim. The other boys no doubt would have questions for him. Questions he honestly did not feel like answering, not until he had a few minutes to rest.

Instead, he saw Scholar Kuno. Lok took two quick steps towards him, but then he saw several notebooks and papers strewn across his bed. Kuno stared daggers at him. Lok froze.

"Close the door," Kuno said, his voice low and harsh.

Lok did so. Why was Kuno glaring at him? He had never seen the Scholar look so angry.

"Did you skip classes again?" Kuno stalked towards Lok.

Lok jolted, pressing his back against the door. He quickly nodded.

Kuno sneered and turned away, resting his hands on Lok's desk. The dark circle where Lok had accidentally burned a candle too brightly marred on the smooth surface. Taking deep breaths, Kuno slowly faced Lok. "How many times have you lied to me?"

Lok stared at him, confused. He hadn't lied. He told the truth about skipping class. Lok took out his pencil and notebook, turning to a blank page.

"Answer. The question. Now."

Lok nearly dropped his notebook. He met Kuno's gaze and shuddered. The Scholar was absolutely furious, anger radiating off him like heat from the sun. And Lok had no idea why. He tried to ask, but the letters were illegible scribbles.

Kuno grabbed a book off the bed and shoved it in Lok's face. "Do you know what this is?"

Lok's heart skipped a beat. Dane Kanton's notebook. But Lok had hidden it underneath his mattress. How had Kuno found it?

"I want the truth, Lok Tolman. Why do you have a notebook belonging to a Captain of the King's Guard? And don't tell me you just happened to find it. The last entry is dated a half week before you arrived at the Academy. Around the time you claimed Kanton was passing through your village."

Kuno's face contorted in mock confusion. "Oh no. That's wrong. Charity says you and her were separated from your friends when Kanton attacked you. But she never explained why. Is this why? Did you steal this book from him?"

Lok was aghast. Steal? He had never stolen anything in his life! He turned to a blank page, trying to write, but no words came. That night was a blur, a half-remembered nightmare.

Kuno flung Kanton's notebook onto the floor. The sound echoed like thunder. "I have risked everything for you! Do you think the Scholars will overlook this because your Thane ability has improved? Do you? Because I guarantee they won't. Four reprimands in one semester. That has got to be a record! Do you want to go down in history as the first Student to be expelled via reprimands in one semester?"

Lok stood frozen. He never realized Kuno could get this angry. The Scholar had always been so patient, always willing to listen to Lok's side of the story. Even when Lok accidentally burned down a tavern, Kuno had not been angry, only disappointed and scared for Lok's safety.

And everyone else's safety.

Perhaps Kuno had only been lenient because the injuries were minor. How would he react if Lok told the truth? Kanton and his cronies attacked them in the middle of the night for reasons unknown, and Lok responded by shoving a man into a fire.

His blood turned to ice, the memory unfolding as though it had been last night. Lok awoke to screaming. Kanton and Callum Haar were fighting. Realta ran to help the thief. Charity stood frozen by the horses. The other three guards surrounded them. Two had their swords drawn, and the guardswoman ran towards Charity, ordering her to get away from the horses. One man ran towards Lok, ready to strike. Lok shoved him away, and the man fell into the fire.

No, that was wrong. Lok planned to shove him, just pushing hard enough so he could get away, but the fire came alive and leapt onto the man's back, eating away his clothes and hair. And skin. The man screamed and ran straight into Kanton, sending both men to the ground. Kanton got up again, but the other man... The second guardsman tried to help him, but the man stopped screaming. He didn't even move...

Oh Great Creator, did Lok kill him?

Kuno was yelling at him. A string of incoherent noises. A shiver ran down Lok's spine, and sounds returned to normal.

"Answer me!" Kuno glared at Lok, seething.

A single thought appeared in Lok's mind. The reason he was searching for his mentor, the reason he was so afraid to remember that horrible night.

"They want to use me as a weapon," he quickly wrote.

Kuno read the words. He slowly reached out and took the notebook, reading them again. He looked like he was going to be sick. "Who wants to use you as a weapon?"

Lok sat at his desk and wrote about Lucan's proposal, his fingers shaking. Kuno sat next to him and read as he wrote. Lok's hand and fingers hurt by the time he was done. The room felt unnaturally cold.

"Damn them to the Abyss. Lok, I'm so sorry." Kuno sighed heavily. "I will confront Lucan and—"

Lok grabbed Kuno's arm, signaling him to stop. He wrote, *"No. If you know, then Lucan will suspect that I was eavesdropping. They will discover the hidden room."*

"You're right." Kuno was silent for a long moment. "We will

have to wait until this is made public and then confront Lucan or go over his head and speak to the Premier. She's busier than ever these days, but... Hmm." Kuno stood and paced along the narrow space between the beds. "You can always refuse. Not even the Garrison forces people to fight."

A thought occurred to Lok. *"They cannot force me to fight if they cannot find me."*

Kuno stopped pacing and folded his hands behind his back. "Explain."

Lok took a moment to gather his thoughts. The idea had crossed his mind a few times, but he never seriously considered it. Not until now. *"What if we go to Vala? It's safe in the Hinterlands, right? We can hide there for a little while."*

Kuno sighed. "Honestly, Lok, I don't think it would be for a little while. This war is going to get much worse before it ends."

Lok frowned. *"How do you know?"*

"Most wars follow a pattern. They start off small. One side declares war on the other side. Then, the fighting begins. Career soldiers only. But then each side experiences casualties. They call in reserves. Sometimes, civilians are called to fight. And when it gets to that point, those civilians don't have a choice. I don't want that happening to you.

"If we go to Vala, it will be to stay. No coming back in a month or two. We will be there for the long haul. Is this what you really want, Lok?"

Lok thought of the armies surrounding Teyrnas, of the fighting growing closer and closer to the Academy. He thought of himself fighting outside the Academy's walls, of fire leaping onto the backs of other soldiers. Of their agonized screams as they died. He then thought of Vala, a place without fighting, and he thought of seeing his mother's smile again.

"Yes. Promise you will go with me."

Kuno smiled, his face lighting up. "Of course. But there are logistical issues. How are we going to cross the Nerin?"

"There are plenty of people crossing near Rangar Forest. We can cross there, travel through the forest, and then take the River Road to Vala."

The smile dissolved into a concerned frown. "Rangar Forest?

Lok, you know smugglers use the forest as a base, right?"

"It's how Charity and I traveled here after Kanton attacked us. And I promise to tell the whole truth about him on the way," he quickly added.

Kuno rolled his eyes. "Fine. But do you realize how much trouble you'd have been in if someone else had discovered Kanton's notebook? They wouldn't have bothered with a reprimand. You would have stood trial in a magistrate's court."

A pit formed in Lok's gut. *"I would have gone to prison?"*

"Or given a twenty-year indentured servant's contract. Either way, life as you know it would be over."

"Are you going to tell anyone?" Lok only knew one indentured servant, and everyone in Vala commented on how lucky Callum Haar was that Sardic Loy had bought the contract instead of the merchant who accused him of theft. Life for him could have been much worse. And if Lok became indentured, how would the contract holder react to him being a Thane? And what about Charity? Would she have gotten in trouble, too?

Kuno picked up Kanton's notebook and thumbed through the pages. "No. I will keep this as a curiosity. And if it happens to accidentally fall into the Nerin…" He shrugged.

Lok stood and hugged his mentor, wrapping his long arms around him. Kuno's head only came up to Lok's chin. He kept forgetting how tall he stood, even though he could reach the top shelf in the pantry when he was ten.

"Just promise me one thing," Kuno said, breaking away from the hug. "Don't mention this to anyone. Go about your day as usual. We will need provisions in order to travel that far, and a lot of things are in short supply. It won't be easy for me to gather them if the other Scholars are watching me. You'll have to be patient."

"I promise."

"Good. Now." Scholar Kuno reached behind the bed and pulled out a quarterstaff. He tossed it to Lok.

Lok just barely caught it. The staff was made of smooth, light brown wood. The same kind Scholar Tell used for martial arts class. He gave Kuno a confused look.

"You aren't getting out of martial arts that easily. First staff form. No shortcuts. Begin!"

6
Memories

Realta was ready to fall asleep the moment her head hit the pillow. She and Serena had worked all day, helping the Jemayrti Scholars and Master Corey rearrange the wagons, gathering extra wood for the firepit, setting up another laundry line and then washing and hanging the clothes, with no help from Master Corey. And finally, when the sun had set behind the trees, they cooked dinner.

Scholar Kambri helped Realta and Serena cook while Corey spoke with Chinasa and Shasta. He asked an endless barrage of questions. Why had the Scholars traveled to see King Nolfri? Why sail all the way to Treilean when the Kereuic land bridge was far more accessible? Wasn't Caman's Pass in Teyrnas still open? To Realta, it seemed like Corey was trying to catch Chinasa in a lie, but Chinasa answered each question diplomatically, sticking to their invented story.

Elliza, Corey's servant, sat by his side all day while Braedan wandered around the camp and the forest's edge. Ezri stuck close to Chinasa, always observing Braedan. Realta and Serena kept their distance from Corey and Braedan. Serena confided to Realta that Corey made her uneasy and didn't like the way he stared at her. Realta also caught Corey and Braedan staring at her a few times.

Why did Braedan lie about me being a Thane? He probably wanted to use it as leverage. But leverage for what?

The Scholars spoke quietly in Jemayrti during the meal. Realta didn't have to understand the language to know they were worried. They never expected to have guests.

And Elliza stared at Realta the entire time. She didn't say anything and barely ate. She merely stared at Realta, her eyes never wavering. Realta was grateful when Shasta dismissed her and Serena.

Pulling the blankets over her head, Realta thought of home, of another, happier summer. She closed her eyes...

And opened them to warm sunlight.

She smiled, seeing the Loy farmhouse. The branches of the sprawling oak tree rustled in the warm breeze. In the fields behind the barn, she saw Callum pulling out weeds with Ander and Lon Millar. The brothers were still in their teens.

She wanted to run to Callum, to hug him, to know that he was alive and well. But this was just a shadow. A day long past.

A peel of laughter sounded behind her. Realta blinked, and the Dream placed her underneath the tree's protective shadow.

Realta spied her younger self running across the yard. She was ten years old in this memory. She, Charity, and Estrid were taking turns chasing Gareth. Younger Realta was one step behind Charity, while little Estrid struggled to keep up. And Gareth ran faster than all of them. The boy wasn't even winded. In fact, he was smiling. A rare time he actually wanted to join their game.

She caught movement in the corner of her eye. Kel walked towards the tree, the sunlight glinting off his leg brace. He always let them have summer afternoons off from lessons, believing that playing was just as important as studying. She and Charity always looked forward to those warm afternoons.

Kel balanced on his good leg and crutch and sat down, resting his back against the trunk. He opened a book and flipped to a marked page. Dog-eared. Aunt Esme constantly berated him for that, insisting that it ruined the paper and that he should use a bookmark instead.

Kel glanced over at the playing children and smiled. He then grabbed a handful of grass and tossed it in the air. Instead of flying away in the breeze, the blades of grass circled back and flew in between his fingers, spinning and dancing. Realta crouched down beside the dream version of her uncle.

"Why didn't you tell us?" she asked though she knew Kel could not answer. "We would have kept your secret."

Esme knew the truth, and Callum likely had figured it out years ago. But what about the Loys? Did they know?

"They took you in when you have nowhere to go. You must

have told them and asked them to keep it a secret. It wouldn't be fair to leave them in the dark."

Kel lowered his hand, and the blades of grass drifted to the ground. He began reading his book. A botany textbook, complete with illustrations.

"Did you get that at the Academy?" Realta asked. She leaned her head against the trunk and sighed. "I wish you could answer me. I wish we were all together again. We're all the way in Kereu, and you're..." She bit down on her lip, sadness creeping over her like a shadow. "I don't know where you are. Or Father."

She drew up her knees and wrapped her arms around them. Her younger self continued to play. Gareth had been caught, and now it was Charity's turn to be chased. Peels of laughter erupted from the group.

Tears pricked her eyes. Would she ever see Charity or her cousins again?

"You have such happy memories."

Realta jumped up, her heart leaping into her throat. A man stood next to the oak tree. A tattered, dark gray cloak was draped over his thin shoulders. The hood hid most of his pale face. The man lifted his head, revealing eyes as black as night.

"Who are you?" Realta had seen him in several Dreams. He always stood off to the side, watching her. Once, he spoken to her, and the Dream ended abruptly. Realta squeezed her eyes shut, willing herself to wake up. She opened them. The Dream and the cloaked man remained.

"Not all memories are happy." The man stretched out his hand. The world around them transformed. Day turned into night. A cramped hallway lined with dark wood replaced the farm and the surrounding forest. A single torch on a metal sconce cast dim, orange light on a set of iron bars.

And behind those bars was her father.

Callum knelt beside a wooden bench, his hands folded in prayer. A linen bandage covered his left wrist. And he was crying.

"Please, Creator," Callum whispered, his voice choked. "I know... I know I don't pray that much, but I need Your help. Please, if You can hear me, help my family." Callum broke down and buried his face in his hands.

A tear fell down Realta's face. She wanted to rush to Callum's side and comfort him, comfort herself. But this was just another Dream. Another shadow.

"What happened?" Realta asked the cloaked man. "Why is he in here?"

"How do you think your father received his servant's mark?" The cloaked man studied Callum.

"He… He never told me."

The cloaked man nodded. His face was even paler in the low light. "Of course. He wanted to protect his only child."

"What did he do?" Realta whispered. Her entire body trembled as though she had walked out into the snow with only a thin dress and no shoes.

A door at the end of the hallway burst open. Esme Haar, a decade younger, rushed inside and ran to Callum's cell. Kel shambled in behind her, his steps forced and awkward. He grimaced with each step, biting down on his lip.

"Callum?" Esme called out. "Callum!"

Callum turned. Recognizing his sister, he scrambled to his feet and held Esme's hands. Tears streamed from his bloodshot eyes.

"What did they say?"

"Sardic Loy volunteered to buy your contract."

"What?" Callum looked her at confused. "Sardic can't afford that. He'd have to sell the farm."

Esme shook her head, long black hair flying every which way. Tears shone in her eyes, but she was smiling. That smile could light up a cavern. "We raised the money. Vera Tolman had half the village in her inn tonight. All of them agreed to help Sardic buy the contract."

"But what about Kiana and the baby?"

"They will live with us. Callum, you won't be separated."

New tears flooded Callum's eyes. He reached through the bars and hugged Esme. "Thank you. Thank you!"

"Hey, what are you doing here?" asked a rough voice. Realta turned and saw a village guard confronting Kel. He held a cudgel, ready to strike. "We ain't giving handouts!"

Kel covered his face with his hood and stammered an apology.

"He's my husband, you ass!" Esme yelled at the guard.

The guardsman jumped. He glanced at Esme, then at Kel, and back at Esme. "Sorry, Mistress Haar." Sparing a second glance at Kel, he hurried away.

Kel shambled over to Esme and Callum. He reached through the bars and placed a hand on Callum's shoulder.

"It took over a year for him to walk again," the cloaked man said.

"How do you know that?"

The cloaked man studied Realta with ink black eyes. "I just know. You are very fortunate to have happy memories, Realta Haar. Even this memory is happy in its own way. If it were not for Sardic Loy and Esme Haar, your father would be contracted to the man he stole eighty gold marks from. You would have never known him."

"My father never stole from anyone!" Realta rounded on him.

"The merchant he was escorting through Caman's Pass claims that Callum Haar stole his money and hid it in the mountains. No one could prove your father's innocence. It was his word against the merchant and three other people traveling with them. They all claim that Callum wandered off for a few hours when the merchant discovered the theft. Eighty gold marks was half his yearly earnings."

"My father was a guide. He likely scouted ahead to make sure the path was safe," she countered, searching for the most reasonable explanation.

The cloaked man sighed. "That was Callum's claim. An easy one."

"How can you say that? Callum never broke the law in his life." Realta looked at her father. Callum, Esme, and Kel were all so happy, so relieved.

The man raised a hand. "I never accused him. In fact, I believe in his innocence. This event was merely meant to be."

Meant to be? "You mean this was fate?"

"In a sense. You needed your father, Realta. We could not risk you growing up without him."

Realta backed away from the man. She bumped against the wall, startling herself. "What do you mean?"

"You are the only Dreamer on Eltriar." The cloaked man

loomed over her, head and shoulders taller.

"Who are you?"

The man smiled. "Someone who was sent to help. You cannot hide in your Dreams forever, Realta Haar."

No, this couldn't be real! This wasn't happening!

Realta ran down the hall, pushing the door open and sprinting into the night. She recognized the mayor's house with its large windows and shady willow trees. Next door to the building she exited. The guardsmen's building, the closest thing Vala had to a jail. Tolman's Inn stood across the street.

The lights in the inn shone brightly. People lingered outside, whispering, wondering if they had done enough to save their neighbor. Callum was a good man and no one in Vala had ever been forced into a servant's contract.

Realta wanted to run to them, to ask for help, but it wouldn't do any good. They could neither see nor hear her.

The cloaked man stood in the light cast from the inn's open door, his cloak moving in the warm breeze like a living shadow.

She spun on her heels and ran towards the market, her heart pounding and her sides beginning to ache. She had already accepted being a Dreamer. Her Dreams transported her to the past, allowed her to relive familiar memories. But the rest could not be true. Valentin Gardyner was a liar and a murderer. Every word he said had been pure manipulation. She was not One of Nine!

"Very well, Realta." Realta skidded to a halt as the man appeared in front of her. "The first Dreamer was reluctant, too. I can give you some time, but not forever." The man snapped his fingers.

Realta jolted. She was lying in bed, coated in a cold sweat with the blankets tangled around her. Pale morning light shone through the wagon's sole window. She glanced around. Shasta's and Serena's beds were both empty, the blankets and pillows neatly made.

She slowly sat upright and wrapped the blankets around her shoulders, trembling all over.

My father is not a thief!

She squeezed her eyes tight, trying to make the Dream go away, but it was part of her memory now. She recalled Callum being in prison as clearly as she remembered playing in the yard with her cousins and Charity.

A board creaked.

Realta's eyes flew open. Had the cloaked man followed her? Could he move about in the waking world as easily as in her Dreams?

The figure standing by the door was small and petite. Elliza, the merchant's servant. How long had she been standing there?

"Hey!" Realta yelled.

Elliza bolted out the door.

7

Resemblance

The Jemayrti Scholars set up a table by the firepit. A series of maps, held down by rocks in the corners so they would not fly away in the breeze, covered the entire surface.

Serena stood by Chinasa's side and peered at the maps, trying to get a better look while avoiding Waylar Corey's attention. She opted to wear her work shirt and trousers today. For some reason, she did not feel comfortable wearing a dress around Corey.

"Hold on," Corey said, frowning. "I thought you were traveling to Treilean. Why does this map show routes to Jemayrt?" He jabbed a finger at one map. It showed the Northern Realm of El-triar and detailed routes from Kereu to every other country in the North, not just Jemayrt.

"That was our original plan," Chinasa explained politely, instead of stating the obvious. "We were going to travel south to Sykeria and then sail west to Jemayrt. But it's impossible to predict how quickly the war will spread. If Kereu joins either side, we will travel to Treilean. I doubt the Eastern Coalition cares about the islands."

Corey's frown deepened. "I don't know. A lot of trade happens between Treilean and Bran Maro."

"Bran Maro trades more with Sykeria. As of now, the Empire is neutral." Chinasa rubbed his chin. "Granted, we can still travel through Sykeria if Kereu does join the war."

"Don't see why not." Corey studied a map of Sykeria. The Empire controlled the entire Southern Realm, an area almost as large as the Northern Realm. Serena didn't understand how the empress effectively governed an entire Realm. Logan constantly got stressed out ruling a single kingdom.

Her throat constricted, as though caught in a vise. Fresh tears stung her eyes. Why did she feel this way? Logan had spent a decade ignoring her and publicly humiliated her in front of Queen Gallia, accusing her of lying and breaking her nose in the process. Her nose was still bent at a slight angle, a permanent reminder of her half-brother. She shouldn't feel anything towards him other than hate and anger. So why was she mourning him?

"Listen, ambassador," Corey said, adopting a placating tone. "The safest bet is Treilean. We can split the cost of a charter."

Chinasa leaned against the table, studying the route. A long stretch of sea lay between Kereu and the island nation. Serena had dreaded sailing across the Nerin River, an ordeal that lasted only a few hours. How many days would it take to sail across an ocean?

"What business do you have in Treilean?" Chinasa asked.

Corey smirked. "I'm a merchant. My business is the same all over the world."

"Not to mention what's-her-name in Barikhir," Braedan laughed, walking up to the table.

Corey shot him a glare.

Serena inched closer to Chinasa, trying not to look at Braedan. Trying not to look at his sandy hair and blue eyes. Features shared by her and all three of her half-brothers. And she could see hints of Logan in Braedan's face. The way his mouth curved when he spoke. The way his hair fell over his forehead. Even the sound of his voice reminded her of Logan.

You're just seeing things, she told herself. *You've been thinking about Logan for weeks. You're only seeing what you want to see.*

Of the half-brother who never loved her?

Serena glanced over at Shasta. The cookfire was burning warmly, creating heat waves in the humid air. Scholar Okorie positioned the hot plate over it while Shasta prepared the tea kettle. The former head of servants had known Logan his entire life. Perhaps she should… Serena bit down on her tongue. No, she was just being foolish. There was no resemblance between Logan and Braedan. It was just her imagination.

"How much would a charter cost?" Chinasa asked.

"Depends on the quality of the ship and the reputation of the captain. And you have to factor in the number of people traveling. Last time we sailed…" Corey knitted his brow. He asked Braedan, "How much did Alcazar charge us?"

"Ten silvers. Sykeria currency. So that would be about two gold Teyrnian marks."

Serena's eyes widened. Most servants earned one or two gold marks in a year. And that was just for three people. How much would it cost to transport all of them?

"You were robbed," Chinasa said.

"Exactly!" Corey smiled widely, revealing his white teeth. "Didn't I tell Alcazar he was a damn thief?"

"Yep," Braedan replied.

Elliza, appearing out of nowhere, ran up to Corey's side. She stood completely still and did not look anyone in the eyes, similar to the way the servants always acted around Logan.

Stop thinking about Logan!

"Where were you?" Corey demanded.

"Sorry. I overslept. Do you want me to help with breakfast?" Elliza spoke in a lilting accent, all the words spoken too quickly, as though each sentence were comprised of one long word. Serena barely understood her. Where was she from? And why did she have that tattoo on her face? Serena had only seen that kind once before, on the Cuchasi in East Bridge. Did that mean Elliza was a Cuchasi, too?

"Yeah, sure." Corey waved her away. Elliza gave him a brief nod and joined Shasta and Okorie by the fire.

"I will have to discuss this with my colleagues," Chinasa said. "Let's have breakfast before we decide anything. Jemayrt is still an option."

Corey agreed. They joined the rest of the Scholars, Shasta, and Elliza around the fire. The Scholars all sat on one side. Ezri never took his eyes off Braedan and Corey, sitting on Chinasa's left. Shasta gave everyone a fried potato cake and a cup of strong tea.

Serena sat on Chinasa's right, but to her dismay, Braedan sat next to her. Elliza sat with Corey, staring directly at Serena. Just like last night. Didn't she realize how creepy that was?

"So, you're an apprentice?" Braedan asked her. Serena stole a glance at Chinasa. The ambassador spoke quietly to Shasta, and the Scholars were deep in conversations of their own, Adanna and Kambri asking Corey questions. The merchant answered them vaguely and asked a few questions himself. Mainly about their areas of study. Elliza, as silent as the wind, continued to stare at Serena. There was no way out of this conversation.

"Um, yes."

"That's cool. Apprentice what exactly?"

"Linguist," she stammered over the unfamiliar word.

"Interesting. What languages do you know? I can speak Teyrnian, Sykerian, Tarodic, and Treileani. Byyarian and Nowani are basically the same as Teyrnian, though some words are different. Is Jemayrti a lot different from Teyrnian?"

"Yes. I just started a few weeks ago. I'm not very good yet."

Braedan smiled, the right side of his face rising a little higher than the left. Her heart skipped a beat. She had seen the same smile on Kel's face. The brother who had faked his death, escaping to a happier life. "Hey, we all start somewhere. Ten years ago, I was lousy at my job. Oh, I could fight, but there was no skill in it. Just punching wildly and hoping to hit something. Most skills take years to master."

Serena took a bite of potato cake. It was burnt on one side and cold on the other. Scholar Okorie must have cooked this one. He was a brilliant physicist but a terrible cook.

Realta emerged from their wagon, her hair in a messy braid and eyes darting around the camp. She spied Serena and hurried over, sparing a quick glare at Elliza.

"Serena, I need to talk to you. In private." She shot another glare at Elliza. The girl averted her eyes and quietly ate her food.

"Is everything all right, Realta?" Shasta asked. All conversations ceased. Everyone looked at Realta and Serena. Great. Just great.

"No, ma'am. Serena." Realta gestured towards their wagon.

"What's wrong?" Braedan asked.

Realta ignored him.

Serena gladly followed Realta into the wagon, relieved to be away from all those eyes and from Braedan. They sat opposite each other on the narrow beds, their knees almost touching. With three beds and several traveling trunks, there was barely enough space to move. Serena never thought she would miss her small bedroom at the palace.

"Elliza was watching me while I slept," Realta whispered.

"What!?"

Realta told her about waking from a Dream and finding the girl in their wagon.

"Do you think Corey sent her to spy on you?" Elliza must have snuck in shortly after Serena and Shasta left.

"I don't know. Probably. We need to convince Chinasa to get rid of them."

"Good luck with that. Corey is determined to follow us regardless of where we go. And his bodyguard…" Would Realta think she was being foolish, too?

"Yeah, a Cuchasi, of all people. I wonder why he lied about my Aura."

Serena shrugged. She had never heard of Cuchasi lying about Thanes, not unless they had been paid off.

"Maybe we should question them. Get Braedan and Elliza by themselves when Corey is speaking with the Scholars," Realta suggested.

"Who should we question first?" She wondered if this was a good idea. Braedan and Elliza might ask them questions in return. Questions they couldn't answer without complicating matters.

"Braedan. I don't trust Elliza. There's something weird about her." Realta stood, acted like she was going to pace, but sat back down. She let out a frustrated sigh. "Why didn't you and Shasta wake me?"

"You were sound asleep. We figured you were having a Dream." Realta was impossible to wake during a Dream. Once, she slept through a thief trying to steal their horses in the middle of the night. Ezri had been on guard and shouted, awaking everyone and running off the thief. "What did you see this time?" Serena leaned forward. Realta's Dreams were always interesting, and Shasta encouraged her to write down each one. Most times, she Dreamed about historical events and memories of her own past.

"Nothing important." Realta adjusted her bracelet, making sure it covered her servant's mark, two diamonds within two dark bands. "I'll question Braedan, and you question Elliza. Deal?"

"Should we tell Shasta and Chinasa first?"

"Might as well. I'm sure they have their suspicions, too." Realta frowned. "I don't like how those other merchants were so eager to get away from Corey. Something is definitely off."

"Yeah." Serena remembered the look on Lagard's face. He had been relieved when Chinasa agreed to stall Corey, even if it meant speaking with a Thane.

Realta stood and headed for the door. Serena followed.

"Realta, do you think…"

"Think what?"

This is foolish. You are just seeing things. But hadn't Realta seen a resemblance between Serena and Kel when they first met? Surely she must see this resemblance, too. If one existed.

"We should study them first," Serena said instead. "Listen to what they say. One of them might reveal information without meaning to."

Realta nodded. "Good idea." She exited the wagon, the morning light illuminating the small space.

The Scholars, Chinasa, and the merchant still sat around the cookfire. Braedan stood off to the side, sharpening a knife. Elliza watched as Realta rejoined the group, never taking her eyes off her.

"It's nothing, you stupid girl," Serena berated herself. "It's nothing, and you should just forget about Logan. He was nothing to you."

No, not nothing. Logan had been a king. A king Teyrnas desperately needed now.

Braedan met Serena's eyes and smiled. Kel's smile.

Pushing Logan and Kel out of her thoughts, Serena returned to the cookfire.

8

Haunted

The Shade returned to haunt him. Logan gripped the windowsill, forcing himself to focus on the street below. Anything to prevent him from looking at the Shade. At first, he believed the Shade was the product of his fevered mind, beckoning him to cross over into the Realm of Stars.

But then the fever broke. He was no longer in danger of dying, but the Shade returned day after day to torment him.

The floorboards creaked as the Shade approached.

Logan O'Kelwyn, the King of Teyrnas, took a deep breath and slowly peered over his shoulder. The Shade of his brother Carwyn stared at him. The Shade was broken. Of course it was. Yestyn had destroyed Carwyn before killing him. The Shade wore a tattered Journeyman's cloak over equally tattered clothes, patched and mended in multiple places. The hood was down, revealing a shock of unruly, sandy brown hair, the same as it had been in life.

Logan shuddered, looking at the Shade's face. The right side had been preserved, but the left side was a network of scars. Dozens of scars with two bisecting the eyebrow and one running from the hairline almost to its neck. And the ears were ruined. Yestyn had ripped the earrings out, claiming that Carwyn did not deserve to be remembered as a Thane.

The Shade shambled forward. Logan's eyes fell on its necklace. A white pendant with two flying ravens. The necklace Esme had given him as a graduation present. The necklace Carwyn had been buried with.

"How are you feeling?" the Shade asked, leaning on its crutch. Strange that such a creature would need a crutch. Or a leg brace.

Logan slowly faced the creature. His side still ached where Valentin had stabbed him. Callum Haar had done the stitches himself and examined it daily to make sure it healed properly. They certainly could not risk visiting a healer. The world believed that King Logan was dead, and his safety depended on that belief.

"Hungry," he replied after a moment. Speaking to a Shade felt so weird, so unnatural. But the others didn't seem to have a problem with it, so why should he? "Ask Callum or Colm to send up lunch."

The Shade studied him with Carwyn's clear blue eyes. The last time Logan had seen those eyes, Carwyn's corpse was staring up at the ceiling.

Logan had rushed to his brother's side, latching onto him, screaming, begging him to live. He was Logan's big brother. The one who protected them. He couldn't be dead. The healers had made a mistake.

Next thing he remembered, the healers were dragging him away. The crown prince, they finally convinced him, was dead. There was nothing he could do except mourn.

"Anything else?" the Shade asked. "Do you still have pain in your side?"

"Go haunt someone else." Logan turned his attention back to the window. The seedy tavern they had hidden in for the last few months was in Tullcrest, the crime-ridden slums near the city's western wall. From this vantage point, he could see the highest towers of the palace. Six flags flew over his home. One for each invading kingdom and one for the Eastern Coalition, displaying the symbols of each member. Nowan's hawk, Tarod's rising sun, Tirshay's stag, Galion's torch, and Bran Maro's stars.

Thousands had died, either from violence or starvation or in failed attempts to retake the city. And thousands more had fled.

Were his wife and children safe? Isla had a good head on her shoulders, good diplomatic sense. If she arrived at the Academy, she would have the Council of Scholars on her side, and access to the Garrison. Did she believe he was dead, too? Did his children believe they would never see their father again? His heart ached.

The floorboards creaked again, louder. The bloody Shade refused to leave.

"Logan, look at me. Please."

Logan stared out the window. A patrol of Marish soldiers dressed in their signature red coats marched down the street.

Civilians cowered, hurrying away. One man had the gall to give them the finger once their backs were turned. Logan smirked.

A bony hand latched onto his shoulder. Logan whirled around, smacking the hand away. "Don't touch me!" he snarled.

"What would happen if someone looked up?" the Shade questioned.

"I'd create an Illusion, making them think I was someone else."

"What if a whole crowd looked up? You could never trick more than two minds at once. If someone in that crowd recognized you, we would all be killed."

"You're already dead." Logan stalked away. He paused in front of the dirty mirror on the nightstand. A half-filled glass of water rested on the stand. He took a sip and grimaced. Warm and stale.

"I know I hurt you, Lo, but—"

White-hot anger surged through him. Lo? How dare this creature call him that! Only his siblings, his two living siblings, were allowed to call him Lo.

He hurled the water glass at the Shade. It shattered against the wall, missing the Shade's scarred face by mere inches. Glass fragments littered the floor. The Shade shambled out of the room, doing its best to run.

The anger drained away, leaving him exhausted. Logan sat on the bed, the mattress sagging under his now gaunt frame, and buried his face in his hands.

✳✳✳

Kel froze as the glass shattered next to his head, pulling his mind back to that horrible night. He had gone to confront Yestyn about Nell Molyns and her baby girl, seven months old and without a father. A baby girl with Yestyn's blue eyes.

"Everyone knows Serena is your daughter. Just admit it," Kel snapped, anger radiating from him, turning his entire body warm. That wasn't good. He didn't think well when he was angry.

Yestyn smirked, the right side of his mouth upturned in a mocking smile. "Are you really that pissed off about one bastard? You've got a lot of nerve, considering you've got a bastard on the way yourself."

Kel's heart skipped a beat. "How did…?"

"Servants talk. Don't worry, boy. You can keep your whore after the wedding. So long as she and the bastard don't cause trouble."

The anger flared white hot, clouding reason and judgment and caution. Every time. Every damn time! He was bloody sick of it! "Stop calling my wife a whore!"

An eerie silence descended on the room. Even Dane Kanton, the guard assigned to attend Yestyn that evening, was silent.

"Wife?" Yestyn's voice was low and dark. "Did you call that little whore your wife?!"

Kel didn't know what to say. Words could not be unspoken. And Kel was sick of hiding the truth, of pretending to care about the arranged marriage.

Looking his father in the eyes, he said, "Yes."

His world descended into pain. Glass shards, the remains of the wine glass resting on the table, ripped his flesh. One sliced through his cheek, embedding itself in his tongue. Kel fell on the hard floor, clutching his face. Blood ran between his fingers.

Then, he felt his leg bone snap, right below the knee. Then above, and then in the center. The names of each bone drifted into his mind.

"The kneecap, also call the patella," Esme had said, reading out of a textbook the night before an exam, "separates the upper and lower leg. Two bones comprise the lower leg. The tibia and the fibula. The femur, the upper bone, is the longest and strongest in the human body."

But not strong enough to prevent Yestyn from snapping it with a well-placed stomp.

The pain was so horrible, Kel barely felt Yestyn ripping out his earrings one by one, saying that Kel did not deserve to be a Thane, did not deserve the privileged of having three abilities.

A cold shiver coursed through him, returning Kel to the present. Logan, his little brother and once best friend, glared at him with their father's cold eyes.

Kel rushed out of the room, relying on his good leg and crutch to propel him forward and into the hallway. He hadn't run this fast since Gareth fell out of the oak tree in the yard. The boy screamed as though he were dying. Thank the Creator it was only a dislocated shoulder and some bruises.

The floor fell out from underneath him, his foot touching open air. The stairs! Kel reached for the banister. His fingers brushed against the wood. He pitched forward.

His arm smacked against a step, his legs against another. Tumbling down, arms and legs flailing, unable to stop. His bed knee contacted the edge of a step. A horrifying pop. Pain seared through his leg as though the bone were on fire.

He landed on his back, knocking the air out of his lungs. He stared up at the ceiling, trying to remember how to breathe.

Wood scraping against wood sounded to his left. He then heard bootsteps, growing closer. Three faces crowded his vision.

"Kel, look at me," Callum said. His brother-in-law's wild black hair stuck out around his head. Callum turned to the other two faces. Deen, formally King Ayrdeen Akardal the Second of Bran Maro, and Colm Byers, the young guardsman from the palace. Another one of Yestyn's bastards. "Help me lift him up."

Callum and Deen lifted Kel by the arms. They carefully walked him over to their table. Colm held out a chair. The guardsman's pet red draig leapt from the table and onto his shoulder. The reptile wrapped its sinuous tail around Colm's neck and studied Kel with curious orange eyes.

Kel collapsed into the chair and gritted his teeth. The throbbing in his knee made him feel sick.

"Stars above, he's lucky to be alive," said Deen. The former king wore a patch over his blue eye. While heterochromia was fairly common in Bran Maro, it was virtually unheard of in Teyrnas. His uncovered brown eye, the more common color, studied Kel. He still did not care for Thanes, but he had grown to trust Kel. Far more than he trusted Logan.

"Are you hurt?" Colm asked.

"Of course he's hurt," Deen snapped. "You think a man falls down the stairs and walks off unscathed?"

Colm shrank back, sinking into a chair. The little draig adjusted itself so that its head rested against Colm's neck.

They had run into Colm while secreting Logan out of the palace. The young guardsman had stepped out of the evacuation queue in order to save his pet. Kel chalked up running into his little half-brother to fate.

"Be nice," Callum admonished Deen. The former king rolled his eyes and took a seat. Callum stood over Kel, examining him.

"Did you hit your head?"

"I don't think so." Kel winced as Callum inspected his arm. He'd have a nice collection of bruises in the morning.

"Nothing feels broken. What about your legs?"

"Left knee," he said.

Callum gently touched Kel's knee.

Kel screamed. Half the people in the seedy tavern's common room glanced at him. The rest were either too drunk or too traumatized to care.

"Damn. We might need a healer."

"No," Kel and Deen said at the same time. Deen gestured for Kel to continue. "Esme taught you basic medicine. Do your best."

Callum frowned, his dark brows knitting together. "Kel, if your knee is dislocated, a healer has to reset it."

"You've reset dislocated shoulders."

"Shoulders are ball and socket joints. Knees are hinge joints."

Kel glared at him.

"What? I'm using what Esme taught me. Just like you asked."

"Esme isn't a smartass with her patients." Kel winced. Callum was only trying to help, and he had a valid point. "Sorry."

"I understand you're in pain. Want me to try?"

"No," he said after a minute, waiting for a wave of nausea to pass. "It can wait another day."

"Kel—"

"No." Kel lowered his voice. He doubted anyone cared enough to eavesdrop, but alcohol tended to loosen lips. Better to be safe than to wind up arrested or worse. "We planned on leaving tonight. We can't risk staying any longer. And Lo…" How could he begin to explain? "We've taken enough risks staying this long."

Callum turned his attention to Deen and Colm. "Well, what do you say?"

"We stick with the plan," Deen replied. "Aska Liddyn has the horses ready. We wait and she might sell them to someone else. Unless you want Kel to continue his successful begging career for another month."

"I think so, too," Colm said. "And the Academy has healers. They can look at Kel's knee when we get there."

"Good point," Kel said. Colm was not the best and brightest the guard had to offer, but he was sensible. Kel only wished Logan could see that. The moment Logan learned their father had sired two bastards, he rejected Colm. Mistress Cray was mistaken. The boy could not be the late king's son, even if he did have Yestyn's blue eyes and tall, thin frame.

Mistress Cray never made a mistake that severe in her life.

Kel let the matter drop. Logan wasn't listening to him anyway. He had waited a month before telling Logan the truth, worried about how he would handle it. And Kel honestly didn't know where to begin. Sarra had accepted him, but Logan was not as warmhearted and slower to trust.

Logan rejected Kel immediately and often ignored him, acting as though Kel were invisible. Today was a rare occurrence of Logan actually talking to him. In Logan's mind, Carwyn was dead, and no amount of proof would change that.

"Shall we inform his majesty?" Deen asked sarcastically.

Callum nodded. Deen headed up the stairs, taking them two at a time.

"Are you sure?" Callum whispered.

Kel finally glanced down at his knee. The straps of his leg brace were loose, but the metal supports were intact. He spied a small, red stain around his knee. The stain began to spread. Callum reached into his pocket and removed a foldable knife. He carefully cut the fabric.

Callum cursed.

A large gash ran along the edge of his knee, blood flowing steadily. Another wave of nausea hit him, accompanied by lightheadedness.

"Should I get bandages?" Colm asked, his face turning white.

Callum nodded, and the young man rushed over to the bar. He pointed wildly at Kel as he explained the situation to Aska. The tavern owner, who dealt with busted lips and knife wounds on an almost daily basis, reached underneath the bar and handed Colm a cloth. Colm hurried back as though Kel had severed an artery.

"Thanks, Colm," Kel said. The boy would be both an excellent and terrible healer's assistant. He placed the cloth over the gash. The white fabric quickly turned red.

"We can wait another day," Callum said.

Kel glanced out the front window. A Marish unit, comprised of seven soldiers, each armed with a cudgel and a short sword, marched past. Their red uniforms were clearly visible through the dirty, cracked glass.

The unit nodded to a passing trio of Tarodic soldiers, dressed in blue uniforms trimmed with red. Both groups stopped, their leaders conferring with one another. A bored Marish soldier glanced inside the tavern.

A pit formed in Kel's gut. If either group decided to conduct a random search...

Don't come in here. Don't come in here.

Mercifully, both groups continued on their rounds.

"No. We leave tonight."

9

Burning Bright

"Are you sure you don't want to come?" Jaim asked Lok. The Academy's bell rang six times, signaling the dining hour. "You might not get a seat."

Lok nodded. The dining hall was always crowded these days, with Students, Journeymen, Scholars, and refugees alike. Sometimes, the seats filled up so quickly that Lok and his friends had to eat standing up. And Lok always felt anxious around large crowds. Hundreds of people moving about. People brushing against him. He always had trouble controlling his ability when he was anxious. Last week, he accidentally caused a wall lantern to flare up, the flames arching dangerously close to their table. Zandon, thankfully, had a Farsight and dowsed the fire before anyone noticed.

"Fine. Starve if you like. What about you?" Jaim asked Gareth. The other boy sat on his bed, the one nearest the narrow window.

"Yes." Gareth placed a paper bookmark in his textbook and set it on top of the neatly stacked pile of books and papers on his desk, arranged in the order of his classes. He donned his Student's cloak, pulling the hood over his head. Gareth still felt uncomfortable around large groups, but his confidence was slowly growing. As long as people could not stare at him directly, he was fine.

Lok grabbed a random book from his desk and opened it to a random page. He sat crisscross on his bed, pretending to study.

"Want us to bring you anything?" Jaim asked.

Lok shook his head. The Council strictly forbid people from hoarding food, and sometimes guards conducted random checks as people left the dining hall. Lok didn't want his friends getting in trouble, especially since he would be gone within the hour.

Jaim shrugged. He and Gareth then left, closing the door.

Lok counted to thirty. He crept over to the door and peered into the hallway. Through the blue-cloaked crowd, he spied them meeting up with Ivar at the end of the hall. They exchanged a few words and turned a corner, followed by dozens of other Students. Lok counted to sixty, making sure they didn't double back.

He then reached under his bed and retrieved the travel bag that Scholar Kuno gave him yesterday. He double checked the contents. Three changes of clothes. Extra pair of shoes. His notebook and pencil. And three books: an Old Eltrian primer, an ancient history textbook, and Dane Kanton's notebook along with Lok and Charity's translation notes stuffed between the pages.

They had translated two-thirds of the book, beginning with the most recent entries. The majority were daily thoughts, routines, and options for tracking down Serena, the thief the Loys had caught in their barn. Kanton did not understand why they had to track down a bastard nobody cared about. Neither did he want to return to the palace empty-handed. And he kept mentioning a secret part of the plan that involved Callum Haar, but Kanton never wrote about it directly.

Lok knew Charity would be disappointed about the incomplete the translation. Both suspected that the attack had something to do with the secret part. But why? Callum had done nothing to Kanton or the king and queen. Lok doubted the man had ever traveled across the Nerin before this year. Oh well. Better for it to remain a mystery than for Charity to get in trouble for having the book.

He slung the bag over his shoulder and pulled up the hood of his cloak. A quick scan of the hallway confirmed that his friends were gone.

No turning back now, Lok thought, his heart pounding.

Dozens of Students provided excellent cover. He knew some of them from class, but most were strangers, too caught up in their own thoughts and conversations to remember seeing him.

Keeping his head low to disguise his height, Lok made his way to the Scholars' rooms.

The hallways in this section were quieter. Only a handful of people walked about, some with white cloaks and others with blue or gray. It wasn't uncommon for Students and Journeymen to visit their mentors in the evenings, so nobody paid attention to Lok.

One Scholar spoke heatedly with a Journeyman.

"Plagiarism is a crime!" the Scholar said, his eyes narrowed and arms folded across his chest.

"I didn't plagiarize anything," the Journeyman pleaded. He was a few years older than Lok and had the ruddy complexion of a Hinterlander. "I wrote every word myself."

"I have no doubt you *wrote* this paper, Silas. But I've read Tenmyn, too."

"He was my main source!"

"Clearly."

Lok hurried on.

Scholar Kuno's door was cracked open. Inside, Lok saw the Scholar with Journeyman Shari. The young woman's blonde hair, a color Lok had never seen before arriving at the Academy, cascaded over her shoulders. Her arms were crossed as she watched Kuno pack.

"How long?" she asked quietly. Tears welled in her eyes.

"I wish I knew."

"Can't you just see him on his way and come back?"

Kuno sighed. "That would lead to questions I don't want to answer." He tied his travel bag shut and faced her, placing his hands on her arms. "It will just be for a little while. A month at most. We will be together again before you know it."

"Can I come with you?"

"I'm pretty sure your uncle would kill me," Kuno said with a smile,

Shari scoffed. "Who cares what that old bastard thinks? We're both adults."

Kuno's hands slid down to her waist. "Adults who have to be careful. Fewer questions get asked if fewer people disappear. I don't want you getting caught in the crossfires."

Shari locked eyes with him and placed a hand on his face. "Kuno, I..."

"Yes?"

She hesitated for a moment and then said, "Just promise me you'll be safe."

"Of course." They kissed. "I love you."

"Love you, too." Shari hugged him and walked towards the door.

Lok back away. His face felt like it was on fire. Oh no, would Shari know he was listening? She did not like him. What would she...?

Shari stepped into the hall and immediately spied Lok. She shot him a venomous glare, which was nothing new, and hurried away, her gray cloak flaring.

Lok counted to thirty, waiting for the blush to go away, and knocked on the door.

"Oh, good timing, Lok." Kuno motioned for Lok to enter and shut the door. "I think I have everything," he said as he inspected the contents of the travel bag. "Guard reports state that more refugees are on the move. They will be here within the hour. We can slip out while they are entering. Hopefully, it's a big group. Easier that way. Are you okay, Lok? You look kind of warm."

Lok nodded vigorously. His blush deepened.

Kuno frowned. "You shouldn't wear your hood up during summer. These walls were designed to retain heat. You might get sun sick."

Lok nodded again. He pushed back his hood and adjusted the travel bag so the strap would not dig into his shoulder.

"Ready?" Kuno asked. The Scholar smiled, but Lok sensed he was worried.

Lok reached into his pocket and handed Kuno a note. It felt wrong to leave without giving his friends an explanation. Especially Charity and Gareth. He had known both his whole life, and he and Charity had gone through so much over the past three months. Too much to simply disappear. He raised an eyebrow, silently asking for permission.

Kuno read over the note. The smile faded. "No. I'm sorry, Lok. If just one person here knows where you've gone, Lucan and his cronies can find you." He handed back the note. "Best to leave them in the dark."

Lok disagreed but didn't argue. He shoved the note in his pocket. *You should have left it in your room. Gareth or Jaim would have found it.* But the idea of Scholar Lucan chasing him to the Hinterlands, and possibly putting his mother and everyone else in danger, unnerved him. He guessed Kuno was right.

The door burst open. Lok nearly jumped out of his skin and cowered behind Kuno. Oh Great Creator, had Scholar Lucan discovered their plan? Was he here to take Lok away?

Kuno adopted a fighting stance, the same one he had taught Lok to use while holding a quarterstaff.

But it was only Brother Malaky, breathing hard and his face flushed bright red. He stumbled into the room.

"Thank the Creator, I'm not too late!"

"Too late for what?" Kuno relaxed. He motioned for the chaplain to sit down at the writing desk.

Brother Malaky placed a hand on his chest, catching his breath. "I haven't run that fast since I was a kid. Car and I were playing in a guest room. Broke a vase. Damn thing shattered into a million pieces. Father thought a servant had been careless. Had her flogged." Malaky shivered. "We felt terrible."

"Why were you running, Brother?" Kuno asked. He glanced at the wall clock. A quarter past six.

A horrible feeling crept into Lok's mind, like storm clouds forming on the horizon, drawing nearer.

"I saw Lok running through a lightning storm. Wind and rain poured all around him, tearing at his cloak. The lightning chased him, but Lok kept running. Ran all the way to the mountains. But the lightning was faster. A bright white flash consumed him and everything around him.

"When the light faded, the rain stopped. Lok stood unharmed, but his Student cloak was gone, replaced by a black military uniform trimmed with red and gold. And his eyes were ice cold. All his warmth and kindness were gone.

"Fire sprang up from his hands, burning bright. He commanded the fire, and it spread across the mountains, burning trees, villages, everything. The fire leapt into the river, boiling away the water. It then reached Teyrnas. The entire city burned to the ground, leaving nothing but ashes. And Lok watched it all with cold, dead eyes."

Lok sank down onto the bed, his entire body going numb and trembling. No. No, he would never do that. He did not want to destroy anything.

His thoughts drifted to Caldeira's pub. He had nearly destroyed it.

No! It was an accident!

"Anything else?" Kuno asked calmly. How could the Scholar sound so calm?

"No, the Farsight ends there. I had to find you before it was too late."

"Too late for what?" Kuno repeated.

Brother Malaky frowned. "I don't know. I had a compulsion to find you and Lok as soon as possible. I felt that something terrible would happen if I didn't tell you."

"Who else did you tell?"

"No one."

"Good. Brother Malaky," Kuno lowered his voice, "Lok and I are leaving the Academy tonight. Scholar Lucan and other Council members want to use him as a weapon against the Coalition."

Brother Malaky jumped to his feet. "That must be it! Oh Lok," he rushed to Lok's side, "you cannot allow them to turn you into that, that creature."

Being turned into a weapon was the last thing Lok wanted. He would rather spend the rest of his life in Vala, being ridiculed and regarded as an idiot, than harm a single person.

"Will you come with us, Brother?" Kuno asked.

Lok's heart sank. Brother Malaky tagging along was not part of the plan. Hadn't Kuno just told Shari that fewer people leaving meant fewer questions? And the Council kept a close eye on Malaky, interviewing him once a week and asking him to summarize his Farsights. They also ordered the guards not to allow him to leave the Academy grounds.

And Lok did not like the chaplain. Every time the man walked into a room, Lok got a strange feeling, a vague sense of wrongness. He especially didn't like Malaky watching while he practiced. He seemed to make twice as many mistakes, and it was harder for him to concentrate. He certainly did not want to travel all the way to Vala with the man.

Lok waved at Kuno, trying to get his attention.

"Well, the Council has me on a short leash," Malaky said reluctantly. "They will be furious once they discover I'm gone."

"No more furious when they discover Lok's absence. And what if you have more Farsights concerning him? We will need you to warn us."

Lok waved his hand in Kuno's face. The Scholar shooed him away.

"I suppose they can't punish me too severely, considering my family connections. Do you think I could leave word with Queen Isla?"

"Absolutely not." Kuno frowned. "Does the queen know about your Farsights?"

"Oh no." Brother Malaky's eyes widened as he shook his head. "I've been too afraid to tell them. I... They wouldn't believe me."

"Then it's settled." Kuno reached into his bag and pulled out a dark cloak. "Put this one. You're coming with us."

Kuno, no! Lok quickly searched his travel bag for a piece of paper. He just needed a single piece.

There's a piece of paper in your pocket, idiot.

Lok grabbed the crumpled note and spied a pen on Kuno's desk. Empty. He checked the ink well. Also empty. He ran his fingers through his hair.

"Lok, what's wrong?" Kuno asked.

Lok pointed at Brother Malaky.

"Yes, his Farsight disturbed me, too. But don't worry. I promise I won't let it happen. Now, put this on." Kuno handed him a dark brown cloak. "Put the blue one in your bag. This one will stand out less."

Lok grudgingly did as instructed. He glanced at the clock. Almost six-thirty. What time were the refugees arriving?

"But I need to pack," Malaky protested.

"I have funds. We'll buy supplies for you on the way." Kuno went to the window. The sun was sinking towards the horizon. They had about an hour, maybe an hour and a half, of daylight. "The refugees are almost here. Let's go."

Donning a dark gray cloak, Kuno slung his bag over his shoulder and hurried out of the room. Brother Malaky followed on his heels. Lok glanced out the window, trembling from head to foot.

He thought about the Chaplain's words and envisioned the

Academy catching on fire, the flames rising into the sky as people fled for their lives. The flames burning, burning, burning.

I will not be a weapon, he vowed.

Grabbing his travel bag, Lok ran after his mentor.

10

Refuge

The sun crept towards the horizon, casting the sky in shades of crimson, as the refugees trekked the last few paces towards the Academy. Men, women, children, and elderly, they wore ragged clothes and carried their merger possessions on their backs. But the weariness that had clung to them slowly melted away. They had made it. They were safe.

Reining his horse closer to Callum, Kel was surprised by how little the Academy had changed. Seventeen years for him had meant nothing to the centuries old structure. The sturdy walls would remain long after he was gone.

I hope. Kel gazed eastward, towards Norgard and the Garrison. Countless ribbons of gray smoke rose from the military camps flying Coalition flags. A hundred cookfires for a thousand soldiers. How many soldiers would it take to bring down these walls?

A line of guards in dark blue blocked the South Gate. They ordered the refugees to halt for inspection. Kel spied a Deirow hawk on one guard's shoulder. As a Student, he'd been fascinated with the creatures and begged the Scholars for one. But the birds were bred as messengers. They were not pets, especially not for Hiraethi runaways. Very few Scholars outside of the Council knew his true identity.

"Form up!" the lead guard ordered, his voice loud and clear. "Family groups and individuals."

Groups quickly formed, both biological and found families. Only a handful truly stood alone.

Colm moved his horse next to Callum and Kel. Deen and Logan, both hidden under ragged clothes and tattered, dark cloaks, stood directly behind them. Neither king complained. They understood the risks.

The guards split up into pairs and spoke to each group, writing names on ledgers. The two who approached their group both had dark hair and eyes and were almost the same height. Kel guessed they were brothers. And he was grateful it was only two. Focusing on their minds, he crafted an Illusion of himself with dark hair, dark eyes, and an unscarred face. Logan, no doubt, created a similar Illusion.

"Dismount," one guard ordered.

Callum and the rest did so with ease.

"Well?" the guard questioned Kel.

Kel gently touched his knee and winced. Callum had done his best to stitch the gash, but he was no healer. It still hurt to walk, even with most of his weight on his good leg.

"Sir, I'm crippled."

"Yeah, right, and I'm King Logan. Dismount!"

Kel grabbed his crutch and slipped his feet out of the stirrups. Okay, first his good leg and then the bad one. An action he had performed hundreds of times. He placed the crutch near the ground and lowered his good leg. His foot contacted the ground. Good. Now, the other one.

His knee buckled and twisted outward as his foot twisted inward, shooting fiery pain up his leg and into his back.

Kel screamed and latched onto the saddle. The spooked horse stamped its hooves and lurched away from Kel. He white-knuckled the saddle and reins, his leg twisting further as the horse moved. Tears burned in his eyes, and he gritted his teeth.

The horse, mercifully, calmed down and stood still.

Oh Great Creator, his leg hurt! It felt like the upper and lower halves were being ripped apart. What if he needed surgery again? What if he had to learn how to walk again?

"What's his problem?" the guard asked.

"He is crippled, your majesty," Callum replied sarcastically.

"I thought he was lying."

"Why would he lie?" Deen asked, careful to hide his Marish accent. Kel heard footsteps approaching. "Do you think he wears a brace for fun?"

"No, sir," the guard stammered, no doubt taken aback by Deen's eyepatch.

"Is everything all right?" asked another voice.

"We have a wounded man, chaplain," Callum said. "Will we be able to get medical help inside?"

"Yes, of course. May I see him?"

Kel's heart skipped a beat. He knew that voice. But it couldn't be. Mal was away when Teyrnas fell. And there were thousands of chaplains in the kingdom. It couldn't be... Taking deep breaths, Kel tried to craft an Illusion. Another shot of pain coursed up his leg and into his spine and arms. Too much pain to focus on his own name let alone another person's mind.

Carefully peeling one hand off the saddle, he covered the unscarred side of his face.

It can't be Mal. But what if it was?

"Brother, we need to go," said another man.

"You can wait a minute."

The chaplain's companion muttered angrily.

A gentle hand touched Kel's shoulder. He flinched. "Please, it's nothing," he tried to say, but the words came out as a low mumble.

"Now, let me see. I..." The chaplain turned Kel's face to look him in the eyes. Kel squeezed his eyes shut. Hot tears streamed down his face. "Oh Great Creator, what happened to you?"

"I was injured," he managed. "Long time ago."

"I'm so sorry," said the too familiar voice.

Kel cracked open his eyes and his heart fell. The shy boy he remembered was now in his late thirties, and the light brown hair was cut short. A pair of glasses framed his clear blue eyes.

"Mal."

The chaplain frowned, confused. His eyes wandered to the unscarred half of Kel's face. "Car?" he whispered. He quickly studied Kel, eyes moving from head to toe and then falling on Kel's raven necklace, the one he was supposedly buried with. Mal gently touched it. His eyes glistened in the failing light.

Kel glanced over at Callum. His brother-in-law, the man who had acted as his surrogate brother all these years, watched, unsure what to do. He knew Kel had siblings, but he only met Logan and Sarra. Did he see the resemblance?

The guard asked Callum a question, but he just stared at Mal. He got that look in his eyes that indicated he was about to fight someone. Logan just pulled his hood lower and turned away.

"Brother, we need to go," said a man on horseback. A dark cloak hid his features. Another rider, a tall man wearing a similar cloak, sat next to him.

"Wait! Please, wait!" Mal turned back to Kel. He lowered his voice, "Car, is that really you?"

Kel locked eyes with his little brother. No, little was the wrong word. Mal was the same height as him, had been since he was eighteen years old. The awkward boy with the glasses had grown into a man.

Malaky, will you forgive me for abandoning you?

"Yes," Kel whispered.

Mal wrapped his arms around him, hugging him tight. Kel hugged him back, the same way he had hugged him when they were children and Mal needed the comfort and love their father refused to give.

"I knew you were alive," Mal said, his face buried in Kel's shoulder. "They all said you died at night. But I heard you talking to Esme. I… She said…"

"I'm sorry we lie to you."

"Guess Yestyn didn't leave you much of a choice." Mal pulled away from the hug. His eyes widened, fearful. "Oh, Carwyn. Esme, is she…?"

"Alive and well."

"And the child?" He whispered so quietly that Kel barely heard him.

"Healthy. He's here at the Academy." Kel smiled proudly. "His name is Gareth, after Esme's grandfather."

Mal smiled brightly and shook his head in disbelief. "I could have seen him. To think, all these months, and he was here all along. Thank the Creator!"

"Chaplain, is this man okay?" asked the guard. The other guards and refugees were waiting by the South Gate, watching curiously. Kel quickly placed a hand over his face.

"Yes, I was just praying over him. Best he sees a healer soon."

"Very well." The guard addressed Kel. "You're free to go inside. Hard to believe all five of you are brothers." He laughed.

"Let me help you." Callum walked over to Kel, keeping a close eye on Mal. Mal took a cautious step back.

"I'm fine."

Callum raised an eyebrow. "You sure?"

Kel's knee felt like it had been kicked by a mule. "Yeah," he lied.

"Wait." Mal whispered into Kel's ear, "What about Lo? Is he really dead?"

Should he lie to his brother or tell the truth? Mal had already lost one big brother, and rumors about Logan's death were now regarded as fact, confirmed by Queen Isla herself. He glanced at Logan out of the corner of his eye. The rightful king had mounted his horse and faced the South Gate, acting as though Mal were not there.

He is not my brother. The quiet, quick-witted young man Kel had grown up with was gone, replaced by a short-tempered king. Kel blamed himself. He knew first-hand how a loved one's death affected a person. Callum rarely talked about Kiana, thirteen years after crimson fever had taken her. And he never spoke about his parents. Mayra had died when he was only four years old, and Drago passed away while Esme was at the Academy and Callum was traveling through Caman's Pass. Callum and Esme lit candles for them at the chapel, and Esme told the occasional story, but only when she wanted to. And only briefly.

He let out a shuddering sigh and sadly shook his head.

Mal looked as though he had been slapped in the face. "I had hoped... Well, he is with Mother now, I guess."

"The sun is setting, chaplain," said the shorter of the cloaked riders. His horse stamped impatiently.

"I have to go. Take care of yourself, Car."

"You're leaving?"

Mal nodded. "I'm needed elsewhere." He placed a hand on Kel's shoulder. "I will see you again. I promise."

"Like you promised not to mess up my algebra primer?" Kel smirked. He touched his necklace, felt the smooth surface, and then tucked it under his shirt.

"Stars above, I was ten years old!" Mal gave him an indignant look.

Kel laughed and gave Mal one more hug. "I wish we'd met again under better circumstances."

"Me, too."

Mal walked back to his two companions and mounted a horse, a sleek brown animal with a coal black mane. Did Mal still watch the horse races? He would have to ask Logan.

Logan will never give you that answer.

Two arms wrapped around Kel's waist, lifted him off his feet, and flung him onto the saddle. Grabbing hold of the pommel, Kel shifted into a seated position and placed his feet in the stirrups. Callum, his face completely blank, handed Kel his crutch.

"I could have done it myself," Kel snapped.

"This saves time. Who was that guy?" Callum gestured towards Mal. He and the riders galloped away from the Academy. Weird. They were heading due west, towards the Nerin River. But there weren't any villages in that area. Unless Teyrnas had changed more than he thought during his time in the Hinterlands.

"I'll explain later. Everything okay here?"

"Sure. As long as you don't mind all of us sharing a room."

"Five people to a room?" Kel peered through the gate. People moved in the deepening shadows, walking down dirt paths and in between rows of tents. Some wore white, gray, or blue cloaks, but far more wore ragged clothes. A trio of barefoot children ran past the gate, laughing, as adults yelled at them to watch it.

"Callum, how many refugees are here?"

"Hundreds living on the Academy grounds. Thousands more in Norgard and outlying villages."

"We can't stand out here all night," Deen said impatiently. The other refugees had already gone inside. The two remaining guards waited outside the gate, glancing furtively eastward.

Callum led their group inside. The normally green fields were overrun with tents, overlapping in places. Campfires dotted the area. And there were people everywhere. Men, women, children. All former residences of Teyrnas and the countless little towns and villages that dotted the Highway. A group of men eyed their horses. Kel rode closer to Callum.

"So, where is our room?" Colm asked. His pet draig, Kalessin, sat primly on his shoulder, surveying the grounds.

"Over here." Callum led them through a narrow maze and dismounted near a cluster of tents. Right next to the stables. "The Academy will give the horses to the cavalry. We're right here." He pointed at the nearest tent. A patchwork of old canvas and oiled tarps.

"Are you joking?" Deen asked.

"Wish I was." Callum grabbed his satchel. "No use in complaining. Deen, help me with the horses. Colm, find a healer for Kel."

✳✳✳

"Who was that?" Kuno asked Brother Malaky once they were away from the Academy. They rode towards the setting sun, twilight at their heels. They had about half an hour of visible light left.

"No one. Well, not no one," Brother Malaky stammered. "Everyone is someone in the Creator's eyes."

"True, but you acted like you knew him."

Brother Malaky flicked the reins, urging the horse to run faster. Kuno cursed and hurried to catch up.

Lok white-knuckled the reins. He had never ridden a horse this fast. If he fell off, he was certain he would break every bone in his body.

"Did you know him, chaplain?" Kuno asked more forcefully. The wind blew off his hood, and the fading light burned in his eyes.

"A long time ago. Why does it matter?"

"I suppose it doesn't," Kuno muttered. "Slow down! You'll kill our horses at this pace."

Brother Malaky slowed his horse to a trot. The other two horses slowed as well, breathing heavily and slick with sweat.

Lok relaxed his hands. The leather reins left red marks on his palms.

He glanced around. They rode in the same empty field that he and Charity walked across on their way to the Academy. Fireflies lit up the field, like dozens of tiny stars. Lok waved at Kuno.

"Everything all right, Lok?"

Lok pointed at the ground.

"We'll stop in half an hour. We need to put as much distance between ourselves and the Academy before morning. When is your first class? First or second bell?"

Lok held up one finger. Teyrnian history. A class he actually liked and rarely skipped. Would Scholar Nycal report his absent or think nothing of it?

"Okay. One more hour of riding."

Lok groaned. He glanced over at Brother Malaky. The chaplain stared straight ahead.

Why are you lying? The chaplain obviously knew the man. Very few men had leg braces and a crutch. Lok's heart leapt into his throat. Master Kel? Was that man Master Kel?

The light had been too low for Lok to get a good look, and he paid more attention to the guards than the refugees. But if that man had been Master Kel, was the other man Callum Haar? He sounded like him. If he didn't have a beard... Yes, it was Callum! He was alive!

Then where was Realta? Shouldn't she have been with her father?

And who were the other men?

Lok peered up at the sky. The first stars shone in the inky blackness, and the first moon Ilana appeared at the horizon.

Those questions would have to wait until morning.

11
Practice

Realta walked into the forest, tucking a knife into her belt. She saw Ezri standing behind Chinasa like a living shadow while the ambassador spoke to Master Corey. The bodyguard never strayed far when the merchant was nearby. Ezri claimed there was something off about the merchant, a strange sense he could not describe with words. Realta agreed. Corey made her feel uncomfortable, similar to the way she felt around Dane Kanton.

She ducked under the leafy branches and walked over a small hill. Countless miles of trees stood before her. The forest here was mostly dry, with a few swampy parts, but closer to the river, it turned into marshland populated by reeds and birds with long, thin legs.

Westward laid the Vogel Mountains. And fifty miles to the south rested the Kereuic Pass, a physical border separating the Northern Realm and the Sykerian Empire.

Will we go there? Realta wished she had an answer. Since crossing the Nerin River into Byyar and venturing south, they followed the same routine: one day of travel followed by two days of rest. They should have moved on two days ago, but Master Corey insisted they remain here until they decided on a destination that everyone agreed on. And by everyone, he meant himself.

Would they really sail to Treilean? The island nation was neutral, but it was right off the coast of Bran Maro. And no one was sure how they treated Thanes. The last Chinasa heard, the Treileani were respectful yet distant. Thanes kept to themselves. But what if attitudes had changed? Should they really take the risk?

Realta came to the small valley where she and Ezri had practiced the other day. Humidity hung in the air, her clothes and hair beginning to cling to her skin despite the early hour. Birds sang as they flitted from branch to branch.

She closed her eyes and inhaled deeply, breathing in the natural scents. She felt safer here. Almost as though she were in the woods back home. At any moment, Charity would come running up, wanting Realta to join her in an adventure, or Mistress Loy would call everyone in for supper. But Charity was at the Academy, and Mistress Loy was far away. Would she ever see them again?

Realta pushed those thoughts away. Dwelling on the past or what might have been would not improve her current situation.

Removing the knife from her belt and positioning her feet, the right slightly behind the left, she gripped the knife by the hilt and threw it with all her strength. The knife sailed through the air, turning over and over. The blade struck the tree and bounced off.

Realta wanted to scream.

"You're throwing it too hard."

She whirled around and saw Braedan leaning against a tree. A collection of knives, all recently sharpened, hung from his belt.

Her heart skipped a beat. She dashed towards the tree, grabbed the knife, and held it tight.

Braedan raised both hands and smirked. "Peace. I won't hurt you."

"What are you doing here?" She didn't know which shook more: her voice or her hand.

"That's a question I should ask you. A young girl heading off into the forest all by herself. Don't all those kid stories end with the girl being eaten by wildcats or kidnapped by bandits?"

Realta glanced behind Braedan. The hill blocked her view of the campsite, and she hadn't told anyone she was going into the forest. No one knew she was here. No one, expect Braedan.

Stupid, stupid, stupid! Why hadn't she told Shasta or Serena? Realta wanted time to practice, but practicing by herself in the woods? She felt incredibly foolish. She gripped the knife tighter in her sweating hand.

"Want me to help?" Braedan pointed at the knife.

"I already have a teacher, thank you."

"The ambassador's bodyguard? Yeah, he's a little occupied right now. My employer has got him all jumpy. I'm sure he won't mind."

"I mind." Realta thought about running, but Braedan was

bound to catch her. She didn't want to imagine what could happen next.

"Maybe we can practice together?" Braedan smiled, but Realta couldn't tell if it was genuine. Her eyes slid to the knives on his belt. Hunting knives, daggers, one with a long, thin blade. And all unsheathed.

"Here," Braedan said, walking closer. "I'll take this tree, and you take that one." He pointed to the one nearest her.

"Um, okay." Realta studied Braedan. He was relaxed and kept his distance. Nothing indicated he wanted to hurt her. And it was her idea to question him and Elliza. Why had he lied about her being a Thane? And why did Elliza spy on her? But she had hoped to question him at the camp with other people around. Not in a forest where it would be too late for anyone to help even if they started running the moment she screamed.

Braedan selected a hunting knife and held it lightly by the blade. "Watch me." Placing his right foot back, he raised his throwing arm, the blade parallel with his ear, and threw the knife as he stepped forward. The blade sunk deep into the tree trunk. Realta didn't doubt that he could sink that knife into a person's back just as easily.

"What do you think?" Braedan asked.

"It was a good throw," she replied quietly.

"Good throw? That's it? No, 'wow, Braedan, you're so amazing'?" He smiled widely, exposing white teeth. Was it just a trick of the light or were his canine teeth longer than normal?

Realta shrugged.

You cannot question someone without asking questions, she berated herself. And Corey couldn't interrupt or eavesdrop while they were out here. She might not get a better chance.

"Very well." Braedan sighed dramatically. "Your turn."

Her heart pounding in her throat, Realta walked ten paces away from the tree, never taking her eye off Braedan. Why was he helping her? Was he just being friendly, or had Corey sent him after her?

Did he tell Corey that I'm a Thane? Was the lie just for show? To trick me into trusting him?

Braedan pointedly cleared his throat.

Realta took a deep breath, trying to calm down. She assumed a throwing stance, held the knife by the blade, and threw it using Braedan's technique. The knife hit the tree sideways and fell into the tall grass.

"How long has Ezri been teaching you?"

"About a month."

Braedan scratched his stubbly chin. "Well, cities aren't built in a day. And practice supposedly makes perfect. Want to try again?"

"Actually, I'd rather practice my Teyrnian. Can you help me?" Perhaps she could get her answers this way.

Braedan blinked. "Um, yeah. But your Teyrnian sounds fine to me. Can't even hear your Lowyrnic accent."

Heat rose in Realta's face. She knew this would happen! Oh, why had Chinasa agreed to delay Corey? Thinking quickly, she said, "I know. Chinasa helped me. But can you help me with Byyarian and Nowani? I know some words are different."

"I don't see why not." Braedan walked over to the trees and retrieved both knives. Realta watched his hands as he gave hers back. "The languages are pretty much the same. Sometimes words sound different because of the accents."

"Like your accent?"

Braedan smiled. "Yeah. Except mine ain't that strong."

"So, you're from Teyrnas?"

"My mother was from Teyrnas. But I was raised in Alennon, Nowan. It's a small town near the confluence of the Nerin and Mallr Rivers. What about you? Which part of Lowyrn are you from?"

"Holtbeinn. Near Caman's Pass." It was the town her mother grew up in. Callum had told her about it. The mountainous town was surprisingly similar to Vala. Probably why Callum had visited so often.

"Yeah, that's a nice place. So, what do your folks think about you being an apprenticed linguist? Couldn't you have studied at the Lowyrn Academy?"

"I don't really like school. And when Ambassador Ekene and the Scholars passed through, it seemed like a good opportunity."

Braedan nodded. "Can't fault taking advantage of opportunities. But I know if I had a daughter, I would worry about her being on the road."

"Well, my mother died when I was little, and my father..." Her voice choked. Had their plan worked perfectly, Callum would be with them. But Val had arrived too early. Realta and Serena had no choice. They ran into the courtyard, losing Val in the chaos, but also leaving without Callum.

She had tried Dreaming about him, but her Dreams took her years into the past. Seeing Callum as a young man was well and good, but what about his present self? Had he and Kel gotten out of the palace in time? Callum would not abandon his brother-in-law, even if it meant risking his own life.

Soldiers had stormed the palace as they fled. Thousands of soldiers hiding in plain sight. What if Callum and Kel hadn't gotten out? What if they were captured? Did the Nowani see Callum's servant's mark and forced him to work, or had they executed him, thinking he was King Logan's loyal servant? What if she could not Dream about Callum in the recent past because he didn't have a recent past?

Was her father dead?

A gentle hand touched her shoulder. Realta glanced up and met Braedan's clear blue eyes.

"I lost my mother when I was thirteen years old," he said softly. "I still think about her all the time."

Realta wiped away a stray tear with her sleeve. "I don't... I don't know where my father is. He went missing. I don't know if..." She didn't dare say it out loud. A bad feeling formed in her gut, and her heart felt heavy.

"You don't have to talk if you don't want to." Braedan glanced at the hill. "Corey will pitch a fit if I'm gone too long. Wanna head back?" He smiled and his eyes brightened to the same color as the summer sky. Warm and comforting.

Realta nodded.

As they walked up the small hill, she asked, "How did you become a bodyguard?"

Braedan laughed. "Sweetheart, I ain't a bodyguard. I'm a mercenary."

Realta's heart skipped a beat, and she nearly tripped over her own feet. She'd heard dozens of stories about mercenaries. Soldiers for hire, they were ruthless and often turned on the people who hired them. Callum had a nasty experience with them shortly after he started working as a guide. They paid him up front, but once they reached Lowyrn, they held Callum at sword point and forced him to give the money back. Callum didn't fight them, but neither did he keep quiet about the experience. Afterwards, nobody in Vala would dare trust a mercenary.

"You're a mercenary?"

"Yep. More fun that way. See, bodyguards are long-term hires. But a mercenary can quit whenever he or she wants. And Corey knows it." His smile widened. Sure enough, his canine teeth were longer. Realta spied fine lines on the teeth.

Did he file them?

A shiver ran down her spine.

They crested the hill, and the campsite came into view. Realta instantly relaxed. If Braedan tried to hurt her now, there would be witnesses.

"Then why work for him?"

"Because he pays twice as much for a Cuchasi." Braedan locked eyes with her. "But being a mercenary and not a professional Hound, I only tell him what I deem necessary."

"So, telling him that I'm a Thane wasn't necessary, but telling him about the others was?"

"I told Corey what he expected to hear. Besides, Elliza asked me not to reveal the girl with the black Aura. Practically begged me on her knees. Dramatic little thing," he muttered.

"Wait. How did she know?"

Braedan motioned for Realta to be quiet as they entered the circle of wagons. The Scholars had gathered near the laundry line, whispering and wearing worried expressions. Chinasa and Corey were arguing, Corey's face dark red and shouting at the top of his lungs. Chinasa rolled his eyes and spoke to Ezri in Jemayrti.

"Anything you have to say, say it in Teyrnian!" the merchant yelled.

"It's not my fault you are monolingual," Chinasa snapped.

Braedan led Realta to her wagon. Serena and Shasta sat on the steps, watching the argument. Serena saw Realta and smiled, but the smile immediately faded as her eyes fell on Braedan. She leapt to her feet, acting like she was going to run. Shasta acknowledged Realta and Braedan with a single nod and turned her attention back to Chinasa and Corey.

"What I miss?" Braedan asked Shasta.

"Perhaps you should ask your employer, Master Sutter. I don't think he will react well to you speaking with us," Shasta replied. Her dark eyes studied the merchant.

The argument shifted. Chinasa wanted to leave Kereu immediately. Corey countered that they would only leave if their destination was Treilean. Chinasa threw up his hands in frustration.

"Corey can shove it. Do you know the truth about this girl?" Braedan cocked his thumb in Realta's direction. Serena's eyes widened.

"What truth?" Shasta asked calmly.

"You know I'm a Hound."

"Hound is a distinctly Byyarian term for Cuchasi. I thought you were Nowani."

"I'm just myself." Braedan crossed his arms. He watched the argument for a minute and then asked, "So, yes or no?"

Shasta locked eyes with him. "Are you trying to bribe us? Our coin for your silence?"

Braedan smirked. "No, just didn't want to spill any secrets."

"How thoughtful of you."

Corey screamed in Chinasa's face, the words too distorted for Realta to understand. Chinasa opened his mouth to speak but closed it. He stormed away, Ezri following on his heels. Corey glared at him and then at the Scholars. The Scholars, as a collective group, went inside their wagons, whispering. Corey's gaze fell on Braedan.

"What in the name of the Abyss are you standing around for?! I don't pay you to stand around. My wagon, now!"

"Yes, sir!" Braedan gave a swiping bow, like an actor before an audience.

Corey scowled and stormed off into his wagon. He slammed the door shut.

"Damn, Elliza's in there," Braedan said, worry creeping into his voice.

"Will he hurt her?" Serena asked.

Realta suddenly felt bad. As much as she wanted to get away from Corey, Elliza was stuck with him.

"Not if I stop him. Oh, Elliza is a Farsight," he said to Realta. "She saw your black Aura a week ago. Thought you should know." Braedan sprinted towards the wagon, pulling the door open and closed in one fluid movement.

"Excellent work, Miss Haar," Shasta said.

"Ma'am?"

"Serena told me about your plan to question those two. Wise thinking."

Chinasa returned to the camp's center with Ezri a step behind. He exchanged a few whispered words with the bodyguard. Ezri nodded and positioned himself next to Corey's wagon. Realta heard muffled yelling. Hopefully, Braedan would calm Corey down.

"I'm calling a meeting in five minutes," Chinasa said to them. "I want everyone present."

"Taking a vote?" Shasta asked.

"Yes." He glanced at Corey's wagon. "Should have never…" He shook his head. "The past is done. All we have are consequences. Five minutes." Chinasa walked over to the next wagon and informed the Scholars. Shasta went with him.

Realta glanced at Serena. The girl shook like a leaf in a storm. "Are you okay?"

"He, um…" She averted her eyes. "The way Corey yelled, it reminded me of Logan."

Realta sighed. She wanted to talk to Serena about her brother's death, but she honestly did not know where to start. She'd been too young to grieve for her mother, so she had no idea what Serena must be feeling. Logan had been indifferent and cold towards her, but Realta suspected that Logan cared about her. He had just been in too much pain to show her love.

"Did Logan yell at you a lot?"

Serena shook her head. "Not a lot. But when he yelled, you didn't want to be in the same room." She paused. "Realta, does Kel yell?"

Realta was taken aback. "No. Well, he yelled at the healer a few times, but Zall had it coming. But Kel never yelled at us. Even when we made mistakes." Kel was always patient and loving, and never so much as raised his voice. How could two brothers be so different?

"And your father?"

Realta shook her head. "Never."

"You're lucky," Serena whispered. She lowered her head, sandy brown hair hiding her face.

"Come on," Realta said. The Scholars gathered around the map table, glancing warily at Corey's wagon. The yelling had subsided. Realta hoped that was a good sign. "Don't want to keep them waiting."

12

Omission

A map of the Northern Realm, weighed down with rocks on each corner, stretched across the table. Serena stood between Realta and Shasta, glancing at the Scholars who whispered nervously to one another in Jemayrti.

She wished she knew the language better, instead of just a handful of phrases. Then she'd have a better understanding of what they were thinking and planning. Better yet, if she were an Empath, she wouldn't have to know the language to know their true feelings.

Serena looked down at the map, studying the colored tiles. The blue tile represented their position in Kereu, near the river. The white one, representing Nowan, rested on the former capital, while the red one, for Teyrnas, rested over the Academy. Green tiles, representing the rest of the Coalition, circled the capital and lined the Highway from Hygate to Norgard, guarding the confluence of the Nerin and Wallach Rivers.

It had been weeks since they heard accurate reports amid a torrent of rumors. They could only guess how the war was progressing.

"Are we leaving soon?" Scholar Adanna asked, pulling Serena out of her thoughts.

"That's up to you," Chinasa replied. He squared his shoulders and spoke in a calm, even voice. "I was asked to delay Master Corey for a few days, and those few days are up. I would prefer to send him on his way, but the man seems determined to travel with us, no matter where we go."

A pit formed in Serena's gut. She always got a bad feeling whenever Corey was nearby, similar to how she felt around Kanton. Always watching, always unpredictable.

"Are we going back to Jemayrt?" asked Scholar Kambri. "Talk

of Treilean was just a rouse, right? A way to get him off our trail?"

Chinasa studied the map, both hands clasped behind his back. Serena looked at the boundary lines. Sykeria was the easiest to reach. There were no mountains to cross, and they could always hire a boat and sail to Averil, traveling to Jemayrt by land. Traveling south and then west seemed much safer than travelling east.

But if the goal is to prevent Val from finding Realta and Chinasa, should we travel east instead? It would be more dangerous, being closer to Bran Maro, but the east is the last place Val would look, right?

"Jemayrt," Realta said. "We should go to Jemayrt."

Chinasa locked eyes with her. "Explain."

Realta paled as every eye turned towards her. "I doubt the war will spread across the mountains. It will be harder to move soldiers through that terrain. My father never guided more than four or five wagons through Caman's Pass at a time. The more people, the more difficult the trip. They had to carry more supplies and take extra care so nobody fell behind. I think going to Jemayrt would be smarter."

"Very good points, Miss Haar. Do we have any arguments for Treilean?" Chinasa looked at each Scholar. Scholar Okorie raised his hand. "Yes?"

"While traveling to Treilean may be a good decision in the short term, it's possible that Bran Maro will solidify its alliance with them. Increase tariffs or threaten to cut off trade if Treilean does not aid the Coalition. If we travel to Treilean, we must make plans to head for Sykeria or another neutral nation."

"Which will add to travel expenses," Scholar Leila chimed in.

"Expenses we don't have." Chinasa rubbed his chin. "Mistress Cray, do you have our numbers?"

"In Teyrnian currency, we have twelve gold marks, twenty-two silver, and five copper," Shasta replied without having to check a ledger. "It should be enough to charter a boat, but what if we need leave in a hurry? We won't be able to afford a ride and none of us have experience sailing across open water. Cut the merchant loose and head for the Kereuic Pass, if you want my advice."

"Always. Shall we vote? All in favor of Jemayrt?"

Every hand rose.

Serena was not surprised. Most of the Scholars had expressed wanting to go home. They only planned on visiting Teyrnas for a half week.

What was Jemayrt like? Until this year, Serena never traveled outside of the capital and rarely left the palace. Only on special occasions with Shasta or Sarra. Sarra and her husband Darrys often hosted dinner at their home, a decent sized mansion near the city's northern wall, and Sarra always insisted that Logan bring Serena, wanting their little sister to be included. Logan did so grudgingly, arguing with Isla on the ride there or muttering under his breath, refusing to speak. Serena came to dread those dinners, though Sarra and Darrys treated her warmly, as though she wasn't a servant's bastard.

Had Sarra and Darrys made it out of the city? They were staying at the palace during the coup. They must have evacuated with Isla.

"Then it's settled," Chinasa announced. "We pack up camp tomorrow at dawn."

"Who will tell Corey?" Ezri asked. He ran his thumb over the hilt of his belt knife.

Silence descended on the group like gray storm clouds encroaching on a summer's day, threatening thunder and lightning. The Scholars glanced nervously at each other. All of them avoided Corey as much as possible, defaulting conversations to Chinasa, much to the ambassador's dismay.

"Who will tell me what?"

Serena's heart leapt into her throat. Corey stormed towards them, his face burning red and his hands balled into fists. Braedan and Elliza were at his heels. The young woman's face was bruised around her right eye and cheekbone. And Braedan watched the merchant like a hawk, one hand on a knife.

Serena tore her eyes away. Braedan looked so much like Logan, but there were just as many differences as similarities. He had Logan's height, sandy brown hair, and blue eyes, but his shoulders were broader, and he was muscular instead of slender. Many men shared *some* of Logan's traits. It was just her mind playing tricks on her.

But his smile. That was Kel's smile. She had only seen it twice, once in Callum's drawing and again when Kel revealed his true identity. Yet, she recognized it. Why hadn't Realta or Shasta recognized it, too?

Because it's all in your head, your stupid girl.

That had sounded eerily similar to Logan's voice.

"Master Corey," Chinasa said, adopting a diplomatic tone, "we've decided to travel to Jemayrt instead of Treilean."

"All right." Corey relaxed a bit. "Would have preferred Treilean. More interesting trade route. But I haven't been through Averil lately. When do we—"

"Without you."

Corey's eyes narrowed. "Excuse me?"

"We are traveling without you. Feel free to travel to Treilean by yourself. We leave in the morning."

"I thought we had a deal," Corey said, his voice low and harsh.

Serena and Realta inched closer to Shasta. Serena stole a glance at their wagon. Would she and Realta be able to make a run for it? Lock the door before Corey chased after them? She had always been a fast runner.

"The deal is off."

"Off?! You listen to me—"

"Sir." Elliza gently tugged on Corey's sleeve.

"Not now. We agreed to travel together. The roads are too dangerous for a single wagon."

"But, sir."

"What?" Corey rounded on Elliza.

Serena's heart rate doubled as a half-forgotten memory surfaced. One from before her mother died. She always stuck close to her mother, even when Nell was working. Serena didn't mind. She liked exploring all the fancy rooms, seeing all the pretty paintings and vases, and sometimes she got to see the princes and princess.

Nell rounded a corner, Serena in tow, when they heard a man yelling. Serena clung to her mother's dress, the scream terrifying her. Nell dropped the basket of laundry she was carrying and picked up Serena, hurrying into the nearest room. Nell whispered a prayer as they hid in a corner.

"Can't you do anything right, you stupid whore?!"

The door burst open, concealing them. Nell held Serena tightly. Serena was so frightened; she didn't make a sound.

The yelling man dragged another servant into the room. He flung her onto the floor. It was Mistress Murand, one of her mother's friends. Mistress Murand covered her face with her hands and sobbed.

"I'm so sorry, Your Majesty. It won't happen again, I swear!"

"You're damn right it won't."

Serena clung to her mother tighter. She recognized the yelling man. He was the bad man. The man her mother was terrified of. He was the reason Nell always wanted Serena to stay close by. The few times Serena had seen him, he gave her and her mother a strange smile, sometimes laughing as he walked away.

The bad man hit Mistress Murand with his belt. Again and again and again...

Cold sweat coated Serena's brow, reliving that awful day. Mistress Murand had been so bruised, she laid in bed for three days, the other servants doing her work so Yestyn wouldn't harm her again.

Yestyn's temper had always been close at hand, forcing the servants and his own wife and children to walk on eggshells. Even Logan took care not to raise his voice to the old king. But once Logan inherited the crown, he inherited Yestyn's temper. Erratic and volatile. As she grew older, she took pains to avoid him. She could not make Logan angry if she was not there.

And Logan's temper always flared in Alet, around his older brother's birthday. And in Zanin, around his brother's death.

Her breath caught in her throat. Today was Zanin nineteenth. The day Prince Carwyn supposedly died. Yestyn brutally beat Carwyn because Carwyn wanted to expose the truth. But a different truth had been exposed: his elopement with Esme Haar. He had endured horrible pain for the woman he loved and for a servant's bastard. The first one was understandable. Most people would die for their loved ones. But the second was just baffling. Why had Kel cared so much?

Tears stung Serena's eyes. Her oldest half-brother, the rightful heir to the Raven Throne, had faced a king's wrath for Serena's sake. He had genuinely cared about her whereas Logan could barely look at her.

"She has a servant's mark." Elliza's small voice rang clear throughout the camp.

Serena blinked a few times, confused. What on Eltriar was she...? Oh Great Creator. Serena glanced at Realta. The other girl covered her wrist. The bead bracelet had slipped off, lying in the green grass.

Corey, his face turning dark red, stormed towards Realta.

"Sir, a word," said Braedan. Corey motioned for him to be silent. He grabbed Realta by the wrist and held it up. Two thin bands with two diamonds marked her ruddy skin.

"You lied to me." Corey glared at Chinasa. "And here I thought the Jemayrti were honest people. But you hid this slave?"

"What I do with my servants is my business," Chinasa replied calmly.

How can he be so calm? Granted, he was an ambassador. He had trained to deal with monarchs and their temperaments. Surely he could handle a single merchant.

"Did you give her that bracelet?"

"It was a birthday gift."

"So you did lie!"

"I said she was an apprenticed linguist. I never," Chinasa gave Realta a pained look. "I never said she was free."

Tears brimmed Realta's eyes. She hated the servant's mark, and Serena hated Logan for giving it to her.

"A lie of omission is still a lie," Elliza said. She held her hands clasped primly in front of her.

"At least you're still good for something." Corey turned his attention to Realta. "So, what did you do, girl? How'd you get that mark?"

"None of your business." Realta tried to pull her wrist free, but Corey's grip was too strong.

Ezri reached for a knife, but Chinasa motioned for him to stop. The bodyguard obeyed but kept his hand close to the weapon.

I should help. But how?

"Take your hand off her, Waylar Corey." Chinasa stalked closer, standing inches away from the merchant. "There is no need for this."

Corey scoffed. "No need. How do I know she belongs to you? The Kereuic government doesn't view harboring runaways lightly. Where are your papers?"

"They were lost," Shasta replied.

"How convenient. Braedan, take her to the wagon. Keep an eye on her while we sort this out."

"You know, sir," Braedan said with a wry smile. "This really isn't any of our business."

"Take her. Now!" Corey shoved Realta towards Braedan.

Serena squeezed her eyes tight. Why did Corey have to yell? Why did he have to sound like Logan? Why did Braedan have to look like Logan? Why in the name of the bloody Abyss couldn't she stop thinking about Logan?!

Corey screamed.

Serena opened her eyes and saw Corey clutching his forehead while the Scholars stared in wide-eyed horror. Realta looked like she was going to cry. Only Elliza was completely at ease.

Corey removed his hand. There was a small cut on his forehead, just above the left eye. Serena spied three colored tiles at Corey's feet.

Braedan cursed.

"Who threw that?" Corey snapped. The camp was so silent, Serena could hear the blood rushing in her ears. Corey picked up one tile, studying it. He then looked at the map table. No one stood next to it. No one could have thrown it.

Serena locked eyes with Realta. She trembled from head to foot. Had she Manipulated the tiles?

Corey glared at Realta and Braedan. "Sutter, why did you curse?"

"I was shocked. Didn't expect them to throw something at you."

"Did you see who?"

Braedan opened his mouth, then closed it. He shook his head. Corey turned to Elliza. "Did you see?"

"Nobody threw the tiles, sir. They flew via a Manipulation."

Corey rounded on the Scholars. "Which one of you is a Thane?"

"I'm a Manipulator," Kambri answered, her voice shaking.

"Did you Manipulate those tiles?"

She stole a quick glance at Chinasa. "I have the ability."

"It was me," Realta admitted.

Braedan squeezed his eyes shut. He looked like he was going to be sick.

"Well, isn't that interesting?" Corey turned to Chinasa. "Did you know about her ability?"

Chinasa said nothing.

"Fine. Be that way. Braedan."

The bodyguard placed both hands on Realta's shoulders. "Yes, sir?" he said quietly.

"Keep a very close eye on that girl. We will discuss your lies this evening. And if anyone," he addressed the group, "decides to run, I will alert the Kereuic militia."

The group stood there, stunned. Nobody moved or whispered. Serena knew she ought to do something, anything. Stars above, she felt completely useless!

Realta broke away from Braedan and ran over to Shasta. Tears brimmed her dark eyes. "I'm so sorry." Her voice trembled. "I didn't mean—"

"You acted in self-defense," Shasta said, placing a gentle hand on her arm. "You and Serena return to the wagon. We will find a way out of this."

"I just got so scared. I don't know why. I just... I felt trapped. I had to get away. Sorry."

"There's no need to apologize. Go."

Serena wrapped her arm around Realta's shoulders and walked towards their wagon. She stole a glance at Braedan. Corey and Elliza were already gone, the door of their wagon slamming shut. The confident bodyguard now looked like a lost child, terrified and alone.

13

The Missing

Charity glanced at the wall clock again. Ten minutes past the hour. Scholar Kuno was never this late. Only a minute or two at most, and very rarely. She drummed her fingers on the desk.

"Where do you think he is?" asked Henson, a boy with eyeglasses.

Tilly, sitting to his right, shrugged.

"Should we practice?" asked Autumn, a timid girl who rarely spoke above a whisper. Scholar Kuno encouraged them to practice outside of class. Speaking a language, even a dead one, made it much easier to remember and learn.

"Maybe someone should check his room," Dunny suggested.

The Students looked at one another, all at a complete loss.

"Doesn't he have a history class before this period?" Charity asked.

"I think so," said Alyn. "One for Journeymen."

"Maybe that class ran late," Charity said.

"Doubt it," said Tilly, turning around in her seat to face Charity. She pushed a lock of unruly black hair away from her face. "Journeymen classes are shorter than ours. Gives them more time for independent study."

"Can't hurt to check," another boy said. Charity was pretty sure his name was Austyn.

"I'll go." Charity stood and collected her Old Eltrian primer and workbook. "Where is the classroom?"

"Third floor probably," Henson replied.

Charity headed out. A handful of Students exited behind her, walking off in the opposite direction. She had a feeling they were not going to study. Many Students skipped classes, using the extra time to work on classwork or to do nothing.

She passed several Students, Journeymen, and Scholars on the way, as well as dozens of people in plain clothes. Refugees from Teyrnas and outlying villages. A lot worked at the Academy, doing odd jobs, cooking food, fixing furniture. Some worked as assistants, helping Scholars with their research and grading exams.

A trio of children, all of them around twelve years old and wearing ragged clothes, ran past her. A fourth child, a skinny boy with reddish gold hair, struggled to keep up. One boy halted at the corner.

"Come on, Morgan!" he called out.

Morgan, gasping for breath, caught up with the other boy. A second later, they took off running again.

Charity climbed the steps to the third floor and entered the Journeymen's wing. A mass of gray cloaks with an occasional white dot crowded the hallway. All the classroom doors were open, and half the classes had spilled out into the hall. Journeymen huddled in groups around a single Scholar, discussing subjects ranging from philosophy to chemistry to political history. Many furiously wrote notes, and more than a few had ink stains on their hands and sleeves. Some Journeymen sat on the floor with stacks of books and papers by their sides. Charity was amazed that any of them could focus in this cacophony.

"Excuse me," she asked a passing Scholar, a man with snowy white hair the same color as his cloak. "Where is Scholar Kuno's ancient history class?"

The Scholar gave her a puzzled look. "That class is for Journeymen."

"I know. He didn't show up to my class. Old Eltrian for Beginners. I'm looking for him."

"Strange. His ancient history class was canceled this morning. Several Scholars are meeting today to discuss the war. Queen Isla is making some sort of announcement this afternoon. He probably forgot to tell you."

"Oh. Where is the meeting?"

The Scholar smiled patiently. "It's only for Scholars. Go back to your studies, young Student." He then walked away. Charity had half expected him to pat her on the head like a kindly old grandfather.

Going back to her studies was sensible, but why hadn't Kuno

informed them that class was canceled? It wasn't like him to overlook that sort of thing.

And why hadn't she heard about the queen's announcement? Even if it was just for Scholars, anything affecting them ultimately affected Students and Journeymen. So why not include them?

Could she sneak in and listen? She hadn't seen the queen in person since the Exhibition, though Gareth visited her from time to time. She was his aunt, after all.

Maybe I can ask Gareth if I can see her.

She quickly pushed the idea away. Gareth wasn't bold enough to ask, and she didn't want him to think she was using his newfound family connections for personal gain. Friends did not use friends that way.

Charity walked up to the nearest Scholar without a class and asked him about the meeting. The Scholar, his eyes bloodshot and his hair in desperate need of a comb, stared at her for an uncomfortably long time. He then shivered as though doused with ice water.

"Queen Isla's meeting? Oh, right! That meeting. Um, good question. Try the Council Chambers. Or the Auditorium. Or maybe the courtyards." He scratched his head.

"I'm sure I can find it." *And maybe Scholar Kuno, too.*

Charity hurried down the hall, dodging people left and right. She had only been inside the Council Chamber once, for Lok's Thane Ceremony, and she'd never been to the Auditorium. If it was like a lecture hall, it was bound to hold scores of people and would be the more logical place for the meeting. She asked a nearby Journeyman, a young man surrounded by a semicircle of books.

"Not likely," he replied. "The Auditorium was converted into a supply station for the guards. There isn't room to hold a crate of dried fruit, let alone a meeting," he added, muttering.

Charity thanked him anyway and asked a Scholar, a woman with hints of gray in her brown hair.

"The queen's announcement is scheduled for noon. But I haven't heard of a meeting for Scholars. Perhaps try the Gorllin Building. We held the last meeting there."

Charity made her way to the main atrium, the Academy's massive twin staircases guarding both wings. Three familiar faces stood out from the crowd: Evelyn, Coryn, and Jaim. She waved and smiled, but the smile faded as she noted the worried looks on their faces.

"Have you seen Lok?" Jaim asked. His eyes were wide, and his hands frantically moved in and out of his pockets. "He wasn't in his bed this morning. Gareth and I've been looking everywhere for him."

"Did he get up early?"

"Not a chance. Gareth woke up before sunrise and saw he was gone. Ivar and Zandon are looking, too. Figured you might know since you've known him for forever."

"No, I haven't seen him today. I was looking for Scholar Kuno."

"Maybe they're studying together," Evelyn suggested, her eyes brightening. "Getting extra practice in. Lok's three-month probation is up in two weeks."

"Oh, right." Charity almost forgot about the Council's probation. Lok was improving so much, both in his Thane ability and his studies. The Scholars had no reason to expel him now.

"Not bloody likely," Jaim muttered. He reached into a pocket and pulled out two silver coins. They twirled around in his palm.

"You don't know that for sure," Coryn replied. She glanced furtively around the crowded atrium and stood closer to her sister.

"I know people in their right minds don't get up at four in the bloody morning to study," Jaim snapped. Coryn shied away.

"Can you help us?" Evelyn asked Charity.

"Of course. Lok is probably with Kuno. You three search for Lok, and I'll search for Kuno. Someone is bound to have seen them."

"Deal," Coryn said a bit too quickly. "Meet us for lunch?"

"Yeah." Hopefully, they would find Lok and Kuno by then.

Her friends faded into the crowd.

The bells rang. Time for Basic Medicine. Oh well. She could afford to skip class. They were discussing how to reset bones this week. Something she had learned from Esme a year ago.

Charity crossed the bustling greens towards Gorllin, a long, rectangular structure that was only two stories tall and had dozens of windows lining both sides.

Hundreds of tents dotted the green. Some were white canvas while others were a patchwork of old blankets and tarps. A well of good those would do in a summer thunderstorm.

A woman sat outside one tent. A little girl, about three or four years old, sat in her lap. The woman wrapped her arms protectively around the child. Both were dirty and clothed in rags. The woman looked up at Charity with vacant eyes. Charity touched the hem of her Students' cloak, the fabric rich and smooth. How many cloaks had been given to the refugees? Had the Scholars run out? She only had three dresses, but she could get by with two. This woman was about the same size as her.

Her eyes then fell on a man. Bone thin and weary. And a head taller than her. What could she possibly give to him? And to the hundreds of others?

Charity averted her eyes and hurried inside the building.

Morning sunlight poured in through the windows, and the atrium branched off in three directions. The building was strangely quiet. No people moved about.

Well, class just started. Then why didn't she hear any muffled voices from the rooms?

She turned left and peered into each room. All empty. Weird. If this building was not in use, then why not open it up to the refugees? Sleeping in a classroom was far better than sleeping in a worn-out tent.

"Where is Scholar Cassandra?" asked a male voice.

Charity jolted. She slowly crept towards the classroom at the end of the hall and peered inside. Five people stood at the front. All five wore long, black cloaks that reached past their feet and trailed onto the floor. Hoods obscured their faces.

"Late as always," said another cloaked figure, a woman.

"No matter. We can start without her."

Charity's heart leapt into her throat. That was Scholar Lucan's voice. What was he doing here? She crouched down, praying they didn't see her.

"Has the Harbinger had any more Farsights?" Lucan asked.

"None concerning us," answered the woman.

"Sir, um…" One of the cloaked men shifted his feet.

"Speak up, Gray," Lucan said impatiently.

"Sir, the Harbinger is missing. The guards stationed at his room have not seen him since last night."

"Then where is he?" Lucan asked, anger rising in his voice.

"We don't know," Gray stammered. "We've searched the Academy grounds. He is nowhere to be found. And we questioned the guards. They claim three people on horseback left the Academy while refugees were arriving. So many people have arrived in the last week, they didn't question people leaving."

"Three? If one was Brother Malaky, then who were the other two?"

Gray glanced at his colleagues. Another cloaked man spoke. His voice was familiar, but Charity couldn't quite place it.

"Scholar Kuno is missing. He didn't show up to either of his classes this morning. And he has spent a lot of time with the chaplain. An unusual amount of time. We think they left together, sir."

"And the third?" Lucan asked. The two men wilted.

"Lok Tolman," Gray stammered. Charity frowned. Did Lok leave the Academy? Why didn't he tell anybody? "We haven't verified it yet, but no one has seen the Elemental since last night. It makes sense Kuno took his student with him."

"Damn him!" Lucan inhaled deeply and stood straighter. "We should have never allowed Kuno to mentor that boy. The only Elemental on Eltriar and the Harbinger were right in our grasps, and Kuno stole them from us."

"Sir, there is still time. The Midnight King has not yet appeared."

Charity's heart skipped a beat. The Midnight King had been defeated during the Thousand Years War, but not before he nearly destroyed the world and killed thousands. Hundreds of thousands. Perhaps millions over the centuries. Why were these Scholars talking about the Midnight King reappearing?

"The Harbinger is proof that our King walks Eltriar again. Send riders. Find Malaky and Tolman and return them to the Academy. Make sure they are unharmed. And bring Kuno to me. Alberik will need to hone his skills, and Kuno will be perfect for practice."

A pair of hands grabbed Charity and pinned her arms behind her back. She screamed. The hands held on tighter. The cloaked figures turned and faced her.

"What is the meaning of this?" Lucan stalked towards her. Her heart pounded against her ribs.

"I caught her spying, sir," said the woman holding Charity. Cassandra, she guessed. "What do we do with her?"

"Depends. How long have you been standing there, girl?"

Charity peered up at his hooded face. Shadows hid the Scholar's dark eyes. She tried to speak, tried to think of an excuse, but her throat was caught in a vise.

"Sir, isn't she Tolman's friend?" Gray asked.

Lucan smiled. "You're right. Charity Loy. That's your name, isn't it?"

Charity stared at him, frozen.

"I remember you now. Where has Tolman gone? Why did Kuno take Brother Malaky with them?"

"I don't know," she stammered.

Lucan addressed the other cloaked figures. "Have the riders inform Tolman that we have his girlfriend once he's found. I doubt he will abandon her." Lucan smiled at Charity.

"What do we do with her in the meantime?" asked the other male Scholar, his voice shaking. "We can't risk her exposing us."

"Of course. Gray, Leland, put her somewhere safe."

The two men lunged at her, grabbing her arms. She kicked at their shins, scoring once. The man cursed and let go. But Cassandra quickly took his place.

She opened her mouth to scream, but something smacked into the back of her head. Stars danced in her vision before everything turned black.

Charity slowly came to. She laid on hard, cold stones, and her eyelids felt like lead. The back of her head throbbed. She reached out, moving her hand along the cold floor.

She cracked open an eye. Faint light filtered in through a narrow window near the ceiling. She slowly pushed herself up. Her vision swam, and her head felt like it was going to split in two.

She tentatively touched the back of her head. Her hair was coarse and brittle. Dried blood. Not a good sign. She could have a skull fracture or a concussion.

Surveying the room, she saw a white basin, chipped and cracked in multiple places, and a long bench bolted to the wall. Metal bars comprise the opposite wall. Beyond stood a dimly lit hallway. And more bars. Prison cells. All empty.

"Hello?" she asked. Her voice was weak and hoarse. She called out again, "Hello?" The word echoed faintly.

"Where am I?" she cried out, praying that someone would hear her.

She waited a minute. Two minutes. Five.

Nobody answered.

14

On the Horizon

A warm summer breeze blew in from the ocean. The beach trees, with their massive, leafy fronds and skinny trucks, swayed gently. Sea mist coated Val's skin and hair. He breathed deeply, committing the scent to memory.

After rescuing West from that abandoned mining outpost in Lowyrn, they travel west to Jemayrt and then north to Saethyr. The peoples of the coastal countries were friendly and happy to see travelers from the eastern side of the mountains, eager to hear news from that side of the Realm. Merchants had been scarce this spring, and the few they encountered always talked of war. Val readily confirmed the bad news, biting his tongue so he wouldn't smile. All the pieces were falling into place.

West was terribly shy at first. Clinging to Val whenever people spoke to them or merely walked too close. Val did not blame the boy. A childhood of abuse was difficult to overcome. A fact Val knew all too well.

They had arrived in Kossa, a port city twenty miles from the Saethyr-Jemayrt border, last week. Val rented a room at the inn nearest the docks. And then the wait began.

"When will the other Nine get here?" West asked two days ago, growing impatient and nervous. Worried that Mida would somehow catch up to them and take West back to Bran Maro.

"Very soon, West. We must be patient."

But Val was starting to feel impatient himself. The Midnight King walked Eltriar again. Val sensed it in his bones, ever since Springtide. The sense grew stronger as he crossed the border into Teyrnas. It was only a matter of time before Alberik regained his powers and amassed his armies. The Nine had to unite before it was too late.

If only Realta and Chinasa had seen reason. But Chinasa was

set in his ways, certain of his beliefs. And Realta… Poor girl. She truly believed that her human father cared about her. If Callum Haar ever discovered her true strength, if he learned what she was really capable of, he would discard her the same way Val's parents had discarded him. As something to be feared, to be hated.

Perhaps she was learning that lesson right now.

Either way, she and Chinasa would come around in due time. Fate would not allow them to sit idly by.

A peal of laughter snapped Val out of his thoughts. He looked at the shore. West, his trousers rolled up to his knees, played in the waves. Chasing them as they receded and racing for the dunes as they rushed forward. Val smiled. It was the first time he heard the boy laugh. He took it as a good sign.

Val stepped over a set of boulders covered with greenish-gray moss. The wet sand felt nice and cool on his bare feet. West continued running up and down, his mop of brown hair slick with sea spray.

"Having fun?" Val asked, clasping his hands behind his back and smiling. He quickly learned to smile when asking West a question, otherwise the boy thought he was in for a beating.

Damn that woman! If he ever found Mida again, he'd—

No, there were more important matters at hand.

West, laughing and grinning, ran up to him. Val didn't know why the Gadyeni had chosen a simpleton as One of the Nine. He could learn, but slowly. He barely recognized letters and struggled to add simple sums. Val spied the long scar near the boy's hairline. A childhood injury that resulted in lifelong damage.

But childlike as he was, Westermor Calbi was not wholly innocent. The boy understood right and wrong, and the ways his gift could be used for good or evil.

"Look, Val. Look!" West threw his hands into the air. A gush of water rose up and started spinning, forming a thin funnel. The water funnel spun around and around, growing taller and thinner. West lowered his arms, and the water funnel collapsed, spraying water all over them. He turned to Val and smiled from ear to ear.

Val clapped. "Wonderful, West!" he said in Teyrnian. While Linked to the boy's mind, his gift translated the words into Marish. "Your ability has grown tenfold."

West cocked his head. "Is that good?"

"Yes, it's very good. Now." Val draped an arm around the boy's shoulders and shepherded him towards the warm, pale white dunes. The handful of people on the beach pointed at West, marveling at his ability. Elementals were believed to be extinct on this side of the mountains, too. "Do you remember what I said about the rest of the Nine?"

"That we have to be patient."

"Well, we don't have to be patient anymore."

"They're here?" West's gray eyes brightened. Those eyes were the same shade of gray as Val's eyes. A lucky coincidence that allowed them to pass as father and son.

There are no coincidences.

His heart felt warm and light. The Gadyeni knew exactly what they were doing.

"Two of the Nine are arriving at port today. They traveled a very long way. One from the Cayuga Islands, and the other from the Konorgree Desert."

"I've never heard of those places."

"They lie far away. Across the Tharys Ocean."

West glanced back at the water and the horizon. Two shades of blue meeting and merging. An endless expanse. "How many miles is that?"

"Too many for me to count. I'm going to meet them once they land and get settled. People need to rest after long trips."

"Are they nice?" West asked hesitantly. Val peered into his mind and gritted his teeth. The boy was thinking about Mida and Argys again. And the people they were supposed to hand him over to. Poor boy. At least Val had found him before Mida found the Wardens.

Val turned his attention to the ship approaching the harbor. Closing his eyes and focusing, he sensed the two Thanes. A man and a woman. They had already created a rapport, despite the language barrier. Thanks to Val, that barrier would no longer be an issue. "I think so. But, West, I have to meet them alone."

The boy's face fell. "Why can't I come? Did I do something wrong?"

"No," Val said, looking into the boy's eyes. "You did nothing wrong. In fact, you've been doing so well that I have a special job for you."

"By myself?"

"Yes."

"But I…" West squeezed his eyes shut and shook his head. "I can't. I'm stupid!"

"No, you are not. Mida lied when she said that. West, I know you are smart. You've already learned a lot of Teyrnian and how to control fire and water."

"But I can't read or write. Why can't I stay with you, Val?" Tears welled in his eyes.

Val paused where the dunes met the stone street. Sea grass waved in the breeze, and people walked up and down the street. They wore brightly colored cloaks that covered the front and back with tightly fitting shirts and trousers underneath. A handful waved at him and Val, recognizing them from the inn. All according to plan.

Val placed both hands firmly on West's shoulders and locked eyes with him. West looked away.

"Look at me, West."

The boy reluctantly met his eyes.

"There is another One of the Nine in Teyrnas. In the Hinterlands. I need you to find her."

"Realta Haar?"

Val sighed. If only. "A different girl. I need you to find her and tell her about the Gadyeni and the Midnight King. This is very important. I would go with you, but I cannot be in two places at once. What do you think, Westermor Calbi?"

West gazed at the beach, at the waves crashing on the shore. "And then we come back here to be with you?" he asked, pointing at the beach. Val didn't need to be a Minder to know the boy loved this place.

"Yes."

"But Teyrnas is a long way away."

"Don't worry. You'll be traveling with the Ullmhir. You remember them, right?"

West shivered and averted his eyes.

"Oh, come now. You aren't afraid of them, are you? They're just people. They only live in a different place. I promise they won't hurt you. They are my friends."

"How?"

"It's easy. First, we go to an abandoned place. Like that old pier with the sign telling people not to walk on it. Then, we call the Ullmhir by name, promising a memory in exchange for the trip. It will only take a few minutes."

"What kind of memory?" West gave him a curious look.

"Well, since they take the memory away, I suggest something you want to forget."

"Argys," West whispered.

"Yes, a bad memory about Argys." Val glanced at the docks. The passenger ship sailed into port. Within the hour, the Two would step foot on Saethyr, and Val would be one step closer to defeating the Midnight King.

"Okay, Val. What's the girl's name?"

Val told him, repeating it twice so the boy would commit it to memory. He was not stupid, but he was not bright, either. Val told West to repeat it. "Good. Shall we send you on your way?"

West looked at the sea. Small seabirds with long, thin beaks walked along the shore on long, skinny legs. They moved up and down, avoiding the waves just like West. "After I find her, can I come back here?"

"Once we defeat the Midnight King, I promise we'll come back and stay as long as you wish."

"Forever?" West's eyes brightening.

Val laughed. "Sure. We mustn't keep the Ullmhir waiting." Val led West down the busy street. A smile tugged at his lips.

Four of Nine.

15

The Stables

The classroom was wrong. The same way that Gareth's dormroom had been wrong this morning. He woke up and discovered an empty bed. Lok sometimes stayed up late to practice controlling fire or to study with Scholar Kuno. Many Students studied with their mentors in the evenings. Gareth's own mentor, Scholar Gormac, met with him twice a week to discuss his studies. Gormac was trying to convince him to continue on as a Journeyman, studying advanced mathematics. Gareth merely shrugged each time the Scholar mentioned it.

But Lok never stayed out all night. No, something was wrong.

Gareth quickly woke up Jaim, much to the boy's dislike, and they started searching. They first went to Ivar and Zandon for help. Ivar readily agreed, but Zandon was reluctant. He was scheduled to leave for the Garrison later this week and couldn't afford distractions.

"Friends aren't distractions," Jaim had snapped. Zandon relented. And the sisters, Evelyn and Coryn, joined the search as well.

No one could find Lok.

A pit formed in Gareth's gut as the first bell rang. He couldn't afford to skip any classes, since he had arrived a month late into the term, and reluctantly went to class. Jaim, Evelyn, and Coryn promised to continue the search. But as he went from class to class, the bad feeling worsened.

And now, sitting in his usual seat in algebra, he sensed the same wrongness. He stared at the door, waiting. More Students filed in and took their seats until all but one were filled. Scholar Lyle entered the room as the wall clock reached the top of the hour.

Gareth glanced at the empty seat.

Where was Charity? She never skipped class.

"Good afternoon, everyone," Scholar Lyle announced as he wrote a series of equations on the blackboard. Gareth solved them all with ease. Kel had taught him algebra a few summers ago, after Gareth complained that multiplication and division were too easy. Except Kel hadn't called it algebra. Just math. And he taught Gareth all the tricks, challenging Gareth to solve the equations in his head before Kel could write it out on paper. By the end of summer, they were competing to see who could solve the equations faster. And it was all in their heads.

Gareth quickly pushed the memory away. Best not to think about his father right now. Not with all the wrongness.

"These are the equations that were most commonly missed on the last short exam. Do I have any volunteers?"

A few hands raised.

Gareth's palms began to sweat. He suddenly felt itchy, as though hundreds of ants were crawling on his skin. He fidgeted, trying to make the feeling go away. His eyes fell on Charity's empty seat again. The bad feeling worsened.

"Don't worry, Gareth. I won't call on you today," the Scholar said lightly. A handful of Students laughed.

How could they laugh and make jokes? Didn't they sense the wrongness, too?

Scholar Lyle called on three Students. The chalk pieces scritch-scratched on the blackboard, hurting Gareth's ears and teeth. He looked at the Thane Students' Auras, drawing his attention away from the grating noise.

The boy sitting in front of him was normal. The girl next to Charity's seat had wisps of gold sparked with red surrounding her skin. So similar to Kel's Aura. All she needed was silver mixed with the gold.

Tears pricked his eyes. His father had promised to meet him at the Academy, and Kel never broke promises. So, where was he? And where were Lok and Charity?

"Gareth, are you okay?" asked Scholar Lyle. The Scholar stared at him. The Students joined in the staring. Every eye on him. Colorful Auras clouded his vision. Too many for him to process. Purple with silver. Bright red. Faint blue with a few gold sparks.

Silver shining like the sun.

"Gareth, what's wrong?"

Gareth jolted. The Scholar stood directly in front of him, dark eyes narrowed and mouth frowning.

"Charity," he said, pointing at her empty seat.

"Yes, I noticed that. But it's fine. She hasn't missed any other classes and her grades are good. You can give her today's notes," he added with a smile.

"No, she isn't here."

"I can see that, Gareth." Scholar Lyle stopped smiling.

"But she... And..." Gareth's head ached. The words were there. They were right there in his mind. He could see them. He could think them. But they refused to be spoken, trapped behind a voice that would not cooperate.

"Would you like to take a break?" the Scholar asked, staring. And the Students were staring, too. A handful whispered. Two boys laughed under their breath. And now more whispering. There was too much. He couldn't focus, couldn't think...

Gareth leapt to his feet, the chair crashing to the floor. Blood rushed to his head, making it ache more.

He wished Charity was here. He wished Lok had been in their dormroom this morning. None of this made sense. People didn't just disappear.

And everyone was staring at him. Twenty sets of eyes. Too many eyes. A cold bead of sweat ran down his spine.

"Gareth." Scholar Lyle placed a hand on Gareth's shoulder. Gareth shoved him away and ran out of the classroom. "Gareth, wait!"

Wait? Wait for what? Two of his friends were missing. He didn't know how or why, but his gut told him this was bad. Very, very bad.

Bad in the same way that Kel breaking his promise was bad.

Should he go to Queen Isla? The woman was his aunt, after all. But Isla was always in meetings, talking to strangers. Gareth did not want to be around strangers. He wanted the familiar. Faces and voices he recognized.

And he wanted to go home.

When Kanton made his false promise, Kel and Esme told Gareth to attend the Academy for a month. If he didn't like it, he could come home. They would not be disappointed.

Well, it had been two months. Twice as long. But how would he get to Vala? The Teyrnas Highway was full of refugees and foreign soldiers. And he didn't like the idea of crossing the Nerin by himself.

The Cuchasi from East Bridge surfaced in his memory. The tattooed man smiled wickedly as he pointed at himself and then at Gareth. A shiver coursed through him, and he shoved the memory away.

Gareth ran down the last flight of stairs and sprinted out the main doors. He nearly ran into another Student, dodging at the last second.

"Watch it!" the Student yelled.

Gareth kept running. The bright afternoon sun warmed him instantly.

Where to go? He slowed to a walk and scanned the greens. Hundreds of tents crowded the space between the Academy and the walls. Guards dressed in dark blue uniforms patrolled the wall, armed with swords and bows and arrows. And hundreds of people roamed about. Hundreds of men, women, and children. All strangers. All unfamiliar. One woman, her dark hair in a messy braid and dark circles under her eyes, stared at him.

Gareth backed away. The bad feeling made his chest feel tight, threatening to crush his ribs. He broke eye contact with the woman and ran away. A long, single-story building came into view. The Academy's stables. Weaving between canvas tents, he reached the stables and pushed the door open.

Cool shadows enveloped him. The scent of sweet hay and worked leather filled his nose. Comfortable, familiar scents. Gareth had worked at the palace stables for a half week. It was the only place he felt safe in that massive structure ruled by a man who looked eerily similar to his father.

He was my uncle. It was so strange, his uncle being a king, despite that fact that his aunt was a queen. But Isla looked and acted like a queen. Beautiful, intelligent, always knowing what to do. It was natural to think of her as one. But Logan had just looked like Kel wearing fancy clothes.

Gareth walked down the long hallway. Stalls lined one side while tack and supplies hung on the opposite wall. The horses whinnied and stamped their hooves as he walked by. A few shook their manes. Motes of dust danced in the light streaming in from the windows, too high and narrow for a person to slip through.

One horse caught his attention. A large, black stallion with a glossy black mane, the same color as Realta's Aura. The horse neighed and bobbed its head. Gareth reached up and stroked the horse's nose, the short hairs fine and soft.

"I don't know what to do," Gareth told the horse. "Two of my friends are missing, but nobody seems to care. We searched everywhere for Lok. He's an Elemental Thane. His Aura is really easy to see, even at night. But he's nowhere. And Charity wasn't in algebra. She never misses that class because sometimes she has trouble and asks me for help. She isn't afraid to ask for help."

The horse nuzzled his hand, no doubt searching for oats.

Gareth sighed. "This isn't fair. How come I can talk to you so easily? I can tell you all about Charity and Lok, how they went missing, but not anyone else. Not like this. How come I can't talk to people like this?"

Footsteps thudded on the wooden floor. He cursed under his breath. A stable hand or a guard must have seen him run in here. He gripped his cloak, running his fingers along the hem, and squeezed his eyes shut. Would this person yell at him? Gareth had a hard enough time talking to friendly people. He always broke down when people yelled at him. He had broken down when Logan yelled at him, causing the king to think he was simple. Would this person assume the same thing?

"Excuse me, young man. Do you know where I can find Queen Isla?"

Wait, he knew that voice.

Gareth slowly opened his eyes and saw his father standing there. Kel smiled warmly.

"Are you…" Gareth's voice caught in his throat. "Are you really here?"

"Yes, son."

Gareth wrapped both arms around his father, clinging to him tightly. Kel hugged him back. Warmth surrounded Gareth.

"Not too tight," Kel said, half laughing. Gareth was afraid to let go. He didn't want his father to disappear again. He reluctantly broke away from the hug and kept both hands on Kel's shoulders, just to be sure. Kel looked so tired, his eyes sunken and bloodshot. And he looked thinner, almost sickly.

"Why...?" Gareth began to ask, but his voice stopped cooperating.

"I'm sorry, son. It took us longer to get out of the city than we expected."

"Us? Realta and Callum are here, too?"

Kel's face fell. Gareth's bad feel got even worse. "Let's sit. I'll explain everything."

Sitting down on a narrow bench, Gareth listened to his father's every word. Kel had gone searching for King Logan and found him bleeding and unconscious. Callum and two other men helped Kel get the king out of the palace, but it was too late for them to use the tunnels or the city gates. Coalition soldiers were everywhere. They stayed in a tavern until the king recovered.

"But where is Realta?" Gareth asked.

Kel let out a pained sigh, massaging his left knee. "She fled the city along with Serena, Mistress Cray, and Ambassador Ekene. Good thing about living in a tavern, people talk more freely when they're drunk. No one mentioned the Eastern Coalition capturing the Jemayrti ambassador. I assume they escaped and headed south like they originally planned."

"But are they safe?"

"I pray they are. Shasta Cray is one of the most capable people I know, and Callum taught Realta about woodcraft. Setting up camp, starting fires." Kel grimaced. He slowly straightened his left leg and leaned against the wall. His face turned deathly pale.

"Are you hurt?" Gareth asked. Kel's bad leg would be fine for weeks only for the pains to return. Sometimes his father was bedridden for days, unable to stand even with his crutch.

Kel managed a smile. "I'll live. How is Queen Isla doing?"

"Okay, I guess. She really misses her husband, and she's in meetings all the time." Gareth shifted on the uncomfortable wooden bench. "Where is Callum?"

"He's around, trying to find odd jobs. Unfortunately, there aren't enough to go around."

"What about helping Sarra and Darrys? Callum helped them at the palace."

Kel's eyes brightened. "Sarra is here?"

Gareth nodded. "She lives in a room across the hall from Isla. I've seen her a few times. She's really nice. And she knows who I really am," Gareth added quietly. "Isla told her." At first, Gareth wished Isla had kept the secret to herself. When she told Sarra, the woman just stared at Gareth. Stared for a very long time. And then she hugged him tightly, crying and thanking the Creator. Strangely, the hug reminded Gareth of Kel. No surprise really. They were brother and sister.

"Good. Sarra deserves to know." Kel glanced around the stable. "I suppose I should visit her. Let her know I'm all right. How many guards are on that floor?"

"Four are stationed there at all times, but sometimes there are more. Depends on how many people are meeting with Isla." Gareth had only seen four guards when he visited Isla the other day. They let him pass, believing that he was the queen's personal messenger.

Placing his crutch firmly on the ground, Kel struggled to his feet. Gareth helped steady him. Kel's left knee bent at an odd angle, and he was already out of breath.

"Did they hurt you?"

Kel was silent for a moment. He then said, "No. I fell down a flight of stairs. Nothing serious."

"We have healers."

"They have more pressing concerns. My leg can wait. Do you want to see your uncle?"

Gareth smiled, the bad feeling vanishing. "Yes!"

Kel draped his right arm over Gareth's shoulder. Usually, Esme supported Kel when his leg bothered him, but his mother was a hundred miles away. How were she and Estrid doing? He wished he could see them soon.

"You've grown taller," Kel said as they walked outside. The bright sunlight temporarily blinded Gareth. He blinked until his vision adjusted.

"Really?"

"Yeah. You're as tall as Callum now."

"I didn't notice."

Kel smiled. "People rarely noticed until they have proof."

"Father, are the Hinterlands safe?" Gareth glanced up at the soldiers on the wall. Several had arrows nocked, ready to be drawn and fired.

"As far as I know, the fighting hasn't crossed the Nerin. Your mother and sister are safe."

"Good." He scanned the tents. Three men stood in front of the one nearest the stables. One man, who Gareth recognized as a guard from the palace, had a red draig sitting on his shoulder. Another had a patch over one eye. Gareth had seen him before but couldn't place him. Probably another guard or servant. And the third was undeniably his uncle. Callum smiled, his white teeth in brilliant contrast to his black beard and wild hair.

"Good to see you, kid." Callum placed a hand on Gareth's shoulder.

Gareth stared at his uncle in awe. Kel was right. They stood eye to eye.

"Now, Gareth," said Kel, breaking away from Gareth and walking towards the young guardsman. "I know you hate surprises, but I promise this is a good one. This is my little brother, Colm Byers."

"Um, hi." Colm waved nervously.

"You're my uncle, too?" He was only a few years older than Gareth, young enough to be Kel's son. But the way the guardsman smiled, that was Kel's smile.

"Yeah. Kinda weird, huh?" Colm replied. The little red draig peered at Gareth with bright orange eyes.

"But weird in a good way." That was how Zandon described Gareth and Lok. A thought popped into his head. "Can you help me find my friend?"

"Which friend?" Kel asked.

"Charity. She wasn't in algebra today."

"Well, it's normal for Students to skip class. I skipped all the time."

"But it isn't normal for Charity."

"The boy has a point," Callum said.

Gareth gave the Creator a silent prayer of thanks. Someone finally understood!

"Colm can help you look," said Kel. "Callum, you and Deen find Lord and Lady Lyr. Tell them I'm at the Academy."

"Why do I have to talk to bloody Thanes?" Deen, the man with the eyepatch, muttered. Gareth raised an eyebrow. Why wouldn't he want to talk to Thanes? They were just people. Only the Cuchasi could see the difference.

"You're talking to a bloody Thane now," Kel replied.

Deen grumbled but relented.

"What about you?" Gareth asked. He wanted his father's help, but Kel needed to rest if he was in pain.

Kel glanced at their tent. A shadow moved within.

Is that the king? A cold shiver ran down Gareth's spine. The man was his uncle, but Gareth did not want to face him. Not today.

"I have a more pressing matter. But it's nothing for you to worry about, son. Go find Charity. I will see you again this evening."

"And see a healer," Gareth insisted. If Esme were here, she would force Kel to see a healer immediately.

Callum laughed.

"Fine," Kel grimaced. "I'll see a bloody healer."

16

Smugglers

Lok white-knuckled the boat's railing as another gust of wind rocked the vessel back and forth. They had no trouble finding a boat once they reached the Nerin. Plenty of other people had crossed the grassy field in order to escape the war. And as soon as one boat left, another took its place.

The real problem was the cost. The captain demanded one gold mark per person. Lok didn't have any money, and neither did Brother Malaky, since the Church paid his expenses. The funds Kuno collected were one silver mark short.

"Tough luck," said the captain, a finely dressed man who stood eye to eye with Lok.

"But I'm a chaplain, and he is a Scholar," Brother Malaky protested. "That must count for something!"

"Maybe over there." He jabbed a finger eastward, towards the Academy and what remained of Teyrnas. "I only take those who can pay."

"Does being a rare type of Thane matter to you?" Kuno asked, his dark eyes burning. He was dangerously close to losing his temper again.

Lok's palms began to sweat. He didn't want any extra attention, not when Scholar Lucan could be right on their trail. All they needed was one frightened person to run back to the Academy, screaming about Fire Elementals. And Kuno had lost his temper once on the ride here, yelling in Brother Malaky's face when the chaplain asked a simple yes or no question. Kuno stormed off, taking half an hour to calm down.

It's just stress, Lok told himself again and again.

"Nope." The captain gave Kuno a smug smile. "But those are some nice horses. Tell you what, I take the three horses to make up for that last silver. Deal?"

"Each of these horses is worth two gold marks." Kuno balled his hands into fists. "Take one."

The captain smirked, looking down at Kuno. "This ain't a negotiation. Pay what I ask or swim."

Kuno grudgingly gave the captain all of their money as well as the horses. They then boarded a boat with a name that made Lok's face turn bright red. A dozen people joined them, all wearing once fine clothes that bore multiple tears and stains. One woman kept reaching for her neck, gripping a necklace she no longer wore.

The captain ordered everyone to stay on the deck. Anyone caught below would have to talk to Bruiser, a massive deckhand who stood a head taller than Lok and was all muscle. The passengers sat huddled to one side, eyeing the captain, crew, and their fellow passengers wearily.

An hour later, they were in the middle of the river, the shores little more than green blurs along the horizons. The boat rocked back and forth, back and forth. Lok closed his eyes. He tasted breakfast in the back of his throat. The waters hadn't been this rough in Alet.

Footsteps walked up beside him. Cracking one eye open, Lok saw Scholar Kuno. The Scholar had exchanged his dark gray cloak for the white one. He looked much better in white, more natural. The cloak fluttered in a gust of wind.

Kuno let out a heavy sigh. "Couldn't have picked a better place to cross?"

Lok shrugged. His notebook was safely tucked in his traveling bag. He glanced at Brother Malaky, guarding their bags. Kuno created a rotating shift after catching a deckhand eying their bags. He didn't want anything to be stolen.

"They've already stolen enough," he muttered angrily.

The chaplain was speaking amicably with two women, one of whom was crying.

"Well, it's better than swimming. Lok, how did you cross the Nerin on your way to the Academy? Was it on a boat like this?"

Lok nodded.

"And did you ever go below deck?"

He shook his head. He and Charity stayed on the deck the

whole time. Charity talked to Captain Kelia, and Lok was lost in his thoughts.

Kuno frowned. "That because the *Keeva's—*"

Lok placed a hand over Kuno's mouth. His face and neck burned.

"The *Keeva's Torso*," Kuno amended, pushing away Lok's hand, "is a smuggler's ship. These people are paid to transport stolen goods across the river. They don't want us to go below because we might find their cargo. I wouldn't be surprised if Bruiser killed us on the spot."

Lok paled. The thought never crossed his mind. He assumed Kelia agreed as a favor to Arnyn. She never mentioned stolen goods to him or Charity.

Why would she? Was that why she was so mad at Arnyn? Did she tell them to wait five days so she could receive stolen goods?

Lok rested his elbows on the railing and cradled his head. He felt like such an idiot. He should have known better.

Scholar Kuno tapped him on the arm. He held Lok's notebook and pencil.

Lok accepted them and wrote, *"I'm sorry."*

"There's no need to apologize. We had no other way to cross. I overheard a crewmember mention Rangar Keep. Have you heard of it?"

"Yes, Charity and I traveled through there after Kanton attacked us."

"Explain that to me. Every detail." Kuno glared at him.

Lok shrank back. He didn't want Kuno to lose his temper again, and he certainly didn't want the Scholar to yell in his face. So he started writing. He wrote until his hand ached and continued writing until every detail was down. Including the fight. And the guardsman whose uniform caught on fire. Lok was pretty sure that was his fault, but he hadn't meant to hurt anyone. He wanted Kuno to understand that.

Kuno read as Lok wrote. When Lok was done, Kuno stared at the last page.

"Why did you wait to tell me?"

Lok shrugged. The writing left him feeling numb, drained.

"No." Kuno jabbed his finger at the notebook. "You can write.

So write. Why didn't you tell me?"

"I was afraid. I had just learned I was an Elemental Thane, and everything had changed so fast. I went to the Academy because I wanted to be normal. To be treated normal." Tears welled in his eyes. He had long since accepted being a Thane, had accepted his abilities. But some part of him longed to be normal. He touched the ring in his right ear.

"Well, you aren't normal, so get over it." Kuno stormed away. Two crewmembers hurried out of his way, watching him warily. He leaned against the railing. The two women speaking with Brother Malaky made an excuse and moved to the other side of the boat. Brother Malaky walked over to Kuno and said a few words. The Scholar brushed him away. The chaplain then spied Lok.

No, do not talk to me! He didn't like being near the chaplain. His Farsights, especially the last one, creeped Lok out. But the chaplain, a Learner and an Empath, and not a Minder, walked over anyway.

"What happened?" Malaky asked, his face a mask of concern.

"We had an argument. Don't worry about it."

"Would you like to talk about it? I mean, discuss?"

Lok shook his head.

"I've never been to the Hinterlands." Brother Malaky adjusted his glasses, peering at the approaching shore. "What is it like?"

Lok sighed. The chaplain was bound and determined to have a conversation. *"They are very green. Not like Norgard with the buildings close together. Everything is spread out, and there are trees everywhere. And lots of hills."*

"It sounds very peaceful. Do your parents know you're an Elemental?"

Lok's heart sank. His parents. The chaplain didn't know that Lok's father was dead. He had mentioned it to Kuno, and thankfully, the Scholar was mindful not to ask too many questions.

Lok glanced at the notebook and pencil in his hands. He could tell the chaplain, but a part of him felt reluctant to explain. Ansonn Tolman had died before Lok was born, so he never grieved for him. But Ansonn's absence was constantly felt. The wardrobe in his mother's room that still had his father's coat and boots. The table with two chairs instead of three. The charcoal drawing of

Ansonn in Lok's bedroom. Parts of him remained, and the parts were all Lok knew.

He simply wrote, *"No."*

Brother Malaky placed a hand on Lok's shoulder. "I bet they will be ecstatic. Thane abilities are rarer in the Hinterlands."

"Why is that?" Lok asked, half out of curiosity and half wanting to steer the chaplain away from personal questions.

The chaplain frowned. "I don't know." His blue eyes suddenly brightened. "Perhaps you can write your Journeyman's thesis on it. If you want to be a Journeyman, that is. And you would have to connect your research to history." The chaplain gazed over the water and said, "A genealogical record would be your best guess. The Academy has information on every Thane that has undergone the Ceremony, as well as information on their families, and the cities and villages where they were born. Of course, some math would be involved. Percentages, things like that. Car would know better than I. He was always good at math. Are you good at math?"

"No." Why couldn't Malaky just shut up and leave? Lok glanced back at Scholar Kuno. The man was as still as a statue.

"Well, I'm sure Mattick will help."

Lok gave the chaplain a puzzled look. *"Who is Mattick?"*

"I... Oh dear." Malaky rubbed his eyes. "I'm sorry. These Farsights are getting me all confused. The Council promised to find an explanation, but they never did. It's honestly had me on edge the last few months. I'm sure you felt the same way when you discovered your ability."

Lok nodded. At first, he thought it was a lie. A clever way for Arnyn to gain their trust. But then Danior saw the Aura, too. And Rune at the Academy.

And Gareth Haar, his oldest friend. Gareth had first noticed the Aura a year ago, faint green wisps that had grown stronger, until they burned like fire. He was afraid to tell anyone because he believed Lok was a Seltachai, just like Master Kel.

"I didn't want you to get in trouble," Gareth explained.

Lok was grateful Gareth hadn't told anyone. Life in Vala would have been ten times worse if people knew he was a Thane. No doubt they'd ask endless questions or ask for demonstrations. Or worse, be afraid of him. Mayor Gan and Master Kel likely hid their abilities for the same reasons.

"If you ever want to talk, I mean write, I'm right here." Brother Malaky stepped away.

Lok quickly grabbed his arm and wrote, *"You're an Empath. Do you know why Scholar Kuno is so angry? Is it my fault?"*

Malaky's eyes softened, a sadness creeping in. "It's not your fault," he replied, nearly whispering. "He blames the Council for wanting to use you. And I know he didn't want to leave his girl-friend. I don't really care for the age gap, but they certainly love each other. Don't think for one second that this is your fault," he emphasized every word. "Kuno could have easily gone along with the Council's decision. But he put your wellbeing ahead of them. Never forget that, Lok."

"I won't."

"Good. Now, how much longer until we land, do you think? None of these smugglers would hesitate to kill us, and I don't like the way their emotions are affecting mine."

"Less than an hour." It was a good enough guess.

Thunder rumbled in the distance, like a wildcat hiding behind the tree, getting ready to pounce. Lok looked up and saw dark clouds heading westward.

"Hopefully, the storm will hold out. Too bad you can't control water."

Control water. If he had that ability, he could have prevented the damage to Caldeira's pub. Kuno should have been furious. In-stead, he responded with patience and understanding. He wished Kuno would be his old self again.

He glanced at the Scholar. Kuno was rummaging through their bags. He took out Dane Kanton's notebook. Kuno met Lok's eyes. He then flung the book over the side. It splashed as it hit the water.

Kuno gave Lok a quick nod.

"Now, why would he do that?" Brother Malaky asked, scratch-ing his head.

Lok smiled, grateful to have Kuno as his mentor.

17

Fate

Nalani, the second moon, appeared above the treeline. Realta stared at its pale face, unable to sleep.

She had been so careful, concealing her Thane ability and the servant's mark on her wrist. But at the meeting, she... She didn't know how to explain it. One moment, she was nervous, worried that Corey would do more than just yell in their faces. And then a stormfront of fear crashed into her, making all other thoughts impossible. She was terrified, trapped, and she had to escape. She spied the tiles and Manipulated them without thinking. Just re-acting.

And in all that mess, her bracelet slipped off. Had it gotten loose while she practiced knife throwing?

Well, it didn't matter how. Master Corey had seen everything. He knew Chinasa lied about her status and Braedan lied about her being a Thane. If he wanted, Corey could land them in a world of trouble. Kereuic law was very strict about harboring runaway slaves. Part of their trade deal with the Sykerian Empire.

A shadowed figure in a dark cloak walked by the wagon's sole window.

Realta bolted upright, her heart leaping into her throat. Was it the strange man from her Dreams? Had he followed her into the real world? Was that possible?

The figure turned around, revealing Braedan's face. Pale moonlight cast him in a deathly pallor. The mercenary muttered to himself and ran his hand over the knives along his belt.

"What is it, child?" Shasta asked, donning a housecoat and stepping closer to the window. Realta hadn't heard her get out of bed. The woman moved like a cat.

"Huh?" Serena, her eyes heavy with sleep, glanced around.

"Braedan. He's just standing out there. Do you think he got in trouble?"

"I have no doubt," Shasta replied. "He deliberately lied to his employer. If word spreads, it will jeopardize his reputation as a mercenary."

"Why did he lie?" Realta gently touched the tattoo on her wrist. "You will have to ask him."

Realta threw off the blankets and pulled a cloak over her nightgown. The nights in Kereu were warm, but she felt more comfortable wearing an extra layer. She also put on her black and gold necklace. Corey had confiscated the bracelet.

"I did not mean right now," Shasta said, raising an eyebrow.

"But what if Master Corey alerts the authorities tomorrow? This might be our only chance."

Shasta narrowed her eyes and sighed. "Just as stubborn as Esme Haar. Once an idea gets in your head, you must chase it down."

A smile crossed Realta's lips. Shasta had told her stories about Esme and Kel while they lived in the palace. How Esme insisted on befriending everybody, both noble born and servant. And how Kel routinely undermined his father in subtle ways that the old king could never prove. Life under Yestyn's roof had not been easy, but Kel and Esme were happy simply by being together.

"Very well." Shasta gestured at the door. "Go on."

Realta slipped into the night. The humid air clung to her like a damp blanket, and insects chirped, filling the night with their songs.

Braedan whirled around, one hand going for a knife. Seeing Realta, he relaxed.

"What are you doing up?" he asked.

"I couldn't sleep. Did you get in trouble?"

Braedan laughed bitterly. "Get in trouble. That's such a kid thing to say. No, I'd say I got royally screwed." He rolled up his shirt sleeve. A bandage covered his right forearm, blood droplets seeping through the white cloth.

Realta's breath caught in her throat. "Corey cut you?"

"You see," Braedan said as he unrolled the bandage, "when a person is made a slave or an indentured servant, they're given a tattoo. On the wrist or the face, depends on the culture. The tattoo can be removed once their servitude ends. Scars, on the other hand, those are permanent." A series of fresh cuts lined his arm. Two ran the length of his forearm, and three were diagonal, intersecting the other two.

Realta looked at her wrist. Two bands with diamonds in between. "What does that mean?"

"That I'm a traitor. My word as a mercenary and a Hound can't be trusted."

"I'm sorry." Realta wished she could take the Manipulation back. An action she barely remembered. She'd been so afraid, and she didn't know why.

"Why? It was my choice, not yours."

"Because Elliza asked you to lie." The girl was the reason Corey knew Realta was a servant. He had been so mad at Chinasa, Realta doubted he would have noticed if it started hailing, let alone notice her tattoo. So, why did Elliza ask Braedan to keep Realta's Aura a secret but then reveal her other secret to Corey?

"Elliza has her reasons."

"And those are?"

Braedan glanced at Corey's wagon. It was completely quiet, and moonlight glinted off the pitch-black windows. He reached into his pocket. "Here. Thought you'd want this." He gave her the bracelet.

She slipped it on. It fit snugly. Too snugly to have come loose on its own. Unless someone had Manipulated it loose. "You said Elliza was a Farsight?"

"Yeah, a real powerful one. Corey paid more for her than I get paid in a year."

Realta winced. She recalled the Cuchasi in East Bridge. The man had the same tattoo as Elliza, and he had been in chains. Elliza wasn't a servant. She was a slave.

Footsteps padded the soft grass. Realta turned and saw Elliza approaching. The girl cradled her left wrist, and long locks of black hair obscured her face. Braedan rushed to her side.

"Did he hurt you?"

"Not badly."

"Let me see." Braedan reached for her. Elliza shied away.

"It's nothing."

"Let me see, damn it!" Braedan grimaced. "Sorry."

"It's okay." Elliza allowed Braedan to push back her hair. The right side of her face was swollen, the tan skin turning darker. Her bottom lip was split and bleeding. Realta stared at Elliza, horrified. Why had Corey hurt her? She told him the truth!

"I'm going to kill that bastard," Braedan said through his teeth.

"No." Elliza grabbed his arm. "That is not his fate."

"Well, fate's gonna change."

"No!" Elliza gripped Braedan's arm with both small hands.

The mercenary took a deep breath. And then another. "Fine."

Elliza's eyes fell on Realta. She smiled despite the busted lip.

A familiar warmth flooded Realta, coursing through her veins and centering around her heart. The same warmth she felt near Chinasa. No, not just near him. She sensed the warmth each time the ambassador walked close, fading as he and Realta separated. She almost mentioned it twice, but she feared Chinasa would understand, that he felt the same warmth around her.

Val claimed they were all being drawn together. The Nine Summit Thanes chosen to fight the Midnight King. It was insane. The ravings of a madman. But he had singled her out in a busy hallway. And hadn't she felt the warmth around him, too?

The cloaked man in her Dreams claimed the same thing.

The first Dreamer had been reluctant, too.

The first Dreamer. Oh Great Creator, did that truly mean she was the second?

"Hello, Realta," Elliza said. She clasped her hands, touched them to her forehead, and then spread her hands outward. "It is nice to officially meet you."

Nice to meet you? After Elliza spied on Realta and then revealed her servant's mark to Corey, this was how she responded? "I wish I could say the same," Realta said flatly. "Why did you show Master Corey my mark?"

"Because it was necessary. You would have left with the Jemayrti uncontested tomorrow. We would have been separated."

"Is that a bad thing?"

Elliza nodded grimly. "The fate of Eltriar rests in our hands."

"What are you talking about?" Braedan asked. He spared a quick glance at the wagons. Save for the chirping insects, the campsite was silent. No one else was awake, except Serena and

Shasta. They should be able to overhear with the window cracked open. She didn't dare look. Elliza might stop talking if she knew someone else was listening.

"I apologize for keeping you in the dark, Braedan. What Auras do you see when you look at us?"

"Yours is bright blue, and Realta's is black with a few gold sparks. Why—" Braedan's eyes widened. "My mistake. There are a couple of purple sparks, too."

Realta's heart skipped a beat. "What?"

"Yeah. I didn't see them before." Braedan smiled, the moonlight glinting off his sharpened teeth. "How about that! Dreamer, Manipulator, and Empath."

"No, that's not possible. I'm not an Empath." Realta backed away. She wished Shasta or Serena would interrupt, tell her to get back to bed. A reasonable excuse to quit this conversation.

"Your Aura says differently. Stars above, girl," Braedan lowered his voice, "do you know how rare it is for someone to have three abilities?"

Kel had three abilities: Manipulator, Minder, and Learner. But he came from a family of Thanes, and it was common for noble Thanes to have more than one ability. But that didn't explain her case. She and Kel were related through marriage.

"But her core ability is Dreamer," Elliza said. "And we are fated to be Two of Nine."

"No, we are not," Realta snapped, heat raising in her face.

Elliza smiled patiently. "Chinasa is one of us as well. I recognized his warmth the moment we met. And yours."

"What if I don't believe you?" Realta crossed her arm.

"It doesn't really matter what you believe. I have seen Nine of us together, though the other six faces are blurry. I cannot tell what they look like, or if they are men or women. Young or old. But we will see very soon."

"Really? You don't recognize any of them?"

"I'm afraid not." Elliza bowed her head.

"What about Valentin Gardyner? Is he one of them?" The heat spread to her neck and ears. Val was the reason they were in this mess. He was the reason Teyrnas was at war and King Logan was dead. He was the reason she and Callum were separated. This was all his fault!

Elliza frowned. "I don't know who that is." The girl's eyes brightened. "How did you meet him? Is he one of us?"

"He claims he is. But the man is insane. You can't trust anything he says."

"Why not?" Elliza gave her a confused look.

Realta dug her nails into her palms. *Be calm. Nobody can think clearly when they are angry.* "He started the war between Teyrnas and the Eastern Coalition."

"Wait, what?" Braedan looked at her incredulously.

"I know how it sounds, but it's true." She told him and Elliza about the events in the palace. Queen Gallia visiting Logan, pretending to want peace while the other monarchs disguised themselves as servants. How Val, acting as Gallia's messenger, manipulated the monarchs and murdered the king. And the way he tried to coerce Realta and Chinasa to join him. "You can ask Chinasa if you don't believe me," Realta finished.

"Don't worry. I believe you." Elliza smiled that patient smile despite her injury. Perhaps Realta was being too harsh with her. "But don't you see? Though you and Ambassador Ekene ran away from Valentin, fate led you to me."

"I'm not sure if I believe in fate." Realta's skin broke out in goosebumps despite the humidity. Fate. The cloaked man claimed that Callum being falsely accused was fate.

We could not risk you growing up without him.

A shiver ran down her spine.

"Have you seen your Gadyeni yet?" Elliza asked.

Realta blinked. "What did you say?"

"Tath, the Gadyeni of Farsights and Justice, is very kind. I'm sure your Gadyeni will appear quite soon. Time for us to find one another is running out."

"Mind explaining this to me, or is it strictly a Thane thing?" Braedan asked. He glanced around the camp. No movement. Realta wished Serena or Shasta would interrupt this insane conversation.

This can't be real.

Elliza bowed her head, dark hair hiding her face. "I apologize. I wanted to tell you, but there was never a good time."

Realta peered up at the moons. Ilana was nearing the horizon as Nalani reached its zenith. "It's getting late."

"Yes. Almost too late," Elliza added grimly.

Shasta opened the wagon door. "Realta, come inside now."

You couldn't have said that five minutes ago?

"Yes, ma'am." Realta walked towards her. Towards safety and familiarity.

"Tell the ambassador," Elliza said, catching up to her. A fervor crept into the girl's voice. "Corey will be angry if I talk to him myself."

"I'll think about it." Realta hurried inside. She closed the door and latched it shut. She sat down on her bed, trembling from head to toe and feeling tired. A night of lost sleep crashed down on her. "How much did you hear?" she whispered.

"Most of it," Shasta replied.

"Do you think she lied about knowing Val?" Serena asked. She sat on her own bed, watching furtively as Braedan and Elliza walked away.

Realta shrugged. Val was an expert liar. There was no reason to assume his allies were any different.

"This can't be real," she said, drawing her knees up to her chest and wrapping her arms around them. Val had lied. The Midnight King had been defeated long ago. And she was not one of the Nine Thanes. End of story.

"Get some rest," Shasta said. "We will discuss this with Ambassador Ekene in the morning."

"We don't have to." Chinasa had too much to worry about. Realta refused to add this madness to the list.

Shasta raised an eyebrow. "Very well. I suppose this is your choice."

"Shasta," Realta asked, "how much do you know about the Midnight King?"

"Only that the Gadyeni defeated him three thousand years ago. We don't have to fear him. Get some sleep, child." Shasta peered out the window. Braedan and Elliza were gone.

This isn't real. It's too insane to be real.

But what if it was?

Shasta and Serena laid down on their beds. Realta crawled underneath the blankets, her mind running through dozens of possibilities. Should they run? What happened if they ran? Would Corey report them to a magistrate? Would the Kereuic militia hunt them down? What if Val and Elliza were telling the truth?

And what about the Wardens of the Night? Queen Isla had seen them in a Farsight. They were supposedly searching for Realta and others like her. Were they still searching?

Shasta said that not all of Queen Isla's Farsights are accurate.

How accurate were Elliza's Farsights?

Realta laid in bed, the blankets wrapped tightly around her, and watched as the moons sunk below the horizon.

18

Shades

"Thank you for your cooperation, Your Majesty," said Scholar Lucan as Isla signed the document. Two days ago, she issued an announcement allowing Thanes to use their abilities as a primary means of fighting. A diplomatic way to turn them into living weapons. The Scholars immediately drew up documents for her to sign. The capital city may be under siege, but that did not mean an end to paperwork.

"As long as it's necessary." Isla felt horrible. A sinking feeling formed in her gut as she made the announcement, and it had only grown worse. Many people at the Academy disapproved of Thanes using their abilities to harm, and more than a few nobles had been very vocal about their opinions. Lady Sarra spoke to Isla in a way that would have driven Logan to tears and stormed off before Isla could respond. Isla did not blame her one bit.

She glanced at the other faces in the room. Una and Gregor stood off to the side, Gregor wringing his hands and Una clutching her notebook close to her chest. And Scholars Lucan and Osian were present to witness her signing. The Premier was meeting with the Madani representatives this morning and could not be present herself.

Isla interpreted the Premier's absence as convenient. She might approve of the Council's decision, but she did not have to be wholly responsible. Better for the axe to fall on Isla's head if things went sideways than on hers.

And Premier Scholar Emera was not the only absent face. Rafael refused to speak to Isla after the announcement.

"Please, Isla, for the love of the Creator, don't do this," Rafael had begged, practically on his knees. "Don't allow Thanes to break their vows. Don't turn us into weapons!"

"But we have Thanes in the King's Guard," Isla counted. It was a weak argument. Those Thanes used swords and arrows to defend themselves and the royal family, not Manipulations or Illusions. But what other choice did she have? The Council approved of this decision. And they counted on her to implement it.

"You can't allow this!" Tears glistened in Rafael's pale blue eyes. "We're supposed to protect people."

"We are protecting them."

"Not like this."

Rafael left soon afterward, realizing that he could not change her mind. She knocked on his door this morning, hoping to see him. Perhaps to say that he was right. Perhaps to just make more excuses. Rafael's personal guard told her that he was not available.

"It's for the good of Teyrnas," Lucan assured her as he inspected her signature. He handed the document to Osian. The other Scholar, who had purple hemming the edges of his cloak, had dark circles under his eyes. At least she wasn't the only one losing sleep over this decision.

"Is there anything else to attend to?" She sincerely hoped not.

"No, Your Majesty," Osian replied. "Not until this afternoon. Or evening. We're not sure how long the Premier will be with the Madani."

"I wouldn't want to rush her." And the longer that meeting took, the more time Isla had to breathe.

Gregor opened the door for the Scholars, bowing as they left. Una glided over and took the seat next to Isla. She placed her notebook, pen, and inkwell on the table. Isla spied the last two entries: a silver crown on Gareth Haar's head, and a raven and a hawk fighting in midair until both were dead. Each was written in shorthand. A code only she and Una could read.

And Logan. The shorthand was his idea, based on a code he and Carwyn created when they were Students and Carwyn was attending under an assumed name.

"Everything will work out, my queen." Una reached into her pocket and gave Isla a handkerchief. Confused, Isla accepted it. She then felt a small drop slide down her face and understood.

"What news is there from Teyrnas?" Isla asked, drying her eyes.

"It can wait," Gregor said.

"No. What are the latest troop movements?" Isla walked over to the bookshelf and removed a map, spreading it over the table. It showed all of Teyrnas, including the Hinterlands. If the Madani harbored only a fraction of the refugees, the rest could shelter in the Hinterlands. Lightly populated villages occupied the space with large swaths of forest in between. Granted, those villages would have to grow more crops to support the added population during the winter. They could order an increase in agricultural trade from Lowyrn and Byyar. But what if there was crop failure? Could they subsist on hunting and gathering?

Isla returned to the bookshelf and selected a volume on harvest statistics containing records for the last thirty years. She shook her head, turning page after page. Too many numbers for her to make sense of. She'd have to consult a Scholar of mathematics.

"Your Majesty," said Gregor.

"One moment." The Summer Solstice wasn't for another full week. Any crops planted now would miss the spring rains, but with the added labor, they could yield a fifty percent harvest. Maybe as much as sixty percent. However, she knew nothing about farming or harvesting. This was just an excuse to focus on other things. Things that did not involve fighting or war or Thanes fighting in war. Thanes breaking their vows, using their abilities to maim and kill. Oh Great Creator, what had she…

"Isla!"

"What, Gregor?" She glared at him. The man had gone completely pale. He backed away from the door, trembling. Una let out a sharp cry, clamping both hands over her mouth.

A man, ragged clothes hanging loosely on his thin frame, walked into the room. His long black hair stuck out at odd angles. Dark brown eyes, so dark they were almost black, studied the room. Those eyes fell on Isla. In the blink of an eye, the hair turned sandy brown, the dark eyes to pale blue.

"Logan?" she whispered. She gripped the back of the chair, her legs suddenly going numb. Was this real, or just a figment of her overtaxed mind?

He smiled at her and nodded.

Isla ran to Logan, wrapping her arms around him. She rested

her head on his chest, listening to his heartbeat, slow and steady. Tears streamed down her face as Logan embraced her. Stars above, she had forgotten how warm he felt!

"They told me you were dead." Tears choked her voice. "Everyone believes you're dead."

Logan guided her to the bed and sat down, holding her tightly. He looked into her eyes and studied her, the same way he had when they first met. Quiet, timid, unsure of where to begin.

"Can we have a moment?" he asked Gregor and Una. Both looked at Isla. She gave them a reassuring nod. They bowed and quietly slipped out of the room, leaving the door cracked open half an inch. Just wide enough for eavesdropping.

"How are you alive?" Isla asked. She looked her husband up and down. Logan had lost weight. He had never been a large man, and now he appeared skeletal. His cheekbones and eye sockets were more pronounced, and his collarbone stuck out. The scar Serena had given him rested just above the bone. Holding onto his hands, she felt every bone. "Did they hurt you?"

"No, I…" Logan paused, gathering his thoughts. "Queen Gallia's messenger attacked me. I blacked out, and the next moment I was in a small room." Logan told her about the tavern in Tullcrest, run by the same woman who sold him the Assassin's fern berries that killed King Yestyn. She had put the money to good use. Colm Byers and two other men cared for Logan over the next two months. "We left the city once I was stronger."

"Who else knows you're here?" This changed everything. Logan was alive. The Teyrnian people had their king again. His leadership could turn the tide of this war. Isla glanced at the wall clock. A quarter to eleven. The Council had to be informed immediately.

"Just you, Isla." Logan pushed a lock of hair behind her ear. "No one can know I'm here."

"What do you mean? You're alive. We have to—"

"Isla, no one can know. At least, not right now." He smiled proudly. "You've done a wonderful job as queen. The people look up to you. I don't want to take that away."

"So, you want people to believe Gallia murdered you?" It didn't make any sense.

"It gives them a reason to fight."

"A false one. Logan, why—"

"Please, just trust me. We have a plan, but it only works if people think I'm dead."

Isla looked into Logan's eyes and wished for a Farsight, assurance that this was the right course of action. But none appeared. She let out a frustrated sigh. Guiding a stubborn mule was easier than changing Logan's mind, so she asked, "Who were the other two men?"

"Callum Haar and a man named Deen. He used to work for Queen Gallia but betrayed her once he discovered the Eastern Coalition's plot."

"I need to meet with him." Deen could be vital to their cause. Even if he was just a servant, he might have overheard meetings, learned important details. A lifetime in noble courts had taught Isla how overlooked servants were and what a terrible mistake it was to overlook someone because of their station. She'd lost count of the number of times Shasta Cray had helped her and Logan simply by listening to people who acted as though she were invisible.

"In a few days. He's very cautious. You have to gain his trust first."

Isla's heart skipped a beat. "Logan, what about Kel?"

"Who?"

She chose her next words carefully. "He helped me organize the evacuation. Nobody had seen you, so Kel went to look…" A horrible feeling formed in her gut. Had Carwyn survived Yestyn's beating only to die during the coup?

Logan shifted, looking uncomfortable. "The cripple?"

"Yes." The horrible feeling faded away. "Did you see him?"

"I saw enough." Logan glanced at the door. Through the small crack, she spied a cloaked man speaking with Gregor and Una. A man leaning on a crutch.

"Do you know who he is?" Isla asked carefully. Carwyn asked her not to tell Logan the truth, afraid of how he would react.

"Yes, I know exactly what he is." Logan's eyes burned, and a harshness entered his voice. "Just a Shade. Nothing more."

"A Shade? Logan," she placed a hand on his cheek and turned

his face towards hers, "Carwyn is alive. Just like you."

Logan shook his head. "That bastard is nothing like me. He lied. He lied to every single one of us."

"Carwyn didn't have a choice."

"Yes, he did," Logan snapped. "He could have told us he was alive. He could have sent a letter through Shasta or... Or..." Logan stood and paced the room, running a hand through his hair.

"He was scared." Isla rose and placed a hand on Logan's shoulder. He shrugged it off and kept pacing. "He and Esme feared for their lives. And the life of their child." A light dawn in her mind. "He's at the Academy."

"Who?" Logan glared at her. Isla took a step back, bumping into the bed. *Why does he have to look just like Yestyn?*

"Gareth. Carwyn and Esme's son. Your nephew. You can meet him, and..." Logan was not listening. He glared at the door, seething. "Lo, talk to me."

"My brother Carwyn is dead." He faced her. "I will visit again this evening. Hopefully, I can convince Deen to join us. The man is surprisingly insightful."

Isla watched as Carwyn walked away from the door, pulling the hood of his cloak over his head. Gregor asked him to stay, but Carwyn shook his head.

"Isla?"

She faced her husband. Logan looked at her expectantly. She held his hand and give it a light squeeze. "Yes, of course. I love you."

Logan smiled, but his eyes were still a mirror of Yestyn's. "I love you, too."

✳✳✳

Logan's words hurt worse than any insult Kel had heard in the last seventeen years. Being called a worthless beggar or a dirty Hiraethi bastard was one thing, but for his own brother to look him in the eyes and say that he was dead, it was unbearable.

Kel hid his scarred face under his hood and walked away.

"Prince Carwyn," Gregor Pym called after him.

"Go help Isla," he said, staring at the floor. He heard the door hinges creak open and close.

Kel slowly walked away. His left leg ached. A healer had examined the knee the other day, popping it back into place and redoing Callum's shoddy stitch work.

"Where are you going?"

Kel saw Callum standing in a doorway. Voices sounded from inside the room.

"Back to the tent. I want to rest." *And to be alone.*

Callum walked up to Kel and shepherded him towards the door. "Rest can wait. What you need is to be around people who give a damn about you."

Kel winced. "How much did you overhear?" Callum's hearing was good, but was it good enough to hear a conversation two doors down?

"I heard enough." Callum led him into a room crowded with furniture. A four-posted bed rested against one wall and two smaller beds lined the opposite wall. Books and papers cluttered the writing desk wedged between a plush armchair and standing mirror. Kel spied the royal seal of Teyrnas on one page, a flying raven in dark blue wax. And various chairs, footstools, and a wardrobe occupied the rest of the space, leaving little room to walk. The wardrobe overflowed with men's, women's, and children's clothing.

And in the middle stood five people. Lord and Lady Lyr and their two small children, as well as one of Logan's sons. The two adults spoke via Linking near the room's sole window while the children ran around the room, jumping from one piece of furniture to the next, trying desperately not to touch the floor. Kel's heart ached, seeing Logan's son smile, his blue eyes shining. He looked just like his father, the young man Kel had abandoned.

Sarra noticed them first. She touched her husband's arm, drawing his attention. Darrys Lyr gave Kel a curious look. Kel backed away. Sarra had been happy to see him at the palace, but everyone was in a panic. Anyone would be relieved to see a friendly face during a crisis. But what did Sarra think now? Was she angry at Kel for abandoning her, too?

Sarra smiled at him, the same smile that lived in his memories.

"Good morning, Car." Sarra glided over, her purple silk dress swishing, and hugged him. He gave her an awkward, one-armed hug. Where did he begin? Their chance encounter had been just that, chance. Kel wanted to tell Sarra everything. She and Esme were good friends, and she deserved to know that Esme was safe and happy. But Prince Carwyn was dead, and with a simple Illusion, Sarra would have continued believing the lie.

But Sarra had been so happy. He couldn't take that away from her.

"Why don't you hate me?" Kel asked.

Sarra's smile faltered. "Why would I hate you?"

"L—" Kel bit his tongue. Sarra was their little sister. She deserved the truth, but Logan insisted that his presence at the Academy be a secret. "Lots of people would be angry if their loved one faked his death."

Sarra rolled her eyes. "You had a bloody good reason." She smiled again. "Now, I don't think you've been properly introduced. Car, this is my husband Lord Darrys of House Lyr. Darrys, this is my oldest brother Carwyn."

"It's an honor to meet you, sir." Darrys shook Kel's hand. The nobleman stood ramrod straight and his brown hair was closely cut in a style common among the nobility. Strange how certain things did not change. Kel had purposely grown his hair long to buck the trend, much to everyone's disapproval. Except Sarra. She thought it made him look more Hiraethi.

"You look just like your father," Kel said, noting the resemblance. Lord Jonas O'Lyr frequently attended royal functions and was a strong supporter of House Kelwyn. Kindhearted and steadfast, he never raised his voice, and he never batted an eye when Yestyn lost his temper.

Darrys blinked. "You met... But of course. Sorry, it's difficult to place you among the nobility."

"I was never truly noble."

"Cock and bull," Sarra muttered.

Kel studied Sarra and Darrys. Despite the recent hardships, both looked well, healthy, and their clothes were in good repair. Clean. And the children laughed and smiled as though nothing were wrong in the world. He wanted to stay, but he knew he did not belong here. "Well, I really should go. The healer said I need to rest my leg."

"Rest it here." Sarra gestured towards the posted beg. One of the children, the only girl in the bunch, stopped bouncing. Her bright blue eyes, identical to her grandmother's, gazed at Kel.

"I don't want to impose." Kel turned to leave. Callum stood in the doorway, his arms crossed. He gave Kel a look that said, "Don't even try."

"Nonsense. You never impose, Illusionist," Sarra teased. She grabbed Kel by the arm and forced him to sit down. The bed was so soft it felt like he was sitting on a cloud. And the bedspread was fine silk, cool to the touch. It had been decades since he sat on a bed this fine.

Callum sat in the armchair, acting the part of the invisible servant. He smiled at Kel, this look saying, "I told you so."

Kel raised his crutch and made a chopping motion, all the while smiling. Callum laughed. For all the times he threatened to hit Callum over the head, he never made good on it.

Sarra gathered the children and shepherded them towards Kel. His chest tightened. Reuniting with his sister was one thing. They had grown up together. They shared countless memories. A trust existed between them. The children were another matter. The last time he had seen Logan's children, they took one look at his scars and screamed. And Sarra's children had cowered from him during the evacuation, as though he truly were a Shade out of a campfire story.

"I don't think…"

Sarra cut him off. "Shandri, Kaden, this is your uncle Carwyn. He's been away for a very long time. I was afraid you'd never get to meet him." Sarra's voice tightened. Her eyes watered, and she quickly blinked the tears away.

"Where did he go?" asked Kaden. Shandri silently stared at Kel, at his scars.

"Someplace safe." Sarra crouched down beside Kaden. "A very bad man hurt him, and he had to run away."

"What bad man?" asked the third child. The boy looked at him with Logan's eyes.

"A man who never loved him," Sarra explained. "He hurt Carwyn every chance he got, but the bad man is gone now. Carwyn doesn't have to hide anymore."

Darrys pointedly cleared his throat.

"Anymore from you," Kel quickly added. "It's a family secret. No one else can know." Kel knew all too well how fast gossip spread among the nobility. An overheard comment, even from a child, could spell disaster.

"So, if you're my uncle, does that mean you're my father's brother?" the boy asked. Mannix. That's right. His name was Mannix. Didn't Isla have an uncle or cousin named Mannix? A man who had died young?

Prince Carwyn officially died young.

Kel nodded.

"Do you know where he is?" Mannix asked.

Sarra sighed and brushed a lock of auburn hair out of Mannix's eyes. "Mannix, your mother already explained this. Your father passed away. He's with the Creator now."

"But I don't want him to be!" The boy's face turned bright red, and tears flooded his eyes. "He promised Mama he would meet us here. He promised!" Mannix broke down sobbing. Shandri edged away as Kaden, the youngest of the three, starting crying, too. The poor child probably didn't know why he was crying.

A flash of anger coursed through Kel. This child's father was alive and well across the hall, but for some obscure reason that he refused to explain, Logan wanted the world to continue believing he was dead. The whole world and this little child.

Kel reached down and picked up Mannix, cradling him. He had comforted his own children countless times. Scrapped knees, insect stings, fights with their friends. But never grief. Children this young shouldn't have to grieve.

"It will be all right," Kel said softly, stroking his nephew's hair. Mannix clung to him, sobbing. "Your mother will always care for you. And your aunt and uncles. I guess that includes me now. You have a big brother, right?"

Mannix nodded.

"What's his name?"

"Morgan. But he doesn't play with me no more. He found new friends."

"Well, you know what that means, right?"

Mannix shook his head, wiping away tears with his sleeve.

"It means you have to find new friends, too. And once you do, you'll be able to play all the time."

Fresh tears fell down his face. "I don't want new friends. I want my father."

Another flash of anger shot through Kel. This one mixed with sadness. A strange longing for his mother, the one parent who actually cared for him. He wished he could have written Owena a letter, letting her know he was okay and happy, and that she had a grandson and a granddaughter. She would have adored them. Her death had struck differently. When guards had traveled from village to village, announcing the old king's death, Kel felt nothing but relief. He was truly free.

News of Queen Owena's death six years ago had felt like a blow to the chest. He spent a full week in a daze, rarely venturing out of the house. He stopped eating, and then stopped speaking. Everyone grew concerned, Aida Loy thinking he was sick. Esme was the only one he could confide in.

He wished Esme was here.

"I can take him," Sarra whispered, sitting beside him. Kaden had quieted down and was playing with Shandri. Callum and Darrys now stood by the window, speaking quietly and glancing now and then at the children. Strange how the head of a noble house and an indentured servant could speak as equals. If only the rest of Eltriar got along so well.

"It's no trouble. I have a lot of catching up to do." An idea quickly formed. "Mannix, did you father ever show you Illusions?"

The boy perked up. "Sometimes," he said, rubbing his reddened face.

"Do you want to see where I live?"

He nodded.

Kel focused on the boy's mind and imagined himself holding the boy while standing up. An action only possible in Illusions. Mannix's eyes widened as the room transformed into an open field surrounding by trees. Songbirds chirped as they flitted from branch to branch. A warm breeze shook the leaves.

Kel shifted the Illusion to show the farmhouse, a sprawling two-story structure with added rooms built for Kel and Esme. Wide windows faced the front porch. He even included the rickety porch steps. Had Sardic fixed them yet?

"Are there horses?" Mannix asked.

"Yes, two horses." Kel added the barn. Two horses appeared. Shadow, a pitch-black gelding, and Dust, a painted brown and white mare, grazed on the bright green grass while Callum stood nearby, keeping a close eye on Shadow lest the horse wander off for the hundredth time.

"It's that other man!" Mannix pointed at Callum.

"Yes, he's your uncle, too. And these are your big cousins." He added Gareth, Estrid, and Realta. And Serena, much to Mannix's delight. He hoped the girl was well. If only he and Esme had brought her with them. Granted, without Serena's appearance, they would have never traveled to the capital. What would have happened then? Would Logan have bled to death during the coup?

He pushed those thoughts away. What was done was done.

He then included Esme, her loose black hair falling midway down her back in waves and her dark eyes shining. "This is your Aunt Esme."

"She's pretty."

"I hope you get to meet her someday."

"Will I get to ride the horses, too? Father always says I have to wait until I'm older."

"You'll be older soon enough." Kel allowed the Illusion to fade.

"Will I be able to do that, too?"

"Create Illusions?"

Mannix nodded.

"You might. Or maybe you will be a Farsight like your mother." It was difficult to predict which Thane abilities a child would inherit, and some abilities, like Farsights and Empaths, were less common than others. Scholars had conducted a few studies, but results were inconclusive. And half the time the math was all wrong. They would have to wait until Mannix reached adolescence to find out, unlike Cuchasi. Gareth seemed to be born with the ability to see Thanes. As a baby, he would move his hand just above Kel's skin, trying to touch lights that only he could see.

Trumpets blared, sending a chill down Kel's spine. Mannix cried out and held onto him tighter.

"What was that?"

Sarra headed for the window. Kaden and Shandri ran after her, clutching her dress. Callum's face was grim while Darrys turned pale.

"The Marish and Galionic soldiers are setting up camp outside the South Gate," Darrys said. "They're blocking the Teyrnas Highway."

"How many?" Kel asked.

"Thousands."

Callum cursed under his breath.

"What about the road to Norgard?" Kel asked. He tried to stand, but Mannix refused to let go.

"I can't see from this angle," Sarra replied.

Callum headed for the door. "I'll go see."

"Find Colm and Deen," Kel told him. "We can't postpone that meeting."

"Got it." Callum slipped into the hall and took off running.

"What meeting?" Sarra asked as she tried to comfort her children. Kaden started crying again.

Kel motioned for her and Darrys to sit down. This explanation was going to take a while.

19

Loyalty

Rain pounded the wagon. The gusty wind rocked it back and forth. Realta sat huddled in a corner, her arms wrapped around her knees. The horses screamed as thunder roared. She closed her eyes, trembling and wishing she could go home.

The storm began shortly after sunrise. Their campsite was flooded in minutes, the nearby swamp rising dangerously high until they reached the road. Chinasa decided to relocate to the nearest village, a small farming community called Aneros. For a wonder, Corey did not argue.

"The slave will ride with me," Corey had said once they hitched the horses to the wagons, the rain pouring down.

"No, she will ride with Serena and Shasta," Chinasa said, yelling to be heard over the storm.

"Nobody leaves unless she rides with us."

The water was ankle deep and growing deeper by the minute. If they waited any longer, the roads would be impassible.

Chinasa gave Realta a pained look. "You don't have to…"

"It's okay," Realta said, a terrible feeling forming in her gut. "It's not that far to the village. And he'll report us if we don't do what he says."

"He might report us still," Chinasa said gravely.

"Better than being trapped here." Realta steeled herself and walked over to Corey's wagon, her cloak soaked through and chilling her. Riding with Braedan and Elliza wouldn't be so bad. She was on good terms with Braedan, and this would give her a chance to question Elliza, to see if she was telling the truth or…

"Braedan," Corey called out. "Take the reins. I'll ride with the girls."

Realta's heart sank. She looked at Braedan and Elliza, but Elliza said nothing, and Braedan just hung his head and obeyed.

With those scars on his arm, he couldn't do anything but obey.

The wagon jolted, hitting a rut. Realta's head smacked against the wall. She rubbed it and glanced over at Elliza and Corey. Elliza sat on one of three narrow beds and watched as rainwater streaked the window. Corey sat on another bed, sharpening a knife and glaring at Realta. The overhead lantern swung back and forth, casting ever-changing shadows.

Corey had kept a very close eye on her the last few days. Never letting her, Shasta, or Chinasa out of sight. And when they went different directions, Corey ordered Braedan and Elliza to follow.

"Don't even think about running," he said each time Realta came within earshot. "Wouldn't want word reaching the magistrate. Unless you want Ekene thrown into prison."

He gave the Scholars similar threats.

"What will happen if he reports me?" Realta asked Shasta.

"They will place you in prison until they can find your master," Shasta replied gravely. "After thirty days, if you are not claimed, you are forfeited and sold to the highest bidder. And since slavery is technically illegal in Kereu, they will most likely send you to Sykeria."

Just thinking about it filled Realta with dread. If Corey reported her, she would never see Callum again. If Callum was still alive. Each attempt to Dream about him in the present failed. Tears pricked her eyes, and she shoved the thought away.

Realta's teeth clicked on her tongue as the wagon hit a hole. Lightning flashed, temporally blinding her. She blinked until her vision returned to normal and screamed. Corey loomed over her, pinning her in the corner.

"What's the matter?" Corey asked, a wicked smile plastered on his face. "Are you scared of a little rain?"

Realta stared up at him, her heart beating in her throat. Kanton had cornered her in a similar way in the palace. In the middle of a thunderstorm. Shasta protected her, and Kanton stalked away once he realized his prey was out of reach.

Corey sneered. "What? Are you too good to talk to me? Talk!"

"No," Realta said. "I'm not scared."

"What about me?" Corey crouched down. Lightning flashed, glinting off the knife in his hand. "Are you afraid of me?"

Realta eyed the knife. Identical to the knife Kanton hid behind his back. He never got a chance to use it on her. But Corey... Realta swallowed. "Yes."

"Why? I thought you were a Thane. You had no problem doing this to me." He pointed to the small red mark over his eyebrow. "Are you going to Manipulate something else?"

Realta shook her head.

"Good. Do you know what they do to slaves in Sykeria when they run away?"

Realta stole a glance at Elliza. The girl sat primly on the bed, making no move to help.

The wagon lurched. Corey cursed and opened the small window at the front. Rain splattered on the wall and floor. "What in the name of the Abyss are you doing?" he yelled at Braedan.

"The road's flooded. It's going to be rough for the next two miles. Hopefully, the village is still standing."

Corey muttered and slammed the window shut. He crouched in front of Realta, closer, until she could feel his breath on her face.

Realta closed her eyes tight, wishing she were back home. Riding to the Loy farm, towards everything warm and familiar. Familiar people. Familiar buildings. And most importantly, familiar terrain. Callum had shown her all around Vala, pointing out different landmarks. Types of trees, which plants were safe to eat. How to tell distances. And how to hide.

Callum had disguised that lesson as a game. He gave them five minutes to hide in the forest. The last one found won a copper penny. Realta and Charity saw it as a grand adventure and pretended they were traveling through Caman's Pass and had to hide from bandits or wildcats. They didn't know it, but that was Callum's reasoning. If they were ever in danger, they could escape into the forest and find their way back home.

I want to go home. Please, Creator, let me go home.

"Hey." Corey grabbed hold of her braid, forcing Realta to look him in the eyes. "Do you know what the Sykerians do to runaway slaves? So everyone knows what they did?"

"Please, I don't—"

Corey yanked the braid. Pain seared her scalp. A second later, the pain faded. Realta's head felt strangely light. She touched the back of her head, and her heart dropped.

Her braid was gone. Short hair hung loosely around her face.

Corey shoved a braided rope of black hair in her face. "They cut off all their hair. Normally, they cut it all off. Every lock. But I'll leave you with a little bit." He tossed the braid at her feet and sat on the bed next to Elliza. He glanced out the rain-streaked window. Dark clouds rolled as lightning flashed.

Tears stung Realta's eyes. She clutched at the short hair. It had never been shorter than her shoulders. Never been cut more than an inch or two at a time. She stared at the braid, tears rolling down her face.

Elliza crouched down beside her. "I'm so sorry he cut your hair," she said, her head bowed. "But it's true, unfortunately. The villagers will know what it means."

"Why didn't you stop him?" Realta mumbled. She wanted to be angry, furious, but she just felt numb. Why didn't Elliza intervene? If she and Elliza were destined to be the new Nine Thanes, why not help her? Yes, Corey would have been angry and possibly hurt her, but being One of the Nine meant she would get away from him soon. Right?

Elliza gave her a curious look. "In all my Farsights, you had short hair. I was confused when I first saw you with a long braid. I understand now." She stood and sat down on the bed next to Corey. The two watched the rain in silence.

Realta buried her face in her knees and cried.

✳✳✳

"We could just run away," Serena said as they neared the village. Chinasa said it was only one more mile. She hoped the roads held out.

"Where to?" Shasta asked. She sat on the bed beside Serena. "You got lucky on your last flight. If anyone other than Callum Haar had found you, they would have handed you over to Kanton without a second thought. You must be more careful if you and Realta run."

"I know where the Kereuic Pass is. And the mouth of the Nerin River. We could hire a boat. I know Treilean might be dangerous but..." Serena closed her mouth, seeing the disapproving look in

Shasta's eyes.

"With what money?"

You stupid idiot! The servants, mainly Shasta, Amzie Fenn, and Gregor Pym, had pooled their money for her. She thought it would be plenty, but she had spent half of it before crossing the Nerin.

And the terrain was so different this far south. The forests swampy and the air unbearably humid, even at night. They wouldn't get far fast, and they would have to hire a mountain guide.

"What about Braedan?" she asked quietly. "Maybe we can convince him to come with us."

Shasta gave her a questioning look.

Serena wanted to explain their similarities, but surely Shasta would have mentioned it if the resemblance existed. It was just Serena's confused mind playing tricks on her. Confused? Yes, she'd have to be confused to think a complete strange looked like her and Logan, the brother who had rejected her.

Choosing her words carefully, she said, "Braedan hates Corey for scarring him. And he hates how Corey treats Elliza. Last time Corey yelled at her, Braedan reached for his knives, like he was going to stab him." Serena thought back to that night in the palace stables, her anger towards Logan at a boiling point. Before she could think, her dagger was in his chest, right above the collarbone. She fled in a panic. She never wanted to hurt Logan, but neither did she want to stick around for the consequences. "And he's a mercenary," she added, "so he can quit working for Corey whenever he wants. Right?"

"Yes, but I thought you and Realta wanted to get away from Braedan Sutter."

Serena bit down on her lip. "No. Just Corey." Simply thinking of the man gave her the creeps.

Shasta glanced out the window. Faint lights, blurred by the rain, shone through the trees. "Choose your words carefully around Braedan, Miss Molyns. You don't know how far his loyalty extends. Remember, Corey gave him a traitor's mark two days ago. He had every chance to leave."

"Because he didn't want to leave Elliza." Reality dawned on

her. Braedan would never abandon Elliza. Not even for a girl who might be his half-sister.

"Don't despair." Shasta placed a gentle hand on Serena's arm. "He may still prove a useful ally."

*** *

The wagon slowed to a halt in front of a wooden, two-story building, the largest along the muddy street. A man wearing an oiled cloak stepped out and introduced himself to Chinasa. A few minutes later, the wagons were placed next to a stable, and the horses were unhitched and led inside.

"Get out," Corey snapped as he and Elliza grabbed their bags.

Realta stood on numb legs. A few tears rimmed her eyes, but there was no point in crying anymore. It wouldn't change anything. She donned her cloak, pulling the hood over her head, and headed out, leaving the rope of hair behind. She couldn't bear to look at it.

The rain fell in sheets. If it weren't for her cloak, Realta would have been soaked to the skin in seconds. Corey cursed as he shoved the bags into Braedan's arms. He grabbed Realta by the wrist and dragged her inside.

At least the common room was warm and dry. A fire blazed in the hearth. Corey let go of her wrist and walked towards the fire.

Realta spied Serena and ran towards her, hugging her tightly.

"What happened?" Serena asked in a low voice. "Did he hurt you?"

"Yes and no," Realta managed. The tears threatened to start all over again. She blinked them away. If Chinasa saw, another fight between him and Corey was inevitable. She didn't want to risk the innkeeper kicking them out.

"What do you mean?" Serena frowned.

Realta pushed back her hood, revealing her missing braid. Short hair got into her eyes. She shoved behind her ears, but it was too short to stay put.

"He cut off your hair?!" Serena gasped, drawing everyone's attention.

Bloody great.

A familiar warmth flooded her. Realta turned to see Chinasa

staring at her in confusion and anger. He stormed towards Corey.

"Did you cut Miss Haar's hair?" he demanded.

"Serves her right," Corey snapped. "She's a damn runaway. She's lucky I didn't cut it all off."

Chinasa began to speak, but Scholar Leila grabbed his arm and gestured towards the innkeeper. The innkeeper looked at Realta suspiciously and then whispered to a passing servant. The servant, a young woman with deeply tanned skin and hair as long as Realta's hair used to be, scoffed and headed for the kitchen, speaking loudly in Kereuic.

Both of them knew what short hair on a servant meant.

Corey said a few words to the innkeeper in broken Kereuic. The man nodded, casting Realta a dubious look.

"All right," Corey announced. "I want that slave in a room with Mistress Cray and the other girl. The room farthest from the stairs. Braedan and Elliza will room with me. We watch the stairs in two-hour shifts. I don't want to risk her running off again. The rest of you can divide the rooms however you like."

"You are not in charge of us." Chinasa locked eyes with Corey.

The merchant smiled wickedly. "But I'm in charge of her." He pointed at Realta. "And unless you want the innkeeper to know you harbored a runaway, you'll do as I say."

The Scholars muttered to each other. They outnumbered Corey, but they were scientists and linguists, not fighters. And even Chinasa's political experience would not aid them in a magistrate's court. The law, unfortunately, was the law.

"Very well," Chinasa said, eyeing the innkeeper who watched the group warily. Chinasa then whispered to the Scholars in Jemayrti. If only Realta could understand him.

"You had no damn right," Braedan snapped at Corey.

"Shut up."

Braedan seethed but said nothing more.

After a few tense minutes, the Scholars decided on a rooming arrangement and headed upstairs.

"We'll find a way out of this," Shasta whispered to Realta. She shot a venomous glare at the back of Corey's head.

They settled their bags in the cramped room. It only had two beds, but one of the serving girls told Shasta that they would find

147

a cot for... She shot a quick glance at Realta and said, "For the third one." She then hurried out into the hallway.

Shasta shook her head disapprovingly and quickly unpacked. She then went to rejoin the Scholars in the common room.

"Are you coming?" Serena asked quietly, seeing that Realta stood in place, her cloak dripping onto the wooden floor. Her bag sat unpacked by her feet.

Realta glanced out the window. The outside world was dark, and rain poured down. A bolt of lightning flashed, followed immediately by thunder that shook the entire inn. As much as Realta wanted to run away, to escape both Corey and Val and maybe find her father, she stood no chance in this weather.

She wordlessly followed Serena downstairs.

Most of the Scholars sat in the common room, keeping a healthy distance from Corey. Realta assumed Chinasa explained the significance of Corey cutting off her hair.

The innkeeper was overjoyed to have so many guests and eagerly spoke to the Scholars in broken Teyrnian. He even offered to give them their meals at half price.

"Scholars. Important Scholars," the innkeeper said to Chinasa. "And good man." He pointed at Corey. "Catch bad server."

Realta noticed Braedan sitting at a table by himself and joined him, much to the mercenary's surprise. Serena acted like she was going to join, but she wavered and sat down with Shasta and Scholars Adanna and Okorie.

Serena always acted so strange around Braedan. She had no trouble talking about him or planning to question him, but when it came to it, Serena always shied away. Realta didn't blame her. Mercenaries didn't inspire any trust, and he carried a dozen knives. Not to mention his sharpened teeth. But he didn't act like the mercenaries in stories. He was kind, and the way he watched over Elliza reminded Realta of Callum. She felt safe around him.

"Are you sure you don't want to sit with your friends?" Braedan asked.

Realta glanced at the Scholars. Their expressions varied from worried to angry to fearful. Only Shasta appeared to be at ease. Granted, she had lived with King Logan and King Yestyn. Corey was probably a minor annoyance compared to them.

Corey himself sat at the table nearest the front door. Elliza sat next to him, her chair pulled so close they were almost touching. The girl's shoulders were hunched, and she stared at the table. Did she feel guilty for not helping Realta or was she just trying to hide the bruises and tattoo on her face?

"I want to sit with you."

"Suit yourself." Braedan leaned back, stealing a glance at Corey. "You know he had no right to cut off your hair, understand? Only your master..." Braedan grimaced. "Sorry."

"What's done is done." She wiped away an escaped tear, wishing she would stop crying.

"Who is your master? If you don't mind me asking."

"I do mind."

Braedan nodded.

The innkeeper and two serving girls passed out drinks. They politely nodded at everyone, the one who spoke Teyrnian asking if they needed anything else. But they acted as though Realta did not exist. One serving girl set two drinks in front of Braedan, smiling. Braedan passed one drink to Realta. She took a sip and grimaced. Spice wine. Far stronger than she was used to drinking.

"So," Braedan said after downing half of his drink in one swig, "when did you discover your abilities?"

"Why do you need to know?" Fire and smoke, she was supposed to be getting information from him, not the other way around!

"Just making conversation. You don't have to answer."

"It's okay." *Stop being so defensive. He will talk to you if you talk to him.* And the more she talked, the less she had to think about her hair and the way Corey called her a slave. "A couple months ago. What about you?"

"The elders in my village discovered me when I was nine years old. They wanted to train me right away, but my mother refused. Said I was too young. And when she died..." Braedan stared into his drink. "Well, I didn't want to be trained, so I left."

"That's how you became a mercenary?"

"It was a step in the journey."

Thunder roared again, causing Realta's teeth to rattle. A few wine mugs fell off tables, spilling onto the floor. The serving girls spoke causally, as though this were nothing more than a spring shower.

"And that's why there ain't nobody else here." Braedan took a sip of wine.

"It always rains like this?"

"Every summer like clockwork. The only good time to be in Kereu is during winter. Get away from the snow."

"Did it snow a lot in your village?" The Hinterlands saw snow every winter. Some years, it was just a light dusting. Others, they got several feet, perfect for making snow forts. And the ponds frozen over. Esme taught her and Charity how to skate...

Realta's heart grew heavy. Were Charity and Gareth still safe at the Academy? And what about the Loys? Had they heard from Charity? Was Estrid a Thane like her father or a Cuchasi like her brother? Would the war reach the Hinterlands?

A dozen other questions flooded her mind.

"Sometimes," Braedan replied.

"Do you like Nowan?" Realta asked, wanting to get her mind off home.

"It's a place."

Realta gave him an annoyed look. "That isn't an answer."

"Sure it is, Thane. Just not the one you want."

A thought occurred to her. "Why aren't you fighting in the war?"

"Pardon?"

"Nowan and the Eastern Coalition are fighting against Teyrnas. Most believe they're fighting to overthrow the Thane monarchs." A shiver ran down her spine. All the reasons people believe the Eastern Coalition started the war were lies. Val had orchestrated most, if not all, of it, using the war as a distraction so the Nine Thanes could defeat the Midnight King without interference. Realta assumed it was the ravings of a madman, but Elliza had confirmed everything. Could it be another lie? Could she somehow be in contact with him?

Realta glanced at Elliza. The girl's gaze quickly returned to the tabletop.

She's watching me again.

"Because I am not loyal to that kingdom," Braedan said slowly.

"I was born there and grew up there, but my mother and probably my father were Teyrnian. Shouldn't have made a difference. We spoke the same language. We looked the same. But we were the different ones. The ones who didn't belong. My mother always had trouble finding work, and none of the village kids wanted anything to do with me.

"Then one day this old geezer realizes that I'm a Cuchasi. Suddenly, Mom can afford to put food on the table and new clothes on our backs. All the kids want to be my friend. Neighbors said hello for the first time. All because I was special. Because I could see the traitorous Thanes." Braedan polished off the rest of his wine. "People like that ain't worth fighting for."

"What about people like Corey?"

Braedan sighed. "I ain't fighting for him. Just collecting a weekly pay."

Thunder roared again. Scholars Leila and Okorie made notations in their notebooks. The other Scholars whispered nervously. Shasta spoke with Chinasa. In Jemayrti, to Realta's surprise. Chinasa spoke slowly, and Shasta stumbled along, pausing between words.

Where is Serena?

Realta spied her standing on the staircase. Serena met Realta's eyes and subtly pointed upwards. Realta shook her head. She finally got Braedan talking and didn't want to ruin it. Serena spared a glance at Braedan and then climbed the stairs, taking them two at a time.

"So, what's that girl's deal?" Braedan asked. "You're the slave, but she's the one who acts like people are going to beat her."

"She was raised by her half-brother. He was mean to her." Word had reached them in Byyar that Queen Gallia had assassinated King Logan. Realta knew it was really Val, but the detail didn't matter. Teyrnas had lost its king and Serena her brother. She was oddly quiet for the next half week. Not talking, barely reacting. Realta asked if she wanted to talk, but Serena merely shrugged. Realta took care not to bring Logan up in conversation.

"Same thing happened to Elliza." Braedan lowered his voice. "Her folks died when she was little, leaving her with two older cousins. Neither of them wanted to deal with her. And being a

Thane, she was worth three times the normal price on the Syke-rian market. Corey bought her before her cousins could ship her off."

"That's terrible." Realta glanced over at Elliza, and that strange warmth flooded her, driving away the chill from her damp cloak. The same warmth she felt around Chinasa.

Does Chinasa sense it, too? She really needed to speak with him. If this was real, then he should sense it as well.

But if it was real, then Val told her the truth.

"Are you okay?"

"What?" Realta jolted.

"You look pale. Are you feeling all right? Sometimes damp weather can make people sick. 'Specially if they ain't used to it. Or is it 'cause?" Braedan pointed at her hair.

"No, I was just thinking." Realta peered at Braedan's emp-ty mug. She focused on the mug, on the shape, on the size, the weight. She Manipulated it, rocking it back and forth, careful not to topple it over. A sense of peace surrounded her. Sure, she was trapped with a man who could send all of them to prison with just a word, and Val might be right about the Nine Thanes, but she felt peaceful. Calm.

Braedan laughed under his breath. "Guess all Manipulators are the same."

"How's that?"

"Gotta move something. It's like it builds up inside them, like a stretched bowstring, wanting to let loose. Eventually, they have to Manipulate something."

"Even by accident?" Realta thought about the tiles hitting Co-rey.

Braedan nodded. "Honestly, that's how Thanes in the East get in trouble. They hide their abilities for so long, but those abilities are meant to be used. I met one man who got really sick whenev-er he went more than a week without a Manipulation. Easier for Empaths, though. Don't have to display knowing another per-son's emotions."

Corey stood and walked over to their table. Elliza followed at his heels. Realta shrank back as the merchant smiled at her. "Well, are we getting along?"

"Yeah," Braedan replied. He took a sip from Realta's wine mug. "Going to try to run away, little slave?"

Realta touched her short hair. It would take years to grow back. "No. Not in this weather."

Corey laughed. "Keep an eye on her, Sutter." Corey walked over to Chinasa's table, exchanged a few tense words with the ambassador, and headed upstairs. Elliza's warmth faded as she followed him.

"Everything all right?" Chinasa asked her in Jemayrti. His warmth surrounded her like a comforting blanket.

"Yes," she replied in the same language.

Lightning flashed, flooding the common room with blindly white light.

"When do you think the storm will end?" she asked in Teyrnian, not knowing all the words in Jemayrti.

Chinasa eyed the staircase and upstairs landing. "Not any time soon."

20

Blue and Green

Dark smoke clouded the valley, casting it in early twilight. Blood coated the once green fields. Some of the fallen men and women wore blue and green uniforms. Others wore black trimmed with red. Not a single one moved, the valley unnaturally silent.

Realta walked across the valley like a Shade. Smoldering ruins stood in the distance, barely visible through the smoke. The few remaining buildings stood many stories taller than any structure she'd seen in Teyrnas. What weapons could have destroyed them?

A hot wind rushed by, blowing her hair. Realta tentatively touched the long braid. The hair felt and looked so real.

Movement caught her eye. A man stumbled along the field, his blue and green uniform frayed and splattered with blood. He shrugged off a metal breastplate, revealing a long gash on his shoulder. As he removed his helmet, Realta noted he looked Teyrnian, with dark hair and eyes, and was in his mid-twenties. Using a broken spear as a cane, he went from body to body, searching.

Realta followed the man through the field. The sight of broken bodies was so terrible, she could only look at him. The brief glimpses of this battlefield were enough to give her nightmares for life.

The man approached a small hill. The smoke started to clear. A single tree with half of its leaves charred black stood at the top. Another man, about fifty years old and wearing the same blue and green uniform, sat with his back against the tree.

The younger man noticed him and scrambled up the hill, casting aside the broken spear. He crouched beside his ally. The old soldier had a gash on his forehead, the blood running down the side of his face and neck. Another gash stretched across his chest, too deep for stitches. This man desperately needed a healer.

"Did you see it?" the older soldier asked in a harsh whisper. Blood trickled out of the corner of his mouth. Realta wanted to look away, but where else could she look?

"The light? Yeah." The younger soldier shot a quick glance at the ruined city. "Does it mean we won?"

The older soldier nodded. He glanced to the left and then to the right. "I guess. The fighting's stopped. First time in a thousand years..." His head listed to the side.

The younger soldier steadier his ally's head, forcing him to stay conscious. Aunt Esme had told Realta and Charity how important it was for people with head injuries to remain conscious. People could die if they went to sleep. "Don't worry. Help is on the way. Hang in there, old man."

"Can't lie to me, Dom." He smiled. Closing his eyes, he leaned his head against the tree.

Realta's heart ached as she listened to the man breathe. It made the same horrible rattling sound that Callum's breathing made when he had a punctured lung. When he almost died. She glanced around the field. No one was moving. No one was coming to save this man's life.

"Domni!" The older soldier's eyes shot open, wide and fearful. He grabbed Domni's uniform, clinging to it like a drowning man clinging to a piece of driftwood.

"What? What is it?"

"You don't know," he said, trembling. "You're the youngest. Leodas, he wanted to tell you, but I wouldn't let him. Hannor. He..." The light in the man's eyes faded. Lifeless hands fell to his sides.

"Tell me what, Jol?" Domni shook his ally, trying to wake him, but the man was dead. "What did Leodas want to tell me? Jol? Jol?"

Domni bowed his head as tears flooded his eyes. Sobs overwhelmed him but only for a moment. Composing himself with a deep breath, Domni closed Jol's eyes and said, "May the Creator shelter your soul, my friend."

A hot wind blew across the field. Realta thought she heard someone crying, but it was hard to tell with the wind.

Domni picked up his head, hearing the sound, too. Someone else had survived this awful battle.

Domni struggled to his feet and cautiously walked around the tree. Realta followed, as quiet and unobserved as a shadow.

"Hello?" Domni called out.

The crying ceased. Domni glanced down. The smoke cleared, revealing another soldier. He was younger than Domni, no older than eighteen. He huddled against the tree, laying on his side. Tears streamed down his face, and he wore a red and black uniform that was tattered beyond repair.

The red-and-black-uniformed soldier glanced up. His complexion was a deep tan, the same shade as most people in Kereu, and his black hair stuck out in places. Seeing the colors on Domni's uniform, he leapt to his feet, but he lost his footing and fell down the hill. His head smacked into a large stone at the base of the hill. He laid absolutely still,

Stars above! Had he survived this battle only to die from an accident?

Domni rushed down the hill as quickly as his injuries allowed. "It's all right. The war is over."

"What?" The younger soldier blinked, looking around until he saw Domni. He shielded himself with one arm while clutching his bleeding head.

"It's over." Domni crouched down beside him. Realta spied scores of small cuts and scrapes on the soldier's arms, legs, and face. And he now had a gash on his forehead.

"I don't understand," he stammered. He saw blood on his hand and touched his scalp again. It came away with more blood, but not enough to be life threatening.

"The Midnight King has been defeated. We don't have to be enemies anymore."

Realta's heart skipped a beat. The Midnight King. She glanced back at the ruined city. Balthazar, the leader of the Nine Thanes, must have fought the Midnight King there, banishing the evil creature at the cost of his own life.

The younger soldier started crying again, his thin frame shaking. Now that she had a better look, Realta guessed he was no older than fifteen or sixteen. Why had a boy so young been forced to fight?

"It will be all right." Domni placed a hand on the boy's shoulder. He flinched but didn't bat the hand away. "What's your name?"

"My name?" The boy wiped his eyes with what remained of his sleeve. "It's... Um... Rien."

Domni gave him a pained smile. "My name is Domni."

"You're one of them," Rien stammered. "One of the Nine Thanes."

Realta's vision lurched as though she were standing at the edge of a cliff, gazing down, and nearly lost her balance.

One of the Nine. This man was one of the original Nine Thanes. One who had fought for years to defeat the Midnight King. She glanced up at the hill. Was the other man also a member of the Nine?

"He was the original Dreamer."

Realta whirled around. The gray cloaked man stood next to her, his inky black eyes fixed on Domni. The soldier helped the boy to his feet and guided him away from the battlefield. A woman with long, black hair joined them, her arm in a makeshift sling. Blood coated her blue and green uniform. They exchanged a few words and disappeared in the smoke.

"Domni was also fifteen years old when he was chosen," the man continued. "A sculptor's apprentice, and the most powerful Dreamer of his age."

"Why him?" Realta asked, tears burning her eyes. *This can't be real. It can't be.* "Why was he chosen?"

The cloaked man raised an eyebrow. "Did you see without observing? Domni could have easily killed that young man. He had every reason to. The Drohkiran were the first people to fall to the Midnight King, and they fought loyally for over seven hundred years. They were enemies."

"But the fighting ended. Balthazar defeated the Midnight King. The war's over."

The cloaked man smiled. "And that is why you and Domni were chosen."

Realta studied the man. His inky eyes made his skin seem paler, and she spied gray hair under the hood. But it was difficult to tell his age. Anywhere between thirty-five and sixty. Maybe. And something Elliza said lingered in the back of her mind. "Who are you?"

"My name is Bas, one of the Gadyeni. It's nice to officially meet you, Realta."

She shook her head. "This is just a dream."

"You know better than that."

"But how can this be real? If Balthazar defeated the Midnight King, then how could he return? How is that possible?"

Bas sighed. "We hoped Alberik would be banished permanently, but he has always been crafty. Three or four steps ahead of everyone. I wouldn't be surprised if he planned this." Bas gestured towards the smoldering ruins.

Realta instead looked at the battlefield. The smoke faded, revealing a pale blue sky. And bodies. Torn and bloodied. Far more bodies than she cared to count. The end result of a thousand years of war. "Then how can we defeat him?"

"Excellent question." Bas snapped his fingers.

Realta blinked. She was lying in bed, the blankets entangling her feet. Rain pelted the window, but it was too big. She sat up, allowing her eyes to adjust. She did not recognize the nightstand beside the bed. The wagon was too narrow for... Oh. Right. She was at the inn in Aneros, and her hair was cut short.

Lightning flashed. Serena and Shasta were fast asleep. Good. Realta really did not want to talk about her Dream. It was too awful for words, and a conversation with one of the Gadyeni? They'd never believe it.

I hope your dreams are more pleasant than mine.

She quietly slipped out of bed and peered into the hallway. Corey was guarding the hall when they went to bed. Elliza now sat in his place, a lantern by her side.

Elliza smiled at Realta and motioned for her to come closer.

Realta stood in the doorway. Was this a trick? Another way to incur Corey's wrath? Or did Elliza simply want to talk?

The door at the far end of the hall creaked open. Chinasa peered out. "What are you doing up?" he asked, walking towards Realta. He eyed Elliza warily.

"The same reason you are up," Elliza answered. "Follow me." Elliza picked up the lantern and headed downstairs.

Chinasa and Realta exchanged an uneasy glance. *What if it's a trick?* Was Corey waiting for them down there?

"Might as well," Chinasa said. Realta followed him as he cautiously took the steps one at a time.

The common room, thankfully, was empty. Elliza's lantern provided the sole source of light. Lightning flashed, bathing the space in blinding, white light. It faded back to near darkness. Realta and Chinasa joined Elliza at the table next to the bar.

"Did you sleep well, Realta?"

"No, I had a bad dream."

"What type of dream?" Chinasa said. He always expressed an interest in her Dreams, marveled by the once lost ability.

"A Thane one," she admitted. There was no point in lying. "Elliza, are we really Three of Nine?"

The girl smiled and nodded.

Chinasa let out a heavy sigh. "I can't believe this. First Valentin and now you?"

"Why do you doubt?"

The ambassador was silent for a moment. "It isn't doubt. Merely surprise. Two people a thousand miles apart who have never met are saying the same thing. It's too improbable to be a coincidence."

Realta's heart sank. She feared Chinasa would say that. "How do we know for sure?"

"Haven't you met your Gadyeni?" Elliza asked.

"I…" Realta started to touch her braid, but her fingers touched air. Her hand fell listlessly onto her lap. "It was just a dream." Anything could happen in a dream.

"Was it?" asked a deep voice.

Realta's heart leapt into her throat. Chinasa shot to his feet, his chair falling over and a knife appearing in his hand. Elliza simply turned around and faced the kitchens.

A tall man strode towards them. He had the same skin tone as a Kereuic with black hair and dark eyes. A dark blue cloak hung from his shoulders. His shirt and trousers appeared finely tailored. And he was completely dry.

How did he get inside? The innkeeper had locked the front door at sunset.

"Who are you?" Chinasa held the knife in a stabbing position. "How did you get in here?"

The man smiled. "You've been having doubts. Last time, we

could allot for doubts. But time is much shorter now."

"Answer the question," Realta said, her voice trembling. *Oh Creator, please, don't let this be real.*

"My name is Tath," the man replied. "The Gadyeni of Justice."

21
War Council

Queen Gallia Toutain of Nowan steadied herself with a deep breath before entering the palace's library. The other monarchs of the Eastern Coalition sat around an oval-shaped, dark wood table. Stacks of books, the upper shelves accessible only by a ladder, surrounded them. Thousands of volumes. Gallia would need two or three lifetimes to read them all.

A new face sat at the table. Liona, the daughter of King Ayrdeen and the acting queen of Bran Maro. The young woman, who claimed to be twenty-five but could easily pass for seventeen, arrived yesterday evening, having received word of her father's disappearance during the coup.

Liona pushed a lock of flaxen hair away from her face, revealing different colored eyes. One brown and one blue, just like Ayrdeen. She met Gallia's eyes and gave her a small wave. The other three turned towards Gallia in unison. King Syleck of Tirshay, rolled his eyes and directed his attention back to the document he was reading. King Eskandar of Tarod, gave her a cursory glance. And Queen Kenda of Galion, the self-proclaimed leader of the Eastern Coalition, scowled.

"Care to join us?" Kenda asked acridly.

Gallia rolled her shoulders back and glided into the library, the silk skirt of her purple and silver dress swishing. She sat between Liona and Syleck. Kenda's dark brown eyes glared at her, as cold as mid-winter ice. Wonderful.

Gallia glanced down at the sprawling map of Teyrnas that covered the length of the table. Dozens of colored tiles dotting the map, symbolizing troop movements. Purple for Nowan, black for Bran Maro, white for Tarod, red for Tirshay, and orange for Galion. A large contingent of white and orange tiles crowded the Teyrnas Highway, cutting off the former capital from the Academy. Gallia frowned. When had they decided that? And her own purple tiles were in a different position. Instead of guarding the capital's southern and eastern gates, they now occupied the grasslands west of the Academy. A good two-days march away.

"Has there been a change of plans?" she asked Kenda.

"How good of you to notice," Kenda replied sarcastically. "Nowan's troops were in a strategically poor location. They will be better suited in the west. In case Byyar's troops cross the Nerin near its confluence. Your generals were notified yesterday."

"I would have preferred to notify them myself." Not to mention keep her troop stationed closer to the city. The best crossing point for the Nerin was between West Bridge and East Bridge, a well-established trade route. In order to cross near the confluence with the Wallach River, soldiers would have to march through miles of dense forest. They'd be exhausted before the fighting began.

But Tirshay's troops held that location now, along with half of Bran Maro's forces.

"Why split the Marish soldiers?" Gallia asked Liona.

"Syleck suggested it," the young queen replied. "Our infantry guards the city while the archers are between the Academy and the Garrison. Better to cover a wide area than have everyone centered in one location."

Not if it means being spread paper thin. Hadn't this girl's father and mother taught her about battle strategy? You only split your forces for two reasons. One, to fight the battle from both sides, as long as both halves have equal strength. Preferably with the two halves positioned back-to-back. And two, to create a weakness for your enemy to exploit and then move in together, trapping them.

But neither was the case here. Teyrnas' forces were concentrated around the Academy and the Garrison, along the Wallach River. Having archers between the two made little sense. Where was their vantage point? Arrows could only fly so high before completing their arcs. Could arrows fired from the ground even reach the top of the Academy's walls? They'd have to be standing directly beside them. Which they weren't.

Gallia sighed. Of course this girl never learned warfare. She grew up in a time of peace, and Bran Maro's involvement in the last war was negligible. Hardly worth mentioning in the history books. Syleck must have mentioned this strategy as a subtle way to keep Bran Maro away from the main fighting, leaving more glory for Tirshay.

I thought we were supposed to be working together.

"I still say we center our forces on the Academy," said Syleck. He pointed to his red tiles.

"Academies are neutral ground," Gallia said, and not for the first time. Their forces originally focused on the capital, but as more people fled and Teyrnas' government reformed at the Academy, tactics changed. They inched closer and closer north, leaving auxiliary troops around the city with the primary forces near the Academy and the Garrison.

"This Academy," Kenda interjected, "is the acting capital of Teyrnas. Queen Isla and half the nobility are there, working side by side with the Scholar Council. And do I have to mention that the Garrison is a mere stone's throw away?"

"I know where it is." Gallia dug her fingernails into her palms, schooling her emotions. Sometimes, she wanted to slap Kenda. A part of her no longer blamed Logan for Manipulating a vase at her head. It was impossible to talk with someone who refused to listen.

She wondered, and not for the first time, if King Logan were alive, if she hadn't stabbed him, would they be in this position? Could they have prevented this war? Logan was willing to negotiate peace. Far more willing than she'd been led to believe. What would the King of Teyrnas say if he could see this mess?

"Are you all right?" Liona asked, placing a hand over Gallia's clenched fist.

Gallia slowly stretched out her fingers. "I'm fine," she lied and immediately hated herself for lying. Liona was a sweet girl. She didn't deserve lies.

Eskandar cleared his throat, indicating that he wished to speak. The man always made sure people were paying attention before he spoke. Kenda nodded and Eskandar said, "I received a report from my spies this morning. Queen Isla is allowing Thanes to fight using their abilities as a primary means instead of secondary. Our forces will now have to deal with Minders, Manipulators, and the Creator knows what else. I propose combing the city for Cuchasi, paying them for their services."

"We don't have to pay them, idiot," Syleck sneered. "We tell them to fight or die. This is a war, damn it!"

"I agree, but not about the Cuchasi," Kenda said. "Eskandar, how accurate is this report?"

"One hundred percent. They're calling it the Thane Regiment. And one spy brought back a flyer asking for recruits."

"So, they've turned the Academy into an active military base instead of a place of learning." Kenda gave each monarch a level gaze. "Every Thane within its walls is a potential weapon. Neutrality no longer applies."

"Yes, it does," Gallia said. "Don't you realize how many civilians are living within those walls? Attacking will only put their lives in danger."

"Funny." Kenda narrowed her eyes. "You did not object to all five of our armies attacking Teyrnas despite over a hundred thousand civilians living within its walls. What's changed?"

"I... I don't know..." Gallia rubbed her forehead. She had not been keen on attacking the capital, not at first. But Valentin had urged her to listen, to heed the other monarchs' counsel instead of rejecting it outright.

"Their ideas deserve to be heard just as much as yours," Val said. Gallia had only been queen for a year and had difficulty getting people to listen sometimes. Except Val. He always listened to her, always validated her ideas and thoughts. "It's only fair," he added.

Val led her down this path. And now he was gone. He left during the initial attack, claiming he had something important to do and promising to return once he was done. She wished he was still here. She missed his smile, his warmth.

I hope you're safe, my love.

"What's on your mind?" Liona asked.

"I was thinking about my adviser, wondering what he would say."

"That bloody Thane?" Eskandar's face contorted as though he had eaten a rotten apple.

"Is that why you don't want to attack the Academy?" Syleck asked. A mocking smile creased his face. "You got a sweet spot for

Thanes now? Or just the ones you take to bed?"

"Shut up," Liona snapped. "She didn't know. That man tricked all of you."

Eskandar averted his gaze. Syleck muttered under his breath, angrily rearranging the documents on the table.

Kenda drummed her lacquered fingernails on the table. Orange and red flames, same as the torch on Galion's flag.

Gallia did not want to believe the rumor. Dane Kanton, one of King Logan's former guards, told everyone the truth after Val disappeared. Kanton described how he survived the ambush on Captain Glasco only to be attacked by Val. The messenger had been in a rage and not only slashed Kanton's leg but mutilated his ears, cutting off the lobes. Val, Kanton claimed, had ranted that the Eastern Coalition would pay for this betrayal in blood and Thanes would soon take their rightful place as the rulers of all Eltriar.

The wounded guard quickly switched alliances, realizing the awful truth: Thanes could not be trusted.

Gallia's allies descended on her, questioning her about Val's employment, his personal history, his family. Gallia then realized that she knew very little about Val's early life, only that he was an orphan. But he was a resourceful, self-educated man who had proven himself capable as a messenger. And the feelings they shared were real. Gallia had even thought about marrying him. Nowani noblewomen proposed marriage just as often as noblemen. And no one would have batted an eye about her marrying a commoner. Nowan's first true king had been a servant, after all.

If not for this war, they might already be engaged.

"I suggest tabling the idea," Kenda announced. She stood and one of her servants materialized from behind a shelf. Gallia recognized him as a former general who had lost his right hand in battle. But only a fool would assume he wasn't dangerous. "Contact your spy networks. This so-called Thane Regiment might be a battlefield mind trick. I want visual evidence before making a decision." Kenda motioned towards the door. The servant opened it, peered into the hallway, and nodded. All clear. Kenda glided out of the library.

Syleck and Eskandar left next. They cast obvious glances at

Gallia and spoke under their breaths. Their servants, armed with hunting knives, met them at the door and escorted them down the hall.

Gallia scowled. They were as subtle as throwing a brick through a window.

Liona stood. "Would you care to join me in the solarium?" The girl, no, the Queen of Barn Maro, had gone to the solarium immediately after her arrival, wanting a private place to play music. She played multiple instruments, just like her father. And just like Ayrdeen, she claimed it helped her think.

Gallia considered it. She needed an ally in the Coalition. Someone who would back her if Kenda tried any more tricks. Getting to know this young woman and learning how her mind worked would be a tremendous advantage. But her own mind went back to Val and to King Logan. She clearly recalled Logan smashing that vase into Kenda's head. She'd been outraged. A blow like that could kill a person, and though she didn't care for the woman, she did not want Kenda to die.

A moment later, King Logan lay on the floor, blood spreading underneath his corpse, staining the carpet dark red. And a bloody dagger, the one her father had gifted her on her twentieth birthday, in her hands. She didn't remember stabbing Logan, nor did she remember Val entering the room. He must have walked in right after. But she could not remember.

Why couldn't she remember?

"No, thank you," she heard herself tell Liona. "Perhaps another time."

The young queen looked disappointed. She went on her way, meeting a pair of servants in the hallways. She spoke politely to them in Marish.

I should have said yes. Liona had looked so lost yesterday, distraught by her father's disappearance and frightened by the fighting. She'd never been around so many soldiers.

Could there be a connection? Ayrdeen revealed his identity to Logan's guards, betraying the Coalition. He then disappeared from his cell around the same time Val told Gallia that he had important work. Had Syleck or Eskandar employed Val to get rid of Ayrdeen? Could the rumor about Val being a Thane merely be a cover-up for their plot? A way to distance themselves? Neither man would talk to a Thane, let alone work with one.

And if they had gotten rid of one monarch, what would stop them from getting rid of her?

A chill ran down her spine.

Gallia glanced around the empty library and felt terribly alone.

22

Time to Think

Charity scrambled to her feet as footsteps approached. Four days had passed since Lucan placed her in this cell. Four periods of darkness and light. She guessed it was almost evening, judging by the waning light.

A cloaked person brought her food and water twice a day, never saying a word. Neither did they respond to her pleas for help. The cloaked figures were always silent. One shoved her away and muttered a curse as she tried to grab the key hanging from their wrist. Since then, they kept the key out of sight.

She glanced up at the window near the ceiling. She tried to reach it the first night, but it was too high and too narrow. Barely more than a slit.

The sky appeared blue. Too blue for the evening. Had Scholar Lucan changed his mind? Was he going to release her?

Or was he going to get rid of her? A horrible dread weighed her down. Lucan placed her here because he could not risk anyone learning about that meeting. Had someone noticed the cloaked figures coming here twice a day? Was she too great a risk to keep alive?

They had discussed the Midnight King, saying that he walked Eltriar again. And worst of all, they had referred to that monster as 'our King'. Lucan said it with the same reverence that chaplains reserved for the Creator and His Gadyeni. She doubted followers of the Midnight King had any qualms about murder.

And what did they want with Lok? She went over their conversation countless times, and she still couldn't puzzle it out. Yes, being the only Elemental on Eltriar was significant, but what did it signify for them? It must connect to the Midnight King, but how?

No matter. Lok was safe. The other cloaked Scholars were certain Lok left the Academy with Kuno and Brother Malaky. Kuno would protect Lok.

The footsteps grew closer, echoing off the cavernous walls. Steeling herself, Charity walked the few paces to the metal bars. What would happen if she started screaming? Not screaming in a terrified way, but just screamed at the top of her lungs? Would that produce a reaction?

Only one way to find out.

Instead of a black cloak, this person wore a blue Student's cloak, and he was a few years older than her. One of the Regor twins, the boys who had mocked her for getting lost and started the fight in Caldeira's Pub. The Scholars punished the wrong Students for that fight, and Charity had to restrain herself each time they mocked Lok, careful never to mock him within earshot of a Scholar.

"What are you doing here?" the boy asked, completely confused.

"I could ask you the same thing." She wanted to snap at him, but her voice was too hoarse.

"They told me to bring the prisoners water," he replied, lifting a water skin. Condensation beaded on the outside. Charity eyed it enviously. "But I thought there would be more than just you down here."

"Scholar Lucan put me here. Which one are you, Yedrick or Edrick?"

"Yedrick," he snapped. He then sighed and said, "Sorry. We get tired of correcting people. So, what did you do? Try to steal something?" A mocking smile crossed his face.

"No. Is that what Lucan told you?" Had the entire Academy heard the lie?

"He didn't tell me anything. Scholar Gray sent me. He's mine and Edrick's mentor. He was supposed to come, but he's busy with the Thane Regiment. Most of them have never fought or held a weapon before. It's a real crap shoot."

"Thane Regiment? What's that?"

Yedrick smiled. "You're really clueless, aren't you?" He leaned against the bars. "How long have you been down here?"

"Four days. I think. Kind of hard to tell." She eyed the water skin. "Can I have something to drink?"

"Oh, yeah, sure." He handed it to her. Charity took a long drink. The water was cool and crisp. She forced herself to stop. This water had to last until morning.

"Do you know why they put me in a cell?"

"Nope." Yedrick snatched the water skin away. "You know Tolman ran away, right? Guess he was too embarrassed to fail in front of the Scholars."

Charity's face burned. "Really? Because I heard he left with Scholar Kuno and Brother Malaky. It was Kuno's idea, actually."

"Good for them. The Council was going to kick out Kuno, anyway. Most of the Scholars are bloody sick of him. And that Brother Malaky guy is crazy. I heard he snapped, and the Church sent him here because they don't want word to spread."

"Doesn't matter. Scholar Lucan can't use any of them to help the Midnight King."

Yedrick's eyes narrowed. "Who said anything about the Midnight King?"

"I overheard Lucan's meeting. He called Brother Malaky a Harbinger, and he talked all about the Midnight King. His king. Didn't Scholar Gray mention that?" she asked, adopting Yedrick's mocking tone.

Yedrick cursed under his breath. "No wonder you're down here. I supposed it's better than outright killing you."

Charity's heart skipped a beat. "Wait. You aren't surprised. You know about their group."

"Yeah, my parents are part of it. They didn't tell me or Edrick until last year. Didn't want us to say anything accidentally." Yedrick lowered his voice. "You could join us. I'm sure Lucan will let you out if you take the vows."

"What vows?" Charity would rather break all of her fingers than serve the Midnight King. She could always lie. Lying was wrong, but what if she lied for a good reason? If lying got her out of this cell and she could warn everyone about Lucan, it was worth it. Right?

"A bunch of crap in Old Eltrian. I didn't understand most of it. But Lucan will know if you aren't serious. Several people in our group are Empaths."

The prison door swung open on creaking hinges. Voices

echoed off the walls. Yedrick spun on his heels and took a half-step backwards.

"What is the meaning of this?" Scholar Lucan's voice boomed. Charity's blood turned to ice water.

The Scholar stood in front of her cell. Yedrick greeted Lucan with a short bow. Two others stood behind Lucan, a woman in her twenties with long, blonde hair, and a skinny man with dark hair in wild disarray. He was the Scholar she'd asked about Kuno. The one who had been confused about the meeting.

All of them wore long black cloaks.

"Well, explain yourself, Student," Lucan snapped.

"Scholar Gray—"

"Scholar Gray instructed you to check on the prisoners, not make idle conversation." Lucan shot a glare at Charity. "What has she said?"

"That you put her in here for eavesdropping."

"Precisely. The Wardens cannot afford exposure. Not at such a critical moment." He fixed his gaze on Yedrick. "Do you understand, Edrick?"

"I'm Yedrick, and yes, Scholar Lucan." He bowed again.

"Very good."

Yedrick stole a nervous glance at Charity. "Scholar?"

"What?" Lucan scowled. Yedrick stepped back.

"Have you considered initiating her? Give her a chance to join us?"

"That could work," said the blonde woman. Charity knew she was a Journeyman but couldn't quite place her. One of Kuno's students maybe. "If she told anyone, she would expose herself in the process."

Lucan shook his head. "Not now. Alberik needs willing Wardens to aid him. Perhaps after he regains his powers."

"What makes you so sure?" Charity asked.

She regretted opening her mouth as three pairs of icy eyes glared at her. She looked at Yedrick, but the boy was too busy studying his shoes.

"The Midnight King walks Eltriar once more, Charity Loy," Scholar Lucan said, his voice calm. "Take this time to reflect and choose your side wisely." Lucan walked down the hallway. His two lackeys followed on his heels.

Yedrick stood by the cell, chewing on his lower lip. He slipped the water skin through the bars. It landed right next to Charity's feet.

"Thank you," she whispered.

"Yedrick!" Lucan yelled.

The boy bolted down the hallway.

The door creaked shut, leaving Charity alone with her thoughts.

23

Prism

Realta reluctantly followed Elliza down the stairs, her chest tight. Elliza said that Corey wanted to speak to her.

"About what?"

"Your abilities," Elliza said matter-of-factly.

As far as the man knew, Realta was a low leveled Manipulator, and she hoped to keep it that way. If Corey learned she was a Dreamer...

Best not to think about that.

Realta glanced at the village through the common room windows. The rain had yet to let up, leaving the roads flooded.

She turned her attention to the common room itself. The Jemayrti Scholars sat off to one side, speaking quietly even though the innkeeper did not understand their language. The innkeeper moved from table to table, asking if anyone needed anything. He was polite to the point of annoyance. He spared a cursory glance at Realta and Elliza and hurried towards the kitchen. Well, he was polite as far as the Scholars and Corey were concerned.

Serena and Shasta sat at their own table. Shasta observed everyone, and Serena acted like the shadows would come to life and attack her. She had been so jumpy lately. Realta assumed Serena was afraid of Corey. They all were to an extent. But her fear seemed to come and go, depending on whether Corey was yelling. Perhaps Corey's temper reminded her of Logan.

Reaching the base of the stairs, Realta saw Corey sitting at the bar along with Braedan and Tath. The Gadyeni, who looked Kereuic with his dark hair and eyes and tan skin, explained that he was traveling through the country when he got caught in the storm. He introduced himself to Savastian Balans and apologized for arriving unannounced. The innkeeper didn't question Tath, nor did he question how Tath had gotten through the locked doors. He was too overjoyed about having one more guest.

"See that, girl," Corey had hissed in Realta's ear. "One more witness. Do anything stupid and he'll alert the militia, too."

Realta, one step behind Elliza, approached the bar. Her heart pounded in her throat.

"There they are," Corey said, smiling from ear to ear. "Take a seat, girls."

Elliza sat down next to Corey and Braedan while Realta took the empty seat next to Tath. She felt much safer having an immortal being between her and Corey. She stole a quick glance at Shasta. The former head of servants studied Tath, her eyes narrow slits. What did she think of this mysterious traveler?

"And they are both Thanes?" Tath asked in a flawless Kereuic accent. His clothes had changed as well, matching the local style. Loose-fitting trousers that were tight around the waist and ankles and a dark green shirt laced up in the front. He took a sip of spiced wine and looked at Realta and Elliza.

"Of course." Corey frowned. "Take that damn bracelet off," he snapped at Realta.

You already cut off my hair, you bastard. What other proof do you need?

Biting her tongue, Realta placed a hand on her bracelet, making no move to take it off. The bracelet was a gift from Chinasa. A way to hide her tattoo and a symbol of her Thane abilities. While Thanes in Teyrnas wore earrings, Thanes in Jemayrt wore bracelets and necklaces. Being gifted with the jewelry was a rite of passage, usually given to a child by their parents on a holiday or birthday. Since Callum was missing, Chinasa presented the bracelet and necklace himself.

And she was not a real indentured servant. King Logan hadn't signed any papers or pressed any charges. He had given her that horrible tattoo purely out of spite.

"Don't anger him," Tath whispered.

Realta relented. The beads clicked as she placed it on the bar. A servant walked by, a handsome but nosy man who was constantly whispering in the innkeeper's ear. He glanced at the tattoo and then at Realta's hair before disappearing into the kitchens. Realta heard him speaking loudly to the cook and did not know whether to scream or cry.

"So, what can the little Thanes do?" Tath asked.

Corey's smile widened. "Elliza is a Farsight. Highly gifted. And Realta is a Manipulator. Low-leveled, if I have to guess. It's hard to get good information these days." He shot a venomous glare at Braedan. The mercenary downed the rest of his wine in one gulp and called out for another.

"Why not test her now?" Tath suggested.

"Is that necessary?" Chinasa asked, turning around in his seat and locking eyes with the Gadyeni. The other Scholars and Shasta watched silently. Ezri reached under the table for a knife.

"Since you lied to me, yes," Corey replied. "Sorry about that, Master Balans. I've heard only good things about the Jemayrti, so I had no reason to suspect them."

"Please, call me Savastian. And I'm certain they had valid reasons. Don't worry, sir," he said to Chinasa. "It's only a simple test. No different from what's performed at Academies."

Chinasa met Realta's eyes, clearly worried. But Tath was a Gadyeni. The Gadyeni needed Realta and Chinasa, so he wouldn't do anything to hurt her. She nodded. Chinasa sighed through his teeth and returned the nod.

"Stand up," Tath instructed Realta. He stood beside her. The Gadyeni was very tall, at least a head taller than Callum. "Right there, yes."

"What do you want me to do?" She could feel Corey's eyes watching her. *Focus on Tath, not Corey.*

"Manipulate something," Tath said gently. "Anything to you. But don't strain yourself."

Realta glanced around the bar. The largest object she had Manipulated was a knife. She hadn't been too keen to practice, worried someone would see and ask uncomfortable questions. Besides, she was a Dreamer. The Manipulator part was secondary. According to Braedan, her Aura was black with little gold sparks, almost too small to see.

He also claims I'm an Empath.

Should she test that ability, too? She looked at Corey. The merchant drummed his fingers on the bar, his eyes narrowed. He only knew about one of her abilities. Best to keep the others a secret.

Realta selected Tath's half-empty mug. She pictured it in her mind. The size, shape, and weight. Focusing on the mug, she made it spin around once.

"Is that it?" Corey frowned.

"She ain't much of a Manipulator," Braedan said, his words beginning to slur.

"Are you just going to drink all day?" Corey snapped. "Get off your ass and do something useful!"

Braedan rolled his eyes. He finished his drink and stalked away, bumping into a table on his way to the front door. A guest of wind sent a torrent of rain into the common room, soaking the floor. The door slammed shut behind him, echoing.

Realta felt a sharp pain in her chest. The horrible sense that she had failed, that she was a no-good screw up who ruined...

No, that pain did not belong to her. It belonged to Braedan.

Stars above, I really am an Empath.

Realta felt strangely numb and tired as Braedan's emotions faded away.

"Wonder where he thinks he's going," Tath mused.

"Who cares? Can't go anywhere in this weather. Well? What else can you do?"

Realta jolted and quickly looked for another small object. A handful of recently polished spoons rested at the end of the bar. She Manipulated one spoon towards her, but she knew it wouldn't be even to satisfy Corey. She then spun it around.

Sweat broke out on her forehead. Her vision blurred, and she felt so tired. Her arms ached and her head pounded behind the eyes. The spoon clanged as it hit the floor. Realta grabbed onto the bar as her legs gave out.

"Stars above," Tath exclaimed. He helped Realta into a seat, standing over her like a mother hen. Tath placed a hand on her forehead and grimaced. "She's overstrained herself."

"What does that mean?" Corey asked.

Realta rested her head against the bar's cool surface. She felt warm, far too warm, as though she had spent all day out in the sun. And her muscles ached. Arms, legs, back. Everything hurt. She wished her father and aunt were here. Aunt Esme would know exactly what to do, how to make her feel better. And Callum would watch over her. He always watched over her when she was sick. Even when she was sick in bed for a full week with a chest cold.

Tears burned her eyes. Why had Callum been late? Why hadn't he joined them?

Callum went to find King Logan, and Val had killed the king. Did he kill Callum, too?

All the horrible, impossible things Val had said slammed into her. The Midnight King returning. The Nine Summit Thanes uniting to fight him. The war in Teyrnas being nothing more than a distraction.

But they weren't impossible. Bas called her One of Nine, and Tath was here in Kereu. They were real. Val's claims were real.

So, why did he destroy her trust by killing the king?

Please, Creator. Please let my father be alive.

"Using a Thane ability is akin to using a muscle," she heard Chinasa explain. "If you exercise a muscle a little each day, it grows stronger. But if you exercise too much too quickly, you risk injury. The strength of a Thane's ability is also a factor. Realta is a very low-leveled Manipulator, and she has had little practice."

"I wonder whose fault that is," Corey replied snidely.

"Do you want some water?" Tath asked her.

Realta nodded. Her head felt like it was full of rocks. Tears leaked from her eyes. And she felt so tired. Stars above, she could fall asleep right here.

Tath handed her a mug, and she took a small sip.

"She will be all right," Elliza said. "She just needs to rest. You can test her more tomorrow."

What makes you think I want to be tested? Realta almost said. She took another sip of water instead.

"Well, we shall have to discuss another topic," Tath said to Corey, sitting between him and Realta. "What items do you have for sale?"

Corey let out a bitter laugh. "All my merchandise is in the stable. But I got something that ain't for sale."

Realta raised her head and saw Corey hand a sheathed dagger to Tath. The Gadyeni inhaled sharply as he removed a dagger.

Thin and long, the dagger shone to a mirror brightness. Its hilt was pure white with a mirror at the base. Tath positioned the mirror so it caught the light. A small, circular rainbow shone on the bar's surface.

"Where did you get this?" Tath asked. Realta looked at the Gadyeni's face and a sense of awe, like bright sunlight emerging from the clouds, enveloped her.

"Bought if off a Treileani trader for a silver mark. He claimed it was a family heirloom, tried to drive up the price, but I ain't stupid. Anyone can make a dagger like this."

"But this is a prism."

"So?"

"They take a great amount of skill to cut. I've never seen one placed on a dagger's hilt. What purpose does it serve?"

"To drive up the price." Corey smirked.

"How much?"

The merchant shrugged. "As much as you can get. Depends on the buyer's intelligence."

Tath's eyes narrowed. "Of course. It's mere ornamentation, after all." He gazed at the prism for a few seconds and then placed the dagger back in the sheath.

A pit formed in Realta's gut as she eyed the dagger. Corey must have hidden it under his coat, armed this whole time. What other weapons did he have hidden?

The dagger inched closer to Realta. She bit down on her lower lip and eyed Corey. She had Manipulated it accidentally. The merchant, thankfully, hadn't noticed, too deep in conversation.

She Manipulated it another inch. It was like swimming with weights tied around her ankles, and she ached all over.

What am I doing? Why Manipulate the dagger closer? She certainly could not use it, not when she was too weak to stand. Could she take it? Corey would have one less weapon to threaten her with, but if he caught her stealing... She shivered.

The front door swung open, drawing everyone's attention.

Must be Braedan.

A figure in a rain soaked, gray cloak stumbled into the common room. He pulled back the hood and gazed around with dark, dark eyes. Realta's heart skipped a beat. Bas. The Gadyeni from her Dreams.

The innkeeper quickly hurried towards Bas, offering to take his cloak. Bas refused.

"Is there a spare room?" he asked.

"Yes, sir. Definitely, sir," the innkeeper replied, bowing.

"Adso!" Tath called out, walking over to Bas and embracing him. "What's brought you to this part of the world?"

"Business as usual. How are you, Savastian?"

"Friend of yours?" Corey sauntered over to the two Gadyeni. How would the man react if he knew these beings were thousands of years old?

Realta's eyes fell on the dagger, completely forgotten. She glanced up and locked eyes with Elliza. The girl nodded. Realta frowned. Elliza's eyes darted to the dagger. She nodded again. *Does she want me to take it?*

Realta glanced at Corey. The merchant shook hands with Bas and introduced himself, his back towards the bar. Realta snatched and dagger and tucked it into her belt. She slid out of her seat. Her legs trembled but held steady.

"I don't feel well," she told Shasta. "I'm going to lie down."

"Very well, child. And try to have peaceful dreams," Shasta added. Realta told her and Serena about the last Dream, excluding her conversation with Bas.

Chinasa stood and intercepted her at the stairs. "Is that other man...?"

Realta nodded. "He's mine, I guess."

Chinasa eyed Bas and Tath warily. "I wonder if mine will appear. I don't like this, Realta. We will get away once the storm ends."

Realta held onto the railing as she climbed the stairs, struggling to not fall on her face. Corey was sure to notice her falling on the stairs.

Once in her room, she hid the dagger underneath the mattress. She sat on the bed, trembling all over. Had she really just stolen from Corey? He would discover the theft as soon as he lost interest in Bas and Tath. How much trouble would she get in? Would the Gadyeni protect her?

And why had Elliza encouraged her?

Realta took a deep breath, forcing herself to calm down. Panicking would only make matters worse.

She had practiced knife throwing for two months. Those lessons had not been for fun. She lied down, praying she would not have to put that practice to use.

24

In the Keep

A tree root snagged Lok's ankle. He stumbled, leaning against the nearest tree to keep his balance, and kept walking. He didn't want to lag behind and give Kuno another reason to be angry.

The boat ride across the Nerin had gone smoothly until the captain upped his prices. Nobody was allowed to disembark until they paid an extra fee.

"And don't worry if you're short on coin," he said with a wicked smile. "You can always work it off."

Scholar Kuno, his eyes blazing, threatened to report the captain for holding a Scholar and a chaplain against their wills. The captain didn't care about authorities, nor about the Academy or the Church.

"And I don't care about titles either," he snapped at two other passengers, members of a minor noble House. The couple cowered.

Lok decided to intervene. Lighting a match, he commanded the fire to grow and swirled a circle of flame over his head. Passengers fled to the edges of the boat, screaming. A few jumped overboard, swimming frantically to shore. The crew also panicked, running for their swords and crossbows.

"Wait!" the captain yelled. Lok collected the flames into a ball, holding it an inch above his palm. The captain stalked closer to Lok and studied the green ring in his ear. "What on Eltriar are you?"

"He's an Elemental Thane," Kuno said.

The captain nodded and allowed the passengers to go, no additional fee required.

Lok, Kuno, and Malaky split off from the others once they were on dry land and headed deeper into the forest. The other passengers followed the shoreline. Several cast fearful glances at

Lok. Had he made a mistake by using his Thane ability? He only wanted to help, and the captain certainly would not listen to anyone.

Two days of constant walking had taken a toll. They had few supplies. Just an extra change of clothes in each travel bag and some camping tools. Kuno gave the captain most of their supplies in exchange for keeping his mouth shut. The captain nodded, handed off the supplies to a crew member, and watched as they walked into the forest.

Scholar Kuno's temper was now at its boiling point. Lok didn't dare look at him. He gave Kuno a note last night, apologizing. The Scholar tossed the note into the campfire without reading it. Brother Malaky, thankfully, said nothing.

He hadn't had any more Farsights, thank the Creator. Lok did not want to hear about the horrible things he might do, people he might hurt. The image of fire leaping onto that guardsman flashed in his memory. The man had shrieked and then collapsed, silent. Lok felt sick.

The forest grew thinner, and human voices sounded just over the hill. Lok crested it and saw the familiar ruins of Rangar Keep. The bases of stone structures and columns stuck out of the foliage. Bits and pieces of a once great city, or so Charity had guessed. A weight lifted off Lok's shoulders.

People milled about, some setting up cookfires and tents while others walked around and talked with other travelers. Or smugglers. Now that he was looking for them, Lok noticed that most people carried weapons. A few even had long swords, weapons that only guardsmen were allowed to own.

"Well, it's about time," Brother Malaky exclaimed. The chaplain adjusted his glasses and peered around. "I've heard of places like this, but never thought I'd visit one. Car and I made up all sorts of adventures..." Malaky's face fell. He had mentioned Car a few times since leaving the Academy. Kuno explained that Car was the chaplain's brother, and that he had died young. "But that's neither here nor there. So, now what?"

"Find the person in charge." Kuno marched past them and into the clearing.

Lok spied Rawni, the unofficial mayor of Rangar Keep, sitting on a slab of stone. A pair of oak trees shaded her. He pointed her out to Kuno. The Scholar gave her a dubious glance and then walked towards her.

Rawni raised an eyebrow as they approached. Lok doubted she had ever seen a Scholar or a chaplain traveling through the Keep. And Kuno's white cloak stood out among the muted browns, grays, and greens most people wore.

"What do you want?" she asked.

"A place to spend the night," Kuno replied. "We're just passing through. And we don't want any trouble," he added.

Rawni smirked. "Scholar, if you're traveling through the Keep, you're already in trouble. But there's always room. I suggest sleeping by a ruin. Might rain tonight."

Kuno thanked her and hurried away. Lok and Malaky jogged to catch up.

"That's it? We don't have to pay a fee?" Malaky asked, his face turning red from exertion.

"Nope." Kuno paused to inspect a stone shelter. It was far too small for all three of them and had a hole near the back corner. Kuno stared at it for several long seconds, let out a heavy sigh, and walked on. The Scholar inspected another set of ruins. It appeared to be part of a house, but only two walls remained. The walls leaned against each other, partially sunk into the ground. Moss grew over them, and there was no roof. "This will do. Malaky, find some leafy branches to cover us. Lok, start a fire."

Lok placed his traveling bag in the ruin's sole corner and took out his notebook. The edges were damp from last night's rain, but the rest was intact.

"How did you know?" Malaky asked. Lok jolted. He was about to ask the same question.

"I wasn't a Scholar my entire life," Kuno said after a moment. "Now, get those branches. With any luck, we can get an early start and arrive in Vala by mid-afternoon."

Malaky adjusted his glasses again and set off into the forest.

Kuno leaned against the ruins and slid down. He closed his eyes, exhausted.

The Scholar looked so much older. His hair was a bit grayer, and the fine lines around his eyes more visible. And he looked thinner. Lok cautiously sat down beside him.

"Fire won't start itself," Kuno muttered.

"*What is wrong?*" Lok wrote. He nudged the Scholar.

Kuno sighed deeply as he read. "Too many things. I hate that Lucan put you in this position. I hate that there is a war, that young men and women have to fight and die again. I just..." Kuno gazed up at the sky. Large, white clouds covered the blue expanse. "I'm just tired. Can you start the fire, please?"

Lok gathered a few sticks and arranged them in a pile. Taking out a match, he lit it and placed it in the middle. Exhaling, he caused the fire to spread, touching every stick at once. The fire burned bright and hot. Perfect for cooking.

"Stars above! I can't believe it. I just can't believe it!"

Startled, Lok looked up and saw Arnyn Teleran standing nearby. Lok blinked. No, he wasn't seeing things. He slowly rose to his feet as the thief hurried over.

Arnyn clasped him on the shoulders and smiled. "Lok Tolman, one of two Elemental Thanes in the world! How are you? I thought you and Miss Loy were bound for the Academy."

Lok began writing but faltered halfway. Arnyn could not read. Charity had to translate for him. He glanced at Kuno. Would the Scholar mind reading his responses out loud?

Kuno stood and eyed Arnyn cautiously. "Who are you?"

"Arnyn Teleran, professional thief and seer of Thanes. And you?"

Kuno introduced himself.

"Well, how about that! Tolman has his very own mentor. So, why aren't you at the Academy?"

"It's a long story. What did you say about Lok being one of two Elementals?"

Arnyn grinned from ear to ear, blue eyes shining. "The Creator has worked His balancing act again! Seeing that only one Elemental in the world was not enough, He graced us with another." Arnyn cupped his hands over his mouth and called, "Westermor! Come over here. There are people you need to meet!"

A boy with a mop of dark brown hair ran towards them, his smile reflected in his gray eyes.

Lok's heart skipped a beat. It was West, the boy he and Charity had met while in Rangar. Charity wanted to help him, but West disappeared, traveling in the opposite direction. Lok's gut told him to help, and he ignored it. Was this the Creator giving him a second chance?

Lok glanced left and right. He didn't see West's aunt or the men they were traveling with. Had West escaped?

West ran up to Lok and wrapped his arms around him, jumping up and down. "Lok! Fire, fire!"

Lok placed both hands firmly on the other boy's shoulders, forcing him to stand still. He appeared to be all right. No bruises or scraps. No signs of abuse. He fumbled for his notebook and pencil.

"He's an Elemental, too?" Kuno asked, his face turning ashen. He muttered in Old Eltrian as he studied West. Lok didn't understand the words, but Kuno sounded worried. Why should he be worried? Wasn't another Elemental Thane a good thing?

Fire. Lok wanted to kick himself. West had pointed to the fire and then pointed to Lok and then to himself. He was trying to tell Lok and Charity about his ability, except he didn't know the words. But he remembered the word 'fire'. Perhaps Kuno could teach him more Teyrnian.

"As I live and breathe," said Arnyn, a proud smile plastered on his face. "Two Elementals in one lifetime. I think that's a record."

"I don't doubt it."

"Lok." West grabbed Lok's wrist. "I talk Teyrnas now. Nice man help." He beamed a smile.

Well, that was a relief. He nodded to Arnyn gratefully. Had Arnyn helped the boy escape? Arnyn prided himself on being an excellent thief. Perhaps he proved it by stealing West from his aunt.

Lok quickly wrote, *"Have you been there this whole time?"*

West's smile faded. "Not read."

Lok sighed. He handed the notebook to Kuno, and the Scholar read the question out loud.

"Friend. Good friend help. Not bad." West smiled again.

"Westermor, what is your native language?" Kuno asked.

West stared at him, his head cocked to one side.

Kuno frowned. "Your language. What did you speak first?"

A light shone in West's eyes. "Marish!"

"Great. The one language I don't know."

"No worries, Scholar," said Arnyn. "The Creator knows exactly what He is doing. He led West into the hands of another Elemental and a capable Scholar. I assume you're capable. Surely the Academy wouldn't allow its only Elemental to be mentored by a fool."

"You'd be surprised by the stupidity of Scholars."

"Is that why you are here and not there?"

Kuno nodded gravely.

"Well, no worries. No one will harm you at the Keep."

Brother Malaky ran towards them, his eyes wide and his face bright red as he gasped for breath. He halted in front of Kuno and grabbed the Scholar by the cloak.

"What happened?" Kuno questioned harshly.

"Hiraeth," Malaky managed after several breaths. He let go of Kuno and adjusted his glasses. "An entire tribe of Hiraeth. Over there." He pointed to the clearing's edge.

A dozen wagons painted with strange black symbols slowly rode into Rangar Keep. The drivers eyed everyone suspiciously. Men and women armed with leather armor over green and brown clothes flanked the wagons. Each one carried bows and arrows or a hunting knife or both. People cleared the way as they rode past, watching from the trees.

"Huh, that's interesting," Arnyn said.

"You don't get a lot of Hiraethi traveling through here?" Kuno asked.

"Maybe one or two, but rarely a whole tribe. Wonder what's brought them here."

"Maybe it's the war," Lok suggested.

"Doubtful," Kuno replied. "The Hiraeth usually stay on the western side of the Nerin. You rarely see them near large cities."

"Unless it's to trade," Malaky added. "That's how my grandparents met."

"You're part Hiraethi?" Kuno arched an eyebrow.

"On my mother's side. But I don't really know much about them. Car was obsessed, though. Learned their language and culture. Even told people he was Hiraethi. I'm honestly surprised he didn't run away to join a tribe." A strange look came over Malaky's face. He frowned and muttered under his breath.

The wagons halted, a long line stretching half the length of the clearing. The horses stamped impatiently. Most of the travelers had scattered. Lok saw only a handful near the ruins. A few inched closer to get a better look. Rawni, eyes narrowed and scowling, walked up to the first wagon and spoke to one of the armed men.

"Westermor, stay here!" Kuno called out.

Lok peered down. West no longer stood by his side. Instead, he walked towards the Hiraeth caravan, a big smile on his face. One man spied West and nocked an arrow. Lok ran towards him.

Two women saw Lok running and raised their bows. An older female voice called out, and they lowered their weapons. They eyed him and West suspiciously, like a new species of snake that might be venomous.

"What do you want?" one woman asked West. Her hair was tied back in a long braid, and a quiver full of arrows hung from her belt.

West just smiled. Lok caught up and tried to lead West away, but he dug in his heels.

"No! Stay here. Person. Person!" West looked into Lok's eyes, pleading to be understood. A pain struck Lok's chest. How many times had Lok struggled to be understood? How many times during the painful years before he learned to write did he burst into tears because he wanted to tell his mother something, but there were no words? There were never any words.

"What do you want?" the woman asked more forcefully.

Lok glanced around. More Hiraethi stared at them. All hostile. He reached for his notebook, but only his matches were in his hand. He must have dropped it.

"Please forgive them," Kuno said. He placed himself between Lok and West and the women. "Both of my sons have difficulty speaking. They don't mean any harm. They're just curious."

"Tell them to be curious somewhere else." Her eyes fell on Brother Malaky. "Have you come to preach to us, chaplain?"

"Um, no," Brother Malaky stammered. "Do you want me to?"

"No."

"Okay." Malaky hid behind Kuno, watching the archers nervously.

"Wait, are you a Scholar?" Another woman, also armed with a bow and arrows, shouldered her way past the other two. They scowled, one rolling her eyes. The third woman was young, about twenty years old, and she had a mass of curly, dark brown hair. Her green eyes stood out like emeralds against her tanned skin.

"Yes, but I'm just traveling through."

"So are we."

"Meredith, opri piird tempt!" said the same elderly female voice.

The young woman squared her shoulders and nodded at the lead wagon. Through the window, Lok saw an old woman, decades older than the Premier Scholar. Snow white hair fell past her shoulders, and she wore several bead necklaces. Rings lined her earlobes. She scowled and Lok.

"Come on," Kuno said, shepherding Lok and West away. "We don't want to interfere."

"Person. Person!" West pleaded.

"Yes, they are people. Obviously." Lok heard traces of anger in Kuno's tone.

"Still, it's strange for a whole tribe to wander this far from the mountains. I wonder if they are relocating," Malaky said.

"Either way, it's none of our business. West, would you like to travel with us to Vala? You will be safe there."

"Vala?" West cocked his head to one side.

"Lok's home village."

The boy's face lit up as he smiled. "Yes!" He pointed at Lok. "I like him."

"It's good to like your traveling companions." Kuno looked at their camp and frowned. "Where did that thief go?"

✳✳✳

Meredith watched as the Scholar hurried away with the two boys. Boys he claimed were his sons, but neither looked like him. One stood a head taller, and the other was far too pale with light eyes. Nor did the boys resemble each other. Were they adopted?

She looked up at her Great Mother, the leader of their tribe and her mother's grandmother. A disappointing scowl met her gaze. She met the scowl head on. She could not back down now.

"I know what you're thinking, girl," her Great Mother said in Hiraethi, her tone neutral. "The answer is no."

"But if they're also heading for Caman's Pass, what's the harm in speaking to him?"

"Those Scholars never come here. He likely stole that cloak."

"He could be a scout." Meredith heard stories of Scholars traveling to remote villages, searching for Thanes and educating them at the Academy, a massive stone building by the river. A building she had dreamed of since she was twelve years old.

"I said no. The tribe needs you and your gift."

Meredith was an Empath Thane, able to read people's true emotions. Not everyone the Hiraeth encountered was friendly. Most wanted them to leave without causing trouble. But sometimes, trouble found them. Stupid villagers who had heard too many stories and believed them. Once, the tribe had to flee in the middle of the night because the locals thought they were Seltachai and wanted to drink their children's blood. As though such a creature could actually exist!

But Meredith was not her tribe's only Empath.

"Perhaps I could speak with him—"

"How many times must you hear the same answer, girl?" her Great Mother snapped.

"All clear!" Lukas, the tribe's spokesman, called out. The man spoke every Vogel language like a native and knew each country's greeting customs. He assured the locals that their intentions were peaceful, and that the tribe would attack only if provoked. Being a low-leveled Empath also helped.

The wagons started moving again. Meredith fell into place, her arrow nocked, ready to draw and fire. She spied the Scholar's white cloak among the forest's greens and browns. Two other men spoke with him and his sons. A chaplain dressed in a brown robe with a white cord tied around his waist, and a plainly dressed man with pitched black hair and a bit too skinny. Probably a regular to the Keep.

Meredith glanced up and down the line. Set up would take hours. First, positioning the wagons in a circle. Then unhitching the horses and gathering supplies. Her mother and older sisters would help organize the set up and evening meal. And her father and uncle would hunt along with a dozen others.

An idea formed. It was difficult to keep track of everyone during set up. Everyone scattered about. She could slip away and explain to the Scholar that she was an Empath. And she was not abandoning her tribe, no matter what the Great Mother claimed. She would use her Academy education to aid them. Perhaps if more Hiraethi were Academy trained, people would have fewer reasons to fear them.

And by the time anyone realized she was gone, it would be too late to stop her.

25

Rumors

Gareth, on his hands and knees, peered through the gap in the Academy's wall. Ivar and Jaim crouched uncomfortably close beside him. Beads of sweat rolled down Gareth's face and neck, the afternoon sun blazing. He wished he didn't have to wear this stupid cloak, but it was the only thing identifying him as a Student instead of one of the countless refugees.

They should be in class, but Charity and Lok were still missing. Nobody had seen them in days. Not their friends or classmates or the Scholars. They vanished, and nobody cared.

"They probably ran away," one Scholar told them. "Stop wasting time and go back to class."

Several Students and Journeymen had left the Academy in desperate attempts to reunite with their families, against the Scholars' wishes. Others had volunteered for the Thane Regiment, including Zandon. The Farsight went to the Garrison yesterday at noon, along with twenty other young men and women, all disguised as refugees bound for Norgard and other outlying villages.

The Coalition soldiers blocking the road ordered them to halt and searched for weapons. Some were forced to remove their clothing. All explained that there was no room left at the Academy and they had to relocate, and none wore their earrings. They had to remove them in order to sell the lie. The soldiers allowed them to pass on the grounds that they would not be permitted to return.

"See anything?" Jaim asked, breathing down Gareth's neck.

Gareth shifted away and crouched down lower, straining to see anything. "Trees. Grass. Horses. Not much else."

"Then move." Jaim dug his elbow into Gareth's ribs. "I can slip through—"

"No." Ivar clamped a hand on the hood of Jaim's cloak, pulling him back.

"You know I can fit," Jaim protested. "Fire and smoke, this gap is big enough for you to fit! The Gadyeni know we've snuck out plenty of times."

"That is not the point. You are wearing light blue. How many others are wearing light blue?"

Jaim gave him a puzzled look. "Uh, all the Students."

"And how many Students have the Scholars allowed outside the walls?"

"None."

"The Coalition soldiers would identify you in an instant," Gareth said, seeing Ivar's point.

"Not if I take the bloody thing off!"

"Still," Ivar said, "it's too great a risk."

Jaim balled his hands into fists. "Well, how else are we supposed to find people who aren't inside the Academy if we don't go outside?"

"Have you considered that they don't want to be found?"

Gareth's heart sank. Charity never ran away from anything in her life. Not even at the prospect of traveling with Dane Kanton. Gareth was the one who run away. He was the coward, not her. And she was like a sister to him. He would not stand idly by if Estrid were missing. He would search to the ends of Eltriar to find her. And Charity and Estrid would do the same for him.

No, he could not take the coward's way out this time.

"You don't honestly think they ran away, do you?" Jaim asked, crossing his arms.

Gareth leaned against the wall and peered through the bushes surrounding the gap. Sunlight glinting off metal caught his eyes. Then he spied a gold Aura and the guardsman attached to it, speaking with another guard. He motioned for Ivar and Jaim to be quiet. All three crouched down low, watching.

"I swear on my father's name," said the guardsman with the Aura. "It was him!"

"You were drunk," the other retorted.

"Drunk?! It was bloody daylight! And he walked right by me. I said his name under my breath because I was so shocked, and he walked faster, almost running."

"Who are they talking about?" Jaim whispered to Ivar as the guards walked away.

Ivar stared intently at the two guards, his silver Aura pulsing like a heartbeat. He explained that in order to read a mind, he pictured a door to the person's mind and opened it. Most times, he didn't have to concentrate, unlike lower leveled Minders.

"Yeah, because he didn't want to deal with a drunk!" said the guard. His colleague let out an exasperated sigh.

"You know what, forget it. Just forget it." They walked out of hearing range.

"Well?" Jaim asked.

Ivar's dark brown eyes were narrow slits, and his mouth was fixed in a pensive frown. "King Logan," he finally said. "The guardsman believes he saw King Logan."

An uneasy feeling settled over Gareth. Kel had sworn him to secrecy. No one could know that the king was alive. It would jeopardize his safety. So, how had the guardsman seen Logan? Was it an accident?

Gareth frowned. No, the guard claimed that Logan walked by him. Out in the open. Shouldn't the king be hiding?

"We have to see my father." Gareth stood and walked towards the stables through the collection of makeshift tents. Jaim and Ivar hurried to keep up, Jaim telling him to slow down. People stared as they walked by. Gareth quickly averted his eyes and focused on the ground. He hated when people stared at him, and with so many new people at the Academy, it was impossible to walk around without someone watching. He felt better around Thanes, though. Their Auras were strangely comforting, and he found them easier to talk to, the main reason he had befriended Jaim and Ivar.

Why is that? He wished everyone was easy to talk to, especially Scholar Lyle. He couldn't properly explain to the Scholar the significance of Charity's absence. If Lyle had understood, maybe the Scholars would have started an official search.

He glanced up for a second and found dozens of eyes staring at him. His skin crawled, and he quickly glanced down.

"Do we have to?" Jaim asked. "Don't get me wrong. Your father is nice and all, but..." He grimaced. Gareth had been so excited to introduce his father to his new friends. But in his excitement, he forgot to mention Kel's injuries, aspects of his father that were as commonplace to Gareth as the sky being blue.

Kel's scars shocked them, making them uneasy and unsure of what to say. Jaim made a real ass of himself, asking Kel if he owned any mirrors. Kel merely smiled and took it in stride.

"Yes, he already promised to help find Charity and Lok. Maybe he can explain what the guardsman was talking about." *And the king is his younger brother.* How shocked would his friends be if they learned that truth?

Gareth led the way through rows of tents, avoiding people as best he could. Most tents were plain canvas, but others were made of old blankets and clothes sown together. Many seams were badly stitched. How well would they hold up during a storm?

He spied Colm sitting crisscross in front of his father's tent. The guard, his pet draig on one shoulder, was intently reading a book, sounding out the words and pausing frequently. The little draig raised her head, recognized Gareth, and went back to sunning herself.

"Where is Kel?" Gareth asked, his shadow falling over Colm.

Colm yelped. He dropped the book and scrambled to his feet, saluting with his fist over his heart. He then relaxed, realizing it was just Gareth. "Sorry," he apologized. "I thought... For a second you sounded like..." Colm glanced at the tent. "Never mind. How are you, Gareth?"

"Where is Kel?" Gareth did not have time for small talk.

"He went to see Lady O'Lyr. Said he'd be back soon." Colm glanced at the tent again. Gareth peered inside. Other than several bedrolls and a mess of tattered clothes, it was empty.

"What are you guarding?" Had they smuggled something valuable out of the city?

Colm looked warily at Jaim and Ivar. "Can I trust them?" he whispered.

Gareth nodded.

"It's an important person. Someone of noble birth."

"I'm of noble birth." Jaim smirked. "What's the big deal?"

"Well, um..." Colm shrugged with his hands.

"Why isn't he or she staying in the Academy's main building?"

Ivar questioned. "The nobles were given first pick of the rooms. The Scholars will see that they are properly housed."

"It's a secret, so…" Colm shifted his feet, glancing from one boy to the next. "Look, I'm just doing what Kel and Callum told me. Is that so bad?"

"No, but the tent is empty," Gareth said.

Colm gave Gareth a weird look, as though he had said there were people living on the moons. He stuck his head inside the tent. He jumped and gave the empty air a quick nod. "No, it isn't."

A light dawned in Gareth's mind. "He's an Illusionist, like my father. I saw his Aura." The king's Aura was gold and silver flames intertwined but lacked Kel's red sparks.

Colm's face went deathly pale. He looked inside the tent again and staggered back, nearly tripping on his own feet. "Stars above! I… I…"

"What's going on here?" Jaim asked indigently. "How is this going to help us find Charity and Lok?"

Gareth placed both hands firmly on Colm's shoulders. He felt awkward touching him, but this was how Esme always calmed Gareth down when he was frightened. He looked down at his half-uncle. *I really am as tall as Callum.* "Calm down. When did Kel leave?"

"About half an hour ago," Colm stammered.

"Was he there when Kel left?"

"Yes."

"Are you sure?" Gareth forced the questions out. If he stopped for just a second, he doubted he could start again.

"Yes, they…" Colm bit down on his lip. "Well, Kel talked to him, but he didn't say anything. He never talks to Kel. Only to me and Callum and sometimes Deen."

"Do you always guard the tent?"

"Most of the time. Deen has been busy, and Callum normally leaves with Kel."

Gareth nodded. He took his hands off Colm and turned to his friends. "The guardsman was not drunk."

Ivar narrowed his eyes and stepped closer to Colm. The guardsman shrank back. Ivar also stood a head taller than him. "King Logan?" he whispered.

Colm looked like he was going to be sick.

"Fire and smoke!" Jaim shouted. "Are you serious? K—" Ivar clamped a hand over Jaim's mouth.

"You weren't supposed to tell anyone," Colm said to Gareth, his face pained.

"I didn't," Gareth replied. "He created an Illusion and snuck out."

"But why?" Ivar asked.

"Is everything all right?" Kel said, walking towards them. His hood was up, hiding the scarred half of his face, and the half that resembled King Logan.

"I'm so sorry," Colm stammered. "I didn't know. I…"

"What's wrong?" Kel shambled towards his half-brother.

"He tricked me." Colm, on the verge of tears, pointed at the tent.

Kel lifted the tent flap and paled. "Damn it! Where is he?" Panic laced his words. A pit formed in Gareth's gut. The last time he saw his father panicking, he just received Callum's letter about Kanton attacking them.

"I'm so sorry." Colm lowered his head.

"It's not your fault." Kel took a deep breath, similar to the one he always took whenever Healer Zall called him a Seltachai. "He cannot have ventured far. He might have gone to see Isla again, but why not tell us?"

"Maybe he wanted to talk about the war?" Colm asked.

"Perhaps." Kel gazed at the rows of tents, towards the Academy. Gareth followed his father's gaze. A figure wearing a black cloak stalked towards them. A horrible dread, like thorns piercing his skin, settled over him. He wanted to run, to hide, but running was for cowards. *I won't be a coward anymore!*

The cloaked man slowed as he approached the tent. Gareth felt eyes watching him from underneath the hood. Logan's gaze shifted to Colm. "You were told to guard the tent," he said, his voice low and harsh.

"I was, but you…"

"You tricked him." Kel rounded on the king, forcing Logan to meet him eye to eye. "He can't guard someone who isn't there."

"Why didn't you send them away?" Logan asked Colm as

though Kel wasn't there.

"Gareth was asking for Kel, and then…" Colm shrank back, averting his eyes. The red draig brushed her head against his chin.

Logan rounded on Gareth and his friends. "Go back to the Academy, Students. Mind your own business."

"And what about me?" Kel asked.

"Go haunt someone else." Logan shoved Kel to the ground.

White hot anger shot through Gareth like lightning. He balled his hand into a fist and slammed it into Logan's face. Logan crashed onto the withered grass, lying beside his brother. Gareth, breathing as though he had sprinted the Academy's perimeter, stood over the king. Then his hands began to tremble. And his arm. The anger ebbed away, leaving Gareth cold and shaky. Jaim cursed loudly. What on Eltriar had he done?

Logan climbed to his feet and brushed the dirt off his clothes. The hood of his cloak fell back, revealing a complete face and ears with two sets of rings, one silver and one gold. The king glared at Gareth, his eyes ice cold. "I'll have you hanged for this, you little…" He blinked. "Wait. I know you. The idiot stable boy." He rubbed his jaw, a dark bruise forming. "How did you get here?"

"He ain't an idiot!" Jaim snapped.

Logan glared at Jaim, but the boy met the glare head on, not even flinching.

"I am your nephew," Gareth said.

"My nephew," Logan strode closer to Gareth until he could feel the man's breath on his face, "is five years old. Get out of my sight before I call the guards."

"Dead men can't call for help." Gareth helped Kel to his feet and retrieved his crutch. His father grimaced as he regained his balance. Gareth regretted punching the king, but no one should treat people that way.

Logan spun on his heels, the black cloak flaring behind him. "Colm, guard the damn tent!" He then slipped inside, tying the flaps shut.

"Man, what an ass." Jaim's eyes widened. "Oh, sorry."

"Don't apologize for telling the truth," Kel said. "Let's talk over here." He gave Colm a reassuring pat on the shoulder and led Gareth, Ivar, and Jaim away. Colm watched for a moment, then settled down and began reading again.

"So, that's how the rumors started," Kel muttered. "What game are you playing, Lo?"

"Father?"

"Just thinking out loud, son. Why aren't you in class?"

"We're still looking for Charity and Lok. Nobody else is."

Kel frowned and ran a hand through his hair. "Fire and smoke, I'm an idiot! You said a Scholar disappeared, too, right?"

"Yes," Ivar replied. "Kuno disappeared at the same time as Lok."

"I saw three men leaving the Academy when we arrived. One must have been Lok Tolman and the other the Scholar."

Gareth stopped in his tracks, trying to puzzle it out. Lok had acted cagey in the days before he disappeared. Did he and Kuno planned this? If so, why not leave a note? "Did Lok run away?"

"What about Charity?" Jaim asked.

"I've never known that girl to run from anything," Kel replied. "The regiments need healers and surgeons. It's possible she joined them without asking permission."

"She can do that?" Gareth asked. Again, why leave without writing a note? This was not like Charity at all.

"If she set her mind to it, yes." Kel gazed at the Academy's walls. Dozens of soldiers and guards in dark blue uniforms and armed with crossbows marched along the perimeter. Deirow Hawks flew from one end to the other, delivering messages.

"Should we do something?" Gareth asked.

"Like what?" said Jaim.

"Zandon joined the Garrison. And if Charity went to work with surgeons..." Gareth shrugged. The rest of the thought was right at the front of his mind, but his voice refused to translate it into words. Again.

"It feels weird to stand around and watch things happen, doesn't it?" Kel ventured.

Gareth nodded. *Thank the Creator my father understands.*

"I know how you feel. Sometimes, I wonder what would have happened if..." Kel shook his head. "The past is gone. But if you decide to aid the war effort, please tell me in person, Gareth. Or leave a note," he added with a smile.

"I promise."

War horns sounded, filling the air. The hairs on the back of Gareth's neck stood on end. Everyone paused, looking at the walls and speaking fearfully. Was it a battle? Were more refugees arriving? A unit of soldiers sprinted towards the wall.

"Fire and smoke, what now?" Jaim groaned.

"Go back to the Academy," Kel said. He went to join the crowd of worried people at the base of the wall. A soldier stood on a crate, preparing an announcement.

"Yes, King Carwyn," Ivar said quietly.

Kel stumbled. He studied Ivar and noted the silver ring in his ear. Kel quickly hid his face with his hood and hurried towards the crowd. Nearly a hundred people gathered around the young soldier. Kel faded into the group.

"What did you call him?" Jaim asked.

"By his true title." Ivar turned away from the gathering crowd.

"That ain't an answer," Jaim protested. "Hey, where are you going?"

"I'm following royal orders. Are you coming, Prince Gareth?"

Gareth froze like a cornered deer. He glanced at the crowd. No one looked at him. None acted like they heard Ivar. Turning back, he saw a weird look in Ivar's eyes. What was that? It was similar to how people in Vala looked at Mayor Gan or Master Loy.

Respect?

Was that respect?

"Did you call him 'prince'?" Jaim asked, confused.

"Yes. Come on. We can't stand here all day." Ivar headed for the Academy.

"Do you know what he's talking about?" Jaim asked Gareth.

"Unfortunately, yes." Gareth kept his head low and followed Ivar inside. Jaim asked a barrage of questions and received no answers.

26

The Battlefield

"No offense, Your Majesty," said Ayrdeen Akardal, sitting by the room's sole window, "but the more time I send with your husband, the less I like him." He pulled a reed flute out of his pocket. "And not because he's a bloody Thane," he added under his breath.

Isla studied the map on the table. Deirow Hawks reported more Coalition soldiers surrounding the Academy. Access to the Teyrnas Highway was completely blocked. And troop movements were seemingly at random. The Marish guarding the highway one day. The Tarodic guarding it the next, with the Marish divided between the Nerin's confluence and the capital. Constant movement without rhyme or reason.

Another detail struck her. They were all spread thin without mixed regiments. Was it strategy? A real-life game of Queens? Or was it a sign of distrust within the Coalition? She hoped Ayrdeen could answer those questions.

"I'm a Thane," she said quietly. Only Callum Haar accompanied her and Ayrdeen. Logan, Una, and Gregor had left after this morning's meeting. Logan returned to his hiding place, and Isla sent Gregor and Una to speak with the other nobles, asking for their input on the war and if they had seen any potential spies. Ayrdeen claimed Kenda had dozens in key places, and Isla needed names.

The errand was half intelligence gathering and half an excuse to be alone with Ayrdeen and Callum. She sensed that Ayrdeen, or Deen as he preferred, was holding back, and she wanted Callum's insight. An indentured farmhand from the Hinterlands was the farthest removed a person could be from the noble court, but the man was smart and caught small details that others ignored. And he was Esme's brother. If he had half of his sister's intelligence, he was an asset she could not afford to waste.

"You're polite about it." Deen began playing. A cheerful melody, constantly rising and falling, like the river tides.

Must be a Marish song.

"What do you think of Logan's plan?" Callum asked. He leaned against the wall, observing her and Deen. He barely said more than a dozen words during their meeting. As silent as a servant. Isla recalled Shasta Cray's incredible mind, memorizing everything she heard and seemingly hearing everything. If only the head of servants was here now.

"It has its merits." Isla honestly did not understand why Logan hid the fact that he was alive. He claimed he was waiting for the opportune time, believing that Teyrnas' soldiers would fight harder to avenge him. He would then reveal himself at a key moment, inspiring the soldiers and leading them to victory. In the meantime, he would stay hidden, searching for Coalition spies and other potential threats.

As a single army fighting against five kingdoms, Teyrnas' soldiers needed all the inspiration they could get right now.

But Logan was the one who was schooled in warfare, not her.

"It is pure idiocy," Deen replied. He fixed his heterochromatic eyes on her. "My soldiers believe I went missing during the coup. If they knew I was alive and well at the Academy and that I've aligned myself with you, they'd abandon the Coalition. They would turn and fight against Galion and Tirshay if I ordered it."

"So, what's stopping you?" Callum questioned.

Deen frowned. "My daughter is in Teyrnas. I can't risk the Coalition turning her into a bargaining chip."

Isla's heart ached. Both of her children were safe, but what if the Eastern Coalition had taken them captive? Would she have the strength to continue the fight, or would she sacrifice a kingdom for the sake of two children?

"I'm so sorry," Isla said. "I didn't know she traveled here with you."

"She didn't. Liona arrived a few days ago. She's the acting queen of Bran Maro."

Isla gave him an incredulous look. "Queen? How old is she?"

"Twenty-five. Doesn't look it, though." Deen resumed playing.

The melody changed, growing somber and slow.

"You have a twenty-five-year-old daughter?" Isla eyed Deen up and down. The man was no older than Logan.

Deen sighed. "Suffice it to say, I was sixteen and stupidly in love."

"What did your parents say?"

"They said," Deen replied, a smile crossing his lips, "that if I was old enough to get a girl with child, I was old enough to take responsibility for my actions. We were married within the month."

"Is she a noble?"

"Noble enough. Her father was my father's senior adviser. She was absolutely gorgeous." Deen's smile brightened, lighting up his whole face. "Still is."

"Then why have your daughter as queen and not your wife?" Callum asked.

"The crown always passes to the firstborn. Besides, Stellanora has zero tolerance for political games. There's no way under the stars Kenda could manipulate her. Liona though…" Deen frowned. "She's a sweet kid, but she has a tendency to be overly pleasing. If Kenda tells her to jump, she will ask how high before asking why. But she will eventually ask why."

"Can we count on her breaking away from the others?" Isla asked.

"If she has a good reason."

"Like her father defecting to Teyrnas?"

Deen peered out the window. "Yeah, that would be a good reason. But how do we get word to her without Kenda and her ilk intercepting it?"

"A Deirow Hawk?" Callum suggested.

Isla shook her head. "They would recognize it immediately."

She barely noticed as the war horns sounded. They had sounded around the clock for the last half week.

Callum went to the window and cursed under his breath.

"What is it?" Isla asked, rising from her seat.

"The flag of Teyrnas is flying outside the walls, and the flag of Galion is rushing to meet it."

Isla's heart dropped. "A battle?"

Callum nodded grimly.

The room's gray walls melted away, stranding Isla in the middle of a field. Blood coated the ground, turning the once green grass red and muddy. Two tattered and bloodstained banners laid at her feet. One bore the ravens of Teyrnas and the other Galion's flaming torch. She turned around and saw more bloodied flags. The silver stag of Tirshay. Bran Maro's seven stars. Nowan's hawk on a field of white and purple. The bloody field stretched towards the horizon, melding with a black, lifeless sky.

A man laughed wickedly.

Isla's skin broke out in goosebumps. She whirled around to face the man, but the Farsight ended. The room was far too cold. War horns sounded once more, sharp and quick.

She bolted out of the room, slamming the door against the wall. She ran down the hallway, the skirt of her dress balled in her hands. Shouts sounded behind her, footsteps on stone. Callum and Deen shouted again, calling for her to slow down, asking what's wrong. Isla ran faster. A strange compulsion seized her. She had to run to the walls. She needed to witness this battle up close.

Callum and Deen caught up with her at the stairs. Callum ran beside her, slowing his pace to match hers. She didn't have the time or the breath to explain. Fire and smoke, she didn't even know how to explain. Her Farsights were always vague, but they were always accurate.

Bile rose in the back of her throat. For the last seventeen years, she believed her Farsights were flawed. But Carwyn and Esme were alive. They had a son with Esme's dark hair and eyes. She could no longer delude herself by thinking that the unpleasant Farsights were not real, that they were possibilities, not eventualities. She could not afford to ignore them. The Farsights were real again.

She spied Gareth Haar and two other Students at the base of the stairs. The silver crown reappeared on the boy's head. A Deirow Hawk materialized on his shoulder and a dagger at his belt. And his clothes changed. Rich, dark blue silk with ravens embroidered on the cuffs. Clothes suitable for a crown prince.

She glanced at the other boys. One wore armor, the flag of Teyrnas flying behind him. The other was covered in blood.

Stifling a scream, Isla kept running. Gareth called after her and Callum, but his voice was lost in the crowd.

Pure summer sunlight blinded her as she ran out the massive front doors. She paused, blinking until her eyesight returned to normal. Callum and Deen stood next to her. Deen rested his hands on his knees. A hitch accompanied Callum's breathing, but he stood upright.

Isla scanned the tents. Hundreds of people hurried in all directions. Scholars shepherded Students and Journeymen back to the Academy, some protesting and other frightened. Several refugees headed for the wall. The guards ordered them to get away. A handful slipped away while the guards were distracted and joined a small crowd at the base of the wall.

The wall. The impulse told her to get to the wall.

She weaved her way through the crowd, thankful for her short stature. Callum and Deen were right behind her. A guard held up a hand, forcing her to halt.

"Where do you think you're going?" he asked.

"The wall..." Isla placed a hand on her chest. Her heart pounded frantically, and a painful stitch formed in her side. "I have to get up the wall. And see..."

"No civilians on the wall, ma'am."

"Does she look like a civilian to you?" Deen questioned.

The guard opened his mouth to retort, but then his eyes fell on Isla's auburn hair, a common trait in Byyar but completely foreign on this side of the Nerin. And the simple gold crown circling her head. He grabbed another guardsman by the collar and dragged him closer.

"What's wrong with you?" he snapped.

The first guard pointed at Isla. "Is she...?"

The second guard's eyes widened. "Stars above! Your Majesty, what are you doing here?"

"I have to get on the wall. I have to..." Have to what exactly? She prayed for another Farsight, a clearer one that would show her what to do. Nothing. Only the memory of bloodstained flags.

"I'm afraid it's too dangerous, Your Majesty."

Isla squared her shoulders and stood as tall as her height allowed. She was a queen. Queens did not have to give explanations. They gave orders and expected them to be obeyed. "Take me and my men to the wall. Now."

The guards exchanged concerned looks and then acquiesced. "This way, Your Majesty."

Soldiers and guards in dark blue ran up and down the wall, forming ranks. All were armed with bows or long spears. A few had newer model crossbows with hand cranks, allowing for faster reloads.

Isla peered over the wall. Soldiers swarmed the field separating the Academy from Norgard. Half wore Teyrnas' dark blue, and the other half wore Galion's orange stripped with white. Everywhere she looked, soldiers clashed and fought until one or both went down in a spray of blood. She tasted bile in the back of her throat, but the strange impulse ordered her to stay and watch.

She glanced at Callum and Deen. Deen was deathly pale and looked like he was going to be sick. Callum watched in horrified silence.

"Move it!" A soldier shoved Callum out of the way, nearly knocking him into Isla. The soldier aimed his crossbow and fired. The arrow found its mark in the back of a Galionic soldier. He fell to the ground. Another Galionic soldier crouched by his fallen comrade, shaking him, trying to make him wake up. A second arrow hit the soldier square in the eye. His body slumped over his comrade's.

Isla squeezed her eyes shut. The impulse ordered her to open them, to watch, to see everything. She felt sick and terribly cold. Why did she have to watch this?

A pair of hands turned her away.

"You don't have to see this," Callum said.

"I have to see something." Isla faced the battlefield again. Her eyes landed on a young Teyrnian soldier, no older than twenty. He fought deftly with a short sword, dispatching his opponents one by one. But the Galionic soldiers were still moving, still alive. An orange clad soldier swung his blade at the Teyrnian soldier. He dodged it effortlessly and sliced the inside of the Galionic soldier's arm, severing muscles. The Galionic soldier fell to his knees, clutching his bloodied arm. He squeezed his eyes shut, no doubt expecting a death blow, but the Teyrnian soldier moved on, fighting two other soldiers at once and dispatching them with ease.

A soldier on the wall cheered. "Give them fire, Jons!"

"Do you know him?" Isla asked.

"Yeah. He's part of the Thane Regiment. A Farsight. See the compass on his uniform?"

Isla spied the emblem on the soldier's right sleeve. A compass divided into eight colored segments. One for each Thane. She then saw the compass on a dozen other soldiers.

One Thane soldier removed a handful of rocks from his belt pouch and Manipulated them at the Galionic soldiers, hitting the weak points in their armor. A few rocks found eyes. Those soldiers collapsed and screamed.

Another Thane soldier stood off to the side. He held no weapons. But any Galionic soldier who came within twenty feet instantly started screaming and attacked his comrades.

So this was her handiwork. Thanes fighting primarily with their abilities. Abilities created to protect. No wonder Rafael stopped talking to her. Watching it in action, it felt so utterly wrong.

"Bloody Thanes," Deen muttered under his breath.

"They're no bloodier than the regular soldiers." Callum pointed out as a Galionic soldier took off a Teyrnian soldier's head. The body dropped to its knees and toppled over, blood spilling onto the Galionic soldier's boots. Deen fell to his knees and retched. A guard ran up to him, but Deen brushed him away, saying he was fine.

Isla peered along the wall. Soldiers lined the perimeter, alternating between those armed with crossbows and those armed with shields. The crossbows let out a volley. Five seconds later, arrows flew at them. The shielded soldiers moved in unison, protecting the archers. Arrowheads bounced harmlessly off metal.

She looked back at the battle. A line of Galionic archers stood at the outer edge. They readied their longbows for another round.

"How much more do you need to see, Your Majesty?" Concern laced Callum's voice.

Isla looked in all directions. Soldiers fought and died. More soldiers lined the wall. The battle continued, but the strange impulse was gone. "No more."

"Get down!"

Something heavy slammed into Isla, driving her into Callum and sending them crashing onto the wall's hard surface. Callum groaned, but Isla did not see any blood. What had hit them?

Shakily, she set up and saw a man lying beside her. Two arrows jutted out of his chest. His eyes were wide and fearful. Blood trickled out of his mouth and nostrils.

"Sorry," he managed. The man grimaced, struggling to breathe.

Callum sat up and studied the man. "You. You were one of the guards working for Kanton. You arrested me and my daughter."

The wounded man winced as though Callum had slapped him. "Sorry. Just following orders. Stupid of me."

"Wills?" Isla studied his face. The hair was too long for regulation length, brushing his ears and shirt collar. Dark circles surrounding his sunken eyes. Eyes she had seen daily for years. "Peydar Wills, how long have you been here?"

"Since the war started. In Norgard. Came here. Hurts." He pointed at the arrows with a shaky hand.

Isla traced the line of sight between where she had been standing and where Wills laid. If he hadn't pushed her out of the way, those arrows would be in her chest. "You saved me. Thank you."

"What is it?" Deen glanced over. His eyes fell on Wills's injuries. "Oh Creator!" He retched again.

"Healer!" Isla called out. "This man needs a healer!"

Soldiers ran back and forth. Shouting orders. Announcing arrow volleys. Reporting movements from below. Too much noise for anyone to hear her.

"Can you help him?" she asked Callum.

Callum placed his fingers on the base of Wills's neck. "Pulse elevated. One arrow landed in the lung. The other just below the sternum." He looked Isla in the eyes. "I can't remove either without risking more damage."

Tears leaked from Wills's eyes. "Sorry."

"Don't apologize." Isla held his hand. It was cold, far too cold. "You were doing what you thought was right." *Just like all of them.* And just like her when she allowed the Council to create the Thane Regiment. How much harder would the Coalition soldiers fighting knowing they now fought against a common, centuries-old enemy?

Isla grabbed Wills underneath the arms. "Help me," she ordered Callum. He took hold of Wills's legs. "Deen, we need you as a lookout. Tell us when the arrows are about to fly."

Deen, as white as mountain snow, stood on shaking legs. "All clear."

Isla and Callum lifted Wills and slowly made their way to the stairs. They crouched twice to avoid arrows. Callum went down the stairs first. Isla stepped carefully. The last thing she needed was to trip on her dress and drop Wills.

Arrows covered the ground surrounding the walls. Several civilians and Students had been struck. People, refugees and Scholars alike, rushed to help them between volleys. A few laid motionless.

Guards rushed by. Deen waved one down, asking for help. The guard pointed at the Academy, saying the Scholars would help before hurrying away.

"Kanton," Wills said in between ragged breaths. "Kanton there."

"Where?" Isla glanced around, but it was pointless. How could she spot one man in this chaos?

"Palace. He snuck back in after..."

"Save your strength," Callum said.

Wills shook his head. "Working for them now. But Marsh with me. Sorry about Logan..." Wills's voice trailed off. His eyes closed, and his head lulled to the side.

"Wills? Guardsman Wills?"

He did not answer.

"Deen, check his pulse," Callum said without slowing down. The Academy was right there. Healers dressed in white tended a row of injured people laying on blankets. More wounded were carried over. Too many.

"How do I do that?"

"Put your finger on his neck. No, right below the jaw. There! Do you feel anything?"

Deen frowned. "No. Am I doing it wrong?"

A healer, her white sleeves splatted with red, rushed towards them. She ordered Callum and Isla to place Wills on a blanket, between a soldier with an arrow in his shoulder and a Student with a wide gash on his forehead. Another woman, her Journeyman's cloak draped over white clothes, joined them.

"Back away," the healer ordered as she and her assistant crouched beside Wills. She placed her fingers on Wills's neck and then on his wrist.

"Casualty," she said to the Journeyman healer. She made a note on a piece of paper. "What was his name?"

Isla's throat tightened. She stared down at Wills. The guardsman laid absolutely still. The fletching of the arrows in his chest fluttered in the warm breeze. Orange and white fletching.

"Ma'am, what was his name? Sir, do you know?" she asked Callum.

"Peydar Wills," he replied solemnly.

"He... No, he can't... He saved my life." Isla looked down at her hands. Blood coated them. There was blood on her sleeves, too. And her dress. *Wills's blood.* She shuddered.

"Then he died well." The healer motioned for two other healers, both men, to step forward. They cut the arrows close to Wills's chest, placed them beside the body, and wrapped the blanket around him. They then carried him away to one of the Academy's outlying buildings.

Isla yelped as a hand touched her. She saw Callum and felt like a fool.

"Let's get you cleaned up, Your Majesty," he said quietly.

"No. I..." She took a deep breath. Tears stung her eyes. "I have to meet with the Scholar Council immediately. The Academy is no longer safe, and it's my fault. Callum, search for Marsh. Tell her..." Her voice choked.

"You're going to meet with the Council covered in blood?" Deen asked sheepishly.

Isla looked at the row of wounded. Soldiers, civilians, Students. The Journeyman healer wrote another name on her list. "This whole place is covered in blood."

27

Chosen

Bright sunlight filtered in through the room's sole window. Realta slowly glanced around. The wooden walls were a lighter color than she assumed. A light brown, almost sand color. The other two beds were neatly made. She sat up, feeling like she had spent the night under water, her head heavy and her throat scratchy. But she no longer felt feverish. A good night's sleep, thankfully a Dreamless one, was just what she needed.

She climbed out of bed and got dressed. Putting on her bead bracelet and necklace, she glanced out the window and saw the village of Aneros for the first time. Neat little houses with sloping roofs made of gray tile lined the muddy streets. Each one had a vegetable garden in the back. The plants thrive despite the recent torrent. Men and women in pale blue and yellow clothes walked by the inn. One man rode on horseback, carefully guiding the horse around the puddles.

The roads appeared almost suitable for traveling. Perhaps a full day in the sun would dry them out enough. Would they be able to leave tomorrow and finally rid themselves of Waylar Corey?

A part of her felt bad for Braedan and Elliza. She didn't want them to be stuck with Corey, but where else could they go? Elliza wore a slave's tattoo on her face, a tattoo that couldn't be hidden with a bracelet. And Braedan had been scarred as a traitor. No one would hire him now.

And there were two Gadyeni at the inn. A creeping feeling, like thorny vines wrapping around her arms, surrounding her. Their presence only meant one thing. Val was telling the truth. She was One of Nine.

Unless it isn't true.

Realta frowned, exploring the idea. Val was an exceptionally powerful Minder. Could this be another one of his Illusions?

But for that to be possible, Val would have to be close by. Had he followed them all the way here? If so, how had he escaped the city? Did he stow away in a wagon? Create an Illusion to make himself invisible? He created an Illusion for Dane Kanton, tricking a hundred minds at once. Tricking their small group would be child's play compared to...

A soft knock sounded at the door. Realta composed herself with a deep breath. "Come in."

Chinasa, dressed in his white clothes with his red necklace and bracelets, entered. Relief flooded the ambassador's face. He rushed to Realta's side and examined her like a trained healer.

"Thank the Creator. We almost sent for the village healer."

"Why?" Realta pushed Chinasa's hands away from her face.

"You've been asleep for two days."

Realta froze. Two days? How could she have slept for two days? She turned back to the window and looked down at the roads. Roads that were flooded when they arrived midway through a storm. They could not have dried this much overnight. And the sun was high in the sky. It wasn't morning. It was just past noon.

"How?" she asked.

Chinasa sat on the bed and motioned for Realta to join him. Doing so, she felt that familiar warmth surrounding her, like a blanket on a winter night, huddled close to the fire. She didn't want that warmth to fade away.

"This is common in young Thanes," he explained. "They are so excited to discover their abilities, they go past their limits. Most times, they develop headaches and fatigue. Nothing a good night's rest won't cure. But a few become severely ill. I saw it plenty of times while at the Jemayrt Academy. This is why Thanes are paired with a mentor. Someone to monitor their progress and prevent overstraining."

"Did anyone ever die?" Realta wished she had a better idea of what it meant to be a Thane. What she could or could not do. If Kel or Mayor Gan hadn't hidden their abilities, she might have learned from one of them. But Realta didn't blame Kel for hiding. His life was in danger. And no one, not even Callum, knew she would develop Thane abilities.

"No one that I met, but there have been incidents. And always with the low leveled Thanes. It seems the stronger the ability, the less chance of overworking oneself."

"Is that why I never overstrained myself with Dreaming?"

"Possibly. I never overworked myself as a Learner, nor has Elliza as a Farsight, though she has no control over when the visions appear."

"You've talked to her? Is she still here?" Realta suddenly remembered the dagger she stole from Corey. Was it still underneath the mattress? Should she tell Chinasa? No, if Corey learned the truth, he would use it against Chinasa. Another crime to report.

I was so stupid. I shouldn't have taken it.

And why had Elliza encouraged her?

"Of course. The roads are in no condition for travel," Chinasa said. "And there is a good chance for rain tonight. Do you want me to get Shasta and Serena? They're both worried about you."

"In a minute." Realta peered into the hallway. She didn't see any shadows or hear any footsteps close by. She lowered her voice anyway, just to be safe. "Are *they* still here?"

Chinasa stiffened, his face like unreadable stone. "Yes."

"Are they really the Gadyeni?"

"As far as I know. Humans don't appear out of nowhere in the middle of a storm." Chinasa studied his hands. "They seem different from what I expected. More human." He laughed quietly, shaking his head. "They've watched over us for thousands of years. Easy to copy the mannerisms, I guess."

"Have they mentioned..." Realta tried to swallow, but her throat was too dry. "Have they mentioned the Midnight King?"

Chinasa shook his head. "They asked a few questions. Questions that haven't raised suspicions, though I think Shasta Cray is on to them. She refuses to speak with Bas or Tath alone. I spied Elliza meeting with Tath last night. I only caught a few words. The girl isn't at all fazed by his presence."

"She's a Farsight. She probably saw them arrive beforehand."

"Good point."

Realta wasn't sure if she ought to ask this question, but she saw no way out of it. "Where is yours?"

"Pardon?"

"Tath is the Gadyeni for Farsights. Bas is the Gadyeni for

Dreamers. Where is the one for Learners?"

Chinasa sighed heavily. "I don't know. I'm not sure I want to meet Esar."

Realta's earlier doubts returned, pounding at the door, demanding to be released. "What if they aren't Gadyeni?"

Chinasa stood and went to the window, his hands clasped behind his back. "You think they are imposters?"

"I was thinking about Val." Realta drew her knees up to her chest and wrapped her arms around them. "He used an Illusion to trick a hundred people into seeing Dane Kanton as another man. How hard would it be for him to trick us? He could be masquerading as Tath and someone else as Bas." A sickening thought invaded her mind. Now more than ever, she wished her father was here. "What if it's Kanton?"

Chinasa's face turned ashen. "I wouldn't say it's impossible. Kanton and Valentin were working together. Seems like a logical step." He locked eyes with her. "The best way to find an imposter is to catch them in a lie. Valentin, unfortunately, is a powerful Minder. He would know our intentions in a heartbeat. Though, it could work. Did you recognize any of Valentin's mannerisms in Tath or Bas?"

"No." Realta shook her head, short hair getting into her eyes. "Forget it. It's a bad idea. I just…" The very idea that Val might be in this inn, just underneath their feet, filled her with dread. She would have to face him someday, but the further in the future, the better.

"It's not a bad idea," Chinasa said, placing a hand on her shoulder. "We have many reasons to be distrustful of strangers. If I had distrusted Corey for half a second… I'll speak with them, ask a few questions. And I'll tell Shasta to be on the lookout."

"Interesting."

Realta yelped, scrambling off the bed. A knife flashed in Chinasa's hand.

Tath stood in the middle of the room, his dark blue cloak swirling around him in a breeze that only touched him. The creature's dark eyes studied them.

"How did you get in here?" Chinasa demanded.

Tath smiled patiently. "Walls are no more difficult to navigate than storms. The first group of Nine had difficulty getting along. Too many personalities clashing. But this is outright suspicion. Why?"

"Valentin Gardyner started a war," Realta snapped.

"Prejudice started that war," Tath replied calmly. "Valentin merely fanned the flames."

"So, the Gadyeni approve of this madness?" Chinasa questioned. He edged closer to Tath, the knife lowered, held in a defensive position.

"Not all of us, but swords are forged in fire. Fighting in this war will prepare you for the fight against Alberik."

Chinasa muttered a prayer under his breath. Realta shivered. Why did Tath call that monster by his real name?

"If it's any consolation," Tath met Realta's eyes, "Bas does not approve of war. Or of Valentin being chosen for the Nine. Then again, I don't approve of you being chosen, Realta Haar. Too young. Too inexperienced with the ways of the world. But you, Chinasa Ekene, are a prime candidate. Intelligent, resourceful, a natural leader. Esar did well in choosing you."

"Then where is he?" Chinasa asked.

"He and Alberik are bitter enemies. He wants to find Alberik first. Though, honestly, I think he'll find him and use the knowledge to avoid him. I doubt Alberik has forgotten that it was Esar's idea to lock him within the Nothingness."

"The Creator locked the Midnight King away," Realta said, the old chapel lesson surfacing. The chaplains rarely spoke about the Midnight King, and always in hushed whispers. Those whispers had given her and Charity nightmares.

"Ultimately, yes."

"Why wasn't it permanent?" Chinasa asked.

"Are you questioning the Creator?" Tath asked, his tone curious and his dark eyes mocking. A smile crossed his lips. "No harm in asking questions, I suppose. We've asked it plenty of times ourselves and have yet to receive the answer."

"Some answers we must learn on our own," replied Bas, materializing out of nowhere. His gray hair was almost silver in the sunlight, and his tattered gray cloak reminded Realta of Kel. But there was nothing of Kel in those ink black eyes.

"Good of you to join us, brother. Your Thane has been asking questions. I think you should be the one to answer her."

Bas glared warily at the sunlight pouring in from the window and hid in the shadowed corner. "I'm not used to speaking with people during the day. Perhaps tonight—"

"Who are you?" Realta shouted. The following silence unnerved her. How loud had she shouted? Loud enough to be heard downstairs?

"We are the Gadyeni," Bas replied calmly. "Who else would we be?"

"Valentin and Kanton." Realta stumbled over the names. She inched closer to Chinasa.

Bas and Tath exchanged looks, Bas concerned and Tath amused, as though watching a child speak before the village council. *I am a child*, Realta thought disparagingly.

"Are you going to answer her?" Chinasa asked after a silent minute.

"Siryn should not have chosen Valentin," Bas said quietly to Tath. "I don't care if he is the most powerful Minder. He is far too volatile."

"Not too volatile for Alberik. Remember the last war? The Battle of Gwyn Dlo Falls? The massacre at Athkendi?" Heat rose with every word. Bas shrank back. "That's what I thought." Tath fixed Realta with a glare. "Rest assured that we are who we claim to be, *child*." He strode towards the door.

Realta gasped as Chinasa hurled the knife. It landed square in Tath's back, directly between the shoulder blades. A killing shot.

Tath staggered, catching himself on the door frame. The Gadyeni then straightened and turned to face Chinasa. Reaching over his shoulder, he pulled out the knife and flung it at the floor. It struck the wood between Chinasa's feet. There was no blood.

"Had I really been Valentin," Tath said, his voice colder than the Vogel Mountains in midwinter, "I would be dead, and the world would be lost." He vanished in the blink of an eye.

"Stars above," Chinasa breathed, staring down at the knife. "Stars above, I just stabbed a Gadyeni."

"He will get over it." Bas walked forward, picked up the knife, and handed it to Chinasa hilt first. "His last Thane, Olita, was very dear to him. She was killed in the final battle against Alber-ik. The fact that she looks just like Elliza…" Bas let out a heavy sigh. "Humans aren't the only ones who let their emotions get the better of them."

"So, he chose Elliza based on her appearance?" Realta asked. "I thought the Nine were the Thanes with the highest ability."

"Oh, they are. But same as last time, there are two or three just below Summit level. We could have chosen one of them instead, but everyone insisted on the best. I always thought we should have selected the highest five of each ability. Increase our odds against Alberik. But Thanes are fewer now. You are the only Dreamer alive on Eltriar. I wasn't faced with a choice."

"And Val? Could another Minder have been chosen? Or be chosen?"

"Perhaps, but his ability far exceeds any Minder that I've en-countered, including Z'Kai. And her ability was phenomenal. Illusions seen by thousands. Intelligence reports received from miles away. Honestly, it was kind of frightening." Bas shook his head. "Apologizes. My mind wanders."

"Did we make a mistake?" Chinasa asked tentatively. "Should we have stayed with Valentin instead of running?"

Bas was silent for a moment, his inky eyes staring at nothing. "Perhaps. But you are destined to meet him again. Running will only make the process more painful. He is meeting two more of the Nine as we speak." A shiver ran down Realta's spine as his eyes fell on her. "I am glad you are well rested. You will need your strength." Bas then walked out of the room, closing the door be-hind him.

Realta sank down on the bed, her knees turning to water. Chi-nasa sat next to her, staring at the knife in his hands. Neither spoke for a long time.

"Are we returning to Teyrnas?" Realta finally asked. Her voice was barely audible, even to her ears. They had spent two long months running, heading south and away from the war. Away from Val and his insane lies. But they weren't lies anymore, were they? The Midnight King walked Eltriar again. Two of the Gadyeni had confirmed it.

They were heading for war no matter which course they took.

"Seems like we don't have a choice."

Something inside Realta, the small portion of Callum Haar's stubbornness that she had inherited, screamed against Chinasa's words. Anger coursed through her. "What if we did?"

"Realta—"

"What if," Realta leapt to her feet and paced around, "there is a way out? Why do the Gadyeni need us to fight the Midnight King? Why can't they fight him on their own? How much do you know about them?"

"Only what I learned in chapel. And very little at that."

"What about history books?"

Chinasa shrugged. "Most records from that time are either lost or collecting dust in an Academy."

Realta tried to think. If only she had more time! "We can go to the nearest Academy. Ask to see their records. Or I can Dream about the Thousand Years War." She had already Dreamed about it once. The aftermath of the final battle. Domni showing mercy to an enemy soldier.

Chinasa stood and placed a gentle hand on her shoulder. "Realta, the nearest Academy is in Byyar. It would take a month to reach it. And we would be heading closer to war. Remember. Queen Isla is Byyarian. If Byyar hasn't joined the war by now, it's only a matter of time."

"But there has to be a way." *Please, I don't want this fight!*

Chinasa glanced at the window. The sun shone brightly, and songbirds chirped as they flew across the clear blue sky. Realta wished she could be just as free. "Perhaps there is one. I will consult with the Scholars and Shasta. In the meantime," he lowered his voice, "be careful of what you say. You never know if one of them is listening."

28

Homecoming

Lok quickened his pace as they rounded the last hill. They left Rangar Keep at first light, Kuno practically forcing them out of their blankets.

"I don't want to spend another minute in this place," he muttered angrily.

Arnyn saw them leaving and accompanied them to the forest's edge. The Scholar spared a cursory glance at the thief and said nothing. Brother Malaky, however, was delighted to speak with Arnyn, discussing theology and the Philosophy of Balance. Malaky was surprised to find a Cuchasi all the way out in the Hinterlands, and Arnyn was thrilled to meet more Thanes.

"Two Elementals and a man with three abilities. Perfect balance!"

Arnyn said his goodbyes at the road. The villages, he explained, were not a good place for him at the moment. "Got caught picking a merchant's pocket. Who knew some people could be so vindictive over a few pieces of silver?"

A surprisingly large number of people traveled on the River Road. Some were merchants going to Caman's Pass, and many were townspeople and villagers from across the river. The fighting had spread all the way to East Bridge. Many worried it was only a matter of time before the war reached the Hinterlands.

The news soured Kuno's already bad mood. Lok kept his distance as they stopped for the night outside of Lothian, and he didn't lag his feet when Kuno kicked them awake an hour before dawn. Malaky also kept his distance and never said more than a word or two at a time. West, however, was completely oblivious, marveling at every rock or tree, as though he had spent his entire life indoors.

A smile crossed Lok's face as the first farm outside Vala came into view. Cows and horses grazed in open fields dotted with farmhouses. Waist-high crops waved in the breeze. A trio of green draigs darted across the road, hiding in a blueberry bush. Two farmers looked up from their chores to wave at them. Lok waved back.

"Is everyone this friendly in the Hinterlands?" Brother Malaky asked, looking around, trying to see everything at once.

Lok nodded. People in Vala always welcomed travelers, eager to hear news of the world.

"That's a relief," Malaky said.

Kuno muttered under his breath. Lok gave him a questioning look. The Scholar said, "Just thinking out loud. It's nothing."

A half mile down the road, they turned off the River Road and walked into the village's center. Rows of houses with tile roofs lined the streets. The mayor's two-story house with its wide front porch, painted with a fresh coat of pale blue paint, stood on the corner. Vendors and buyers crowded the marketplace. Many were people who they passed on the road, buying what they needed and continuing on.

And across the street stood the inn.

When he left for the Academy, Lok doubted he would see his first home again. At least, not until his education was complete. Three months passed, and nothing changed. Except himself.

"Lok Tolman?"

Lok turned and saw Esme Haar standing on the front porch of the healer's house. Estrid, who had Esme's dark hair and ruddy skin, studied him with Master Kel's blue eyes. A man stood behind them. He looked vaguely familiar, but Lok couldn't place him. Probably a traveler who had taken ill.

Esme ran to Lok and embraced him. "Thank the Creator! When we heard Kanton attacked you, Kel and Gareth went searching. And then the war started… How did you get back?"

Lok got out his notebook and pencil and started writing. He told Esme that he and Charity reached the Academy safely, and Gareth had arrived shortly after Teyrnas fell. Lok explained he wanted to come home. All the fighting frightened him. The Scholar and chaplain had volunteered to escort him and West, another Student.

He hated lying to Esme. She had always been kind to him, but the truth would take hours to explain. And he didn't want anyone to know he was an Elemental.

"What about Callum and Realta?" Esme asked. Estrid stood by her side, glancing anxiously at Malaky and Kuno.

Lok shook his head, shrugging. He thought two of the men Malaky spoke to were Callum and Kel, but he wasn't sure. He didn't want to give Esme good news that turned out to be wrong.

Esme let out a heavy sigh. "Callum and Kel have survived worse."

Brother Malaky stepped forward, his eyes glistening with tears. "Esme? Is that really you?"

"Stars above! Mal?"

They embraced, silent tears running down their faces. Lok stared at them, unsure of how to react. The chaplain knew the midwife? How? Malaky said he'd never visited the Hinterlands. Had they met at the Academy?

"Friends?" West asked.

Esme laughed, wiping away the tears. "Yes, we were friends. A long time ago."

"I saw him," Malaky replied, lowering his voice. "Don't blame Lok. The boy didn't see him. Car…" Malaky coughed. "He has changed so much. I didn't recognize him at first." He grimaced, as though someone had punched him in the ribs. "What kind of man doesn't recognize his own brother?"

Brother?

Esme placed a gentle hand on Malaky's face. "A man who doesn't know the truth. Kel felt so bad about leaving you, but Yestyn didn't give us a choice. Where did you see him?"

Malaky explained seeing a group of refugees outside the Academy. One man was injured, and Malaky went to help.

"That's when I saw him," he whispered.

So, the chaplain did know Kel. Why lie about seeing his own brother? Wait. Hadn't Kuno said that the chaplain's brother was dead? And Malaky called Master Kel a different name. What was it? Car? Did Kel change his name?

"I guess this is a good day for reunions." Kuno slowly pushed back his hood. "Hello, Esme."

Esme placed her hands over her mouth, suppressing a laugh.

"What's so funny?" Kuno asked as a warm smile spread across his face. "Journeymen ought to have more respect for Scholars, Miss Haar."

"That's Mistress Haar to you, Historian." Esme and Kuno shared a quick hug. "Lok Tolman, how on Eltriar did you find this man?"

"He is my mentor."

"Thank the Creator for small miracles," Esme said.

"Friends?" West pointed at Esme, Kuno, and Malaky. He titled his head to one side, just like a little bird.

"Believe it or not, yes," Kuno said. "We were at the Academy together. Though I don't recall seeing you there," he said to Malaky.

The chaplain shifted his feet. "Well, I was a few years behind Esme. I, um, I kept to myself. Didn't really venture out of the theology department."

Esme smacked herself on the forehead. "Stars above, where is my head? Mal, this is your niece. Estrid," she said, wrapping her arms around the girl, "this is your father's little bother. Your uncle Mal."

Brother Malaky faltered, almost falling to his knees. He stared at Estrid for a long minute, tears brimming his eyes. "She... She has Carwyn's eyes." He tentatively held out his hand. "I am so happy to meet you, Estrid."

The girl timidly shook his hand. "I'm happy to meet you, too."

"Estrid," Malaky said. "That's a name fit for a princess. A wonderful name."

Esme then faced Kuno. "Estrid, this is Scholar Kuno. He was mine and your father's best friend at the Academy."

"Hello, Estrid," Kuno said, smiling and looking just like his old self.

"Hello." Estrid eyed him up and down and then smiled shyly.

"When Lok told me that you and Kel were living out here," Kuno said, "and that you had two children, I almost didn't believe him. It was too good to be true, you know? And I met Gareth. He's a good boy. Very quiet, though."

Esme smiled. "Gareth isn't one for words. Is he happy there?"

A bit of concern crept into her voice.

Lok wrote, *"Yes, he and Charity have made a lot of friends."*

Esme's eyes widened. "Wait, Lok. Does your mother know you're here?"

He shook his head.

"I have to tell her. Henry!" she called over her shoulder. Lok expected the man on the porch to reply. Instead, a younger man with short brown hair and a ruddy, Hinterlander complexion poked his head out the door. "Keep an eye on Darran. I'll be back in a minute."

"Yes, ma'am."

Esme grabbed the skirt of her dress in both hands and took off running for the inn, just like a girl rushing to the village dance. Estrid spared a quick glance at Malaky and then ran after her mother.

Malaky laughed quietly. "It's incredible. Here we thought we would be among strangers, and we find a mutual friend. The Philosophy of Balance is surely at work today."

"So, Carwyn goes by Kel now?"

The chaplain paled. "I… Well, you see. I thought…" He frantically ran a hand through his hair, his eyes darting fearfully. Far more fearfully than when they were surrounded by smugglers and thieves. "Don't tell anyone. At least… I think…"

"I understand," Kuno assured him. "People are allowed their secrets." He glanced at the inn. "It is wonderful to see her again. And that girl has her father's eyes."

The door of the healer's house creaked open. Henry exchanged a few words with the man leaning against the porch railing, eyeing Lok and the others cautiously. He slowly walked down the steps. "Um, hello."

"Good afternoon. Do you work for Mistress Haar?" Kuno asked.

"Yes, sir. I mean, Scholar. I'm the assistant healer. You see, the old healer fell terribly ill last month, and I was called up to help. I'm originally from Kessal. It's a small village near the border with Byyar." Henry's eyes brightened. "I never expected to learn so much from Mistress Haar. Did you know she studied medicine at the Academy?"

"Yes," Kuno and Malaky answered simultaneously. Malaky started to smile, but it faded the instant he saw Kuno's stern look. *"Is Healer Zall still sick?"*

Henry read the question and nodded grimly. "I'm afraid he's getting worse. Hey, why are you writing? Does your throat hurt?"

"He not talk," West said loudly enough for everyone on the street to hear.

Henry gave him a curious look. "You're a mute?"

Lok's face burned. Damn it, he just wanted people to treat him normally. Why did he always have to be different?

"No, I mean, are you the innkeeper's son? The one studying at the Academy?"

Lok nodded, studying Henry. The young man was barely into his twenties, and though ruddy, he looked pale for a Hinterlander. He seemed friendly, smiling at Lok and the others.

Footsteps thudded on the road. Lok turned and saw Vera Tolman running towards him. Esme Haar, Estrid, and Ellis Brun, the brewer, ran after her. Vera halted a few paces away from Lok. Her eyes glistened with tears, but she was smiling.

Lok felt tears picking his eyes. One fell, and the rest followed in a torrent, blurring his vision and tightening his throat. His mother. He wondered about her all the time, hoping she was okay. He had never been truly homesick. Hard to be homesick for a place where everyone looked down on him. Everyone except Vera. She had only shown him love. His heart ached.

Lok held out his arms, and Vera embraced him, holding him tight and crying.

"I never thought I'd see you again," Vera said, her voice shaking. "Callum's letter said you and Charity were separated. Nobody knew what do to. And then the war…"

Lok broke away and wrote, *"Charity and I sent letters once we reached the Academy."*

"The Loys got Charity's letter. Yours must have been lost." Vera dried her eyes with her sleeve. "But you're here and safe again. Where is Charity?" she asked. Ellis walked up to Vera and placed his hands gently on her shoulders.

"She is still at the Academy. She wanted to stay."

"I suppose that's her choice. She's always been a strong-willed girl." Vera then noticed Ellis standing behind her. She placed a hand over his. "Lok, you know Ellis, right?"

He nodded. Why was the brewer here? And why were he and Vera touching hands?

"Well, we married two months ago."

Lok felt like he'd been slapped in the face. Married? His mother got married to Ellis Brun? The brewer was nice, he guessed. Always starting conversations with villagers and travelers alike. But why had she married him?

She reached up and placed a gentle hand on Lok's face. "It was a long time coming, sweetheart. We talked about it for years, and with both of his daughters grown and married and you heading for the Academy, it seemed like the right time."

Lok was certain he would have been rendered speechless if he could speak. He ought to write something. Congratulate her, if nothing else. But his fingers felt numb. His entire body and mind felt numb.

"Congratulations, Mistress Tolman," Kuno said, shaking hands with her and Ellis. "Lok has told me all about you."

"Thank you, sir, and you are?"

"Scholar Kuno Surylin. I'm Lok's mentor. He asked me to accompany him back home."

"That was very kind of you, Scholar."

"Say, you didn't run into any Hiraeth on the way, did you?" Ellis asked, pointing at Lok's green earring. Lok immediately covered his ear, his face burning. The earring felt so normal now, he rarely noticed it.

"Actually, it's a tradition at the Academy," Kuno explained.

Ellis frowned. "Then why doesn't Esme have one?"

"Because I'm not a Thane." Esme pulled Lok's hand away, studying the earring. Her eyes grew wide, excitement lighting her face. "Lok, why didn't you tell us?"

Lok averted his eyes. He wished he could run away, vanish into thin air. But the truth was out. No point in avoiding it.

"Fire!" West shouted excitedly. "Fire, fire, fire!"

"What is he talking about?" Henry asked.

"Lok is an Elemental Thane," said Kuno. "He can control fire."

Lok wished he could turn invisible. Ellis and Henry stared at him like he had two heads, while Esme stared at him in awe. And his mother just stared, her face completely blank.

"Is that a good thing?" Vera asked Kuno.

"Yes, your son is one of two living Elementals. West is the other one."

Vera smiled gently. The smile she reserved for the armed guards of haughty merchants, hired to rough up anyone who got within fifty feet of their employers. "And the Academy is teaching him to control fire?"

"It was." Kuno frowned. "All the fighting was negatively affecting Lok's concentration. It's safer for him to continue his studies here."

"As long as my son is safe." She gave Lok's hand a reassuring squeeze. Though reassuring for him or for her, he didn't know. "Your room is just the way you left it."

His old room. Did he really want to return to that small attic room? He was very different from the boy who had lived there. Lok frowned. Had he really changed so much in three short months?

"I'll come back with you in a minute. I want to look around a bit more."

"You know where to find us." Vera exchanged a glance with Ellis, and they walked back to the inn hand in hand. Ellis Brun. His stepfather. Lok honestly did not know what to make of that. But his mother seemed happy.

A scream sounded from the healer's house. Henry dashed up the steps and hurried inside. Estrid grabbed hold of Esme's arm, eyeing the house fearfully. Esme sighed.

"What was that?" Malaky asked.

"Healer Zall," Esme replied. She smoothed down Estrid's hair.

"What illness does he have?" Kuno asked.

"I honestly don't know. We've read every medical book available and tried every treatment, but he keeps getting worse."

"Could I pray for him?" Malaky asked.

Esme did her best to smile. "Darran isn't religious, but I'd certainly appreciate it. And afterwards, we need to talk." Her tone turned serious.

Malaky looked like he was going to faint. "About what?"

"Your brother."

"Oh, yes!" Malaky laughed nervously. "Yes, of course." His eyes fell on Estrid. "Just like Carwyn," he whispered.

"I'd like an explanation, too," Kuno added.

"Him first, you second. Right now, I have a patient to tend to." Esme said to Estrid, "I think it's best if you go to the inn and wait for Master Loy. He should be here in about an hour. Okay, sweetheart?"

"Yes, Mother." The girl spared another glance at Malaky, this one curious, and walked across the street to the inn.

Esme walked up the steps. "Patyn, go with Estrid. Unless you want to stick around?" She smiled wryly.

"I'll pass." Patyn hurried away from the house. Lok noticed a series of wooden splints wrapped around his right arm. He looked familiar, but Lok could not place him.

"Are you coming, chaplain?" Esme called over her shoulder. Malaky took the steps two at a time and followed Esme inside.

"She nice," West said, a big smile plastered on his face.

"And smart. Too smart to be baffled by an illness." Kuno walked up the steps. Lok grabbed him by the cloak and vehemently shook his head. "What's wrong?"

Where did Lok begin? He had been terrified of Healer Zall for as long as he could remember. The man was insane! Most people in the village believed Zall ought to retire and promote Esme to healer, but the stubborn old man would yell and curse until everyone ran away. And then he had the gall to wonder why they preferred Esme over him.

Kuno snatched his cloak out of Lok's hand and walked into the house. West went inside after him, acting like this was a grand adventure. Lok, letting out a heavy sigh, followed. It was either this or return to the inn. And his new stepfather. He guessed that meant he had two stepsisters. And two stepbrother-in-laws, and half a dozen stepnieces and stepnephews. Great.

The healer's house was vastly different from how he had imagined. He'd never actually been inside. Instead of being filled with bloodied knives and other horrors, the little house was neat and tidy. Bottles of medicine lined the shelves on the far wall, and herbs tied in bundles hung from the ceiling, providing a clean, natural smell. Chamomile, garlic, feverfew, milk thistle.

Three beds occupied the back room. Darran Zall, his face gray and haggard, laid in the bed nearest the windows. Sweaty, snow-white hair clung to his forehead. He tossed and turned, muttering.

"Pulse eighty-seven," Esme said. She held the healer's hand, her fingers on the base of the wrist. Henry jotted down the number on a notepad. Neat rows of numbers with dates and times in separate columns covered the page.

Brother Malaky sat on the middle bed. Holding a small, bronze compass, his lips moved in silent prayer.

"How long has he been like this?" Kuno asked.

"Five weeks, tomorrow," Esme replied.

Zall's eyes shot open and darted around the room. He latched onto Esme's wrist. "Seltachai! Seltachai!" he cried. He held onto her like a man hanging over a cliff and clinging to a fraying rope.

Lok cowered behind Kuno.

Esme crouched beside him. "Kel isn't here, Darran. He went looking for Realta, Charity, and Lok." She smiled brightly. "And one of them came home. Lok." She motioned for him to move closer.

Lok's heart pounded in his throat. Zall terrified him, but the healer was sick in bed. He couldn't hurt anyone. Lok took a step closer. Then another.

"Seltachai," Zall repeated. He looked all around the room, searching. Esme smoothed down his hair, brushing the strands away from his face. His eyes focused on Lok. "What? Tolman boy?"

Lok nodded.

He glanced at Lok's cloak. "Academy?"

Lok nodded again.

"Good place for you. Scholar?" He pointed at Kuno's white cloak. The Scholar nodded. "That's what I thought." His eyes clouded over, and his face contorted into a grimace. "Esme, where...?"

"I'm right here, Darran. And so is Henry."

"What? Who...?"

"That's Brother Malaky. He's a chaplain."

"I can see that, woman!" Zall snapped. "Tell him to go away."

"He will go away in a minute."

"Tell him to go away now! Get out, all of you. Damn Scholars. Too damn smart." Zall sneered. "And bloody Seltachai. I'll kill him! You should have let me kill him," he snarled at Esme, his teeth clenched and eyes burning.

Esme let out a patient sigh. "Henry, make the sedative. Lok, it's almost suppertime. Why don't you and your friend go to the inn? Vera has missed you terribly. Kuno and Mal will join you shortly. We have a lot to discuss," she added gravely.

"Your mother nice?" West asked. He huddled behind the door, clutching the frame and trembling. Lok didn't blame him. Healer Zall scared everybody.

Lok nodded. Yes, no matter what else changed in his life, he could always count on his mother's kindness. Thinking back, Ellis had always been nice to Lok. Waving hello and giving him copper pennies from time to time. And he never mocked Lok behind Vera's back. He also talked highly about Ansonn Tolman, commenting on how Lok resembled him. Perhaps having a step-father wouldn't be so bad, as long as it was Ellis.

"We go now?" West asked anxiously.

Lok smiled and nodded. He cast a quick glance at Zall. The healer had calmed down, though he still held onto Esme's hand. Brother Malaky finishing praying and placed the bronze compass in his pocket. Scholar Kuno stared out the window. The sun was at the treeline. It wouldn't de dark for a few more hours, but they'd had a long day. It would be good to rest in a familiar place.

Lok shepherded West out of the healer's house and towards the inn.

✳✳✳

Villages were strange. Buildings in neat little rows. Fields full of crops, bright green this time of year. And always in the same place. No movement. Same view every single day. And most villagers boasted that they never ventured more than twenty miles from home. Meredith could not understand it. She would go mad staying in one place for so long.

Sneaking away from her tribe had been weirdly easy. Everyone had a task during setup, and people crowded Rangar Keep.

Many, despite being bandits and smugglers, kept a healthy distance from the Hiraeth. The result of believing too many stories. Granted, some of those stories were true.

Chavi, Meredith's cousin on her father's side, said they had plenty of hunters and sent her to collect firewood. Her second-best option. Meredith brought back one bundle, but before she could venture into the forest again, her Great Mother caught her.

"Don't think I don't know what you're thinking, girl. You're on sentry duty. First and third shifts. I've more than one set of eyes on you," she added, leaning on her dark wood cane.

But there was more than one way to catch a fish. Meredith cornered Mattin, a young hunter who was not terribly bright, while supper was cooking.

"If you take the third shift, I'll take your place hitching the wagons when we leave."

"Deal," Mattin said with a smile and a wink. He'd been smitten with her since they were ten. Too bad Meredith wasn't interested in idiots.

Once third shift began, Meredith collected her bow, arrows, a hunting knife, and an extra change of clothes. She found the Scholar's campsite and waited. Mercifully, the Scholar and his group left at first light, a half hour before the shift ended.

She stayed on the outskirts of the River Road, just behind the trees. The men were none the wiser. The chaplain jumped at every sound or movement, even the tiniest birds flitting from branch to branch. At least the Scholar knew what he was doing. She doubted the chaplain ever ventured out of a city.

A city. Many times larger than a village and packed with thousands of people. The capital city of Teyrnas boasted a hundred thousand people. Or it did before the war.

Her tribe originally planned to cross the river and settle in the flatlands for a time, trading with villagers along the Highway. There was no real reason other than a new experience. The war canceled those plans.

So, they were heading back to the Vogel Mountains.

But Meredith felt compelled to follow these men, and not solely for the chance at an education. An invisible tether drew her towards the young man with gray, storm cloud eyes. His speech was strange, never speaking in complete sentences and growing confused when someone spoke too quickly. But a warmth surrounded him. Similar to the warmth given by a fire on a cold winter night. She had never felt that kind of warmth, not even from her own mother. There was something different about this boy, and she was determined to figure it out.

She hid in the shadows as they entered the village. The villagers greeted the men warmly, but kindness like that was not reserved for the Hiraeth. A black-haired woman greeted the men, gathering more people around her, and then led the men into a small house. Meredith crouched between the porch and some bushes that were more twigs than leaves. And then she waited.

Meredith excelled at waiting. You couldn't properly stalk a deer if you did not have patience. The deer would take off running before you could draw a bow, disappearing into the woods. And you'd have to return to camp empty-handed. Even the smallest child wanted to avoid that shame.

The two boys left the house, heading for the long, narrow building across the street. She sensed a strange mixture of emotions from them. The taller, silent brother felt both happiness and sadness. The shorter one, still radiating warmth, was fearful. But as he gazed around, curiosity replaced fear. He pointed at various people and buildings, the villagers nodding or waving, some smiling. The taller one strode towards the building, eyes fixed dead ahead.

The invisible tether tugged at her, urging her to follow the strange boy, but she had another quarry.

The door opened, and the chaplain, the woman, and the Scholar walked onto the porch. The Scholar leaned against the railing, letting out a heavy sigh. A great weight rested on his shoulders, and he was on the verge of breaking. She could not focus on him for long without the emotion infecting her own.

The chaplain, as always, was nervous. Why? Weren't chaplains supposed to trust the Creator in all things?

"Carwyn's name is Kel," the woman said. "Kel son of Owena."

Meredith arched an eyebrow. That sounded like a Hiraethi name.

"I see," said the chaplain. "How did he survive?"

"My questions first," said the woman. She felt tired, so tired…

Meredith broke away. Being an Empath was useful, but sometimes she wished she only had her own emotions to deal with.

"You said Gareth and Kel are at the Academy," the woman continued. "How are they?"

"Gareth is doing well," the Scholar replied, studying his fingernails.

"Doing well," the woman repeated. "My son panics whenever someone unexpectedly visits for dinner. Tell me the truth, Kuno."

"Truth is, I don't really know. The boy is quiet. I never heard more than a few words from him. For a while, I thought he was a mute. You'll have to ask Lok. He and Gareth stuck close together."

The woman breathed out slowly, relieved. "And Kel?"

"I think he was hurt," replied the chaplain. "I only saw him for a few minutes. And there were others traveling with him."

"Describe them."

"Well, um, two of the men wore cloaks. Couldn't see their faces. Another was young, maybe twenty years old. And the last was tall and black hair and dark eyes."

"Callum?"

"Your brother?"

"Yes."

"I don't… Maybe?"

"Well, at least my son and husband are safe." She smiled. "I shouldn't worry so much about my little brother, but…" She shrugged.

"How did Kel survive?" the Scholar asked. "It was no secret he and Prince Carwyn were the same person. Everyone had figured it out by that point. Did you help him fake an illness?"

"I wish that were the case. Yestyn beat him so badly, I feared he would die before we reached Vala. But Kel survived because he wanted to live. Stubborn bastard," she said lovingly.

"It's late," the chaplain said. "If I come back in the morning, will you tell me more? About you and Kel. And your family." His voice faltered.

"Of course, Mal."

She and the chaplain hugged, and he headed for the chapel, a little building with wind chimes hanging in front of the door.

Likely to burn candles and speak in whispers. They had very strange ways of worshipping the Creator. Always so quiet. And some mistakenly believed that the Hiraeth, because they worshipped differently, believed differently. The chaplains they'd encountered spoke at length, admonishing them and pleading for them to change their ways. Always talking, but never listening.

The Scholar also said goodbye to the woman.

"It's good to see you," he said. "I'm glad everything worked out well for you and Kel."

"So am I. And I missed your lectures. Maybe you can give me and Henry one tomorrow?"

"On what subject?" he asked, lifting his chin and clasping his hands behind his back.

"Scholar's choice."

"It's a deal."

The woman went back inside the house.

The Scholar looked up at the sky and let out a heavy sigh. Day was quickly heading into twilight. He muttered under his breath in strange words that Meredith did not understand. Anger now radiated off him in waves, and a deep sadness laid at the foundation of that anger. Sadness that had taken a lifetime to build. What had created the sadness? That was the frustrating part. Meredith could read emotions like words on a page, but she didn't know their cause.

She slowly stalked towards him. People could react the same as deer, running at the slightest hint of danger.

The Scholar's dark eyes fell on her, widening. Embarrassment bloomed and quickly mixed itself with anger.

"Where did you come from?" he snapped.

"I followed you." Best to tell the truth. Too many people believed the Hiraeth told nothing but lies.

"You followed…" His eyes narrowed. "You're the Hiraethi girl from Rangar. Did you follow us all the way here?"

She nodded. "My Great Mother didn't want me to speak with you, but I'm a Siltelmai. I mean, a Thane. Empath. The Scholars educate Thanes at their Academy, right?"

The Scholar let out an exasperated sigh. "The Academy is no longer safe."

Right, the war. Of course the Academy would not be excluded.

"You'll be in a mess of trouble," the Scholar said suddenly.

Meredith jolted. The Scholar changed. He now stood with one foot slightly behind the other, and his hands loose at his sides, ready to strike. He stared at her with a hunter's eyes. She met the hunter's stare with her own, ready to move if he leapt off that porch.

"Perhaps."

"No perhaps, girl. The Hiraeth don't take runaways lightly. How often have runaways been welcomed back into your tribe? Or any tribe?"

"Sometimes." Runaways were extremely rare. A few years back, a young archer named Nadia had fallen in with a group of thieves. The Great Mother forbid her from associating with them, knowing the danger they posed to the tribe. Nadia was too stubborn to admit her mistake and turned her back on the tribe. The tribe had responded in kind. No one had seen or heard from Nadia since. Meredith's last memory of Nadia was her standing side by side with her new brothers, glaring daggers at the Great Mother. "No one is lost forever," she found herself saying. "If they truly wish to return, we will allow them." It was always an option, but asking a Hiraethi to admit they were wrong was more difficult than pulling a tooth.

The Scholar relaxed. The hunter's eyes disappeared. "What is your name?"

"Meredith, daughter of Ramyra, daughter of Meralda," she said, squaring her shoulders.

"My name is Kuno Surylin, son of nobody." He studied her. "You said you're an Empath?" Kuno Surylin stepped off the porch. He only stood a few inches taller than her.

"Yes."

"And you followed us all this way without me noticing. That's impressive. I'm afraid I can't take you to the Academy, but I can educate you. If you want to study history. I'm useless at natural science and law."

"Are you a Thane?"

Kuno shook his head. "But I will do my best. Only if you truly want to learn. My time is valuable."

"Yes, if you will answer one question."

"Sure."

"Why are you angry?"

Kuno sighed. He glanced at the building his sons had entered. "Everything had been going so well. I'd found a good place..." He shook his head. "I don't want to trouble you with my personal problems. Would you like something to eat? I'm sure there's plenty of food at the inn."

An inn. So that's what the building was called. She had heard of inns but never stayed in a village long enough to see one up close.

Meredith smiled and nodded. A sense of relief washed over her. She was not going to the Academy, but she would be educated by a Scholar.

And when she was ready, she would return to her tribe and admit her fault.

No one, after all, was lost forever.

29

Alcove

Isla's feet moved of their own accord as she climbed the grand staircase. One after another, after another, after...

The healer who had pronounced Peydar Wills dead informed her that the Council was meeting in the Chamber, but it was a closed session. Not even the nobility was allowed to interrupt. If she wished, she could make an appointment...

Isla hadn't bothered to hear the rest.

She halted in front of the ornately carved doors. Polished, dark oak. So dark it was almost black.

Almost the color of dried blood.

Isla looked down at her hands and dress. Blood coated the skirts and sleeves. Cold water mixed with vinegar would remove the stains, but she'd never been able to wear this dress again let alone look at it. Better to burn it. But not yet.

Holding her head high the way her mother taught her, Isla pushed open the doors and strode into the center of the Chamber.

Scholars huddled together in groups of threes and fours, all deep in conversation. The trio nearest the door wondered if they should send additional messengers to the Madani. They were supposed to arrive within the week, but with the war right outside the walls...

Isla walked by. None of the Scholars noticed.

The Premier Scholar sat in her usual seat, two white cloaked women hovering over her, blocking her view of the Chamber.

Isla stood on the central mosaic, a compass with the ancient symbols for each type of Thane at the cardinal points, and waited. A dark line bisected the colorful tiles. A scorch mark. Was it there before? She couldn't recall.

Scholar Domhnall, an elderly man with pure white hair and soul piercingly blue eyes, finally noticed her. He quickly alerted the Scholars nearest him. Scholar Niona, a woman in her mid-forties, gasped, and Scholar Osian, whose hair was almost the same shade of auburn as hers, stared at her, at the blood on her dress. Niona alerted the next group.

Scholar Ealee rushed to Isla's side, her face turning ashen. "Are you injured, Your Majesty?" She fretted about, hands and eyes darting all around but accomplishing nothing.

"I need to speak with the Premier." For a wonder, her voice did not shake.

Scholar Ealee nodded frantically and led her towards the seats. All conversation ceased, replaced by furtive whispers. One by one, the Scholar took their seats. All of them stared at her. Isla's palms began to sweat.

But I want them to notice me. That's the whole point.

The Premier Scholar stood, Scholars Lilia and Bronwyn stood by her side, steadying her. Emera seemed much older, her white hair thinner, the lines around her eyes deeper, and blue veins visible underneath pale skin. If she had aged so much in a few weeks, how much had Isla aged? Would the noble friends she had left behind recognize her?

"What happened to you, Queen Isla?" the Premier Scholar asked, concern lacing her voice.

Isla took a deep breath and told her about the battle outside the walls, the soldiers on both sides fighting and dying, and Thanes using their abilities to maim and kill. She included her Farsight at the end, and her interpretation of the flags covered in blood.

"I came here straight away," she finished. Tears picked her eyes, and she blinked them away. Queens did not cry in public.

"Whose blood is that?" the Premier asked.

"His name was Peydar Wills. He died saving my life." Her voice wavered.

"What would you have us do?" asked Scholar Lucan. He stood and stepped closer to Isla and the Premier. "There are battles and bloodshed in every war."

Isla was bloody sick of this man. Couldn't he keep his mouth shut for once? Schooling herself, she replied, "Recall the Thane Regiment. If soldiers have to die, have them die from swords and arrows, not from Manipulations and Illusions."

More than a few Scholars muttered nervously.

"We can't, Your Majesty," Lucan replied. "You signed the document approving of the Thane Regiment."

"I made a mistake. Recall the Regiment. That is an order."

Several Scholars averted their eyes. The nervous muttering grew louder. Isla's heart pounded in her throat. Why did she get the feeling that she was outnumbered?

"This is not an order you can give, I'm afraid," the Premier said, choosing her words carefully. "The decision was proposed to the Council and approved by the Council. Your signature was merely a formality. I hope you understand, Queen Regent."

Isla blinked. She looked at Scholars Ealee and Bronwyn, sitting on both sides of the Premier. They refused to meet her eyes. As did Scholars Jori and Domhnall and Osian. None so much as looked at her, except Lucan and the Premier.

"Queen Regent?" she tested the words. "Since when do you address me as such?"

"It has always been your title," the Premier said. "And will be until Prince Morgan comes of age. The proposal for Thanes to fight was met with much scrutiny. This decision wouldn't have been made if the situation weren't so dire. Teyrnas could be lost if we do not turn the tide soon. Is there anything else we can do for you, Your Majesty?"

Isla looked to the Scholars again. They remained silent. She stood alone. "I didn't understand the implications of this decision until it was too late." No, she must not lie to herself. She knew it was wrong from the beginning. They all knew it was wrong. She could see the guilt in Jori's eyes as plain as day. But guilt wouldn't persuade all of them, especially not Lucan. "By allowing Student and Journeymen Thanes to fight, you remove the Academy's neutrality," she said, using politics and logic. "Instead of a place of learning, this Academy is now a military base, full of potential recruits. Nothing will stop the Eastern Coalition from attacking these walls. Every civilian life is now in danger. How much longer until the reserves from Madan Och arrive?"

"They should arrive round the Solstice," Scholar Adhran replied.

A little more than a half week. Maybe longer if they were delayed. And five armies were moving in for the kill. May the Creator and His Gadyeni preserve them.

"Send word to their scouts across the Wallach," Isla ordered, recalling the latest maps. "They will transport civilians to Madan Och as planned, and their soldiers will aid any battles fought near the Academy until everyone is evacuated." The representatives had not agreed to fight, but the Madani would act to defend themselves. Surely they could extend that defense to unarmed refugees.

"Your Majesty, you don't give the orders here," Lucan reminded her. She wanted to slap him across the face, but queens, regents or not, did not resort to violence.

Isla stepped closer to the Premier, forcing the older woman to look her in the eyes. "Then I make this proposal to the Council of Scholars. Contact the representatives and send messengers to Madan Och. They will escort the civilians to safety. Teyrnas will compensate them. And since Representative Elinya said that this is not their fight," she added, "they should have no qualms with aiding civilians."

"This proposal has been accepted," Premier Scholar Emera replied. "We shall discuss it and vote tomorrow afternoon."

Isla wanted them to discuss it here and now, but she felt that her good relations with the Premier were on thin ice and took the Premier's answer as her cue to leave.

Once outside the doors, she leaned against the wall and sank down. She wanted to cry, to scream, to grab the Council by the throat and force them to act.

All she could do now was wait and hope. She started to brush a strand of hair away from her face but stopped, seeing Peydar Wills's blood on her fingers.

Grief crashed into her like an avalanche. Wills had been a civilian. A civilian who should not have been near the fighting. Who had no business on the wall. Isla did not give a penny for what the Council said. She was still the Queen of Teyrnas, and these civilians were her responsibility. She would protect them no matter what the Council decided.

A soft creak sounded as a door opened. Had the Scholars changed their minds? Or was the meeting merely over?

Isla quickly wiped away her tears and stood up, smoothing down her dress. But the ornate doors were still closed. A narrow door adjacent to the Chamber opened wider. A shadowy figure concealed by a long, black cloak met Isla's eyes and stalked towards her.

She braced herself. If need be, she could scream, and all seventeen Council members would hear.

But how many will actually help me?

Her blood turned to ice.

The cloaked figure removed his hood, and Isla wanted to smack him.

"What are you doing here?" she asked her husband. "Are you trying to scare me to death?"

"Sorry," Logan whispered, glancing around. "I was listening. There's a small alcove up there. You can hear every word without being seen. Good for eavesdropping." His eyes fell on her blood-stained dress. "What in the name of the Abyss were you doing on the wall? You almost got yourself killed!"

"I was doing your job," she snapped.

Logan chewed on his lip, looking just like a kid. Just like the young man she had first met. Quiet, unsure of himself, untested. Back then, Carwyn was set to inherit the throne. A position he did not want but was willing to accept in order to serve his people. Serve, not rule.

And now, the world believed that both brothers were dead.

"What drove you to the wall?"

"A Farsight. I thought you were listening." She jabbed a finger at him.

Logan glanced furtively at the door.

Oh, are you worried someone will see you and ruin your bloody plans?

"What part did you leave out?"

Damn the man. "It was every flag. Not just Teyrnas and the Coalition. But every flag in the Northern Realm." An image flashed before her. A sky-blue flag with a golden eagle. The flag of the Sykerian Empire. "And the South. The fighting won't end here."

"Unless we force it to end."

"How? According to the Council, I'm powerless and you're

dead."

Logan gave the door a sideways glance, thinking.

Isla grabbed his arm. "Why don't you tell them? Manipulate the doors open and proclaim to the world that Logan O'Kelwyn, the Raven King, is alive."

"I can't."

Isla wanted to scream. Instead, she shoved a bloodied hand in Logan's face. "This is Peydar Wills's blood. He died protecting me. He died believing that he failed you."

"Of course he failed me. He tried to murder my sister." Heat rose in Logan's voice. His eyes flashed, turning him into a perfect copy of King Yestyn.

"Because he was acting under Dane Kanton's orders." A light shone in her mind. A piece of information she almost forgot. "Kanton is at the palace."

Logan gave her a confused look.

"Wills told me right before he died. Kanton went back to the palace after you banished him. He's working for the Eastern Coalition. What if he has been working for them this entire time?"

"Why would a bunch of monarchs hire a guard to kill my bastard sister?"

"How should I know? But it makes sense, doesn't it? They order Kanton to kill Serena, and you're too grief-stricken to properly deal with Queen Gallia. They wanted to guarantee a war."

"Perhaps." Logan cast a furtive glance at the door so quickly that Isla almost missed it.

"What's stopping you?"

Logan hooked his arm around Isla's elbow and led her to the hidden door. They climbed a narrow flight of stairs, so narrow that only one person could fit at a time. It was a wonder Isla didn't trip on her dress, or Logan trip on his long cloak.

"How did you find this place?" she asked.

"I didn't. Carwyn…" Logan cleared his throat. "Just don't tell anyone, okay?"

The stairs ended in a small, dimly lit room. Logan crouched down beside the wall. Isla sat next to him, folding her legs under her dress. In the low light, her husband looked pale, the dark circles underneath his eyes more pronounced. When was the last time either of them got a decent night's sleep?

Logan brushed a strand of hair away from Isla's face. "How many Farsights have you had about random people at the Academy?"

"Define random." Guilt stabbed her heart. She saw that silver crown over Gareth Haar's head every time she looked at the boy. How could she explain that Gareth, the boy who looked like Esme Haar, and not Morgan, the boy who looked like Logan, was the heir to the throne?

"Random people. People you've never met. The people you pass in the hallways."

"A few."

"Anything concerning the Nine Summit Thanes or the Gadyeni?"

"No. Logan, what are you talking about?"

"Students have gone missing. The first was Charity Loy. Do you remember her from the Exhibition? The girl who assisted Scholar Maryn?"

"A little." The only thing Isla recalled was her fear for Logan's safety. Scholar Maryn's device had injured him, and he laughed as though it were the world's greatest joke!

"At first, I thought nothing of it. The Academy is a big place and overcrowded with refugees. But then I overheard more Students ask about classmates. Students who didn't show up for a class, or didn't return to their room one night, and are never seen again."

"Runaways?"

Logan shrugged. "Perhaps, but I've heard twenty names so far. All Students, and all good Students. I think... Isla, last night, I saw two people wearing black cloaks."

"So? You're wearing a black cloak." Where had he found it? Surely the one he owned was still at the palace.

"But this was in the middle of the night. They went into a building that's closed for renovations. The doors should have been locked. I followed them." Logan squeezed his eyes shut, grimacing. "I heard one call the Midnight King by his true name."

An ice-cold shiver ran down Isla's spine. "What else?"

"I don't know. I was so shocked, I just froze. Thank the Creator neither of them turned around. I would truly be dead."

"Who else have you told?"

"Just you. Isla, I have to figure out what's going on here. Something... Something's wrong. Something other than the war. If people knew King Logan was alive, I would be followed everywhere. As a dead man, I can move around freely."

"The Wardens of the Night," Isla said quietly.

Logan looked like he was going to be sick. "What did you say?"

"I don't know. It just..." Isla rubbed her arms, feeling colder. "They are called the Wardens of the Night."

Logan cursed under his breath. "Now, do you understand why I can't walk into the Council Chamber and announce myself?"

Isla nodded. She didn't want to, but if the group from her Farsight was real... *Stars above.* "Realta Haar. I had a Farsight of the Wardens hunting her."

"Should I tell Callum?"

"What good will it do? Realta must be in another kingdom by now, and Mistress Cray is with her." Isla considered the girl lucky. She certainly could use Shasta Cray's insight right now.

"And so is Serena," Logan whispered.

He's thinking about Carwyn again. Logan always thought about Carwyn whenever Serena's name was mentioned. For years, he blamed Carwyn's death on his honesty, confronting Yestyn about a bastard better left forgotten. But Carwyn wasn't dead anymore. He could talk about him. Fire and smoke, he could talk *to* him! But her husband was too stubborn to make things simple.

"Peydar Wills died to protect you, huh?" he asked quietly.

She nodded.

"He deserved better than a banishment. Isla, do me a favor. Tell me every Farsight you have from now on. Write it down in a code, if you have to. We cannot afford followers of the Midnight King to get the upper hand."

Voices rose from the Chamber, echoing up the walls. Isla recognized Scholar Lucan but could not place the other two. A pit formed in her gut. How long had the Wardens been here? Did they arrive disguised as refugees? Or had they been here from the beginning?

"Do you think they're influencing the Council?"

"They barred your orders with a technicality that hasn't been used in centuries," Logan said. "It would be foolish to assume they aren't."

✳✳✳

Callum stalked the tents, peering down each row, studying each face, searching. Kel kept pace with him. He ran into his brother-in-law shortly after Isla had gone to confront the Scholars, setting him on this grim task. Deen returned to their tent. Witnessing the battle left the King of Bran Maro pale and weak. Best for him to lie down. Callum was grateful to find Kel. Two sets of eyes were always better than one, a lesson he had learned well as a mountain guide. And this camp was just another type of wilderness, filled with its own unique dangers.

I'd rather deal with wildcats, Callum thought solemnly as more war horns blared. The men on the walls cheered. A victory for Teyrnas. For now.

"Have you seen anybody matching Marsh's description?" he asked Kel. Callum had related the events on the wall as they walked, concluding with Wills claiming that Kanton now worked for the Coalition. Kel paled, hearing the disgraced guardsman's name, but the news did not shock him.

"Do you know how many women with black hair and fair skin live in this kingdom?" Kel asked, favoring his right leg more. Callum frowned. Kel had gone to a healer to fix his knee, but Callum spied yellow-ish purple bruises on Kel's arms and torso last night. Bruises that were too fresh to have resulted from that fall down the stairs. Was he posing as a beggar again? That trick had worked in Teyrnas, but the Academy grew more hostile every day.

"How about women who worked with the Guard?" Callum studied every person he passed. More than a few averted their eyes and hurried along. "She studied at the Garrison, right?"

"Yes, but she's probably disguised herself. Isla didn't recognize Wills until the man spoke to her, and he worked at the palace for years. Marsh is likely keeping a healthy distance from the guardsmen. What's her first name?"

"I think it's Eirica."

Kel raised an eyebrow. "Are you sure? That's more of a Byyarian name."

"Well, it's what Logan called her." A group of refugees stared at him as though he were a wildcat stalking their flocks. He slowed his pace and motioned for Kel to walk closer. People who could not chase you tended to be less threatening.

"How would you like to proceed?" Kel scanned the tents. The people barely glanced at him. He was just another beggar in their eyes.

Callum looked down at a woman sitting outside a tent. She was half his size and looked like she had lived through a nightmare. Putting on his friendliest smile, he walked over and crouched down, meeting her eyes. "Excuse me, ma'am, I'm looking for my sister. Her name is Eirica. We were separated while escaping the city. Have you seen her?"

The woman stared blankly at Callum. Staring right through him, he realized. He then noticed the bandages on her feet. Blood stained the dirty linen. Broken blisters ripe for infection.

"Have you seen a healer for your feet, ma'am?" Callum asked.

The woman continued to stare.

"The healers helped my brother." He gestured towards Kel. "They're very good."

The woman made no sign that she understood him.

Does she speak a foreign language?

The tent flaps burst open. Callum leapt to his feet, hands balled into fists. But it was just a boy. No older than Gareth. A bit on the skinny side, but he stood as tall as Callum, and board shoulders indicated the man he would become in a few years.

The boy's dark brown eyes burning like a bonfire. "What in the Abyss do you want?"

Callum relaxed, holding up his empty hands. "We were just looking for someone."

"We can't help you." He positioned himself between the woman and Callum.

"Have you seen a woman named Eirica?"

"I said we can't help you," the boy snapped. "My mother isn't well. Get away from us!"

The air rushed out of Callum's lungs as he lurched backwards. He hit the ground hard. A throbbing pain spread across his chest.

Were his ribs broken? First a punctured lung and now this. Esme was bound to give him a lecture if they made it home.

"Stars above, you're a Thane!" Kel said.

The boy glared daggers at Kel.

"No, no! It's okay." Kel removed a few copper pennies from his pocket and twirled them around in his palm. He smiled. "See? We're the same."

Callum slowly rose to his feet, taking exploratory breaths. Nothing felt broken, but Kel couldn't take the same treatment unscathed. He placed himself between Kel and the boy.

"No!" the woman cried. She leapt up and wrapped her arms around her son. "Don't take my boy. Please, don't take my boy!" Tears made clean tracks down her face.

"Nobody is going to take your son," Callum said a little too forcefully. The woman cried harder. Great. He looked at Kel.

"Why aren't you a Student?" Kel asked, his voice gentle.

The boy scowled. "They wanted me to go, but Father died two years back, and I'm all my mother has. She begged the Scholars to let me wait another year. I never wanted to come here." He glared at the Academy as though it had beaten him bloody, robbed him, and then burnt his house down.

"But you're a Manipulator, right?" Callum still wasn't clear on the types of Thanes, even after Kel's explanations.

"And a high-leveled one," Kel added, "if you can knock down a grown man."

"I don't care. Look, if people find out, the guardsmen will make me fight."

"The Thane Regiment is volunteer only," Kel replied.

The boy scoffed. "Ain't what I heard. They'd mark me with a stupid earring and force me to fight." He looked at Kel's ears and frowned. "Shouldn't you have earrings?"

Pain flashed in Kel's eyes. "I did, once."

"Did you rip them out?"

Callum looked at the boy aghast. Rip them out? What Thane on Eltriar would purposely rip out their earrings?

"Would you rip yours out if the Scholars forced them on you?" Kel asked.

The boy nodded. "You said you were looking for your sister?"

he asked Callum.

"Yes." He gave the boy Marsh's description. He should have drawn a picture. Much easier than repeating the same information over and over. And more accurate. "She was traveling with a man named Peydar."

"Yeah, I've seen them. They have a tent over there." He pointed down the row. "They don't talk much. Promise you won't tell the Scholars about me?"

"We promise. My name is Kel, and this is my brother Callum. If the guards give you or your mother any trouble, our tent is near the stables."

"Thanks. I'm Deklan, and my mother is Amira." He gently took hold of his mother's hands. "Let's get inside. The sun's too hot this time of day." He shepherded her inside the tent and tied the flaps shut.

Callum walked on, following Deklan's directions. "How many more do you think are like him?"

"Impossible to tell. The Academy tries to find every Thane, give them proper training, but there are so many small villages. Some are so remote they don't remember they're part of a larger kingdom. And city slums... In many ways, slums are worse than forests. Most Scholars are too afraid to venture into them, especially Tullcrest. Let's say," Kel adopted his tutor voice, "there are a hundred villages east of the Nerin, and a hundred more in the Hinterlands. With only one unaccounted for Thane in each, you have two hundred. Minimum. And this is just speculation. Not to mention the number of Cuchasi. Remember your thief friend?"

Callum smirked. Arnyn Teleran had just been a kid when he tried to pick Callum's pocket, not realizing that indentured servants weren't allowed to carry money. Sardic despised that rule, but Callum knew the consequences for both of them if they broke it.

Another man might have boxed Arnyn's ears, but Callum saw something of himself in the boy. He had nowhere to go, and Callum couldn't bear to see another person with a servant's mark on their wrist. So, he taught Arnyn how to properly pick a person's pocket and made a friend for life.

Running into Arnyn in Lothian was pure chance.

Callum had been reluctant to believe Arnyn when he named Realta and Lok Tolman as Thanes. There were no Thanes in the Haar family, save Kel. But Arnyn never lied. Not to the man who taught him to be a better thief.

A deep-seated anger rose in Callum's chest. Realta was his daughter, his only child. Her safety was his responsibility, and he was powerless to help her. If he hadn't gone searching for the king, he could have left with her, could have done something, instead of just sitting around in a dirty tavern for weeks, praying they weren't caught.

But Kel was not strong enough to carry Logan. They would have been trapped in the palace, and Deen might have turned coats again. Callum had to be there to save Logan. And Realta was fifteen years old. Old enough to care for herself though it pained him to stand by and just watch.

Can't watch out for her if I don't know where she is. Any place was better than here, he guessed.

"What about Thanes born in the east?" Callum asked.

"Most probably live in hiding, afraid they will be banished or imprisoned. But a few are more vocal. Years ago, before…" Kel touched the scarred half of his face. Callum and Esme had observed the tick each time Kel hinted at his past. Kel never noticed, so they never mentioned it to him. "Before Esme and I moved out west, we heard news from Bran Maro. A Thane named Etragian Calbi had gone insane, destroying everything. Entire villages burned to the ground before the Watch killed him. But before that, messengers from Bran Maro asked Yestyn for help. None of them knew how to deal with a Thane. Yestyn thought it was propaganda and sent them away."

"Do you think it was real?"

"Perhaps. I never got a chance to investigate. Besides, there are plenty of Cuchasi in the east. They would have identified whether he was a Thane or just a madman."

"Your son is a Cuchasi."

Kel averted his eyes.

"When were you and Esme going to tell us?"

"We…" Kel grimaced. "Never. We saw no point. There are no Thanes in Vala, save for myself and Mayor Gan. And Gan is harmless. Besides, you know how much Gareth hates attention."

"Very true." Callum rarely understood his nephew. The boy seemed to live in his own head, rarely speaking, even to family members. Often, he was too nervous to speak. And he hated loud noises. Hated yelling. Callum's mind wandered back to Dane Kanton. The guard had yelled and raved, threatening to harm Serena. Gareth panicked. Callum did not have Esme's way with the boy and couldn't calm him down. He ran away instead of facing his fear.

Callum understood his nephew's actions now. Hares hid from hawks in order to survive. There was nothing wrong with that. It was their nature.

Kel motioned for Callum to stop. A small circle of tents stood around a dead campfire, an iron tripod hanging over the center. Two women sat near the fire pit, talking. One woman had a shawl wrapped around her shoulders, clinging to it as though she were freezing. A purple bruise covered her cheekbone, and her left eye was swollen shut. The second woman wore a tattered dress and men's work boots. Her black, shoulder-length hair hung loose instead of in a tight braid.

"This is the diaphragm," Eirica Marsh said, pointing just below her sternum. "One swift punch, and he'll go down. Won't be able to breathe."

"But I don't want to hurt him," the other woman stammered.

"Why not? He already hurt you."

The woman wrapped the shawl tighter. She sobbed quietly.

"Look," Marsh said with a sigh. "Why don't you stay in my tent tonight? My husband will talk to—"

"No! I mean, I don't want any trouble. I—" Her good eye fell on Callum and Kel. "I've got to go. Edard will wonder what's keeping me." She scrambled to her feet and hurried off.

Marsh exhaled through her teeth. Shaking her head, she stood and almost went inside her tent. She spied Callum and took a tentative step forward, studying him. "You."

"Hello, Marsh."

Her eyes darted left and right, but the rest of her body remained still. "Actually, my name is Eirica. Eirica Danell."

"I understand. Friend of yours?" He cocked his head in the direction the other woman ran.

"Yes and no. Her husband is a no-good jackass who…" Marsh clenched and unclenched her fists. "I'm trying to help, but she's been with him since she was eighteen. Doesn't know how to live without him."

Callum's mouth and throat suddenly went dry. Marsh had mentioned a husband. "Eirica, have you heard about the battle? About what happened on the wall?"

"No. Well, Coalition soldiers haven't stormed the Academy, so I guess we won."

"At a cost." Fire and smoke. Callum had prepared his speech. Every word. But seeing Marsh now, looking her in the eyes, all those words were just tripe. What if Wills was her husband? Was he going to inform this woman that she was a widow? Esme had the horrible task of telling Callum that Kiana had died from crimson fever. She broke down crying, blaming herself. Callum understood that Esme did everything possible to save Kiana. Crimson fever was deadly. Every villager in the Hinterlands feared it. Callum had come close to dying himself.

And it was still hard for him to talk about Kiana. He wanted his daughter to know about her mother. Words failed him again and again, so he drew. Realta might not know her mother's favorite songs or that her perfume smelled like star lilies, but she knew Kiana's face.

"What cost?" Marsh glanced from Callum to Kel and back again. "Who is this man?"

"Why don't you sit down?"

"I'd rather stand. What cost?" Her eyes widened. "Did something happen to Queen Isla?"

"It would have, if Wills hadn't saved her." The words, by some miracle, flowed freely. Callum told her every detail, starting with the queen's Farsight and ending with Wills dying in Isla's arms. Marsh listened silently. Tears brimmed her eyes, but she held them at bay, a soldier fighting to hold the line in a losing battle.

"Peydar is dead? Are you sure?"

"I saw his body. I'm sorry for your loss." Sorry for your loss. He despised that phrase. Hated that people he had known his entire life could not think of anything better to say. A man loses his wife and you're sorry?! But what else could Callum say? No words would bring Wills back from the dead. "How long were you married?"

"Three weeks. We fought it, tried to. Guards aren't supposed to have personal relationships, but we weren't guards anymore. Where is he?" Her voice choked.

"The healers took him away, along with the other causalities," Callum replied.

"They probably won't perform burials until tonight," Kel said. "You can ask to see him."

Marsh studied Kel warily. Her eyes narrowed, tears forgotten. "You look familiar. Who are you?"

"It's a long story."

"I have time." She reached for her belt, only to realize that she didn't have a sword or a knife. She cursed under her breath.

"King Yestyn had a lot of bastards," Kel said simply.

Callum kept his mouth shut. A simple lie was better than the complicated truth, he supposed. Hopefully, this lie wouldn't come back to bite them.

Marsh relaxed a bit. "I thought it was just Serena. But I see the resemblance now. Kinda eerie. What happened to your face?"

"I told Yestyn the truth, and he decided it was better to get rid of me than face the consequences."

"Yeah, I believe that, too." Marsh glanced upward as new tears threatened to spill over. The sky had darkened as storm clouds moved in from the west. "I want to see Peydar now. Will you take me?"

"Of course." Callum silently led the way.

30

Errands

Lok leaned against the second-floor railing and peered down. The common room was almost empty. Most of the guests left shortly after breakfast, either traveling towards the Pass or going to the market to buy supplies. His mother and two serving girls swept the floors and dusted tables. Scholar Kuno sat at a table near the window along with West and that strange Hiraethi girl Meredith.

Ellis had left at dawn to work at the tavern. The man was nothing but friendly towards Lok, smiling as he commented on Lok's height. "Almost as tall as Ansonn." And he was happy to have a Thane in the family. Lok hadn't minded the compliments until Ellis invited his daughters and their families over for dinner last night.

Maci and Hope were as amicable as their father, and their husbands were polite enough not to make too many comments. Their seven small children crowded around the table. The oldest reached Lok's waist while the youngest could barely walk and sat in Maci's lap. They smiled at all the right moments and asked Lok too many questions about being a Thane. He quickly finished eating and asked to be excused, claiming that he had a lot of schoolwork to catch up on.

"Kind of quiet, huh?"

Lok glanced to the side. One of the guests sauntered towards him. The man resembled most people on the eastern side of the Nerin with light brown hair and pale blue eyes, and he was quite tall, only an inch shorter than Lok. He moved with a strange grace, as though he were prepared to dance with every woman who came his way.

The man casually placed a hand on the railing. "I don't think we've been introduced. I'm Luckson."

Luckson? Strange name. Lok took out his notebook and introduced himself.

"Oh, the innkeeper's son. I've heard of you," he said with a smile. "Sorry things at the Academy didn't work out. Nobody plans for a war, unfortunately."

Lok sighed heavily. Life was throwing him one change after another, and he feared it wasn't done yet.

"Is there anything to do around here?" Luckson asked. "The folks staying here ain't much for conversation."

"You can go to the marketplace."

"I went there yesterday." Luckson peered down. "What about the Scholar? Think he'll be up for conversation?"

Lok studied Kuno. The Scholar watched in awe as West caused the water in his mug to spin around in a funnel. Yesterday, when West first demonstrated his ability, Vera, Ellis, and all the serving girls rushed over to watch. Now, the serving girls watched from afar while Vera carried on with her work. Lok was thankful his mother hadn't asked him to demonstrate his ability yet.

"You can try." It was the best answer Lok could give. Kuno's mood had improved considerably, but his moods changed so quickly nowadays. Why? Was it the war, or Scholar Lucan wanting to use Lok as a weapon? Or both?

Luckson headed down the stairs. Lok cautiously followed. The man strode up to Scholar Kuno's table. Kuno nearly choked on his drink.

"Sorry," Luckson said. "Didn't mean to startle you."

Kuno coughed, clearing his throat. "It's fine. Can I help you?"

"I am in dire need of a decent conversation. Would you and your Students mind if I join you?"

"Hi!" West leaned across the table and waved his hand in Luckson's face. The man smiled, taking it in stride.

"If the Scholar allows it," Meredith replied. Her hand rested on the sharpened hunting knife on her belt. She always reached for a weapon and then had the audacity to wonder why the other guests avoided her!

"It's fine, as long as you don't mind them practicing," Kuno said.

"No problem at all." Luckson sat between Kuno and West.

"Thanes are great. Always full of surprises. Are you going to join us?" he asked Lok.

Lok glanced over at his mother. Vera had her head in the kitchen door, talking to the cook. If he hung around any longer, she might rope him into chores, and working near her might draw her to ask questions. About him being a Thane. The real reason he left the Academy. And his real feelings about her getting married. He was happy that she was happy, but he did not want a stepfather or stepsisters or a dozen people crowding around a table every night and pretending to be polite.

"I want to get some fresh air."

"Don't wander far," Kuno said.

Wander far? Lok could walk every street in Vala twice and be back in time for lunch.

Warm morning sunlight greeted Lok as he stepped outside. The sky was clear blue with puffy, white clouds. Songbirds flitted in the air. Bees hummed in the morning glory bushes his mother tended to every spring. And people, faces he had known his whole life, went about their daily tasks.

Perhaps living in Vala again wouldn't be so bad. Thanks to Brother Malaky, half the village knew Lok was a rare type of Thane. It would have been a mistake to hide his ability, he realized. People were less likely to bother someone who could control fire. Even Reder Yorath had greeted him nicely yesterday.

And the Loys were overjoyed to see him. Sardic Loy gave him a crushing hug while Aida constantly touched Lok's arm or held his hand, making sure he was truly there. They and their two older daughters asked question after question.

"Why did you leave the Academy?"

"Is Charity still safe?"

"What about Realta and Callum? Did they escape Kanton, too?"

Lok assured them that Charity was safe, and that she loved the Academy. They both made a lot of friends and were learning a lot. And Gareth Haar was at the Academy, too. Safe and sound. Brother Malaky confirmed that Callum and Kel were also at the Academy, but he didn't know where Realta was, only that she escaped the capital.

He omitted the part about Charity examining a skeleton up close, though he told Esme. She laughed until tears rolled down her face.

"Of course Scholar Wik donated his body!" she said once the laughter subsided.

The Loys thanked Lok for the reassuring answers. There might be a war, but as long as their little girl was safe, that was all that mattered. He promised to tell them more about the Academy next time they were in the village, and he would keep an eye out for any letters from Charity or Realta.

"You can visit any time," Sardic told him.

He thought about writing Charity a letter. He still felt bad about not leaving a note, and there was so much to tell. Her oldest sister, Nina, was engaged to Ander Millar, and the wedding was scheduled for autumn. But part of him doubted the letter would arrive. Last he heard, the fighting had spread to East Bridge.

And plenty of people asked Lok to demonstrate his ability. They were genuinely curious, only hearing about Thanes in stories. Mayor Gan still kept his ability a secret. He steered clear of Lok and Brother Malaky and wore a wide-brimmed hat, covering his earring. A purple earring identical to the chaplain's.

"I don't understand why he keeps it a secret," Malaky had confided to Lok and Kuno. "Empaths are quite rare these days. Not as rare as Farsights, but—"

"Let the man have his secrets," Kuno interrupted.

But Lok understood. He saw fear in some people's eyes. Control fire? What exactly did that mean?

Lok showed them little things. Causing a flame to jump from one candle to the next. Snuffing out a fire by snapping his fingers. Simple things. Nothing to fear.

Most clapped their hands or complimented Lok, but others just smiled tensely and excused themselves.

Lok heard footsteps running towards him. Henry Saxon, the healer's assistant, skidded to a halt, panting and coated in sweat.

"Lok, listen, I need a favor." Henry placed his hands on his knees, took several rasping breaths, and then said, "Esme left this morning to visit the Cambel farm. Both their boys have fevers. But she forgot to deliver some pain medicine to Tirnan Hagan.

He broke his leg a few days back. Anyway, he lives on the other side of the village. I have to take it to him, but I can't leave Healer Zall by himself. I'd ask Estrid or Master Patyn, but they aren't riding into town till this afternoon. Will you watch him for me, please? Oh, and he's asleep. I gave him a sedative. Should stay that way until I get back. It will only be a half hour. Please, Lok. Mistress Haar is counting on me."

Lok held up his hands, motioning for Henry to calm down. He stole a glance at the healer's house. Silent.

Being in the same room as Healer Zall sounded worse than torture, but the man was asleep. What harm could he do? And doing a favor for Henry was the same as doing a favor for Esme. Yeah, he could watch a sleeping man for Esme. He nodded.

"The Gadyeni bless you, Lok." Henry shepherded Lok inside the healer's house. Dread settled in Lok's gut like approaching storm clouds.

No! Healer Zall was asleep. A sick, unconscious man could not hurt him. And he was a Fire Elemental. He had no reason to fear anything.

Except being turned into a living weapon.

"Just sit by the bed," Henry whispered, pointing at a high-backed wooden chair. The healer laid on the bed, muttering softly. Henry grabbed an envelope and hurried towards the door. "It will only be thirty minutes. Forty at most. Mistress Hagan tends to ask questions. Doesn't really trust medicine." He glared at Zall. "Guess we have him to thank for that." Henry left, closing the door.

Lok moved the chair farther away and sat down. Bright sunlight streamed in from the windows, making the place seem friendlier. He glanced around. Bundles of herbs hung from the ceiling. Jars of powders and medicines lined the shelves. Charity must know all of those by now. Names, how to make them, which ailment they treated.

What if Charity had returned with him? She loved the Academy, but she could learn just as much from Esme. And she would be safe. Kuno wouldn't have liked it, but...

Healer Zall shifted, muttering.

Lok froze like a deer in a hunter's crosshairs, eyes fixed on the healer. His skin was deathly pale. Blue veins lined his thin arms, the wrist bones clearly visible. One eye cracked open.

No, don't wake up, don't wake up!

"Tolman boy," Zall muttered, his voice groggy. He peered around. "Where's Esme?"

"She went to help someone. She will be back soon." He hoped.

The healer squinted his eyes and scoffed. "Course she's helping someone. It's her damn job. What about the other one? The one here yesterday?"

"Running an errand."

"And you're the best replacement Esme could find?"

Lok nodded.

Zall cursed under his breath. "Fool boy. Don't know a damn thing about medicine, do you? Well, do you?" he snapped.

Lok shook his head. He stole a glanced out the window. No sign of Esme or Henry. His palms began to sweat.

"Didn't think so. You look like him, you know? Your father."

Lok blinked. He never expected to hear this from the healer. A drawing of Ansonn Tolman hung in his bedroom, and he saw a few similarities. A thin face. Dark, round eyes. But it was hard to compare yourself to someone you never met.

"Good man, Ansonn. Helpful. Folks said he could fix anything. So, this fool agrees to mend somebody's roof. Goes up, falls off, breaks his bloody spine." Zall swallowed, catching his breath. "Should have killed him then and there, but he hung in there. Four days. Said he had to make it. Had to see you. Never did. Died in his sleep. Your mother was by his side the whole time. She cried and cried. Then, two months later, you came along. Damnedest thing. You didn't cry." Zall looked at Lok curiously. "Not a sound. Just looked at everything, then fell asleep in Vera's arms."

Zall tried to sit upright, but his arms gave out. Lok propped him up on a pillow.

"Thanks. I hear there's a new war raging. That's true?"

Lok's blood turned to ice. He nodded.

"Bloody fools. Didn't they learn nothing from their fathers and grandfathers? I was in the last one, you know? Worked as a field surgeon. Wanted me to fight at first, but I was better with a scalpel than a sword." Zall closed his eyes, and his breathing grew slow and steady. Lok thought he was asleep, but Zall continued. "Doesn't mean I didn't see battles. Lots of them. Out in the Caslan Valley where there ain't no hills or forests to hide in. All open country. Bad for hiding."

Zall fixed his eyes on Lok. "I was with a group of civilians. Their village got caught in the crossfires. They were originally Nowani, but we had won that land a month earlier, so the Nowani wanted it back. The villagers didn't care if they were Nowani or Teyrnian. They just wanted to be left alone.

"Lots of people got hurt. People on both sides. The villagers wanted to get away. We agreed to help. Snuck out in the middle of the night so the Nowani patrols wouldn't see. But we couldn't make any noise. A twig snapping meant death. This one woman had a cat." Tears shimmered in Zall's eyes. "Refused to leave it behind. Treated it like it was a child. Some people are like that with animals. Never understood why. Anyway, we were creeping along, so quiet I could hear the blood rushing in my ears. And that damn cat started meowing. I told her to shut it up. That bloody thing was going to get us all killed. Shut it up! And the cat shut up. Once we got someplace safe, safe enough to light a lantern, I saw the woman crying, cradling the cat. It was too quiet. I… She broke its neck…"

Zall's face contorted as sobs racked his frail body. Lok stared to back away, but Zall latched onto his shirt collar, pulling him closer, their noses almost touching.

"I didn't mean for her to kill it!" he cried. "I just… We would have all been killed. I didn't… It was a cat, damn you!"

Lok, his heart pounding in his throat, tried to pry away the healer's fingers, but the man's grip was too strong.

"It cried and cried! I didn't… And you. Not a damn sound. Why?!" The healer's eyes flashed white hot. "Why didn't you cry?!"

Lok's heart skipped a beat. He jerked away, his shirt tearing, but Zall held on, glaring hatefully.

The door slammed open. Esme Haar, like a hero out of a story, rushed into the room. She latched onto Zall's hand, pressing her fingers into his wrist. His grip faltered. Lok stumbled backwards, falling onto the other bed. Esme crouched beside Zall, holding his hand.

"It was a cat, Esme." Tears choked Zall's voice and streamed down his face. "You don't get sent to the Abyss for making someone kill a cat, do you?"

"Of course not. You need to rest." She gently smoothed down Zall's white hair. The healer closed his eyes, crying softly. The crying soon subsided as his breathing steadied. Zall, thankfully, was asleep. Esme turned her attention to Lok. "Where is Henry?"

Lok showed her the note about Henry running an errand.

Esme frowned. "For what?"

"Delivering medicine for Tirnan Hagan's broken leg."

"I delivered that medicine on the way to the Cambel farm. Why did…?" Esme sighed through her teeth. "What are you doing here?"

"Henry asked me to watch Healer Zall. Did I do something wrong?" Would Esme get mad at him? He had never heard her yell or curse, not even when the healer called her husband a monster. But Kuno never yelled before the war began. What if the war had changed Esme, too?

"No, Lok. Henry should have been more thoughtful." Esme looked at Zall, counting under her breath in time with his breathing. "Next time, I'll tell Henry to get a chaplain, or better yet, communicate my schedule with him. Did Darran hurt you?"

Lok shook his head.

"I think you should head back home. I don't have any more house calls today."

Lok slowly rose to his feet, both legs numb and shaking. The moment he stepped out the door, he took off running.

✳✳✳

The Scholar was nervous, but he hid it well. Better than most people Meredith knew. The other man, Luckson, a traveler from East Bridge, sat between the Scholar and West, facing her. He smiled politely, even at her. Didn't he know she was Hiraethi? The other guests kept their distance, eyeing her and the knife at her belt suspiciously. Meredith rolled her eyes. She wouldn't stab anyone unless they gave her a reason.

"So, what brings a Scholar all the way out here?" Luckson

asked.

Kuno watched as Lok left the inn. His Student, not his son. And neither was West. Why had the Scholar lied about their relationship? The Hiraeth might live in forests, but they knew about the Academy. Lying only cast him in a bad light.

"We wanted to get away from the war. The fighting is getting worse," Kuno explained calmly. He clasped his hands tightly, anxiety threatening to overwhelm him.

Meredith kept the observation to herself. She had learned early on not to reveal people's true emotions. Villagers pretending to be nice became embarrassed or angered when a little girl caught them in a lie. Her Great Mother always admonished that she was slow to learn.

But those who were slow to learn were most in need of schooling, right? She never understood why the Hiraeth didn't send their Thanes to be educated. Shouldn't an educated Empath be more valuable to the tribe than an uneducated one?

Luckson grimaced. "Have other Scholars followed your example? Yours is the only white cloak I've seen in Vala."

"Most Scholars believe the Academy's political neutrality will protect them."

"Well, shouldn't it?"

Kuno stared at the table. "It did in the last war. But Teyrnas was still the capital. Now that Queen Isla is living at the Academy and so many other refugees, people are treating it like the new capital. And Lok..." Kuno shifted uncomfortably. "My Student is a special case. Both of them."

"Yeah. Elementals. I thought they were extinct."

"You and everyone else." Kuno forced a smile. It quickly faded. He eyed Luckson warily, a hunter realizing he was not alone in the woods. "Why are you traveling through Vala, Luckson? Heading to Caman's Pass?"

"I'm looking for someone. My brother." Luckson chewed on his lip. Meredith tried to read him, but his emotions changed, as though a letter had shifted to another language halfway down the page. "We... Well, there's bad blood in the family. I kept trying to reach out to Rikard, but he always shoved me away."

"Why not leave him, then?" Meredith asked.

"Do you have siblings, miss?" Luckson leaned forward, folding his arms on the smooth table.

"Two older sisters and a little brother."

"Do you love them?"

"Of course I love them! What kind of question is that?" Heat rose in her face. Yes, her sisters had constantly hovered over her growing up, getting her into trouble more times than she cared to count, but they were her family. Her flesh and blood. And they had acted in her best interest. Of course they told Mother that little Meredith climbed the massive oak tree, attempting to jump from one branch to another. She likely would have broken her arm or worse if Mother hadn't interrupted and Father hadn't climbed up to carry her down.

She had been furious. She was eight years old. Perfectly capable of climbing down by herself, thank you very much. Father tried and failed not to laugh, smiling at her tirade. Her little brother had inherited that wonderful, warm smile. A heaviness settled over her heart. How long before she saw Mahai's smile again? Months? Years?

Too hasty, her Great Mother's voice said. *Always acting. Never thinking. Just like your fool of a father.*

Was her twenty-year-old self just as rash as her eight-year-old self?

Of course I can climb this tree and jump from one branch to the next.

Of course I can run off and join the Scholar.

"That's the same question you asked me," Luckson replied.

Meredith's face burned red. "I… I apologize for asking a foolish question."

"There is no such thing. Right, Scholar? I didn't catch your name."

"I didn't give it." Kuno grimaced. "I'm sorry. It's Kuno Surylin. Have you met many Scholars? Scholar Lucan Kalgan, perhaps?"

"No, can't say I have."

Kuno's anxiety faded, but a thin layer of nervousness, like ice coating a pond, laid over his calm demeanor. "I was just curious. I hope you find your brother."

"Thanks. So, is this young lady your Student, too?"

Meredith jolted. Young lady? Young ladies wore silk gowns and adorned themselves with emeralds and diamonds and sapphires. Not trousers made of tanned animal hides and shirts of homespun wool. Nor did they carry knives on their belts.

"Yes," Kuno replied without hesitation. "Meredith is an Empath."

"I see. Care to give a demonstration? If that's all right," he quickly added.

"Your call," Kuno told her.

"West, too?" West asked, his eyes wide and bright.

"Ladies first," Luckson said.

Again calling her a lady. Did Luckson need eyeglasses?

She focused on Luckson. His emotions were surprisingly easy to read now. Strange. A minute ago, it was impossible. "You are curious and happy to have people to talk to. It has been a long time. And you're sad." Tears pricked Meredith's eyes. The emotions latched onto her, invading, turning into her own. No! These emotions did not belong to her. "You... You're so sad." Stars above, had this man ever been happy? His smile was nothing more than a mask.

Luckson merely nodded, the mask never slipping. "Very good, Miss Meredith."

"What happened between you and your brother?" *And how come I couldn't read you a minute ago?* Was he a Thane, too? A kind that could block Empaths? A Minder?

"I think that's a bit personal," Kuno admonished, but Luckson waved him away.

"No, it's fine. Rikard and I were once very close. We did everything together. But one day, he started to change. I..." The mask almost slipped. "We all tried to help him, but he went further and further down the wrong path. Everyone says I should give up, but I want to help. And if Rikard puts up another fight..." He shrugged and turned his attention to West. "So, what can you do, young man?"

Kuno pointedly cleared his throat, getting Meredith's attention. He whispered, "No more personal questions."

Meredith nodded. She vowed to learn this lesson quickly. And she could still feel Luckson's sadness. She looked at West.

"Fire and water," West said happily. He stood, grabbed a candle from the nearest table, and set it next to the one on their table. He pointed at the fire burning in the fireplace, large enough to boil a kettle of water, but small enough not to add to the summer heat. "Fire." He gestured, and a small flame separated itself from the fire and flew in a wide arc over the common room. One of the serving girls dropped the mug she was polishing, and it shattered. The flame jumped onto the wick, lighting the candle.

"That was—" Luckson began, but West cut him off, motioning for the fire to jump to the next candle. The flame leapt back and forth, back and forth. West smiled, his gray eyes shining like stars. The two flames merged into one midair and then split into three. They flew to the bar, lighting a small candelabra. The serving girl who dropped the mug screamed. West beamed a smile at Kuno and Luckson.

"How did you learn that?" Luckson asked. Pure awe overpowered his sadness. He locked eyes with Kuno. "Did you teach him?"

"I wish I could take the credit, but West already knew how to do this and more by the time I met him. And Lok is just as talented."

"The innkeeper's son. She must be so proud."

Meredith wasn't so sure. Vera Tolman and her new husband said all the right words, but deep down, they were afraid. She stared at her son as though he were a stranger. A potentially dangerous one.

The inn's front door opened, spilling bright light into the room. Henry, the healer's assistant, sauntered over to the bar.

"Hey, Laurel, can I get a mug of cider?" he asked the serving girl with a smile and a wink.

Laurel giggled, her fear disappearing. "No problem, Henry."

Henry turned around, facing Meredith's table. "Hello, Scholar Kuno. How are you this morning? And you, Master Luckson? Has your headache improved?"

Kuno replied that he was well, and Luckson said that his headache was gone, thank the Creator. Laurel handed Henry a mug of cider. He joined them at the table.

"How is Healer Zall?" Kuno asked.

Henry took a long drink of cider and sighed heavily. "Honestly, he isn't better, and he isn't worse. I just need a break. You understand?"

"Then Esme is watching him?"

A guilty smile crept onto Henry's face. "Not exactly. I asked Lok to watch him."

"You what?" Kuno raised an eyebrow.

"Zall is asleep. And Esme will be back soon. Five minutes tops." He took another sip.

Meredith sensed a weariness from the young man, but very little concern.

"What if he wakes up?" Kuno asked.

"Doubtful. Esme gave him a sedative before she headed out. He'll sleep like a dead man for hours."

Kuno muttered under his breath.

"Like a dead man is not a phrase I would use for a severely ill person," Luckson said.

Henry shrugged and finished his cider. "Have you tried the cider yet?" he asked the group. "Master Brun is an excellent brewer."

"I don't care for strong drinks," Luckson replied, a hint of disdain lacing his words.

The door burst open, and Lok stumbled in. His eyes were wide, fearful. He immediately went to Kuno but halted, seeing Henry. White hot anger evaporated the fear.

"Lok, what's wrong?" Kuno asked.

Lok stormed towards Henry and punched him square on the jaw, knocking the healer's assistant out of his chair and onto the floor. Henry stared upwards, dazed. His lower lip bled.

"Lok, stop! Stop, Lok!" West cried, gripping Meredith's arm. She started to shrug him off, but then she saw the candles. The flames burned as hot as a kiln, the wax melting in seconds. Flames shot into the air, long and thin, and burning hotter. Stars above, he could burn down the whole inn!

"Lok, calm down," Kuno said. "Did something happen with Healer Zall?"

"Scholar, control your Student." Luckson edged away. The candles burned down to the stands. Molten metal coated the table, and the flames charred the wood. Laurel ran into the kitchen, calling for Mistress Tolman. West gripped Meredith's arm tighter.

Kuno placed a gentle hand on Lok's arm. The young Thane just stared at Henry. His mind swirled with anger and confusion and fear. Too many emotions for anyone to think clearly.

West, whimpering like a kicked dog, clapped his hands together. Air rushed around them, meeting at the table, and snuffed out the flames. West pointed at the fireplace, and the wind rushed up the chimney. The common room grew strangely quiet and still.

Meredith caught West as he slumped forward. The boy seemed to weigh half of what a person his height should.

Lok blinked and looked down at Henry and his bleeding lip. Fear banished anger. He started shaking and looked at Kuno and the table. Dark char marks and liquid metal stood in the candles' place.

"Lok, it's okay. Write down what happened—"

Lok took off running, climbing the stairs two at a time. Meredith heard a door slam.

Vera Tolman, the cook, Laurel, and another serving girl rushing into the common room.

"What happened?" Vera asked. "Is everything all right?" Her eyes fell on the burned table. "Did Lok...?"

"It was an accident, Mistress Tolman," Kuno said reassuringly. "He just needs some time to rest."

"But he hit Henry!" Laurel cried. Henry blinked and looked around, dazed.

"A misunderstanding. Nothing more," Kuno said. "Please, it's fine."

Vera stared at Kuno for a long moment, searching. Searching for the lie, Meredith had no doubt. Vera sighed, finding no evidence, and retreated to the kitchen. The others followed her, whispering.

Luckson slumped down in a chair, his blue eyes as wide as the moons. "How did...? Air. He controlled air."

Kuno reached down and helped Henry to his feet. The young man tentatively touched his busted lip and winced.

"You should be able to help yourself, healer," Kuno said acridly.

Henry glared at him. "Does he always attack people? Should I tell Mistress Tolman the type of man her son really is?"

"No." Kuno met the glare head on. "Here's what is going to

happen. You heal yourself, and I will speak with Esme. Make sure she hears the truth." Kuno strode out of the inn, his white cloak billowing out behind him.

"Whoreson," Henry muttered. Meredith wanted to give him a black eye to match that busted lip, but she restrained herself.

Vera peered out of the kitchen door and scanned the room. She slowly walked towards Henry, eyeing his bleeding lip. "What really happened?"

"Just a fight," Henry relented. "Just a stupid fight, Mistress Tolman." Henry hurried outside.

Vera glanced at Luckson, Meredith, and West. The poor woman was conflicted, love and fear fighting for dominion. Love won over, and Vera went up the stairs, calling for Lok.

West still clung to Meredith, as weak as a newborn deer. His skin felt warm, almost feverish. She helped him into a chair and sat next to him.

"You saw that, didn't you?" Luckson asked. "He controlled air. Young man, you said you can control fire and water. Why didn't you mention air?"

West titled his head like a little bird. "Too fast. Slow, please. Slow Teyrnas."

Luckson repeated himself, making the sentences clearer.

"Air?" West stared at the burned table. His eyes widened. "Air! Fire and water and air." He glanced up the stairs. "Lok just fire. Why?" he asked Meredith and Luckson.

"Do I look like a Scholar?" Meredith asked.

"I have no idea," Luckson said, running a nervous hand through his hair. "I have no bloody idea."

Fear crept into Meredith, making her skin crawl.

Luckson was lying.

31

Three of Nine

Val folded his hands on the table and waited. He had introduced himself to Alani and Jerryk a few days ago, pretending to run into them at the docks and recommending that they stay at the same inn. Both readily agreed, no doubt sensing the same warmth from him as they sensed from each other. He made sure to see them often, saying a friendly word and then moving on, acting like a curious traveler. People were more apt to believe someone they were familiar with than a complete stranger.

He made that mistake with Ambassador Ekene, thinking the Learner would be able to fully grasp their roles. But Ekene had dismissed Val as a madman at best and a heretic at worst.

And Realta had been so trusting until she learned that Val worked for Queen Gallia. Should he have kept that secret? Earned her trust first? No, despite being a rare Thane, she was one of King Logan's servants. She would have learned the truth eventually.

Roping Kanton into his plan had backfired spectacularly. The man terrified Realta. Any chance of her believing and trusting Val shattered. By now, the Eastern monarchs had discovered Kanton was a Thane, hiding in their midst. And probably Val as well. The infighting would begin any day now, like a spark in a sun-dried field. The sooner, the better.

He hoped they went easy on Gallia. He tricked her, too.

"I don't want to believe it," Alani said slowly. Via Linking, Val translated everything she and Jerryk said into Teyrnian and his words into their languages. Alani, a prominent historian in the Cayuga Islands, was familiar with Linking and routinely hired Minders when meeting with foreign Scholars. But Jerryk was harder to convince. Minders were very rare in the Konorgree Desert, regarded as little more than legends.

"But I've had this feeling the past few months," Alani continued, "drawing me here. Drawing me to you and Jerryk. We both felt it the moment we boarded the ship." Her dark brown eyes, shining like stars, met Val's gray ones.

Alani Kisei, a Manipulator Thane, was in her late forties, and she wore it well with just a touch of gray at the edges of her dark, wavy hair. And she was completely devoted to her work. Until Springtide, or the Vernal Equinox as Cayugans called it. To her colleagues' shock, she abandoned the archaeological dig she had spent the last two years researching and booked passage to Saethyr.

"The Wise Ones of my village said I was destined for greatness," Jerryk Ordaryk's Son said. "I thought they meant as a Healer." Jerryk lived in a small village in the Konorgree Desert, an isolated region of Eltriar that rarely saw outsiders. The villagers lived in vast cave systems, growing crops in underground cisterns that opened up to the sky and venturing out in the cool of night.

The Wise Ones, their term for Farsights, had instructed Jerryk to journey first north, across the open desert, and then east across the ocean in order to fulfill his destiny. A journey that meant leaving behind his wife and two young daughters.

"But you believe me?" Val asked tentatively. West believed, but the boy was so trusting. Val could have told him that humans lived on the moons and traveled between the stars on winged horses, and he would have believed. Probably. The boy was not as stupid as he appeared.

Alani sighed and brushed a long lock of hair away from her face. "All evidence points to you telling the truth."

Val's heart soared. She believed him!

"But why has the Lost One returned now?" Jerryk frowned, his pale eyebrows knitting together. "Don't get me wrong. I believe your words, and I feel that strange warmth you described. But why me? I'm a Healer. I have no desire to fight anyone."

"Who said you had to fight? Perhaps your role is to prevent death. If any of us are injured, you will Heal us. And not suffer the side effects," Val added, smiling.

Jerryk shrank back, pulling the hood of his sand-colored cloak over his face. He was the only male Healer in his village. The first one in four generations, though the ability was prevalent among women. His mother and grandmother were powerful Healers, able to mend broken bones and banish fevers with a touch. But they experienced horrible fatigue and spent days, if not weeks, in bed after each Healing. Jerryk, however, felt nothing. No fatigue. Not even a simple, tired feeling. He wasn't even hungry or thirsty. Identical to Elizar, the original Healer.

"So, where are the others?" Alani asked, glancing around the small tavern. A handful of other patrons occupied the room, all lost in pleasant conversation. And none of them were drunk. The Saethyrians viewed drunkenness as a moral weakness. The notion dated back to King Anselmo, who had been famous for his drinking. So famous that word had reached Queen Amachi of Jemayrt. The queen invited Anselmo to the capital, a diplomatic meeting disguised as a friendly visit.

She waited until the king was thoroughly drunk before broaching a new treaty: Jemayrt would aid Saethyr in all wars as long as Saethyr paid a yearly tribute. Anselmo agreed, woke up the next morning with a skull splitting hangover, and forgot about the new treaty until Queen Amachi's generals marched into the palace and demanded the yearly tribute.

The king tried to nullify the treaty, saying that he hadn't signed it in a clear state of mind. His own council turned on him, saying that he was never in a clear state of mind. The Saethyrian government honored the tribute every year for the next two hundred and eighty-seven years. And no one in Saethyr moved to abolish it, even after an elected council replaced the monarchy, citing it as a reminder to remain sober. The Jemayrti used the tribute to fund orphanages and hospitals, so at least the money was put to good use.

The wine, as a result, was watered down to the point that it was merely colored water. Barely a hint of alcohol. Val would have to wait until they returned to Teyrnas to get his hands on the real stuff.

A light dawned in his mind, as clear as the sun on a cloudless day. Teyrnas. They were returning to Teyrnas. He knew it as certainly as he knew he was One of Nine. The only question was when.

"What are you smiling about?" Jerryk asked, his sky-blue eyes studying Val from underneath the hood.

"I know where to find the others. Teyrnas. Two of them are there already. And I believe I can convince two more to join. The Learner and the Dreamer."

Alani shook her head. "I just can't believe you found a Dreamer. Historical records state they died out centuries ago."

"Alani, the Creator allowed the Gadyeni to give humans Thane abilities in our hour of greatest need. Why not gift another human with the ability to Dream?"

"I guess." A hint of doubt remained, but Alani sounded intrigued.

"Not to mention the histories say the same thing about Healers." Val pointed at Jerryk. The man was shocked when he learned that Healers no longer existed outside of the Konorgree Desert's foothills. Alani made a note to research it once they found a decent library. When confronted with a puzzle worth solving, her mind latched on, refusing to let go.

Val hoped she would set that brilliant mind to defeating the Midnight King.

Jerryk pushed back his hood, revealing hair so blond it was almost white. The same shade as King Syleck's hair. He pointed to the three of them. "Healer, Manipulator, and Minder. And you mentioned a Learner and a Dreamer. What are the two in Teyrnas?"

"An Elemental and an Empath." Had West found her yet? He was certain Meredith would sense the connection, but would West be able to communicate their mission to her? Would she believe a simpleton?

"How do you know this?"

Val frowned. "What do you mean?"

"You are a powerful Minder," Jerryk said. "You've already proven your capabilities. But how do you know the ability of Thanes you've never met while Alani and I do not? Aren't we all Summit Thanes?"

"I don't know." A darkness overshadowed Val, like a well-traveled path obscured by a sudden fog. Familiarity turning into uncertainty. He could not explain it. He just knew. The same way he knew how to breathe. "Maybe it's because I was the first to realize my position."

"How? Who told you?"

Again, Val did not have an answer. Neither for Jerryk nor for himself. He gulped down watery wine. *Damn it!* He needed to find a real drink and fast.

"Perhaps it's different for all of us," Alani said. "I felt a compulsion to drop everything and travel across the Tharys Ocean. You were told to travel here by the Wise Ones. Val, your knowledge appears to be intuitive. How did the others discover their positions?"

"I told them." Val drummed his fingers on the polished table. He hoped that Realta and Chinasa would recognize him the same way he recognized them. But both viewed him as a stranger, fighting him every step of the way until they fled the palace. A smile crept onto his face. The palace. "Meeting them was not a coincidence. We were all at the Teyrnian palace at the same time. Practically arrived on the same day. As for West, I merely followed a hunch. The Ullmhir led me to him."

Jerryk leapt to his feet, the chair crashing to the floor. Every head in the tavern turned their way. He made an X across his chest and muttered under his breath, glaring daggers at Val.

What had...? Val glanced into Jerryk's mind. *Fire and smoke!* The Konorgree villagers believed the Ullmhir, called the Shadow's Children, were monsters created by the Midnight King. They lurked in shadows and captured people on moonless nights. Three people going missing from the village during Jerryk's childhood only strengthened the belief.

Val slowly rose to his feet. He kept his face neutral, calm. He needed this man on his side. The Nine must be united. "It's not what you think, Jerryk. The Ullmhir mean us no harm. In fact, most of them are curious about our world. Think of them as Scholars."

"You consort with the Children of Shadow," Jerryk said in a low, harsh voice. The daggers in his eyes glowed red hot. "And you dare try to gain our trust?"

"Calm down." Alani stood and placed her hands on his shoulders, standing on her toes. Alani was a head shorter than most women, and Jerryk stood two inches taller than Val. "The Ullm-hir are just a story. A myth."

"They are no myth," Jerryk said through his teeth. "My people know they are evil."

"Well, your people are wrong. Sorry." Val stepped forward. Jer-ryk drew a curved dagger from his belt, holding it at eye level. One patron screamed and others ran for the door. Jerryk claimed he didn't want to fight anyone, but there was murder in his eyes. He remembered the people who went missing. Names, faces. The loved ones left with no explanations other than superstitions. Fighting against another human? That went against Jerryk's vows as a Healer. But fighting the ally of evil monsters? Yes, willingly.

Val held up his hands nonthreateningly. *Yeah, probably not a good idea to insult the man's beliefs.*

Taking a deep breath, he tried again. "I had to find you as quickly as possible." Val reached out to the remaining patrons. The tavern owner. The servers and cooks. In their minds, he translated his words into Saethyric. "The Midnight King walks Eltriar once more." Furtive, fearful whispers spread like smoke, filling every corner, seeping out. "You can feel it. Don't deny it, Jerryk Ordaryk's Son. Yes, I traveled with the Ullmhir, but only so I could find you in time. Had I traveled by horse, Eltriar would have lost the war against the Midnight King long before I found you. If I thought for one second that the Ullmhir were evil, I never would have taken the risk. The fate of the world is too important."

Jerryk studied Val. He grimaced, muttering under his breath. A prayer? "You traveled into their Realm?"

Val nodded. "It's not so bad. Just darker. They only have the stars to see by. I saw other people there," he quickly thought up a lie. "Other travelers. None of them were afraid. None of them were in pain. The Ullmhir treated them as you would treat a guest. They might look like shadows, but that does not make them creations of the Midnight King. In fact, they're much older than the Thousand Years War."

"That's right," Alani chimed in, her dark eyes softening. "My colleague is an expert on ancient mythology. Only a few frag-ments remain, but stories predating the Thousand Years War mention the Ullmhir. The stories called them Star Children, or something similar. Doesn't that prove they aren't monsters?" By the question's inflection, Val didn't think Alani was convinced by her own explanation.

Jerryk glared at Val, the dagger posed to stab him in the eye or the neck. "I cannot trust a man who consorts with Shadows."

Fine! Time to play the guilt card. "Okay. It's okay, Jerryk. You don't have to join me or the other Thanes. But can you really sit out this war and allow the Midnight King to conquer Eltriar? Would you allow your daughters to grow up in a world of shadows? If they survive. The Thousand Years War claimed hundreds of thousands of lives. Perhaps millions." Val slowly inched closer. Jerryk's knife hand trembled. "Do you think your village will be safe because it's small and out of the way? The Midnight King won't leave any part of Eltriar untouched."

The nervous energy in the tavern increased tenfold. Frantic whispers turned into panicked shouts. Some people started crying. Several ran out of the tavern, word of the Midnight King escaping his prison on their lips. Val bit down on his tongue. Smiling would put Jerryk back on guard. But it was hard not to smile. The plan was working perfectly!

"This is your destiny, Jerryk," Val continued. "You cannot walk away from destiny. Realta and Chinasa tried to run, but fate will force them down this path, and it will be more painful for them. Don't make the same mistake. Don't allow Yaila and Evian to live in a world of darkness."

"I…" Jerryk exhaled through his teeth and returned the knife to his belt. "My daughters' lives are more important than my opinion of you. If I must work with a man of shadows in order to protect them, then may the Old Ones forgive me."

Val smiled. A soft, relieved smile. The Old Ones. The Konorgree people believed the Gadyeni were gods, a belief Val plan to use to his advantage. He looked at Alani. "What about you?"

"You have my word. I will fight the Midnight King alongside you." She laughed bitterly. "And here I thought I was making a historical discovery."

"Better. You're making history." Val placed a firm hand on her shoulder. Pride shone in Alani's eyes, a Scholar seeing the culmination of her life's work. They were the words every historian wanted to hear.

Now he just had to find the words that Chinasa Ekene and Realta Haar wanted to hear.

32

Interrogation

Gallia quickly closed her notebook as the door to her private sitting room opened and shut like a gust of wind. Liona, her long skirts swishing, strode over to Gallia and halted in front of the desk. Her eyes were bloodshot.

"Is everything all right?" Gallia asked. She placed the notebook in a drawer. The ink wasn't dry, but she did not want Liona to view her journal, to read what she really thought of Kenda and the Coalition. Thoughts that could land her in a well of trouble.

As though I'm not in trouble already!

The Coalition had convened three times in the last half week, and Gallia had only been invited to one meeting. She learned of the other two through the guardsmen talking as they patrolled the halls. She immediately went to confront Kenda.

"Don't worry yourself," Kenda said, dismissing Gallia with a wave of her hand. A trivial annoyance soon forgotten. "The war is going in our favor. We don't need you to complicate matters."

Translation: she did not want Gallia's potential weak spot for Thanes to influence the Coalition.

Syleck and Eskandar had stopped talking to her. Eskandar always averted his eyes and made a half-hearted excuse whenever she walked into the room. And Syleck glared at her murderously.

She saw no point in explaining for the hundredth time that Val had lied about his ability, that he tricked her the same way he tricked all of them. No one listened.

And to think she almost married Valentin!

Liona locked eyes with Gallia. "Guardsman Kanton will be here to escort us to the dungeons in a few minutes. Don't panic," she said as Gallia opened her mouth. She closed it, and the younger woman continued. "The others won't lock us in there. Not now. You must go along with whatever they have planned.

Your loyalty is in question."

"Is that what the other meetings were about?" Her palms began to sweat. Who had influenced who? Syleck with his hated for Thanes or Kenda with her need to be in control? Or had they influenced each other, sowing more distrust?

And why meet in the dungeons? Had they decided to get rid of Gallia the same way they got rid of Ayrdeen? Did Liona know the truth about her father's disappearance? Did anyone?

Liona gave her a small nod.

A sharp knock sounded at the door.

"That's him," Liona whispered. She sat down on a divan by the window, smoothing down her dress and tucking a lock of hair behind her ear. She motioned for Gallia to sit.

Gallia half sat, half collapsed onto her chair. Her knees had turned to water, and her heart pounded in her chest and throat. She took a deep breath. King Cedric did not raise a coward.

A sharp pain tore at her heart. She wished Cedric were here. She could use his guidance. His quick, calculating mind. Cedric never tolerated people who tried to intimidate him.

The knock sounded again.

"You may enter," she called. Thankfully, her voice held steady.

Guardsman Dane Kanton sauntered into the room, one hand resting on the hilt of his sword. He still wore the dark blue uniform of the King's Guard, but he had ripped off the raven symbol. And the collar was turned upwards, drawing the eye to the burn scars lacing the left side of his face. They had faded to white and pale pink, hardly noticeable at first glance. Gallia's eyes traveled to the man's ruined ears. The lower halves of the lobes were hacked off.

A sickening feeling formed in her gut. She could not imagine Val, the man she loved, committing such violence.

Strange. Did she still love him?

"Your Majesty." Kanton gave her a low bow. The guard never failed to be polite. But why did she get the impression that he was mocking her? "I am to escort you to a meeting on Queen Kenda's behalf." His eyes fell on Liona. "Oh, Queen Liona, I didn't realize you were here."

"Am I needed as well?" she asked, staring out the window.

"Queen Kenda didn't say. She only asked for Queen Gallia."

"Then I shall stay here." Her voice sounded choked. Gallia took a half-step closer and saw that she was crying. By the stars, what happened at the last meeting? Had Kenda strong-armed her as well, or was Liona merely thinking about her father? Her own father had passed away a year ago, and she thought about him constantly.

Creator, why couldn't you have waited one more year before taking my father to the stars?

Cedric, she knew, had had his fill of war.

"Queen Gallia," Kanton said. "We mustn't keep Her Highness waiting."

"Very well. Lead the way."

Gallia followed Kanton down the long corridors, the guard limping slightly. Val, supposedly, had slashed the guard's leg as well.

She pulled her mind away from Val and gazed at the paintings and sculptures as she walked. She hadn't paid attention to them when she first walked down these halls, escorted by King Logan and leading an entourage of hundreds. Servants, personal guards, and dozens of soldiers hidden in their ranks, waiting for Kenda to break character and give the signal to attack.

Logan didn't know it, but he had led the way to his own death.

Bile rose in the back of her throat.

Guards lined the halls, men wearing the white and black of Tirshay, the orange of Galion, and red and blue of Tarod. Only Kanton wore dark blue. But that did not stop the others from deferring to him. A few even bowed.

This man is a traitor.

Kanton switched sides the moment he learned that King Logan was dead. What did that say about loyalty? Looking at the uniforms, she saw none of her own guards.

Kanton led her down a winding staircase to the palace's lowest level. The dungeons. Walls of cold, gray stone narrowed, closing in on her. Her throat tightened.

"Why meet here?" she managed.

"It's Kenda's idea," Kanton replied, as though it were answer enough. Queens did not need to explain themselves, especially not the Queen of Galion.

At the base of the stairs, Kenda stood with Eskandar and Syleck. Their eyes were ice cold.

The queen wore a red and orange silk gown, mimicking the torches burning on the walls. The kings wore plainer clothes. Simple trousers with wool coats. They could have passed for villagers.

A quartet of Galionic soldiers stood against the wall.

"What is this?" Gallia asked. Each member of the quartet carried a long sword, the same as Kanton. Muffled weeping echoed from down the hall. A prisoner? Gallia tried to get a better look, but Kenda blocked the way.

"Gallia, my dear, we have a very important question for you." Kenda's gaze snapped to Kanton. "You are dismissed. Wait at the entrance. We wouldn't want anyone to get cold feet."

Kanton bowed low and marched up the stairs, a hand on his sword.

"What's going on?" Gallia's voice echoed off the walls. Heat rose in her face. She hadn't meant to speak so forcefully, but she wanted an answer.

Kenda glared at her. "Is King Logan dead?"

Gallia blinked. "Pardon?"

"Have you become hard of hearing?"

"No."

"Then answer my question."

Nausea crept up her throat as her mind went to King Logan, lying dead from a knife to the heart. Blood pooled under the body, staining the carpet. Some had stained the soles of her shoes. She had burned them and thrown away the ashes.

"Yes, of course he's dead. You saw his body."

Kenda shook her head. "I was rendered unconscious, remember? I recall you and your pet Thane saying that Logan was dead. Was he?"

"Yes, I…" Gallia squeezed her eyes shut, but that only brought the memory into sharper focus. "I stabbed him. He is dead."

"Did you check his pulse?"

"No." Gallia didn't know what a pulse was, but she refused to look ignorant in front of Kenda. "I saw his body, and the blood…"

She swallowed. "What is this about, Kenda?"

Kenda turned to Syleck and Eskandar. "Did either of you see King Logan's body?"

"No," both men replied in unison. Syleck's glare grew colder.

"And do you know what became of his body? Where was it taken?"

"I don't know." Gallia assumed the guards took it away and buried it. She'd been too distraught to think, and with Val leaving…

"You don't know," Kenda replied mockingly. "How very convenient." Turning on her heels, she motioned for Gallia to follow her deeper into the dungeon. Gallia followed. She didn't have a choice. Eskandar and Syleck trailed behind them, Eskandar breathing down her neck.

Kenda snapped her fingers. The guards changed formation, standing between each cell. Gallia peered into one. People clothed in dirty rags cowered in the shadows. One man bled from a fresh cut above his eye.

"What happened to them?" Gallia asked. Her eyes went to the guards. To their weapons. The swords and daggers were sheathed. Were they bloody? No, she shouldn't jump to conclusions.

"These people," Kenda spat, "claim King Logan is still alive. Now, how is that possible when you killed him?"

Gallia had no words. Kenda… Kenda had tortured these people. She stared at one woman. Blood matted her hair, and her lower lip was split. And the way she cradled one arm suggested that it was broken. Gallia glanced at the nearest soldier and spied blood on his sleeve.

"Did you hurt her?" she demanded. The guard stood at attention, as silent as stone.

"He only speaks Galionic," Kenda said. She walked up to the cell. The woman shrank back. "This will end once she tells us the truth. So, Aska Liddyn, what do you know about King Logan? Is he alive?"

The woman looked at Kenda with blank eyes.

Kenda spoke to the guard in Galionic. He unlocked the cell and drew a knife. The woman did not move, did not scream as the guard sliced her arm.

"Stop it!" Gallia screamed. She grabbed Kenda's arm. The other queen flung her away, her eyes full of fire.

"This woman owns a tavern in Tullcrest." Kenda pointed at Aska Liddyn as though she were an insect. "Five men stayed in her rooms for two months. One man was tall with dark hair and eyes. Another wore a patch over one eye and spoke with an accent. The third was a cripple. A worthless beggar likely sticking around for a hot meal. The fourth was little more than a boy. And the fifth never showed his face. Never left the room or said a word.

"All five fled Teyrnas on the same night. Less than a week later, rumors about King Logan being alive began circulating. Starting in Tullcrest. What should we conclude?"

"That five men stayed at her tavern. And like thousands of others, they fled the city. Are you suggesting that one was Logan O'Kelwyn?"

Kenda smiled coldly. "Do you know how long it takes to recover from a stab wound?"

"No." She didn't like where this was going.

"Let's say one month. Or a month and a half to recover full strength. The bartender stated that these four men carried the fifth into the tavern late at night. The fifth badly injured. He was bedridden for three full weeks. The others brought him food and water. He never mentioned his name. None of them did."

"When was this?"

"The same day we took the city. The same day you claimed King Logan died. Did he?"

Gallia suddenly felt very small, surrounded by enemies on all sides. "Who was the bartender? How do you know he told the truth?"

"Trust me. Every word was true."

She shuddered, squeezing her eyes shut. "You tortured him."

"We encouraged truthfulness."

"Where is he now?"

Kenda gave her a patient smile. "He outlived his usefulness. So tell me, Gallia Toutain, what really happened between you and Logan?"

"I already told you! What more do you want from me?" Surely

Kenda didn't plan to torture her, too. She would call her guards and...

What guards? Where are they?

She only saw one of her guards in the last two days, and he had deferred to Kanton, bowing low. Kanton, who stood at the top of the stairs, just in case she made a run for it.

"Long live King Logan!" a man cried.

Kenda motioned to a guard, flicking her fingers rapidly. The man drew his blade and marched towards the cell.

"Long live King Logan!" Aska Liddyn yelled. Her dull eyes were now wide and full of life. She smiled at Gallia. The smile tugged at Gallia's memory. Something about the way one side was higher than the other...

Kenda glared at Gallia. "Eskandar, Syleck, escort Gallia to the library. I will join you momentarily."

Before Gallia could protest, they grabbed her arms, pinning them to her sides, and forced her up the stairs. They passed Kanton at the top. The guard greeted her with a smug smile.

Gallia tried digging in her heels, but the wooden floor was too slick. Every time she jerked her arms back, Eskandar dug in his fingers. She felt bruises forming.

Syleck shouldered the library door open, and he and Eskandar shoved Gallia into the nearest chair.

Her eyes darted back and forth. The library appeared empty, but guards could be hiding behind the stacks, waiting for her to make a move. She rubbed her arms and looked up at her former allies.

Syleck sneered and stalked out of the library.

"Where are you going?" Eskandar asked.

"I need some air." The door slammed shut, echoing.

Blood rushed in Gallia's ears, in rhythm with her racing heart. She bit down on her tongue. This was not the time to give into panic. She had to be strong. She had to be the woman her mother and father raised her to be. "How long has Kenda been torturing people?"

The King of Tarod looked down, studying his boots. "A few days. We... I don't know how she found those people, but all of them claim King Logan is alive. Until they were brought here."

Eskandar grabbed a chair and moved it closer, the legs scraping the floor. He sat in front of her. "Gallia, tell the truth. What really happened after Logan knocked Kenda unconscious?"

"I already told you." But was it really true? She didn't remember stabbing Logan. Only her and Val standing over the body. And Val left suddenly, just before everyone discovered he was a Thane. But which type of Thane? Some could alter people's memories or cast Illusions. Others were just smarter than average, more at home with books than people.

Had Val tricked her? Had he confided in Logan, exposing the plot? Did Logan use Val to fake his own death, tricking the Coalition into thinking they won? It made sense. Val must have lived his entire life in hiding, fearful of being thrown into a prison or exiled. Or executed. In Teyrnas, as an ally of the king, he would be free.

Did Val secretly hate her?

Could she blame him if this was true?

The library door opened, and Liona strode towards Eskandar. "Kenda told me to watch her. She needs to speak with you."

"About what?"

"She didn't say," she replied acridly.

Eskandar rolled his eyes.

Liona watched the door close and stood there, silently.

Gallia wished the younger queen would speak. She understood why Liona was upset. Kenda must have shown her the dungeons, informing her that Logan might be alive. Should Gallia speak first? But what to say? If Liona was on Kenda's side, there was no point in conversing with the enemy.

A numbness settled in Gallia's heart. When had Kenda turned from ally to enemy? Was the change so subtle that Gallia missed it? No, more likely the woman was never Gallia's ally. She had been played like an infantryman in a game of Queens, moved across the board, believing her role was more important than mere arrow fodder.

Liona grabbed Gallia's wrist and hurried her through the maze of stacks. She shoved open a narrow door and led the way down a flight of stairs.

"Where are you taking me?"

"You're getting out of here."

"Hold up." Gallia yanked her wrist out of Liona's grasp. Liona looked at her impatiently. "Where are we going?"

"Kenda isn't the only one asking questions. My father went missing the same day King Logan was presumed dead. The same day four men escorted an injured one into a tavern. The bartender said one wore an eyepatch. Not many people in Teyrnas have different colored eyes. Too easy to spot." Liona took a deep breath. "I think Logan and my father are both alive. And I want you to find them."

"Why me? Why not you?"

"Because Kenda still trusts me."

Gallia's heart sank. "Is she planning to…?" She didn't want to say it. Didn't want to imagine the fate Kenda intended for her.

"She said nothing specific. But we all know what she's thinking. Come. We don't have much time." Liona hurried down the stairs. A few servants, all loyal to the Eastern Coalition, passed by and gave respectful bows. Gallia's heart pounded in her throat. What if they told Kenda? Would she punish Liona?

They paused at an outer door, facing the courtyard and the palace's imposing walls. The sun shone brightly on the tiled walkways. A trio of Marish soldiers in red coats marched by.

Liona held her head high and walked towards the stables. Gallia followed a step behind. The soldiers saluted Liona and continued their rounds. The cool shadows of the stable enveloped them.

Two men wearing Bran Maro's seven stars on their coats greeted them. One was about fifty years old and thin as a whip. The other was around Liona's age and also had different colored eyes. One brown and one bright green.

"Salti, Reina Liona," said the older man.

Liona gave a formal bow. The men retrieved a brown and white mare, already saddled and bags packed. The younger man handed Liona the reins.

"Grattai, Lari ey Silvamor. Pon darinist ra."

The men bowed deeply and went to check on the other horses. Several other men worked in the stables, absorbed in their work.

"Can you trust them?" Gallia asked, studying the men. She only knew a handful of phrases in Marish and only recognized the word 'grattai'. 'Thank you'. But thank you for what? For helping Gallia escape? Or for helping trap Gallia in a ploy to determine her loyalty? Fire and smoke, why hadn't she agreed to spend time with Liona? She knew nothing about the girl. For all she knew, those tears were the product of lemon juice.

"With my life." Liona handed Gallia a bundle of papers. "Take this. They will get you past the Marish soldiers guarding the Highway. And hopefully into the Academy. There are changes of clothes in the bags. They're ragged, so you'll blend in."

Gallia was at a loss for words. "Why are you doing this? Why align yourself with me?"

"Because you're the only one I trust." Liona lowered her voice. "The guards at the North Gate will let you pass, but they change shifts in half an hour. Go to the Academy. Find King Logan and my father. Tell them what's happening here."

Gallia looking into the girl's eyes. Bright and determined. And a sense of longing. To go with Gallia?

No, this was not a trick or a test of her loyalty. This was Gallia's chance to escape. Perhaps her only chance.

"What will you do?"

A smile crossed Liona's lips. King Ayrdeen's smile. "All I can to undermine Kenda and her ilk."

Gallia climbed into the saddle. The horse tossed her head once and looked at Gallia with big, brown eyes. She smoothed down the horse's mane, reassuring the animal. The horse turned towards the door and stamped a hoof. She flicked the reins and led the horse into the light.

The North Gate was up, the guards glancing around anxiously. *I should be afraid. How come I'm not afraid?*

Instead, she felt a strange exhilaration. A sense of determination. She was finally acting like the daughter King Cedric had raised.

She spared a final glance at Liona. The young queen smiled despite tears brimming in her eyes.

Gallia sharply flicked the reins. The horse galloped out of the gate and into a ruined city.

33

Ravens

A sinking feeling settled in Braedan's gut. First, two travelers showed up in the middle of a summer storm that turned the roads to mud, and these travelers just happened to know each other, acting like this was some big coincidence. And now, a battalion of Averillian soldiers marched in.

War horns sounded just after daybreak. The entire village was in a panic. Everyone feared the Nowani or the Tarodic had crossed the Nerin, but the soldiers did not attack. They stood in formation while the commander met with the mayor's council. The commander explained they had marched across the mountains in order to defend Kereu when the Eastern Coalition attacked.

Not if. When.

The council allowed the battalion to set up camp in front of the inn.

Five hundred soldiers and an equal number of camp followers covered every available inch of green.

Corey, not wanting to miss an opportunity for business, went out to greet the soldiers, along with the eager innkeeper and those two strange men. Elliza claimed the strangers were harmless, but Braedan wasn't buying it. Elliza had acted funny the last couple of days. Kinda jumpy. Not listening to conversations. And it wasn't because they were trapped with Corey.

Braedan blinked. Trapped? He never associated that word with his employer before.

He's more than that now. Braedan's arm itched. He'd never find respectable work with these scars. He had no choice but to continue working for Corey.

He was now a slave as much as Elliza.

I should have run away with her when we had a chance.

Too late now.

Unless the Jemayrti considered harboring two more runaways.

Speaking of the Jemayrti, Chinasa Ekene and two of the white cloaked Scholars, Adanna and Kambri, stepped outside and halted, seeing the size of the battalion. They exchanged a few words and walked closer, the Scholars holding up their cloaks so the mud wouldn't ruin them. Chinasa glared at Corey as they walked by. He and Corey were not on speaking terms, and the ambassador actively avoided the merchant.

And Elliza and Braedan.

Fire and smoke, how would Braedan bring up the idea of running away if Chinasa refused to look at Braedan? Could he use Realta as a go-between?

"Greetings!" the innkeeper said to the battalion's commander, a man dressed in shining armor with a dark green cloak draped over his shoulders. Averil's oak tree was painted on the metal. He carried a board sword on his belt, and judging by the scars displayed on his bare arms, he'd had a lot of experience using it.

Bare arms covered in scars. Braedan eyed the other soldiers. A lot of them had similar marks. He could sneak away and join the Averillians. But his skin was too light. He'd have to lie in the sun all summer to get tan enough to blend in.

And what about Elliza? If it weren't for the tattoo on her face, she could blend in with the camp followers. Could they cover it with makeup? No, terrible idea. Makeup was bloody expensive, and sweat or rain would wash it off. Perhaps they could find a tattooist. How much would they charge to remove it and then keep their mouth shut?

Granted, if he could find and afford a tattooist, he'd have the impossible task of getting Elliza to agree.

The Averillian commander addressed the innkeeper in Kereuic. The innkeeper smiled and nodded the entire time.

"Doesn't he know we aren't Kereuic?" Corey complained, arms crossed over his chest.

Braedan just shrugged. It was the safest response.

The two men shook hands, the innkeeper bowing. The commander then shouted orders in Averillian, too fast for Braedan to understand. The nearest soldiers saluted and hurried into the camp to pass the order along.

The commander then approached Corey and Chinasa. "What languages do you speak?" he asked in Averillian. A common phrase that Braedan understood.

"We both speak Teyrnian fluently," Chinasa replied before Corey spoke. Corey scowled and quickly turned the expression into a smile. Blink and you miss it. Braedan had missed it for the first year he worked for the man. If only he had seen the warning signs sooner.

The commander nodded. "Okay. I am not fluent. But it will work." He took off his helmet and bowed. "I am Commander Adri Maddrel. My company was sent across the Vogel Mountains to aid Teyrnas. Rumors said the Tarodic will cross the river in Kereu and travel north. They will attack Byyar if that kingdom aids Teyrnas, which I think they have. Have you seen anything suspicious? Spies maybe?"

"I'm afraid not," Chinasa replied. Again speaking half a second before Corey. "This village is remote, and we've spent the last few months trying to avoid the war."

Commander Maddrel frowned. "I fear that is no longer possible. Forces in Averil and Lowyrn are crossing the mountains now. We are the first. Are you loyal to Teyrnas?" he asked dubiously.

"Of course," Corey said, placing himself between Chinasa and Maddrel. "I'm Teyrnian, born and raised. And Ekene is the Jemayrti ambassador to Teyrnas. We had to leave the capital when those damn Nowani invaded. Honestly, we're lucky to be alive."

The commander raised an eyebrow.

"It's true," Chinasa said. "I was in contact with King Logan before…" He sighed heavily. "Before his assassination. Would you care to speak inside? King Logan's personal adviser, Mistress Cray, is with us."

Commander Maddrel's eyes widened. "The king's personal adviser?" He addressed the soldier nearest him, speaking rapidly in Averillian. Braedan caught a few words. 'King', 'adviser', 'understand'. The commander then said, "I would very much like to speak with her."

Chinasa led him inside the inn. The front doors were opened wide to let in the warm summer air. Mistress Cray sat at one table with Realta and Serena. Realta had made a full recovery. Not gonna lie, Braedan was worried about her. Overstraining oneself was no joke. Most Thanes in the East got caught because they either hid their abilities for too long or they lashed out, fearing imprisonment or worse, only to fall ill afterward, making it easier for them to be captured. Academies prevented a lot of that, Braedan guessed. Being a Hound, he had no desire to set foot in an Academy and find out. Too many Auras at once.

Braedan waved at them. Realta waved back, her black Aura sparked with purple and gold. Serena just stared at him. He couldn't get a read on her. Serena was always jumpy and acted like Braedan was going to hit her. Granted, mercenaries didn't inspire a lot of trust, but he never threatened her. Not intentionally.

As Chinasa and Commander Maddrel walked inside, Elliza slipped out. Her face was ashen, and she trembled from head to toe.

"I'm sorry, sir. I cannot find it."

Braedan's hands went to his knives. Corey's prize dagger went missing during the storm. Around the same time those strangers arrived. Corey could not help dragging the damn thing out. He always did. Tricking people into thinking it was a valuable prize instead of a cheap trinket, and that his goods, by extension, were far more valuable. The ploy worked four times in five. Not everyone was a gullible villager.

Braedan assumed the strangers were thieves and stole the dagger.

Corey was incensed. But instead of confronting them, he ordered Elliza to find the dagger. She bore bruises from yesterday's failure.

The merchant grounded his teeth. "You stupid girl. Can't you see where it will be found?"

"I tried. But I don't know. I'm sorry." She bowed her head. Long black hair obscured her face and the faint bruises along her jaw.

"Maybe it wasn't Savastian or Adso," Corey muttered, glaring at the Scholars. His eyes blazed. "The Scholars! One of them must have stolen it as leverage. The dagger in exchange for their freedom."

"I honestly don't think—"

"You are not paid to think," Corey snapped. "Conduct another search," he told Elliza. "Tear up their wagons if you must. I need that dagger!"

"Why?" Braedan asked. "It's just a trinket. Have a new one made."

The murderous look in Corey's eyes made Braedan regret every word. Why was Corey acting like his house was robbed in the dead of night and his loved ones held for ransom? The dagger was worthless. He said so himself. Just a cheaply made dagger, the leather hilt lacquered white and a bit of glass to mimic a diamond. Sure, it looked like it cost a small fortune, but it was all for show. A merchant's trick.

Corey grabbed Elliza's hair, yanking her closer. "You care about her?" he asked Braedan. "Then help her look. Or I'll make you watch next time." He shoved Elliza into Braedan's arms and strode into the inn. He sat at the same table as Chinasa, Shasta, and Commander Maddrel. Chinasa stared at Corey hostilely, and Shasta raised an eyebrow. The commander gave him a confused look. Who did this man think he was, joining without permission?

You'll find out soon enough, he thought bitterly.

He glanced at Realta and Serena, now seated at the bar. The two girls watched Corey warily. Two deer who had spied the hunter first.

Elliza stifled a cry and clung to Braedan. He smoothed down her hair and realized that they were alone. The soldiers had better things to do, and the two strangers were nowhere in sight. Great. If they really were thieves, they likely saw the battalion and bolted. They'd never find that bloody dagger.

What does it matter if we ain't here either?

"We don't have to put up with him anymore. We can leave right now. Hide among the soldiers."

"No."

"I know blending in will be hard for you, but we can cut your hair or buy makeup from a camp follower."

"No."

Braedan let out an exasperated sigh. "Do you want him to keep hurting you?"

"He won't be hurting me after much longer."

"Did you have a Farsight?" *Don't get your hopes up.* Elliza's Farsights were always accurate, but she waited for things to happen instead of making them happen.

So do you, idiot. The scars itched maddeningly.

"The dagger does not belong to Waylar Corey," Elliza said quietly. "It never did. It merely needed him to bring it closer to the true owner."

"Come again?" The sickening feeling in his gut worsened. *Oh no. Elliza, please tell me you didn't steal it.*

"Realta took it," she continued, as though reading his thoughts. "I told her to. She will bring it to the Windrose. It is his to wield."

"Do you mind speaking Teyrnian?" Fire and smoke. She stole it! No, she told Realta to steal it. Same thing, really. But why? Why do something she knew would earn her a beating?

Elliza shook as though she had awakened from a deep sleep. "I'm sorry, Braedan. I can't explain it right now. But it's very important. Do you believe me?"

"Yes. But Corey beat you black and blue last night. Why—"

"It must be."

"No, it must not be. Elliza, what…?" Elliza looked at Braedan, eyes wide, but she didn't see him. The faraway look only meant one thing. "What do you see?"

"Shadows. Men and women of shadows. Everywhere we turn. We cannot escape. The City of Lights. The Eternal City. We must reach it before they can find us. Nine of Nine in one place." Tears streamed down her face. "The Midnight King," she whispered. "He… His people are searching for us. They want to destroy us before we can stop him. Braedan, help us, please!" She broke down sobbing and clung to him. He wrapped his arms around her. Her slight frame shuddered, a sapling in a storm.

"It's okay. I'll help you. But you have to tell me what's going on."

"The ravens."

"What ravens?" Braedan stole a glance inside the inn. Corey was deep in conversation with the commander. And by conversation, Corey was talking incessantly while the commander listened. So long as Corey didn't overhear this Farsight, Braedan didn't care.

"You are one of them. So is Serena."

"Okay. Is that a good thing or bad?" Ravens were the symbol

of Teyrnas, but the Nowani viewed them as carrion feeders. Bad luck. Braedan hadn't felt terribly lucky as of late.

"You and Serena must decide for yourselves. So must the other ravens."

A trio of Averillian soldiers walked by, studying Braedan and Elliza. Did they understand Teyrnian? Braedan glanced around, seeing more soldiers and camp followers eyeing them. Two people who obviously were not Kereuic. Fire and smoke, what if Corey told Commander Maddrel that Braedan was Nowani? Would the commander treat him as an enemy spy? Kill him before he could explain?

Yet another threat to keep everyone in check.

He led Elliza to the other side of the inn, near a stand of shady trees. Their branches swayed in the warm breeze. Summer always came early in the south, and most years it refused to leave until half the Northern Realm was coated in snow.

"What do ravens have to do with the Midnight King?" Braedan asked once he was certain they were out of earshot.

"One sits in his left hand. One is tempted, and the rest are free."

"The rest. How many, exactly?"

"Eight, including you and Serena. Two hide from the world, and one does not know what she is. And the one in Alberik's hand." Elliza shivered. "He might be lost forever. Only time can tell."

"Alberik? The Midnight King?" Braedan wished Elliza would shut up. His mother always prayed for protection against the Midnight King, and she believed speaking about him drew his attention, cursing you with bad luck. But if it concerned him, then Braedan needed to know.

"His wardens search for us. Me, and Realta, and Chinasa. We are safe here, for the moment. But the Wardens sense our presence. If it were only one or two, perhaps we could evade them, but three in one place draws too much attention."

Braedan's blood raced through his veins, every muscle ready to fight. "Savastian and Adso. Are they—"

"No. They are allies. We can trust them. I've already said that," she added, a bit exasperated.

"The battalion, then? Are they hiding among them?"

"The Farsight did not reveal any faces."

Bloody great. An enemy they could not identify. And working for an entity that had been defeated millennia ago. *Wait a minute.*

"Why are they working for the Midnight King?"

Fresh tears streamed down Elliza's face. She breathed deeply, trying to compose herself, but the tears kept flowing. She finally told him. It was weird. She was crying her eyes out, but her voice was so calm. Determined, even. She told him about Nine Thanes, and the second war between them and the Midnight King. The current war was just a preview.

"Do Realta and Ekene know?"

She nodded. "That's why Realta must be protected. Don't tell Corey she has the dagger, even if he hurts me again."

Braedan balled his hands into fists. "I'll keep your secret. But if Corey lays a hand on you, I'll cut it off."

"It is not his fate to die at your hands, Braedan Sutter."

"Who said anything about dying? I want the bastard to suffer."

Elliza sighed. "Perhaps two ravens are lost."

The words hurt. Braedan didn't understand why, but they hurt. The same way everyone in the village saying that little Braedan Sutter was special after treating him and his mother like dirt for years hurt.

Footsteps tread on the soft grass. Braedan spun around, reaching for a knife. He halted, seeing Realta and Serena. Serena, watching Braedan's hand, hid behind Realta. It didn't accomplish much. She stood half a head taller than the other girl.

"What now?" Braedan asked, relaxed his hand.

"Tarodic soldiers are gathering across the Nerin," Realta said. "The Averillians plan to attack them."

"Okay, then we're leaving?"

"They won't let us," Serena said. She glanced at Realta. The girl prompted her to continue. "The commander wants this to be a surprise attack. He thinks we will spread the word if we leave."

"That's ridiculous," Braedan said. "None of us are Tarodic."

"So we claim," Realta said bitterly. Chinasa, Braedan guessed, had tried and failed to convince Maddrel of that simple fact.

"Then we're stuck here?"

Realta nodded grimly.

Braedan looked at Serena. Another raven, whatever that meant. Did Serena know? She was an apprenticed linguist. Maybe the word held symbolic meaning. He could ask... No, he couldn't just ask. The girl always acted jumpy around him, searching for an excuse to leave. But he caught her staring at him a few times. Maybe she did know. He had to find a way to ask without frightening her.

Adso, wearing his tattered gray cloak, rounded the inn. From this distance, the man looked like a Shade from a campfire story.

Realta muttered under her breath.

"What's that?" Braedan asked.

"Nothing." Realta walked towards Adso. The man spoke softly, too softly to overhear. Realta whispered heatedly, and Adso replied, his face calm and gentle. The girl hung her head and followed him inside.

"Does she know him?" Braedan asked Serena.

Serena nearly jumped out of her skin. "What? I..." Her eyes darted to the corner and then back to him. "He spoke with her and Chinasa. I, um... Why does it matter?"

"I guess it doesn't."

Serena hurried inside.

That did not answer his question, but he let it slide. The girl wanted to be secretive, fine. He'd find an answer. Maybe Shasta Cray knew something about ravens.

Thunder rumbled in the distance.

"Another storm," Elliza said.

Bloody great.

34

The Stuff of Dreams

Realta sat in the middle of a long, semi-circular bench, Dreaming about the original Nine. She Dreamed about them individually a few times, and tonight she succeeded in Dreaming about all Nine at once, meeting for the first time.

The massive room contained twenty rows of benches, all curved with a walkway in the center that descended into the ground. The benches were craved from dark wood, polished to a mirror-like shine. Even the white floors were polished. Large windows lined one wall, providing ample sunlight. The bottom level ended in a half-circled shaped platform with a lectern and a slate board covering the entire wall. The Nine sat on the lowest bench.

Nervous energy radiated off them. Some paced around. Another picked at her fingernails with a thin knife. Revin. A young warrior who had lost her village when the Midnight King's army attacked, leaving her with two choices: fight or die.

She recognized the others from previous Dreams. She spotted Domni and Jol immediately. Domni looked younger than fifteen, and he sat huddled, clinging to his coat and eyes fixed on the floor. And Jol's hair was black without a trace of gray. He spoke as a paced.

"This is insane. Don't get me wrong. I understand why you two are here." He pointed at Revin and Z'Kai, a tall woman with curly black hair and a dark complexion similar to Chinasa's. She was an army messenger who had grown up in a warrior society, created out of necessity to fight the Midnight King. Before the war, her people had been farmers and poets.

"But he," Jol jabbed a finger at Domni, "is a child!"

Domni shrank as every eye fell on him.

"Son, how old you are?" Jol asked.

"Fifteen," he whispered. A tear fell down his cheek.

"Fifteen," Jol repeated in disbelief. "And you, young lady, how old are you?" he asked Olita, who sat on Domni's right. Realta was shocked by how much she resembled Elliza, like a long-lost sister with the same small frame, dark hair, and oval-shaped eyes.

"Nineteen," she said, smiling and meeting Jol's gaze.

"I'm nineteen, too," said Faryna, the Elemental of the group. She wore flowing green robes embroidered with wind, fire, and raindrops on the sleeves. She tucked a stray lock of blonde hair behind her ear.

"Great. Three children. Tell me I'm not the only one who thinks this is madness!"

"The entire world is falling into madness," said Balthazar. Standing a head taller than most men and wearing a blue and green uniform, the leader of the Nine Thanes cut an impressive figure. He looked and acted like a proper king. Strong, noble, willing to defend his people, and without a trace of noble blood. His dark brown eyes surveyed the group. "I don't understand why the Gadyeni chose three teenagers to number among us. Nor do I understand why they chose a world class complainer to be our Empath."

Jol crossed his arms and mumbled under his breath.

"But I trust their judgment." Balthazar turned to Domni. Folding his hands behind his back, he asked, "Tell me, young man, how vivid are your Dreams?"

Domni slowly glanced around the room. He faltered as his eyes fell on Balthazar. He stared at the hands in his lap. "I see them as clearly as I see everyone here."

"And how tired are you when you awake from a Dream?"

"I'm not tired at all."

"Not tired at all," Balthazar intoned. He addressed the group. "Most Dreamers awake feeling fatigued. Others act as though they hadn't slept at all. But this boy can Dream every night for a week and experience no ill effects. That is why Bas chose him. And you, Elizar, do you experience fatigue the same as other Healers after you mend a bone?"

"No," he said, shaking his head. He was a skinny man with thinning, brown hair who wore eyeglasses. Not most people's image of a hero, either.

"And Leodas, what is the limit of your ability?" he asked the Manipulator, a man with fiery red hair.

Leodas fidgeted. "Well, I work in construction."

"That doesn't answer the question," Revin said, pointing at him with her knife.

"Well, maybe I don't have an answer." Leodas licked his dry lips. "Look, my job is to lift heavy materials with my mind. It's not like I have a set of scales in my head that tells me one beam weighs two hundred pounds and an arch's keystone weighs four hundred. I just do my job."

"I think you will find," Balthazar said, pacing around the platform, "that none of us experience ill effects. We don't become fatigued or overstrained or burn out. We are at the height of our powers. The Summit. That is why the Gadyeni chose us. Age has nothing to do with it."

"But I don't want to fight anyone," Domni said, almost too quietly to hear. Jol shot him a hostile glare, a far cry from the friendship he showed the young man as he laid dying.

"I don't think we have a choice," Olita replied.

"But I can't fight. I'm an artisan's apprentice. I don't know how to use a sword or..." Tears welled in his eyes.

"And you think I do?" Faryna questioned. "I'm a priestess. My job is to worship the Creator and help others along their spiritual paths. I don't know how to fight, but I know the Midnight King doesn't care. Sooner or later, he will bring his fight to my country. To my parents and sisters. And to you."

Tears leaked out as Domni squeezed his eyes shut. Two nights ago, Realta Dreamed about Domni and his older sister fleeing their village when the Midnight King's army attacked in the dead of night. The people had expected an attack. All the other villages along the highway had been destroyed, and they were next in line. Instead of running, they prepared, handing out weapons and stocking supplies. And then they waited. And waited.

Three months passed. Word spread that the Midnight King was marching north, away from their village. They had been spared.

Or so the Midnight King led them to believe.

He attacked without mercy, ordering soldiers to set fire to the houses and create barricades on the roads, shooting down anyone who tried to escape.

Domni and his sister Dyna ran as their parents shielded them.

"Don't look back," Dyna screamed as they ran and ran.

They made it to the next town. It too had been attacked but not as badly. They were taken to an orphanage. A temporary shelter until they were transported to Luroradi, the ancient capital city. A city of thousand, millions. Teyrnas paled in comparison. A rural village with a wooden gate. Domni and his sister were separated within a day. He never saw her again. The people in charge of orphans promised to look for her and set up Domni with an apprenticeship in the meantime. The artisan, an older man who had lost his family in the war, treated Domni as his own son and gave him more responsibilities, seeing his innate talent.

Balthazar placed a large hand on Domni's shoulder. The hand was calloused and tanned by long hours working in the sun. The same as Callum's hands. Realta's heart ached. She didn't want to see these faces anymore. She just wanted to see one face. Her father's. Would she see him again, or would they forever be separated like Domni and Dyna?

"If we win this war," Balthazar said, "no one will have to fight again. But we cannot win without your help."

"How? I can only Dream when I'm asleep. What good will that do in a battle?"

"You think battles just happen? They take planning. You will Dream then."

"Dream about what?" Fear crept into his voice.

"The Midnight King."

Domni stiffened. The room grew eerily silent. The Midnight King, the entity they were destined to fight. But only Domni had seen him. He caught a glimpse of a tall man on horseback as he ran for his life. A man shrouded in darkness.

The young Dreamer swallowed and slowly nodded. "I will try."

The Nine Thanes froze, turning into living statues.

Realta stood, completely baffled. Glancing out the window, she saw a bird frozen in flight, like a painting. What on Eltriar...?

Soft footsteps padded the polished floor. Realta sighed through her teeth as Bas, the Gadyeni of Dreamers, walked towards her bench and sat down.

Wasn't seeing this creature every day in waking life not enough?

"What do you make of them?" Bas asked.

"Most of them don't want to be here, including Jol." The man worked as a lawyer, using his Empathic ability to determine whether people in court cases were lying. What would have happened to Callum if an Empath had presided over his trial? Would he be living as a free man, or would the Gadyeni have interceded again?

Bas smiled. "I think the only willing participants were Revin and Elizar. She wanted to avenge her people, and Elizar was tired of putting broken bodies back together." His smile faded. "None of them realized how long they would have to fight."

"Ten years," Realta whispered. She reached up to grab her braid, but it was gone. Her Dream self now matched her real self. Her hand fell listlessly at her side.

"Ten years, five months, twenty-two days." Bas looked Realta in the eyes. His own eyes reflected the night sky, a blue so deep it was almost black.

"How long will we have to fight?" Realta hated asking. She hated that Val had been right. The Midnight King had returned, and she, unfortunately, was One of Nine. A shudder ran down her spine. *I don't want to face Val again!*

How could she after all Val had done? After he murdered King Logan?

"I don't know," Bas said solemnly. "But I know that time is running short. Alberik's powers are returning, and his loyal followers grow bolder."

"The Wardens of the Night." Queen Isla's scream echoed in her mind.

Bas nodded.

"But how can they exist? The Thousand Years War ended three thousand years ago."

"Three thousand years ago, two-thirds of Eltriar belonged to him. If the Nine had not been selected to fight, the entire planet would have fallen to him within the next century. Their leader was defeated, but their beliefs endured."

Realta gripped her skirt with both hands. "How do you know the Midnight King's powers are returning?" she ventured.

"The storms." Bas snapped his fingers, and the massive room transformed into the inn's common room. She and Bas sat near the window, a single lantern providing a small island of light. Storm winds battered the inn, the shutters rattling. Roaring thunder shook the foundation and made Realta's ears hurt.

"I thought summer storms were normal for Kereu."

"One or two a week is common, but four? Five?" Bas shook his head. "And the storms are raging all over the Northern Realm. Soon, the Tharys Ocean will be too dangerous to sail."

"Then, he's an Elemental?" She thought about Lok, the only Elemental on Eltriar. Did being the only Elemental make Lok one of the Nine, too? She was afraid to ask. She didn't want her friend trapped in this madness.

Bas shook his head. "Our powers are different from Thane abilities. Alberik has some power over storms, but only to create. Once created, he cannot control them. Thankfully for you, we are not infallible."

"So, how do we defeat him?"

"You have Hannor, the Sun Dagger. You tell me."

The dagger appeared on the table. The metal shone red and orange in the faint light.

"So, it really is valuable." Realta inspected the dagger. She could just barely see the prism reflected on the table. "Does Elliza know?"

"She has an inkling."

"Why didn't she steal it herself?"

"That is a very good question."

"My uncle Kel says it's good to ask questions." She placed the dagger between her and Bas.

The Gadyeni gave her a curious look. "Crown Prince Carwyn O'Kelwyn. Strange. Not many people would prefer being a tutor in a rural village over living in luxury, the heir to a throne. He loves you very much."

Realta narrowed her eyes. "Have you been watching me?" She recalled what Bas said about Callum, how the Gadyeni could not risk her growing up without him.

"Yes. For quite a while. But that is a conversation for later. Your uncle is right, Realta. It's very good to ask questions. It's the best way to learn." Bas rose from his seat. "Continue Dreaming of the Nine, Realta Haar. You will find your answers."

"Only if I know my father is alive."

The storm froze. Everything grew deathly silent. Bas studied her with those dark, dark eyes. Had she stepped too far?

No, he needs me. I'm the only Dreamer on Eltriar. He won't harm me.

I think.

"Realta," Bas said gently, "your father does not factor into this fight."

"But I do." Tears pricked her eyes, but she fought them back. Crying would only make her look like a child. "And if you want me to fight, you will show me a memory of him from today." Realta saw how Bas convinced Domni to join the Nine. He said all the right things and always spoke gently. Domni had been through too much pain. Yelling caused him to shut down, to draw inward. In some instances, he wouldn't speak for days. The artisan and his employees quickly learned to tread carefully with Domni's emotions. And Bas knew all of this.

Realta would not be swayed the same way. Bas would not coerce her with kindness, only to have her dance on his strings. Having diamonds on her wrist did not make her a slave!

Bas smiled, as though reading her thoughts. He waved his arm, and the inn disappeared, replaced by an open sky and hundreds of patchwork tents crowding a field. The sun shone warmly, and a massive building stood in the distance. A building as large as a palace. Her heart skipped a beat. The Academy!

She blinked, and hundreds of people appeared. Men, women, children. All dressed in ragged clothes. A handful wore cloaks of blue, gray, or white, and always moved in groups, casting furtive glances at the ragged people. A guardsman in dark blue stood nearby, leaning against a tree.

"Where is he?" she asked.

Bas pointed towards a row of tents near a long, wooden building. Callum sat in front of one tent. Realta's heart soared as she ran to him, arms outstretched.

She stopped, arms falling to her sides.

This was just a Dream. No matter how badly she wanted to, she couldn't hug Callum. She walked the rest of the distance, a strange mixture of heaviness and joy settling over her heart.

Callum sat crisscross on the ground along with a young man and a woman with short, black hair.

Realta's breath caught in her throat. Marsh. One of the guards working for Kanton. What was she doing here? And why was Callum talking to her?

On second glance, she noted that the guardswoman's eyes were bloodshot and puffy. Marsh stared at the ground, tearing out blades of grass as she spoke. Callum and the young man, Colm, a guard from the palace, listened.

"He nearly shot himself in the foot." Marsh managed a small laugh. Colm leaned forward. A small, red draig lounged on his shoulders, soaking up the sunlight. "He didn't touch a crossbow for a full week."

"Her husband," Bas whispered, though only Realta could hear him. "This memory is from a few days ago. A battle occurred outside the Academy's walls. Her husband was a casualty. Eirica Marsh finds talking about him the easiest way to cope. Callum is an excellent listener."

"Who was her husband?"

"Peydar Wills. Another guard who worked for Dane Kanton before realizing the man's true motives."

Realta glanced around the Academy, searching the faces. "Is Kanton here?"

"No, and neither is Valentin."

Realta rounded on him. "Are you reading my mind?"

"I am guessing your thoughts based on your facial expression and past experience. Rest assured, I cannot read minds."

That was a small comfort. "But you know where Val is?"

"With two more of the Nine. We're impressed by how quickly the new Nine are uniting. I know you dislike him, but it is vital that you work together."

Realta jolted as the dagger appeared in her hand. "And this? What are we supposed to do with it? Stab the Midnight King?"

Bas smiled. "I already bargained with you once this evening,

Realta Haar." He gestured towards Callum, alive and well. But he hadn't fulfilled his promise. Not entirely. Realta asked for a memory from today, not a few days ago. Why? Had something happened to Callum? Before she could ask, Bas said, "Please don't strain my patience." He snapped his fingers.

Realta blinked and found herself lying in bed. Shasta and Serena were both sound asleep despite the raging storm. Rain pelted the window as the wind howled.

She reached underneath the mattress and touched the hilt of the dagger. It felt warm, as though someone had left it out in the sun all day.

Can the Midnight King be defeated with a simple dagger? It sounded too easy. But Bas wouldn't lie to her, right? The Gadyeni wanted the Midnight King defeated just as much as everyone else.

She faced the window. Lightning flashed, blinding her for a second. The afterimage faded to gray.

Is the Midnight King really causing this storm?

Would Lok be able to stop a storm? Charity said he was a Fire Elemental, but if he was also One of Nine, shouldn't he have control over all four elements?

Her eyes suddenly felt heavy. She wished Bas had shown a more recent memory. Anything could happen in a few days, and with the Academy right next to the fighting...

No, she couldn't think that way. Callum was safe. And he would keep Charity and Lok safe.

She hoped.

35

Keys

Charity memorized the pattern. One cloaked person with a hood over their face and gloves on their hands arrived each morning right before daybreak with food and water. Another arrived just after sunset with food, a small washbasin, and a towel, presumably for her to wash with, but there was little she could do with them staring.

These people never spoke, but each was distinct. Two of them were almost perfect. The first was short and on the skinny side. Probably a man. The second was Charity's height and size. Either would work, so long as Yedrick or Edrick did not accompany them.

At first, only Yedrick visited her. Each time, he told her about the Midnight King and the Wardens of the Night. Each time trying to convince her that the history books were wrong. The Midnight King tried to save humanity, to unite Eltriar under one banner. The Midnight King only wanted humans to live in peace.

"Then how come the Thousand Years War happened?" she questioned. "Doesn't sound very peaceful to me."

"The war wouldn't have happened if the Gadyeni had left well enough alone," he countered. "There are plenty of other worlds for them to conquer. If they'd just let Alberik have this one—"

"What do you mean other worlds?" Surely there weren't people living on the moons.

"I, uh... Look, I don't know, okay? This is just what our parents taught us."

They taught you a well of lies!

Charity brought up the subject again the next time Yedrick visited. Except the boy had no idea what she was talking about. After a round of questions he couldn't answer, Edrick admitted to posing as his twin. Yedrick had failed to persuade her, so maybe

Edrick would have better luck. She soon figured out the subtle differences between the twins. Edrick stood half an inch taller. Yedrick's eyes were a darker shade of brown. In less than a half week, she knew each boy by sight. The twins were impressed. Most people in their home village could not tell them apart.

The prison door creaked on rusty hinges. Charity hurried to her feet and stood beside the bars, listening. Only one set of foot-steps. The cloaked person was alone.

Please, let it be the right one. Please, please…

The figure came into view. Relief washed over Charity. It was the one with her height a build. They carried a covered tray and a small flask of water. The person slid it underneath the bars.

"Wait," Charity said as they turned to leave. She bit down on her tongue as hard as she dared, drawing tears. She hoped it was convincing. "How do I join the Wardens?"

The figure stared at her. "Are you serious?" It was a woman's voice. A little deeper than Charity's, but she could fake it. Her freedom depended on it.

Charity nodded, her tangled hair falling into her face.

"So, those boys convinced you?"

"I…" She inhaled sharply and released a shuddering breath. "I don't like fighting. And the Midnight King's reign is inevitable. There's no point in fighting. Do I have to swear an oath?"

"We will know if you are insincere," the woman warned.

Charity dug her nails into her palm, summoning more tears. "I don't want to fight this anymore. I will do anything you ask." She stepped forward, placing her hands on the bars. "Please."

The cloaked woman studied her silently.

Stars above, what if she's an Empath?

"Very well," she said. "I will inform Lucan."

Charity lashed out, grabbed the woman's cloak, and yanked back. The woman's forehead smacked against the bars. She crum-pled to the floor.

Charity froze, watching, listening. Blood rushed in her ears. The woman lied completely still. She crouched down and felt the woman's pulse. Still alive. Good. She didn't want to kill anyone.

She quickly searched the woman's pockets. Her fingers touched metal. A ring. She pulled out a set of keys.

Thank the Creator and all Eight Gadyeni!

She tried the first key. No good. She tried the second, and the lock gave way. The cell door swung open. Free. She was free!

Well, not quite, she reminded herself. She still had to get out of here.

Charity took the cloak off the woman. She immediately recognized her. The blonde woman who accompanied Lucan the other day. What was her name?

Figure it out later.

She donned the cloak. The black material covered her from head to foot, trailing a few inches on the ground. She also put on the gloves. Every detail had to be perfect. For all she knew, Lucan and a small cadre of Wardens were waiting outside.

Pulling the hood over his face, she realized that the material was thinner, allowing her to see while concealing her face. Perfect. Now—

"Shari, are you still in here?" Yedrick called.

Charity muttered a curse she had learned from Lon Millar. Yedrick and his twin, both wearing black cloaks, walked down the hall. They saw Charity and the unconscious woman.

"What happened?" Yedrick rushed forward, but Edrick grabbed his arm and pointed at Shari.

"Charity?" Edrick asked.

Her entire body froze, including her tongue. She could not lie. Neither boy would fall for it. But she refused to spend another day in this bloody prison. She was useless in a fight, but she would punch and kick and scream. All the things she had been too afraid to do the night Kanton attacked them.

Steeling herself, Charity removed the hood and glared at the twins.

"Fire and smoke," Yedrick muttered. "What did you do to her?"

"Lucan is going to kill you," Edrick said, half angry and half terrified.

"Being dead is better than being in this Abyss," she spat.

"Is she...?"

"Alive."

"We can fix this," Yedrick said to his brother.

"Really? How are we going to explain this to Lucan? That the prisoner knocked out his niece and escaped?"

"You won't," Charity replied. She walked up to the boys. "You're going to get me out of here."

Edrick scoffed. "It's two against one. Do you even know how to throw a punch?"

"I know where all your arteries and veins are located. And I know how quickly you'll bleed to death if I sever one."

"With what?" Edrick smirked.

Drat. If only Shari had a knife.

Kanton raised the knife and plunged it into Callum's chest. Callum screamed. She had never heard Callum scream. Not even when he fell and sprained his ankle. The knife was embedded in Callum's chest to the hilt...

She shuddered. No, best that Shari did not have a knife. Charity doubted she would be able to touch the bloody thing, let alone use it.

"Hold up." Yedrick lowered his voice. "What if she takes the vows, right here and now? It's always been an option."

"She won't be genuine. Lucan will know."

"Lucan ain't a Thane. Besides, we can get her out of the Academy later. During the night. No one will know."

"She will expose us." Worried crept into Edrick's voice.

"Is that really a bad thing? The Midnight King—"

"I bloody know!" Edrick exhaled through his teeth. He glanced at Shari lying on the ground and then at Charity. "Can you keep your mouth shut for an hour?"

"Yes." Anything to get out of this horrible place.

"I don't like this," Edrick said to his brother.

"Too bad. We—"

"What is the meaning of this?"

Charity's heart leapt into her throat. The twins spun around as another black-cloaked figure stalked towards them.

Stars above, Lucan...

No, this man was taller and thinner than Lucan, his shoulders less defined.

But he was a Warden. He could throw Charity back in that cell and report the escape attempt to Lucan.

"The meeting starts in five minutes," the man said. "We cannot afford to be late."

"We were on our way, Master... Um, what is your name?"

The men seized Edrick's cloak, pulling him closer, their faces barely an inch apart. "You don't need to know my name." He looked at Charity and then at Shari. "What happened here? Did the prisoner try to escape?"

"She is the prisoner, sir." Edrick pointed at Charity, his hand trembling.

The man released him and stalked towards her. Every muscle in her body screamed to run, but she stood her ground. She was not going back in that cell without a fight. A poor fight, but a fight, nonetheless.

"You escaped on your own?" the man asked, clasping his hands behind his back.

Charity nodded.

"Well done. The Wardens admire resourcefulness. Alberik will reward you greatly." The man headed for the door, brushing past the twins. "Let's go."

"What about Shari?" Yedrick asked.

"Leave her. We cannot tolerate incompetence."

"But she's Lucan's niece," Edrick protested.

"So?" The man waited at the doorway. "Aren't you coming?"

Charity moved first. She had no clue where this prison was located. She would allow the man to lead her outside, and then she would slip away. Hide among the refugees until nightfall and then look for Scholar Maryn or Scholar Roseen, someone she could trust, and tell them the awful truth. The Wardens of the Night were at the Academy.

If she could slip away.

And if they believed her.

The twins fell in step behind her.

"You're just going to let her join?" Edrick questioned the cloaked man. "You know she was imprisoned for eavesdropping, right?"

"Eavesdropping is not a crime." The man's long strides carried him down the corridor and up a narrow flight of stairs. Charity jogged to keep up.

"Scholar Lucan wanted her—"

The man rounded on Edrick, looming over him from several steps up. "Do you believe Lucan Kalgan is the Head Warden here?"

"He is at the Academy," Edrick stammered.

"And in Teyrnas?"

Edrick stared at him slack-jawed.

The man continued up the stairs.

What have you gotten yourself into now, Charity Loy? The Head Warden? That implied he was in charge. But when he said Teyrnas, did that mean the city or the kingdom? A chill ran down her spine. What did the leader of the Wardens have in mind for her? Would he force her to take the vows?

Would it be a choice between life and death?

At the top of the stairs, the man ushered them down a long hallway lined with windows. Charity pulled the hood over her face in case other Wardens were nearby. But the hall was empty and silent, save for the sound of boots treading the dusty floor.

Daylight shone through the windows, and birds sang outside, but Charity derived little comfort from either. She walked closer to Yedrick, two steps behind the Head Warden. Could she slip away now? She glanced at both boys. No, they would alert him, and all the Wardens would join the search. They'd find her before nightfall.

Faint voices touched Charity's ears. She wanted to be happy. It had been days since she heard a real conversation. But she knew they were other Wardens. People who would not hesitate to throw her back in that cell if Lucan ordered it. Fire and smoke, was Lucan there, too?

The man opened the last door on the right and shoved the twins inside. He clamped a bony hand on Charity's shoulder and ushered her forward. The door clicked shut.

Black-cloaked people filled the room, every single one with their hoods down. A tall man who might have been Scholar Lucan stood at the front. He bowed to the cloaked man, and the man returned it.

The twins stood in the middle of the crowd. Charity went to join them, but the cloaked man tightened his grip and forced Charity to stand with him against the back wall.

Her heart pounded in her throat. What was his plan? Would

he expose her to the Wardens? Force her to take the vows? She supposed she could say them without meaning it.

Unless the Head Warden was an Empath.

Unless this was his plan all along.

Why else visit Charity if not to deliver an ultimatum? Join the Wardens or starve to death in a cell.

No, she would die of dehydration long before she starved.

"Do you recognize my voice, Charity Loy?" the man whispered. His voice wasn't as deep now. He adjusted his hood so Charity could peer inside.

She glimpsed an angular face and blue eyes. Blue eyes that reminded her of Kel. Then the man smiled.

Charity bit down on her tongue, stifling a scream.

King Logan. The cloaked man was the King of Teyrnas!

But how could he be here? Queen Gallia had assassinated him.

Well, clearly he survived. But why was he here instead of with the Council or Queen Isla? Why hide among the Wardens?

Logan let out a relieved sigh. "Glad to see you, too. Were there others in the dungeon with you?"

"No."

The smile faded. "Guess they're all here."

"Who?"

Logan shushed her.

The man she assumed was Scholar Lucan raised his hands. The room fell silent. All eyes turned his way.

Charity's chest tightened. What would the Wardens do? What was the purpose of this meeting? Stars above, they might kill her and Logan if they learned they were in disguise.

Logan wrapped his arm around her, holding her close. The sensation felt strangely familiar, similar to a hug from Callum or Kel. And the king did look like Kel.

There will be some things you cannot explain, Kel's warning echoed. He told her that before the Exhibition. Before she met King Logan, a man who strongly resembled him. Was there a connection? Should she ask the king, or would he be just as confused?

"I call this meeting to order," Lucan intoned, his deep voice resonating. For once, Charity hated being right. "Let all who stand here do so in loyalty to our true King."

"We stand in loyalty to Alberik, the Midnight King," everyone except Charity and Logan replied. She huddled closer to him.

"Before us stand four who wish to join us, to be counted among the faithful. I call forth Makson Parr, Alie Mylnar, Nala Alcor, and Ollyn Danlyn."

Charity's heart skipped a beat. Nala Alcor? She was in Charity and Gareth's algebra class. What on Eltriar was she doing here?

Swearing her loyalty to the Midnight King, obviously.

"Which ones do you recognize?" Logan asked.

"Nala."

"You aren't the only Student to go missing in the last month," Logan whispered as Lucan conducted the ceremony. The four initiates stood in front of him. "Your friends have been looking for you. Jaim, Evelyn, Coryn, and Ivar. It's important you know that. They never stopped looking."

"Thank you." Real tears pricked her eyes. And a smile, the first smile in weeks, crossed her face. It felt so good to smile.

"Most of the others were brought here," Logan continued. "A few are still unaccounted for. Either the Wardens sent them away to join groups in other cities, or they got rid of them."

"Why not get rid of me?" Charity wondered.

"Good question. And if anybody asks, my name is Tull."

"So, is anyone else here in disguise? Are a bunch of guardsmen doing to draw their swords and arrest the Wardens?"

Logan sadly shook his head. "Everyone here is loyal. I'll take you to Callum Haar after the meeting. He will keep you safe."

"Callum is here?" Charity bit her tongue. Lowering her voice, she asked, "What about his daughter Realta?"

"No. I…" Logan glanced at the ceremony. The four initiates were on their knees. Lucan talked about the virtues of serving the Midnight King before switching to Old Eltrian. Charity barely understood him. His pronunciations were different from what Kuno had taught her. "We were separated from her while leaving the palace."

"And Master Kel?"

Logan stiffened.

"Did he make it out of the city?" Her chest and throat tightened again. Gareth had been so distraught, so worried about his father.

How would he react if Kel was... *No, don't think that. Not until you know for sure.*

"Are you referring to a crippled beggar?"

"He isn't a beggar. He is my tutor." But plenty of people in Vala treated Kel like a beggar, taking advantage of the Loy's kindness. It wasn't as though he had a choice. His injuries prevented him from helping in the fields or working a trade. And she could not image life without him. He was like an uncle to her and her sisters.

"Yes," Logan replied after a long minute. "He's lurking around somewhere. I wish he just go away."

"Why? He's a good man. I'm sure he will help you."

Logan scoffed. "The dead can't help anyone."

"I thought you said he was alive."

"What? No, someone else. Your tutor is alive."

"We swear to serve the Midnight King in body, in mind, and in soul," the four initiates said in unison.

Lucan bid them to rise and face the group. "Remove your hoods, so that the faithful may know you by sight."

They obeyed without hesitation. Charity was surprised by how young they were. All round her age, except one man who appeared to be in his thirties. After a minute, they donned their hoods.

"May we all walk the True Path," Lucan intoned. The Wardens echoed his words. He then spoke in Old Eltrian, using the same weird pronunciations. Charity only understood a word here and there.

Lucan bowed his head. The cloaked figures bowed and filed out of the room. Logan ushered Charity towards the door. She kept her head down as they passed Scholar Lucan.

"Shari," Lucan said, motioned to Charity. "A moment, please."

Charity's blood turned to ice. She glanced up at Logan. The king nodded. He stepped into the hall and stood against the wall. Lucan waited until the last person exited.

"How did the prisoner seem?"

"She did not speak," Charity replied, hoping her imitation sounded legitimate.

Lucan cupped her face in his hands. Fire and smoke, if he removed her hood... "Have you been crying again?" he asked gently.

Charity wanted to shove his hands away and run, but Shari

would not react that way. And Wardens swarmed the hallways. Running would alert all of them, and she could not risk Logan exposing himself in order to help.

She nodded.

Lucan sighed, shaking his head. "How many times do I have to tell you to get over that man? It was never meant to be anything serious. We needed access to Kuno's research, that's all."

"I understand," she whispered. The pieces finally clicked into place. Shari was a Journeyman. Charity had seen her and Kuno together a few times, discussing Kuno's research and ancient history. She spied their fingers brushing together but thought little of it. A quick gesture. Blink and you miss it. Were they secretly a couple?

Lucan placed a hand on her shoulder. "He was never right for you. You will find a man who is loyal to our cause." He led her into the hallway. Leaning down, he whispered, "Gray is a good man. I think he likes you."

Charity's skin crawled, but she managed a nod. Lucan patted her on the shoulder and walked down the hall. He nodded at Logan and met the other Wardens at the corner. They exchanged a few words and walked away.

She sagged against the wall, placing a hand on her chest. That was too bloody close.

"What did he ask?" Logan said.

"Something about Scholar Kuno's research."

"The Scholar who disappeared?"

"He's still missing?" It made sense now. Kuno must have suspected that Shari was a Warden and left with Lok in order to get away from them. He certainly could not go to the Council with his suspicions. Lucan was on the Council.

Were there others? The very idea made her feel cold.

"Do you think he and Lok knew about...?" She gestured towards the room.

"I don't know. I wanted to find you and the other missing Students first. What was the nature of Kuno's research?"

"He is a historian. Ancient history. He mentioned the Gadyeni Cycle and the Thousand Years War a few times, but never in detail. Could the Wardens want information about that era?"

"Perhaps." Logan muttered to himself, too low for Charity to hear. "We need find out exactly what Kuno was researching. The library is our best bet."

"Wait. What about the cloaks?" Not that Charity wanted to walk around in a dress that hadn't been washed in a full week.

"Lose the hood." Logan strode down the hall, his own hood still obscuring his face. "Are you coming?"

Charity quickly followed, not wanting to be alone in this horrible place.

36

Recognition

Gallia blinked, a small stream of light shining in her bleary eyes. Where on Eltriar...? Her eyes adjusted, bringing a small hole in the ceiling into focus. A missing piece of slate shingle.

She glanced around and saw a brown and white painted mare eating a bit of hay. The painted mare Liona had given her. Right, she was in the stables. At the Academy.

Gallia's arm gave out as she tried to sit upright. A shooting pain lanced up and down the limb. Her head smacked against the wood floor, bringing additional pain.

Using her other arm, Gallia slowly sat up and inspected her left arm. A large gash crusted with ugly red scabs tore across the upper half. Blood stained the sleeve.

Memory returned in a flood.

Gallia had ridden fast at night and rested during the day. The ragged clothes Liona packed helped her blend in. Only a handful of refugees traveled the Highway, along with a small battalion of Marish soldiers. The soldiers stopped people at random, asking questions. Some people were stopped more than once. She almost showed them the papers Liona had given her, but instinct told her not to. After a cursory glance, they left her alone. Just another refugee.

Another night of riding brought her in sight of the Academy's gray walls. And in sight of two clashing armies. Teyrnian and Tirshic soldiers fought and died in front of the South Gate, blocking the Highway. Gallia, her heart in her throat, tried to ride between them, but the soldiers did not care that she wasn't in uniform. She had more than a few close calls with a sword. One Teyrnian soldier almost stabbed her, but he stopped just in time. He called out to the guards at the gate, announcing a civilian.

The guards waved at Gallia, the gate opening inch by inch.

Gallia urged the horse on. An arrow grazed her arm and embedded itself in the wall. Once she was through, the gate slammed shut.

The soldiers never questioned her. The battle raged, and every person able to wield a sword or shoot an arrow was on the wall or outside it. A line of guards forced curious civilians away, including herself.

Instinct told her that these soldiers would show no mercy to the queen who started this war, so she hid in the stables. Her legs trembled so badly that she nearly collapsed as she dismounted.

She sat down on a bale of hay, away from the door. She just needed to rest for a few hours, and then she would find Queen Isla, somehow, and explain—

Gallia never completed the thought. She fell into a dreamless sleep.

And now the cut on her arm burned. She really ought to see a healer. But what if someone recognized her? Would they execute her? Throw her into a cell and let the infection finish her off?

Was the cut infected? She knew nothing about medicine, but she had seen infected cuts. Red and puffy and sometimes oozing a yellow liquid. Her cut wasn't oozing, but it was certainly red. And it itched terribly.

Then again, perhaps it wasn't infected. She could wait it out and see if...

You did not come here to hide, she berated herself. Liona had entrusted her to find Ayrdeen and Logan. If either man still lived. Hiding in a stable and succumbing to infection accomplished nothing.

Gallia looked around the stable, thinking. Her best course of action was to find Queen Isla. But would she welcome her husband's murdered? Even if Logan was alive, Isla had no reason to trust her. She had led an invasion and laid siege to their home.

But she had to start somewhere. Doing nothing accomplished nothing.

The painted horse stared at her with big brown eyes. She had been so exhausted that she hadn't removed the saddle and reins.

Speaking with Isla was a massive step. Almost too big to complete. What if she started with something small? Her mother always approached problems in steps. First, take the easiest step, and then work your way up to the hardest.

Removing the saddle would be an easy step. The harder step, meeting with Queen Isla, would come later.

Gallia slowly rose, her legs still a little shaky, and walked towards the horse. Her arm throbbed as she undid the saddle straps. At this rate, step two would be to see a healer.

Laying the saddle and reins next to the window, Gallia gazed at the Academy. The massive building rose into the sky, far larger than the Academy in Nowan. Granted, that institution was reserved for noble families and the few commoners who could pass the rigorous exams. Gallia had been an average Student, breezing through her classes thanks to her family's status. She'd been far more interested in practicing politics than studying political history in musty old books.

And there were no Thanes. All mention of Thanes being educated at the Nowan Academy had been struck from the records, relegated to the whispers of Students late at night. The terrible Thanes used to walk these halls. Here, Scholars taught Thanes to read minds, to cast Illusions, to control the four elements and hundreds of other horrible things. Here, Thanes learned how to dominate the world.

She wondered how much was true.

Yes, Thane had abused their powers, using them to conquer instead of protect. And where history books and records were full of gaps, oral stories filled them in. Generations of Nowani children heard tales of Symon the Great who raised a rebellion and overthrew the Thanes. Tales of wars fought between Nowan and the Thane monarchs, desperate to recapture what they had lost.

The tales spread eastward, inspiring others to overthrow their corrupt Thane tyrants and govern themselves. First Galion, and then Tirshay. Within a century, the eastern half of the Northern Realm was free.

How were those same stories taught here?

Did the Students at this Academy even care what happened in other kingdoms hundreds of years ago?

People walked by the stables. Most wore ragged clothes and stared ahead with vacant eyes. One person turned, walking towards the stables.

The door! Gallia hadn't thought to close it. Anyone could have walked in and discovered her asleep. It was a miracle she hadn't awakened in a cell.

She spied a stack of crates near the wall. She barely reached them as the person's shadow filled the doorway.

Hiding from a single man, are you? What was wrong with her? A few weeks ago, she would have never cowered at the sight of a single man. She had sauntered into Logan's palace, right in the middle of his exhibition, and met his enraged glare with a smile.

What had Kenda done to her?

A ragged man with a tattered gray cloak draped over thin shoulders shambled inside. His breathing was labored, and he leaned against a crutch, one leg wrapped in a brace. He sat on a wooden bench.

This was what she was so afraid of? A cripple?

Then why are you still hiding?

She stared at the man. A beggar, she guessed. She could run right now. He wouldn't be able to chase after her, not with a bad leg. But what if he alerted the guards? Would they listen to a beggar?

"Esme, I wish you were here," the beggar said with a heavy sigh. He glanced up at the ceiling and rested his head against the wall. The hood of his cloak fell away, revealing a collection of scars on his face. Messy, light brown hair obscured the scars nearest the hairline.

"I don't know what to do," the beggar continued softly. "I've tried everything. He still won't listen. I know I messed up, but how do I ask forgiveness from someone who won't listen?" He covered his face with his hands. "Maybe I deserve it."

The painted mare lifted her head, ears twitching. She walked over to the beggar and nuzzled his messy hair.

"What on…?" He looked at the horse and sat upright. "Dust?" He stroked the horse's nose with a skeletal hand, smiling brightly. "How did you get here, girl?" He glanced around. The smile disappeared as his eyes fell on Gallia.

She quickly sized him up. Yes, she could make a run for it. And countless women were short with black hair. Even if he alerted the guards, it would be nearly impossible for them to find her.

The beggar looked at her strangely. Did he…? Fire and smoke, he recognized her! But how? It didn't matter. The guards might not be able to find a single refugee, but if word got out that Queen Gallia was here, every guard, soldier, and civilian would be searching. No, running was not an option.

Never run from a fight, Cedric had advised. *Is your opponent stronger? Use his strength against him. Is your opponent smarter? Discover how she thinks.*

Fulcrums of the mind, Cedric had called it.

So, on what fulcrum did this beggar's mind rest?

Shouting sounded outside. A man's voice. Another man spoke. Younger, judging by the pitch. The first man's voice grew hostile.

The beggar raised a finger to his lips, signaling for her to be quiet. She crouched down as the shouting man marching into the stables, his white cloak billowing. A Scholar!

Was he a Thane? Gallia glanced at his ears. No rings.

"What is the meaning of this?" the Scholar demanded. He loomed over the beggar. The beggar shrank back, fumbling for his hood, hands shaking. "You again! How many times do I have to tell you to stop begging? Do I have to beat you myself?!"

"No, Scholar. I…" He bowed his head. "I won't beg again, sir."

The Scholar grabbed the beggar's chin, forcing him to meet his eyes. He studied the beggar's scars. "What are you doing in the stables? How did you slip past the guards?"

"I just wanted a place to be alone, Scholar," he stammered.

"Alone?" The Scholar scoffed. "And what do you plan to do *alone*, beggar? Steal a horse?"

"No!" He squirmed, but the Scholar's grip was too tight. "I just wanted a quiet place to think."

"Think? And what do rabble like you think about?"

"Scholar, please, I…"

The Scholar shoved the beggar onto the floor. The beggar screamed, holding his bad knee close to his chest. He laid completely still, eyes squeezed shut.

The painted mare reared her head and stamped, one hoof almost crushing the Scholar's foot. He side-stepped out of the way. "Not stealing, huh? Guard!" he bellowed.

A young guardsman rushed inside.

"Yes, Scholar?" The guard saw the beggar laying on the floor. He lurched forward but stopped himself.

"Put this horse with the others," the Scholar said, jabbing a finger in the guard's face. "And see that no more beggars enter the stable. Understand?"

"I... Um, I mean, yes, sir. I mean, Scholar." The guardsman saluted, a hand over his heart.

The Scholar kicked the beggar's legs. The beggar curled up into a ball, trembling. The Scholar huffed and sauntered away.

"Fire and smoke!" The guard rushed to the beggar's side and helped him stand up. "Are you okay, Kel?"

"I'll be fine. Take care of Dust." He pointed at the mare. "I have another errand."

"Another?" The guard frowned. "Don't you want to lie down?"

"I just did," he smirked. Gallia saw pain in his eyes.

"All right." The guard guided the horse towards the stalls. Kel the beggar watched for half a minute. Once the guard was out of sight, he walked towards the crates.

"Colm is a good lad," Kel said, motioning for Gallia to come closer. "He won't tell anyone about you on purpose. But he gets flustered. Almost gave me away a few times."

"Do you recognize me?" Gallia asked tentatively. He must have spent time around the palace stables. How else would he know the mare's name?

He might know if Logan is alive. If the rumors were true. Always *if.* For all she knew, this man viewed her as a murderer.

"I..." Kel shook his head. "You look familiar, but I've seen a lot of faces lately. When did you get here?"

"Yesterday. During the battle." The cut on her arm burned. She realized she was scratching it and stopped.

Kel stared at her incredulously. "It's a miracle you survived. What's your name?"

Gallia's throat tightened. "Catarina." It had been her little sister's name.

"It's nice to meet you, Catarina. My name is Kel." He frowned. "You're hurt."

She clamped a hand over the cut. "It's nothing." *Nothing, huh?*

You were just debating whether to see a healer. And now the cut burned like someone had stabbed her with a molten metal spear. "Just a cut."

"Have you cleaned it out?" Kel eased her hand away and inspected the cut. The skin was a brighter red. Part of the scab was cracked and bleeding. "It's infected," Kel said, confirming her fears. "I'll take you to the healers."

"No." A single beggar not recognizing her meant nothing. Dozens of noble families were taking refuge at the Academy, many of whom attended the Exhibition. If one of them recognized her before she could speak with Isla, her plan would unravel.

"You could lose the arm."

Gallia grimaced, imagining a healer walked towards her with a bone saw. "Where are the healers?"

It was a risk, but a calculated one. If Kel had spent time in or around the palace, he might know where Queen Isla was staying. The tricky part would be getting past the royal guards. And the Scholars. That one Scholar had it out for Kel. They needed to be careful.

But the risk was worth it if it meant stopping the war before it worsened.

Stopping the war. Was that what she was doing now? Logan pleaded with her, wanting to prevent warfare, but Gallia killed him. And she did not remember any of it, only her and Valentin standing over the king's body. Blood pooled underneath the corpse. She shuddered.

"Are you okay?" Kel asked.

"Actually, no. Can you take me to the healers now?"

Kel smiled, his blue eyes soft and kind. Val smiled at her that way. She wished he was here. Thane or not, she loved him.

"Right this way."

***

Dane Kanton stalked the rows of tents. All these people crammed within the walls of the Academy, once a place of learning, now a place of fear and anxiety. People cowered as he walked by, eyeing the sword at his belt. He placed a hand on the hilt and smiled. Logan had taken his sword away, stripping him of his rank. The few days without the sword felt unnatural, as though a part of his soul had been stolen. The Eastern Coalition corrected that mistake. So what if he had to hide his Thane ability? He had a sword again.

He glanced around. These people all looked the same. All ragged. All lost and frightened.

Once the Coalition discovered Gallia's disappearance, he volunteered to search for her. The monarchs, after all, were not complete idiots. They would connect Dane Kanton the guardsman to Dane Kanton the Leaner Thane eventually. Best to be away when they did. And he hated hiding his power and intelligence.

It was all Valentin's fault. His and Callum Haar's. Val had convinced him to work for the Eastern Coalition, with the guarantee that he would get a second chance at killing Haar. But then Val led him into a trap. Of course it was a trap. Why else would Val flee the palace and cause the Illusion to fail?

It had taken Kanton three full weeks to heal from Haar slicing his hamstring. And he still walked with a slight limp. No matter. This time, he would take Haar by surprise.

And Prince Carwyn.

Kanton grounded his teeth. That bastard always caused trouble. He always undermined King Yestyn, consorting with servants and even dressing like a damn beggar at royal gatherings. The nobility chalked up his behavior to eccentricity. Prince Carwyn was heir to the throne and a three-fold Thane. He could act however he wished.

Fools! Didn't they recognize open rebellion when they saw it?

Yestyn did Teyrnas a favor by getting rid of Carwyn. Logan had always been a better fit for the throne.

And Kanton would love nothing more than killing two birds with one stone. Three, if he could find Gallia. The monarchs only stated that they wanted Gallia found. They never said to bring her back alive. The bitch deserved it for turning his home into a war zone.

A skinny boy, no older than fifteen, walked Kanton's way. He wore a blue Student's cloak and kept his head down. Kanton snagged him by the collar.

"Hey, let go!" the boy cried. He kicked Kanton's shins and

threw wild punches, but there was no skill behind them.

"Be quiet," Kanton snapped. "I am a member of the King's Guard."

The boy scoffed. "Yeah, right."

Kanton's face burned red hot, but he forced the anger down. "I'm looking for some people. Have you seen them?" He gave the boy descriptions for Gallia, Haar, and Prince Carwyn. Carwyn would be easy. Few people had scarred faces and walked with a crutch.

The boy squirmed. Kanton tightened his grip and inched the sword out of its sheath. Sunlight glinted off the metal. The boy's eyes widened.

"I ain't seen none of them." The boy quickly glanced eastward. Towards the wall. The opposite direction from where he was heading. What was over there? Kanton recalled the Academy's stables and a stairway leading up to the wall. But the memory was twenty years old. A lot could change in twenty years.

Was the boy looking for someone? The guards patrolling the wall were too far away to hear a cry for help.

Had he seen Haar or Carwyn near the wall? Hiding within the maze of tents? He needed to investigate this further.

"What is your name, boy?"

"None ya!" He landed a kick, and pain shot up Kanton's leg.

Little bastard! Scaring the information out of him was no longer an option. Perhaps Kanton could motivate the boy with greed. He pulled a gold mark out of his pocket. "Tell me your name, and this is all yours."

The boy smirked. He reached into his pocket and pulled out five gold marks. The coins spun around in his hand. "I already got coins."

Kanton noted the boy's gold earring. A Manipulator. And one with plenty of pocket money.

"That's quite a fortune," Kanton said, pretending to be impressed. "Are you a noble, young Thane?"

"My parents are."

"Which house? I'm good friends with House Lyr. Are you related to Lord Darrys?"

The boy pocketed the coins. "I need to go to class."

"Are your parents here, too?"

"No." The boy wilted. "They headed for East Bridge. Mother's family lives there. They figured I'd be safer here."

"Look at my ears." Kanton pointed at the missing lobes. "The Nowani soldiers captured me and cut off my ears because I'm a Thane. They will do the same to you if you're captured."

"Can't be captured if I stay inside the walls. Did they mess up your face, too?"

Kanton ignored the barb. "What if they breach the walls? Last night's battle was a narrow victory. Barely a victory at all, if you ask me. Our soldiers managed to drive the Nowani back to their starting position, nothing more. I hear they'll try again tonight."

"Well, we got Thanes fighting now. And..." The boy squirmed again. "Fire and smoke, what do you want from me?"

"I want to know if you've seen those people."

"I already said no."

Kanton locked eyes with the boy and lowered his voice. "The woman is Queen Gallia."

The boy narrowed his eyes. "Are you serious?"

"Yes. What is your name?"

"Jaim O'Siarlwyn. Fire and smoke. Queen Gallia is here? Right here at the Academy?"

"Yes. Now lower your voice." O'Siarlwyn, huh? Perhaps the boy was safer here. Lord Tymons was a notorious drunk, the main reason he wasn't invited to this year's Exhibition. Placing Tymons in the same room with alcohol was just asking for trouble. And with Lady Nadia's reputation, the boy might very well be a bastard. He certainly did not look like Lord Tymons. In fact, he looked eerily similar to the Siarlwyns' coach driver. A short, wiry man who always greeted Lady Nadia with an affable smile. And the boy's dark brown eyes, a color neither the lord, the lady, nor their three older children possessed, were identical to the servant's.

"Listen, Jaim. Queen Isla instructed me to be cautious. We believe Gallia arrived here in disguise. A way to learn our military secrets. It's vital that I find her. Do you understand?"

"Sure. But what about the two men?"

"Spies. The few we intercepted disguised themselves as refugees. They revealed how they sent coded messages to the Coalition. These men are their leaders. Have you seen either? Think!"

"No." Jaim again looked towards the wall.

Kanton grounded his teeth. The boy was lying, but Kanton couldn't force the truth out of him. Bastard or not, the boy belonged to a noble house. If the boy complained to the Scholars, they'd find Kanton in a heartbeat and question him to no end. He'd miss his chance to kill Haar. "Please contact me if you do," he said gently. "Both men are very dangerous."

"Even the one with the crutch?"

"It's part of his disguise. Don't be fooled. This man is very dangerous." Not a complete lie. Carwyn was a skilled Illusionist. Kanton once remarked to King Yestyn how much of an embarrassment Carwyn had become. In the blink of an eye, Kanton found himself trapped in a dark forest, dense fog threatening to suffocate him. He ran away and tripped on a table leg, upsetting an ornate vase from the Cayuga Islands. The vase shattered into a thousand pieces. The Illusion ended, leaving Kanton face to face with the enraged king. Carwyn, of course, had been eavesdropping. And this was twenty years ago. Thane abilities improved with age.

"Yeah, sure. Hey, what's your name?"

"Dane Kanton, Captain of the King's Guard. I doubt you'll have trouble finding me." He gestured at the burn scars.

"Yeah, I can remember that. The guy with the crutch has scars, too, right?" Jaim raised an eyebrow.

"Good lad." Kanton gave him the coin. "Keep an eye out for them. The future of Teyrnas depends on it."

"I will. Thank you, sir." Jaim dashed off, weaving between tents in a random pattern. But the general direction led him eastward.

Kanton smiled. The boy definitely knew something. He might even lead Kanton directly to Callum Haar.

Kanton touched the dagger at his belt and imagined plunging it into Haar's heart. Keeping a healthy distance, he followed Jaim.

✳✳✳

"Healer Sanna." Kel waved at a woman wearing all white. Her pitch-black hair was tied in a tight bun, and her eyes were sunken and bloodshot. "This woman was injured in yesterday's battle."

Gallia shrank back as the healer approached. Rows of cots lined the walls of the infirmary, most of them occupied. The injuries ranged from minor cuts and bruises to soldiers with amputate limbs. Scholars and healers moved from bed to bed, tending to the grievously wounded first and shouting for aides to bring bandages or medicine. The aides were young, all in their late teens and early twenties, and they wore gray cloaks over white clothes. Many looked exhausted.

"Let me see." Healer Sanna inspected the cut. "I need disinfectant. Wait over there." She pointed at an empty cot. A young soldier with his arm bandaged from wrist to elbow slept on the cot to the left, and a mother and child sat on the one to the right. The mother cradled the little girl, about five years old, whose ankle appeared broken. "How are you feeling, Kel?" Sanna asked.

"I'm fine," he said a bit too quickly.

The healer pursed her lips and nodded. She glided down the long room and spoke with an aide.

Gallia sat down, her entire body trembling. The healer hadn't recognized her, thank the Creator. Granted, she was not dressed like a queen, in her ragged clothes and her hair a tangled mess.

Kel sat next to her and stretched out his leg. Gallia got a better look at the brace. Two thin metal rods ran up both sides and were jointed at the knee, allowing it to bend. A series of belts secured the leg at the ankle, shin, knee, and thigh. Well-cured leather belts. Where had a beggar gotten such a well-made brace? Did Logan or Isla have it made so he could continue working?

"How long did you work at the palace?" Gallia asked.

Kel gave her a confused look. "Pardon?"

"Well, you knew that mare's name. I figured…"

"Oh, right. I gave her to my son. He worked as a stable hand."

"I see. Is he safe?"

"Yes." Kel smiled, his eyes shining. "He's a Student now. Though I don't think he likes it."

"Why not?" Many Nowani teenagers dreamed of attending the Academy. They studied for years to pass the exams. All the commoners she had known as a Student took pride in their education and didn't let a single minute go to waste. Unlike herself. How big of a fool was she for wasting her education?

The healer returned with a small jar of ointment. She cut away the sleeve and applied the ointment. Gallia shivered. It felt like ice. So cold it almost burned.

"Clean the cut with fresh water twice a day for a half week," Healer Sanna instructed. She placed the lid on the jar. "If you experience any discomfort, return here immediately. We cannot afford to have the infection spread."

"Yes, healer."

Once the healer was out of earshot, Kel replied, "Gareth has always been a quiet boy. Keeps to himself. But he's so smart. His mother and I want him to have a proper education, but school isn't for everyone."

"Is his mother here?"

"No, she's in the Hinterlands. Away from all this madness." Kel gazed at the rows of patients. Half civilian, half soldier. A man screamed as a healer reset a broken leg. Kel grimaced.

"What happened to your leg?" Gallia immediately regretted the question. This man's personal life was none of her business.

"I was hurt by someone who should have loved me," Kel replied quietly. He touched the scarred half of his face. "I… It wasn't until I met Esme that I truly understood what love was supposed to look like. What about you? Are you married?"

"No. There was one man. I hoped he would…" Gallia stared at the hands in her lap. Yes, she loved Val, but did he love her? How could he love someone who hated his kind? "It's not really a good time to get married."

"There's never a wrong time." Kel smiled at her.

A trio of aides, all young women, flocked towards the door. Gallia peered over her shoulder, and her heart leapt into her throat. Lady Sarra O'Lyr, King Logan's sister, greeted the aides with a smile as she walked into the infirmary. The lady wore a fine silk dress, dark blue with silver and purple embroidery at the sleeves and hem. She stuck out like a bluebell in a field of star lilies.

A healer, an older woman with gray and white hair in a braid, shooed the aides away, telling them to get back to work. The aides did so, bidding the lady good day. The healer exchanged a few words with Lady Sarra and then continued her work. Lady Sarra then noticed Kel and sauntered over, smiling.

Gallia quickly pulled the hood of her cloak over her face. What would Lady Sarra do to her? She couldn't imagine the hatred this woman must feel towards her.

"What trouble are you in this time?" Lady Sarra asked as she sat next to Kel. She hugged him. Gallia blinked. A noblewoman hugging a beggar? Lord and Lady Lyr were well known for their charity work, but hugging? It was far too familiar a gesture. "Making friends?"

"In a sense. Sarra, this is Catarina. Catarina, this is Lady Sarra. Bet you didn't expect to meet any nobles today."

Gallia stared at Kel and Sarra. Her throat was in a vise. Why was Kel introducing her to Logan's sister? She was bound to recognize... Fire and smoke, Kel did recognize her. Pretending not to know, taking her to the infirmary at the same time Lady Lyr walked in, it was all a ploy to trap her.

Lady Sarra glimpsed under Gallia's hood and jumped to her feet. Her clear blue eyes burned like torches. A healer, a woman with pitch black hair and ruddy skin, walked over.

"Is everything all right, my lady? My lady?"

"What? Yes, fine. I..." Lady Sarra glared at Gallia. "Never mind."

The healer shrugged and turned to the mother and child on the next cot, inspecting the girl's ankle.

Should Gallia confess? Explain why she ran away? But Lady Sarra would never believe her brother's assassin.

"Sarra." Kel tapped his forehead.

Lady Sarra nodded.

They looked at each other for several long minutes, neither speaking. Gallia's mind raced. Lady Sarra O'Lyr was an Empath and Minder Thane. Was she reading Kel's mind? The very idea sent shivers down her spine. Wait, was Kel a Thane? She didn't see any earrings. There was barely any space for rings. The lobes were torn to pieces, as though mauled by a wild animal.

Lady Sarra nodded and sat back down. Her face was deathly pale, and she intertwined her fingers to keep them from shaking. "Bloody Abyss," she breathed. "Bloody Abyss, Car."

"Watch your language," Kel said half mockingly.

"But she…" Sarra sneered at Gallia. "You!"

Kel held up a hand. "Catarina is here seeking shelter. Same as you and I."

"She is responsible for all of this. She's the one…" A healer and his aide walked by, carrying blankets. Sarra waited until they were out of earshot. "She's the one who killed Lo."

Kel cupped his hand around Lady Sarra's ear and whispered.

"What?!" Lady Sarra jumped to her feet again. A dozen faces turned her way. A woman shouting once in an infirmary was nothing noteworthy. But a noblewoman shouting twice in five minutes? More faces turned to stare.

Gallia felt uncomfortably warm. What would these people do to her? Lady Sarra was right. She was responsible for this war. She should have fought harder when Kenda first approached her to join the Coalition, used the bullheadedness she inherited from her father. But Gallia hadn't been in the right frame of mind. Cedric passed away a month earlier. She'd been almost thirty years old but felt like an orphan, alone in the world.

Her stomach twisted in knots. Had Kenda waited for Gallia to be at her most vulnerable before proposing the idea? It made so much sense, Gallia felt like a fool. Kenda was a skillful ruler, but she was no match for Cedric. And if Cedric and Gallia had a chance to collaborate? To dissect Kenda's proposal word by word? In all likelihood, Nowan would be an ally of the Coalition but not a member.

Lady Sarra slapped Kel across the face, forcing Gallia back to the present. "You son of a bitch!" she said through her teeth as she sat down. "You deserved that. Don't talk your way out of this. You deserved that." Tears spilled down her face. She hugged Kel, holding him tight. Kel hugged her as well. "Why didn't you tell me?"

"Is everything all right?" asked another healer, a stern-looking woman with a white Scholar's cloak over her white clothes.

"Yes," Lady Sarra said, wiping away tears. "Everything is fine, Scholar Roseen."

The Scholar gave her a questioning look and mercifully walked away, tending to other patients.

Lady Sarra gave Kel a wry smile. "I love you. But I also kind of hate you right now. Does that make sense?"

"Absolutely."

"I, um…" Gallia regretted speaking the second Lady Sarra's eyes fell on her. But they didn't burn as intently, and she did not expose Gallia to the Scholar. What fulcrum did the lady's mind rest on? "I feel kind of lost."

Kel and Sarra exchanged a knowing look. "I think it's time you explained why you're here, *Catarina*."

"So, you do recognize me."

"I didn't want to alarm you. And I was surprised. Never expected to see you again."

"Again. Then, you were at the palace when…"

Kel nodded grimly. "Please, tell us the truth."

Gallia took a deep breath, reminding herself that she was King Cedric's daughter and that he did not raise a coward, and told them everything. But not in the right order, and she was sure she missed a few details. She was never good at speeches without writing a script beforehand.

She concluded with the Eastern Coalition's plan to attack the Academy, and how Queen Liona of Bran Maro helped her escape.

"There are rumors that King Logan…" She tried to swallow, but her throat was bone dry. "That King Logan is alive. They… They tortured people, trying to get information. I'm sorry." She buried her face in her hands. Bile rose in the back of her throat. "I begged them to stop, but they kept hurting them. I… I don't even remember stabbing Logan. I'm so sorry."

Kel placed a gentle hand on her shoulder, far more gentle than she deserved. "You didn't kill him," he whispered.

"What?" Gallia glanced up at him.

"You didn't kill Logan."

"I don't understand." She searched his and Lady Sarra's eyes.

"Did you check Logan's pulse after he was stabbed?"

That bloody word again. "No. I was so shocked. And Val led me away…" Kel grimaced, and Lady Sarra looked like she was going to spit. "What's wrong?"

"Valentin Gardyner isn't who he claimed to be. He's a Minder Thane. A very powerful one. He likely created an Illusion to make Logan's injury appear lethal. We suspect he also influenced the Coalition. Manipulating them."

Gallia's heart felt heavy. She understood Val lying about being a Thane. That was a matter of survival. But to lie to her this way... To make her believe that she killed a man... It was almost unbearable. "I can't believe it," she said sadly.

Lady Sarra scoffed. "He sent Kenda's guard to kill me and my family. We're alive because he was sloppy and Callum Haar is a better fighter."

"Callum Haar? Realta's father?" She almost forgot about the little Thane. What had the Cuchasi called her? A Dreamer? Yes, Dreamers saw the past. "Logan sent her to spy on me."

"No, that was Val's doing. He wanted Realta close." Kel balled his hands into fists and exhaled heavily. "He wanted her for his schemes."

"What schemes? Was he planning to undermine the Coalition?"

Kel grew silent, thinking. "Queen Liona is right. Her father is alive. He's here and meeting with Queen Isla in secret. You should meet with her, too."

"No, I..." Well, this was unexpected. Almost too easy. Was this a trap? "I killed..."

"No one. Isla knows the truth. And she needs to know about this attack. You started this war, but now you have a chance to end it."

"Or we can call the guards," Lady Sarra said casually.

"Sarra."

"What? Don't act like that isn't an option, Car."

"Car?" Gallia asked. "I thought your name was Kel."

Lady Sarra cursed under her breath.

"We all have secrets," Kel replied. He glanced around the crowded infirmary. "Best not to tell them here." He tried and failed to stand, falling onto the cot. Lady Sarra helped him to his feet. Testing his balance with the crutch, Kel thanked her. "What do you say, Catarina?"

Gallia studied Kel and Lady Sarra. A beggar and a member of the royal family. What a strange pair. "How do I know you aren't taking me to the guards?"

"You have to trust us." Kel held out his hand.

Gallia tentatively took it, but not solely out of trust. Cedric would have like this man. Most beggars were too afraid to look people in the eyes, let alone protect them from vengeful Scholars and take them to see healers. "Okay. Take me to Queen Isla."

37

Shades

Charity and Logan hurried towards the Academy's main building, keeping their heads low. Turns out, the Wardens' dungeon was underneath the same building they caught her eavesdropping in. And little wonder nobody thought to look for her there. A sign on the door stated that the building was closed for renovations. New housing for refugees.

But she did not see any workers, despite it being a bright summer morning. Just a ruse to keep curious eyes and ears away while the Wardens plotted to aid the Midnight King.

An air of heaviness hung around the Academy, like a lodestone tied to a person's neck. Everywhere Charity looked, people walked as though stepping on eggshells, casting furtive glances and avoiding eye contact. Several cowered away, seeing Logan and Charity in their long, black cloaks. Soldiers in dark blue patrolled the area, hands on their weapons, ready to draw.

I missed a lot more than a week of classes.

The library's wall clock struck nine as they walked through the door. Relief swept over Charity. They had made it. And not a single Warden in sight.

That you know of.

Charity pushed the sickening thought away. Only a handful of Students and Journeymen were in the library, too focused on their studies to notice two people, however strangely dressed. One girl wiped away silent tears with her cloak while reading a book. Another Student looked like he hadn't slept in days, his eyes bloodshot.

"Is it the war?" she whispered.

"Hmm?" Logan kept walking, taking long strides towards the history section.

"Has the fighting gotten worse?"

Logan stopped in his tracks. He gave Charity an inquisitive look which faded into a frown. "Of course they didn't tell you anything. The war is right on our doorstep. There was another battle for the walls last night." He sighed heavily. "Causalities were high. Several volunteers were killed."

Charity's heart sank. A battle for the walls? Did that mean the Coalition was trying to invade the Academy? But what about the neutrality law? And who were the volunteers? Her mind immediately went to Zandon. He talked about joining the Garrison, and... "I thought Academies were neutral."

"Not anymore." Logan moved farther into the library, away from the handful of Students. "Do you know where Scholar Kuno kept his research? Could he have taken it with him?"

"I don't know. There was a small corner he and Lok used to study in. It's over here." Charity, forcing her mind to focus on the here and now, led the king past the private study rooms to a small corner that was more dust than books. It felt weird having one of the most powerful people on the planet walking side by side with her. But weird in a good way, Zandon would say. Comforting. Similar to the way she felt around Kel. The fact that both men looked nearly identical helped.

Should she ask King Logan about that? He had spent time with Kel. He must have seen the resemblance.

She glanced up at him. A pensive frown creased the king's face. Perhaps she should just ask Kel instead. He was the one who warned her not to ask too many questions. Questions he likely had answers to.

Reaching the corner, Charity saw a Student sitting at the sole table. He rested his head on folded arms and breathed deep, even breaths.

"Should we wake him?" Logan asked.

Charity stepped closer. "Gareth?"

The Student jolted, his mind still half asleep, and glanced around. He saw Charity and blinked several times, as though he didn't believe his eyes. Gareth then jumped to his feet, nearly knocking over the chair, and hugged her.

Wait, a hug? Gareth never hugged her!

"How are...?" Gareth eyed her up and down. "We looked everywhere. No one could find you." He noticed the king standing behind her, and his face turned ashen.

"It's okay, Gareth. He helped me get away from…" How to explain this without leading to a million questions? "From some very bad people. And he wants to help us find Lok and Scholar Kuno."

"But he's…" Gareth staggered backwards, bumping into a shelf. He shook his head, unable to speak.

Logan stared at Gareth for a moment and then turned his attention to the books, searching the titles. "Do you know if Kuno used any of these texts for his research?" he asked Charity.

"Maybe if they're about ancient history." Honestly, there were so many books, it would take hours just to read the titles. Perhaps they should ask a librarian. Discreetly, of course. Scholars were required to publish at least one paper each year. They could ask for Kuno's papers and read the books he referenced.

Charity yelped as Gareth grabbed her arm and pulled her away. She yanked her arm out of his grip.

"What's wrong with you?" Charity looked Gareth in the eyes and saw fear. "Did something bad happen?" *Oh please, Creator, don't let it be Zandon.* Or any of their other friends.

"Don't you know who he is?" Gareth whispered.

"Yeah, he's the king. He's still alive. Isn't that amazing?" A few days after Teyrnas fell, Queen Isla arrived at the Academy with horrible news. Queen Gallia of Nowan had assassinated Logan. Everyone mourned for days, Students, Scholars, and refugees alike walking around in a daze. Many feared the kingdom would be lost without him. But Queen Isla proved herself a capable leader, leading Teyrnas towards victory. Together, she and Logan could win the war in a matter of weeks. Maybe sooner.

"Amazing. Not the best word." Gareth eyed the king warily.

"Then what word would you use?" Why was Gareth acting so strangely? He looked at the king as though he were a wildcat that had wandered too close to the farm. Shouldn't he be happy that King Logan was alive?

"Same eyes. Half a face," Gareth muttered. He edged away, never taking his eyes off Logan.

"This will go a lot faster if you help, Charity," Logan said, glancing over his shoulder. The hood had fallen back, revealing his face. Thin and angular, just like Kel's. And his eyes were the same shade of blue. Charity wanted to kick herself. Gareth had been worried sick about Kel, and here stood a man who looked just like him. No wonder he was confused.

"Yes, sir." She then said to Gareth, "I'll explain later." What she would explain, she wasn't sure. But for now, she just wanted to put her friend at ease.

Hundreds of books with titles in gold or silver leaf lined the shelves. All pertained to recent history. Within the last five hundred years. She doubted they would be helpful.

"How do you know that boy?" Logan asked. He leafed through one book, *Gwallter of Hygate's Account of Captain Solman's Voyage to Treilean, Academic Era 312-313, a Critical Analysis*, and placed it back on the shelf.

"We grew up together. His father was my tutor."

Logan bristled, muttering under his breath. He selected another book, read the table of contents, and slammed it back into place.

"Is everything okay? Gareth doesn't really talk, so you don't have to worry about him revealing your secret."

"I'm not worried about that." Logan glanced over at Gareth. "His eyes..." The king shook his head. "Never mind. Did Kuno have a private room or office he worked in? We're getting nowhere fast."

Charity shrugged. Kuno rarely referenced his own work in class and only briefly. "Gareth, did Kuno ever tell Lok where he kept his papers?"

Gareth stared silently at the king.

"I don't think we should ask him," Logan whispered. "He doesn't seem too bright."

Charity gave the king a confused look. "Gareth is really smart. He's just shy and doesn't like talking with new people."

"It's because he doesn't want to look at me," Gareth said, walking closer. He glared at the king, looking like a younger version of Callum. "You see my mother when you look at me, right?"

Logan glared at Gareth, eyes burning. He turned back to the books, selecting another volume.

"Wait, Gareth, how would the king know Esme?" Esme only

ventured out of the Hinterlands when she attended the Academy. Granted, Esme and Logan were about the same age. Had they been Students together?

Gareth lunged at the king, grabbing his arm and knocking a book out of his hands. The king swung a fist. Gareth dodged, the blow missing his face by a mere inch. He staggered back, standing between Charity and the king. Logan seethed.

"I can have you imprisoned for that," Logan said through his teeth.

Charity just stared, every muscle frozen. Gareth, the boy who did not like being touched, had just grabbed someone. And not just someone. The King of Teyrnas!

"Everyone thinks you're dead," Gareth said, his voice eerily similar to Callum's. "Just like they thought my father was dead. You can't do anything to me."

"Is that what you think, bastard?" Logan smiled wickedly, white teeth flashing.

Gareth mirrored the smile. "Manipulator. Minder. Gold and silver flames intertwined. My father is the same, except he has the red sparks of a low-leveled Learner. Not much, but enough to make him smarter than you."

Logan reeled. "A Cuchasi? You're a bloody Cuchasi?!"

"What's wrong with that?" Charity wondered. There were plenty of Cuchasi at the Academy. It was nothing unusual—

A light dawned in her mind. "Wait, Gareth, what did you say? Is Master Kel a Thane?"

His smile disappeared. Gareth glanced around, his dark eyes widening, fearful. "I… I'm sorry. He asked me not to tell…"

"Makes sense," Logan muttered, rubbing his forehead. "One parent a Thane, the other a normal human. Common among noble bastards."

"Gareth is not a bastard," Charity snapped. She instantly regretted it. Logan had helped her escape the Wardens and here she was yelling at him. But he tried to hurt Gareth. And why would Master Kel hide his abilities? Being a Thane was a wonderful gift, and people would have treated him more respectfully if they knew.

And more importantly, why had Logan called Gareth a bastard? Kel and Esme were married!

She studied the king's eyes again. The same blue as Kel's eyes. The same blue as Brother Malaky's eyes. It could be a coincidence, but...

"You and Master Kel are brothers," she hazarded a guess.

The king rounded on her, eyes like fire. The books rattled on the shelves, and a few fell onto the floor. Charity held her ground. The king had risked his own safety to help her escape. He wouldn't harm her now.

Would he?

The king sighed and sat down at the table, his anger draining away like water through a sieve. Charity took a tentative step closer. Gareth remained frozen in place.

"I'm sorry," Logan said quietly. "Carwyn, I mean Kel, had us all convince he was dead, and when Realta and that boy walked into the palace..." Logan's eyes flickered towards Gareth. "She looks just like Esme, and that boy has his mother's eyes."

"Did you know Kel and Esme were married?" Charity asked.

"I was at the ceremony." Logan shifted uncomfortably. "Carwyn knew our father would never approve, but they loved each other. And with a child on the way, they didn't want to wait. I was wrong to call you a bastard, Gareth."

Gareth continued to stare silently at Logan.

"Well, say something!" Logan snapped.

Gareth winced as though Logan had slapped him.

"Don't yell at him," Charity said. "He hates it when people yell." She motioned for Gareth to step forward, but he shook his head, black hair flying in every direction.

"My father is alive," Gareth said. "Say it."

Logan balled his hands into fists.

"Do you want Scholar Kuno's research?" Gareth asked. "I know where his room is. I will take you there when you say that my father, your older brother, is alive."

Logan's face was like stone.

"What are you waiting for?" Charity asked. "You already told me that Kel is alive. Why can't you say it now?"

"Go with the boy," Logan replied. "We need that research."

Gareth merely nodded and turned to go.

"No, wait." Charity faced the king. "Why won't you acknowledge that Master Kel is alive?" It was so simple. A single sentence. Stars above, it didn't have to be a sentence. Just a simple 'yes'.

"His name was Carwyn," Logan said, his voice harsh. "He was my brother and my best friend, and you have no idea how much he hurt me. How much his death hurt all of us. He… He abandoned us. Left us with that monster. I…" Tears welled in Logan's eyes. "Get away from me!" he yelled at Gareth. "I don't want to see your face again!"

"Fine." Gareth rounded the corner and walked away.

"Gareth!" Charity called, but he ignored her. She gave Logan an incredulous look. "Don't you want Scholar Kuno's research?"

"Of course I want it," he said in a tone that suggested her question was idiotic. "You're going to get it for me."

"But you can come with us."

"No!" Logan closed his eyes and took a deep breath. "You get it and bring it to me. Understand?"

Charity could not believe this. If she thought that one of her sisters had died and then discovered that she was alive, she'd be overjoyed. She'd be thanking the Creator with every breath in her body. But Logan was hateful, angry. And the way he treated Gareth, his own nephew, made no sense. "Why are you acting this way?"

Logan studied her with cold eyes. "Just because a person grows up in luxury does not mean they have an easy life. I spent the first thirty years of my life in fear. Carwyn protected us, taking the blame for our mistakes. But after he died, Yestyn turned his wrath on us."

"The old king hurt you?" Charity sat down in the other chair. "Why didn't you tell anybody?"

Logan scoffed. "Who would have believed us?" He rolled up his sleeve, revealing an old scar on the outside of his forearm. "Yestyn Manipulated a kitchen knife at me when I was fourteen. I don't remember what I said or did, but it angered him. All four of us have scars from him."

The blood in Charity's veins turned to ice. "The scars on Kel's face. Did you father do that to him?"

Logan nodded. "Crushed his leg and dislocated his shoulder,

too. He had scars on his back as well. Scars that should have been mine." He let out a shuddering sigh.

Charity placed her hand on the king's hand. Strange. He had comforted her when they confronted Dane Kanton, and now she was comforting him.

"Has Kel talked to you?"

"Some. But," Logan moved his hand away, "it doesn't change anything."

"He's your brother. And Gareth is your nephew."

Logan stood and returned his attention to the bookshelves, selecting a few volumes. Charity waited for him to speak. The king glance at a few books, then returned them to the shelves, selecting more. Realizing she was still there, he said, "Go with the boy. We need that research if we're going to stop the Wardens."

Charity opened her mouth to speak, but what could she say? There had to be a way to mend Logan and Kel's relationship. They were brothers! Maybe she could arrange for them to meet and have them talk...

One problem at a time.

She left to find Gareth.

***

Gareth paced back and forth in front of the library's entrance. What was taking Charity so long? He should not have left her with that man. He should have waited close by, but that man... Fire and smoke, he felt cold.

He went to the library looking for a quiet place to think. So much was happening at once, and he didn't want to be around people. Not even his new friends. And he barely slept last night, the sounds of battle raging until an hour before dawn. He must have fallen asleep.

Seeing Charity had been more than wonderful. Like waking up to a dream. She was safe and sound, and he didn't have to worry about her anymore.

The dream ended when he saw the king with her. The man terrified him, but he wanted to be brave, so he revealed he was a Cuchasi. He thought it would give him some leverage, but the king grew enraged and tried to hit him. Actually hit him! Gareth only dodged the blow because Callum forced him to learn how to fight two summers ago.

And instead of admitting that Kel was alive, he denied it and called Gareth a bastard. He wasn't the first to call him a bastard, but he was the first to say it to Gareth's face.

He honestly did not care. He knew the truth. Both truths.

Gareth nearly lost his balance as something collided into him.

"Sorry," Jaim said, steadying Gareth. The other boy looked like he had seen a Shade.

"What now?" Gareth sighed.

"Kanton." Jaim's voice trembled. "Guardsman Kanton is here. Looking for your father and Master Callum."

Gareth's heart skipped a beat. First a run-in with the king and now Dane Kanton? He could not decide which was worse. "Where did you see him?"

Jaim explained how Kanton had grabbed him and tried to bribe him for information. Gareth glanced over his shoulder, hoping to see Charity. What was taking her so long? If the king hurt her...

"And Queen Gallia is here, too."

Gareth felt like he was going to be sick. "Why?"

"Kanton thinks she's spying. We have to warn Queen Isla, and you being her nephew and all..."

Gareth groaned. This day had gone from bad to worse in a heartbeat. At least the guards stationed on that floor knew him, believing he was a messenger. But what if Isla was meeting with a lot of people today? He went to the library to avoid people!

Charity finally exited the library. She saw Jaim and her whole face brightened. "Jaim!"

"Charity!" Jaim gave her a big hug and kept hugging. A little too long. Charity didn't seem to mind. She liked hugs, and she looked like she needed one.

"What's going on?" she asked after taking one look at Gareth's face.

Jaim repeated his story, a bit more coherently.

"I'll warn Isla," Gareth said. Might as well get it over with. Maybe he would get lucky, and she would be alone. "Charity, you and Jaim go to Scholar Kuno's room and look for his research.

339

Charity will explain everything else, Jaim."

"I hope so. Why do you need Kuno's research?"

"Charity will explain," Gareth repeated, annoyed. He really did not want to talk to people today. He headed for the main staircase.

"Gareth, be careful," Charity called out.

"I will." Dane Kanton's face surfaced in his memory. A wicked smile and cold, hateful eyes. Gareth had been so terrified that he ran away, throwing away his parents' wish for him to get a real education. But he was done running. Running away was for cowards. If Kanton and Gallia were here, it meant everyone was in danger.

And he, unfortunately, had to warn them.

38

Thieves

Realta and Serena stepped lightly on the creaking floorboards in Chinasa's room. She doubted anyone below would hear, but she refused to take the risk. As an added precaution, Shasta Cray was in the common room, discussing potential plans with the Scholars should Aneros turn into a battlefield. And Elliza sent Braedan to keep an eye on Corey. The man had spent the last two days in the camp, selling his goods to camp followers for more than they were worth. But he was still searching for his dagger. Realta checked this morning to make sure it was underneath her mattress.

The only variables they could not account for were Tath and Bas. The Gadyeni could appear in the blink of an eye. Realta didn't view this meeting as going behind their backs. She just wanted to get her bearings before committing to this fight.

"Why is she here?" Elliza asked as Realta and Serena joined her and Chinasa at the small table.

"She's my cousin," Realta said. She sat next to Chinasa, with Serena sitting between her and Elliza. "And I want her to be here." Technically, Serena was her aunt, but with an age difference of only two years, it felt more natural to label her a cousin. Besides, she could easily pass as Kel's daughter.

"I vouch for her," Chinasa added. "She won't repeat anything said here."

"And I promise not to tell," Serena said. Realta told her about the Dreams. About the original Nine Thanes, and the Midnight King returning to conquer the world. And about the two Gadyeni masquerading as normal humans. She needed to tell someone. She could not keep all of this to herself and remain sane. Serena had taken it in stride. A lot better than Realta hoped.

"Very well," Elliza said in her quiet voice. "Then let's not waste any more time. I think we should ask Tath to take us to the others."

"No," Realta said a bit too loudly. She accepted her role as the Dreamer, but she would not be forced or coerced. If she joined, she would do so of her own accord.

"We must unite." Elliza gave Realta a confused look. "We don't have the luxury of time that the original Nine had."

"Why not?" Chinasa questioned. "The original Nine fought him for ten years. Granted, he had centuries to prepare. Perhaps that's it." Chinasa steepled his fingers. "They want us to defeat him before he can amass an army. If only I'd paid better attention in history class," he added under his breath. "Then I'd have a better idea…"

"Why don't the Gadyeni fight him themselves?" Serena asked.

"Good question," Realta said. Bas was always cryptic about how the Nine would defeat the Midnight King. His only hint was for Realta to give the dagger to the Windrose, a Thane with all eight abilities. Should she bring that up now or wait?

"Humans are different from the Gadyeni," Elliza said. "We think differently, living for such a short time. And we react to the same situations unpredictably. That was how the Original Nine defeated Alberik."

Chinasa said a prayer under his breath and touched his fingers to his forehead. None of them had known the Midnight King's true name until Elliza told them. A name almost lost to history. "Don't speak his name."

"Names only have power if you give them power." Elliza turned to Serena. "You know all about that, don't you, Miss Molyns?"

Serena stared at the table.

"Leave her out of this," Realta snapped. Stars above, did Elliza know that Serena was King Yestyn's bastard daughter? Did Tath tell her? And what would Master Corey do if he learned Serena's real identity?

"Why?" Elliza asked innocently. "You're the one who brought her here."

Realta sighed through her teeth. "This is pointless. We're supposed to figure out our next move, not argue."

"Agreed," said Chinasa. "I suggest traveling north, towards the

Teyrnas Academy."

"But the war—"

Chinasa raised a hand, signaling Realta to be quiet. "The Academy is the acting capital. We can use our abilities to assist Queen Isla and end this war before fighting the other."

Elliza shook her head. "We must unite with the others. Alb—" Chinasa glared at her. "The Midnight King," she amended, "is our priority. Not some petty war."

"That petty war killed my brother," Serena said, eyes glistening with tears. The room grew eerily silent. Realta's mind went back to the palace, seeing a man run down the hall, hoping it was her father. But it was Val, proclaiming King Logan's murder. Had he been laughing? Val always laughed in her nightmares.

Why does that murderer have to be One of the Nine? Bas's explanation of Val being the most powerful Minder was logical, but he killed a king! The man should be in a prison cell, waiting for the hangman's noose.

"This war," Elliza said, "will only be the first of many if we don't stop the Midnight King."

"How are we going to unite if we don't settle on a location?" Chinasa asked.

"The Gadyeni will transport us," Elliza replied matter-of-factly.

"How?"

"The same way they travel on their own."

"That is not an explanation," Chinasa said, exasperated.

Elliza frowned, thinking. "I can't really explain it. It's something better experienced than explained."

"Can they take us anywhere?" Realta asked.

"Of course."

"Then it's settled. We'll go to the Academy." She glanced around the table. Chinasa nodded solemnly. Serena looked worried, but she nodded.

"Why are you so insistent on the Academy?" Elliza asked. "None of the other Nine are there. Three are in Saethyr, and two are in the Hinterlands of Teyrnas. We—" Elliza's eyes grew wide and glassy. She shuddered as though an icy wind had blasted through the room. "Nine of Nine." She shivered and blinked several times. "The Academy it is."

"Just like that?" Realta questioned at the same time Chinasa asked, "What did you see?"

"I saw all of us." A smile brightened Elliza's face. "All our faces. I saw us all!"

"Did you see Val?"

Elliza nodded. "You never said he was so handsome."

I was too busy running for my life to notice.

Chinasa stood and walked towards the room's sole window. Below, the battalion's camp stretched for half a mile. "What about my colleagues? Will the Gadyeni transport them, too?"

"I'm afraid not."

"I won't abandon them." Chinasa rounded on her.

"We are going somewhere far more dangerous. They will be safer here. Trust me, it's better this way." Elliza hurried towards the door. "I will tell Tath the good news."

"Wait," Realta called out. "What about Mistress Cray and Serena? Are the Gadyeni going to transport them?"

"Why should they? They aren't important."

A pang, as sharp as an arrowhead, pierced Realta's heart. She looked at Serena. The other girl stared at the table, hair hiding her face. How many times had Serena been told that she was not important? That she was unwanted? Just a bastard.

"They are important to me," Realta said more to Serena than to Elliza. "And I won't leave without them."

"Tath does not need your permission."

Heat rose in Realta's face. She already told Bas she would not be pushed around. If the Gadyeni went back on his word, she'd... She'd... Well, she didn't know what she would do, but she would prove to be every bit as stubborn as Callum Haar.

"What about Braedan?" she asked, an idea taking shape. "You're just going to leave him here with Master Corey? The man is already pissed off about losing his dagger. What will he do when he discovers that you're gone, too? Who do you think he's going to blame?"

A small wave of guilt trickled from Elliza.

Realta smiled. She could get used to being an Empath. "Do you think Tath will make an exception for Braedan?"

"Braedan can care for himself. And so can Serena." Elliza

quickly slipped out of the room.

"That girl is a terrible liar." Chinasa returned to his seat. "Good job exploiting her weak spot. Perhaps when this is over, you can have a career in the magistrate's court."

"I don't want to exploit her weak spot." Great, now she was the one who felt guilty. "I want her to think. I don't trust Tath."

"What about Bas?"

Realta thought back to her Dreams. The way Bas spoke. He wanted her cooperation, and he was willing to meet her halfway. Was it just a ploy? "I want to."

"You won't leave me, will you?" Serena asked. Looking into her eyes, Realta saw that Serena accepted it. She was nothing special. Logan had only sent Kanton after her because he couldn't have a potential assassin running around. If she had run away as planned, if she hadn't stabbed Logan, would he have cared enough to search?

"Of course not." Realta placed a comforting hand on her shoulder. "You're my family. I'd never leave you."

Serena tried and failed to smile. "I... I don't think we should leave Braedan either."

"Having a trained mercenary on our side would be an advantage," Chinasa said.

"Not to mention he's a Cuchasi."

"And I..." Serena bit down on her lip.

"Speak up, girl," Chinasa said.

"I think he looks like me."

Realta stared at her, confused. What was Serena talking about?

"He and I have the same eyes," Serena began, almost whispering. "I know it's silly. Lots of people have blue eyes. But when he smiles, it looks like Kel's smile, and Kel looks just like Logan. I'm being foolish." Serena covered her face with her hands. "I'm just seeing things because Logan is dead, and I don't want him to be. He treated me like dirt, but I don't..." Serena started crying.

"You've known King Logan your whole life," Chinasa said. "If a resemblance exists, you're the one to know."

"King Yestyn fathered three bastards," Realta said, remembering Shasta's words. "Perhaps Braedan is one of them."

Serena shook her head vehemently, wiping away tears. "No, it's nothing. Forget I said anything."

A knock sounded at the door. Was it Corey? No, Corey wouldn't bother knocking. Probably a Scholar.

Realta answered the door. Mistress Cray stood in the hallway.

"Master Corey would like a word with you and Serena." Shasta peered inside the room. "Is everything all right?"

"Yes, ma'am," Serena said, wiping away the last tears. "We were just talking about the war."

"I see." Shasta turned to Realta. "Tread lightly, Miss Haar. The man is in a mood to rival King Logan's temper."

"Yes, ma'am."

"Hold on," said Chinasa. "Why does Corey want to see the girls?"

"He did not say, and I did not ask," Shasta replied tersely. "Do you mind if we speak, Ambassador Ekene? Privately?"

Chinasa looked at Realta. She nodded. Corey was likely surrounded by people. What was the worst he could do? "Very well."

"What do you think he wants?" Serena asked as they walked down the hall.

"I don't know." A bad feeling formed in her gut. *It must be about the dagger.* Why had she been so stupid? She shouldn't have stolen it.

She and Serena passed Tath and Bas on their way through the common room. They wore blue and dark gray cloaks, respectively. Tath was dressed as a wealthy Kereuic merchant, and Bas resembled a poor traveler who had to repair his clothes more than once. They were deep in conversation, speaking a language Realta didn't understand. It sounded more like music than words. Bas gave her a surreptitious nod as she headed out the door.

Tents crowded the once green field. Men in forest green uniforms conducted drills with practice weapons while other sharpened spears and swords. Camp followers hurried about, carrying supplies or cooking food or mending armor. No one paid attention to the two girls amid the orderly chaos.

Realta spied Corey speaking with Commander Maddrel. The commander wore a helmet with large, dark green feathers cresting the top, as well as his cloak and sword. Braedan leaned against a nearby tree, sharpening a knife on a whetstone. He eyed Corey as though he were a rabid wildcat.

"Ah, there's one of my servants now," Corey told the commander. The servant's mark on Realta's wrist itched. Corey had snatched away Realta's bracelet the other day, ripping it apart, the black and gold beads scattering. He threatened to report her to the magistrate if he caught her covering up the tattoo again. She doubted the commander would believe her side, that King Logan had given her the tattoo out of spite because she looked like his dead brother's lover.

It was too unlikely a story to believe.

"Now, Realta," Corey said, "have you found my missing dagger?"

Realta felt an ounce of relief. Corey hadn't found it yet. She shook her head.

"The girl doesn't speak much Teyrnian," Corey said to Maddrel.

"That makes two of us," he replied in a thick Averillian accent and laughed.

"What about you, girl?" Corey addressed Serena. "Have you seen it?"

"No, sir," she stammered and averted her eyes.

Corey frowned. "That's too bad. Because the last time I saw it, I was talking to Master Balans. Around the same time his friend arrived. Now, I know Scholars are above stealing. But you aren't a Scholar, are you, girl?" Corey loomed over Serena.

"She didn't take it," Realta said a little too quickly. She bit her tongue.

"How do you know?" Corey snapped.

"She isn't a thief."

"She dresses like a thief." Corey pointed at Serena's trousers and work shirt. Serena was the only woman in their group who wore trousers, and only because Corey had her feel uncomfortable. "Easier to sneak around dressed like that." He said to Maddrel, "Has anything gone missing during your stay?"

"Um, some coin. But soldiers like to gamble and don't like to admit when they lose." Maddrel smiled at Serena. "Are you a good card player, miss?"

Serena shook her head, keeping a nervous eye on Corey.

"You see. Not her. Can't play cards." Maddrel stopped smiling. "Now, about those horseshoe nails."

Corey waved the commander away. Maddrel scowled, strained patience emanating from him. "Now, I want the truth out of you two. Do either of you girls know who stole my dagger? Before you answer, know that it is worth more than your lives." His tone grew ice cold. "And I will trade anything to get it back."

"Even your life?" Realta snapped. *Fire and smoke, why did I say that?* Where had the thought come from? She stole a glance at Braedan. The mercenary glared murderously at Corey. Stars above, she really needed to learn how to control her Empath ability.

Corey narrowed his eyes. He lashed out to smack Realta. She ducked, and the blow missing her by inches. Her heart leapt into her throat as Corey lashed out again. She was too slow. He grabbed a fistful of hair and yanked her towards him. Pain seared Realta's scalp.

"Let go of her!" Serena yelled. She grabbed Corey's arm. He shoved her away.

"Was it you?" Corey demanded, yanking her hair. Tears stung her eyes. "Did you take my dagger?!"

"It's just a dagger," Maddrel said. "You can buy a new one."

"A new one? It's centuries old. It's irreplaceable!"

"It was me!"

The field grew silent. Through tear-blurred eyes, Realta looked at Serena. The girl trembled, but she stood firm and met Corey's gaze.

"So, now we have the truth," Corey said calmly. Too calmly. Realta's heart pounded in her throat. And she thought they would be safe because of witnesses! "Braedan!" Corey snapped. The mercenary stood at attention. "Take this thief to my wagon." He jabbed a finger at Serena. "Make sure she doesn't escape."

"Are you sure?" Braedan asked, tucking the knife in his belt.

"Just do as you're told for once, damn it!"

"Think, Corey. You are hurting her cousin. How do you know she isn't lying to protect her?"

"Are you lying?" Corey rounded on her. He gripped Realta's hair tighter. It felt like her scalp was being torn off.

"No! Stop hurting her!" Serena screamed.

Realta had to escape. Had to get away. But she couldn't run without Corey ripping out her hair.

Her eyes fell on Braedan's knife. Recently sharpened. And the same size as the knives she practiced throwing. Knives she could Manipulate.

She focused all of her will on the knife, imagining it flying towards her and Corey. *Please work, please.*

Sunlight glinted off metal. Corey screamed and let go of Realta's hair. She half ran, half stumbled away. She glanced back and felt sick. The knife was embedded in Corey's hand, in the soft tissue between his thumb and forefinger. He pulled it out and glared at Realta, teeth clenched.

"Ma ryonnai!" Maddrel yelled, pointing at Realta. "Thane! Your servant is a Thane!"

"I am not his servant!" Realta grabbed Serena's hand and ran. Corey cursed and ordered Braedan to stop them. Realta and Serena ran faster.

They raced through the camp, weaving between tents and dodging soldiers and camp followers. A woman yelled them in Averillian as they ran past, upsetting a basket of clean laundry.

The forest came into view. Miles and miles of trees. And hundreds of places to hide. Corey would never find them in there. And where they would go afterwards, she honestly did not know. Right now, she and Serena just had to get away.

Hooves thundered behind them. Realta and Serena ran faster, neither daring to look back. The forest was so close. Just another hundred yards.

A horse charged in front of them and reared its legs. Realta halted. Serena crashed into her and almost knocked her down.

Braedan dismounted and stalked towards them.

Realta, her heart pounding, focused on the knives along his belt, ready to Manipulate them. She did not want to hurt Braedan. He'd been nothing but nice to her and Serena. But he worked for Corey. The scars on the arm guaranteed that. She refused to go down without a fight.

Braedan reached behind his back and threw a white sheathed dagger on the ground.

"Take it."

Realta and Serena exchanged wary looks. What kind of trick was this?

"Where did you find it?" Realta asked. She snatched up the dagger and tucked it into her belt.

"Under your mattress," he said, annoyed. "You seriously couldn't think of a better hiding place?"

Realta shrugged.

Braedan rolled his eyes. "Corey wants you two found. But he said nothing about giving you a head start. Take the horse and head for the river. I'll try to find you later after Corey's temper cools. Right now, he's fit to order every soldier in the battalion to search for you."

"Thanks." Realta held onto the reins, but she did not climb into the saddle. "Do you know the dagger is valuable?"

Braedan mulled it over. Shouting sounded from the camp. "Yes and no. Look, Corey talks a good game. He can convince you that a rock is a priceless artifact. But I've had my suspicions. He bought it from Elliza's cousins. Part of the deal he made to get her. And he rarely lets it out of sight. That's all I know."

The fine hairs on the back of Realta's neck stood on end as the shouting grew closer. Serena huddled next to her.

"Go now." Braedan selected two daggers, holding them loosely in each hand, ready to fly. "I'll tell Chinasa where find you. Just get to the river and hide."

"But isn't the Tarodic army marching there?" Serena asked.

"We'll find you before the fighting starts. If there's fighting." Braedan shifted his feet, glancing back. Another horn sounded. "I'll figure it out. You and Realta need to go. Now!"

Realta and Serena climbed into the saddle. She ran a finger over the small piece of glass embedded in the hilt.

I have to give it to the Windrose. Whoever he was.

"Thank you," she said to Braedan.

"If Elliza's Farsights are right, then I'm the one who should thank you. And Serena…" Braedan paused, staring at her. In this light, his eyes resembled Logan's. "Be safe."

"Wait, Braedan, do you know—"

"I know we're connected," he interrupted. "Now, go!" He

slapped the horse's side, and the animal took off at a gallop.

Keeping her head low, Realta maneuvered the horse into the forest, the branches and shadows sheltering them. Behind, she heard men shouting and the swift sound of knives piercing the air.

39

War Games

Queen Isla studied the map. The Coalition armies surrounded the Academy, every gate and roadway blocked. Red tiles along the Highway. Purple and white tiles to the east and west, respectively. Soldiers stretched thin. An advantage she sought to exploit.

"They weakened their defenses around Norgard," she said to Deen, Gregor, and Una as she pointed at the map. The latest reports from their Deirow Hawks stated that Tirshay's army had moved away from the city and the river, closer to the Academy to reinforce Galion's troops, weakened from yesterday's battle.

"There are still plenty of soldiers near the Garrison," said Deen. Black tiles represented the Marish soldiers. They circled the Garrison and Norgard.

"Why don't you send them a message to stand down?" Una asked. Poor woman. She had no experience with military tactics, but she was bound and determined to help.

"They think I'm either dead or missing." Deen gave her an exasperated look.

"Forge your daughter's signature," Una suggested. "I read that in an adventure novel once."

"A work of fiction. Great." Deen rubbed his temples. "Have the spies intercepted any messages from my daughter? Anything to indicate she's okay?"

"Most of those messages were signed by Queen Kenda," Gregor replied.

"Forge her signature," Una said.

"This is what I'm thinking." Isla moved her finger along the map. "The reinforcements from Madan Och should arrive within the next two days. Gregor, when is the next storm prediction?"

Gregor leafed through a stack of papers. Though she had been relegated to Queen Regent, that did not stem the endless flow of papers and reports. Gregor found the right one. Thanks to research conducted by Scholar Maryn, they could predict storms with some accuracy. Lately, storms seemed to occur every other day, but she needed to be certain.

"Tomorrow. Sixty percent accuracy," Gregor read.

Could she gamble thousands of lives on a prediction that was slightly higher than a coin toss?

"These planning sessions work better when you think out loud," Deen said, his different colored eyes as hard as stones.

"Right. If there are no delays, the Madani should arrive tomorrow, during the storm. We will divide their forces in half. The first half will divert attention away from the North Gate, pushing the Coalition closer to the Garrison, acting as hammer and anvil. We won't order the Madani to fight." The representatives had been adamant. Elinya told her yesterday that this was not Madan Och's war, therefore they would not fight unless it was in self-defense. "They will keep the soldiers at bay while the second half evacuates the civilians."

"And the storm is important how?" Deen asked.

"The rain will prevent archers from firing. Even those who risk ruining their bows will have little to no accuracy. And the increased activity around the Garrison should draw attention away from the gates. It's not perfect, but it ensures that some civilians will be evacuated safely."

"If there are no delays." Deen let out a heavy sigh. "Too many ifs. Have you cleared this plan with the Scholars?"

Isla sadly shook her head. "They won't listen to me." It was a small miracle that she was able to meet with the representatives without the Scholars finding out. "And there is little chance they would listen to you, either."

The King of Bran Maro scowled. He had lived in disguise for a full week, sometimes disguised as a refugee and sometimes as a servant. Two Scholars had met with her unannounced the other day, at the same time she was meeting with Deen. Her heart was in her throat the entire time, but they regarded him as a servant and paid him no attention, leaving the king fuming.

"They'd likely put you in chains," Gregor said, not unkindly. The former stable master was prepared to fight Deen when he discovered the man's identity. Isla talked him down, explaining that Ayrdeen was now on their side. Gregor still did not completely trust Deen, but he trusted Isla's judgment.

"What about the rest of the nobility?" Deen asked. "Lord and Lady Lyr will listen to you. They can rally the others to your side. Force the Scholars to adopt your plan."

"I doubt that." Isla didn't want to admit it, but she already tried that. It failed spectacularly. Most nobles had no experience with fighting and feared losing favor with the Scholars. A handful who had pushed too far, demanding special privileges and accommodations, were kicked out of Academy's main building and forced to find shelter with the other refugees. And though few would admit it, a lot of nobles were afraid of common people, viewing them as thieves and opportunists. They would not back Isla. The risk, if they failed, was too great.

And Rafael still refused to speak with her.

Will he ever forgive me?

"What about one key member of the nobility?" Deen asked.

Isla's throat tightened. "No, Carwyn officially died seventeen years ago. No one would believe it's really him. Certainly not the Council."

"I'm not talking about him. Logan's death was never made official, and there are plenty of rumors circulating around that he's alive. Why not convince him to appear before the Council and retake his title? Their whole stupid argument hinges on you being the regent. Well, we don't need a regent if we have a king."

Isla stared at the table. Everyone needed to believe that Logan was dead so he could safely investigate the Wardens. He suspected several members of the Council, and he needed to collect evidence. Something a king, surrounded by servants, guards, and other nobles every hour of the day, could not do. Isla wanted to argue, but her last Farsight changed her mind. Men and women of shadows infiltrating the Academy and spreading like a disease to every major city in Teyrnas.

She shuddered, remembering the ending. The Wardens attacked a small group of people made of light. Nine people against thousands. One of the light people looked eerily similar to Realta.

"I respect his decision," she said flatly.

Deen let out an exasperated sigh. "This is madness! Why allow the world to believe your husband is dead?"

"Because there is more going on in the world than this war."

Deen spread out his hands. "Oh really? Like what?"

Would Deen believe that followers of the Midnight King existed right here at the Academy, or would he think she was making it up? The fact that he, a man who had been raised to fear Thanes, was speaking to her was amazing. But he never spoke with deference. Always using a tone that suggested she was slightly less than his equal.

And Farsights could only be seen by one person. Yet another reason people in the East did not trust Thanes. Too many Farsight advisers had given their newly installed monarchs advice based on false visions. Within a generation of King Symon claiming the throne, Nowan had outlawed Farsights, giving them two options: exile or death.

Would Deen believe her Farsight?

Would he believe Logan's testimony?

A knock sounded at the door.

"Una, see who that is." Isla stood up and smoothed down her dress. Might as well look presentable. She felt Deen glaring at the back of her skull.

"Good morning, Lady Sarra and Master Kel," Una said, opening the door wider.

A weight lifted off Isla's shoulder. She half expected it to be a Scholar. Instead, it was two people she trusted.

Lady Sarra, dressed in a gorgeous blue silk gown with a matching cloak, glided into the room. She greeted Isla with a warm smile. Carwyn entered a step behind, still wearing his ragged clothes and old Journeyman cloak. She had offered him new clothes, but he refused.

"It's all right, Catarina," Carwyn said into the hallway, his voice gentle. Always gentle. The antithesis of his father's voice. "No one will harm you."

A woman peered into the room. She clutched her cloak tightly. The hood covered her face.

"This will be interesting," Sarra muttered in Isla's ear.

"Interesting how?" she asked, noting the irate look on her sister-in-law's face.

"You'll see."

"Greetings, Kel," Deen said once Una closed the door. "Perhaps you can lend your opinion on Her Majesty's battle plans."

"I don't have a mind of warfare." Carwyn escorted the woman closer to Isla. The poor woman trembled from head to foot as though she had been caught in a winter storm. "Isla, there is someone you need to meet."

"Very well." She didn't have time to speak with individual refugees, but Carwyn would not waste her time. If he thought it was important, it likely was. "It's nice to meet you... Catarina, is it?"

"Um, not exactly," the woman murmured.

Deen cursed in Marish. He rushed over and yanked back Catarina's hood, revealing Queen Gallia Toutain of Nowan.

Isla's head spun. She staggered against the table, upsetting the tiles. Queen Gallia, right here at the Academy, in her private rooms! Why had Carwyn brought her here? How did she get inside?

Gallia shrank back, huddling against Carwyn. She stared at Deen like a trapped deer.

"What is...? How is she...?" Gregor stammered. Una looked like she was going to faint.

Sarra crossed her arms. "Told you this would be interesting."

Isla forced herself to stand upright. She was the queen and, regent or not, she was going to bloody act like it. "What brings you here, Your Highness?"

"She's a damn spy, that's what!" Deen sneered. "Who sent you? Kenda? Syleck?"

"Be quiet," Isla ordered.

Deen glared at her, but he relented. Through his teeth, he said to Carwyn, "I hope you know what you're doing, Your Former Majesty."

"What did you say?" Gallia asked. Deen ignored her.

"Queen Gallia," Isla said, walking up to her and Carwyn, "why are you here?"

"Queen Liona sent me, asking me to find her missing father." She glanced nervously at Deen.

"Liona?" Deen's eyes softened. "How is she? Does she look well?

Kenda didn't hurt her, did she?" The softness instantly hardened. "If that bitch hurt my daughter—"

"Yes," Gallia interrupted. "I mean, no. Liona is well, but she…" Gallia breathed deeply, composing herself. "She doesn't trust the Eastern Coalition. She believes they are responsible for your disappearance."

"Then why not come here herself? Why send—"

Isla pointedly cleared her throat.

"Apologies."

"You traveled across a war zone at the request of another queen?" Isla questioned. She thanked the Creator and all eight Gadyeni that Logan was alive. If Gallia had really killed him, Isla doubted she'd be able to control her anger.

"It wasn't just for her. I don't trust the Coalition either." Gallia paled. "They started torturing people. Civilians. I… This is not what I agreed to."

"Why are they torturing people?" Deen asked, his own face turning pale.

"They believe King Logan is alive. And now I know it's true." She looked at Carwyn and Sarra.

"You told her?" Isla asked Carwyn.

"It made things easier."

"I see. What will you do with this information?" Isla's heart pounded in her throat. Was this another one of Gallia's tricks? Pretend to run away and gain Isla's trust just to stab her in the back and open the gates for the rest of the Coalition?

"I want to help you. I don't care if you are Thanes. This war was a mistake. When Kenda first approached me, I wasn't thinking clearly. I still wasn't when Logan vied for peace. Is Logan here?" she asked apprehensively. "I'd like to speak with him. Apologize, though I doubt it will do much good."

"Logan is in hiding." Isla refused to let this woman anywhere near her husband. She chose her next words carefully. "The Eastern Coalition is not our only enemy here."

"What do you mean?"

How would Gallia react to a Farsight?

Only one way to find out.

Isla explained the Wardens of the Night. First a blurry vision and now a genuine threat operating out of the Academy and possibly dozens of other locations across the Northern Realm. The last Farsight showed shadow people moving eastward to all the major cities and capitals. She did not pause for a second and included every detail. Gallia just stared at her, her face blank. Isla prayed the woman would not reconsider her alliance.

"Val mentioned the Midnight King once," Gallia said quietly. "It was offhanded. I said that humans got along fine without Thanes for centuries. And then Val said, until the Midnight King arrived. I thought he was being witty."

"That doesn't mean the Midnight King is back," Deen said. "Just that his followers still exist."

"They are still a threat," Carwyn said heavily. If her Farsights were correct, then the Wardens were hunting his niece. He asked Isla, "How long has Logan been investigating them?"

"Since he arrived here."

"Did he mention any names?"

"No. I think he wants to be sure before he starts naming people."

Carwyn was silent for a moment. "Did you know that Val stalked my niece?" he asked Gallia. "He told Realta all these wild stories about them being the new Nine Thanes. And they were destined to fight the Midnight King."

"Of course not. Val..." Gallia faltered. "He left during the coup. Said he had something important to do. Could that be it? Did he know about the Wardens?"

"This is madness," Deen groaned. He removed his flute from his coat pocket and began polishing it. "The Midnight King is gone. Bloody stars, most of the stories from that age are more myth than fact. You don't honestly believe this, do you?"

"Isla's Farsights are never wrong," Carwyn said with more confidence than Isla felt. "Where is Logan now?"

"Who cares?" Deen sat in the window seat and began playing a tavern song.

"I'm not sure," Isla replied. She hadn't seen Logan since yesterday. They met briefly after the battle. Logan told her that the Wardens were meeting this morning, and he would have more information tonight. She wished desperately for him to stay away. She already lost him once. But Logan was adamant, so she kept her thoughts to herself.

"Gregor," Carwyn said. "Can you find Callum Haar and ask if he's seen Logan today?"

"Of course." Gregor hurried out of the room, casting an uneasy glance at Gallia.

"We can ask Realta," Gallia said. "If she's really part of this, then she'll know, right?"

The room grew eerily silent. Deen stopped playing, his eyes flicking back and forth between Isla and Carwyn.

"Realta Haar isn't here," Isla replied. "She went missing during the coup. She was trying to escape Val."

"Escape Val? Why?" Gallia looked terribly lost. "Val never hurt anyone."

"He hurt my brother," Carwyn said softly. "And he hurt you."

Gallia shot him an icy glare. "Val never hurt me."

"He lied to you about being a Thane. A very powerful *Minder* Thane."

Tears welled in Gallia's eyes. "I don't care. You're all Thanes. If I'm going to work with you, then it doesn't matter."

"He still lied to your face," Sarra muttered.

"Who is your brother?" Gallia asked Carwyn, growing defensive. "Why did Ayrdeen address you as Your Former Highness? How does a crippled beggar know the Queen of Teyrnas?"

Isla's muscles tensed. Gallia was skirting dangerously close to a truth best left a secret.

"I wasn't always a beggar," Carwyn said.

"What does that mean?"

"He's Prince Carwyn," Deen announced. He resumed playing, a soft, almost somber melody.

Isla did not know who was more shocked: Gallia, Carwyn, or herself. Sarra glared at Deen, as though she wanted to beat him with that flute. And Carwyn... Poor Carwyn looked terribly lost, as though the entire world had fallen out beneath him.

"Prince Carwyn died," Gallia said slowly, studying him.

"Technically, yes," he said.

The door burst open, slamming against the wall. Isla's heart leapt into her throat as Gallia replaced her hood and Deen reached for his eyepatch.

Gareth Haar, his hair disheveled and his eyes wide, ran inside and latched onto Carwyn, holding him tight.

Isla released a breath. Stars above, that boy nearly sent her into a panic!

"Son, what's wrong?"

"Kanton is here!" the boy cried.

A bottomless pit formed in Isla's gut. "Captain Dane Kanton?"

Gareth nodded.

Peydar Wills claimed that Kanton sided with the Coalition as revenge for Logan banishing him. If Kanton was here, he was acting under the Coalition's orders.

Orders to what? To win back Isla's favor, hoping she didn't know about his treason and acting as a spy? Or to confirm the rumors about King Logan and assassinate him?

A pair of guards rushed into the room, their swords drawn. One, Eryn, a guard who had served at the palace, grabbed Gareth by the collar and dragged him away from Carwyn. The other, a young guard named Ruben, who was fresh out of the Garrison, gave Isla a bow.

"Your Majesty, are you all right?"

"We tried to stop the boy, but he ran past us," said Eryn, struggling to hold Gareth still. The boy jabbed Eryn in the ribs, knocking the breath out of him. He slipped out of Eryn's grip and returned to his father's side. "Ouch! Damn it, boy." Eryn rubbed his ribs. "I've never seen someone run that fast!"

"Are we interrupting?" Ruben asked, glancing around the room. Gallia had retreated to the back corner with Una, and Deen played quietly, his eyes closed and the eyepatch halfway out of his pocket. Ruben saw Lady Sarra and gave her a quick bow.

"As a matter of fact, yes. You are interrupting," Isla replied.

"Apologies." He bowed again. "We will take the boy—"

"The boy is my messenger. He has news from the wall. Confidential news," she added gravely.

"Why didn't he give today's password?" Eryn questioned.

"We had to change it at the last minute," Isla said quickly. "It was compromised. Some guards, it seems, cannot keep their mouths shut. You two, I assume, are more careful with information regarding the throne?"

360

"Yes, Your Majesty," they answered in unison. Eryn looked pale. He was a good man, but Isla recall how he liked to impress the female servants with his 'brave acts of courage' as a guardsman, and old habits died hard.

"I believe an apology is also in order," Isla said.

"Sorry, Your—"

"Not to me."

The guards sheepishly turned to Gareth. "Sorry, young man," they said. Gareth just stared at them.

"You are dismissed."

The guards bowed once more and left.

"He followed me," Gallia said. All the blood had drained from her face. "The other monarchs must have sent Kanton once they discovered I was gone."

"Where did you see Kanton, Gareth?" Carwyn asked.

"Jaim saw him near the tents. He's looking for you and Uncle Callum. And her." He pointed at Gallia.

"Why Callum?" Sarra questioned.

"Kanton blames Callum for his burn scars and banishment," Carwyn replied. "Son, go warn your uncle. And keep your head low. Kanton is bound to recognize you, too."

"Yes, Father."

"What about me?" Gallia asked.

Isla placed the colored tiles back in their correct position. The purple tiles, representing Nowan, were mainly by the West Gate, cutting them off from the Nerin, with a small group near the Garrison, between Bran Maro and Tirshay. And she had two of the three monarchs right in this room. A smile crossed her lips.

"You, Your Majesty, are going to help me win a war."

40

Hiding Places

Charity felt overwhelmed as so many friendly faces surrounded her. She and Jaim went to his room after Gareth left to warn Queen Isla. She didn't want to be out in the open, not when the Wardens were lurking around. Jaim left for a few minutes and returned with Ivar, Evelyn, and Coryn.

They asked her question on top of question. Too many for her to answer.

"I'm okay, really," she assured them. "I'll explain everything when Gareth gets here." She really did not want to repeat the story more than necessary. For the moment, she just wanted to be with her friends.

Half an hour later, Gareth arrived with Callum. Callum gave her a crushing hug. He looked well. He still had a beard, though, and he needed a haircut, his hair sticking out in every direction.

The only ones missing were Lok and Zandon.

"Zandon is fighting with the Thane Regiment," Jaim said.

"The what?" Yedrick had mentioned it but never gave her an explanation.

"Queen Isla and the Council created the Thane Regiment to aid Teyrnas," Coryn said. "A lot of Thanes were against it, but with armies surrounding us on all sides…" She shrugged.

"They even tried to recruit Coryn," Evelyn said with disgust. Charity didn't blame her. She didn't want her sisters fighting in battles, either.

"So, where were you?" Coryn asked. "We all…" She looked away sheepishly. "Some people said you ran away."

Charity composed herself with a deep breath and ordered events in her mind. She started with accidentally eavesdropping on the Wardens' meeting and being caught and locked in a dungeon.

"Since when does the Academy have a dungeon?" Jaim interrupted.

Ivar shushed him.

"I don't really know how long I was down there. I hoped someone would find me or that the Wardens would change their minds, but..." Tears stung her eyes. Long nights waiting, unable to sleep, thinking about a hundred possible futures, none of them good. Once, when Shari and Yedrick visited her cell, she genuinely thought about taking the vows just to get this ordeal over with. She told herself to hold out for one more day. And then one more, and one more until she decided to escape. If no one was coming to rescue her, she had to rescue herself.

"We never stopped looking for you," Callum said, placing a hand on her shoulder.

"Thank you." Charity wiped away a tear. She didn't want to ruin the happy reunion by crying.

She continued, explaining her escape. Jaim interrupted again, cursing the Regor twins' names. Ivar once again told him to hush. She concluded with today's meeting and King Logan helping her.

That prompted a dozen more questions. King Logan was alive? Right here at the Academy? Jaim and Ivar did not seem as happy as Evelyn and Coryn, Jaim muttering under his breath and Ivar merely nodding in acceptance.

Callum then told his side of events. Rescuing King Logan from the palace and hiding in the city until he recovered.

"I hate keeping it secret," Callum said. "These people need their king."

"Should we tell the Scholars?" Evelyn asked.

Callum shook his head. "Logan doesn't want anyone to know yet."

"That's bloody stupid," Jaim muttered.

"Do you know what the Wardens want with Kuno's research?" Coryn asked Charity.

"No idea, but it can't be good."

"Have you checked Kuno's room?" Ivar asked.

"No," Charity said. "Gareth and I were going to, but Jaim warned us about Kanton. I wanted to wait until Gareth found Callum." Images flashed in her mind. A dark forest clearing. People running, screaming. A man on fire. Kanton plunging a knife into Callum's chest. Blood.

Charity shivered. *That was months ago. Callum is fine now.* Looking at him, it was hard to believe he had been injured.

"Maybe we should wait until tomorrow," Callum suggested.

"No, we have to find the research first."

"The fighting will start again soon," Gareth said. "I overheard Isla talking with my father and another woman."

"What other woman?"

Gareth shrugged. "I didn't see her face. Isla asked her to look at a battlefield map."

She must be a spy, Charity assumed.

"So, where do we start?" Coryn asked.

"I think Ivar has the right idea," said Callum. "Search the Scholar's room first."

"The Scholars don't allow certain books to leave the library," Evelyn said. She was a history Student, focusing on the interactions between Vogel Kingdoms. She complained on multiple occasions about the librarians refusing to let her see the oldest books because they were not part of her curriculum, and many were too fragile to handle. "The head librarian makes everyone sign a log." Her eyes brightened. "We can ask to see it. We won't be able to read the books if they are old, but we'll know the titles."

"But he's there," Gareth whispered.

Charity sighed. She wished the meeting between Logan and Gareth had gone better. He was Gareth's uncle just as much as Callum was, but they refused to acknowledge one another.

No, that wasn't right. Logan refused to acknowledge that Master Kel was alive. His own brother. A prince. Did that make Gareth a prince, too?

"What if Kuno didn't ask for permission?" Callum suggested.

Evelyn looked at Callum as though he told them to jump off the roof and fly away. "Scholars do not steal. Especially not rare texts."

"They aren't supposed to worship the Midnight King either. And stealing isn't that hard. Not if you're smart, and it's something you need."

Charity eyed the servant's mark on Callum's wrist. Two diamonds, now striped to mark him as a runaway. Rumor said he stole from a merchant he was guiding through Caman's Pass, hiding the money in the forest. Nothing was even proven, but the merchant lost a small fortune and needed someone to blame.

It was all hearsay.

Or was it?

Yes, of course it is. Callum is not a thief!

Gareth stood up. "Scholar Kuno's rooms are this way."

The group followed Gareth to the Scholars' rooms, moving wordlessly through the halls. A few people milled about. A pair of Scholars discussed whether they should flee.

"I got a bug-out bag stashed…" one said. His eyes fell on the seven of them, and their conversation halted. They gave polite hellos and plastered on smiles. The one who mentioned the bug-out bag eyed Callum warily. They hurried down the hall, whispering.

"Here." Gareth stopped in front of room number twenty-seven. The door was slightly ajar. Gareth pushed it open.

Charity's heart dropped. The room had been ransacked. Clothing strewn across the floor. Blankets tossed off the bed. The mattress and pillows ripped open.

"We're too late." This was all her fault. If she hadn't waited for Gareth and Callum, if she had gone to the Scholar's rooms right after leaving the library, then she could have gotten here in time.

"Not necessarily." Callum pushed aside a toppled chair and studied the room. Charity and the others followed close behind. "Close the door," Callum said to Coryn, the last one in line. She did so, but it swung back on broken hinges. Callum grabbed the chair and used it to hold the door shut. "Kicked in."

Maybe waiting wasn't a mistake. If the Wardens had arrived while she was alone… No, best not to think about that.

"Evelyn, Coryn, and Jaim," Callum said as he surveyed the rooms, "search the back room. Charity, Ivar, and Gareth, search the front room. Leave nothing unturned."

"Too late," Jaim said under his breath, but he did as instructed.

"What are you thinking?" Charity asked as Callum inspected the writing desk. Every drawer had been thrown out, laying in a haphazard pile. And dozens, possibly a hundred, of papers were scattered. A spilled inkwell stained several, making them unreadable.

"Scholars are smart people," Callum said. "Esme and Kel were a year away from becoming Scholars themselves. Where would they hide something important? Someplace obvious like a desk or inside a pillow cover?"

"Of course not. I..." Charity bit her tongue. Last summer, she purchased a novel at the marketplace. She had very few opportunities to read fiction, and judging by the title, *The Conquests of Lady Freya*, she assumed it contained grand adventures across the world. Instead, it was mostly romance. Very detailed romance. She hid the book underneath her mattress, only reading it when she was certain no one would see.

Oh dear. That novel was still in her bedroom. What if her parents found it?!

Callum laughed. "Under a mattress is a very poor hiding place. Even for a short book."

Charity's face burned red hot. Callum knew! Did her parents know? Her sisters? Bridget would never let her live this down, and Nina was sure to give her a lecture about what a young lady ought to read. And her mother... Her face burned as hot as the sun.

"Don't worry." Callum smiled. "Esme put it back."

"But she told you? Did she tell my parents?"

"Tell them what?" Gareth asked, completely lost.

"Mind your own business," Callum said gently. "Anyway, Scholars are smarter than teenagers. If this research is secretive, he wouldn't just hide it anywhere."

Charity jolted as Ivar smashed a flower vase. Pottery shards scattered across the floor. And a bundle of papers rested in the center.

"What in the bloody Abyss was that?" Jaim called out from the other room. Evelyn yelled at him to watch his language.

"Everything's fine," Ivar replied. He picked up the bundle and handed it to Callum.

Callum undid the ties and folded out the papers. He flipped through them, frowning. "I don't know this language."

"Can I see?" Charity glanced at the first page. "It's Old Eltrian."

Callum raised an eyebrow.

"It's the language people on Eltriar spoke during the Thousand Years War."

"The whole world spoke one language?" Callum shook his head. "Doesn't seem possible."

"Scholar Kuno is fluent," Ivar added. "He must have written in that language as a precaution."

"All right." Callum gave the papers to Charity. "Keep searching."

An hour-long search yielded two more bundles. One hidden in a hole in the wall behind the wardrobe, and another in a hollowed-out leg of the bed. Every page was written in Old Eltrian. Charity, Ivar, and Evelyn knew some, but none of them were fluent, so they took turns with the first bundle, helping each other with an unknown word or difficult syntax. The dinner bell rang. They were all hungry, but none of them wanted to stop. Not when they were so close.

"I can bring you food," Callum said.

"They won't let you take food out of the dining room," Jaim said. He sat on a chair with his chin propped in his hands. Knowing zero words in Old Eltrian, he sat and waited. Charity caught him sleeping once. "Don't want people hoarding it."

"They deliver food to the tents twice a day. They don't seem to care what we do with it."

"But Kanton is out there," Gareth protested. "He wants to kill you."

"Gareth, you don't know that."

"Why else look for you?"

Callum didn't have a response, so he stayed and acted as a lookout. Charity was glad he stayed. She had seen Callum break up fights and knew that if the Wardens showed up, he would protect them.

"I don't know this word," Evelyn said, halfway through the second bundle. The first bundle had been a list of military tactics used by the Nine Thanes. Charity could not make heads or tails of it and some words were strange, describing weird weapons. One sounded like a crossbow that fired rocks instead of arrows.

Ivar glanced over. "Prince?" He looked to Charity for confirmation.

"I guess so. That suffix means 'little', and it's on the word for king. So, little king? Prince?"

Evelyn paled.

"What is it?" Coryn asked, sitting on the bed next to her sister.

Evelyn swallowed and read the paragraph, "And when the Midnight Sun eclipses the Moon, and when the Raven sits upon his left hand, so shall the Prince join his King, and the two shall rule as One."

Charity's blood turned to ice water. She glanced at her friends. Evelyn was paper white, and Gareth and Jaim looked terribly confused.

"What does that mean?" Jaim asked. "Is this what the Wardens are looking for?" He dug into his pocket for coins and began twirling them in his palm.

"Yes. I mean, I think. This is all about the Midnight King," Evelyn said, her voice shaking. "All the notes Kuno could find about him. About him escaping from his prison and taking over Eltriar."

Callum pointed at the third bundle. "What about this one? Does it say anything about the Nine Thanes?"

"Some," Ivar said. "It calls them by their old names." He frowned and recited, "So it was, so shall it be. Nine to nine, all against one. Faces, names, these shall change, but the essence all the same. All must stand or all must fall to the court of the Midnight King."

Callum cursed and ran a hand through his hair.

"What's wrong?" Charity shot to her feet, a few papers falling onto the floor. She had never seen Callum so worried.

"That bastard was telling the truth. Where is King Logan?"

"He might be in the library. But that was hours ago. Callum, who are you talking about?"

Callum gathered up the three bundles and went to the door.

"Give them to Isla!" Gareth shouted. He grabbed Callum's arm and pulled him back. Callum stared at Gareth. So did Charity. Not only did Gareth raise his voice, but he was touching someone. Twice in one day.

"Gareth is right," said Ivar. He joined them at the door. "The queen needs those papers. We are fighting something much more dangerous than the Eastern Coalition now. And she needs someone who can translate them." He motioned towards Charity and Evelyn.

"Will you please explain what's going on?" Coryn pleaded.

"A much larger war is coming to Eltriar," Callum said. "If those papers are correct, if Valentin was telling the truth." Callum gritted his teeth. "We need to warn Queen Isla. And King Logan," he added, looking at Gareth.

"Who is Valentin?" Charity asked.

"He was Queen Gallia's messenger. A Minder Thane, pretending to be loyal to Nowan. He tried to rope Realta into his schemes. That's why she isn't here. She and Serena ran away from him, escaping the city before we were trapped." Callum balled his fist, crumpling the papers. "He said that she was One of Nine."

"Nine? The same Nine mentioned there?"

Callum nodded grimly.

Charity sat down, her body going numb. This was crazy. First, followers of the Midnight King were at the Academy, and now her best friend was involved? Her head hurt, trying to put all the pieces together.

"So, if the King is the Midnight King," said Evelyn, tried to keep calm. "Then, who is the Prince? And why does it mention a raven?"

"Isn't Logan called the Raven King?" Ivar asked.

"It's an old term," Callum said. "Dating back to Caslana splitting into Nowan and Teyrnas. It has nothing to do with the Thousand Years War."

"That we know of," Coryn said quietly. The room grew so silent, Charity could hear her heart beating.

"We have to give them to Isla," Gareth repeated.

Callum moved the chair away from the door and peered into the hall. "Scholar Lucan is also looking for these papers. Evelyn and Coryn, you take this one. Ivar and Jaim, take this one. And Gareth and Charity, the last one. Tell the guards that Master Haar sent you to speak with Queen Isla. If that fails, tell them that ravens fly at dawn. It's an old code, but it might work."

"Why not go together?" Jaim asked.

"Better for one group to get caught than everyone."

"Aren't you coming with us?" Charity asked.

"I have other work."

"Don't look for Kanton," Gareth said, locking eyes with Callum.

Callum raised an eyebrow. "If I didn't know better, I'd think you were a Minder. And Kanton needs to be found," he said as Charity began to protest. "You cannot talk me out of this. Now, take those papers to Queen Isla. Don't leave at the same time!"

The sisters left first, heading towards the main staircase. Five minutes later, Jaim and Ivar left in the opposite direction. Charity ticked off the minutes in her head, anxiety rising like a river during a flood, threatening to drown her.

"What is Realta involved in, exactly?" she asked Callum.

He sighed. "It's complicated. I don't understand half of it, but Val wanted this war as a distraction so the Nine could face the Midnight King without outside interference. We are going to put it front and center. If the Midnight King is trying to conquer Eltriar again, people should have a chance to fight." He studied her. "Are you going to be okay?"

"Yes," she said despite her fear. She imagined the Midnight King attacking Vala, destroying everything and everyone she loved. She shoved the thought away. The Midnight King hadn't returned yet, according to Lucan. They still had time.

She and Gareth divided the papers and tucked them into their pockets.

War horns split the air, sending chills up Charity's spine.

"More fighting," Gareth said.

"Don't waste time," Callum said. He gazed out the window, blocking their view. "Take those papers to Isla now."

41

Prognosis

Lok and West stood in front of the healer's house, tossing a ball of fire back and forth. After each catch, they took a step back, testing how far the fire could fly. A handful of villagers stopped and watched, but only for a few minutes. The two Thanes were now commonplace, and afternoon was rapidly turning into dusk. West caught the ball, the flames less than an inch from his fingers. He smiled brightly at Kuno and Meredith who sat on the porch steps.

"Well done, West," Kuno said and then resumed his lesson. It was a dual lesson. He would say a word in Old Eltrian and translate it into Teyrnian. Meredith then translated it into Hiraethi. "This way, we teach each other," Kuno explained. Meredith readily agreed.

"Can you teach me history next?" Meredith asked.

Lok caught the ball and took another step back. He felt the heat, but it did not burn his fingers. His skin wasn't even red. Thinking back, he never got sunburned, and the few times he burned himself in the kitchen, the injuries were minor. But according to Gareth, Lok's Aura appeared last year. Had the ability protected him before it manifested? Something to research if they returned to the Academy.

He launched the ball, arching it so its apex was parallel to the roof.

"Which part of history?" Kuno asked, glancing over his shoulder. Esme and Noal Patyn, the guardsman who was injured at the Loy farm, stood on the porch. The guardsman now lived with the Loys, sleeping on the couch, and traveled to Vala with Esme for daily exercises. His arm was broken in two places, but according to Esme, they were clean breaks. The bones mended properly, and Patyn regained most of his mobility, though the muscles had weakened.

"Guess I won't be using a sword any time soon," he had joked a few days ago when he noticed Lok watching. Lok wasn't sure what to make of the guard. He always joked and laughed. Nothing at all like Kanton.

"I don't know." Meredith shrugged. "Just history."

"Hiraeth history?"

Meredith rolled her eyes. "I already know my people's history. What about yours?"

"Sure, I can teach you Teyrnian history. Do you want to begin with the war between Emitia and Merart?"

"No, I meant your history."

Confusion clouded the Scholar's face. "What do you mean?"

"You're obviously not Teyrnian. Your skin is too dark. Where is your family from?"

"Well, I was born in Teyrnas, so Teyrnian history is my history," he said defensively.

"And your parents? What's their history?" Meredith asked carefully.

Kuno folded his arms over his knees and kicked a small mound of dirt. "I never knew my parents. They died when I was an infant."

"How?"

"Nobody told me."

"Then how do you know they were really your parents? Someone must have told you."

"Why in the Abyss do you care?" Kuno snapped.

"Catch, Lok! Catch!" West called out.

Lok glanced up. The ball of flame dove towards him, like a hawk striking down on its prey. He quickly splayed his fingers. The flames dispersed.

Meredith stared at Kuno, aghast. "I just…" She swallowed. "We care for our own. Even orphans. If you were Hiraethi, you would know your parents' history. Their names. I… I'm a fool. Sorry." Meredith hung her head.

"You're not a fool," Kuno said softly. "There are just some things I don't want to discuss. Now, the war between Emitia and her twin brother Merart." He stood, folded his hands behind his back, and started pacing as though he stood at the front of a lecture hall. "It began after the death of their father, King Garno."

Esme laughed. "Always the historian."

"Always the healer," he replied, smiling.

Lok and West joined them at the steps. They had enough practice, Lok supposed, and fire was the only Elemental he could control. West could control three: fire, water, and air. Lok had experimented with air, water, and earth, but each attempt failed.

"Do you still find injured animals to nurse back to health?" Kuno asked.

"Only sick and injured villagers. With the occasional guard or Journeyman." Her bright smile reminded Lok of Realta and Charity. He wished he left Charity a note. What must she think of him, running away in the middle of the night?

Would he ever see her or Realta again?

"Why are you worried now?" Meredith asked Lok as Kuno walked up the steps to speak with Esme and Patyn, his lecture on the Caslanic war forgotten. The Scholar asked Esme about Patyn's exercises and the nature of his injury. Patyn reluctantly admitted to falling out of a hayloft. "I'd be more worried playing with fire."

Lok shrugged. He didn't want to talk about his friends or think about the Academy. Sometimes, he wondered if he should have stayed and fought Lucan. The Council could not force him to fight. Granted, they could have threatened to expel him if he refused. Which would have landed him back in Vala, anyway. But perhaps Charity would have traveled with him.

"Is it Luckson?" Meredith whispered. She glanced over her shoulder. Esme, slowly extending and rotating Patyn's arm, explained that she used a similar technique to help Master Kel relearn how to walk. The guard met Meredith's eyes for a split second and quickly looked away. He respected the Hiraeth for their skill as fighters, but he wasn't too keen on being in the same village as one.

"Why?" West tilted his head to one side.

Meredith stood and led them to a shady tree by the main road. Too far away for Esme and Kuno to overhear. "I know Scholar Kuno always gets nervous around him. I assumed he was with the people you're running away from."

Lok shook his head. He never had a reason to be nervous around Luckson. The traveler was friendly. Genuinely friendly. Not the forced politeness Lok's stepfamily displayed.

"Why you nervous?" West asked.

"He lies. Little lies, but I can sense them. He also lied about your abilities, West."

The boy gave her a confused look.

Lok took out his notebook and pencil. *"He knows why West can control more than one Element?"* Kuno mentioned that ancient Thanes could control all four Elements. He simply assumed West was like them.

Meredith nodded. "Are you sure he isn't some sort of Scholar?"

"Maybe he is from the Lowyrn or Byyar Academy."

"Not a chance. He has a Teyrnian accent, and most Byyarians have reddish hair."

Lok peered around the tree. Kuno and Esme were deep in conversation, talking and laughing about their days at the Academy. In the waning sunlight, Kuno's tan skin seemed darker. Too dark for a native Teyrnian.

"Where do you think Scholar Kuno's family is from?"

"I assumed he was Kereuic or Sykerian. I just thought it was strange for him to end up in Teyrnas. Did he ever mention his family to you?"

"Only that he's an orphan."

The door burst open. Estrid, crying, rushed to Esme and clung to her. Patyn reached for his belt and scowled. He had neither a sword nor a knife.

"What is it?" Esme asked. She smoothed down the girl's dark hair and wiped away tears.

"I just fell asleep for a minute. He was fine, but now he's bleeding! I don't know what happened!" Estrid cried.

Esme guided her to the bench and sat her next to Patyn. The guardsman moved over and tried to peer inside the house. "Where is Darran bleeding?" Esme asked her.

"On his neck. I don't know how it happened. I shouldn't have closed my eyes. I'm sorry." Estrid buried her face in her hands, sobbing.

"It's all right, dear. It isn't your fault." Esme turned to Kuno. "Stay with her." She then rushed inside.

Lok walked up the steps, curiosity overriding fear. Bleeding? The healer was asleep most of the time. How could he have injured himself?

"Stay out here, Lok," Kuno said.

But Lok felt compelled to enter. Ducking his head, he followed Esme into the bedroom.

"Great Creator," Esme muttered as she inspected Healer Zall. "Darran, what did you do?"

Lok stepped closer. Bloody scratches lined the side of Healer Zall's side. Dark red stains coated the pillow and the healer's shirt. Bile rose in the back of Lok's throat.

"Get me bandages and sterile water," she said to Lok, pointing at the shelf. Lok retrieved linen bandages and a skin of water.

"Is he all right?" Scholar Kuno called.

"Yes," Esme replied. "Superficial wounds. Likely did it in his sleep." She cleaned the cuts. "Lok, hand me that ointment. Red jar, second row." She pointed at a cabinet. Lok found it easily. She coated the inside of the bandages with the ointment and gently applied them to Healer Zall's neck. Zall didn't move. Didn't even open his eyes.

"Did he really scratch himself?" Lok wrote. The scratches seemed too deep to be caused by fingernails.

"Most likely. He probably had another nightmare." Esme placed her fingers on Healer Zall's wrist, counting. She sighed and tucked the thin wrist under the blankets. Heavy wool blankets. Far too warm for summer. Esme motioned for Lok to follow her outside.

"He will be all right," Esme said with a smile. She gave Estrid a comforting hug. "It was an accident. Nobody's fault."

"Hurt?" West asked.

"Nothing serious."

Meredith frowned. She met Lok's eyes and subtly shook her head. A pit formed in Lok's gut. Did that mean Esme was lying? Why would she lie?

"Have you seen Henry?" Esme asked.

"Not since you sent him on that errand," Kuno replied.

Esme asked Henry to make house calls that afternoon, and

Lok hadn't seen the healer's assistant since. He didn't mind. He regretted punching Henry and was afraid of how he would react the next time they were face to face.

"Would you mind taking Estrid home?" she asked Kuno. "She's an excellent rider, but I don't want her taking the trip alone so late in the day."

"I can go by myself, Mother," Estrid said, her voice shaking. "It's still daylight."

"There are rumors of bandits closer to the mountains," Kuno said. "It's always better to be safe than sorry."

A pensive look formed on Estrid's face, a mirror image of Master Kel. "Okay."

"Thank you," Esme told him quietly. "The horses are stabled at the inn."

"Sorry to cut the lesson short," Kuno said to Meredith.

"It's no problem."

Esme watched silently as Kuno and Estrid walked across the street.

"What about me?" Patyn asked.

She gave him a half serious smile. "Don't think you can get out of exercises early."

The guardsman rolled his eyes.

"Is he dying?" Meredith asked, sending a jolt through everyone. A guilty expression creeped onto Esme's face.

"The girl deserves the truth," Patyn said, his voice somber.

Esme bowed her head, as though in prayer. "Yes. I've tried every medicine, searched for every know illness. It's as though his body has betrayed him. I didn't want Estrid watching him, but with Henry out... I was afraid that Darran had died."

"Henry is a jackass," Meredith scoffed. "I would trust the tribal idiot before I trusted him."

Esme sighed heavily. "Henry is a little difficult to get to know."

"Did he tell you how he got that busted lip? That he and Lok got into a fight?"

Lok was grateful that Kuno had been supportive instead of angry. Lok ran into his room and bolted the door, fearing that Kuno would abandon him or return him to the Academy.

"Guess he's a weapon after all," Kuno would tell Scholar Lucan.

But it never happened. Kuno greeted him with warmth when Lok gathered the courage to open the door. Neither of them talked about the fight, nor did his mother bring it up at supper that evening. He caught her staring at him once, but it happened so quickly a part of him thought it was his imagination.

The other part knew better.

Esme crossed her arms. "No, he didn't. Lok, you aren't one to lose your temper. What caused the fight?"

Lok reluctantly wrote, *"He lied to me about delivering medicine. He just wanted an excuse to get away from Zall and drink."*

"Drink what?"

"Ale."

"Of all the stupid!" Esme schooled herself. "That boy knows better than to drink alcohol when he has a patient. Thank you for telling me, Lok. Perhaps I need to find a new assistant."

"Or just take over as healer yourself," Patyn interjected.

Esme waved the comment away.

"Esme!" Zall yelled. "Esme, help! Seltachai! The Seltachai is trying to kill me!"

"Fire and smoke." Esme turned to Patyn. "Congratulations. You're getting out of exercises early today."

"Great." Patyn stood. "Are there any rules against patients having alcohol?"

"You've earned one drink." Zall yelled for Esme again. She hurried inside.

"What about your three?" Patyn asked. "Will your Scholar allow you to drink?"

"It's more fun to watch people get drunk," Meredith replied.

"Depends on the people," Patyn muttered. He spared a quick glance inside the house and then made a beeline for the inn.

"Are you coming?" Meredith asked.

Lok shook his head. He spied Ellis and his son-in-law walk into the inn an hour ago. Lok really did not feel like being near his stepfamily.

"Suit yourself."

Lok walked down Vala's main road. The handful of vendors in the marketplace were finishing up business and closing for the night. The carpenter, Mister Ritt, waved as Lok walked past his shop.

It was hard to believe Lok ever thought this village was big with all its people and buildings and farms. Everyone in Vala could live inside the Academy, and there would still be room for all the Students, Journeymen, and Scholars.

The wind chimes outside the chapel sang as a warm breeze rushed by. Should Lok say a prayer for the healer? He never particularly liked the man and feared him more than anything else. But Healer Zall was dying. People always prayed for a dying person, that the Gadyeni would guide their soul to the Creator.

Perhaps he could ask a chaplain to pray for Zall.

The chapel door burst open. Brother Malaky looked around wildly, his hair messed up and glasses askew. His crazed eyes fell on Lok.

Stars above, no! Why did he think about chaplains? Brother Malaky had kept his distance, spending most of his time at the chapel. But the other chaplains began to talk about Malaky and his Farsights. Visions of fire and destruction. Soon, other villagers started avoiding him and quickly made excuses to leave if he happened by.

"Lok Tolman!" Malaky exclaimed. He ran up to Lok and embraced him, his sweaty hair resting against Lok's chest. Lok tried to squirm away, but the chaplain held on tight. "Thank the Creator! I saw you surrounded by flames! You were dressed all in black. A raven sat on your left shoulder. And your eyes! Great Creator, I wish I never saw those eyes!"

Malaky held Lok at arm's length, studying him. "Thank the Creator and all Eight Gadyeni. Your eyes are still brown."

Of course they were brown. What other color would they be?

"Where is Scholar Mykell?" Malaky asked, eyes darting. Passersby glanced nervously at Malaky and hurried along. Lok wished he could hurry along. He didn't not care if Malaky was Master Kel's brother. The two men were nothing alike, and he did not want to be associated with him. Or his Farsights.

Malaky grimaced. "Kuno. Sorry. Scholar Kuno. For the life of me, I can't understand why I'm always forgetting his name. Must be these Farsights. Can't think right."

Lok pulled away from the chaplain and pointed at the inn.

"Oh, do you have to go home?" Malaky almost sounded sad.

Lok nodded, not that he wanted to confront his stepfather and his forced kindness. He wished he had volunteered to ride with Kuno and Estrid. Mistress Loy's smile would be a welcomed sight.

But Lon Millar is there, too.

Who cared? Lon Millar tormented a scrawny boy who couldn't defend himself. There was no way Lon would mess with an Elemental Thane.

A weird feeling surrounded Lok, like a shadow creeping over his heart. Would Lon Millar leave him alone out of respect or out of fear? He didn't want anyone to fear him, even a childhood bully.

"Well, I need to go, too," Malaky said. "I need to speak with Mayor Gan. I keep having Farsights about Vala. All these buildings on fire, burned to the ground. I fear the war is going to reach us soon." The chaplain paled. He adjusted his glasses. "But Watchtower isn't far from here. We can send for recruits, if nothing else." He then hurried down the road.

Lok doubted Mayor Gan wanted to see Malaky. His Farsight were so frequent that they were more troublesome than interesting. Gan started inventing errands, going on his rounds at the same time Malaky arrived. He always instructed him to return to the chapel, much to the other chaplains' collective dismay. Malaky had yet to catch on.

A flash of black caught Lok's eye. He glanced up and saw a raven perched on the chapel's roof.

Why did so many of Malaky's Farsights include ravens? Weren't ravens the symbol of the royal family? If anything, it meant Teyrnas was involved.

But why is the raven on my shoulder?

The raven cawed loudly and flew away. A single black feather floated down and rested on Lok's left shoulder. He swatted it away and ran towards the inn.

42

Sacrifice

Realta cursed under her breath as she awoke in the Dream. It was her turn to keep watch.

She and Serena had followed Braedan's instructions and rode towards the river. By the time they reached it, it was almost too dark to set up camp, and they spent an hour finding a suitable place. The forest here was different from the Hinterlands. It was more akin to a swamp, with soft, spring earth that gave way to patches of marshy rivulets. Realta's boots were soaked by the time they finished.

At least they got a small fire going. The nights were warm, but walking in wet boots led to blisters.

Once that was done, Realta put everything Callum had taught her about forestry to use. Everything she had been too frightened to remember as they fled from Kanton. Bending branches to create shelter. Boiling water before drinking it even though it tasted horrible. And setting traps. With a ball of string from the horse's saddlebag, Realta set up three around their camp. Anyone who came within twenty yards would trip and fall into a pile of dry twigs. She hoped it would give them time to run.

"We can swim downstream," Realta said as they ate a meager supper of berries and dried meat.

"I don't know how to swim."

Water splashed behind them. Realta and Serena crouched low. Under the light of the moons, they watched as several large boats crossed the Nerin. The sailors lowered smaller boats, each carrying twenty men, into the water. Moonlight glinted off their weapons. Over twenty boats docked on the shore. Commanders barked orders in a language Realta did not understand, and the soldiers set up camp.

Her heart sank. They must be the Tarodic.

"Should we move away?" Serena whispered.

"No," she said after a moment, thinking through possibilities. "Corey won't risk a confrontation just to find us. We should be okay."

"But why if they find us?"

Realta did not have an answer. The camp was well camouflaged, and a patch of swampland separated them from the Tarodic camp. And the fire was reduced to embers. Impossible to see from the river.

Serena took the first watch, until the two moons were past their zenith, and reported that one unit had broken away, moving closer to the village.

Realta tried to stay awake for her watch, but her muscles ached, and her eyes were so heavy, begging to go back to sleep. She felt them close. Opening them, she discovered she was struck in another Dream.

She glanced around. It was too dark to make out details.

Can't see the sky. Must be indoors.

"Not everything goes as planned," Bas said, appearing behind her. His inky eyes shone like stars underneath his hood.

"You got that right." Realta touched the back of her neck, where her braid belonged. It would take years to grow back. If she lived that long. A shudder ran down her spine. "Why didn't you and Tath help us?"

"We could not show our hand. Not with all those soldiers present. But don't worry. Tath informed Chinasa and Elliza of your location. They should be here by morning."

"What about the Tarodic soldiers?"

"What about them?" Bas replied, his face blank.

Realta glared at him.

"Perhaps you should focus on your current surroundings first."

"Fine." Realta glanced around, and the Dream came into focus. She and Bas stood in a long hallway made of dark stone. Torches burned every ten feet, providing small pockets of light. There were no windows. She covered her nose with her sleeve as a musty, metallic stench filled the air. "What is this place?"

"It was a dungeon." Bas's eyes dimmed, his face downcast.

Realta spied a series of steps cut into the wall, leading upwards into darkness and giving her the impression that she would never see sunlight again.

"This definitely is not the dungeon at the palace." That place was downright cheerful compared to this hole.

"No, it's far older."

"The Thousand Years War?" Realta ventured.

Bas nodded solemnly.

"Are the original Nine here?" Realta cautiously walked down the hall. Barred cells lined the wall opposite the torches. All were empty. At the end of the hall stood a metal door, protected by a series of locks. The metallic stench worsened, twisting her stomach into knots. "Is someone in there?"

"Realta." Bas motioned for her to stand by his side. He placed a gentle hand on her shoulder. "In your Dreams, you've seen the original Nine and most of the Gadyeni. You've even seen members of the new Nine, though you probably did not realize it. There is someone else you need to see."

"Okay. Who?"

The air grew ice cold. The torches guttered, some going out. Realta shivered and wished she had a cloak. Half a second later, a warm, dark gray cloak covered her shoulders, but it did little to stave off the cold.

"The person Valentin Gardyner warned you about."

The door at the top of the stairs creaked on rusty hinges and slammed shut. Realta's entire body went numb, an icy fear invading her mind, making all thought impossible. Bas held her in a protective embrace.

"Remember, this is just a Dream. A window into the past. He cannot hurt you."

"I want to wake up," Realta pleaded. Heavy boots descended the steps, like a hammer striking an anvil. Her heart pounded in her chest, in her throat. No, she did not want to see the Midnight King. She did not want this fate!

"Please, let me wake up!"

"Not yet," Bas said gently. "You must understand what you are fighting against."

"I don't want to fight," she said, her voice barely more than a whisper. Tears stung her eyes.

"The best soldiers are the ones who want peace. Now look."

Realta blinked away the tears, and confusion replaced fear. Instead of a hideous monster, what stood before her was one of the handsomest men she had ever seen. A head taller than Callum with broad shoulders and a muscular build, the Midnight King sauntered into the dungeon. He had fair skin, devoid of any blemishes or scars, and rich, reddish-brown hair that fell to his shoulders in waves. He wore a pitch black uniform with red trim, and red embroidery in the pattern of flames decorated the collar and cuffs. Gold buttons went down the front of his coat in two rows. His black, knee-high boots were polished to a mirror shine.

Fear crept back into her as she met his eyes. They were the same blue as a cloudless summer sky, but they held none of the warmth. The longer she looked into those eyes, the colder she felt.

The Midnight King stalked down the hallway, a predator with easy prey in his sights. Realta huddled closer to Bas.

"His past self cannot hurt you," the Gadyeni assured her.

But those eyes... Oh great Creator, would she ever feel warm again?

"Good morning, Rudi," the Midnight King said as he undid the locks on the metal door. "Pleasant dreams?" He laughed, a deep, rich sound that echoed off the walls. A faint moan came from behind the door.

Bas moved closer, dragging Realta with him. She bit down on her tongue.

This isn't real. It's just a Dream. This isn't real.

But it had been real.

The door swung inward. Snapping his fingers, the Midnight King summoned a blueish white flame. The area behind him darkened, the meager light absorbed by the unnatural flame.

The white light fell on a young man chained to the wall. Rags covered his skeletal frame, and his wrists bore bloody cuts from too-tight manacles. He winced, turning away from the harsh light.

The Midnight King grabbed a handful of matted black hair and forced the prisoner to look him in the eyes.

Realta gasped. The prisoner was just a boy, only a few years older than herself. Dried blood covered his face, and one eye was swollen shut. His lips had been split multiple times, never given a chance to properly heal.

"Feel like talking today?" the Midnight King asked. He suspended the flame next to his head.

The boy spat bloody saliva at him.

Sighing through his teeth, the Midnight King wiped the saliva away. "I'm disappointed in you, Rudi. Everyone else submitted weeks ago. Listen. You're the only one left."

"I'm not afraid of you," Rudi said, his voice weak and hoarse.

The Midnight King smiled patiently. "Of course you aren't. I've watched over Drohkira for centuries, tended to your people's every need. I've even helped you conquer your enemies so you have nothing to fear. I want to help you, Rudi."

"Everything you say is a lie. You enslaved us."

"I warned you not to listen to Balthazar and his cronies. And now look what's happened. They've got your mind all twisted."

"No." Rudi locked eyes with the Midnight King. "They told us the truth. You're a monster!"

The Midnight King snapped his fingers, and his forefinger burned white hot. "Don't make me hurt you again, Rudi. I know you spoke with the Nine last month. I know you traded information. But I need details. What did you tell them?"

"The Creator shaped the worlds and set them in motion," Rudi said. "He set the stars in the Heavens to guide their ways."

The Midnight King touched Rudi's face with his burning finger. The boy shrieked. A thin tendril of smoke rose from the burning flesh.

Realta hid her face in Bas's cloak, shuddering each time Rudi screamed. She wanted to wake up. She bit down on her tongue, pinched her arms, thought of the small camp in the forest. Nothing worked. She was trapped, same as Rudi.

The last scream faded to a hoarse whimper.

"What did you tell Balthazar?" the Midnight King demanded.

Rudi muttered, too low for Realta to hear.

He seized Rudi by the chin, forcing him to look up. "Where is Hannor?"

Realta's heart skipped a beat. Hannor. The Sun Dagger. Was it really the same dagger that rested at the bottom of her saddlebag? Could it really be over three thousand years old?

"Balthazar will kill you," Rudi managed.

The Midnight King back handed Rudi, and his face smacked against the wall. His head lulled to the side. The Midnight King felt the boy's pulse and nodded. Satisfied that his prisoner was still alive, he stalked out of the dungeon.

Realta blinked. She and Bas now stood outside a massive stone structure, many stories taller than the palace in Teyrnas. The sun shone through a misty haze. Soldiers in black uniforms trimmed with red and gold walked through the camp. No, camp was the wrong word. It was more like a city with large stone buildings and paved roads. One soldier with hints of gray in his dark hair stood outside the largest building. He shifted nervously.

The Midnight King walked outside, making a beeline for the soldier. Realta quickly stepped out of the way. The soldier saluted, his fist over his heart. The Midnight King gestured for the soldier to follow. They disappeared within the maze of buildings.

"Do you understand the type of creature you are fighting against?" Bas asked.

Realta nodded. She felt like she was going to be sick. "Who was he?"

"His name was Rudimund e Raric i Tagern. He was a soldier in the Drohkiran army, recruited on his nineteenth birthday. Before that, he spent time on the front lines as a messenger. Even met Balthazar a few times. He started to wonder if all the magnificent tales about the Midnight King, the protector of his people, were true. On his last mission, his unit was entrusted to deliver Hannor, a weapon that could kill someone with a single scratch, to the Midnight King's top generals.

"The dagger went missing, and everyone blamed Rudi. They sent him to the Midnight King for questioning." Bas let out a heavy sigh. "He survived for forty-seven days. Forty-seven days of torture. Most people would have broken down long before then. Admitted anything just to make the pain stop. But Rudi refused to admit his theft."

"Did he really take it?"

"Yes. He gave it to Balthazar, told him how it was made and how it worked."

"Who made it?" Realta asked. If it was the same dagger, she

needed to learn everything she could about it.

"Metallurgists working under the Midnight King's direct supervision. We suspected he made several weapons. All resembling normal weapons but far deadlier. We tried to see how he created them, but he set wards against us. We could not enter this camp without experiencing extreme pain."

"The Gadyeni can feel pain?"

"To an extent. The men and women who created Hannor were executed once it was complete, and all their notes were destroyed. We do not know how Alberik created it, only that it worked very well."

"How do you know?"

"Balthazar used it to defeat him."

"Wait, is it the same dagger I have? The one Master Corey…" Realta's mind raced. Too many questions to voice at once.

"Hannor weakened Alberik enough for him to be imprisoned again."

"So, Balthazar just stabbed him? That sounds too easy."

"Agreed. Using the dagger killed Balthazar. It drained him of all his energy, and his organs failed one by one over the course of a half week. He died in agony. We tried to save him, to counteract the dagger's effects, but Alberik created the dagger to kill mortals and severely wound Gadyeni. We could only watch. Do you think you can endure the same, Realta Haar?"

Realta grimaced, tasting bile in the back of her throat. "No. Could a Gadyeni use the dagger against him?" she asked.

"We fought Alberik directly the first time and won, but the same methods failed the second time. He learned all of our tricks, and he's had plenty of time to review our tactics, plan our strategies before we even thought of them.

"And the Midnight King will regain his full power during the Summer Solstice. Two days from now. Just as he did three thousand years ago. Do you think you can unite with the rest of the Nine and find him in time?"

"No." Realta glanced around the hazy area. "Didn't you say one of the Gadyeni was looking for the Midnight King?"

"Yes. Esar, however, has yet to report back." Worry crept into his voice.

"But the dagger will defeat him? Are you sure it will work a second time?"

"There is a possibility it will weaken him. We recovered two other weapons he created and noted that they weaken over time. One lost all its strength slowly over two centuries. And the other just stopped without warning after a thousand years. Hannor, mercifully, retains some of its power. And it is the Windrose's to wield." Bas's face fell. "He might die, the same as Balthazar."

The Windrose, a Thane with all eight abilities. The one destined to be their leader.

Val's face appeared in her mind. He only had one ability, so he couldn't be the Windrose. But he was crafty. Would he allow the Windrose to lead, knowing he would ultimately sacrifice himself, and then seize leadership for himself?

Regardless, Realta would have to confront Val again. Would have to work and fight side by side with him. The very thought made her shiver.

"I want to wake up now."

"Very well. We will direct Chinasa in your direction at first light. And keep a close eye on that dagger."

Bas snapped his fingers, and Realta woke up.

43

Vows

Chinasa was done. He was done running, done being stuck in the middle of nowhere, and he was done dealing with Waylar Corey and his insipid temper.

Unfortunately, he was also done being the leader.

He called Shasta Cray into his room. None of the Scholars had strong leadership skills. Place them in a laboratory or in front of a lecture hall, and they were in their element. But putting them in charge of a group of people? Scholar Kambri or Scholar Okorie might do well for a day or two, but not long-term.

So, he met with them before sunup and explained how fate had dealt its hand. The vote was unanimous.

"The Scholars are at a consensus," he told Shasta before she had a chance to sit down. "They want you to lead them."

The short woman arched an eyebrow, the equivalent of another person dropping their jaw. "And what prompted this decision?"

Chinasa exhaled slowly. He didn't want to believe Val Gardyner. His words were those of a madman. Borderline heresy. The Nine Thanes defeated the Midnight King millennia ago, and there were no records or Farsights about him waging war a third time.

And Valentin was Nowani. The information he presented about himself and Chinasa seemed too good to be true. A fabrication to make himself seem important and prove the Nowani government wrong about Thanes.

Tath's arrival in Aneros changed everything. Chinasa tried to fight it and earnestly prayed for the first time in years, hoping the Creator would make his path clear. The next day, Bas arrived during a storm. Two Gadyeni in the same place. If that was not a sign, Chinasa didn't know what was.

"I have to find Realta and Serena," Chinasa replied. He tucked his red necklace inside his shirt collar. A green and brown hunting shirt, complimented by brown trousers and sturdy boots. Two of Ezri's hunting knives hung from his belt.

"How do you hope to accomplish this?" Shasta intercepted him at the door.

"I promised to protect them, and by sitting around here and waiting, I am failing that promise." His sole meeting with Callum Haar had been brief, barely long enough to exchange names. But he promised to protect Realta should they be separated or, Creator forbid, Callum died.

"And the two Gadyeni in the common room? Why not ask them for help?"

Chinasa stared at Shasta incredulously. Of course she knew. She was King Logan's head adviser. No secret could escape her knowledge.

"You will never cease to amaze me, Mistress Cray."

"Not a great accomplishment if you get yourself killed out there." Word reached the village this morning that the Tarodic docked on this side of the river. Some of the villagers spied scouts in the forest. Commander Maddrel placed his men on high alert.

"I doubt the Gadyeni will allow us to come to harm." He was One of Nine. If his life became endangered, Tath would intervene. *Unless he is still mad about me stabbing him in the back.* Was it too late for the Gadyeni to select a new Learner? Was that why Esar hadn't introduced himself?

"How did the Scholars take it?"

"Well enough." Chinasa had prepared a speech, but looking them in the eyes, the words sounded hollow. He never meant to grow so attached. Chinasa had spent his entire adult life traveling. Different cities, different languages, different faces. Never the same group for months on end. He felt like he was leaving his childhood village all over again.

Ezri was the hardest to convince.

"I am sworn to protect you," the young man protested. Judging by the look in his eyes, he was prepared to follow Chinasa into the depths of the Abyss.

Chinasa placed a firm hand on Ezri's shoulder. "And now it's my turn to protect all of you."

A few voiced dissent. Chinasa was running headlong into a

war they spent two months fleeing from. Was it logical to run back? But Chinasa's mind was already made up. They respected him for that and quickly voted. Better to rip out a hangnail than let it hurt all day.

Now that he set a foot on this path, there was no turning back.

An ambassador in his fifties and a little girl going to fight a supernatural entity for the sake of the world. May the Creator help them.

A look of resignation came over Shasta. "Find those girls, Ambassador Ekene. And be safe."

"I promise." It was a promise he hoped to keep.

He walked out of the inn and entered a madhouse. Averillian soldiers marched throughout the village. Saddling horses, putting on armor, checking weapons for any defects. Kereuic civilians were also being outfitted for battle. Anyone from boys barely into their teens to old men with gray and white hair. Most looked like they had never held a sword in their lives. Chinasa didn't doubt they would make up the bulk of the casualties, those who didn't run away in a panic once the fighting began in earnest.

Braedan Sutter reined his horse in front of Commander Maddrel. The commander wore polished armor and a dark green cloak with Averil's oak tree embroidered in gold, shining in the sunlight.

Sutter dismounted. He was coated in sweat, and the sleeve of his shirt was torn, and the frayed edges were stained dark red. A close call with an arrow.

Why isn't he wearing armor? Chinasa wondered. Granted, a person needed a certain amount of insanity to stay in close proximity to Waylar Corey.

The commander gave Sutter a nod. Half a second later, Corey himself appeared, red faced and scowling.

Chinasa sighed through his teeth. He did not want to deal with the merchant, but he really needed Sutter's horse.

"Mind if I borrow this?" Chinasa asked the mercenary as he grabbed the horse's reins.

"I do actually," Sutter replied. His eyes darted to Corey.

"Do you know where those thieves are?" Corey demanded. He jabbed a finger in Chinasa's face. "Is that why you're sneaking off?"

"If I were sneaking, I wouldn't have bothered to ask permission." Chinasa turned to Maddrel. "Commander, it is imperative that I find Realta Haar and Serena Molyns. Both girls are my responsibility."

"Responsibility?" Corey sneered. "Haar is a runaway slave. I don't know about Molyns. Where did you find her? A cheap whorehouse?"

Chinasa took a deep breath, exhaling slowly. He would get nowhere fast by punching Corey in the face. "I admit both girls are runaways. But slavery, to an extent, is illegal in Kereu. By breaking the law of one land, I am upholding the law of another."

Maddrel just stared at Chinasa. Stars above, the man was completely confused! If only his Teyrnian were better. A thought occurred to him. Why didn't he think of it earlier?

"Does Corey know Lower Vogellian," Chinasa asked Sutter, using the official term for Averillian.

"No, sir." The mercenary smirked.

"What did he ask?" Corey rounded on Braedan. "Lower what?"

"Lavair sora," Sutter added in Averillian. *Speak freely.*

He certainly catches on quick. Perhaps more than his appearance reminded Serena of King Logan. He made a note to ask Shasta if he returned.

"I understand," Chinasa said to the commander in his native language, "that breaking a vow is a source of great sham. Is this correct?"

"Yes. I would rather die than break my vows."

"Well, I took a vow to protect Realta and Serena. You can report me to a magistrate for harboring runaways if you wish. But I need to take this horse and find them before the Tarodic army attacks."

"I don't give a flying leap for magistrates," Maddrel sneered. "They cause more trouble than they're worth. Take the horse. If any of the men give you trouble, use my name."

"Thank you, sir." Chinasa climbed into the saddle.

"Hey, what are you doing?" Corey demanded, his face turning a darker shade of red. "What did you say?" He rounded on the commander. "What did he say?"

"My Teyrnas no good, sir. So, sorry. I must go now." Commander Maddrel marched away, calling out orders. The soldiers formed ranks, the civilians lining up behind them. The second in command, a grizzled man with red, Byyarian hair, translated the commands into Kereuic.

"Get back here!" Corey yelled, but no one listened.

"I can help you," Sutter said to Chinasa.

He looked the mercenary in the eyes, eyes that seemed wholly familiar. Eyes that belonged to the King of Teyrnas and to Serena Molyns. And those eyes belonged to a man who had proven he was a better person than Corey time and again.

Chinasa could use a person like that on his side.

Corey scoffed. "So, you do know where those thieves are hiding. I should have known not to trust you."

"Go to the Abyss." Sutter flagged down a young cavalry soldier.

"Down, soldier!" he ordered in Averillian. "No time for questions. On your feet!"

The confused soldier dismounted. "What's going on? Who are— Hey!"

Sutter climbed into the saddle. He flicked the reins, leading the horse to Chinasa. "Commander Maddrel's orders."

"Like the stars, they are!" The soldier ran off, calling for the commander.

"Do you think anyone will hire you, traitor?" Corey asked.

Sutter bristled.

"I thought not." Corey smiled wickedly. "Place Ambassador Ekene under arrest. We'll sort this mess out."

Sutter sat motionless, staring at the ground, white-knuckling the reins. Chinasa waited.

Come on, man. Prove me right! You're better than him. Now prove it!

The mercenary drew a knife and cut off his shirt sleeve, revealing the scarification on his right forearm.

"I'm not a mercenary anymore."

"What about Elliza?" Corey asked mockingly. "Are you going to abandon her?"

Chinasa maneuvered his horse between Corey and Sutter. "Elliza is far more important than your pathetically small mind can comprehend. The Gadyeni will not allow you to harm her."

"The Gadyeni?" He laughed nervously. "Why would they care

about some slave girl?"

"Why don't you ask them? Tath and Bas are in the common room. You know them better as Savastian and Adso."

Sutter smirked.

Elliza must have told him.

"You've gone mad!" Corey shouted. His eyes darted towards the inn. "He's insane!" He jabbed an accusatory finger at Chinasa, but the soldiers paid him no heed as they marched towards the forest.

"Perhaps." Chinasa turned to Sutter. "Well?"

War horns sounded. A flock of startled birds erupted from the trees. The Averillian soldiers halted, murmuring.

Chinasa spied the flag of Tarod, a yellow sun rising over the water, at the forest's edge.

Sutter cursed under his breath. Corey ran back into the inn, slamming the door.

"We've wasted too much time." Chinasa flicked the reins, steering the horse towards the forest, away from the approaching army. Sutter kept pace as the smooth dirt lanes transformed into dense underbrush.

Behind them, the Averillians shouted a war cry.

44

Nowhere to Run

"Wake up!" Serena shook Realta as another series of war horns sounded. Soldiers shouted, giving and relaying orders. Peering through the branches of their shelter, she spied soldiers marching closer, closer.

Please wake up!

Serena shook her again. Was she in another Dream? Realta was next to impossible to wake during a Dream. But Serena couldn't leave her here. Could she carry her? No, it would slow her down, and the soldiers were bound to spot one girl carrying another through the forest.

Realta's eyes fluttered open.

Thank the Creator!

"We have to go," Serena whispered, pulling Realta to her feet.

Realta shoved her away and leaned against a tree. Her face was deathly pale in the morning light. Bright light that would give them away in seconds.

"Was it a Dream?" Serena asked tentatively. She glanced over and saw a column of soldiers in red and blue uniforms bearing the flag of Tarod march through the forest. Five yards away and heading towards the village. Away from them. Serena felt some relief, but there were more soldiers by the river. They wouldn't stay hidden for long.

"I don't want to talk about it." Realta's eyes widened, seeing the marching column. She shoved Serena down and hid underneath their shelter. "How long have they been there?" she whispered.

"They started moving a few minutes ago. Realta, what do we do?"

"I don't know. How far are we from the river?"

"I told you I can't swim." Serena nearly had a panic attack when Realta suggested swimming downriver. She was fine crossing the

Nerin in a boat. Boats were designed to float, and on such a large vessel, she forgot they were on the water. But she never learned to swim. Never had a reason. There were no ponds or lakes in the capital, and she rarely ventured outside the palace.

"Not what I'm thinking. How big are their boats?"

Serena shrugged. "Big enough for twenty people, I guess."

"Do you know how to row?"

"No. Do you?"

"No better time to learn. Same goes for swimming."

"That will never happen," she replied adamantly.

"We can't risk going back to Aneros. We have to make it to the river. And we don't have to row. We can let the boat follow the current downstream." Realta crept towards a row of large, flowering bushes. They left the horse tied up there. Far enough away that, if spotted, would give them time to run, but not too far to reach quickly. She retrieved the stolen dagger and hurried back to their camp. The white hilt shone brightly in the light, as if it were made of glass. Serena noticed strange patterns decorating the sheath. Were they letters? It certainly wasn't Teyrnian script.

"Have you seen Braedan?" Realta asked, tucking the knife into her belt.

"No."

"Eh, vas reterom hyr?"

Serena and Realta crouched down. A soldier pointed at their horse, alerting the next man in line.

Fire and smoke. They should have left the horse behind. There was no way they could ride in this dense forest, not with moss covered swamp every five feet. The soldier walked up to the horse, one hand on his short sword.

Serena crouched down lower, her heart in her throat. What if the soldier saw them? Would he let them go or would he draw his sword and...

Twigs snapped. The horse neighed fearfully.

A second soldier called out to the first.

The first replied in Tarodic.

Serena's blood rushed in her ears. What were they saying? Did they see the camp? Branches did not curve naturally. They were bound to notice.

A third soldier shouted. The first soldier's footsteps retreated, absorbed into the column. The marching faded away.

Realta rose to her knees and glanced around. "It's clear," she whispered.

Serena slowly stood on shaking legs. She saw nothing but trees in every direction. This was worse than the coup. At the palace, she knew where to hide, how to escape. Out here in the woods, they were exposed with no clear path. There could be scouts hiding in the trees right now, watching her and Realta, and they wouldn't know until it was too late.

"Come on," Realta walked over to the horse and untied the saddle bag. Slinging it over her shoulder, she untied the horse's reins. The horse stared at her with big, brown eyes. She nudged it towards the village and the horse started walking. Realta headed in the opposite direction, towards the water. And countless Tarodic soldiers.

Serena steeled herself. It would be fine. She had ridden in a boat before. This would be no different. Just smaller and much closer to the water.

What if they posted guards?

She dug her nails into her palm. *Reach the river first, then worry about guards.* Maybe they didn't bother posting guards. They were miles from a major city, and most villagers did not know how to use weapons. They might not know about the Averillian battalion.

A root snagged her foot. Serena bit her tongue, suppressing a scream. Realta steadied her and kept walking.

Why couldn't Serena be just as brave? She knew Realta was afraid. It was impossible to be lost in the woods surrounded by hostile soldiers and not be afraid. But her steps never faltered. Was it because she'd been raised by a mountain guide? Or was it because she was a Thane? Were Thanes inherently braver than normal people?

It made some sense. Ambassador Ekene was always brave, and he never let anyone, not even Waylar Corey, intimidate him. In that sense, he reminded her of Logan.

What would her half-brother have done in this situation?

He would not be cowering behind a girl who's younger than him.

And he would not be making excuses for himself.

Was she making excuses?

Serena's heart sank. Yes, she was making excuses. Shasta Cray was the bravest woman she knew, and the head of servants was not a Thane. She had confronted Logan at his worst, not once but countless times. Even when the King's Guard was too hesitant to be in the same room as him, Shasta marched in without batting an eye. Logan raged and fumed, proving he was every bit Yestyn's son. He always thanked Shasta for her honestly afterwards and even apologized in public a few times. He rarely treated nobles with the same curtesy.

Shasta was just as brave as Chinasa, and she was as normal as Serena.

And Serena herself? She had run away from home, from everything and everyone she knew, hoping to start a new life and maybe finding her lost half-siblings. What happened to that girl? Why couldn't she summon that bravery now?

The trees thinned out, replaced by river grass and reeds with feathery plumes on the ends. The marshy soil turned to sand. Water lapped on the shore.

Realta signaled for Serena to halt.

Serena peered through the tall grass and saw an entire fleet. Massive war ships, their central masts rising a hundred feet in the air. The canvas sails displayed the rising sun of Tarod. Men hurried along the decks as commanders and captains shouted orders.

Ten smaller boats lined the shore. Boats designed to carry ten or twenty or a hundred people judging by the rows of benches. Two were laden with supplies: sacks of food, wooden crates, and a variety of weapons. Soldiers armed with short swords patrolled the shore.

"What now?" Serena whispered.

"I'm thinking."

"Think fast." One of the soldiers spotted them. He wore plated armor over his red and blue uniform. Drawing his sword an inch out of the sheath, he stalked towards them.

"Don't run." Realta grabbed Serena's arm.

The soldier shouted at them in Tarodic.

Serena tried and failed to swallow. She didn't know a single word in that language. He could be asking their names or demanding they follow him to the boats.

He shouted again. Completely unintelligible.

The soldier, muttering angrily, then spoke in Kereuic. Serena recognized the sounds, but not the words.

Some apprenticed linguist I would have made!

"Teyrnian?" the soldier asked in a heavy accent.

"Yes," Realta replied.

"Step forward. Stand where I can see you!"

Realta obeyed. Serena followed one step behind. Her legs felt like they were made of water.

"Let me see your hands."

Serena jolted as something kicked her leg. She saw Realta's raised hands and raised her own.

"What are you doing here?"

"We got lost. We're trying to find our way back to Aneros," Realta replied, her voice trembling.

"But you are Teyrnian. Why are you in Kereu?" The soldier's eyes went to Realta's servant's mark. He scowled. "You are a servant?"

Realta's face reddened, but she nodded.

"Who do you belong to?"

"Her older brother," Realta said. "He sent us south to avoid the war, sir."

"Where in Teyrnas are you from?" he asked Serena.

"West Bridge, sir," Realta replied. "We—"

"I am not addressing you, servant," he snapped. "Where are you from?" he asked Serena.

"West Bridge," she stammered. Her eyes darted to the boats. The nearest was a ten-seater. Could they outrun the soldier and take it?

The other soldiers on patrol watched attentively, hands on their weapons. Serena's heart sank. No way they could outrun them all.

"Who is your brother? Some Teyrnian noble?"

Serena nodded.

The soldier grabbed Serena by the chin. She almost slapped his hand away but stopped just in time. Assaulting him would land her and Realta in a world of hurt. He brushed her hair away, studying her ears. He did the same with Realta. "Not Thanes. Good. Where is your brother now?"

"I… He sent us ahead. I don't…"

"Vas tubel, Veltan?" asked another soldier as he walked towards them. He was older, with creases at the corners of his eyes. Two golden knots adorned his right shoulder.

The soldier replied in Tarodic, gesturing at Serena and Realta. The older soldier nodded, never taking his eyes off them.

"One has a servant's mark," Veltan finished in Teyrnian. "I believe they are spies."

"We weren't spying," Realta said.

"Speak when spoken to!" Veltan yelled in her face. Serena shuddered, memories of Logan and Corey flooding her mind.

"Calm down, major," the older soldier said, his accent so thick Serena barely understood him. "Neither girl is armed."

"She has a dagger."

The soldier smiled. "She also has skinny arms. Tell me, Major Veltan, do you think a skinny girl is a match for Tarod's best?"

"Of course not, Captain, but—"

The captain raised a hand. Veltan clamped his mouth shut. "What harm can two young girls cause? Now, little one, hand over the dagger, and we will get this matter sorted out."

"I can't. He will beat me if I lose it." Realta hung her head, and her lip trembled, as though she were going to cry.

"Will your master really beat you?" the captain asked skeptically.

Realta nodded, her short hair getting in her eyes. "He already cut off my hair for losing his grandfather's pendant. And this knife is much older. Please don't take it away."

Serena didn't know how to react, awed by Realta's performance. She created that lie so easily. Had Callum taught her, or was it the result of fear? Serena had heard servants create quick lies to escape Logan's wrath.

"Fine, keep it," the captain replied. "But if that dagger comes out of its sheath, I will beat you myself. Is this clear?"

"Yes, sir. Thank you, sir." Realta wiped away imaginary tears.

Serena turned and nearly jumped out of her skin. Major Veltan glared at her, studying her clothes. Clothes that were not the attire of a young noblewoman.

"What is your brother's name, miss?" Veltan asked.

"It's um…"

A soldier on the massive warship shouted, pointing upstream. The soldiers on patrol ran towards the disturbance, weapons drawn. A man on horseback approached. A tall man with light hair. Braedan!

"It's Braedan O'Sutter. Of House Sutter. And my name is Serena O'Sutter."

"I have never heard of that House," Veltan sneered.

"Since when are you familiar with Teyrnian nobility?" the captain asked. "Where is your brother, miss?"

Serena glanced upstream, and her heart soared. Chinasa Ekene rode side by side with Braedan. A quartet of Tarodic soldier blocked the shore, ordering them to halt. A third man wearing a tattered gray cloak rode up behind them.

"There," Serena pointed, tears brimming her eyes as she smiled. Chinasa and Braedan were both here. And with Bas by their side, what did she have to fear? "That's him. The tall one with light hair."

The captain ordered them to follow, and they obeyed. Serena felt a lightness in her steps, a lightness she hadn't felt in… She honestly did not know. Major Veltan breathing down her neck ruined it a bit, but she'd be away from him soon.

Veltan eyed Braedan and Chinasa warily. Braedan, as usual, was armed to the teeth. And Chinasa wore a hunting knife. The major spoke to the captain in Tarodic.

The captain gave him a curt replied. Veltan muttered angrily.

"Now, miss, which of these men is your brother?" the captain asked.

"The one with sandy hair and blue eyes. The one who looks like me." Strangely, Serena did not feel foolish saying it out loud. The first time, she was filled with doubt, believing her mind was playing tricks on her. Now it felt natural.

"Oh yes, I see the resemblance."

Serena's smile brightened. A tear fell down her cheek. A tear? But she wasn't sad. This was the happiest she had felt in weeks!

Realta lightly squeezed Serena's hand and smiled.

Major Veltan muttered a phrase in Tarodic over and over. Fear crept its way into Serena's mind, threatening to suffocate her happiness. If only she knew what the man was saying!

The captain waved Braedan over. Braedan dismounted and walked towards them. Chinasa also dismounted, but two soldiers bared his way with their swords. Bas remained seated on his horse.

"Sir, he has a traitor's scar," one soldier informed the captain.

The captain scowled. "Show me."

Braedan obeyed.

"How did you get this?" the captain asked. He flicked the fingers on his right hand. The soldiers formed a loose circle around them, weapons drawn.

"By being a fool," Braedan replied.

"I've no doubt. What was a member of the Teyrnian nobility doing as a mercenary?"

Confusion clouded Braedan's face.

"Like my employer said," Chinasa intervened, "he was acting foolish. A lesson he learned too late."

"And you are?"

"I am Master Sutter's private Scholar." Chinasa gave the captain a short bow. "And this gentleman is my colleague." He pointed at Bas.

"Scholar Adso of Lowyrn," the Gadyeni replied, bowing with a hand over his heart.

"Why aren't you wearing white cloaks?" Veltan asked.

"We are private Scholars, sir. We don't adhere to a dress code," Chinasa added with a smile.

Veltan scowled.

"Why are you here, Lord Sutter?" the captain asked Braedan.

"Looking for these fool girls, that's what." Braedan went up to Serena and hugged her. "What did you tell them?" he whispered.

"That we are siblings. Nobles on the run."

Braedan, one hand on Serena's shoulder, addressed the soldiers. "I will pay handsomely if you would transport us down the river. As far as the border of the Sykerian Empire. We want nothing to do with this war."

"Sorry," the captain replied. "We are stationed here until further notice. So, unless you are good friends with my commanding officer, we are going nowhere. And neither are you." The captain relaxed his stance. "I'm curious. Why does your servant have short hair? It's odd to see short hair on girls."

"Well, it's just easier," Braedan replied, adopting a confident posture, as though he truly were a noble. "She spends more time on cooking and cleaning and less time on washing and brushing."

"And she is a good servant? Doesn't lose things?"

A pit formed in Serena's gut. She tapped Braedan on the arm, but he ignored her.

"Lose things?" Braedan looked aghast. "Course not. Realta is too careful to lose things."

The captain snapped his fingers. Rasping metal filled the air. A dozen swords glimmered in the morning light.

Serena edged closer to Braedan.

"I knew they were spies!" Veltan yelled. He fixed his blade on them.

"Fire and smoke," Braedan muttered.

"I believe there is a misunderstanding," Chinasa said calmly. But no one was listening.

"Men, place them on board the flagship," the captain ordered.

The soldiers advanced, tightening the circle. Braedan drew his knives. One soldier placed a sword at his throat. Tears welled in Serena's eyes as Veltan pointed his sword at her throat, the metal touching skin. Some rescue this turned into.

"Are you going to let this happen?" Chinasa asked Bas. Anger, true anger, rose in his voice. "I thought Realta and I were important."

"You are important," Bas replied, sitting calmly on his horse. Even the animal was calm.

"Then prove it! Help us now or we allow them to arrest us. We will watch this war from afar."

"That is not possible. Fate won't—"

"Help us or find another Dreamer!" Realta shouted. The soldiers drew closer. The tip of one sword brushed Realta's hair.

Bas sighed. "Esar just had to pick someone as stubborn as himself. And I've followed his example." The Gadyeni raised his hand into the air and said, "Dream!"

Every Tarodic soldier fell to the ground.

Serena stared at the soldiers. They laid motionless. What had…? She looked at Bas. "What did you do?"

Braedan crouched down and placed his fingers on one man's neck. "He's asleep. How on Eltriar—"

"The perks of being a Gadyeni."

Serena nudged Veltan with her boot. The man breathed deep and easy. Fast asleep. She knew the Gadyeni were powerful, but putting a dozen men to sleep with a single word? *Not just them.* She glanced up at the warship. No men shouting or feet running. *He put them to sleep, too.*

If Bas could do this, what could Tath do?

"Do those perks include bringing Elliza here?" Braedan asked.

"No. We must hurry. The fighting in the village is worsening." Bas pointed to a line of horses. The soldiers guarding them were also asleep. How many people did that make? Fifty? A hundred? And all asleep. The horses stamped their hooves nervously. Bas placed a finger to his lips. The horses quieted.

"Come. Time is growing short. The Midnight King will regain his full power at sunset. You won't have a chance to confront him before then, but you must unite with the rest of the Nine immediately."

"This is really happening," Serena said to Realta as they climbed into a saddle, Realta taking the reins. "All this running just to go backwards."

Realta bit down on her lip. "We don't have a choice." She cast a wary glance at Chinasa. The ambassador's face was ashen.

"What about me?" Serena asked. "I'm still coming with you, right?" Realta had never broken a promise to her, but dread crept into her mind, telling her that she was not good enough. And even if Braedan was her brother, they were just bastards. The voice sounded less like Logan and more like Yestyn.

"We're a part of this," Braedan replied. "Don't know how or why, but Elliza saw that we're connected. Do ravens mean anything to you?"

Serena's heart skipped a beat. How much had Elliza seen? Did she know the truth or only part of it? She nodded quickly.

"Explain later," Chinasa said. He led the way through the forest, following the path cut out by the Tarodic column.

Shouting and clashing metal rang through the forest, but Serena could not pinpoint it. The sounds grow louder. She fixed her gaze on the Gadyeni. Bas slumped forward, his breathing labored. Forcing the soldiers to sleep must have tired him.

Can the Gadyeni get tired?

The question never crossed her mind. Getting tired seemed so human, and the Gadyeni were always so much more than human. One step below the Creator.

She began to ask Realta if she knew, but her head hung low, and she held onto the reins loosely. Serena could not see her face, but she sensed that Realta was crying.

Serena sighed through her teeth. Was there any way to help Realta? Something she could say to make a bad situation better?

Bad? We're riding to a battlefield and then traveling into a war zone so Realta can reunite with the man who started the war. The same man who murdered Logan. This is absolutely terrible.

A part of her wished she agreed to swim downriver. Swimming couldn't be too hard, and it was better than riding through a forest with enemy soldiers fighting nearby.

Why couldn't she be brave again?

Less than a year ago, she planned on running away and mapped out her entire route. She was afraid to leave everything familiar, but she knew she could not stay. The palace was no place for her.

She was brave enough to confront Logan.

Perhaps she could summon that bravery again. She had lost it somewhere along the way, but standing alongside Realta, Chinasa, and Braedan, maybe she could find it again.

Find it again? a voice asked. *You're running into a fight instead of away from it. That sounds very brave to me.*

The voice sounded strangely like Logan's.

45

Rightful Heirs

Isla leafed through the papers those Students gave her last night. She hadn't known how to react. Two girls arrived with a bundle of papers, giving an old code. "Ravens fly at dawn." The royal family hadn't used that code since Logan ascended the throne.

"Callum Haar told us to use it," said one girl, who had a red earring.

They then explained that the papers belonged to Scholar Kuno and contained information about the Wardens.

Isla accepted the papers, though the guard on duty told her to be cautious, eyeing the girls as though they were assassins in disguise. She thanked them and dismissed the guard.

Not two minutes later, the same guard escorted two boys, also with the same code and also with a bundle of papers from Scholar Kuno.

And five minutes after them, Gareth and Charity Loy presented her with a third bundle.

Isla never met Scholar Kuno and didn't know anything about his research. But far better for her to have these papers than the Wardens of the Night.

A chill went down her spine, just thinking about the name. First, it had been a vague Farsight. A strange title with no faces, and no way for her to confirm whether it was real. Back then, she had the luxury of thinking some of her Farsights were flawed. These papers and Charity Loy's account confirmed that Farsight and validated Logan's search.

She called Ayrdeen, Gallia, and Logan to her room at sunrise. It took longer for Gregor to reach Deen and Logan's tent. Soldiers patrolled the walls and gates, setting up barricades and directing civilians to move closer to the main building. The East Gate, leading to Norgard, had nearly collapsed during last night's battle. Work crews comprised of soldiers, Manipulator Thanes, and refugees busily made repairs.

Deirow Hawks reported that the Nowani and Galionic soldiers were preparing for another fight. Whether it would be today or tomorrow, no one could accurately say.

With any luck, the war would end soon. They just had to hold out a little longer.

Isla placed the papers on her desk. All the furniture had been pushed to the side, making room for a semi-circle of chairs facing her desk. Deen and Logan sat opposite her, two chairs between them. Deen cleaned his flute, casting surreptitious glances Logan's way. Logan stared out the window. He wore a long, black cloak that fell past his feet. She had seen him dressed this way a few times. The first was shortly after Yestyn's death. Logan stood in front of a mirror, studying himself. He acted like a kid who had been caught trying on his father's clothes when he noticed Isla standing in the doorway.

The second was the night Serena ran away. He had worn the cloak to confront and possibly frighten her. There were a handful of times in between. Quick glimpses. She half suspected it was camouflage, a way for him to walk the streets of Teyrnas without interference.

The cloak's hood was down, revealing uncombed hair and bloodshot eyes. When was the last time he got a decent night's sleep?

Can you blame him? Isla was lucky to get two or three hours a night.

A sharp knock sounded at the door. Logan pulled the hood over his face.

"Enter," Isla called.

Gallia, her face hidden inside her cloak, walked in, escorted by Carwyn. She surveyed the room, looking warily at Deen. The King of Bran Maro shot her a venomous glare.

Carwyn held Mannix by the hand and Morgan cowered behind him. The boy looked at Logan as though he were a bandit out of a story, ready to rob him in the dead of night. Isla's heart ached. Morgan was afraid of his own father and didn't know it.

Didn't even know his father was alive.

"The boys wanted to be with you," Carwyn said.

Mannix let go of Carwyn's hand and climbed into Isla's lap. The child wrapped his arms around her, shaking. Isla gently stroked his hair. Frequent nightmares plagued Mannix, keeping him up half the night. Isla spent hours at a time calming him down, convincing him that they weren't real.

Morgan quietly sat on the bed. The boy looked drawn and haggard.

No twelve-year-old should look like that. Isla knew he was worried about his new friends, a group of refugee boys. Most were orphans. Three had gone missing in the last week. Isla assumed the worst. Civilians were ordered to avoid the walls, but children were naturally curious. Soldiers weren't the only ones killed in battles. She didn't have the heart to tell Morgan that his friends might be dead.

She shuddered, remembering Wills's blood on her hands and clothes. She had stowed the dress in the back of the wardrobe, not bothering to have it cleaned. Why didn't she just burn it? She would never wear it again.

"Please, take a seat," Isla said, returning her thoughts to the present.

Carwyn sat next to Deen while Gallia sat between Carwyn and Logan. Logan shifted away, the chair scraping against the stone floor.

We're supposed to be working together. But could she really blame him? Gallia and Val tried to kill him.

"Who is this?" Gallia asked, edging away.

"One of my spies," Isla lied. It had become so easy to lie. She held onto Mannix a little tighter. "He has new reports on a faction operating inside the Academy."

Deen frowned. "Which faction is that?" He glared at Gallia.

"The Wardens of the Night," Isla said tersely. She would not allow this meeting to devolve into an argument. "I've told you about my Farsights, and now we have proof." She placed a hand on the papers. Thank the Creator her parents forced her to learn Old Eltrian. Some of the words were obscure, but she understood enough. And it terrified her. "The Wardens believe the war is a sign that the Midnight King's powers are returning, and he will try to conquer Eltriar again."

"I still say it's a load of cock and bull," Deen spat. "Where did you get these papers?"

Isla explained Gareth Haar, Charity Loy, and their friends bringing the papers last night.

Deen scoffed. "A bunch of stupid teenagers. You honestly believed them?"

"I believe them and my spy." Heat rose in her face. Those Students had been frightened, terrified that the papers would fall into the wrong hands. One boy, a Manipulator Thane, had questioned her extensively, to the point of being disrespectful. His friend, a Minder Thane, assumed him that Isla was trustworthy. Only then did the boy hand over his share of the papers. And Gareth had no reason to lie to her.

"Stupid teenagers *and* a pathological liar. Tell me," Deen said to Logan, adopting a mocking tone. "Have you told those boys your real name?"

Logan sat as still as a statue.

"He wishes to remain anonymous," Isla replied coldly. *Ayrdeen, if you know what's good for you, leave my children out of this.*

Deen rolled his eyes and leaned back in his chair. "Sure. Doubt he wants to get stabbed again. What does that feel like, anyway? Does it hurt?"

"Would you like to find out?" Logan asked, pitching his voice low.

Mannix started crying.

"That's enough," Isla snapped. "Ayrdeen, have you and Gallia worked on a treaty?"

"We tried," Gallia replied. She glared at Deen out of the corner of her eye.

Deen crossed his arms over his chest. "I refuse to work with unreasonable people."

"You're unreasonable!" Gallia yelled. "Every time I make a suggestion, you either shoot it down or change the subject."

"Stop." Isla held up a hand, silencing them. Both monarchs looked at her. Good. At least they recognized somebody's authority. "All we need is a document to stop the Nowani and Marish soldiers from fighting alongside the Coalition. Both of you left the Coalition and allied yourselves with Teyrnas. Put that in writing, and we will present it to the Council."

Gallia fingered a lock of hair while Deen studied his flute.

"What?" *They decide to be quiet now?!*

"What will the Scholars do to us?" Gallia asked, sounding like a lost child.

"It's not as though they'll welcome us with open arms," Deen added.

"Petition for asylum," Carwyn said. "The documents are easy to draw up. All you need is Queen Isla's signature and seal."

"Sound like a plan?" Isla asked. Gallia nodded, but Deen didn't look convinced.

"What does it guarantee?" he asked. "We get to live in Teyrnas, but what about our soldiers? What if they decide their loyalty is to the Coalition, not to Bran Maro or Nowan? And if they choose to follow us, what will the other soldiers do to them? Do you think the Galionic soldiers will just let them go home? Do you think Kenda will allow them to live?" Anger rose in his voice. "My daughter is still trapped with that bitch!"

Isla's throat tightened. For each solution they found, a new host of problems arose.

"Could we spare some of our soldiers to aid them?" Carwyn asked.

"Not bloody likely," Deen replied. "They've been fighting for months. Hostilities don't magically cease by signing a piece of paper."

"The Madani." Isla felt a weight lift off her shoulders. Finally, a solution! "The Madani are scheduled to arrive today. They can protect the Marish and Nowani soldiers from the rest of the Coalition."

"And the refugees?" Logan asked, keeping his voice low. "Who will escort them to the ships? The Tirshic soldiers guard the North Gate."

"We can redirect the Thane Regiment to the North Gate," Isla said, thinking quickly.

"A regiment that does not answer to you," Deen interrupted. "And good bloody luck convincing the Scholars to listen."

"They'll listen to all of us," Gallia said. She met Isla's eyes and smiled, mirroring the woman Isla had met at the Exhibition. "When is the Council meeting?"

"This morning at ten." Isla glanced at the wall clock. Just past nine. They had less than an hour to prepare. "We can sign a document by then."

"Are you sure this will work?" Deen asked skeptically. "My bet, they will order their guards to detain us before we can speak a single word."

Isla looked at Logan. A single word from him would solve half their problems. Instead of adhering to an obscure law, the Scholars would have a king to answer to. King Logan would never stand for the Council's games, and the Council knew it.

But he still had the Wardens to deal with.

You don't have to deal with them alone. Let us help you.

Shouting echoed in the hall. Morgan shot to his feet and froze. He, and everyone else, looked to Isla.

"It's just the guards," she said, recognizing the voices.

"Why are they shouting?" Gallia asked.

Furious pounding shook the door. Isla's heart leapt into her throat. Mannix cried, clinging to her. The two confident monarchs looked like frightened children. Had someone recognized them? No, Gallia wore a cloak, Deen dressed like a servant, and Logan... Isla glanced around. Where had he gone?

"Who is it?" Isla called out. She walked the short distance to the bed and handed Mannix over to Morgan. The boy immediately clung to his older brother. Morgan's eyes were wide and glassy, simultaneously staring at the door and at nothing.

"Should we hide?" Gallia whispered, eyes darting to the small side room. Isla followed her gaze and saw Logan hiding behind the door, cracked just wide enough for him to peer out.

Isla shook her head. "The guards aren't allowed inside without my permission."

"Just an intruder, Your Majesty," called out of the guards, a young man named Lloyd. "Nothing to worry about."

"Let go of me!"

"Gareth?" Carwyn rose to his feet.

"Let him go," Isla ordered.

"I can't. He was caught stealing from one of the Scholars." Feet scuffled on the stone floor. Another guard cursed. Someone got slapped. "We chased him here," Lloyd said between breaths.

"Let go!" Gareth shrieked.

Isla flung open the door. Lloyd held Gareth's arm twisted behind his back while another guard massaged his hand, small red marks appearing between the thumb and forefinger. Gareth screamed again, his face bright red.

A man in a white cloak ran up to them. Isla's heart caught in her throat. Scholar Lucan. The man Charity Loy identified as the leader of the Wardens.

"What is the meaning of this?" Isla demanded.

"The bastard broke into my room," Lucan replied, seething. His bushy eyebrows were knitted together, and his eyes burned like coals. "I caught him before he could steal anything."

"What do you want us to do with him?" the second guard asked.

"Let me go!" Gareth cried.

"Lock him away."

"No!" Isla and Carwyn said at the same time.

"Why not?" Lucan's dark eyes fell on Carwyn. Anger melted away, replaced by confusion. "Aren't you the beggar I caught lurking in the stables?"

"Yes," Carwyn admitted. "Please, Scholar, this boy is my son, and he's a Student."

"Where's his cloak?" Lloyd asked.

Gareth balled his free hand into a fist and punched Lloyd in the ribs. The guard let go, clutching his torso. Gareth made it two steps before the second guard grabbed him, wrapping muscular arms around his torso and neck. The boy looked at Isla, pleading.

"Son, look at me," Carwyn said calmly. "Please, let him go. He won't run away, I promise."

The guard and Lloyd exchanged glances. The guard then looked at Lucan. The Scholar's face was like stone.

"I order you to release him," Isla said.

The guard, thank the Creator, obeyed.

Gareth ran to his father's side, rubbing his shoulder.

"Tell me what happened," Carwyn said. "How did you lose your cloak?"

"And what were you trying to steal?" Lucan demanded.

"One question at a time."

"You don't give me orders, beggar," Lucan rounded on him. "What is a beggar like you doing in Queen Isla's presence?" He grabbed Carwyn by the cloak and shook him. Carwyn splaying his fingers, and Lucan stumbled backwards. His head smacked into the wall. He stared at Carwyn, stunned.

"How did…?" Gallia began. She quickly shut her mouth.

"Gareth, it will be okay," Carwyn said. Gareth trembled, staring at his boots. "What happened to your cloak?"

"How do you know this beggar?" Lucan asked Isla without a single ounce of deference. The Scholar touched the back of his head and winced.

Isla pictured the Scholar in a long, black cloak. It suited him.

"He works for me," Isla replied.

"Why? What good is a crippled beggar?" He looked warily at Carwyn.

"That is none of your business." *And yes, Lucan, he is a Manipulator. How nice of you to notice.*

Carwyn gently placed a hand on Gareth's shoulder. "Please, son."

"I left the cloak in my room," Gareth replied quietly. He pushed a lock of hair out of his eyes. "I didn't want to be seen."

Lucan jabbed a finger at him. "So, you were stealing! I will have you expelled for this!"

Gareth raised his head and glared at Lucan. Isla's heart skipped a beat. The boy looked like a younger version of Callum Haar.

"I'm sure it's a misunderstanding—" Carwyn said.

"Misunderstanding," Lucan scoffed. "No doubt he learned to steal from you. What happened to your leg? Punishment for theft? Answer me, you damn thief!"

"He is not a thief," Isla said.

"Then who is he?" Lucan finally noticed the other people in the room. He paled. "What…? What are…?" Lucan rounded on the guards. "Arrest them!"

"Who are they?" Lloyd asked, completely confused.

Gallia stood side by side with Isla, holding herself regally. "I am Queen Gallia Toutain of Nowan, and I formally surrender to Her

Majesty Queen Isla Margents O'Kelwyn."

"And I, King Ayrdeen Akardal the Second of Bran Maro," Deen announced, standing and adopting a military posture, "also surrender. Again."

Lloyd's eyes nearly popped out of his skull. The other guard tried to speak, but only a strangled sound escaped his lips.

Lucan quickly composed himself. "How did you get inside the Academy?"

"We disguised ourselves as refugees," Deen replied matter-of-factly. "You know all about disguises, don't you, Scholar?"

"I want all of them taken in for questioning," Lucan addressed the guards. "And have this beggar and his son placed in custody. I want the truth out of them."

"You can't arrest them," Deen said.

"Why not?" Lucan asked, as though speaking to an unruly Student instead of a king.

"Because that beggar is Crown Prince Carwyn O'Kelwyn, the rightful heir of Teyrnas, and the boy is his son, Prince Gareth."

Carwyn looked as though Deen had punched him below the belt and then kicked him for fun while he was down. He looked to Isla for help, but what could she say? That Deen was lying? The Council would never believe another word the man said!

"Crown Prince Carwyn," Lucan muttered, testing the words. He grabbed Carwyn by the chin and studied his face. "The scarring is extensive, but I knew I recognized those eyes. Yes, I remember you." He scowled. "Always asking too many questions. Always getting into trouble. It seems trouble found you, boy."

"If by trouble, you mean King Yestyn beating him half to death," Isla interjection. The world might as well know the whole truth.

"What do you want us to do with the boy? I mean, the prince. Is he really a prince?" Lloyd asked Isla.

"Let him go," she replied. "You have no proof of a crime. The Council is meeting at ten o'clock. All five of us will be present." Isla turned to Lucan. "Scholar, you are on the Council, correct?"

"Yes, Your Majesty," he said through his teeth.

"Inform them that we will be present. Be sure to include our titles."

"I will do so." Lucan glared daggers at Carwyn. Carwyn met

the glare head on. It was nothing compared to the way Yestyn had looked at him. The Scholar stalked away, the guards flanking him.

Carwyn shepherded Gareth towards the bed, and he sat next to Morgan. Mannix cried softly.

Isla noticed a bright red mark on Gareth's face. She made a mental note to find the guard's name and put a reprimand on his record.

"Well, that went well," Deen said with a smug smile.

"What were you thinking?" Isla rounded on him. "Carwyn has been in hiding for seventeen years. You've jeopardized everything he worked to protect."

"Calm down. It's not like I revealed your spy's identity," he pointed at Logan. Logan stepped through the side door. At least Lucan hadn't seen him.

Regardless, Isla wanted to slap Deen.

Carwyn shambled past her and slammed his crutch into Deen's kneecap. He screamed and collapsed onto the floor.

"You son of a bitch!" he yelled through gritted teeth.

"I'm a son of a bitch?" Carwyn snapped. "You idiot, you have no idea what you've done!"

"I told the truth," Deen sneered. He huddled into a ball, clutching his knee to his chest.

"You called Logan's reign into question," Carwyn continued, looming over Deen. "People didn't care about him taking the throne because I was dead, and he was second in line. But now, people will start wondering. Did Yestyn conspire to get rid of me? Was it a plot between Yestyn and Logan? Between Logan and me? And King Nolfri will be furious. He created that marriage arrangement so his grandchild could sit on the Raven Throne. What happens when he discovers I'm alive with two children? Do you want to risk Byyar ending their alliance?"

"I... I just..." Deen shot a hateful glare at Logan. "I'd rather have you as king than him!"

"Well, good for you. You got what you wanted." Carwyn closed his eyes and breathed deeply. The anger ebbed away. "Isla, have there been any cases like this in Teyrnas' history?"

Isla's head ached behind the eyes. They were so close to making progress, and thanks to Deen's grudge, they were two steps back. "Not Teyrnas, but other kingdoms." She racked her brain, trying to recall history lessons from twenty years ago. "In most cases, the rightful heir was crowned after the current monarch stepped down. Sometimes willingly and sometimes by force. There was one case in Lowyrn in which the rightful heir abdicated, allowing his sister to continue to rule. But the abdication process takes months."

"We don't have months." Logan stepped into the center of the room and removed his hood.

Gallia gasped, hands covering her mouth.

Morgan stared at him. "Father?"

"Hello, boys." Logan smiled weakly. Morgan and Mannix leapt off the bed and ran to him. Logan held Mannix with one arm while hugging Morgan with the other. Morgan stood as tall as Logan's shoulders now. As tall as Isla. The boy sobbed quietly. "I've missed you so much."

"Where did you go?" Mannix asked.

"I had to hide, and I still have to hide. Your uncle Carwyn is going to be king for a while. Let's see how well the crown fits him."

Isla sensed hostility in Logan's tone. *Why can't they get along like they used to?* Carwyn and Logan had been thick as thieves, always protecting each other's back. She made another mental note: repair the brothers' relationship. If she could accomplish that, the Coalition would be no match for them.

The wall clock chimed the half hour.

"Ayrdeen, stand up," Isla ordered.

"My bloody kneecap is broken!"

Isla didn't have time for this. "Help him," she told Gallia.

Gallia, never taking her eyes off Logan, helped Deen to his feet. He leaned against her while balancing on one leg. He glared at Carwyn, but Carwyn ignored it.

"I don't want to be a prince," Gareth whispered.

"It's only temporary," Carwyn assured him. "What were you trying to steal from Lucan?"

"Nothing. Charity wanted to find proof that Lucan is a Warden. She didn't want him to catch us, so we waited 'til he got back. I was the distraction."

Carwyn smiled. "Clever girl."

"Charity? Is she the Student from the Exhibition?" Gallia asked.

"Yes," Isla replied. She hadn't paid the girl a second thought at the Exhibition. Just one Student out of hundreds. She would not repeat that mistake. "Is Callum Haar with her?"

Gareth nodded.

"Good. Let's not waste any more time," Isla said.

46
Son of Midnight

"Damn, he's fast," Jaim said as Gareth sprinted down the hallway. Scholar Lucan shouted at him to stop. They had timed their arrival perfectly, in the small window of time between Lucan returning to his room after breakfast and before the morning Council meeting.

"He's one of the fastest kids in Vala," Charity replied. She, Jaim, and Coryn dashed across the hall when no one was looking. Charity closed the door softly.

"What evidence will convince the Council that Lucan is a Warden?" Coryn asked, peering around the spacious room. It was three times as large as Kuno's with two smaller rooms off to the side. A large window faced the East Gate. And shelves of books and artifacts lined the walls. The perks of being a Council member.

Charity went to the window and spied two units advancing towards the wall, one of Nowani soldiers and one of Teyrnian soldiers from the Garrison. Was Zandon with them, or was the Thane Regiment stationed elsewhere?

"What about those creepy cloaks?" Jaim suggested. He rifled through the wardrobe.

"No, anyone could own a black cloak," Charity replied. "We need something more solid."

"Books?" Coryn asked, pointing at the bookshelf. All the volumes were about political theory and economics, Lucan's areas of research and subjects that were way above Charity's head. "Did you see any books at the meeting?"

Charity shook her head. The plan included Gareth distracting Lucan so they could search freely, but Lucan's rooms were much larger than they expected. It would take twice as long, and they had half the people. Callum went to the refugee camp to see Kel, and Ivar and Evelyn returned to the library so they could view the books Kuno had checked out.

She wished Callum was with them, an extra set of eyes to act as a lookout. Or King Logan. He likely knew more about Lucan and the Wardens, but he disappeared. And Callum advised against enlisting the king's help.

"Keep his presence here a secret," Callum said when she mentioned the king.

Before he left, she asked, "Are Kel and Logan really brothers?"

"Yes," he said after a long moment. "For both their sakes, don't tell anyone."

Charity agreed despite having more questions, mainly about how Esme could keep being married to a prince a secret, but she refrained. She would ask Kel the next time she saw him.

"Check behind furniture or inside furniture," Charity said.

She and Jaim moved the wardrobe away from the wall, and Coryn overturned chairs and desks. Quietly, of course. A well of good it would do them to get caught in a Scholar's room without permission.

War horns sounded. Charity and Coryn shared an uneasy glance and continued searching. They were safe inside the Academy. No matter how bad the fighting got, they were safe. The Coalition breached a wall, but the Teyrnians fought them off. The wall was fixed now. It was just a fluke. Nothing like that would happen again. They were safe…

Charity reached for a book and found that her hands were shaking. She quickly balled them into fists.

Pretend you're in a surgery. Remember what Esme and Healer Zall taught you.

The first piece of advice was not to panic. Panicking led to mistakes, and mistakes led to disaster.

The second piece of advice came from Esme. You can be terrified on the inside. You can be afraid, uncertain, completely in over your head, but don't let anybody see it. If you're performing surgery with another healer, your fear will infect them faster and deadlier than any disease.

Yes, it was okay for her to be afraid, but she had to look brave for her friends.

Taking a deep breath, she slowly relaxed her hands. Still shaking, but a little steadier. Yes, she could do this.

"What about this one?" Coryn removed an old book from a false bottom in a desk drawer. The pages had yellowed with age, but the leather cover was well cared for, with just a little fraying on one corner. "A book this old ought to be in the library."

Charity examined it, gingerly turning the pages. The book was written in Old Eltrian.

"Let me see." Jaim stood on his toes to peer over Charity's shoulder. "What's that name?"

"The author is Mab Alberik." Charity's blood turned cold.

"Does that mean anything?"

"It means Son of Alberik. The Midnight King." Charity wanted to hurl the book at the wall, run away, and wash her hands in lye. But running away solved nothing. *Be brave on the outside.*

"The Midnight King's true name is forbidden to write," Coryn said, her voice shaking. "If we show this to the Scholars, they'll know something is wrong."

Charity placed the book on Lucan's spacious writing desk and rubbed her hands on her dress. Great, now she had two things to wash.

"Can you prove Lucan owns that book?"

Charity whirled around, her heart leaping into her throat. Shari stood in the doorway. A large purple bruise rested in the center of her forehead.

"I, um…"

With one fluid movement, Shari closed the door and strode towards them, arms crossed over her chest. "Do you think my uncle will simply imprison you again? When he catches you, he will make sure nobody finds your body. Or your friends'."

"I'd like to see you try." Jaim pulled out a handful of nails and screws. The bits of metal spun around his hands.

Shari rolled her eyes. "Go ahead. You're so low leveled a Manipulator it's a wonder the Scholars gave you an earring in the first place."

Jaim's face reddened. The nails spun faster, blurring.

Charity forced herself to meet Shari's eyes. "Why are you doing this?"

"You knocked me unconscious, and those two morons just left me there. How did you convince them to let you go?"

"Another Warden intervened." Let Shari mull over that. "What I really want to know is why you're a Warden."

"My family has served the Midnight King since the Thousand Years War." Shari stood tall and proud. "We have remained faithful, and when Alberik returns to claim this world, we will be rewarded."

"You're delusional," Coryn said. The poor girl had gone completely pale.

"Oh, really? And what do you believe, Learner? Do you really think the Gadyeni are your protectors?"

Coryn shrank back. "Um, yes."

Shari smiled mockingly. "Did you know Alberik was one of the Gadyeni? One of the Nine. The others betrayed him."

"Where's your proof?" Jaim snapped. The nails spun so fast, that if Jaim lost concentration, they would go flying in all directions. Fast enough to take out an eye. Charity shuddered, recalling Evelyn's story about Ailyssa and Padraig. But this was different. Ailyssa couldn't control her temper, and this was a self-defense.

Shari eyed the spinning nails warily. "Why don't you join us and find out?"

Another volley of war horns sounded, followed by shouting. A thousand voices joined as one.

"Does the Midnight King approve of this war?" Charity asked, an idea forming.

"Alberik approves of fighting. Wars determine who is the strongest. Who is the most worthy to rule."

"And that's why there was a war between him and the Gadyeni." Charity chose her next words carefully. "He proved himself to be the strongest."

"Obviously."

"The Gadyeni could not defeat him on their own. So, they created Thanes to defeat him. But it was only temporary. He proved he is stronger than us. That gives him the right to rule us."

"We are weaker than him. That's a given."

"But it's more than that. He thought we were weak to begin with."

"Charity, what are you doing?" Coryn whispered.

"He thinks," she continued, hoping she said all the right words, "we are too weak to rule ourselves, right?"

"People need a strong hand to guide them. Alberik offers us guidance, gives us direction."

"Threatening people with war isn't guidance."

"Yes, it is," Shari replied. "The Drohkiran were the first to bend to his rule, and they soon proven themselves worthy by fighting in Alberik's name. By conquering all who were weak or foolish."

"Right. Exactly. So, what will Alberik," she tasted bile in the back of her throat, "think of you when he gets here? I knocked you out without really trying."

Shari's face flushed red. "You caught me off guard, you little—"

"Does Alberik care?" Charity interrupted. She locked eyes with the older girl. "I doubt it. You were weak once, so you'll be weak again."

"My uncle is the Head Warden of—"

"And what about Scholar Kuno? He's another one of your weaknesses."

"Shut up!" Shari yelled. She drew in a shuddering breath, and tears brimmed her eyes. "Don't you dare talk about Kuno."

"Why not?" Jaim asked. The nails and screws spun slowly around his fingers.

Shari's face became stone. She glared at Charity.

"Does Kuno know about the Wardens?" she asked softly.

"No, he…" Shari tried and failed to take a deep breath. "I wanted to tell him, but the way he talked about his research… He loves history. Loves teaching history."

"Ancient history." A smile stole across Charity's lips, recalling Kuno's enthusiasm. The way his eyes lit up during a lecture, making him look twenty years younger. "What does he think about the Midnight King? Does he think Alberik wanted to help Eltriar?"

"No, Kuno…" Shari blinked back tears. "He describes Alberik as a tyrant. A monster. Sometimes, he looked like he was going to be sick. I wanted to tell him that he was wrong. Alberik would have helped Eltriar if the other Gadyeni hadn't interfered. But I couldn't."

"Why?"

"Because…" Shari looked up at the ceiling. "Fire and smoke. I feel so stupid, but I love him, and he loves me. When he first told me, I didn't know what to think. The man's twice my age, and I only got close to him for his research. But I love him so much. I couldn't ruin that by telling him the truth."

"Why do the Wardens want his research?" Charity asked.

"A lot of old texts were lost when the original Academy burned down. The ones that survived were placed in special archives. Only a handful of Scholars have access, including Kuno. Some were written by Farsights, describing visions of Alberik escaping the Abyss and returning to our dimension."

"Our what?" asked Coryn, equal parts horrified and confused.

"Our world," Shari amended.

"Why couldn't Lucan just take them?" Charity asked. "He's a member of the Council."

Shari shook her head. "Doesn't work like that. Being on the Council does not grant special favors. Not where the archives are concerned. So, he sent me to Kuno."

"He never expected you two to fall in love."

"Lucan thinks I'm being foolish. But why not? In time, Kuno can see that Alberik is not the evil creature history portrays him as."

"But what if he is?" Charity asked, keeping her voice low and gentle. They didn't have time for an argument. Lucan could return any minute, and he might bring guards.

"Guess we'll find out." Shari eyed the book. "What are you going to do with that?"

"Take it to the Council. Unless Lucan isn't the only Warden among them."

"There are two more," Shari replied, smiling.

"Who?"

"I'm not going to make it easy for you."

"Give the book to Queen Isla," Jaim said. "We can trust her."

"Are you going to tell Lucan we were here?" Charity asked.

Shari stared at Charity, drumming her fingers on her arm. Another volley of war horn sounded.

What if they break through the walls? Everyone in the Academy would be trapped, at the mercy of the Coalition soldiers. What would happen to her? To her friends? The Nowani hated Thanes.

Would they be imprisoned, or would Jaim, Coryn, and Ivar suffer a worse fate?

Would all these old books written in a dead language matter if Teyrnas fell?

"Give the book to the queen," Shari said. "I doubt she'll understand it, anyway. On one condition."

A pit formed in Charity's gut. "What?"

"Help me find Kuno."

"We don't know where he and Lok went." Perhaps it was a good thing Lok didn't write a note. One less clue for the Wardens to follow.

"Doesn't matter. You, Charity Loy, will help me find Kuno Surylin, or I will personally hand you and your friends over to the Wardens. Got it?"

"It's a trick," Jaim said. "It's got to be."

"Can you really trust her?" Coryn whispered. "Scholar Kuno left weeks ago. There's no way you can find him."

"And how will you get past the soldiers?" Jaim added.

Charity handed the book to Coryn. "It's worth the risk. Give the book to Queen Isla." The last thing she wanted was to see her friends behind bars.

"But—"

"No buts. She needs to know what we're fighting against."

Coryn relented and held the book close to her chest.

"Charity, don't go." Jaim pleaded. "It's a trick. You know it is."

It was possible. Shari could be leading Charity right into the Wardens' hands.

But what if it wasn't a trick? If their search led them to Kuno, then who better to help them fight the Midnight King? Kuno was an expert on the Thousand Years War. His research might hold the key to defeating that monster.

And, if it truly was a trick, better for just her to be captured than all her friends.

"I'll take the risk." She gave Jaim a quick hug and turned to Shari. "Okay."

"Let's go." Shari latched onto Charity's wrist and dragged her into the hallway.

47

An Evened Field

The village erupted in chaos. Soldiers clashed, swords emitted sparks as metal contacted metal, arrows rained down, blackening the sky in waves. Some hit the inn's windows. One cracked the glass, the arrowhead embedded within it. The innkeeper, his family, and the servants sought shelter in the basement.

Elliza counted her breaths. Inhale, exhale. Calm and even. She experienced many Farsights that included herself. She was not fated to die here. So why was she afraid?

The Scholars, led by Shasta Cray, carried their meager possessions down the stairs and headed for the basement door. Elliza hadn't experienced any Farsights concerning the Scholars, but she had one about Mistress Cray. She stood beside a throne, whispering into the ear of a king dressed in rags. Elliza filed that one away as being very odd, and she didn't mention it to Shasta Cray. The woman was amiable towards Thanes, but would she believe Waylar Corey's supposed ally? Should she explain her actions? No, her actions would not make sense. Not now. Perhaps after the battle...

"Aren't you coming?" Shasta Cray asked as the last Scholar walked through the narrow door.

Elliza glanced around the common room. She had never seen it so empty. So strangely quiet. Sounds filled the outside world, muffled by the thick walls.

"No, ma'am," she replied quietly. "I will be all right."

Shasta Cray studied her shrewdly. "Very well." As she closed the door, Elliza had a strange feeling they would soon meet again.

She heard Corey mutter under his breath. The merchant sat at the table nearest the door, watching the battle through the window, a knife at his side. The poor fool had no idea what lay in store for him today. And Tath sat at the bar, calmly sipping a pint of ale. Though alcohol had no effect on the Gadyeni, Tath explained that he liked the taste.

The Gadyeni wore his long, dark blue cloak over finely tailored dark clothes. The time for them to leave drew near.

"Get away from the window," Tath said.

Elliza moved to the bar and sat beside him.

Two soldiers, one Averillian and one Tarodic, crashed through the window. Glass shards flew everywhere. Their swords showered sparks, metal clanging in Elliza's ears. The fight was not how she pictured a duel. Instead of a fluid dance, each soldier complimenting the other until one got the upper hand, it was brutal and chaotic. Each man desperately hacked at his opponent. The Averillian soldier sliced the Tarodic soldier's arm. The man screamed, dropping his blade and clutching his bleeding arm. In one swift movement, the Averillian slashed the Tarodic man's throat.

Elliza screamed and covered her face as blood sprayed out, coating the floor.

The Averillian nodded towards Elliza and Tath and then jumped out the window, rejoining the battle.

"Disgusting," Corey muttered. He walked around the body and sat down beside Elliza.

Why couldn't he piss off for five minutes? She and Tath had important matters to discuss before Bas returned. Matters that did not concern Waylar Corey.

Well, this was his last day on Eltriar. What was the harm?

"Are we going to the Academy?" Elliza asked.

Tath nodded. "About time you made up your minds," he muttered.

"I was willing to go anywhere, so long as we united with the others."

The Gadyeni glared at her through the corner of his eye. "Nobody likes a bootlicker."

Elliza's face reddened. "I only meant—"

"What are you talking about, girl?" Corey interrupted, knitting his gray eyebrows. "Kereu doesn't have an Academy."

"We are meeting the rest of the Nine as well as Master Savastian's associates at the Teyrnas Academy," Elliza said tersely. She did not have time for pointless questions.

Corey shifted uneasily. "The Nine, huh? Nine what?"

"The Nine Summit Thanes," she replied.

"Where did you get that ridiculous idea?" he scoffed. Elliza spied a bead of sweat on his brow. "Another Farsight?"

Afraid I'll reveal your secret? Elliza smiled on the inside while keeping her face neutral.

The Gadyeni took another sip. "This is good stuff. Why don't you help yourself? You never know when it will be your last drink."

Elliza's heart skipped a beat. Did Tath know? She glanced at him. The Gadyeni gave away no emotions.

She then looked at the busted window. The outside world was awash with chaos. Soldiers fighting left and right, dark green blurs mixing with red and blue ones.

A volley of arrows embedded themselves in the wall. Another volley found softer marks. Several Averillian soldiers, including the one who had crashed through the window, fell. Red and blue fletching stuck out of their chests.

This must be, Elliza reminded herself. *A lot of fighting now to prevent worse fighting later.*

All would balance out in time. They still had until sunset before the Midnight King fully regained his power. Going to the Teyrnas Academy made more sense now. Its library was full of ancient texts, some dating back to the Thousand Years War. One was bound to contain information about Hannor, the Sun Dagger. How the weapon worked. Why it killed Balthazar, and if there was a way around that.

Her cousins had instructed Corey to never use it, not even to cut food. The dagger was death itself. Her parents had learned that the hard way. They had been fools. Choosing the wrong side. Her cousins were smarter, getting rid of the dagger and Elliza simultaneously. Both were valuable to the Wardens, and who better to safeguard them until the right time than another Warden?

"What are you thinking?" Tath asked.

"About what must be."

"Plan all you want," Tath whispered in her ear, making her skin break out in goosebumps. "It won't do you any good. Not with my brother."

"What are you talking about?" Corey asked.

"Nothing that concerns you," Elliza snapped.

Corey grabbed a fistful of her hair. She had lost count of the number of times he grabbed her hair. *I swear on my parents' names, this time will be the last!* "Don't think you can get smart with me, girl. Don't forget about the mark on your face."

How could she forget? She saw it every time she looked in a mirror.

"I apologize," Elliza forced out the words. "I am afraid, and I forgot myself."

Corey released her and grinned. "At least one of you has an ounce of sense."

Elliza squeezed her eyes shut. Now was not the time. The time was close, so very close. She just had to be patient.

She opened her eyes and saw a massive stone building. The flag of Teyrnas flew from the highest turret. The Teyrnas Academy. Elliza smiled. She had one Farsight of her and the rest of the Nine at the Academy a few days back. Nine Thanes drawn from every continent on Eltriar.

But this Farsight only contained the Academy. No people, no walls. And no sky. Just a dark expanse, stretching towards eternity.

The Teyrnian flag widened, occupying her entire field of vision. Two ravens flying on a field of blue, a silver stripe crossing the blue diagonally. Two more flags joined it. The hawk and silver keys of Nowan and the seven stars of Bran Maro dancing on a field of black. The constellation of Rosmerta's boat, sailing to explore the open sea. Strange that a people who hated Thanes had one of the Gadyeni as their national symbol.

All three flags flew side by side. Elliza frowned. That wasn't right. Bran Maro and Nowan belonged to the Eastern Coalition. They were supposed to be fighting Teyrnas. This was not the same as the other Farsights, the ones in which Teyrnas was wiped off the map.

The flags faded away, and Elliza found herself in the common room. Tath and Corey looked at her expectantly.

"What did you see?" Corey asked, a slight tremor in his voice.

"More fighting." Elliza didn't understand. This was a five against one fight. Not three against three. The odds were too even.

But we're supposed to unite at the Academy. Are we going to save Teyrnas? Why? This conflict was worth more than a single kingdom. And not an ancient or advanced one at that. *It makes no sense.*

"What did you really see?" Tath whispered.

"Where are Realta and Chinasa?" she asked, her chest tight. Something was wrong. Terribly, terribly wrong. Her Farsights never changed. Never! She glanced at Corey. Did that mean his fate would change, too?

"Those damn thieves are probably dead," Corey spat. He rounded the bar. "You know, I think I will help myself. You never know when it will be your last one!" He laughed.

Tath raised his mug. "Cheers!"

Elliza wrapped her arms around herself, feeling very cold.

✳✳✳

Val stole one last glance at the sea, committing it to memory. He had dreamed of seeing the ocean since he was a little boy, and it was more beautiful than he imagined. Something eternal that no war could touch. Only the Creator knew if he would see it again.

Alani and Jerryk stood off to the side, talking quietly. The same uneasiness from the villagers surrounded them. Word of the war beyond the Vogel Mountains had reached the Tharys Ocean. Every merchant told a different story. Teyrnas had gone up in flames. King Logan was publicly decapitated by the Queen of Nowan, who was then shot with an arrow fired by Queen Isla. The Eastern Coalition wanted to conquer the whole world, including the Sykerian Empire.

And his personal favorite: King Logan and Queen Gallia had orchestrated the war, manipulating the other monarchs in order to reunite the ancient kingdom of Caslan.

"Why is that?" Val had asked the thick-headed merchant.

"Isn't it obvious?" he said, one hundred percent serious. "Logan and Gallia are secret lovers. Have been for years."

Val bit his tongue to keep from laughing.

A familiar warmth, the same warmth he felt from the other Nine, enveloped him. Val glanced over and saw the most beautiful woman in the world. Tall and lean with dark skin, curly black hair crowned her head, framing a heart-shaped face. And her eyes were as dark as the night sky. A man could drown in those eyes.

"Well, it's about bloody time," Val said, smiling.

Siryn, the Gadyeni of Minders, rolled her eyes. "Is that the best greeting you can give me, Valentin Gardyner?"

"I've been waiting to see you since Springtide," he replied, a bit irritated. "Since I realized what I am."

"Is this such a bad place to wait?"

Val gazed at the ocean, where sky and water blended together and created the purest blue. No, he supposed not.

"Alani, Jerryk, come here please," Siryn called out. Her silver cloak waved in the ocean breeze, glittering like stars. "I don't have time to repeat myself."

The two walked over. Alani's eyes darted all over. "Where did you come from?" She glanced at the dunes. There were no footprints save their own.

"Mistress of Stars!" Jerryk fell to his knees and bowed.

"What's gotten into you? What's going on?" Alani asked Val.

Val held out his hand, and she took it. "Alani," he said, drawing her closer, "this is Siryn. Perhaps you've heard of her?"

"Siryn? Isn't that one of the Gadyeni?"

"Yes," Siryn replied, a small smile tugging at the corners of her mouth.

Alani's confusion transformed into embarrassment. "But I... I thought..." She bowed her head. "Forgive me. I always viewed the Gadyeni as archetypes. Ideals. It wasn't until the Equinox that I... Please forgive me."

"Of course. We haven't been as active in human affairs as we ought. Jerryk, stand up."

Jerryk obeyed, keeping his head bowed. "Great Mistress of Stars, what do you want of me?"

"You already know the answer to that question, Healer." She motioned for Val, Alani, and Jerryk to come closer.

"What's going on?" Alani asked.

"We are going to Teyrnas," Val replied. His heart soared. The Nine would finally unite. He hoped Realta and Chinasa would be more amenable.

"Right now?" Alani looked at him uneasily.

He nodded.

"I have to pack my bags. My research—" Alani turned, but Siryn raised her hand. Alani froze mid-step.

"We will bring it to you later," Siryn replied. "We must not waste time."

Val smiled. "This is going to be fun."

"What is?" Jerryk asked, eyeing Val warily. The man still did not trust him.

"Remember how I traveled with the Ullmhir?" Alani nodded, and Jerryk made a sign to ward off evil, touching his heart and then both eyes before pointing skyward. All these pointless superstitions. No matter. Val had the favor of the Gadyeni. Jerryk could not deny that. "This is similar."

"How do you know what I'm going to do?" Siryn asked.

"I read a lot of old books."

Siryn narrowed her eyes. "Good for you." She waved her hand, and a silver disk appeared in the air. It spun around and around, lengthening to the size of a standing mirror. The silvery surface changed, showing an image of a large building made entirely of gray stone. Hundreds of tents dotted the field between the building and its walls. Soldiers in dark blue uniforms and armed with swords and crossbows ran along the wall, taking their positions between the crenellations.

Jerryk back away, muttering under his breath.

Alani's jaw dropped. "What is this?" She studied the image curiously.

"A form of traveling," Siryn replied. "It's nothing to worry about," she assured Jerryk. The man studied the image as though it were a stranger in the night, full of potential danger. Shaking his head, he backed away, again making the sign against evil.

"I suggest an empty room within the Academy," Val said. "Somewhere we cannot be seen. Won't do Eltriar any good for us to be riddled with arrows."

"You're quite clever, Valentin," Siryn said.

"Thank you."

"Almost too clever." The Gadyeni shot him an icy glare. "Don't make me regret choosing you."

Val flashed a smile. "As though there is a stronger Minder on

Eltriar."

"Eltriar is a big place. You'd be surprised by what you will find."

What does that mean? Did the Gadyeni have two or three of each Thane they could choose from? Alternatives in case one died?

No, Realta was the only Dreamer alive, and Val had done a lot of traveling, read hundreds of books. He was the strongest and most skilled Minder in the world. He created Illusions that fooled hundreds at once! No Minder had been capable of such a feat since the Thousand Years War when Z'Kai worked side by side with Balthazar.

Siryn was merely bluffing in order to keep him in line.

He hated these kinds of games.

"Shall we?" Val gestured towards the mirror. The image switched to a study with an oval-shaped table and bookshelves lining two walls. And not a person in sight. Perfect.

Alani, smiling like a child at Festival, nodded. "Yes."

"If the Mistress of Stars requires it," Jerryk replied. He closed his eyes and whispered a prayer.

"Minders first," Siryn said. Val, smiling brightly, took a single step and traveled halfway across the continent.

48
Broken

Going to the chapel to gather his thoughts was a mistake.

Lok only wanted a few minutes to himself. A few minutes away from Meredith and West. Away from his mother, and especially away from his stepfamily.

He ate breakfast with them this morning in the inn's back room. The small table with three chairs had been replaced by one large enough to seat a dozen people uncomfortably. Lok sat between his mother and Hope's husband Denny. The man worked as the assistant brewer and seemed fit to take over when Ellis retired.

Lok ate while everyone else talked, nodding now and then to prove he was paying attention. Hope and Maci talked about their children, who all stared at Lok with expressions ranging from fascination to horror.

"Will we control fire, too?" asked Reed, Hope's oldest son. The boy was an eerie combination of Ellis and Denny.

Hope plastered on a smile and explained that Lok was their step-uncle, meaning they weren't related by blood and weren't Thanes.

Reed seemed disappointed, but his little sister Rosie looked relieved.

Conversation then shifted to work and which job would be best for Lok. He nearly choked on his drink.

"Well, with you taking a break from the Academy," said Ellis, "you should start thinking about a career."

Lok shook his head. He wasn't staying in Vala permanently. Just until the war ended. He was still Kuno's Student.

But Ellis continued, "If you don't want to work at the inn, you can help me at the tavern. You can work in the back. That way, you won't have people bothering you," he added with a smile.

"Or you can work with the blacksmith," suggested Stone, Maci's husband, who had the intelligence of his namesake. "You can stoke the fires."

"Let's not talk about that anymore, dear," Maci said, patting Stone on the hand. She had always acted wary around Lok, commenting on his inability to speak and wondering if he had suffered an injury. Now, she was terrified of him. There was no point in Lok denying it. Maci always watched him closely, as though he were a rabid wildcat and never allowed her children to be alone with him. Lok responded by avoiding Maci as much as possible.

Stone, unfortunately, did not take the hint.

"Or lamp lighting. I hear bigger villages have streetlamps. We can build some, and you can light them. Be much easier to see at night."

"Most people are home by nightfall," Vera said curtly. "We won't have any use for lamp lighters."

"Yeah, but…"

Maci kicked Stone's leg. He finally shut up.

"Does it hurt?" asked Iris, the oldest of Ellis's grandchildren at ten years old and Reed's older sister by two years. She stared at him with big brown eyes. "When you start fires. Do you ever burn yourself?"

Lok shook his head. He asked Kuno the same question a few days ago. Kuno could not confirm it without checking official records, but it seemed his ability protected him from burns. Same for West.

Maci gave her sister a pleading look.

"It's almost time for school," Hope reminded the children, plastering on a smile. "Wouldn't want to keep Mistress Pross waiting."

Six of the eight children neatly stacked their plates and left for the schoolhouse, saying goodbye to Ellis, Vera, and Lok on their way out. Maci collected her two youngest and went back home, kissing Stone goodbye and casting Lok a dubious look.

"You know," Hope said to Lok. "We've been meaning to bring this up, but some of the parents are talking, and they wonder if your Scholar would help teach school. We have so few Academy education people, save for Mistress Haar and…" Hope paused for half a second. "And her husband. But Mistress Haar is helping

Healer Zall in addition to her other duties, and her husband…" A worried look creeped into her eyes.

Just go ahead and say it. Master Kel is a dirty Hiraethi. It's not like he can hear you. Master Kel was at the Academy, and he was Brother Malaky's older brother. How would Hope react if she learned that Master Kel was more than a dirty Hiraethi beggar?

No, she would never believe it. Let her keep her prejudice.

"Well, mention it to him when you get the chance," Hope said, smiling sweetly.

Lok nodded, but decided he would 'forget'. As much as Scholar Kuno loved teaching, Lok doubted he would care for a crowded room full of young children.

"Why don't you help me and Denny today, Lok," Ellis suggested. "We would really appreciate it."

Denny covered his face with his hand. Lok knew that gesture all too well. Denny was hiding a mocking smile. Ellis might want to help Lok, but Denny certainly did not.

"Lok still has his studies. Don't you, dear?" Vera said.

Lok nodded, grateful that his mother could still read his face. At least one thing hadn't changed.

"I just want to help the boy," Ellis said to Vera as Lok headed out.

"Some people don't want to be helped," Hope replied, not bothering to lower her voice.

The words stung Lok's heart and made him think. He first thought of this idea back at the Academy. A simple notion, nothing serious, but it grew more substantial as time passed and refused to leave, no matter how silly he told himself it was. He almost brought it up on the way here, but Kuno's temper turned volatile, flaring up unexpectedly.

Now that things had calmed down, Lok took the idea more seriously.

So, he went to the chapel to think. He just needed to put his thoughts into words and pray that it worked. He honestly did not know what he would do if this idea failed. He wouldn't be able to look himself in the eyes, let alone Scholar Kuno.

Sitting on a bench, he began to write. One page, then two. No, no! The words were all wrong. He furiously scratched them out and wrote new ones. Too many, too few, too stupid. This whole idea was stupid. He was stupid.

Lok buried his face in his hands.

Creator, why did You make me this way?

Lok paused. He never asked that question before. Had never thought to ask it. Of course he said prayers in chapel whenever he and his mother lit a candle for his father, but to question the Creator? The thought never crossed his mind.

But the Creator made him this way, made him a mute, so why not ask?

Creator, why can't I speak? Why did You make me different? Arnyn said You balanced out my life by making me an Elemental, but people are either afraid of me or laugh behind my back. I'm still an outcast!

Tears burned Lok's eyes. *Why didn't You make me normal?!*

"Lok, is everything all right?"

He glanced up and saw Brother Malaky standing nearby. Of course it was Brother Malaky. Who else?!

And what an absolutely stupid question. No, Lok was not all right. People didn't cry in chapels when everything was all right.

"Is there anything I can do to help?"

Yes, you can go away and take your bloody Farsights with you.

Lok just shook his head.

"I can get Scholar Serxio."

His name is Kuno, you stupid idiot!

"Apologies. Kuno." Malaky rubbed his forehead, frowning. "I don't understand why I'm so bad at names lately. Did you know that I've confused Brother Hamish and Brother Robin three times in the last half week? It must be these Farsights messing with my head."

Lok wiped his eyes with his sleeve. His eyes fell on the crossed-out pages in his notebook. None of the words were good enough. He was not good enough.

He tore out the pages and snapped his fingers. A small flame alighted on his fingertip, and he lit the pages. Fire ate away paper. A handful of crumpled, gray ashes fell onto the stone floor. He grounded them with his heel.

"Why did you do that?" Malaky asked.

None of your bloody business.

Lok put his notebook and pencil in his pocket. Well, he was good at one thing. Starting fires. Perhaps he should have stayed at the Academy and allowed Lucan to use him as a weapon. He would have been miserable, but it was better than being here.

Better than finding West?

Lok frowned. Finding West, another Elemental, had been wonderful, elating. A sense that he was no longer alone in the world. And West, in his own way, was different, too. Why had the Creator made West that way?

Another question without an answer.

He glanced at the tapestry depicting Abhainna, the Gadyeni who created Elemental Thanes. A beautiful woman who looked like a Hinterlander, wearing a dark green dress. In her hands danced the four elements: water, fire, earth, and air. Everything about her was perfect. What would she think if she met Lok and West? Would she be disappointed?

"Well, if you ever want to talk, I'm right here, Lok."

A burning anger coursed through him. He furiously wrote, *"I can't talk."* Ripping out the page, he shoved it at Brother Malaky and ran out of the chapel.

"I'm sorry, Lok," the chaplain called out. "I didn't mean—" The door slammed shut, cutting off his words.

Lok's feet moved of their own accord. He didn't know where he was going, only that he had to get away from the chaplain. And he certainly could not return to the inn or the tavern or the blacksmith's shop. Stone might have already told Master Dyllin about his idiotic plans.

Could he go to the healer's house? Esme might be there. She never asked Lok stupid questions. She treated him like she would treat any of the other boys in Vala.

Is it because her husband is broken, too?

Broken? Was Lok broken because he could not talk? A lot of villagers viewed Master Kel as broken, unable to work because of his injury.

Maybe Esme had been around broken people so long that she didn't view them as different.

A flash of white caught Lok's eye. He spied Scholar Kuno in the marketplace, speaking with Master Lanlin, a vendor who specialized in paper and writing supplies. Lok had bought his first notebook from Lanlin when he was six years old and learning how to write. The vendor smiled and shook his head when Kuno handed him a coin for new pens and an inkwell, insisting that this purchase was free.

Well, this was Lok's chance. If Kuno thought he was an idiot, better to find out now than to waste anymore of the Scholar's time.

Lok tugged on Kuno's cloak. The Scholar smiled.

"Hello, Lok." He pocketed the pens and inkwell. "Ready for another Old Eltrian lesson?"

He motioned for Kuno to step away. Kuno did so, bidding Master Lanlin a good day.

"Yes?"

Lok took out his notebook and pencil. A voice in the back of his mind told him to put them away. He was being foolish. This idea would never work, and... He forced the unwanted thoughts away. His fingers shaking, he turned to a blank page and wrote, *"Will you be my father?"*

Kuno stared at the words, his mouth slightly open.

Oh, no. This idea was stupid! Should he just run away now and save himself the embarrassment?

"What do you mean?" Kuno asked slowly, meeting Lok's eyes.

Lok's hand trembled as he wrote, *"I want you to be my father."*

"What about Ellis Brun?"

"No, he is my stepfather. Can you be my father?" Sweat beaded on Lok's forehead. His hands shook, almost too much for him to write clearly. Should he write that it was a joke? A stupid prank?

But it wasn't a joke. He really did want Kuno as a father. He wanted this since the night he burned down Caldeira's pub and Kuno responded with kindness and patience, the way a real father would.

"Lok," Kuno said, confused, "why do you want me as a father?"

"Because you care about me. You helped me at the Academy. You defended me in front of the Scholars, and you are protecting me now. Those are things that fathers do. And since I never met my real father, can you be my father instead?"

"Well, I..." Kuno cleared his throat. "Have you discussed this with your mother?"

"*No. She did not discuss getting married to me. Why should I discuss this with her?*"

"This is very unorthodox." Kuno ran a hand through his graying black hair. "People your age are usually considered too old for adoption. Do you really want me to be your father?"

"*Yes.*"

Kuno smiled, his eyes bright. "Then, yes, Lok. I would love to be your father."

Lok hugged Kuno, joy replacing fear. It worked! His silly, stupid idea worked! Thank the Creator, one thing in his life had gone right.

Kuno laughed. "Okay, Lok, don't choke me. We'll have to draw up some documents, and tell your mother."

Lok shook his head. He loved his mother, but he did not think Vera would understand.

"Eventually, we will tell your mother. I don't think Vala has a magistrate's office, so we will have to travel to get the adoption papers."

"*There is a magistrate in Lothian.*"

"I can ride out today and get the documents. But Lok," the Scholar locked eyes with him, "do you really want me as a father?"

Lok nodded. "*Yes, you don't care that I am broken.*"

"You're not broken, Lok. Don't ever think that." Kuno smiled, his eyes shining. "I never thought I would be a father. Thank you, Lok."

This time, Kuno hugged him. Tears stung Lok's eyes. Why was he crying? People didn't cry when they were happy.

"I'll try to be back by nightfall," Kuno said, heading towards the inn's stable. "Tell Meredith and West they have the day off from lessons."

Lok felt wonderful. He felt like he could jump off the roof and fly across the world. He had a father!

Strangely, he felt like telling someone. Meredith and West were likely at the inn. He didn't want to go there, not yet.

Esme Haar? Yes, he could tell her. She would understand.

Lok walked across the marketplace, smiling brightly. The day had started out terribly, but now it was wonderful. One of the best days of his life. Arnyn would say it was the Creator balancing out his life again. Perhaps it was true. If he hadn't been born mute, he wouldn't have dreamed of going to the Academy. If he hadn't been an Elemental, the Scholars would not have accepted him. He had to be both in order to meet his father.

The door to the healer's house was propped open with a stool. The warm summer breeze brushed the herbs hanging from the ceiling. He peered around. Esme was not here. He checked the small lean-to where Zall kept his horse. The animal was gone. Esme must be on a house call.

Then who was watching Zall? The curtains were drawn, casting the room in shadow. Estrid would not be sitting in darkness. She would have the curtains open so she could read. And he hadn't seen Patyn since yesterday. Was Henry inside? Lok grimaced. He didn't want to confront the healer's assistant again.

But what if Healer Zall was alone?

Henry had shirked his responsibilities before. No reason to think he wouldn't shirk them again. And if Esme had ridden to a farm, she might be gone for hours. Henry would have all day to waste drinking at the inn or chatting with the village girls.

And Healer Zall was dying. Esme had admitted it herself.

A dying person should not be alone.

Lok ventured inside.

Every room was dark, the curtains drawn tight. A faint moan sounded from the back room. Healer Zall must be having another nightmare. Lok heard another sound, strange and wet, as though someone were drinking messily. If Henry was drinking ale while watching over Zall, Esme would be livid.

Lok snapped his fingers, lighting a small flame, and walked into the room.

Zall laid on the bed, his face deathly pale. He muttered in his sleep. A shadow stood over the bed, holding up Zall's arm. The weird drinking sound grew louder.

Lok increased the flame. Light fell on Henry. The healer's assistant held Zall's arm up to his mouth. A red line ran down Zall's arm.

Henry's head shot up, eyes wide, and he dropped the healer's arm. Seeing Lok, he smiled, revealing teeth and lips stained with blood. Healer Zall's blood.

"Oh, hello, Lok."

49

Justice

Storm clouds darkened the sky as they rode towards Aneros. Everywhere Realta looked, Averillian and Tarodic soldiers fought, swords clashing, arrows flying. She and Serena ducked as a volley of arrows flew at them and embedded into trees with sickeningly close thuds.

Braedan cried out as an arrow grazed his leg. The mercenary gritted his teeth and kicked his horse, forcing it to run faster. Chinasa flicked his horse's reins, riding side by side with Braedan. Realta and Serena struggled to keep up, dodging trees and ducking to avoid branches.

"Can you make them fall asleep?" Chinasa asked Bas.

"I am already overstepping myself," he replied. "My goal is to keep you and Realta safe, not stop this battle."

"They'll start fighting again when they wake up," Braedan added.

"You're bleeding." Chinasa pointed at Braedan's torn trousers, stained dark red.

"I'll live."

A blinding flash of lightning lit the sky. Thunder cracked, shaking Realta's bones and making her teeth rattle. She white-knuckled the reins and kept her head low.

The trees thin out, revealing the village's outlying farms. Several houses were on fire, the tenants scrambling to put out the flames while dodging arrows and fighting soldiers. Two fell in the crossfires.

A drop of rain hit Realta's head. Roaring thunder heralded a torrent. Within seconds, freezing rain soaked her.

Realta squeezed her eyes shut as lightning struck a tree. It exploded in a blast of sparks and wood.

The horse reared its legs. Serena screamed as her hands slipped off Realta's waist. Realta reached out for her, their fingers almost touching…

Serena fell off, disappearing into the underbrush as the horse galloped away.

"Stop!" Realta yelled to Braedan and Chinasa, but her horse recklessly charged past them, neighing and rolling its eyes. "We have to stop!" She pulled on the reins, but the panicking horse didn't respond.

"Can't," Braedan said. "More soldiers are coming." He pointed towards the village. A unit of Averillian soldiers ran towards the trees, weapons drawn.

"Serena fell. I think she's hurt." Realta pulled on the reins again. The horse finally stopped, breathing heavily. She wiped the rain out of her eyes and looked back at the forest's edge. Where was Serena?

Braedan glanced over his shoulder and muttered a curse. Turning his horse around, he said, "I'll find her. Keep going. Stay together." He kicked the horse in the side and rode off.

"Come on," Chinasa said, urgency building in his voice. "Serena will be okay."

"What if she broke a bone?" Esme and Healer Zall once treated a man who had fallen off his horse during a simple ride. The animal had been spooked by a draig. The man landed on his back, breaking his spine. He never walked again. And Lok's father died from a broken spine.

Don't think that way. Serena will be okay. She has to be.

She was the closest thing Realta had to a sister all the way out here.

The rain soaked Realta to the skin by the time they reached the inn. Her short hair was plastered to her scalp, and she shivered, the summer heat banished by the storm. Chinasa was equally soaked, but Bas did not seem bothered by the rain.

Barrels and sacks of dirt surrounded the inn, stacked too high and too precariously to climb. A line of Averillian soldiers guarded it.

Bas raised a hand and slowly dismounted. Realta and Chinasa followed his lead.

Shouts rose from the forest. Screams. Realta's skin broke out in goosebumps. Who screamed? It sounded like a man. Braedan?

"State your business!" yelled a young Averillian soldier. He leveled a spear at Bas's chest. His hands shook.

"We are civilians. Please, let us take refuge here."

"Show me your weapons!"

"We have none," Chinasa replied.

"I have a dagger," Realta said, her teeth chattering. "But I don't know how to use it."

The soldier called out to another stationed in front of the barricade. They exchanged a few words in Averillian, casting furtive glances at Realta, Chinasa, and Bas.

Realta peered over her shoulder. Where were Serena and Braedan? Serena fell off near the forest's edge. Braedan should have found her by now. Unless Serena was too injured to be moved. Or the Tarodic soldiers captured them. Or killed them. Realta bit down on her tongue.

No, don't even think about that. They're fine. They just got turned around in the rain. They'll be here soon.

Any second now, they would ride through the trees, perfectly fine.

Any second now.

Thunder roared, shaking the ground and hurting Realta's ears. She recalled Bas's explanation for the storms. The Midnight King's powers were returning, and though he could summon storms, he could not control them. She shivered.

"You can enter, but we must take the horses," the soldier said.

They handed over the reins and rushed inside.

The common room was eerily quiet and empty save for a stash of supplies and weapons by the door. One window was smashed to bits, glass littering the floor. Rain poured in, soaking the floor and overturned furniture.

Heavy footsteps descended the stairs. Tath marched towards them, his dark eyes narrowed. Impatience radiated off him in waves, making Realta feel even colder.

"It's about time," he snapped.

"Where is Elliza?" Bas asked.

"Saying her goodbyes. Oh, you still have the dagger," Tath said, spying Hannor on Realta's belt. "Very good. We might actually have a chance."

"Esar found him?" Bas asked.

"He has a good idea, but he wants to make sure. Always leaving things to the last minute," Tath muttered.

"Hold on," Chinasa said. "Esar knows where the Midnight King is? Is he at the Teyrnas Academy?"

A shiver ran down Realta's spine. Callum and Charity were at the Academy. She didn't want them anywhere near that monster.

"No," Tath replied. "Elsewhere."

"Where?" Chinasa questioned.

Bas gave Tath a concerned look.

"Like I said, Esar wants to be sure. And the Nine must unite first. We're taking you to the Academy."

"Right now?" Realta asked. She glanced at the door. Thunder mixed with fighting, making it impossible to hear anything else. Where Serena and Braedan close?

"Obviously," Tath said. "Amsera is there. She reports that the fighting has worsened. The Academy might fall to the Eastern Coalition."

"But you won't let that happen," Realta said. When neither Gadyeni replied, she said, "Right?"

"It depends," Tath said. "Alberik has broken free, and the Wardens are active again. There will be worse battles to fight. And worse decisions to make." He pointed at the dagger.

Realta placed her hand on the hilt. Hannor belonged to the Windrose, the new leader of the Nine, but she had a sinking feeling that Val would claim leadership for himself, reducing the Windrose to a puppet on a string.

She tasted bile in the back of her throat. Was Val at the Academy? Suddenly, she didn't want to go. Didn't want to face Val again. He started this war. He was responsible. But instead of being punished, he was one of the Nine Thanes. If they defeated the Midnight King, the world would praise him as a hero.

"We shouldn't waste time, then," Chinasa said.

"Wait. Serena and Braedan aren't here."

Bas and Tath spoke in their strange language, arguing. Realta glanced at the busted window and saw nothing but fighting and rain. How could anyone ride through that chaos?

"We did not come for them," Bas said calmly. "We came for you, Chinasa, and Elliza."

"But we can't leave them." Realta refused to break her promise to Serena. And Bas had promised not to force her along, to meet her halfway. How was this meeting her halfway?

"Yes, we can," Tath snapped. "This conflict is far more important that two bastards."

Realta's heart sank. "But she—"

"Enough prattle. Where is Elliza?" Tath whirled around. "Elliza!"

✱✱✱

Elliza felt the edge of the blade against her fingertips. Smooth and sharp. One of dozens that Corey sold to the villagers in Aneros. Each for far more than it was worth. But the villagers were too terrified to gauge a fair price, and many were likely dead, caught up in a fight they were woefully unprepared for.

She met her own reflection in the small, hanging mirror. Long black hair framing a thin face. Dark eyes. And the mark of slavery on her face. A mark she could never escape.

Corey told her to wait in his room. He took Tath's suggestion regarding free drinks and was halfway through his third pint when he ordered her out of the common room. Her chest tightened. Braedan wasn't here to protect her. Corey could have his way, free of repercussions.

But that was okay. She had seen this room many times before. This was fate.

The door slammed open, and Corey staggered into the room. Lightning flashed, revealing the drunken smile on his face. He closed and locked the door. He made it two steps before his eyes fell on the black cloak laid out on the bed.

"Why'd you drag that out?" he asked, voice slurred. He picked up the cloak, feeling the smooth material, and smiled. "Well, never was a secret. Not between us."

Elliza said nothing.

Draping the Warden's cloak over his shoulders, Corey loomed over her. "Did I ever say how much I appreciate you?" He kissed her on the cheek, in the center of her tattoo. She tightened her grip on the knife's hilt. She just had to be patient for a little longer.

"Yes, sir," she whispered.

"I didn't understand why your cousins handed you over with the dagger, not at first. The dagger was what I wanted. Safe keeping. You were just extra. A scrawny little thing. But you grew up beautiful. And useful." He pushed a lock of hair away from her face. "Guess that's why Braedan is so protective. Wants you all to himself."

Corey sat on the bed next to her. Elliza resisted the urge to run away. This had to be. She had seen it again and again. She glanced out the window, waiting.

He laid down and pulled her closer. She kept one hand behind her back, ready to strike.

"Why are you being so shy?" he asked, his words growing more slurred.

"Because this is fate. I've seen this moment."

Corey smiled.

A bolt of lightning struck a tree. Sparks and bits of wood flew upwards. The soldiers guarding the inn screamed, exactly as it happened in her Farsights.

Elliza seized the dagger and plunged it into Corey's heart. His eyes widened.

"I saw myself killing you," she whispered in his ear.

Corey gasped, trying to speak. Blood trickled out of the corner of his mouth. He grabbed her neck, but he had no strength left. His arms fell away as his eyes turned glassy. Corey laid completely still, the dagger embedded in his chest.

Elliza slowly sat up. It was done. She had killed him, just like in all her Farsights. Strangely, she didn't feel anything. A bit relieved, yes. But nothing else.

It had been so easy.

"Elliza!" Tath called from downstairs.

She quickly stood and inspected her hands. No blood. She spared a final glance at Corey. Should she remove the dagger? No, let everything see how he died, and let them know he was a servant of the Midnight King.

Smoothing down her hair and dress, Elliza calmly walked down the hallway and took the steps one at a time.

Realta, Chinasa, and Bas accompanied Tath. Hannor, the Sun Dagger, hung from Realta's belt.

"Where is Braedan?" she asked, and thankfully her voice was even. Why shouldn't it be? It wasn't as though she'd done anything wrong. Corey was an evil man and would have continued to commit evil acts as long as he lived. All the same, she was grateful none of them were Minders.

"Looking for Serena. We were separated," Realta said. She was on the verge of tears.

"Don't worry. Braedan is sure to find her." He was also sure to find Corey's body, but they would be far away by then. And nothing indicated that she was responsible. No one looked at her as though she were guilty. Even Tath, the Gadyeni of Justice, did not give her a second glance.

"We have to go," Bas said.

Elliza nodded. She would finally fulfill her destiny. Her cousins wanted her as a tool for the Wardens, using her Farsights in their favor. She had prayed for a way out, for a nobler path. And the Gadyeni answered.

Tath waved his hand. An oval-shaped mirror, six feet high and two feet wide, appeared in the air. The silvery surface transformed into a battlefield. Soldiers on both sides of a wall fought and died. The building within the wall flew the flag of Teyrnas.

A sinking feeling formed in her gut. Why had that Farsight changed? Was this the only one, or would more prove to be false? She wanted to ask Tath, but what if the Gadyeni regarded her as defective and chose another Farsight? How would she fulfill her destiny then?

"How did you...?" Chinasa shook his head. "Is this how we're going to the Academy?"

Bas nodded.

"Not without Serena," Realta said adamantly.

"Yes, you are." Tath seized Realta's arm and dragged her towards the mirror. Realta kicked Tath in the shins, but the Gadyeni was unfazed. Chinasa grabbed Tath, trying to break his grasp. The Gadyeni shoved him away, eyes flashing.

"Stop!" Bas said. "This is not the way."

"You said you wouldn't force me," Realta cried at Bas. "You

promised!"

Bas sighed heavily. "That I did. Tath, let her go."

Tath glared at him but relented. Realta rubbed her wrist.

"Realta, we must go now. There isn't any time," Bas pleaded.

"Will you come back for her?" Realta asked.

"Yes."

Realta studied him for a long moment.

"I promise in the name of the Creator," Bas added.

Tath muttered under his breath.

Realta nodded. She held out her hand and Chinasa took it. Together, they followed Tath through the mirror, into the image of a spacious study.

This is bad. Already fighting. Would they waste so much time fighting amongst themselves that Alberik would conquer the world without them realizing it?

"Well?" Bas asked.

Elliza blinked. How long had she been standing here?

"Is everything all right, Elliza?"

"Yes, Master Gadyeni." She gave him a quick bow. Did Bas know? Some said that the Gadyeni of Dreams was also the Gadyeni of the Dead. Did he know that Corey was dead? He didn't say anything to the others. And surely Tath, the Gadyeni of Justice, would approve of her killing a servant of the Midnight King who abused her for years.

She hoped.

Before Bas could say anything else, Elliza quickly stepped through the mirror.

50
Help

Charity mapped out the maze of hallways and corridors that Shari led her down, dodging people as they hurried by. Terrified Students, Journeymen, and refugees clogged the halls. Family and friend groups huddled together.

Shari dragged her into a conference room on the second floor. A massive, oval table made of dark wood rested in the center. Bookshelves filled with leather-bound tomes lined one wall while the opposite wall had floor to ceiling windows.

Lok and I gave Scholar Lucan our statements here. And she thought the Scholar had been nice!

Charity looked out the window. Dark clouds lumbered in from the west. Soldiers in leather armor and chain mail lined the wall. Archers pulled their bows, ready to fire. Beyond the wall, thousands more lined the field between the Academy and Norgard, the flags of Nowan and Bran Maro flying in their midst. Charity could barely see the flag of Teyrnas flying over the Garrison. She hoped Zandon was okay.

"What did Scholar Kuno tell you?" Shari asked, rounding on her.

Charity held her ground, meeting the other girl's eyes. "Tell me about what?"

"I don't have time for games," she snapped. "What did he tell you about his research? About the Gadyeni Cycle?"

"Nothing. He's Lok's mentor, not mine."

"Then what did Lok tell you?"

"Nothing. He's mute, remember?" Charity smirked.

"Don't make me hit you!"

Charity studied her. Shari's eyes were bloodshot with dark circles underneath. When was the last time she slept? And her cheeks were hollow. Probably not eating regular meals. Was it the result of emotional stress, or was it a punishment? Charity did not see any signs of bruising, but Scholar Lucan was smart enough to conceal injuries. "Does he hurt you?"

"Kuno never hurt me," Shari said, absolutely shocked.

"I meant Lucan."

Shari averted her gaze for a second. Just a second, but it was there. "He has a temper. The Wardens demand excellence. Second best is not good enough for the Midnight King. And you cannot stop us by stalling."

"I'm not stalling. I told you the truth. Scholar Kuno told me nothing about his work."

"Then why were you and your friends in his room last night?"

Charity's heart skipped a beat. "We weren't—"

"Don't lie. I heard you talking, moving stuff around. It was clever to leave separately. I'm guessing it was the man's idea."

"It was just an old map," Charity lied. Shari already knew Jaim and Coryn were taking the book to Queen Isla. She could not allow her or the Wardens to discover those papers.

"A map to where? Did you see any names?" Shari gripped Charity's shoulders.

"It was all in Old Eltrian. I couldn't read it. It…" *Think, Charity, think!* There had to be something that Shari would believe. "Luroradi. I think one of the cities was called Luroradi."

"The Eternal City," she said reverently. "Are you sure?"

Charity nodded, a bit ashamed. Her mother and father raised her to always tell the truth. What would they say if they were here? Would they understand?

Shari relaxed. "That's where Kuno went. He and the Elemental left to find the Eternal City. Perhaps to find the Midnight King."

"Why? Kuno isn't a Warden."

"No, but he's a historian. If he is following the Cycle, he must have gone to witness Alberik regain his powers."

"Is that really a good thing?" Charity questioned.

"Kuno is smart. He won't waste an opportunity to speak with someone who lived through the most important eras in history." Shari glanced outside. Rain coated the window as the sky darkened. Torches designed to burn in the presence of water hung on the crenellations. War horns sounded, making Charity's skin crawl. "Where was Luroradi?"

"I told you. I didn't recognize any other names."

"But what about landmarks? Rivers? Did you see the Nerin?"

"I..." *Come on, Charity, where is a logical place for Kuno and Lok to go?* She assumed Lok went to Vala to get away from the fighting. She wanted to find him, but she also needed to get away from Shari. Perhaps she could kill two birds with one stone. "I think it was on the other side of the Nerin. Between the river and the Vogel Mountains."

"How close to Teyrnas?"

"Somewhere in the Hinterlands."

"The Eternal City could be right here," Shari said more to herself than to Charity. "Kuno made us think he left the kingdom, while staying close by." She latched onto Charity's wrist. "Come on. We need—"

The door burst open. Charity screamed and clamped a hand over her mouth, feeling foolish. Dozens, if not hundreds, of people were close by. The Wardens could not ambush her here, not with so many witnesses.

Instead of a cloaked Warden, a tall man with coal black hair and gray eyes sauntered into the conference room. He wore a silver cloak over travel-worn clothes. He smiled at Charity.

"Uncle Lucan," Shari exclaimed. "Is everything all right?" She turned pale.

Charity frowned. This man looked nothing like Lucan.

The man took on a dignified air. "What is the meaning of this?" he demanded, crossing his arms.

"I found Charity Loy." She grabbed Charity's arm. "She was rifling through Kuno's room. Uncle, there is a map—"

"Enough. We shall discuss your findings later. I am glad to see you are still loyal to the Wardens."

A pit formed in Charity's gut. Wardens might worship the Midnight King, but they weren't completely stupid. They wouldn't send a group in black cloaks to capture her. They only needed to send one person. She glanced at the man's ears. No rings. Strange. Wouldn't they send a Thane?

And why does Shari think he is Lucan?

"Of course I'm loyal." Shari looked as though the man had

slapped her for no reason.

"We feared you had gone astray. Charity agreed to test you."

Charity's heart skipped a beat. *Wait, what?!*

"Test me?" She looked at the man, aghast. "But... But why?"

"We had to be sure. Don't fret. Others were similarly tested. Isn't that right, Charity?" *Play along,* she heard the man's voice in her head.

"We had to be sure," Charity replied. "Like you said, Alberik does not want the second best." She felt like she was going to be sick. What was wrong with her? Speaking the Midnight King's true name!

"Go and join the others, Shari. Charity and I have an important matter to discuss." The man flashed a smile.

A light dawned in Charity's mind. She saw this man at the palace. He was Queen Gallia's messenger. Her blood went cold. Why was he here? Did Gallia send him as a spy?

But he spoke to me in my mind. Only Minders Thanes can do that. And Nowan had no love for Thanes.

Don't worry, Charity, the man said into her mind. *You are among friends.*

Two more people joined the messenger. On his right stood a woman who was about forty years old with bronze skin and dark hair and eyes. A golden cloak lighted her shoulders. The other was a man with pale skin and hair so light it was almost white. He wore a white cloak similar to the ones worn by Scholars, but it had strange symbols embroidered along the edge in silver. The woman glanced around nervously until her eyes fell on the books. She immediately went to them and scanned the titles, smiling. The man just stared at her and Shari, looking a bit lost.

Shari bowed to the man and woman, though the woman's attention was fixed on the books. The man raised an eyebrow and spoke in a strange, guttural language.

"Hm?" the woman asked, selecting a volume.

Shari cast a wary glance at Charity and then hurried out of the room.

"Bloody Wardens," the man muttered. "They think they know everything about the universe. They couldn't be more wrong."

"Who are you?" Charity asked, walking up to the two men.

The woman, a small stack of books in her arms, rejoined them. "Why did she think you were Scholar Lucan?"

The man smiled warmly. "A simple Illusion. I believe we've already met. I'm Val Gardyner, and these are my associates Alani Kisei and Jerryk Ordaryk's son. We are Three of Nine."

"Nine? As in the Nine Thanes?" Did that mean Realta was with them?

The smile brightened. "That saves one explanation. And your friend Realta Haar will be here presently."

At the far corner of the room, a silvery line split the air. Charity stood between Val and Alani, her skin breaking out in goosebumps. The line widened, forming a large, mirror-like object. No, it was more like a window, revealing an inn's common room on the other side. A tall man stepped through. He wore a dark blue cloak over finely tailored clothes and had dark skin, the same shade of brown as Scholar Kuno. The man nodded curtly to Val.

A second later, Ambassador Ekene stepped through. The ambassador's white clothes were replaced with browns and greens, though he still wore his red necklace. A young woman followed him, standing a head shorter than Charity. The girl stared at the floor, shivering.

And then Realta appeared. Her long braid had been cut off, and numerous scratches covered her face and arms. Water dripped off her soaked clothes.

Where had they come from? What was the mirror-window thing? Did it matter? Realta was here! She was alive!

Charity, tears stinging her eyes, ran to Realta and hugged her.

"I knew you were alive!"

Realta held onto her, trembling.

"Where were you? How did you create that?" Charity pointed at the mirror. Another man stepped through. A dark gray cloak obscured his features. He waved his hand, and the mirror disappeared.

"Tath is a very skilled traveler," the man said.

Tath? He was one of the Gadyeni, depicted as a brown-skinned man with black hair and a blue cloak...

"You are in the presence of greatness, Miss Charity Loy," Val said. He bowed to Tath and the gray-cloaked man. "May I present

Tath and Bas of the Gadyeni. Siryn is also here, but she has more important matters than small talk."

A thousand thoughts swarmed Charity's mind. First, Realta and Ambassador Ekene appeared literally out of thin air. And now, two of the Gadyeni... No, three of the Gadyeni were at the Academy! "Realta, how is this possible? How can the Gadyeni be here?"

"Because everything Val said is true," she said in a small, hollow voice.

"It's so good to see you again, Realta." Val walked towards her and Charity. "Have you been well?"

"Where is my father?" Realta asked Bas. "I want to see my father."

"In due time. Where did you get that dagger?" Val asked, his eyes growing wide.

Charity noted the dagger on Realta's belt. The hilt was made of silver, and the sheath was pure white and decorated with strange symbols. The same symbols as the ones on Jerryk's cloak.

"From her," Realta pointed at the other girl. The girl's face was ashen, and she had a tattoo on her face in the shape of a compass.

"Hello, Elliza," Val said gently. "It's so nice to meet our Farsight."

"Hello, Valentin," she said, finally looking up. An old bruise lined her jaw.

"And Ambassador Ekene. How has our Learner—"

Ambassador Ekene took three quick strides towards Val and punched him square in the jaw. Val crumpled to the floor.

"Why did you do that?" Alani cried. She handed the books to Jerryk and crouched beside Val, helping him sit up. His lower lip was split. Blood trickled down his chin, a few drops staining his silver cloak. He gingerly touched his jaw and winced.

"He deserved it," the ambassador said coldly.

Jerryk laughed.

"I don't see what's so funny," Alani snapped.

Jerryk laughed until tears rolled down his face.

"We don't have time for this," Tath said through his teeth. "Where is Siryn?" he asked Alani and Val.

"She went to the wall," Val replied. Alani helped him to his feet. Wiping the blood off his chin, he glared at the ambassador. "Still think I'm yelling blasphemies?"

"I don't trust you. I don't care what they say." He gestured towards the Gadyeni.

An idea formed. The Nine Thanes would unite here so they could defeat the Midnight King, and the Gadyeni would aid them. Could they also aid Teyrnas? Stop this war before fighting the next?

"The Wardens of the Night are at the Academy!" Charity exclaimed. "You have to stop them!"

Tath smirked. "They aren't a threat."

"Not at the moment," Bas amended. "We appreciate the warning, Charity, but there are more important matters to attend to presently. Shall we leave them to get acquainted?" he asked Tath.

Tath sighed heavily. "We don't have time."

"An untrained army is no army at all. They can have ten minutes."

"Fine." Tath turned to Val. "Battles need plans and leaders to implement them. I elect you. You have ten minutes." He and Bas headed for the door. "Charity, come with us."

"Charity stays here," Realta said, holding onto Charity's hand. Her voice shook, but that wasn't fear in her eyes. She was livid, angrier than Charity had ever seen her.

Tath gave her an exasperated look. "No."

"Then let me see my father."

"This is not a negotiation, Dreamer." In the blink of an eye, Tath loomed over Realta and Charity. Charity shrank back. The Gadyeni were supposed to help the Nine Thanes. Why were they arguing?

"Tath, calm down."

Every eye turned towards the doorway. A dark-skinned woman with curly, black hair decorated with silver beads sauntered up to Tath, the train of her silver dress trailing behind her. Charity had never seen such a dress. Cut low in the front and the back with diaphanous sleeves hanging from a series of rings on her arms. And the material sparkled like stars.

"She is no older than Domni," the woman said calmly.

"That's no excuse."

"You will be allowed to see your father after the Solstice," the woman said. "He is on the wall, fighting alongside Teyrnas' soldiers. Soldiers who are depending on him. But I promise you will see Callum again. As for your friend," she fixed her dark brown eyes on Charity, "she is studying to be a healer. Can you show our Healer to the infirmary?"

Jerryk said something in his language.

The woman smiled brightly. "Don't worry. Charity will vouch for you with the other healers." She said to Charity, "The number of causalities is growing. Go now."

"What about us?" Alani asked. A series of war horns sounded at the same time thunder roared.

"Valentin will discuss the plan with you."

"I will not take orders from him," Ekene snapped.

"Unfortunately, this is not up for negotiation. With the Windrose absent, you need a leader, and we need you to work together. Use your time wisely." She turned to Charity and Jerryk. "Why are you two still here? Go!"

"Bryththwil," Jerryk said, holding up his index finger. He placed his hand on Realta's forehead. Realta shivered. All the cuts on her face and arms healed in seconds.

Charity opened her mouth to speak, but no words formed. She wanted to kick herself. A Healer. Jerryk was a Healer Thane!

"Hlafa hea and rest."

Charity jolted, hearing the sentence change to Teyrnian. How on Eltriar...?

"Water and rest will have to wait," Siryn replied. Charity assumed she was Siryn. Who else could this regal woman be? "Now, go with Charity, Jerryk."

Charity locked eyes with Realta. She did not want to leave her friend. They had just found each other again. But winning this war was important. Once they won, she and Realta could spend all day together. Just like back home.

She and Realta hugged one last time. She felt awful, tearing herself away, but Realta would be here when she got back.

Charity led Jerryk out of the room. She looked at him in complete awe.

"So, a Healer Thane." She couldn't help smiling. She wished Esme could meet him. The midwife would be overjoyed and have a hundred questions. "Are you the only one, or are there more?"

Jerryk just stared at her. "Many more," he replied. "And you are?"

"A Student, studying to be a healer."

"But not a Thane?"

"No."

"I see. Where is this infirmary?" Jerryk frowned. "What is an infirmary?"

"A place for healers." Strange. Didn't they have infirmaries or hospitals where he was from? Where was he from? *Save those questions for later.* Right. Jerryk had people to Heal. "You'll see." Charity took Jerryk by the hand and led him to the infirmary. She could not wait to see the look on Scholar Alia's face!

51
Two Ravens

The world slowly came back into focus. Serena blinked as raindrops splashed in her eyes. Her left arm burned as though it were on fire. She tentatively flexed her fingers and screamed as pain shot up her arm.

Rolling onto her side, Serena propped herself up into a sitting position. She glanced around the forest. Countless trees stretched for miles. Sounds rose around her. Men shouting, screaming, metal striking metal. The sounds faded, lost in the rain.

No sounds, and no people.

Realta, Chinasa, and Braedan were nowhere in sight.

Tears stung her eyes. Where had they gone? Why hadn't they come back for her? Realta promised not to leave her alone.

What if the Gadyeni forced her and Chinasa to leave? Elliza told Serena that she was not important. That the Gadyeni had no need for a king's bastard in their plans. She shouldn't be surprised. She was born useless. Not a Thane or a Cuchasi. Just an embarrassing mistake.

But Realta never cared that she was a bastard. From the moment she learned that Serena was Kel's little sister, Realta had treated her as family. As an equal. She would have ridden back for Serena if she could. Did Bas force her to keep riding? If the Gadyeni could force people to sleep, what else was he capable of?

Hooves thundered through the trees. Metal struck metal. A call for help was cut off as the hooves rode towards her.

The Tarodic! Serena crawled underneath the nearest bush. Twigs and thorns pricked her skin and snagged her clothes, tearing off little pieces of fabric. She reached to snatch them, but her arm gave out. White hot pain coursed through her. Did she scream? She didn't think so.

Backing up against a tree, she inspected her arm. Fresh bruises were forming, but the skin wasn't cut. Was it broken? How would she get back to the village with a broken arm and soldiers fighting all round her?

A horse burst through the trees, the hooves inches from her.

Serena scrambled to her feet and ran, dodging trees and branches. A root snagged her ankle, but by some miracle, she did not fall and kept running. The rider chased her. Serena could feel the horse's breath on her neck.

She turned a sharp corner, but the rider steered his horse expertly, not giving Serena an inch.

The rider reached out and grabbed her. Serena slapped his hand away.

Stars danced in her vision as she collided with a tree. Next thing she knew, she was on the ground, her head throbbing in tandem with her arm.

"Don't move." The rider dismounted and crouched down beside her. He removed his hood, revealing light hair and blue eyes. Braedan. He came back for her! "Calm down," Braedan said. "It's just me. Are you hurt?"

"My arm feels broken," she said, voice trembling. "Where is Realta?"

"She's with Chinasa and Bas. They sent me to look for you. Damn, your arm doesn't look good. Definitely fractured. You're lucky you didn't break your spine."

Braedan helped her to her feet. Serena leaned against him as relief washed over her. Realta had kept her promise. She hadn't abandoned her. Now, she and Braedan just had to get to Aneros while avoiding the fighting.

"Don't move!"

Serena whirled around and locked eyes with Veltan. The Tarodic soldier aimed his spear at her and Braedan. His clinched teeth and wide eyes reminded Serena of a rabid dog.

"Hold on. We aren't armed." Braedan drew Serena closer to him.

"You're covered with knives!" Veltan seethed. Serena noted that his helmet was missing, and his uniform was torn and bloodied in several places.

"Well, not covered," Braedan replied. "But none of them are

drawn. We are not a threat to you."

"But you were with that pale man. He made us…" Veltan's eyes darted around the forest. He gripped the spear tighter. "One second, I was confronting you and the next, I was back in basic training. Except, I wasn't really there. I was watching myself learn maneuvers. How did he do that?" Veltan demanded.

Braedan smirked. "You wouldn't believe me if I told you."

"He's a Thane, isn't he? A bloody Thane! And you are Thanes, too."

"No, we're not." Braedan nudged Serena behind him and slowly backed away.

"Prove it!"

"Braedan is a Cuchasi," Serena stammered. The pain in her arm pulsed in rhythm with her racing heart. "And he is from Nowan."

"Nowan? You said you were Teyrnian." Veltan leveled the spear at her eyes. "Tell me the bloody truth!"

"We were betrayed." Braedan showed Veltan the traitor's scar on his forearm. "A Teyrnian merchant hired me. When he discovered I was Nowani, he did this to me. Said I was a traitor for not telling him a truth he never asked for. He just did it out of spite." Braedan spat on the ground.

"And her? Where did she come from?"

"I'm his sister," she said. "We already told you—"

"Shut up!" Veltan took a series of deep breaths. He studied Braedan curiously. "A merchant gave you that scar?"

"Yes."

"Where is he now?"

"In Aneros. His name is Waylar Corey."

"Take me to him. He can tell me the truth. About both of you." He shot Serena a glare.

"You'll have to get us through the Averillian soldiers first," Braedan said.

Veltan scoffed. "The Averillians are a farce. Most of them have been captured or killed."

Serena's heart sank. No, they couldn't have lost. Not so quickly. Veltan was lying. He had to be. She glanced up at Braedan. The mercenary's face was like stone.

"Fine. It's your life," Braedan said nonchalantly. He guided Serena to his horse.

Veltan rounded them, keeping the spear leveled at Braedan's chest, and grabbed the horse's reins. "I'll ride. You two walk."

"Look, man—"

Veltan jabbed Braedan's shoulder. Braedan yelled and clutched a large gash. Blood ran through his fingers.

"No!" Serena rushed Veltan, driving her elbow into Veltan's chest. The soldier grabbed her shirt, pulling her down as he fell. An exposed root smacked against her head. Stars danced in her vision again.

A heavy weight pressed down on her chest. She blinked the stars away and saw Veltan looming over her. His knee dug into her abdomen, making it hard to breathe. He grabbed her neck with both hands and squeezed.

Serena tried to fight back. But her left arm was useless, lying on the ground and throbbing, throbbing. Her heart raced, blooding rushing in her ears. She couldn't breathe.

She slapped his face, but Veltan wasn't fazed. She slapped him again, aiming for his eyes. Her vision grew gray and fuzzy.

"Damn Teyrnian bitch," Veltan said through his teeth.

Braedan bowled into Veltan, sending him to the ground. Serena gasped for air, coughing, and rolled away. Braedan wrestled Veltan, each man trying to gain an advantage. Veltan broke away and leapt to his feet. Braedan grabbed Veltan's wrist as the soldier threw a punch. He tried to twist the wrist behind Veltan's back, but the soldier twisted with Braedan, wresting his hand free.

Braedan then reached for a knife. Veltan kicked his hand and sent the knife flying into the underbrush. He then kicked Braedan in the knee. Braedan lost his balance and fell onto his side. Veltan jumped on him, pinning him down, trying to choke him.

A flash of metal caught Serena's eye. Veltan's spear rested forgotten on the ground. She picked it up and felt the weight. The haft was surprisingly light. Light enough for her to use. Gripping it one handed, she smacked Veltan on the head with the spearpoint.

The soldier cried out, clutching the back of his head and rolling onto his side. Braedan scrambled to his feet and kicked Veltan in the ribs, once, twice. The soldier curled into a protective ball.

"Thanks," Braedan said.

Serena handed him the spear. "I think you should have this."

"Good idea." Braedan leaned on the spear, catching his breath while looking down at Veltan. "I think we got ourselves a prisoner. You wanted to meet Corey. Now's your chance."

Veltan muttered something in Tarodic as Braedan pulled him to his feet and tied his hands with a length of rope from the saddlebag. He shoved Veltan onto the saddle, his head and feet dangling.

"Now what?" Serena asked. Her arm ached, the pain worsening by the second.

"We go back to the inn, leave this one as a prisoner of war, and get your arm checked out. Maybe the Gadyeni have a way to heal broken bones."

"Gadyeni? What are you talking about?" Veltan asked.

"Shut up."

Braedan gripped the reins and led them through the forest. The fighting had all but stopped, save for a few pockets of violence. Two soldiers clashed less than ten yards from them. The Tarodic one gained the upper hand and quickly disappeared into the forest. Serena walked closer to Braedan. Fighting with Veltan had left her tired and shaking, and she felt strangely warm, as though she were coming down with a fever.

"I really am your sister," Serena said quietly as Aneros came into view. Or rather, what remained of Aneros. Burnt buildings greeted them. Villagers, their clothes reduced to rags, stared at their ruined homes with vacant eyes and barely acknowledged them.

"Really?" Braedan surveyed the inn. A handful of Averillian soldiers guarded it, and none of them had weapons. Serena then noticed Tarodic soldiers close by, watching everyone and everything like hawks.

One of the Averillians signaled for her and Braedan to halt.

"I…" How could she begin to explain? "Well, we look the same. Same hair and eye colors."

"And?"

A lump formed in her throat. *You are a fool. You are a foolish bastard girl and…* No, Realta saw the resemblance. And she recognized Serena as Kel's sister the moment they met. This could not be a mistake. "My father was married to another woman when I was born. He was unfaithful a lot of times. Mistress Cray said he had at least three bastards. I think you're one of them."

"Interesting." Braedan yanked Veltan off the saddle. The soldier landed roughly on his feet. Braedan then punched him in the face. Blood dripped from his broken nose. The two Averillians looked at Braedan, aghast.

"What was that for?!" Serena demanded.

"That was for my shoulder. Now," he grabbed Veltan by the collar and led him inside the inn, "what were you saying?"

"I..." A thought dawned in her mind as a wry smile crossed her lips. "Logan would have done the same thing. He had a spiteful streak."

"Who's Logan?"

"One of my brothers. One of the legitimate ones." Silence struck Serena as they entered the common room. Several villagers sat at the tables along with the Jemayrti Scholars and Shasta Cray. A few eyes turned their way and quickly looked away, seeing Veltan's red and blue uniform. Shasta stood and walked up to Serena.

"Are you injured?" she asked.

"My arm. Shasta, tell Braedan that we're siblings." Tears stung her eyes. She hadn't discussed this with Shasta, worried the older woman would explain it away as grief clouding her judgment. What if it was just grief, and Realta had agreed in order to comfort her?

"And somebody put this one in a safe place," Braedan said. Ezri appeared out of nowhere and quickly disarmed Veltan, handing the hidden weapons to Braedan.

"Commander Maddrel died in the battle," Ezri said. "The new commander will be here shortly." He seated Veltan near the Scholars, hovering over him.

"I told you we won," Veltan called out.

"Is it true?" Braedan asked.

Shasta, her face impassive, said, "Yes. The new commander signed a declaration of defeat. He and the Tarodic general will be here momentarily. I assume we are prisoners of war."

"Where are Realta and Chinasa?" Serena asked. Neither they nor the two Gadyeni were present.

"They left with Bas, Tath, and Elliza about ten minutes ago. I saw them leave." Shasta's eyes narrowed. "It was most unusual."

Serena's heart sank. But Realta promised!

"Realta wanted to wait for you," Shasta continued. "Tath didn't give her a choice."

Well, that was a small comfort. But surely the Gadyeni could have spared ten minutes.

"Is Elliza safe?" Braedan asked, urgency gathering in his voice. His shoulder still bled, but he didn't seem to care.

"As safe as she can be. Master Sutter," Shasta, unmoved by the worst of Logan's outbursts, turned pale, "what do you know about that girl? About her temperament?"

"She's quiet. Keeps to herself. Why? Did she look upset?"

"After she and the others left, we discovered Master Corey's body in Elliza's room. He was stabbed in the heart. Elliza is the only one whose movements cannot be accounted for during that time."

"You think she did it?" Braedan's face turned paper white.

Serena didn't know how to react. Corey was a terrible person, threatening the Jemayrti, cutting off Realta's hair, and carving up Braedan's arm... Serena shuddered. It was all terrible, but did he really deserve to be murdered?

"We have our suspicions. Do you think she is capable of such an act?"

"No," Braedan shouted. He took a deep breath and said, "But she always said it was not Corey's fate to die by my hands. The Creator knows how much I wanted to kill him but... Fire and smoke, did she really kill him?" Braedan looked like he was going to be sick.

"If so, then Realta and Chinasa are traveling with a murderer," Shasta concluded.

"The Gadyeni will protect them, right?" Serena asked.

Elliza said that she and Realta were Two of Nine. She won't hurt her or Chinasa. Not if the Gadyeni chose them to fight the Midnight King.

"Given their importance, yes," Shasta replied.

"And Elliza?" Braedan asked. "She's supposed to be one of those Nine, too."

"So she claims. Did she have any Farsights concerning Corey?"

"Not…" Braedan cleared his throat. "None that she told me."

"What about you, Master Sutter?" Shasta raised an eyebrow.

"Just that I was a raven. Whatever that bloody means."

A small smile crossed Shasta's lips. "Ravens. The symbol of the throne of Teyrnas. Let's sit down."

"I prefer to stand."

Voices sounded outside, a man shouting orders. It sounded like Tarodic. Serena watched red and blue uniformed soldiers march past a broken window.

"Don't think you can fight your way out of this, Master Sutter," Shasta said. Serena turned around and saw Braedan reaching for a knife. The mercenary balled his hand into a fist. "Those soldiers will cut you down before you can throw a single knife. I already lost your brother." Tears welled in Shasta's eyes. "I don't want to lose you, too."

"I don't have a brother. I'm just a bastard…" His eyes narrowed, studying Serena. "A bastard. Serena, who was your father?"

"King Yestyn O'Kelwyn of Teyrnas. And my brother was King Logan."

Braedan staggered. He grabbed hold of a nearby chair. "Are you… Are you serious?"

"Yes, Master Sutter," Shasta answered. "How old are you?"

"Twenty-eight."

"Then your mother was Celyna Sutter."

"Yeah, did you know her?" A bit of color returned to Braedan's face.

"Briefly. You and Serena are indeed half-siblings. The children of King Yestyn O'Kelwyn."

Braedan laughed. The joyful sound echoed off the walls. Tears streamed down his face. The villagers gawked at him as though he had gone insane.

"A king! My father was a bloody king!" Braedan, still laughing, wiped his eyes with a sleeve. He glanced at the gash on his shoulder, gave it a puzzled look, and laughed again.

"Sit down, Master Sutter," Shasta instructed. "Let me have a look at that cut. Also, you mustn't breathe a word of this. Being a prisoner of war is one thing. Being a *royal* prisoner of war, quite another."

"Don't worry," he said, fixing his clear blue eyes on Serena. "My little sister and I will keep our mouths shut."

A warmth surrounded Serena. A warmth she should have felt every day but rarely experienced. Little sister. Words Logan said in anger or bitterness. Words Sarra said a little too often, making it awkward, and words Malaky was too afraid to speak.

And Braedan used them immediately, naturally.

She sat beside her older brother, wrapping her good arm around his, and smiled, knowing that no matter what happened next, she would not face it alone.

52

Seltachai

Glass jars rattled as Lok backed into a shelf. One jar crashed onto the floor, causing him to jolt and lose the flame over his hand.

Henry... Henry was drinking Healer Zall's blood!

He snapped his fingers, creating a new flame, in time to see Henry lunged at him. Henry grabbed him by the shirt and threw him across the room as though Lok were a rag doll. Lok's head smacked the hardwood floor. Stars danced in his eyes. He blinked them away and saw the healer's assistant looming over him. Blood dripped from his wide smile.

"You really should have knocked first, Lok." Henry, his teeth bared, grabbed at him. Lok scrambled to his feet and ran for the open door. Bright sunlight blinded him, and he smacked his ribs against the porch railing, knocking the breath out of him. Henry laughed.

Lok whirled around and snapped his fingers, recalling the flame.

"What are you going to do, Lok?" he whispered. "Burn me to death?" His smile turned into a mocking sneer. "Good bloody luck."

Lok struggled to wrap his head around this. Henry was drinking Zall's blood. Why would he do such a thing? How could he do such a thing? Lok recalled the scratch marks on Zall's neck. Esme assumed the healer had injured himself during a nightmare. Were those scratches actually bite marks?

Henry cornered Lok against the railing. His irises were as red as his pointed teeth. Every single one resembled a canine tooth. Henry smiled all the time. Why did Lok never notice they were pointed?

He never showed his teeth. Each time Henry smiled, it was a toothless smile.

"You can keep a secret, can't you, Lok?" Henry leaned closer, their faces almost touching. Lok smelled blood on his breath. "I bet you're great at keeping secrets. Nobody has to know. Healer Zall is a madman, after all. Nobody will miss him."

Nobody except Esme. She was always kind towards Zall, even when he was at his worst. Even though he believed her husband was a Seltachai.

Seltachai. A monster that drank human blood. Lok suddenly felt cold.

"What are you thinking, Lok?" Henry's smile vanished, replaced by a rictus sneer. "You know, maybe Zall's condition is contagious. Maybe you'll succumb to it, too. You have been spending an awful lot of time with Zall. Mistress Haar and I will have to care for two patients." He placed both hands on the railing, trapping Lok. "Maybe it will infect Mistress Haar, too. And her daughter. And that Scholar. Who knows?" He shrugged. "The whole village could be lost. These kinds of things happen, you know."

The cold feeling fled Lok, replaced by white hot fire. This monster wanted to hurt his entire village! Esme, Estrid, Scholar Kuno. His mother.

The small flame in Lok's hand blazed to life. He shoved it into Henry's face. Seltachai shrieked, a high pitched, almost metallic sound that made Lok's ears feel like they were bleeding.

Lok leapt down the porch stairs and spread the flame to both hands.

Henry frantically beat at the flames. He fell down the stairs, rolling and screaming. The fire died away. Henry, his skin burned red and black, glare daggers at Lok.

"You shouldn't have done that." A char piece of skin peeled away, revealing healthy pink skin underneath.

"What was that?" Lok turned and saw Meredith and West running towards him. She skidded to a halt. West nearly ran into her.

"What happened?" Meredith asked.

"He tried to kill me!" Henry jabbed a finger at Lok. "He set me on fire!"

Meredith gave Lok a horrified look. "What did he do? Why did you—"

Henry lunged at her, tackling her at the waist. He pinned her down and tried to bite her, but Meredith got a hand underneath his chin and held him at arm's length. She reached for her belt knife. Henry grabbed her wrist and twisted it.

West screamed, jumping up and down and waving his arms frantically.

Lok balled up the flame and kicked Henry in the ribs at the same time Meredith shoved him off her. Lok threw the fire at Henry. The Seltachai shrieked again, the sound splitting the air. He frantically tore off his coat and beat out the flames.

Meredith leapt to her feet, a knife in her hand, and stood beside Lok. West cowered behind them.

"What's going on?" someone shouted.

Henry staggered to his feet, his clothing charred and his face covered in patches of red welts and new skin. Part of his hair had burned away. "Help!" he screamed, a normal human scream. "The Elemental is trying to kill me!"

West cried, "Wind, wind!" and a massive gust blew past the healer's house and swept Henry off his feet. He sneered at West, sharp teeth bared.

A small crowd gathered along the road. Someone pointed at Henry, at the burns on his face and clothes. Another pointed at Lok. One person screamed. The rest just stared, too shocked to act.

"Help me!" Henry staggered to his feet. A second gust knocked him down. A few people took off running, calling for the village guard.

Lok tapped Meredith on the shoulder and pointed at the mayor's house. They had to reach the mayor and the guard first and explain... Explain what? That Henry was a Seltachai? It was too crazy to believe, but Lok didn't want people thinking he attacked Henry unprovoked.

"Get the mayor?" Meredith asked.

Lok nodded.

"What about him?" Meredith pointed at Henry. A whirlwind pressed him to the ground, the swirling air rising higher and higher.

Lok pointed again at the mayor's house. He didn't have time to explain.

Is Healer Zall still alive?

He would check on him later. First, he had a monster to deal with.

Meredith sprinted towards the mayor's house. Worried villagers tried to stop her, tried to ask what was going on, but she ignored them.

Lok glanced at West. He grimaced, his arms shaking. The whirlwind began to slow.

"Help, Lok. Help!"

Henry slowly rose to his feet as the wind whipped at his clothes and hair. Lok snapped his fingers, calling the flame back, and forced it to burn hotter and brighter. Balling it, he threw the flame at Henry. The whirlwind caught it. The flame flew off course and landed on a nearby roof. The building instantly caught fire. The crowd starting yelling, panicked. Two people ran to get water.

The people inside the building rushed out, among them Mister Ritt. Lok squeezed his eyes shut. Of all the buildings in Vala, he had set the carpenter's shop on fire. Master Ritt asked what caused the fire as people tried to save some of the furniture. Black smoke billowed skyward. A man pointed at Lok and West, his eyes full of venom.

"Help me!" Henry screamed as he ran across the street to the marketplace.

Lok chased after him. If Henry escaped, he would be a danger to everyone. He had to catch him, take him to the guards, and lock him up before he hurt someone else.

But how could Lok convince the guards that Henry, the healer's assistant who had lived in Vala peacefully for months, was a monster?

Would Esme believe him?

A pit formed in Lok's gut, a sense of dread filling his veins, telling him that this was futile. There was no way to stop a Seltachai. In stories, Seltachai were always stronger and faster than humans. They could be shot full of arrows or set on fire and still they would not die.

But maybe Lok could stop him long enough to explain, to show people Henry's real teeth.

His teeth! Henry never showed his teeth. If Lok could hold him down long enough for the guards to see, they would have to be-lieve him!

Henry ducked behind a stall.

"Hey, what's going on?" asked the merchant. His eyes darted to the carpenter's shop. The fire had spread to a nearby tree, turning the wood into char.

"Please, you have to hide me," Lok heard Henry say. "Those Elementals are trying to kill me!"

The merchant glanced up at West and Lok. He stepped out of the booth and raised his hands for them to stop. "Now, what's this about, boys?"

"Bad man! Bad man!" West shouted. Flames danced between his fingers. The merchant stumbled back.

"Hey, I don't want any trouble."

Henry grabbed a spade off the merchant's display and hit him in the back of the head. The merchant crumpled to the ground, his head bleeding.

"See what you did, Lok? You need to stop hurting people!" Henry shouted so loud he could be heard all the way to the inn.

Guess that's the point.

West shot flames towards Henry, but he couldn't hold his hands steady. The flames flew in every direction. Henry easily dodged them. The stall, unfortunately, caught on fire. The fire leapt to the next stall and the next.

Holding his palms flat, Lok lowered them. Some of the flames died down, but there were too many. The roof of one stall col-lapsed, billowing smoke and orange-red sparks. People screamed for help. Others shouted for water.

Water.

Lok grabbed West and pointed at the well on the street corner. West gave him a puzzled look.

One word. Lok just had to say one word, but no sound escaped his throat. Damn it, why was he broken?

You're not broken, Lok, Kuno's voice said.

West stared at the well. His eyes widened. "Water?"

Lok nodded. *Yes, water. Get water!*

"Water!" West ran towards the well. Lok quickly lost sight of him in the growing haze.

Heavy footsteps thundered behind him. All five members of the village guard, cudgels in hand, rushed towards Lok. Meredith was right on their heels. Lok smiled. Help had finally arrived.

"Stand down, Lok Tolman!" one of the guards yelled.

Fire and smoke!

"Not him, you idiot!" Meredith yelled back.

The guards ignored her. They spread out, forming a semi-circle around Lok. One guard drew an arrow.

"Oh dear," said Henry. "Looks like nobody believes you." He flashed his pointed teeth. The last bit of burned skin peeled off, and the missing patch of hair grew in. "I wonder what Thane blood tastes like. Your kind is so rare out here."

Henry lunged at him. Lok crouched low and drove his shoulder into Henry's chest, mimicking Scholar Kuno. He never understood why Kuno wanted him to learn how to fight. He was studying to be a historian, not a soldier. But Kuno had been adamant. Lok was suddenly grateful for the lessons.

He knocked Henry off his feet, but the Seltachai grabbed Lok by the shirt. Lok fell on top of him.

Henry punched Lok in the ribs three times in quick succession. Lok rolled onto his side, his chest aching. It hurt to breathe. Had Henry cracked his ribs?

Lok glanced around and saw flames. Fire engulfed the entire marketplace. The guardsmen abandoned their positions and ordered the villagers to get water.

Water. West was getting water. What was taking him so long?

And where was Henry?

Lok rose to knees and peered through the smoke. He could barely see five feet away.

"What are you thinking, Lok?" Henry's voice echoed from all directions at once.

Lok stood, his ribs aching as he coughed. The smoke made it hard to breathe.

"Some stories," Henry said, "claim Seltachai can read minds. Complete nonsense. Only Thanes can read minds."

Is he trying to distract me?

Of course he is, you idiot. Think!

But it was hard to think. Hard to breathe.

Footsteps sounded behind him. Lok whirled around, drawing fire to his hands, making it burn so brightly it hurt his eyes.

"It's me, it's me!" Meredith yelled, halting a pace from him. She had an arrow ready. "So, what caused this fight? Drinking on the job again?"

If only Meredith knew.

Meredith drew her bow, the arrow fletching parallel with her cheekbone. She scanned the smoke-filled market.

"Lok Tolman," said Henry's mocking voice. "I see you've got a friend. Did you know that Hiraeth blood tastes the best? It's true."

"What is he talking about?" Meredith tried to aim her arrow at Henry's voice, but it kept moving. First behind them, then two stalls over.

Lok reduced the flames to a single ball and pointed at his wrist. At the vein just visible underneath the skin. He pretended to bite his wrist, and then he pointed at Healer Zall's house.

Meredith gave him a baffled look. "Henry bit you?"

Close enough.

"Why?"

A gust of wind knocked Lok off balance and caused Meredith to drop her arrow. She quickly replaced it with another from her quiver.

Lok heard shouting. A large number of people shouting, yelling, wondering what to do. One of them sounded like Ellis. Someone else, it sounded like Mayor Gan but Lok wasn't certain, shouted for everyone to remain calm.

"Where is West?" Meredith whispered.

"West was delicious," Henry replied in Lok's ear. Lok froze, the flames in his hand disappearing.

Meredith pivoted on her heel and loosed the arrow. The bolt flew past Lok's face, the fletching brushing his cheek. Henry let out an unearthly scream and fell to the ground.

Lok turned and saw the arrow sticking out of the Seltachai's eye. Relief washed over him. It was over. They killed the Seltachai. Now they just had to...

Henry sat upright and calmly pulled the arrow out of his eye. "Now, I'm going to make you bleed," he sneered and flung the arrow away. The eye regrew as Henry rose to his feet.

"Stars above." Meredith stepped back, reaching for another arrow. A nearby stall collapsed in a heap of ashes. Fire and smoke darkened the already hazy air. "What are you?"

"Really? And here I thought you were the smart one."

"Get away from them!"

The smoke cleared enough for Lok to see Scholar Kuno approaching. His white cloak billowed in the wind. Lok's heart sank. What was the Scholar doing here? Had he seen the smoke on the way to Lothian?

Henry laughed, low and mocking. "Glad to see you, Scholar. Can't have too many loose ends."

No, don't hurt him! Lok directed a massive wave of fire at Henry. The Seltachai's skin burned, and his clothes were reduced to tatters. Henry rolled his eyes as new skin formed.

"I told you, Lok. You can't hurt me. Perhaps you are as stupid as you look."

Fire burned inside Lok. He was bloody sick of people calling him stupid!

Lok raised his hands, forcing the fire to burn hotter, but the heat died away. The air grew colder. Far too cold for the middle of an inferno. Lok edged closer to Meredith, shivering. An icy wind blew through the marketplace, expelling most of the smoke, and the sky darkened. He and Meredith huddled together. Lok snapped his fingers, drawing a flame, but it disappeared in an instant.

"What are you doing?" Henry asked, his voice faltering. He spun around and faced Kuno. The Scholar stretched his arms towards the darkening sky. "What are you doing?!" Henry shrieked.

"Lok, what is he doing?" Meredith said through chattering teeth. Icy wind whipped through the marketplace, drawing away every degree of heat. The flames died away.

Lok frowned. No, the flames weren't dying. They were growing darker. Yellow and orange turning a deep red. And the sky... It might as well have been midnight. He huddled closer to Meredith.

Scholar Kuno met Lok's gaze. "Close your eyes!"

A second later, a bolt of lightning shot down. Henry screamed as the bolt struck him.

The force knocked Lok and Meredith backwards. Lok's head

smacked the ground hard. His chest ached with each breath. Blinking, he slowly sat up. The world came into focus.

Where Henry stood was nothing but a pile of ashes. And the marketplace was gone. Every building, save for a handful along the periphery, had been flattened. Black streaks charred the few remaining pieces of wood.

Lok spied Kuno in the middle of the wreckage. Soot covered his face and white cloak, turning it gray and black. The Scholar wavered, his eyes wide and breathing unsteadily. He collapsed onto a heap of ashes. Lok ran to his side.

"What was that?" Meredith asked, crouching beside him. Lok cradled Kuno's head in his lap. The Scholar was unconscious, bleeding from his nose, ears, and eyes. His breathing was no more than a faint wheeze. "How did he... Is he a Thane?"

Lok rocked on his heels, his mind reeling. Oh Creator, what should he do? Kuno wasn't moving. He didn't want to lose his new father.

"How did he do that?"

Lok wished he knew. Kuno... Kuno had called down lightning on a cloudless day.

Murmuring crept towards him, making the hair on the back of his neck stand on end. Within seconds, a crowd circled him, Kuno, and Meredith. The village guards drew their weapons. Mayor Gan looked like he was going to pass out. His mother and stepfather stood behind the guards, Vera clutching Ellis's arms. They both stared at Lok and Kuno, terrified. Nobody spoke above a whisper.

Two figures pushed their way through the crowd. Brother Malaky and Luckson. Both men froze when they saw Lok, Meredith, and Kuno. Luckson began to speak, but no sound escaped his lips. Very slowly, he nodded.

Brother Malaky let out a horrified scream. "Alberik! Alberik! The Midnight King walks Eltriar!" The chaplain ran away, shoving people aside. "Alberik walks Eltriar! The Midnight King!"

The words sent shudders down Lok's spine. The crowd murmured louder. People looked at the chaplain and Kuno, terrified. A few ran after Malaky, demanding answers. The guards looked to Gan for guidance, but the Empath Thane just stared at the ruined marketplace, no doubt overrun by emotions.

"What did he mean?" Meredith asked. "Why did he mention the Midnight King?" Her voice faltered on the last two words.

"Get the midwife," someone said. "She might…"

The murmurs grew fearful.

Lok looked at Kuno. Why had Brother Malaky mentioned that horrible creature? Was it another Farsight?

But he was looking at Scholar Kuno.

And Kuno had called down lightning on a cloudless day. Only an Elemental Thane could have done that. And Kuno was not a Thane. The Cuchasi at the Academy would have known. Did that mean Kuno was something else?

A shadow fell over Lok. Meredith leapt to her feet, gripping a knife tightly. Lok held Kuno close to his chest.

Luckson stared at the Scholar in awe.

"Found you, brother."

53
Cooperation

Realta's mind reeled. She was finally at the Academy, but it was not the happy reunion she imagined. Yes, Charity was alive and well, but Siryn forced her away with that strange man with hair so blond it was almost white. The same shade as King Syleck's hair.

And a war raged outside the walls. A war Val had created.

Chinasa stood by her side, glaring at Val. The Minder Thane smiled pleasantly despite the busted lip. As though they were old friends who just happened to run into each other.

"Would you care to take a seat?" Val asked. He sat down at the oval-shaped table between Elliza and Alani. She had introduced herself as a Manipulator Thane, but she didn't wear any earrings or gold jewelry.

Realta stole a glance at Bas, Tath, and Siryn. The three Gadyeni stood by the door and whispered in their strange language.

She wanted to scream. Didn't the Gadyeni know what kind of person Val was? Didn't they care? Bas claimed the war was inevitable. The Eastern Coalition would have attacked Teyrnas within a few years, and the Midnight King would have used it to his advantage.

That doesn't erase Val's crimes. He was still a murderer.

"I prefer to stand," Chinasa said. He took a step closer to Realta. She was grateful for his familiar warmth. If only Charity were here. She ought to be safe at the infirmary. Unless she never made it to the infirmary. The strange man might hurt her, use her as leverage so Realta would have to work with Val. He...

Realta pushed the thoughts away. The Academy was full of people. The man could not hurt Charity without witnesses.

"Jerryk would never dream of hurting anyone," Val said, massaging his bruised jaw. "It's against his religion."

"Stay out of my head!" Realta snapped.

Val held up his hands nonthreateningly. "Fine. Have it your way, Realta. But I cannot help being a Minder any more than you can being a Dreamer or Alani being a Manipulator. So, we might as well set our differences aside and work together."

Realta walked towards the Gadyeni, singling out Siryn. "Is there any way to contact my father? Can you bring him here for just a few minutes?"

Siryn gave her a patient smile. "Realta, people are looking to your father for guidance. To remove him, even for a minute, would put their lives in danger."

"They wouldn't be in danger if it wasn't for him." She jabbed a finger at Val. "This is all your fault!"

"What is she talking about?" Alani asked.

Chinasa scoffed. "Of course he didn't tell you. Valentin only deals in lies."

"Oh really, Chinasa Ekene?" Val asked. "What about when I told you that you are One of Nine? Was that a lie?"

Chinasa grounded his teeth.

"Val is responsible for this war," Realta said, locking eyes with Alani. "He murdered King Logan!" *My uncle*, she almost said. She bit down on her tongue.

Alani gave Val a questioning look. "I heard about the assassination. Queen Gallia took credit."

"Because *she* is responsible. Realta," Val gave her a leveled look, "those monarchs would have banded together and attacked Teyrnas with or without me. I merely pushed their timetable up a few years. If I hadn't intervened, they would have gotten in the way while we fought the Midnight King. This way, no one will hinder us."

"They could have been allies," Chinasa said.

Val rolled his eyes. "Come on, ambassador. Bran Maro and Nowan helping Thanes? You'll have an easier time reversing the Nerin's course than convincing either of them to help us. Odds are, they would lock us away out of fear, and Alberik would be free to conquer Eltriar."

Alani shuddered and muttered under her breath. A prayer, Realta assumed.

Assume? I'm an Empath now. I don't have to assume. Focusing on Alani, Realta sensed fear but also determination. She would not stand down from this fight, even if her knees were shaking.

"Apologies," Val said to Alani. He then addressed Realta and Chinasa. "We must work together. You don't like me. I understand. But don't let that stop you from helping Eltriar. Think about your father, Realta. Do you really want him to fight in this war?"

"No," she said quietly. Callum was a skilled fighter. He could take on any man in Vala. Most stopped fighting when they heard Callum approaching. Half the time, he could end a fight before it started just by staring at the other person. But he wasn't fighting against farmers and merchants this time. These were trained soldiers. They wouldn't stop until their opponents were dead.

"What about you, Elliza?" Val asked. The girl suddenly bolted upright, as though she had been half asleep. "What do you think?"

"Sometimes, sacrifices must be made," she replied quickly. "The monarchs of Eltriar are too petty to band together, even to fight a common enemy. I've seen the Eastern Coalition fracturing. It will no longer exist at the year's end."

Val nodded gravely. "You see, Realta? We must work together."

Was King Logan just another sacrifice? Serena and Shasta had told her a few good things about Logan. His sharp mind. His ability to read between the lines of a document. And, in his own way, he cared for Serena. Logan could very easily have cast her aside, but he ensured that she was always clothed and fed and had a bed to sleep in.

"It's more than Yestyn would have done," Shasta commented. "Far more."

Logan had been a good king. Not necessarily a good person, but a good king. A leader people willingly followed. What would Logan have said and done in Realta's place? He certainly would not allow Val to intimidate him. So, why should Realta?

"I will work with Chinasa," she said after a moment. "And I will work with Elliza, Alani, and Jerryk. But I won't work with you. Not yet. You have to earn my trust." *And good bloody luck with that.*

Val smiled. "Fair enough. And you, Chinasa?"

"I will follow them." He gestured towards the Gadyeni. "They've fought the Midnight King before and won."

"Don't mistake that as a guarantee," Tath said. "Alberik is too clever by half. It's impossible to guess the number of tricks up his sleeves."

"Regardless, I trust you far more than I trust Valentin."

"Wait, where are the others?" Alani asked, glancing around the room. "There are only six of us. Where are the Elemental, Empath, and…" She frowned. "All of the above? What type of Thane was Balthazar, exactly?"

"All of the above is an apt description," Siryn said. She glided over to the table, her silver cloak flowing like a river of stars. "They will be here when they are here. And this battle is worsening by the minute."

Realta looked out the window. The rain slackened, revealing a row of soldiers fighting to protect a broken section of wall as other soldiers fought to get inside. Was Callum there?

"What can we do?" she asked.

"Queen Isla has already contacted the Madani," Val said. He stood and walked to her side, peering out the window. She felt the same warmth emanating from him as from Chinasa and Elliza, but it felt wrong. It was too warm, like standing near a large fire in the middle of summer. Uncomfortable and unwanted. "They will aid the evacuation effort this evening."

"This evening?" Chinasa questioned. "Night fall is hours away. Do you really think Teyrnas can fight that horde for so long?"

"They can with our help. You don't want to work with me, Chinasa. Very well. Work for them." Val pointed at the wall and the battlefield beyond. "There are thousands of civilians at the Academy and Norgard. Thousands of people who want to live in peace. The Eastern Coalition will not give them peace. And the Midnight King will turn them into slaves. Do you want them to suffer that fate?"

Chinasa hung his head. "No. I assume you have a plan?" he asked grudgingly.

Val smiled, flashing white teeth. "Of course. Please, sit."

Chinasa sat next to Alani, his eyes never leaving Val. Alani smiled brightly, excitement radiating off her. Elliza stared at the table's surface as Val resumed his seat. Realta focused on Elliza. The girl was afraid. Terrified. Was she afraid of Val?

"Are you joining us, Realta?" Val asked.

Realta watched the battle. Soldiers in dark blue clashing with soldiers in orange and white, too far away to make out any details, save colors.

Her eyes went to the wall. Soldiers in makeshift armor and tattered bits of blue tied to their arms ran up narrow flights of stairs. Other soldiers handed them arrows and bows as they ran by. They took aim and fired.

But she saw no sign of Callum.

Realta reluctantly tore her gaze away and sat down next to Chinasa. The three Gadyeni nodded, satisfied their selected Thanes were working together.

But why did they have to select Val?

"So, here's what I'm thinking," Val said.

Realta had no choice but to listen.

✳✳✳

People ran away from the wall, screaming and crying, carrying their meager possessions. Children clung to their mothers and fathers as they ran across the rain-soaked field.

Two Scholars flanked the Academy's doors, escorting people inside and urging them to remain calm. But people never acted calmly during a crisis. The civilians pushed and shoved their way inside. One Scholar was nearly trampled.

Kanton laughed as the other Scholar, barely thirty years old, tried to maintain order.

Turning away from the civilians, he gazed at the wall. The East Gate had fallen. A massive pile of rubble stood in its place. Teyrnian soldiers and the newly formed Thane Regiment fought to keep the Coalition at bay. Too bad the Regiment hadn't been formed sooner. They would've had time to drill and act like a real regiment instead of a bunch of clueless civilians with swords. At least there were some Manipulators in the lot.

One soldier caught Kanton's eye. A tall man with wild black hair and a beard. Neither were army regulation. And though he didn't have earrings or the symbol of the Thane Regiment on his makeshift leather armor, the soldiers rallied to him. The man gave an order, and they obeyed. Brandishing a bow, a quiver of arrows, and a sword, the man scaled the walls, the soldiers hot on his heels.

Kanton recognized him instantly.

Callum Haar.

Kanton touched the burn scars on the left side of his face. First, Haar had disfigured him, and then he helped Logan banished him from the guard. Kanton should have never sought the slave's help, regardless of Isla's letter.

Not Isla. Eltzy.

According to Valentin Gardyner, Eltzy used her ability to make Isla write that letter and deliver it to Kanton right before leaving to track down Serena. Did Isla ever learn that she had been used like a puppet? And how had Val known about Haar? He must have read Logan's mind and saw memories of Esme Haar with Carwyn. The Creator knew those two were inseparable.

After he killed Haar, Kanton planned to track the Minder down and question him.

Haar stood on the wall. He noted the slackening rain and called out to the archers. They took aim and fired as one. Judging by the cries, several hit their marks. Haar exchanged a few words with a skinny soldier. The soldier saluted and ran for the guard post near the gate. What was left of the guard post, Kanton should say.

Wait a minute. That soldier wasn't a skinny boy. It was a woman.

Eirica Marsh?

What on Eltriar was she doing here? And why was she taking orders from Haar? He had ended her career just as much as he ended Kanton's.

Did that mean Wills was here, too? Kanton hoped not. That weak-willed little worm wasn't good for anything. He'd just get in the way.

And he had the gall to blame Kanton for that disastrous recovery operation! Sure, when things went well, Peydar Wills took the credit, but when things failed, it was always someone else's fault.

Kanton glanced around. The battle raged on all sides now that the rain stopped.

Behind him, civilians continued to pour into the Academy. Would all of them fit?

They didn't matter. Kanton looked upwards. Haar stood in the middle of the fray, speaking to an Academy guardsman. The man nodded, listening to Haar's every word.

Kanton's blood boiled. Haar was a slave! The marks on his wrist were as plain as day. He didn't even bother to cover the tattoo. And not only did this guardsman listen to Haar, he obeyed him. Had the entire world gone mad?

Kanton touched the hilt of his sword. Queen Kenda had given him this sword for one purpose. Find Gallia. Not bring her back alive. Just find her. Killing Haar was his reward. And Prince Carwyn, if he was lucky.

Gripping the hilt with his good hand, Kanton stalked towards the wall.

54

A Crown of Gold

Kel rested his head against the stair railing. His leg throbbed, sending a pulsing pain throughout his body. How long had he been climbing?

Isla wrapped her arms around his thin torso, urging him onward.

"It's only a few more steps," she whispered. Scholar Lucan, Gallia, and Deen were already at the top of the stairs, standing in front of the Council Chamber's ornate doors. Deen looked ashen, favoring his right leg. His kneecap was not, in fact, broken, just severely bruised. But facts didn't stop the King of Bran Maro from complaining under his breath the entire way.

"We don't have all day." Scholar Lucan frowned, his dark eyebrows knitting together the same way Kel remembered. He only had one class with the Scholar, thank the Creator. An introductory economics course discussing Teyrnas' imports and exports. It was more mathematics than anything else, and Kel passed with minimal effort. Did Lucan still hold a grudge against the Hiraethi boy who turned out to be a king's son?

Kel, with Isla supporting him, climbed the final steps. He leaned against the door, thankful the ordeal was over. How did the Council members manage these steps every day? Most were old enough to be his parents.

Lucan led them into the Council Chamber with no ceremony. No one noticed. The Scholars were neck-deep in conversations, some on the verge of hysterics. One council member spoke to an elderly colleague, but the old man just stared at the walls. Several vied for the Premier Scholar Emera's attention. Her sharp eyes locked onto Isla.

"Queen Isla, I did not realize you were invited to this meeting."

One by one, the council members fell silent and turned towards them. The air grew uncomfortably warm.

"Premier Scholar," Isla said, taking a deep bow, far too deep for a queen to give, "I came at Scholar Lucan's insistence. We have a way to stop the war. At least in part."

Kel stared at Isla in amazement. She met the Premier Scholar's gaze with her head high, and her voice held steady. Isla had been so shy when they first met. Her mannerisms so timid. She only spoke when spoken to and always deferred conversation to her father, King Nolfri. Weeks later, Kel learned about her Farsight concerning his and Esme's marriage. No doubt that contributed to her shyness.

But that shy young woman was gone now. Replaced by a true queen.

"Explain," the Premier demanded. The Scholars quickly took their seats. Lucan glared down at Kel and Isla.

"I propose a treaty between Teyrnas and the kingdoms of Nowan and Bran Maro. A way to break the Eastern Coalition."

"A treaty?" asked one Scholar, a woman with gray and white hair in a braid that fell to her waist. "How will you get them to listen?"

Isla smiled. "Scholars of the Council, I present to you Queen Gallia Toutain of Nowan and King Ayrdeen Akardal the Second of Bran Maro." She paused and met Kel's eyes. His stomach was in knots. No going back now. No returning to his quiet, anonymous life. "And my brother-in-law, Prince Carwyn O'Kelwyn, the rightful heir to the Raven Throne."

The Council erupted. Some Scholars jabbed accusatory fingers at Deen and Gallia, demanding for their arrest or their heads. Others believed it was a trick. Isla had found convincing lookalikes to pose as the monarchs. And the rest stared at Kel, some thinking it was another trick and some wondering if he was truly the crown prince.

Kel pulled his hood over his head. Isla immediately pulled it down.

"But more hiding."

"But Logan—"

"Has his own tasks." Isla shot a wary glance at Lucan. If those accusations against him were true…

Great Creator, preserve us all.

Premier Scholar Emera raised a hand, and one by one, the Scholars fell silent. "One matter at a time. Crown Prince Carwyn O'Kelwyn, step forward."

Kel stood in the center of the colorful mosaic, now marred by a dark streak. Every eye stared at him, and the knots in his gut tightened. He glanced over his shoulder. Isla, Deen, and Gallia stood a pace behind him. And behind them stood a host of guards armed with crossbows, blocking the door. The Minders on the Council must have summoned them.

At least Lucan isn't a Minder.

"Prince Carwyn."

Kel faced the Premier, studying her. Emera's hair, a rich brown color when she was elected to the Council twenty years ago, was now snow white, and her hands were so thin Kel could see the veins. Her dark eyes, though still alert, held a wariness, an invisible shadow lying underneath the surface.

The years have been unkind to us both.

"Are you truly Prince Carwyn?"

"Yes, Premier," he said hoarsely.

"Speak up!"

"Yes, Premier Schola Emera."

"Prove it!" another Scholar snapped. Was that Scholar Gormac? Gormac had been his academic mentor, and Kel took three of his mathematics courses, loving every minute. Gormac had urged Kel to stay on as a Journeyman and study advanced mathematics in addition to honing his ability as an Illusionist Minder under Scholar Zuzanna's tutelage. Kel readily agreed, half for his love of math and half to stay close to Esme who was continuing as a Journeyman in order to study medicine.

"Calculus is easy," Kel said with a ready smile.

"Calculus is one of the hardest mathematical disciplines to learn," Gormac replied.

"For you."

Gormac's mouth opened and closed, struggled to speak. The old man then rushed from his seat and embraced Kel. "Oh my boy! What did they do to you?"

"It might be a trick," Lucan cautioned.

"No, this is not a trick." Gormac smiled at Kel warmly, in a way Yestyn never did. Another reason Kel stayed on as a Journeyman. Only a twist of fate landed him back at the palace.

"Scholar Gormac, you will display self-control during meetings," Premier Scholar Emera said in a neutral tone.

Gormac lightly squeezed Kel's shoulder and resumed his seat. Scholar Jori, seated to his right, whispered in Gormac's ear, staring furtively at Kel.

Yes, Jori. I am the beggar from Teyrnas. How kind of you to remember.

"Prince Carwyn, you were pronounced dead seventeen years ago," the Premier said. "How are you standing before us today?"

"Yestyn's attempt to kill me failed." The Scholars whispered loudly. Prince Carwyn officially died of a wasting disease, necessitating a closed casket funeral without the traditional two-day wake. "I was secreted out of the palace without the knowledge of my family. My parents and siblings assumed I was dead."

"Who aided you?"

Kel touched the necklace Esme had given him as a graduation gift. Two ravens soaring into the sky. He quickly tucked it inside his shirt. "You don't need to know."

"Prince Carwyn," the Premier continued, "you were close to another Journeyman, Esme Haar, who disappeared around the time of your supposed death. Did she aid you?"

"Leave my wife out of this," he snapped and immediately regretting speaking. He didn't want Esme dragged into this mess. It was bad enough that Lucan knew Gareth was his son.

A small smile crossed Lucan's face as murmurs rose from the Council. Fire and smoke.

I swear on my mother's name, if you hurt my son, Lucan, I will tell the entire world your secret.

The Premier motioned for one Scholar, a man in his forties and relatively young for the Council. She whispered into his ear. The Scholar nodded and exited the Chamber, sparing an uneasy glance at Gallia and Deen. The guards parted just long enough for him to slip through the door.

"Queen Isla," the Premier addressed her, "were you aware of Prince Carwyn's fate?"

"No, Premier." She walked forward and stood beside Kel. "Not until a few months ago."

The Scholars' mutterings turned hostile. They glared at Isla as though this was all her fault. Kel heard the word 'conspiracy' more than once.

"Why did you hide this fact?" The Premier's voice remained level.

"Because Carwyn asked me to keep it a secret. Logan didn't know, and we didn't want to jeopardize his reign."

"And now that Logan is dead and you've been relegated to queen regent," Lucan said, rising to his feet, "you decide to bring this secret to light."

"What? No, it isn't like that."

"Carwyn has no diplomatic experience, unlike yourself, Your Majesty," said another Scholar. Was that Iosaph? If the years had been unkind to Emera, they'd been downright cruel to him. "How do we know Carwyn will not dance on your strings?"

"Don't worry. I'm a terrible dancer." Kel pointed at his leg brace. Nobody looked assumed.

That's two times your mouth has gotten you in trouble, Kel. Want to try for a third?

"King Ayrdeen told Scholar Lucan the truth against mine and Carwyn's wishes," Isla explained. "Carwyn wanted to remain anonymous."

Lucan scoffed. "Why would anyone prefer to be a beggar?"

"Silence!" The Premier cleared her throat. "This brings us to our next problem. King Ayrdeen, Queen Gallia, step forward."

Deen walked up and stood beside Isla. Gallia stood beside Kel, gripping her dress and staring nervously at the Council. Kel doubted she'd ever been around so many Thanes, let alone Thanes in a position of power. He gently touched her hand. She took hold of it, gripping it tightly.

"Prove your identities," the Premier Scholar ordered.

"How?" Deen asked. "You can refute anything we say."

"Not necessarily. Scholars Ealee and Adhran, read their minds. Ensure they are telling the truth."

Deen looked like he was going to be sick.

"Very well," Gallia said, a slight tremor in her voice.

Gallia testified first. She explained her involvement with the Eastern Coalition and how Kenda manipulated her from the beginning. She also included stabbing Logan. Tears choked her voice, but she kept speaking, holding onto Kel's hand. She ended with the Coalition torturing civilians.

"I wanted no part of it, so I ran away. Kel, I mean Carwyn, found me hiding in the stable. He was kind to me. The first kind person since Liona." She looked at Deen. "Your daughter is an amazing young woman."

Deen beamed a smile.

"She is truthful," Scholar Ealee announced.

"Now you, King Ayrdeen."

"There isn't much to tell. Syleck is an idiot, that's why I left. Hid out in the city with Kel and his friends until we came here. Hid out some more, and then met with Isla. So, are we going to sign a peace treaty or not?"

"He is truthful," Scholar Adhran said grudgingly. He crossed his arms and glowered at Deen and Gallia.

"Scholar Osian will return momentarily." The Premier fixed her gaze on Isla. "Why did you wait so long to bring this information to us?"

"I feared you wouldn't listen. You stopped listening to me, and…" She let out a heavy sigh. "I was afraid I couldn't trust you."

"I'm sorry we weren't worthy of your trust. None of us expected another war in our lifetimes, and never one outside our walls. Our decisions were rash, but we only did what we thought was best."

Scholar Osian returned, carrying several books, a wooden box, papers, and ink and pens. He handed the books and papers to the Premier. The Scholars broke out in whispers, and Isla tensed, eyeing the box in Osian's hands. It looked familiar, but Kel couldn't place it.

The Premier gave the papers to Isla. She read over them and frowned.

"These are generic treaties. Why do you have them?"

"Just in case we faced surrender."

"You mean if I faced surrender," Isla clarified.

Ignoring her, the Premier said to Deen and Gallia, "Sign these papers. More formal documents will be drawn up tomorrow."

Gallia read the papers silently. Deen rolled his eyes and scoffed at every other sentence.

"Is this really the best—"

Isla elbowed him in the ribs.

Deen rolled his eyes again and then signed. Gallia signed as well, and Isla countersigned them.

"Make this known to the soldiers," the Premier said to the guards. "Nowan and Bran Maro have surrendered to Teyrnas. Any soldier who surrenders will be granted amnesty." Three of the guards bowed and hurried out of the Chamber.

Will this work? Kel wondered. Would every soldier in the Nowani and Marish armies stop fighting or would they decide their true loyalties lie with the Coalition?

He feared this war was far from over.

"Now," the Premier said, opening a large tome bound in dark leather, "a legal formality. Prince Carwyn, you are alive and well, and you are King Yestyn's firstborn."

"Yes, Premier." A sinking feeling formed in his gut, remembering Logan's words. *Your uncle Carwyn is going to be king for a while. Let's see how well the crown fits him.*

"Did you abdicate?"

"No, Premier." The pain in his leg throbbed in tandem with his racing heart.

"In the light of King Logan's death and the inability for either Brother Malaky O'Kelwyn or Lady Sarra O'Lyr to inherit the throne, as well as Prince Morgan being under the age of eighteen, you Prince Carwyn, are the rightful heir, making you King Carwyn."

"I abdicate," he said hurriedly. "I renounce my title."

The Premier gave him a patient look. "An abdication requires a magistrate and the signature of the one you abdicate in favor of. Is Prince Morgan present?"

"Obviously not. You just said he's too young. I name Isla Margents O'Kelwyn as my heir." No way he would name Gareth. He was only sixteen and too nervous to speak in front of the whole family let alone issue royal decrees.

"That is all well and good. But where is the magistrate?"

"Don't you have one?"

"We are at war, Your Majesty," the Premier replied matter-of-factly. "We do not have time to play political games."

"Judging by the way you've treated Isla, you have plenty of time for games." Heat rose in his face.

"Carwyn, just do it," Isla said. "We can straighten this out later." She looked at him pleadingly.

"Did you have a Farsight?" Kel whispered.

Isla looked into his eyes, saying nothing.

Fire and smoke.

Kel turned to the Premier. "Are you declaring me King of Teyrnas?"

"Yes, Your Majesty."

The title made his skin itch. "So, the power you took away from Isla on a technicality, the power that is still rightfully hers, you're giving to me?"

The Premier stared at Kel, weighing him. "Correct."

Stars above, Kel hated politics. One of the many reasons he loved his quiet life in the Hinterlands. But it this was the only way...

"Fine."

Scholar Osian opened the box. Kel's heart stopped. Inside the box rested his father's crown. Not the simple gold circlet that Logan wore, but the true crown of the Raven King. A heavy gold band, three fingers thick, and inlaid with golden oak leaves. Two ravens adorned the front, wings stretched back, ready to soar into the sky.

Osian, the crown held reverently in both hands, walked towards Kel. He bowed deeply and placed the heavy crown on Kel's messy hair.

Kel swallowed bile and fought down the urge to fling the damn thing against the wall. His father's hateful sneer surfaced in his memory, mocking Kel, mocking the child he refused to love.

Logan, I hope your plan is worth it. Kel glanced at the Premier and then at Lucan. The Scholar seethed.

"All hail King Carwyn O'Kelwyn, the Raven King!" the Premier intoned. The Scholars repeated the words. The sound echoed off the walls and hurt Kel's ears.

"Now," the Premier said once the echo died away, "our first

order of business—"

"Our first order of business," Kel interrupted, "is to grant amnesty to King Ayrdeen and Queen Gallia. They surrendered to Teyrnas in good faith, and they are to be treated as citizens of the realm. Not as prisoners."

The Scholars stared at Kel, shocked. Gallia breathed a sigh of relief and gently squeezed Kel's hand.

"Are you sure?" Scholar Jori asked tentatively. His colleagues muttered, worried. Two noted the way Gallia held Kel's hand.

"Yes."

"Your Majesty," Lucan began, "I—"

"You declared me king." Kel refused to let Lucan push him around. Shoving away a nameless beggar was one thing, but Kel was a king, and Lucan was going to treat him like one, damn it! "Are any of you shocked that I issued a decree?"

The Scholars were silent for a minute. Then two.

"Treat them as you would any Teyrnian," Kel ordered. It felt so wrong to speak this way, but Deen and Gallia were too valuable to put in chains.

"As Premier Scholar, I ratify this decree. Ayrdeen Akardal and Gallia Toutain will not be imprisoned and will be treated fairly, as citizens of Teyrnas."

"Wait, what?" Deen asked.

"I just saved your ass," Kel whispered through his teeth. "Play along."

"I am very grateful to King Carwyn and the Scholar Council," Deen said, putting on a smile.

"I am also grateful," Gallia said sincerely.

Kel's aching leg began to stiffen, and his head felt unnaturally heavy. He needed to sit down but couldn't show weakness in front of the Council.

"Where are you going?" the Premier demanded as Kel turned towards the door. Kel whirled around, jolted by her tone, and saw every Scholar watching him. Osian and Gormac looked at him respectfully, but others... Fire and smoke, he was just a dressed-up beggar in their eyes.

So, that's how this game is going to be played.

"I and my advisers," he pointed to Isla, Deen, and Gallia, "are

492

going to meet in private and discuss war strategies."

"What about us?" Lucan asked, his words acidic. Words that would have earned an outburst, possibly a beating, from Yestyn.

"We will tell you once a decision is made." Kel would be damned if he allowed a Warden to overhear their plans. "Isla, your rooms will do." *Now I just need to get down those bloody stairs.*

"Yes, King Carwyn," Isla replied with a smile. "I thank the Premier and the Council for meeting with us today and for granting King Carwyn his rightful place." She hooked an arm around Kel's elbow and walked towards the door. Gallia and Deen followed on their heels.

"Should we help him?" one guard asked his colleague, pointing at Kel's brace and crutch. The other guard shrugged.

Kel Manipulated a dagger from the guard's belt. "No need," he said, the dagger gliding into his hand. "I can help myself." He needed the guards' loyalty, not their pity.

The guard stared, mouth agape. He quickly remembered who he was staring at and bowed. The rest of the guards followed suit.

Outside the Chamber doors, Kel said to Deen, "Find Gareth, but don't tell him what happened. Just that I want to see him."

"Worried the Council will find him first?" Deen asked jokingly.

Kel glared at him.

"Fire and smoke, you are worried. You don't trust those bastards at all."

"Gormac is a good man. I can't speak for the rest."

"Understood, Your Majesty." Deen gave him a half-mocking bow and headed down the stairs, his bruised kneecap forgotten.

"Now what?" Gallia asked.

Kel looked at Isla.

"Why are you looking at me?" she asked. "You're the king."

"Don't remind me. Fire and smoke, what have I done?" He started to run his fingers through his hair, but instead he touched cold metal and shivered.

"The right thing. Come on, King Carwyn." Isla led him down the stairs. "Let's end this war."

55

The Wall

Hundreds of people crowded the Academy's atrium, families and friend groups huddling close as the battle raged outside. Each cry from the war horns sent a wave of terror rippling through the crowd. Realta gripped the stair railing, the collective fear threatening to overwhelm her.

"I don't know if I can do this," she said to Chinasa. The ambassador placed a comforting hand on her shoulder, though she could sense an underlying fear coming from him. *I wish I was just a Dreamer.*

"Listen, Realta. The Gadyeni need us to fight the Midnight King. All nine of us. They won't allow us to be harmed. We shouldn't have to fear."

Realta wasn't so sure. She glanced up and saw Val, Alani, and Elliza a few steps back. Val gave her a wink and a smile. His plan was ridiculous, but they had no choice. Val ignored all of their input and questions, and the Gadyeni were too absorbed in their own conversation to intervene. They were still talking when Realta and the others left.

She kind of wished Bas had gone with them. She did not completely trust him, not after he broke his promise and allowed Tath to force her along. But he did promise to go back for Serena and Braedan. She wanted to believe him.

"Chinasa, Elliza, you first," Val said, pointing towards the North Gate. The gate and the surrounding wall were intact, but a horde of Coalition soldiers stood between the gate and the Wallach River. According to Val's plan, Elliza would report her Farsights to the Teyrnian soldiers while Chinasa Learned the enemy's battle tactics in addition to looking out for the Madani's arrival.

Chinasa said nothing. He took the final steps two at a time and disappeared in the crowd.

"Do you still have the dagger?" Elliza asked Realta as she walked by.

Realta nodded. "But I can't exactly use it."

"Not right now." Elliza glanced over her shoulder at Val. The Minder Thane arched an eyebrow. A smile then crossed his lips.

"He just read your mind," Realta said.

"I know. I don't understand why you're so opposed to Linking. It's just like talking."

"No, it isn't."

"Well, see you after the battle." Elliza grew quiet, staring at nothing. She shivered and hurried after Chinasa. The crowd parted for her.

Realta glanced up at Val and Alani. A pit formed in her gut. Why couldn't she have gone with Chinasa instead of Elliza?

Because Val wants to keep you close. Trick you into trusting him.

"No tricks, Realta. I promise."

Realta grounded her teeth. *This war is bigger than me. I can't let my opinion of Val get in the way of helping these people.* Even if it meant standing side by side with a murderer.

"Head for the East Gate," Val said. "I'll meet you there."

"What?" Alani asked. "But you said—"

"Plans change. It's good to be flexible." Val rushed up the stairs. For a split second, he looked worried. Realta brushed it away. Let Val play his games so long as he played them far away from her.

Realta and Alani slowly made their way through the crowd. She bit down on her tongue, focusing on the door and not on the terrified people. Glancing at someone for more than a second caused their emotions to flood her, banging at the invisible door in her mind and demanding to be let inside.

How do Empaths function?

A line of Scholars guarded the door. They wore makeshift leather armor under their white cloaks and were armed with dagger no longer than kitchen knives. On second glance, Realta realized they were just kitchen knives.

"We cannot allow you to leave," said one Scholar, a woman in her forties with touches of gray in her brown hair. Dark circles surrounded her eyes. "All civilians are to remain inside until the evacuation begins."

"We're with the Thane Regiment," Alani said calmly, repeating the words Val had fed her.

The Scholar frowned. "Then you should be on the wall. We—"

Alani raised a hand, and the door Manipulated open. A gust of wind pushed the Scholar out of the way. A few final drops of rain lighted on Realta's face. She and Alani quickly exited, the door closing behind them before the Scholar or her colleagues could react.

Realta's heart dropped as she gazed at the field. The battle had spilled through the walls. The East Gate was no more than rubble. Stone slabs and twisted metal were strewn about as soldiers fought and died. And beyond the wall, thousands more fought.

Alani grabbed her by the hand and pulled her along.

No, this was wrong. Realta should not be here. None of these soldiers should be here. She didn't care about the Gadyeni's excuses. Val had designed this war as a front. If the true war was between the Nine of them and the Midnight King, why involve so many people? Why turn half the countries of the Northern Realm against Teyrnas? Why drag her family into this chaos?

Before she could voice protest, Realta found herself standing beside the ruined wall. This section, including a stairway at the top, was still standing. But several slabs were loose, ready to collapse. Soldiers in dark blue ran towards her and Alani. Each one wore Thane earrings.

"Who are you?" asked a young soldier, only a few years older than Realta. He wore a blue earring, and a compass adorned the left arm of his uniform.

"Reinforcements," Alani said calmly. Far too calmly for a historian with no fighting experience. "Hope we aren't too late."

The young soldier glanced behind them. "Just you two?"

Alani nodded.

"Well, can't complain. I'm Infantryman Jons. You?"

"Alani Kisei," she said over the shouting soldiers. "I'm a Manipulator. And Realta Haar is an Empath and Manipulator as well." Val had instructed Alani not to mention that Realta was a Dreamer, if anyone asked. That type of Thane had been extinct for centuries, and they couldn't afford extra distractions.

Jons's eyes widened. "Realta Haar? Do you know Charity Loy

and Lok Tolman?"

Realta's heart skipped a beat. "Yes, we grew up together. How do you know them?"

"We were Students together. Still are, I guess." Jons eyed her up and down, smiling. "Stars above, a two-fold Thane. That's incredible. They never mentioned it."

"I asked them to keep it secret."

"Why?"

A soldier standing on a ruined part of the wall shouted orders, pointing at the massing soldiers on the other side.

Alani raised her hands and Manipulated a large section of wall, positioning it above them. Several soldiers ran for cover. Realta shivered as dozens of arrows rained down, metal hitting stone. Two soldiers who didn't reach the stone shelter were hit multiple times. One screamed, but the other laid completely still.

Alani then Manipulated the stone away in a wide arc over the wall. It landed with a thud, and men screamed. Alani's face turned ashen. She stumbled back, trembling.

How many are dead? Realta wondered, staring at the dead Teyrnian soldier. Arrows with red and blue fletching stuck out of his body. Bile rose in the back of her throat.

"Thanks," Jons said to Alani.

Alani blinked a few times, her eyes darting around until they found Jons. "What do you need us to do?"

"You can stay down here with us. Secure this opening. How strong is your ability?"

"I can easily Manipulate objects three times the size of that stone," Alani replied.

"Excellent. And you?"

"I'm very low-leveled," Realta said.

"Are you any good with a bow and arrow, then?"

"Kinda." Callum had taught her and Gareth how to shoot, using apples as targets. Realta was never really good, only hitting one apple in five. Her skills improved some as they traveled south, doing her share of hunting while they traveled between villages.

And now she was back in Teyrnas. Had all that running been for nothing?

"Good." Jons grabbed a bow and a quiver full of arrows from a wounded soldier and handed them to her. "Get up on the wall."

Realta recoiled as though Jons had handed her a snake. "I don't want to kill anyone."

Jons gave her a pained look. "I understand, but these soldiers won't hesitate to kill you. Just slow them down a bit."

Realta slung the quiver over her shoulder and tested the bow. Lightweight and made of flexible wood. Tears stung her eyes, remembering Callum crouching down beside her and Gareth, neither of them older than ten.

"Pull back until your bow arm is perfectly straight." Callum watched Realta test it. "Good. Now with the arrow. Pull until the fletching touches your cheek." Realta did her best, coming a few inches short. Callum smiled proudly. "Great start. Now let your cousin try."

Gareth hadn't done any better, but Callum encouraged them, practicing every other day. By the end of that summer, she shot an apple right out of the tree, and Gareth shot three apples in a row, only requiring a few seconds between shots. Everyone cheered. Gareth quickly handed the bow to Realta and hurried inside the house, barricading himself in his bedroom. He emerged several hours later, and everyone was quieter with their praise.

"Hurry," Alani said, pushing Realta towards the steps. "We have to hold until this evening."

Realta looked up at the overcast sky. Gray clouds hid the sun, making it impossible to accurately tell the time. Evening was hours away, but how many hours?

White knuckling the bow, Realta ran up the steps, taking them two at a time.

***

Gareth searched for Auras. A large rainbow of Auras belonging to the Thane Regiment stretched along the wall, between the South and East Gates. Or rather, what was left of the East Gate.

He crouched between deserted tents with Jaim and Ivar by his side. Both boys wore pieces of spare armor. A breastplate and helmet for Ivar, and a leather jerkin and arm guards for Jaim. Gareth only wore a dark cloak over his regular clothes. The added weight from the armor felt weird, unnatural. He decided to take his chances, not realizing how close they would come to the fighting.

"See anyone?" Jaim asked, peering through the tents.

Per the Premier Scholar's orders, all civilians were to take refuge inside the Academy until the evacuation. They expected the Madani to arrive this evening, but nobody had seen any sign of them. Gareth overheard two Scholars wondering if the Madani were delayed and if they should plan to surrender. They immediately stopped talking when they saw Gareth, plastering on smiles.

Gareth, Ivar, Jaim, and several other Students and Journeymen had volunteered to search for civilians who were hiding or foolhardy enough to join the fight. What would his father say if he knew Gareth was here? Would Kel be proud of Gareth's bravery or think he was also being foolhardy?

"Yes, there's one," Gareth said, spying a gold Aura. Very strong. Stronger than some of the Thane Scholars. He moved closer and saw a teenaged boy with a woman. The woman's skin was pale and stretched thin over her bony features. They huddled together, shuddering each time soldiers yelled or a horn sounded.

Jaim and Ivar approaching them, Gareth walking a pace behind. His friends were better at talking to strangers. Best for him to act as a lookout.

"Hey, you guys have to get inside," Jaim said.

The boy leapt to his feet, his hands balled into fists. "No, you won't take me away from her!"

"You'll stay together, idiot."

Ivar motioned for Jaim to step aside. "You must get inside. The Coalition soldiers have broken through the wall."

The pale woman groaned.

"And then what?" the boy asked. "We just wait inside for them to kill us?"

"Of course not. The Madani will arrive around nightfall. They will help you and your mother evacuate."

"How do you know we can trust them?"

"I am Madani. We keep our promises."

The boy bit his lower lip. He looked at his mother and then at the wall. A half second later, his head whipped around, glaring daggers at Ivar. "How do you know she's my mother?"

"I'm a Minder Thane. Sorry for reading your mind without

permission."

"Then you…" He stood in front of his mother protectively. "Then you know what I am?" he asked, lowering his voice.

Ivar nodded.

"I ain't going with you!" He raised a fist, ready to strike.

Gareth stepped between him and Ivar. "Your secret is safe with us. We promise."

The boy glared at Gareth. Sweat beaded on Gareth's forehead and neck as he forced himself to look the boy in the eyes. A bead slipped down his back. The boy sighed heavily and lowered his hand. "We can't stay out here, can we?"

Gareth shook his head.

"But those Scholars, they'll find out…"

"Not if I intercede," Ivar said. "I'm no good at Illusions, but I can place thoughts in people's heads. Make them forget seeing an Aura."

"Deklan," said the woman, her voice a hoarse whisper. "It's okay."

The young man relented.

Ivar helped Deklan raise his mother to her feet. "Keep looking," Ivar said to Jaim and Gareth. "And be careful."

"That goes without saying," Jaim retorted. Once they were out of earshot, Jaim muttered, "What was his problem?"

"He's a Thane," Gareth said. "But he doesn't have an earring." Strange. Scholars went to great lengths to find every Thane in Teyrnas. How did one slip past them?

"Really? Weird. What kind?"

"Manipulator. Very high leveled."

"Huh. Do you think—"

The hairs on the back of Gareth's neck stood on end as shouting rose into the air. They stood dangerously close to the wall. He and Jaim watched as a pair of soldiers Manipulated a volley of rocks, likely pieces of the broken wall, in a wide arc. Soldiers on the other side screamed as rock contacted flesh and metal. Two more volleys arced over the wall, each with the same effect.

"Must be the Thane Regiment," Jaim said. He shifted his feet uneasily. "Hey, think we should get back?"

Gareth gazed up at the wall and froze. "Black." A small black Aura stood out like a drop of ink on a clean page. "Black Aura."

Only one person had a black Aura. "Realta?" Yes, it was her. But her hair was cut short. What was she doing here? And why in the name of all Eight Gadyeni was she on the wall?

"Realta? As in, your missing cousin?"

Realta ran down the wall, her black Aura trailing her like a kite. She had a bow in her hands and a quiver of arrows slung over her shoulder.

Gareth took off running.

"Hey, where are you going?!"

"Helping!" was the only word he could manage. Thoughts and half-formed plans swarmed his mind. Too much to explain verbally.

"Wait for me!"

***

Guiding merchants through Caman's Pass was easy. One entrance, one exit. Stay on the path and you'll be fine. Leaving the path invited danger, and no sane person would invite danger to their dinner table.

And yet, here Callum Haar stood in the middle of the most dangerous situation of his life. On top of a wall surrounded on all sides by people who wanted to kill him.

Oh well. At least his life wasn't boring.

"Commander, they have siege engines!" shouted a young soldier, a boy barely into his twenties.

Marsh had addressed Callum as Commander Haar in front of a unit of soldiers, and the soldiers accepted the title without question. He doubted if any had noticed the lines and diamonds on his wrist: a runaway slave, twice over. But as the battle progressed and more and more soldiers deferred to him as Commander, Callum realized that there was no one else to answer to. The previous commander, the commander of the Thane Regiment no less, had been killed shortly before he and Marsh arrived. And someone had to lead these people.

Callum followed the soldier's line of sight. Slow-moving siege engines lumbered across the field. A siege? The Coalition already felled a section of wall. What would siege engines accomplish other than causing a panic?

Causing a panic, obviously.

"Manx, have archers target the wheels. Jam the mechanisms."
A benefit of living with two Academy educated family members:
they read a lot of books and felt compelled to share what they
learned. A few years back, Kel bought a book on military technol-
ogy, including siege engines and their mechanics. It was a pretty
interesting book, Callum had to admit. Lots of illustrations and
diagrams. Maybe if he survived this war, he could finally become
an illustrator and get Esme off his back.

The Creator gave you an artist's hand for a reason, she always
said.

A smile creased his face. At least his sister and niece were safe
in Vala. And Realta and Serena were miles away, probably at the
border of the Sykerian Empire by now.

The smile faltered. Two kingdoms separated Teyrnas from the
Empire. And they might have changed course and headed west,
towards Lowyrn or Jemayrt. They could be anywhere by now.
Would he ever see his daughter again?

The twang of snapping bowstrings rang in Callum's ears as
a volley of arrows darkened the sky. The majority found their
marks. One of the siege engines halted, arrows jamming the
gears and the soldiers operating it lying motionless.

Marsh ran up to Callum. The former guardswoman wore
makeshift armor, just like Callum. Leather breastplate with metal arm and leg guards. She found a metal helmet as well, a size too
big. She kept having to push it away from her eyes. "Commander
Haar, we've received word via Deirow Hawk. The Council has
signed a preliminary treaty with Nowan and Bran Maro."

Callum frowned and watched the battle from the corner of his
eye. Marish and Nowani soldiers continued to fight Teyrnians.
"Explain."

"Nowan and Bran Maro have surrendered, sir," she replied.
Glancing at the battle, she added, "At least, their monarchs have."

"How?" Callum directed his attention to the siege engines.
They flew the flag of Galion, and a smattering of Nowani and
Tirshic soldiers aided them.

"Somehow, Queen Gallia and King Ayrdeen arrived at the
Academy. They met with Queen Isla and the Council. Signed

a treaty."

"It's about damn time, Deen," Callum muttered under his breath. Deen was one of the stubbornest men he'd ever met. Convincing him to speak with Isla had been like shoeing a mule. And Queen Gallia... She ordered men to kill Callum. He wasn't sure if he should trust her.

How did she slip inside? The walls were tightly guarded. Anyone entering was questioned thoroughly. A handful of refugees were turned away the other day because one got frustrated and said he was from West Bridge instead of East Bridge. Despite the others vouching for him, the guards ordered the entire group to leave. How could Gallia have talked her way inside? Did she have more than one Minder in her retinue?

"Commander, there's another development."

"What?" Callum scanned the battlefield. Coalition soldiers swarmed the field, but there was a thin patch. Between the Academy and the river. Could they use that as an advantage?

"Queen Isla isn't the ruler of Teyrnas anymore," Marsh said slowly, testing the words. "The Council crowned Prince Carwyn as king."

Callum's head whipped towards her. "I'm sorry?"

"I had to hear the message twice myself, Commander. But there is a man who claims to be Prince Carwyn. He was crowned as Logan's heir. Do you think it's a ploy?"

"No, it's no ploy." Callum lowered his voice. "Do you remember my brother? The man with the crutch?"

"Yes, Commander. He's kind of hard to forget." Marsh paused. "No, he couldn't..." She studied Callum's face. "Great Creator, you can't be serious."

Callum nodded. "Isla must have been in dire straits for Kel to reveal his identity. What else did the message say?"

"Not much. Only that the Madani are two hours out."

Callum peered at the sky. Still overcast. Impossible to accurately judge the time. "Let's pray they arrive early."

"The Council will send more Hawks to the Nowani and Marish commanders within the hour, proclaiming the surrender."

The disabled siege engine began lumbering towards the wall. The Galionic and Tirshic soldiers cheered.

"We don't have an hour. Tell the Council to send the message within the half hour."

"Yes, Commander."

***

Realta huddled against the wall, the bow clutched to her chest. Tears threatened to overwhelm her, and her legs were frozen, unable to move an inch. There was so much fighting. So many soldiers dying. Men and women on both sides. Every time she glanced over the wall, new horrors greeted her.

It was too much.

"You cannot stay here, Realta."

Bas crouched beside her, the familiar warmth radiating from him. For once, she was glad to see him.

"Where were you?"

"Our meeting took longer than expected," he replied apologetically. "Tath has his ideas, and Siryn has hers. Rarely do they agree."

"What ideas?"

"I can't discuss them in the open. Just know that you aren't alone in this fight. And the other Nine are doing wonderfully."

"There aren't nine of us. Only six."

"Seven, actually," Bas replied, smiling. His inky black eyes shone despite the lack of sunlight.

Realta sat up a little straighter. "Then who is the seventh?"

"For his safety and yours, I must keep his identity a secret. Alberik has regained his abilities ahead of schedule. Esar is very concerned." Bas's already pale face turned snow white.

Realta's heart sank. "Then we're too late."

"Of course not." Bas placed a comforting hand on her shoulder. "We just need a change of plans."

"Then pick a different Minder." Realta swatted his hand away. "Val—"

"Valentin Gardyner is a very complicated man. Most people are. And Val has been through a lot. Perhaps too much. You don't have to like him, Realta, but you must find a way to work with him. Even if he did push this war forward a few years."

Realta bit down on her lip. "So, the war was unavoidable."

Bas sighed heavily. "Queen Kenda has had Syleck and Eskandar in her pocket for years. All she needed was Ayrdeen and Gallia's support. Val pushed Gallia in that direction, and Ayrdeen sided with his neighbors. War with Teyrnas has long been on Kenda's agenda. A guarantee of putting her name in the history books."

"And the Midnight King would have been free at that point. With all his powers?"

"Correct. Your forces would have been divided. Teyrnas and its allies breaking away to fight the Coalition. Once weakened, Alberik would have gone for the kill. He..." Bas swallowed a lump in his throat. "He used a similar tactic during the Thousand Years War. We thought we had him on the run, but it was all a diversion. Tricking us into looking north while he moved south, so to speak."

"So, Val causing a war helped us?"

"In a sense."

"That's really messed up."

"Alberik wants to subjugate and rule an entire planet. That's even more messed up."

"Tell me what to do," Realta pleaded. "Val's plan didn't involve me shooting arrows from the wall. This was Jons's idea." Originally, she, Alani, and Val were to assist the Thane Regiment and prevent the East Gate from falling. Then Val ran off without an explanation, and the Gate had collapsed by the time she and Alani arrived. Val, so confident that his plan would work perfectly, never told them what to do if the gate fell. This was worse than walking through the woods blindfolded.

"Who is Jons?" Bas asked.

"He's in the Thane Regiment."

"I see." Bas gazed around.

Realta heard shouting, screaming, metal contacting metal. She squeezed her eyes shut. She wished she was home, wished she was with her father.

She thought about her Dreams. About Domni wandering the aftermath of a battle, finding a young soldier among the bodies. An enemy soldier. An adherent to the Midnight King. But Domni had shown him kindness.

Her mind then went to the Midnight King torturing a soldier to death. She wished she could forget, but that was not the point of her Dreams. They were meant to be remembered. To be learned from.

"Can I be like Domni?" She slowly opened her eyes, meeting Bas's gaze.

"Yes, you can. Domni did not like fighting either, but he was always loyal to his friends. Always wanting to help."

"How can I help without fighting?"

"Help her."

Realta glanced up and saw a woman dressed in leather armor with a helmet tucked under one arm. She had short, black hair in a braid, and her sharp eyes observed everything.

Realta's heart skipped a beat. It was Eirica Marsh, the former member of the King's Guard.

Did that mean Kanton was nearby? Marsh had worked side by side with the man, hunting down Serena, attacking them in the dead of night. The woman said nothing when Kanton lied to King Logan's face, earning Realta a servant's mark and Callum the mark of a runaway slave.

How could she trust such a person?

"Hey, you're the one who wants to help," Bas said.

Gritting her teeth, Realta stood up. Marsh skidded to a halt, nearly running into her. Recognition shone in her eyes.

"Realta Haar?"

She nodded.

"Thank the Creator. Your father is worried sick about you!"

"My father?" Realta's heart raced. "Is he here?"

"Yeah. He's my acting commander."

"Can I see him?"

Marsh glanced over her shoulder, frowning. "The fighting is worse in that section. How good is your handwriting?"

Handwriting? "Um, pretty good. Why?"

Marsh beamed a smile. "Come with me." She led Realta down the wall, towards one of the few remaining guard posts. Slipping through the narrow doorway, Realta spied extra swords and bows on the walls and a table covered with newly fletched arrows. Soldiers moved about the small space, exchanging damaged weapons for new ones. Two soldiers had Deirow Hawks on their shoulders.

"What's going on?" Realta asked as Marsh went to the table and cleared away the bowstrings and arrowheads. She then pulled a rolled piece of paper from her pocket and spread it flat. The seal of Teyrnas, two flying ravens imprinted on dark blue wax, adorned the page.

Marsh grabbed a nearby chair and motioned for Realta to sit. "A way to end this bloody fight."

***

"Okay, we're at the wall. Now what?" Jaim asked, standing at the base of the partially destroyed wall.

Gareth looked at every person. At every Aura. Silver, gold, red, mixtures of two colors in every combination. But no black. He glanced up at the wall, looking left and then right. Panic built in his chest, an invisible hand threatening to crush his ribs. Where was Realta?

"What are you doing here?" a familiar voice demanded.

Gareth saw Zandon stalk towards them, his blue Aura flashing. He scowled at them as though they were beggars at the palace gates. Gareth's chest tightened. Zandon was their friend. Shouldn't he be happy to see them?

"You haven't gotten tired of fighting people yet?" Jaim asked, smirking.

Zandon looked like he wanted to punch that smirk off Jaim's face. "I am tired. But I don't know if you've noticed or not, Siarlwyn, but we're in the middle of a bloody war!"

"No need to shout."

"Where is Realta?" Gareth asked. He didn't have time for an argument.

"Up on the wall. Why didn't you tell us your cousin was a Thane?" It sounded more like an accusation than a question.

Gareth flinched, fear invading his mind. Fear? No, he didn't want to be afraid of his friend. But what could he say? He already lied about being a Cuchasi, and judging by Zandon's temper, admitting the truth would only enrage him.

Zandon shook his head. "I don't have time for this. At least her friend is helpful. More than helpful."

Gareth noticed a dark-skinned woman Manipulating massive slabs of rock and setting them into place, blocking the collapsed gate. Two soldiers, both with gold Auras, Manipulated a canopy of wood over the woman's head, protecting her and the other soldiers from arrows.

"Who is she?" Jaim asked.

"Damned if I know. But she's on our side, so I ain't asking questions." Zandon fixed them with a leveled look. "You two need to get inside the Academy. No civilians are supposed to be out here."

"We know, but Gareth thought he saw Realta."

"She's a Thane, and she's here to fight. So, unless you're joining the Thane Regiment…"

"No way. Thanks for the offer. Come on, Gareth." Jaim tugged his cloak.

A flash of white caught Gareth's eye. A dagger in an ornate white sheath lay on the muddy ground beside the wall. Gareth picked it up. It was surprisingly light and had a bit of glass embedded in the hilt.

"That's Realta's dagger," Zandon said. "It must have fallen off her belt."

Gareth climbed the stairs. Some steps were damaged, but it was no more difficult than climbing the oak tree back home.

"Where are you going?" Zandon questioned.

"I have to give the dagger back to her." Gareth didn't know why, only that Realta needed this dagger.

"You'll bloody get yourself killed up there!" Jaim shouted.

"He's right. Get down!" Zandon lunged for Gareth. His fingers missed Gareth's cloak by inches.

Gareth kept climbing as an invisible string tugged him along, compelling him to find Realta.

***

A triumphant yell filled the air as the third siege engine grounded to a halt. Callum smiled, watching the Galionic and Tirshic soldiers scramble to remove dozens of arrows from the machinery.

The gray clouds parted, and warm, summer sunlight poured down on them.

It's about time.

"Where is Haar?" someone shouted.

"Right here." Callum turned towards the voice's owner, and his heart stopped. Dane Kanton stood five paces away, his sword drawn and murder in his eyes.

Callum reached for the borrowed sword at his belt.

"Commander," said one soldier, a grizzled veteran who had fought in the last war between Teyrnas and Nowan, "is everything okay?"

Before Callum could respond, half a dozen hooked ladders affixed themselves to the wall. Callum cursed under his breath as Marish soldiers scaled the ladders. An endless flow of men armed to the teeth.

Stupid idiot! All this time and energy spent on siege engines, and they hadn't noticed the soldiers directly underneath them. Those siege engines were never meant to reach the walls. They were just a distraction.

The Teyrnian soldiers drew their swords, meeting the Marish head on. Cutting, hacking, blocking. Soldiers in blue and red fell. Some screamed while others went silently. And for every Marish soldier who died, two more took his place.

Callum fumbled for his sword. The damn thing was caught in the sheath.

Dane Kanton, blind to the fighting, stalked forward.

Callum worked his sword free just as a Marish soldier leapt in front of him. He countered the soldier's quick slash, batting the sword downwards and then slashing up. Metal sliced flesh. A spray of blood. The dead soldier fell to the ground.

He was grateful his daughter was half a world away. He did not want her to watch while he killed.

Kanton fought two soldiers at once, dispatching them with practiced ease.

"Callum Haar!" Kanton yelled, his blue eyes like fire.

The former guardsman raised his blade. Callum lunged, attacked first. But Kanton swiped low. Callum leapt backwards, the blade scoring his leather armor. Too damn close. He needed to be smarter than this. Gripping the hilt tighter, he waited for Kanton's next move.

Kanton lashed out, aiming for Callum's neck. Callum blocked high and then blocked low. Kanton's powerful strokes nearly knocked the sword out of Callum's hands. If Kanton had wielded a sword instead of a dagger that night in the woods, Callum would be a dead man.

Kanton attacked in quick succession. Neck, torso, neck, legs. Callum struggled to keep up. He was not a swordsman. Not a soldier. He trained to fight wildcats and bandits, not men trained from adolescence to fight and kill in the name of the king.

A light dawned in his mind. Callum was going about this all wrong. That look in Kanton's eyes was more reminiscent of a rabid wildcat than a trained soldier. He found his advantage.

Callum struck first. Kanton blocked each stroke with easy. And with each strike, Callum inched him closer to the ladders. Closer to the edge and the endless flow of Marish soldiers.

Kanton backed into a soldier as the man scaled the edge. The poor soldier, however, did not stand a chance. He likely never saw the face of the man who killed him. While Kanton's back was turned, Callum rammed into him. The guardsman collided with the wall. The sword escaped his grasp.

Callum raised his blade, but Kanton was faster and slammed into Callum. The back of his head smacked against hard stone. The sword slipped out of his hand and clattered away as soldiers fought around them. Callum's vision swam, blue and red uniforms blurring together as bright sunlight glinted off armor.

Kanton dragged Callum to his feet.

"You damn slave," Kanton hissed in his ear. "I should have killed you at the palace. You and that damn cripple."

"That cripple is your king."

Kanton's eye twitched. A rictus smile slowly spread across his face. "Maybe I should let you live. Long enough to watch Carwyn die. And your little bitch of a daughter."

Fire raged inside Callum. Damn this man for threatening his family!

He jabbed Kanton in the eye. The guardsman screamed. Tightening his grip on Callum's shirt, he threw a wild punch. Callum dodged it and drove his thumb into Kanton's eye. Kanton screamed as blood leaked out of the tear duct.

Two fighting soldiers slammed into them. Kanton, half blinded, reached for a dagger and slashed at the Marish one. The blade connected with the Marish soldier, scoring him on the shoulder. The soldier screamed and lunged at the Teyrnian. The Teyrnian slammed his shoulder into the Marish's sternum, driving him into Kanton.

Kanton lost his balance and fell over the wall, dragging Callum with him.

Callum reached out, his fingers brushing the wall's edge, but the stones were slick with blood and rain. He felt himself falling, falling, and then the world went dark.

***

Gareth wanted to scream, but no sound escaped his throat. He had been so close.

He searched everywhere for Realta, but her black Aura was nowhere in sight. And the fighting grew worse the farther he went. The cowardly part of his mind told him to go back, find Jaim and Zandon, and get somewhere safe. He told the cowardly part to shut up. He was done running away. Even if a hundred fighting soldiers stood between him and Realta.

A bright red Aura then caught Gareth's eye. Dane Kanton.

Kanton stalked through the chaos, his eyes fixed on one man. Callum.

Gareth tried to reach Callum first and warn him, but there was so much fighting. He almost got cut a couple of times, dodging swords and daggers. One soldier yelled at him to get out of the way.

He tried to call out, but his voice refused to work.

And now it was too late.

Gareth peered over the wall, gazing downward. Marish and Nowani soldiers swarmed the field, a sea of red and purple and white uniforms. The sea parted for two pairs of Nowani soldiers, their uniforms more white than purple. Each pair lifted a man and carried him away. Both were bloody and broken. Neither moved.

No. Callum could not be dead. He was the strongest man Gareth knew.

Gareth refused to believe it. Not until he saw with his own

eyes. Callum might just be stunned, knocked unconscious. He couldn't be dead!

A myriad of thoughts clouded his mind. He had to get below and find Callum, but how? The East Gate was blocked by a new wall and surrounded by the Thane Regiment, and neither could he ask Jaim or Zandon for help. Jaim might understand, but not Zandon. The young man had changed so much in a few short weeks that Gareth no longer recognized his friend.

But other exits remained. A small hole hidden by a row of shrubs. A hole so small, the Scholars and soldiers never bothered to guard it.

Gareth raced down the wall, avoiding soldiers and swords and arrows, and ran down the narrow stairs. He passed the Thane Regiment, but Zandon and Jaim were arguing, Zandon yelling in Jaim's face. Neither boy noticed him. Good. He could not waste time.

The shrubs lined the wall, untouched by the fighting. Parting the branches, Gareth spied the hole. Just large enough for him to slip through.

Is this a good idea?

He knew the answer the moment he asked. Going beyond the wall meant going closer to the fighting. No one would be able to protect him. And he had no armor or weapons except Realta's dagger.

But Callum was hurt. Someone had to save him. And Callum would not hesitate to save Gareth.

Praying that his uncle was still alive, Gareth slipped through the wall.

56
Messages

Marsh weighed down the paper with a broken sword hilt and an inkwell.

Realta glanced around the cramped space. About twenty soldiers, all in dark blue, moved to and fro, grabbing weapons, issuing orders. And all, to an extent, were scared. She took comfort, knowing she wasn't the only one.

"Baltyn," Marsh waved to one soldier. He jogged over. "Do you have your hawk?"

"Of course. Why?" He removed his helmet, revealing a mass of unruly black hair, and wiped sweat off his brow.

"We need to send messages. Lots of them."

"Sure. To whom?" Baltyn gestured around the room. None of the other soldiers paid attention, too focused on the battle.

A sharp pain tore into Realta's forehead, like a thousand wasps stinging her at once. She sat down in the nearest chair and nearly fell out of it.

A large hawk, far larger than she had ever seen, glided into the room and landed on the table. The hawk studied her with piercing, gold eyes.

"Injured?" the hawk asked.

Realta leapt to her feet, knocking the chair over, and retreated to Marsh's side. The pain in her head spread and dulled at the same time. As quickly as it arrived, the pain disappeared.

What was that? Something to do with being an Empath? She had to be careful not to overstrain herself.

Baltyn smiled. "Never seen a Deirow Hawk, huh, kid?"

"This is Realta. Commander Haar's daughter."

"Who?" Baltyn asked.

Realta almost asked the same question. Her father was not a soldier. *Siryn said he was fighting on the wall, leading soldiers.* It seemed one of the Gadyeni was truthful.

"Not important. Only that my orders come from him." Marsh placed her hand on the paper. "How many hawks do we have available?"

Baltyn frowned. "Six, I think. We lost three to archers, and two hawkers were killed on the wall. Their hawks... Well, they aren't good for anything right now."

Marsh nodded gravely. "Realta, can you write out six copies of this document?"

Realta read it and was taken aback. It was a peace treaty between Teyrnas, Nowan, and Bran Maro. Signed by all three monarchs. "I can write it, but I don't know if I can copy the signatures." Queen Gallia's signature was easy to read, just her name with a few elaborate loops, but King Ayrdeen's was barely more than a scribble. As though a child had grabbed hold of the pen. And Queen Isla's signature...

That isn't Isla's name. Instead, it belonged to King Carwyn of Teyrnas. But there was no King Carwyn. He...

He died, and Kel son of Owena took his place. A crippled Hiraethi man living in the Hinterlands, far away from Thanes and noble courts.

How had Kel become king? Did Queen Isla step down, or did something worse happen?

"Realta?"

"Yes?" Did Marsh know the king was her uncle?

"Is everything all right?" she asked.

"I think so." Realta studied Carwyn's signature. It was definitely her uncle's handwriting. Neat and precise.

"You can sit here." Baltyn righted the chair. "Hey, Tyson, get some paper," he called out to another soldier with a hawk.

"Why?" Tyson gave him a weird look.

"Commander Haar's orders."

Tyson saluted halfheartedly and rummaged through a trunk near the doorway.

"Now what..." Baltyn's eyes fell on Realta's wrist. On the servant's mark. "Um... You're a servant?"

"I was." Realta pulled down her sleeve. She wished the bloody tattoo would just disappear.

"The man she and her father were indentured to died when the Eastern Coalition invaded Teyrnas," Marsh skirted the truth.

Baltyn nodded. "Well, I guess that stuff won't mean much if Nowan wins this war."

Tyson placed papers, a pen, and a fresh inkwell on the table. Some ink had spilled on his hand. The hawk on his shoulder spread out its wings and flapped them, creating a small windstorm.

"Stay here, Tyson," Baltyn said. "The girl has messages we need to send."

"No problem." Tyson nudged his shoulder. The hawk flew across the room and perched on a wooden peg embedded high on the wall. He leaned against the wall, crossed his arms, and closed his eyes.

Realta rubbed her eyes as Tyson's fatigue knocked on the door of her mind, asking to be let in.

Why do I have to be an Empath? None of the other Nine Thanes had more than one ability. None that they confessed to. And one Thane was supposed to have all eight abilities. Bas had refused to reveal his name.

His name.

Realta relaxed a bit. At least it wasn't her.

This Thane, the Windrose, would be their leader. The one to use the Sun Dagger against the Midnight King.

Bas is protecting him. That's why he can't say his name.

But why? Balthazar wasn't hidden away. He was the leader from day one.

Granted, this person would only be their leader if Val allowed him to be. She couldn't imagine Val giving up his position easily.

Sitting down at the small table, Realta read the treaty again. There were a lot of legal words she didn't understand, but most of it was straightforward.

Dipping the pen into the inkwell, she started to write.

***

Val stood atop the North Gate and smiled. Chinasa and Elliza worked together wonderfully. Helping soldiers, directing the wounded back to the Academy's main building. Chinasa was a fast study, learning the enemy's tactics and figuring out how to

515

outmaneuver them, like pieces on a game board. And Elliza's Farsights had saved a group of soldiers from being riddled with arrows. These soldiers were more than grateful to have Thanes on their side.

The smile faltered. Was Val wrong to press the Eastern Coalition into attacking Teyrnas? The kingdom was open to Thanes. Ruled by them. Educated by them. A Minder of his capabilities would hold a place of honor.

On second thought, he should have tricked the Coalition into attacking itself. Strong personalities could only coexist peacefully for so long, and his plan included them turning against one another.

But even if the Coalition attacked itself tomorrow, the damage to Teyrnas was done. The kingdom would need generations to recover, and there were good men and women in this army. Good soldiers tested for battle. The strongest and smartest would survive. They would aid the Nine in the war against the Midnight King.

Yes, that was the reason. This war was a proving ground. The strongest always survived.

He always survived.

A pair of soldiers pointed at the Wallach River. One held a spyglass up to his eye. And not just any spyglass. The one presented to King Logan by Scholar Leila of Jemayrt at the Exhibition. Designed to study the stars, it provided sharper images than a standard spyglass. How on Eltriar did it end up here?

Val strode over, creating an Illusion of a commanding officer.

"Report, soldiers," he said.

The soldiers saluted, fists over their hearts. "Sir, the Madani ships are arriving." He pointed at the river.

Val motioned for the spyglass. The soldier handed it over without comment or question. Val smiled. He should masquerade as a commanding officer more often.

Holding the glass to his eye, Val saw dozens of long boats sailing down the Wallach and docking due north of the Academy. They had arrived a few hours ahead of schedule. But, since this was not their war, they were useless in the battle. They had only come for the civilians. All of those boats were run by lightly armored skeleton crews.

"Alert the Council," he said to one soldier. "Tell them the Madani are in sight. Prepare to evacuate."

The soldier saluted and ran off.

Val turned to the remaining solider, a man in his thirties with dark hair and eyes. He looked vaguely familiar. "Carry the message down the line. Make sure every soldier on the wall knows."

"But, sir, what about the Galionic and Tirshic soldiers?" the soldier asked. Val recognized him now. One of the palace guards who was present at the Exhibition when Gallia made her entrance. Good thing Val was using an Illusion.

Val gazed down. Thousands of soldiers blocked the way to the river. "Are the troops in the Garrison ready to attack?"

"I don't know, sir."

Val fixed the spyglass on the Garrison, a massive stone structure situated between the river and Norgard. He focused on the people within, searching for one specific mind.

Found you!

Syleck's niece Eltzabet had been stationed in the Garrison months ago, spying on the soldiers and helping Kenda and Gallia single out Dane Kanton for their schemes. The girl was an extraordinary Minder, able to influence people from miles away. Had Isla discovered the letter she wrote to Kanton as Eltzabet's puppet? Val made a mental note as he Linked with the girl.

Eltzabet, do you recognize me? He sent an image of his face.

Who is this? replied the girl's startled thought. Poor thing. Her family had kept her in isolation after discovering her ability and only allowed her to practice while spying on unassuming guests.

This is Valentin. Queen Gallia's messenger. Turns out I'm a Thane, too. Where in the Garrison are you?

A long pause. Too long. Val feared she had broken off the Link, but she replied, *With the scribes. Why?*

I need you to send a message to whoever is in charge. Have the Garrison's reserves attack the Galionic troops. Clear the way to the river. Did you get that? We don't have much time.

Will they believe me? she asked timidly. Always so timid. Val made another mental note to find her after the battle and take her under his wing. The Nine needed all the Thane allies they could get.

They are accustomed to Thanes. Prove your ability and say the message came via Linking from a Thane Commander.

Okay. I'll try.

Thank you, Eltzabet.

Val hoped it worked. How had Syleck discovered his niece's ability? Probably an unfortunate accident. The scar along Val's right shoulder blade itched. A reminder of his own unfortunate accident.

"How did this happen?" Gallia had asked one quiet night as they laid in bed, watching the stars shine like the firebugs that populated Nowan's endless fields.

"It's nothing," he lied. "Know how kids like to jump out of trees?" He smiled and kissed her. She accepted the lie, having no reason to suspect him.

A shadow fell over him. Val turned and greeted Chinasa with a smile. The ambassador scowled.

"What?" Val asked.

"Alani just arrived. Realta is not with her."

"Realta can take care of herself." The plan called for Realta to stay with Alani, but the Gadyeni would not allow her to be harmed. Besides, she was old enough to look after herself.

Val looked at the river through the spyglass. More boats docked on the riverbank. Who would be evacuated first? The common people or the nobles? Or the Scholars?

Chinasa grabbed Val by the shoulders. "You told Alani and Realta to stay together, and she left her the Gadyeni know where!"

"Plans change all the time, Chinasa. And the Gadyeni will protect her. Trust them. You sure as the Abyss don't trust me," Val muttered.

Chinasa sighed through his teeth and shoved Val away.

Taking another look at the river, he saw more ships. But instead of Madani long boats, they were river ships, flying the flag of Byyar.

Stars above! How could he be so stupid? Queen Isla was King Nolfri's daughter. And he had no love for Nowan. It was only a matter of time before Teyrnas' western allies joined the fight.

Trumpets blared from the battlefield. They differed from normal war cries, the sound longer and lower pitched.

Val frowned, a pit forming in his gut.

"What is that?" Chinasa asked.

"I don't know." The feeling in his gut worsened, and his vision swam as though he stood on the edge of a bottomless pit. Val shoved the spyglass into Chinasa's hands and hurried off to find Elliza.

***

"Here's the last one." Realta handed the paper to Baltyn. He rolled it into a tight scroll and tied it on the hawk's leg.

"Take it to the Nowani commander," he said for the third time. Three messages were sent to Bran Maro's commanders and three to Nowan's.

Realta hoped the commander received the message. The Marish shot down the first hawk. Its handler screamed as it fell. The man had to be carried to the infirmary, shivering and muttering incoherently as wide eyes stared at nothing.

"Each hawker forms a bond with a Deirow chick when it hatches," Baltyn had explained. "The two are bonded for life, each feeling what the other feels. And when one dies…" Baltyn faltered. "Sometimes, the other recovers. Most aren't so lucky."

A series of trumpets sounded low and slow. The sound repeated twice, leaving an empty stillness.

Marsh smiled. "That's a rallying cry. The soldiers are being recalled one unit at a time. Someone believed us."

"Or they think it's a trick and want to plan for the worst," Baltyn replied. Marsh shot him a glare. "What? Wars are unpredictable."

Realta peered out an arrow slit. The sun was almost at the horizon. Soldiers in red uniforms formed ranks and marched away from the wall.

A soldier, a young man about twenty years old, ran up to Marsh and saluted. "Lieutenant Marsh," he said, pausing to catch his breath, "we can't find the commander."

"What do you mean, Manx?"

"Commander Haar. One second, he was on the wall. But then all chaos broke loose. The Marish tried scaling the walls. Took nearly an hour to fight them off. We thought Haar was with us, but he's gone!"

"Is he hurt?" Realta asked, her heart racing as she hurried to Marsh's side.

"I don't know. We looked for him, but he's just gone!"

A pit formed in Realta's gut. That weird pain. When had she felt it? An hour ago? Two hours? Had she sensed her father's pain? It had faded away so quickly…

"People don't disappear into thin air," Marsh said calmly. "We will find him."

"Where could he have gone?" Realta asked. It wasn't like Callum to abandon a fight. *Unless he was injured.* Or dead. *No, don't think that!*

Trumpets sounded again, repeating the low tone.

"What does that signal mean?" Manx asked, his voice trembling.

"They're withdrawing. I think this battle is almost over." Marsh walked towards the door. Realta and Manx followed. The sun sank below the tree line, dyeing the sky bright orange and red. And below, dozens of boats lined the river. Some flew a flag with a white bear on a blue field while the other flew a flag striped red and yellow.

"That's the Byyarian flag!" Manx said, hoping rising in his voice.

Realta wished she could share the feeling. Callum never ran from a fight. Never abandoned the people who needed him.

Great Creator, if you can hear me, please keep my father safe.

All around her, soldiers cheered.

57

Consequences

The hallways were eerily quiet. Countless thousands huddled together. Some peered out of windows. Others had their eyes squeezed shut. And all of them, even the smallest children, were silent. Kel hurried along, hoping nobody noticed the crown on his head.

Deen waited impatiently outside of Isla's room, eyeing the refugees warily.

"What are you doing here?" Kel whispered.

"Couldn't get outside. Bloody Scholars barred the doors. Tried looking for your boy, but there's too many. Sorry."

"Gareth will be all right." Kel hoped. A Warden, wearing a Scholar's cloak, could easily approach Gareth, saying that Kel wished to see him and lure him into a trap. But the boy was smart. He'd likely see through the ruse.

Deen ushered Kel, Isla, and Gallia inside and quickly shut and locked the door.

A small lantern burned on the table, filling the room with a soft, yellow glow as the sunlight faded. A red draig lounged next to the lantern, its tail curled over its head. Colm rose from his seat at the window and reached for his dagger. He relaxed, seeing Kel and Isla, though he cast an uneasy glance at Gallia.

"What are you doing here?" Kel asked. He saw Morgan and Mannix sleeping on the bed, Morgan's arm wrapped around his little brother. Isla glided over and gently brushed a lock of golden-red hair out of Morgan's face.

"Logan asked me to keep watch," Colm replied. "Said he had an important meeting to go to. Didn't explain anything else. I thought he meant the Council..." Colm bit down on his lip. "Did he trick me again?" Colm had felt terrible after Logan tricked him with an Illusion, thinking he was good for nothing. Just a stupid bastard. It took Kel and Callum an hour to assure the young man that was not the case. Even the simplest Illusion could trick the best and brightest.

Colm frowned. "Why are you wearing a crown?"

The two boys stirred. Morgan sat up and rubbed his eyes. Mannix latched onto Isla, crying softly.

"What's going on out there?" Morgan asked.

"A lot of fighting and dying," Deen replied. He sat in the window seat and retrieved his flute.

Isla glared at him.

"What? The boy's old enough to hear the truth."

Gallia joined Deen and Colm at the window. "The soldiers aren't fighting anymore. They're just standing on the wall. Watching. Have you gotten any reports?" she asked Colm.

Colm started to salute and then stared to bow. He then settled with a salute. "Well, not officially, Your Majesty. Gregor was here about half an hour ago, asking for you, Isla. He said the Scholars will start evacuations soon."

"Good." Kel sat down at the desk and selected a blank piece of paper and a good pen.

"What are you doing?" Deen asked as Kel started to write.

"Writing a formal peace treaty. One that guarantees we won't be played."

"Don't you trust the Council?" Gallia asked. She sat in the chair nearest the desk, hands gripping her dress tightly. Noticing this, she stretched out her fingers, laying her hands flat in her lap.

"I don't like that they accepted me as Prince Carwyn with minimal proof." He dipped the pen into the inkwell. "Nobody in Vala, the village I live in, would believe that I'm a prince. Not even if Logan and I were standing side by side."

"Scholar Gormac and the Premier recognized you," Isla said. "Isn't that proof?"

"Eyewitnesses are one thing. Some can be bought, and people lie. And my face isn't actually..." He gestured towards his scars.

"Yes, you are obviously hideously disfigured," Deen replied, rolling his eyes.

"They accept your authority as king," Isla said. She then sighed. "It's more than they offered me."

"Wait, you're a king?" Colm's eyes widened.

"You're a sharp one," Deen said.

"Shut up," Isla snapped. She told Colm about the Council meeting, concluding with the peace treaties and Kel's informal coronation. Colm stared at Kel with awe. It made Kel's skin itch, and he focused on writing.

"But I thought Isla and Morgan were Logan's heirs," Colm said, still a bit confused.

"It's complicated," Kel replied. "A lot of legal jargon. I think the Council and the Wardens just want someone on the throne who isn't a threat."

"Someone they believe they can manipulate." Isla shook her head in disgust. "Logan would never stand for their games. And I can always write to my father and get Byyar involved. But a conflict among allies is the last thing Teyrnas needs."

"So, you're their puppet king," Gallia surmised. A small fire burned in her eyes.

"So they think. They'd be amazed at how stubborn I can be." Kel needed to be stubborn to survive. He adamantly refused to let Esme and Darran Zall amputate his leg, even after they explained the numerous surgeries he'd need and the possibility that the limb would be useless. And he refused to lie in bed and live as an invalid. He lost count of the number of times he had fallen. All the cuts, bruises, the pains that plagued him each night, making sleep impossible. But the years of stubbornness paid off. He learned to walk again. And if he needed to learn how to be a king, so be it.

Kel read over the new treaty. Something was missing. *Shouldn't have slept through that law class.*

"Can you make sure this is legitimate?" he asked Isla.

She walked over, Mannix in her arms, and peered over Kel's shoulder. "It's close. Add clauses ensuring full amnesty for Marish and Nowani soldiers who surrender, as well as clauses for Deen and Gallia's residential status."

"Clauses?" He knew the word but for the life of him, he didn't remember the meaning.

Isla gave Kel a patient smile. She handed Mannix over to him and rewrote the treaty on a fresh sheet of paper. The little boy clung to Kel as though he'd known his uncle his whole life instead of a few weeks.

Holding Mannix close to his chest, Kel thought about Gareth. He wished Deen had time to properly search. But the Academy was a big place. Gareth was probably hiding in a quiet corner with Charity Loy and their friends. Kel made a mental note to ask Callum to draw a map of the Academy. One with all the hiding places Kel had discovered as a Student.

"There," Isla announced. "Sign here."

Kel wrote his full name: Carwyn of House Kelwyn, King of Teyrnas. He felt as though he had nailed his brother's coffin shut, with Logan kicking and screaming to be let out.

Isla handed the pen to Gallia and Deen.

"How is this different from first treaty?" Gallia asked as she made the last flourishes on her signature.

"It guarantees that you are now private citizens," Isla explained. "Anyone from your armies or kingdoms who surrenders are now under Carwyn's protection and authority. Not the Council's."

Gallia frowned. "But how much authority does Kel really have?"

"As much as Logan. But he will have to fight the Council every step of the way."

"Part of the Council," Kel amended. "Did we ever get a definitive list of Wardens on the Council?"

"Just Lucan."

Kel drummed his fingers on the table. He wished Logan would give them a full list or explain the Wardens' plans. Why was he being so tightlipped?

"Who are the Wardens?" Morgan asked.

Kel and Isla exchanged an uneasy glance.

"Some very bad people," Isla said. "Don't mention this to anyone, Morgan, but the Wardens are the reason your father is in hiding. They won't hurt you as long as you stay close to us. Same goes for you," she said to Gallia and Deen.

"Very well." Deen tested a note on his flute and began playing.

Gallia laughed.

"What?"

"You and your daughter are so much alike."

Deen cursed in Marish. "I forgot about Liona! Those bastards still have her! What will they do to her after the treaty goes public?"

"She's a smart girl," Gallia said. "She'll—"

"Smart?" Deen rounded on her. "Smart means nothing when dealing with Kenda. She will kill her!"

"You don't know that," Kel said. "And it would be stupid. Right now, Liona is a bargaining chip. Once Kenda knows you're alive, you're locked in a stalemate. You cannot make a move without her harming Liona, and she cannot make a move without you retaking control of your army and turning against her."

Deen gave him a weird look. "Where in the Abyss did you get that idea?"

Kel wished he could take it back. He was already starting to sound like a king. "I read a lot of history books. A lot of military tactics." He glanced at the window, but he couldn't see anything from this angle save for the red and orange sky. Red and orange? Was it sunset already? Where had the day gone? "Unfortunately, I have no real-world experience. Colm, what's going on out there?"

Colm, with Morgan trailing, glance out. "Can't see much. But I don't see any fighting."

Trumpets sounded low and slow.

"I think I hear fighting," Morgan said.

Isla joined them. The room grew absolutely silent. Slowly, sounds drifted in. Men shouting. Metal striking metal.

"There's fighting," Isla replied. "But not on the wall."

***

Realta stayed close to Marsh as they walked along the wall. Chaos had erupted in the Eastern Coalition's ranks. Nowani and Tirshic fighting another one. Marish against Galionic, setting a massive wooden structure with wheels on fire. In some places, the Nowani fought each other. Commanders shouted for order. One commander was cut down by his own soldiers. Realta squeezed her eyes shut.

"Look!" Baltyn pointed towards the city. Soldiers from the Garrison marched towards the Academy, splitting into two columns. One headed for the North Gate while the other for the East Gate. The North column attacked the Galionic soldiers from behind, turning their attention away from the gate.

The East column halted a hundred paces from the gate. A Marish commander, who wore a red crest on his helmet, rode out to meet them. The Garrison commander exchanged a few words with him as soldiers on both sides readied arrows, waiting for the signal to fire.

Miraculously, the two commanders shook hands. Two armies merged into one and charged the Tirshic and Tarodic units.

The North band pressed the Galionic soldiers towards the wall, forcing them closer to the second band of Garrison troops. The road, reduced to torn up gravel and mud, slowly cleared.

Realta spied several ships docking on the riverbank. Half flew a flag displaying a white bear on a field of blue, and half flew a flag with red and yellow stripes. Soldiers disembarked. The ones from the red and yellow flag ships marched westward, meeting a unit of Tarodic soldiers who had circled around, and held them at bay. The ones from the bear flag ships marched towards the Academy.

"Thank the Creator," Marsh said, breathing a sigh of relief.

"Who are they?" Realta asked. She glanced up and down the wall, hoping and praying for any sign of Callum. Marsh assured her that Callum was fine. Battles were messy, confusing things. He likely either got separated and joined another unit or was aiding the Scholars and healers on the ground.

But a small voice in the back of Realta's mind told her that something was terribly wrong.

"Soldiers from Byyar and Madan Och," Marsh replied. "The Madani will transport civilians across the river while the Byyarians keep the Coalition at bay."

"Nobles will probably get evacuated first," Baltyn said, a hint of bitterness in his tone.

"What about Queen Isla?" Realta asked.

"She might stay and aid the Council," Marsh said, shrugging with her hands. "The Council are the ones really ruling Teyrnas, from what I hear. But it's hard to tell."

A trumpet blared four times. Realta turned and saw people slowly exit the Academy, escorted by Scholars and soldiers. Some people carried bags, but most only had the clothes on their backs.

A group of Galionic soldiers broke away, running for the North Gate as it opened. The Madani met the charge and held them back until a unit of Byyarians rushed from a newly docked ship and attacked ruthlessly. They drove the Galionic soldiers towards the Garrison troops, trapping them. A few threw down their weapons and placed their hands on their heads, kneeling.

"I'm sorry about earlier," Marsh whispered. "I was following orders without thinking. We all knew Kanton had a temper, so most of the time, we were too afraid to question him. I'm sorry we hurt you and your friends. And Serena. We should have known something was wrong by the way Kanton treated her. Bastard or not, she is still Logan's sister."

"Thanks," Realta said quietly.

"Where is Serena?"

"She's in Kereu with Shasta Cray. We…" Tears stung Realta's eyes. "I didn't want to leave her, but we didn't have a choice."

Marsh nodded. "That's a good place for her, I guess. Mistress Cray will look after her, and she has a chance to be free of her family." Marsh smiled. "I wonder if she'll find any of Yestyn's bastards. That's half the reason why she ran away."

A smile stole across Realta's lips. "She might."

The sun sunk low, nearing the horizon. The first moon would rise in a few hours.

Tiredness stole over Realta, weighing her down. Part of her wanted to lie down and sleep right here, but she still had work. She had to find Callum.

And Charity, and Lok, and Gareth. Charity, no doubt, was still in the infirmary with Jerryk. What was he like? Would he mindlessly follow Val, or would he think for himself?

"Should we help?" Realta pointed at the refugees. The Madani and Byyarians formed a loose line to the river, ready to defend the civilians. Soldiers from the Garrison joined them, their weapons drawn. Most of the Galionic and Tarodic soldiers had retreated.

Marsh shook her head. "The Madani will care for them. And we have new allies." She pointed at a group of Marish soldiers. They placed their weapons on the ground and approached the Madani. The Madani looked uneasy, but a Garrison commander vouched for them.

"Does this mean the war is over?"

"No, the Coalition still exists," Marsh said. "Last I heard, they turned Teyrnas into their de facto capital. We'll have to retake the city before the war ends."

And we will have to defeat the Midnight King, Realta thought but did not dare say aloud.

"You should get some rest. We can look for Commander Haar in the morning. Who knows? He might find us first." Marsh led Realta back to the guard post. A handful of soldiers were sleeping, their backs against the walls while others stood watch.

"But I—"

Marsh cut her off with a wave of her hand. "If you are going to help soldiers, you might as well take orders like one. Now," Marsh pointed at an empty corner, "I order you to sleep until sunrise."

Realta wanted to protest, but she felt so very tired. She suspected the soldiers' exhaustion was affecting her. *I can't overstrain myself again.*

"Chinasa," she said as she sat down. "I have to talk to Ambassador Chinasa Ekene first." She failed to keep her eyes open.

"I'll find him. Tell him you're here. Now sleep."

Realta leaned her head against the wall and fell into a deep, Dreamless sleep.

58

The Midnight King

Lok hardly noticed as the first pale lights of dawn filtered through the window. He sat beside Scholar Kuno's bed since the fire. Since Kuno called down lightning on a cloudless day.

The villages were at a complete loss. The marketplace was reduced to cinders, and some villagers suffered from burns and eye pain. Esme readily treated the burns and gave people linen bandages coated in salves to place over their eyes.

The guards searched for Henry, wanting to hear his side of events, but they never found a body. The lightning had utterly destroyed him.

And then came the questions. First by Mayor Gan in the presence of a guard armed with a long sword, a weapon the village guard never carried. Then the magistrate from Lothian arrived, along with a quartet of guards. The magistrate, seeing the aftermath of the fire, was shocked that only Lok and Meredith were being questioned. Judging by Mayor Gan's message, he assumed a gang of bandits was responsible.

"Who started the fire, boy? You or the Hiraethi?" the magistrate, a stern-looking man with slate gray hair and a short beard, asked.

Lok's hands shook so badly that the words were illegible.

"Why is he writing?" the magistrate asked Gan.

"The boy is mute."

The magistrate nodded tersely and directed his questions at Meredith. She explained everything calmly. One of the guards wanted to discredit her because she was Hiraethi.

"Everyone knows those damn savages are liars," he spat.

"I'm telling the truth," she protested. She fixed Mayor Gran with a level gaze. "Should I tell everyone what that earring really means?"

Gan paled. "That won't be necessary, young miss," he stammered. "I'm good friends with a Hiraethi man," he told the magistrate. "He never lies."

The magistrate nodded and asked about West.

Two villagers found West on the other side of the market, knocked unconscious by a blow to the head. He also had scratch marks on his neck, same as Healer Zall. His blood loss, thankfully, was minimal. Esme patched him up and sent him to bed at the inn, ordering Gan and the guards not to bother her patient.

"Well, without Henry Saxon's testimony," said the magistrate, making a final note in his journal, "I cannot determine whether Lok Tolman caused the fire. We will search for Master Saxon. If he isn't found within a full week, we will close the case, ruling it as accidental. Until then, Master Tolman and Miss Meredith are prohibited from leaving Vala." He fixed both with a stern look, but Lok was too worried about Kuno to care.

A pair of guards escorted him and Meredith out of the mayor's house, leading them towards the inn. Lok pointed at the healer's house.

"He wants to see Kuno," Meredith explained.

The guards relented, one leading Lok to Zall's house and the other taking Meredith to the inn.

Kuno laid on the middle bed, Healer Zall to his left. Esme had given him a full exam. Bleeding from the eyes, nose, and ears. Potential hearing loss from ruptured eardrums. Difficulty breathing, cause unknown. And Esme cautioned Lok that Kuno likely had internal damage.

"We will have to wait and see," she said solemnly. She cast an uneasy glance at Kuno, a mixture of concern and fear. She had witnessed Kuno call down lightning, something no human being, not even an Elemental Thane, could do.

Lok sat beside Kuno's bed and waited.

"I can watch over him," Esme said when the two moons were high in the sky. "You need to rest."

Lok shook his head. Best for him to stay here. His mother and stepfather were likely asleep, and he didn't have the courage to face either. Vera and Ellis had stood at the edge of the marketplace, staring at the smoldering ruins. Lok saw fear in his mother's eyes. She flinched and huddled closer to Ellis as Lok walked up to her.

"Lok, did you…" Vera bit down on her lip.

Lok wanted to explain, but the village guards marched up and grabbed him by the arms, pinning them behind his back.

"Mayor Gan wants to see you," one said.

Lok looked at his mother and stepfather, pleading, silently begging them to understand. Yes, he started the fire, but he acted in self-defense, protecting the village from a monster. Vera refused to look at him.

"Best see what the mayor wants," Ellis said quietly.

How could Lok ever face them again? What if the fear in his mother's eyes never disappeared?

The floorboards creaked. Lok looked up, expecting to see Esme, but Meredith stood in the doorway, watching Kuno.

"How is he?" she asked softly.

Lok shrugged. Kuno hadn't moved at all during the night, and there was a strange hitch in his breathing.

Meredith sat at the foot of the bed. "I talked to the mayor again. He understands it was self-defense. He still has a lot of questions. Most of them for him." She looked at Kuno.

Lok grabbed his notebook off the nightstand. *Is Esme awake?*

"Yeah. She's outside with Patyn. She says Healer Zall is doing better. He definitely looks healthier." Meredith glanced at Zall. The healer slept easily, the ruddy tint returning to his face. "I guess since Kuno killed that Seltachai…" She shrugged. "I don't know. Seltachai were just campfire stories. We never imagined they were real."

Lok sighed. Healer Zall always called Master Kel a Seltachai, desperately trying to convince everyone that he was a monster. How had he mistaken Henry for a normal person? Were Seltachai clever enough to trick people?

He tricked an entire village.

"What type of Thane is Kuno?" Meredith whispered. "Is he an Elemental, too?"

Lok shook his head. Elementals only controlled the four elements, not lightning. And the air had grown colder. The sky turned darker. Lok shivered.

"They found Brother Malaky," Meredith continued. Lok's skin prickled. "He ran all the way to Watchtower. The guards detained him. He was raving about the Midnight King, saying he walked Eltriar. That he was here in Vala." Meredith swallowed. "He's in the jail. The guards asked Esme to look at him. They're terrified."

Lok held Kuno's hand. It looked thinner, the bones more prominent. The Scholar's face was thinner, too. He called down that lightning at a great cost, and he did it to protect Lok and Meredith. The Midnight King never protected anyone. Brother Malaky was just crazy. He had been crazy this whole time. His Farsights were nothing more than the ravings of a lunatic.

"The villagers are worried," Meredith continued. "The chapel is full of people. The chaplains are concerned, too." She shivered and rubbed her arms. "Stars above, I can sense them all the way here. Anyway, if it weren't for the guards and Esme's reputation, some would storm in here."

Lok's head whipped towards the door, his heart racing.

"There's a guard posted outside. Asked me a hundred questions before he let me in. He's been there all night."

Lok frowned. Esme never mentioned a guard. Then again, she had two sick patients here, one at the inn, and a very worried Elemental to care for.

"How much do you know about Scholar Kuno?"

"He is a historian. He and Esme attended the Academy together." A light dawned in his mind. Kuno had been young at the same time as Esme and Kel. He had aged. The Midnight King was thousands of years old. They couldn't be the same person. It was impossible!

A pensive look crossed Meredith's face. Lok wished Ivar was here so he could know exactly what she was thinking.

"Anything else? What about his family?"

"He doesn't have one. He's an orphan." Meredith already knew this. Why bother asking again?

"An orphan from where? His skin is too dark for Teyrnas. Even out here in the Hinterlands."

Kuno never mentioned where he was born. It wasn't important. The Academy was his home.

A shadow fell over Lok, turning his blood to ice. Meredith leapt to her fee and reached for her belt knife.

Luckson stood in the doorway. The man wore a crimson cloak over his clothes, and a board sword at his belt. Flames and words in Old Eltrian decorated the scabbard, lacquered a dark red. The sword's hilt was tied to the scabbard with a long, red ribbon, making an intricate knot. It was impossible for Luckson to draw the blade. That was a small comfort. But how did he get past the guard?

"Already has you eating out of his palm, huh, little raven?" Luckson's voice was steady and cold, like frost creeping over a pond. He stepped closer. The door… The door was closed. Lok tightened his grip on Kuno's hand.

Luckson turned his attention to Meredith. "What are you doing here, Thane?"

Meredith glare at him. She gripped the knife tightly, prepared to fight.

Luckson sighed and shook his head. "You and Westermor shouldn't even be here. The rest of the Nine are at the Teyrnas Academy."

"Nine what?" Meredith asked.

"I'll explain later. West is awake, in case you were wondering. But what am I to do with you, raven?" Luckson looked at Lok sadly.

"Leave my son out of this, Esar," Kuno muttered.

Lok crouched by Kuno's side, his heart racing and falling all at once. Son. Kuno had called him son!

Kuno cracked open his eyes. The whites were bloodshot. He tried to prop himself up on his elbows but collapsed. Lok adjusted the pillow, helping Kuno sit upright. Kuno's breathing turned ragged.

"Your son?" Luckson studied Lok. "Didn't think it was possible," he muttered. "He doesn't look like you. Though, he is tall. About the same height."

Lok frowned. What was Luckson talking about? Lok stood a head taller than Kuno.

"He's adopted, moron."

A smile quirked over Luckson's face. He relaxed visibly. "So, you're adopting your pets now. I guess that adds another layer of blind loyalty."

"Why are you here?" Meredith demanded.

"I am here to find my brother." He glared at Kuno. "Found you."

Brother? Lok studied both men. They had different builds, different hair and eye colors, and different complexions. No shared similarities. Nothing to indicate that they were related. And what had Kuno called him? Esar? The name sounded familiar, but Lok couldn't place it.

"Esme!" Meredith yelled.

Footsteps thrummed on the floorboards. Luckson rolled his eyes. "This is unnecessary," he said as Esme burst into the room.

"Thank the Creator you're awake!" she said to Kuno. She rushed to the Scholar's side, shooing Lok out of the way.

Lok kept one eye on Luckson, who had moved to the far corner near Zall's bed. The healer was fast asleep.

"Are you in any pain?" Esme asked.

"My head and chest hurt. How is Zall?"

"Better. He slept most of the night. The one time he did wake, he was lucid. But his memory is blurry. He doesn't remember Henry at all."

"Not surprised," Luckson said.

Esme spun on her heels. "Who let you in here?"

"I let myself in, ma'am." He gave her a short bow, his hand over his heart. "Sorry for the disturbance. I'm here to collect the man who calls himself Kuno Surylin."

"You can't. He suffered a trauma. He..." Esme gave Kuno a searching look. "What exactly did you do?"

"Something foolish. Esar, take me if you must, but leave them out of it. They don't know the truth."

"You and your lies." Luckson shook his head in disgust. "Nothing changes."

Lok placed himself between Luckson and Kuno, glaring at the armed man. Adopted or not, Kuno was his family. If he could face a monster to defend his family, he could face Luckson. Or Esar. Where had he heard that name?

"What has he told you?" Luckson demanded.

"*About what?*" Amazingly, Lok's hand did not shake.

"His true identity. Granted, you can just ask the Harbinger. He will tell you. Where did they put Brother Malaky?" he asked Esme.

"He's in the jail. One of the chaplains and a guard from Watchtower are with him." Tears welled in her eyes. "They say he went mad."

"But he speaks the truth. You heard what he said, right?" Luckson rounded on Lok, trying to loom over him, but Lok stood an inch taller.

Lok glared at Luckson, refusing to answer. It was not true!

"Well, Alberik, should I tell them or you?"

"What did you call him?" Esme demanded. Meredith shifted uneasily, switching her knife to an underhanded position. Lok stumbled backward, his legs hitting the bedframe. Luckson... Luckson called the Midnight King by his real name!

Kuno let out a weary sigh. He pushed off the blankets, and with some difficulty, sat upright. His chest was bare, revealing the strange scar on his sternum. It radiated outward, like a starburst. He looked at Esme and Meredith and then met Lok's eyes.

"Sit down, Lok. I..." He grimaced, as though the words caused physical pain. "I have something very important to tell you. Esme, Meredith, you are free to listen, if you wish."

Nobody moved.

Kuno sighed. "I lied to you, Lok. I lied to everyone. I don't expect you to forgive me. I only ask that you listen." Kuno swallowed, tears glistening in his eyes. He gestured at the chair. Lok slowly sat down, his heart pounding.

No, it can't be true. It can't!

"My real name..." Kuno looked like he was going to be sick. "My real name is Alberik, the Midnight King."

59

Solstice

It was the first Summer Solstice without a celebration. In Vala, people would flock to the village green, greeting neighbors, listening to music, dancing. Some years, they set off fireworks as the stars appeared, lighting the sky for another hour.

But no one at the Academy felt like celebrating. They were just thankful to be alive.

The Madani spent most of the evening and morning evacuating civilians to the other side of the Wallach, pausing in the dark hours to rest. The Byyarians and Marish protected the gates at night. Half of the Marish forces still fought for the Coalition, but the rest surrendered, declaring their loyalty to King Ayrdeen. With the Garrison's help, they drove the Coalition forces away, forcing them several miles downriver.

A handful of Students and Journeymen chose to remain at the Academy, aiding the Teyrnian soldiers. All classes were canceled indefinitely. And the Academy would continue to provide shelter as long as people required it.

Though Madan Och did not have an Academy, many villages had private libraries. Students and Scholars were invited to use them, provide they shared the responsibilities of their host families.

The Council and Premier Scholar were going to make an announcement at noon, along with King Carwyn, King Ayrdeen, and Queen Gallia. So far, none of them had evacuated. Rumor said they were going to convert the Academy into a temporary capital.

Realta struggled to wrap her head around Kel being the King of Teyrnas. She tried to visit him this morning, but a cadre of guards turned her away. No civilians were allowed in the royal wing without written permission.

So, she headed for the infirmary, formerly the mess hall. Rows of patients lined the walls, a seemingly endless sea of cots and blankets. Scholars and healers dressed in white moved about, changing bandages, administering medicine, and writing notes. A woman in a dark purple, silk dress spoke with a young woman in a dark blue uniform. With a start, Realta realized it was Lady Sarra, Logan and Kel's sister.

Glancing around, she noted that most patients were dark blue. A few Marish in red and Nowani in white and purple also occupied cots. Fear wafted off the Marish and Nowani. One man in a bright red coat shied away as a Scholar with silver earrings approached his bed. Realta did not blame them. They were taught to fear Thanes, but they had nothing to fear now. Kel had ordered—

No, not Kel. King Carwyn, she reminded herself.

King Carwyn had ordered that the Nowani and Marish wounded be treated with the utmost care.

Her eyes fell on a familiar face.

Charity Loy wore a white smock over her dress. She sat beside a wounded Teyrnian soldier. The young man Realta and Alani had met at the wall. His right leg was bandaged around the knee, and he had several cuts on his arms and face.

Realta sat next to Charity and hugged her. Tears stung Realta's eyes as Charity hugged her tightly.

"Thank the Creator!" Charity exclaimed. "So many people are missing. I didn't know if…" She composed herself. "Well, you're here. And you get to meet Zandon. Zandon, this is my friend Realta."

"Yeah, we met on the wall. Glad to see you're in one piece." Zandon Jons tried to smile, but it looked more like a grimace.

"You, too. Where is Jerryk?" Realta glanced around the infirmary. The pale Healer was nowhere in sight.

"The Scholars wanted to talk to him," Charity replied. "They all believed Healers were extinct, so they're asking him a hundred questions instead of letting him Heal people." Bitterness laced her voice.

"Hey, you know how the Scholars reacted when they discovered Lok's ability," Zandon said.

"But people are dying! People Jerryk could have Healed." Charity bit her lip as tears ran down her face.

A young woman with blonde hair and wearing a gray Journeyman cloak walked past. She made eye contact with Charity, giving her a slight nod. Charity wiped the tears away and returned the nod. The Journeyman walked away, inspecting the wounded.

"Is she a healer, too?" Realta asked, sensing anxiety from Charity.

"Just, um… Just someone I know."

Zandon muttered under his breath.

Realta peered at the nearest soldiers. Young men in their twenties and early thirties. All clean shaven, and most with fair skin. "Charity, have you seen my father? Was he brought here?"

She shook her head. "I haven't seen Callum since yesterday morning. Why? Was he hurt?"

"He's missing. The last place anyone saw him was the wall. During the battle." Realta had awoken in the early hours of the morning. Marsh sat at the desk, cradling her head. All the other soldiers were gone.

"Did you find him?" Realta asked groggily.

"Hm?" Marsh glanced up. Exhaustion clouded her face. "Who?"

"My father."

"No. I'm sure he'll turn up."

Hours passed. Still nothing. Realta got tired of waiting and when to the Academy's main building, hoping to see Kel. And Marsh went to join a unit of soldiers. Alani had prevented the Coalition from spilling into the Academy, but the East Gate was completely blocked. Repairs were desperately needed.

"He might be helping the remaining civilians. Or maybe he's with Kel." Charity's face brightened. "Can you believe it?" she lowered her voice. "Kel is a king!"

"Who?" Zandon asked.

"I'll explain later. Promise." Charity smiled.

"Honestly, I don't know what to think." A strange feeling crept over Realta, like insects crawling over her skin. "Have you seen Gareth?"

"Not since yesterday morning."

"He was at the wall," Zandon replied, propping himself up on an elbow. "He was looking for you, Realta. I told him to get down, but he didn't listen."

"Gareth was on the wall?" The wall had been pure chaos. Realta barely managed to keep her head while up there. Why had her cousin, who hated large crowds and loud noises, voluntarily gone there? "Where is he now?"

"I was hoping you knew." Zandon's face fell. "Jaim and I went looking. That's how I got hurt. Bloody Tirshics jumped us. No idea where Jaim ended up."

"We will find them," Charity said, the words a bit forced. "They can't have gone too far."

"There you are."

A chill ran up Realta's spine. She whirled around and saw Val looming over her, a bright smile painted on his face.

"What do you want?" Realta spat. Val was the last person she wanted to see. Just behind him, she spied Bas, his hood drawn over his face. The Gadyeni walked up to one of the healers, a young woman with wavy black hair and ruddy skin. The two spoke quietly.

"I wanted to see how you're holding up. Everyone else is in a conference room. Second floor. Decent view. I hoped the other two would have joined us, but Tath reports they're delayed." He shot an icy glare at Bas. "And that one hasn't said a word about the Ninth. But I digress." The icy glare melted. "Hello, Charity Loy. Remember me?"

"Yeah. Are you really on our side now?" Charity asked.

Val smirked, no doubt reading Charity's mind. "Yes, and Queen Gallia is on our side, too. I should know. I am her personal messenger."

"Really?" Realta raised an eyebrow.

"Well, she doesn't know I'm here yet. She's currently in a meeting with Carwyn and Ayrdeen. I'm glad your uncle is king, Realta. It will make things a lot easier."

"Uncle?" Zandon sat up straighter. "King Carwyn is your uncle?"

"Oh, a Farsight." Val eyed Zandon's blue earring. "You will be very useful. I will tell Jerryk to Heal you first."

"There are men and women with more serious injuries than

me."

Val nodded. "And a good heart. Yes, you will be a wonderful ally. So will you, Miss Loy."

"Can you just go away?" Realta was too tired to deal with Val's games.

"We can't begin our meeting without our Dreamer," Val said, placing a hand on her shoulder.

"Dreamer?" Zandon's eyes widened. "You're a Dreamer?"

"The only one on Eltriar," Val answered for her.

"But you... Alani said you're an Empath and Manipulator. Why didn't she—"

"For Realta's protection," Val interrupted, "she is keeping her core ability a secret. Now, I believe you have something for us," he said to Realta, holding out his hand.

Realta glared at him.

"Hannor, Realta. The dagger Elliza helped you steal. Where is it?"

"It's right..." Realta reached for her belt and touched torn fabric. Her heart skipped a beat. When had her belt snapped? An hour ago? Five? "It's gone!"

"What?!" Val seized her by the shoulders. "Where is it? What did you do with Hannor?" He glared at her, their faces almost touching. Anger radiated from him, as sharp as a slap to the face.

"I don't know," she stammered. "My belt snapped. It must have fallen off."

"Fallen off where?" Val dug his fingernails into her skin. "Near the wall? In the Academy? In Kereu?" His gray eyes burned white hot.

"She does not know, Valentin," said Bas. He walked over and pried Val's hands off Realta. "And hurting her will not reveal the dagger's location."

"But we need it!"

Several patients and healers stared at Val. Realta huddled closer to Charity and Zandon. Both placed protective arms around her.

Bas looked at Val curiously. "Perhaps. Perhaps not. There is more than one way to win a war."

"What is he talking about?" Charity whispered. "Why does he

need a dagger?"

"It's very old and powerful." Realta didn't dare say anything else. A small voice in the back of her mind told her that Val would get angrier if more people knew about Hannor. *But what do we do now? How will we defeat the Midnight King?*

"Come along, Realta." Bas held out his hand. He looked at her with soft, kind eyes. "We mustn't keep the others waiting."

Realta wanted to be angry at Bas. He broke his promise, forcing her and Chinasa to leave without Serena and Shasta, stranding them and the Scholars in Kereu. But it wasn't completely his fault. Tath had strong-armed them, including Bas. And Bas promised to go back for Serena. A promise he might fulfill.

"It's okay," she said to Charity and Zandon. They reluctantly let go of her. She held Bas's hand. Warmth flooded her.

"Look for Callum," she told Charity.

"I will." She stood and gave Realta a quick hug.

Realta followed Bas out of the infirmary. She felt Val's eyes glaring at the back of her head and walked closer to Bas, holding his hand tightly.

"Siryn wants you to meet with the monarchs," Bas said. "She believes it will be good for you to work together."

"What good will they do?" Val muttered.

"King Carwyn—" Realta rounded on him, but Bas cut her off.

"Is very cooperative. You should give him a chance, Valentin. And Gallia will be there, too."

Val didn't respond.

"What about the dagger?" Realta whispered to Bas as they walked up a massive staircase. A few soldiers passed them.

"Think of Hannor as a failsafe. One of many possibilities. The Nine of you will find a way."

Realta prayed that Bas was right.

Epilogue

Gareth dreaded the sunrise. At night, he was just another shadow. Nothing to see.

Now, hiding was next to impossible.

A lot of Marish and Nowani troops had stopped fighting Teyrnian ones. Now, they fought Tirshic, Tarodic, and Galionic soldiers. Gareth witnessed a band of Marish soldiers ambush the Galionic soldier they were marching side by side with. One moment, they moved in two silent columns. Then the Marish commander whistled sharply. The Marish attacked the Galionic swiftly and brutally. Gareth watched from his hiding place within a broken-down siege engine.

Part of him wanted to return to the Academy. But he could not run away again. He had to find Callum.

He crept along a copse of trees. The city of Norgard, reduced to ruins with black plumes of smoke rising into the air, stood half a mile down the torn-up road. The flag of Nowan flew overhead. Had the soldiers taken Callum there?

A chill ran down Gareth's spine. Would Kanton be there, too? What if Kanton wasn't badly injured? What if he attacked Gareth while he tried to rescue Callum? Or worse, what if Kanton had already killed Callum, or...

Don't be a coward!

A coward would not have scaled the wall, nor would a coward have come all this way to search for his uncle. No, it was too late to be a coward again.

Gareth touched the hilt of the dagger at his belt. First, find Callum. Second, give Realta her dagger. He did not know why Realta had a dagger, or how she ended up at the Academy. Those were questions for later.

A hand grabbed his shoulder.

His heart leaping into his throat, Gareth whirled around and balled his hand into a fist, ready to strike. He stopped in time, seeing Jaim crouched beside him. The boy grinned.

"What are you doing here?" Gareth whispered. Had he

screamed? He didn't think so. He peered around the trees. Nobody looked his way.

"Looking for you, obviously. Why did you leave?"

Gareth told Jaim about Callum. "Then he... He fell..." His throat tightened, cutting off his speech.

"Fire and smoke. I'm sorry, Gareth. Do you think he was captured?"

"I saw soldiers carrying him away." He glanced at Norgard. The purple and white flag was just visible through the smoke.

Jaim stood and headed for the road.

"Jaim, no!" Gareth grabbed Jaim's wrist, but the other boy slipped away.

"We can't find Callum just sitting around. We can look in Norgard."

Gareth frowned as dozens of possibilities crowded his mind. What if they were caught? Would the Marish know they were Teyrnian and escort them back to the Academy? Would Tirshic soldiers find them instead? What if Callum wasn't in Norgard? What if the soldiers moved him and Kanton to a different camp?

You cannot answer those questions by standing still. The voice in his mind sounded vaguely like his father's.

He joined Jaim and walked down the road. The torn-up path was deserted and eerily quiet. He spied a few soldiers in the fields, but either they didn't see the two boys, or they were too preoccupied to care.

"Hey, that's a cool dagger," Jaim said. "Can I see?"

Gareth handed it to him.

"Wow! This looks really valuable. It's even got a prism in the hilt."

"A what?"

"A prism. See? I hold it up to the light, and it shows the color spectrum. Fire and smoke, Scholar Maryn would love to get her hands on this!"

Gareth glanced down. A small, circular rainbow danced on the road.

"Where did you get it?"

Hooves thundered on the road, kicking up a plume of dust. A man on horseback charged towards them. A dozen men on foot raced behind him. All wore white uniforms striped with purple. They cut off the road, surrounding Gareth and Jaim in a loose semi-circle.

Gareth froze, his heart pounding against his ribs.

"Halt!" ordered the rider as the soldiers drew arrows and swords. His dark brown hair was matted with sweat and dried blood. And his armor was dented in several places.

"Who are you?" Jaim stammered.

"State your countries!" the rider snapped.

"What?" Jaim gave him a confused look. Gareth stood completely still, trying to think, but the man's yelling hurt his head.

"Your countries!"

"Teyrnas," Jaim said.

"Both of you?" His dark eyes were like ice.

"Yes, sir."

The man sneered. Half of the men drew their bows, ready to fire. Sweat beaded on Gareth's forehead.

Should they run? The trees were twenty paces away. Too far to reach before these men fired their arrows.

"What are you doing here?" the rider asked.

"We were just—"

"He's got a weapon!" One soldier pointed at Jaim.

"It's just a dagger." Jaim held up the dagger and sheath so they could see. "I'm not—"

"Thane!" Another soldier pointed at Jaim's earring.

Gareth's heart skipped a beat as half a dozen arrows flew towards them. Four arrows embedded in Jaim's chest, and he fell to the ground.

Gareth slowly looked down. Jaim didn't move. Didn't scream. His friend laid absolutely still. Silent. Jaim's dark brown eyes stared at the sky. Blood pooled underneath him.

He... No, he can't...

"Please," Gareth whispered. "Please, get up."

"Damn it, why did you fire?" the rider demanded. His horse snorted and stamped its hooves.

"He's a Thane, sir." The soldier spat on the ground.

"He was a kid." Flicking the reins, the man rode closer to Jaim. He shook his head in disgust and then turned his icy eyes on Gareth. "What about you, boy? Are you a Thane?"

Gareth tried to speak, tried to think. Jaim couldn't be dead. He was just stunned. That's right. His mother told him about people going into shock when they were badly injured. Some didn't speak or move for hours afterward. Jaim was just in shock. He was...

"Hey, can you talk?" The rider tapped Gareth on the shoulder.

Gareth jolted, but he didn't take his eyes off Jaim. *Come on, Jaim, move!* But Jaim's eyes were glassy, and his gold Aura slowly faded away.

"Take him." The rider shoved Gareth. Two soldiers grabbed him roughly by the arms and bound his hands with a piece of rope.

No! Fight back. Callum taught you how to fight. His arms and legs refused to listen.

Another soldier, a man with shaggy brown hair and gray eyes, picked up the dagger. A few specks of Jaim's blood marred the white sheath. He gave it to the rider.

The rider inspected it, frowning. "It's a bloody ornament." He angrily shoved it into his belt.

"Sir?"

"It ain't much use as a weapon." The rider glared at the six archers. They averted their eyes. One had turned deathly pale.

"What should we do with the body, sir?" the soldier asked, shifting his feet nervously.

The man spared a momentary glance at Jaim. "Leave it." Flicking the reins, he trotted past the other soldiers, heading towards Norgard. "Bring the boy."

Another soldier shoved Gareth. His feet moved automatically to prevent himself from falling. The soldier shoved him again, forcing him down the road.

Gareth looked back at his friend. Purple and white fletching swayed in the breeze.

No, stop! He wanted to scream at the soldiers, but his voice refused to cooperate. *Don't leave him there. Take him with us. We have to bury...* Tears burned his eyes.

The Nowani soldiers led Gareth away. The sun rose higher in the cloudless sky as they reached the ruined city.

The End of Book Two

About the Author

Beck Todd was born and raised
in South Carolina and currently lives
in Charleston with her family.